The Fu Manchu Omnibus

a&b

The Fu Manchu Omnibus

Volume 4

SAX ROHMER

This omnibus edition first published in Great Britain in 1999 by
Allison & Busby Limited
Suite 111, Bon Marche Centre
241-251 Ferndale Road
London SW9 8BJ
http://www.allisonandbusby.ltd.uk

The Drums of Fu Manchu
First published 1939 by Doubleday & Company, Inc

Emperor Fu Manchu
First published 1959 by Herbert Jenkins Ltd

Shadow of Fu Manchu
First published 1958 by Crowell-Collier Publishing Company

A catalogue record for this book is available from
the British Library.

ISBN 0 7490 0232 8

Design and cover illustration by Pepe Moll

Printed and bound in Spain by
Liberduplex, s.l. Barcelona.

SAX ROHMER was the pen name of Arthur Sarsfield Ward, who was born in Birmingham in 1866 of Irish parents. For many years he lived in New York. He worked as a journalist on Fleet Street before he made his name as the creator of the Dr Fu Manchu thrillers. He died in 1959.

Contents

Contents

The Drums of Fu Manchu

Mystery comes to Bayswater

"Damn it! There is someone there!"

I sprang up irritably, jerked the curtains aside and stared down into Bayswater Road. My bell, "Bart Kerrigan" inscribed above it on a plate outside in the street, was sometimes rung wantonly by late revellers. The bell was out of order and I had tried to ignore its faint tinkling. But now, staring down, I saw someone looking up at me as I stood in the lighted room: a man wearing a Burberry and a soft hat, a man who signalled urgently with his arms, indicating: "Come down!"

Shooting the bolt open so that I should not be locked out, I ran downstairs. A light in the glazed arcade which led to the front doer refused to function. Groping my way I threw the door open.

The man in the Burberry almost upset me as he leapt in.

"Who the devil are *you*?"

The door was closed quietly and the intruder spoke, his back to it as he faced me.

"It's not a holdup," came in coldly incisive tones. "I just *had* to get in. Thanks, Kerrigan, but you were a long time coming down."

"Good heavens!" I stepped forward in the darkness and extended my hand. "Nayland Smith! Can I believe it?"

"Absolutely! I was desperate. Is your bell out of order?"

"Yes."

"I thought so. Don't turn the light up."

"I can't; the fuse is blown."

"Good. I gather that I interrupted you, but I had an excellent reason. Come on."

As we hurried up the semi-dark staircase, I found my brain in some confusion. And when we entered my flat:

"Leave your dining room in darkness," snapped Nayland Smith. "I want to look out of the window."

Breathless, between astonishment and the race up the stairs, I stood behind him as he stared out of the dining room window. Two men were loitering near the front door—and glancing up toward my lighted study.

"Only just in time!" said Nayland Smith. "I tricked them—but you see how wonderfully they are informed. Evidently they know every possible spot in which I might take cover. Unpleasantly near thing, Kerrigan."

In the lighted study I gazed at my visitor. Hat removed, Nayland Smith revealed a head of virile curling hair, more grey than black. Stripping off his Burberry, he faced me. His clean-cut features, burned by a recent visit to the tropics, looked almost haggardly thin, but the fire in his eyes, the tense nervous vitality of the man must have struck a spark of animosity or of friendship in any but a soul dead.

He stared at me analytically.

"You look well, Kerrigan. You have passed twenty-seven, but you are lean as a hare, clean-cut and obviously fit as a flea. The last time I saw you was in Addis-Ababa. You were sending articles to the *Orbit* and I was sending reports to the Foreign Office. Well, what is it now?"

He stared down at the littered writing desk. I moved towards the dining room.

"Drinks? Good!" he snapped. "But you must find them in the dark."

"I understand."

When presently I returned with a decanter and syphon:

"Look here," I said, "I was never happier to see a man in my life. But bring me up to date: what's the meaning of all this?"

Nayland Smith dropped a page which he had been reading and began reflectively to stuff coarse-cut mixture into his briar.

"You are writing a book about Abyssinia, I see."

"Yes."

"You are not on the staff of the *Orbit*, are you?"

"No. I am in the fortunate position of picking and choosing my jobs. I did the series on Abyssinia for them because I know that part of Africa pretty well. Now, I am doing a book on present conditions."

As I poured out drinks:

14

"Excuse me," said Nayland Smith, "I just want to make sure."

He walked into the darkened dining room, carefully closing the door behind him. When he returned:

"May I use your phone?"

"Certainly."

I handed him a drink of which he took a sip, then, raising the telephone receiver, he dialed a number rapidly, and:

"Yes!" His speech was curiously staccato. "Put me through to Chief Inspector Wessex' office. Sir Denis Nayland Smith speaking. Hurry!"

There was an interval. I watched my visitor fascinatedly. In my considerable experience of men, I had never known one who lived at such high pressure.

"Is that Inspector Wessex? . . . Good. I have a job for you, Inspector. Instruct Paddington Police Station to send a party in a fast car. They will find two men—dark skinned foreigners—hanging about near the corner of Porchester Terrace. They are to arrest them—never mind the charge—and lock them up. I will deal with them later. Can I leave this to you?"

Presumably the invisible chief inspector agreed to take charge of the matter, for Nayland Smith hung up the receiver.

"I have brought you your biggest story, Kerrigan. I know you can afford to await my word before publishing. I may add"—tapping the loose manuscript on the desk— "that you have missed the real truth about Abyssinia, but I can rectify that." He began in his restless way to pace up and down the carpet. "Without mentioning any names, a prominent cabinet minister resigned quite recently. Do you recall it?"

"Certainly."

"He was a wise man. Do you know why he retired?"

"There are several versions of the story."

"He has a fine brain—and he retired because he recognised that there was in the world one *first-class* brain. He retired to review his ideas on the immediate destiny of civilisation."

"What do you mean?"

"The thing most desired, Kerrigan, by all women, by all sensible men, in this life, is *peace.* Wars are made by few but fought by many. The greatest intellect in the world today has decided that there must

15

be *peace!* It has become my business to try to save the lives of certain prominent persons who are blind enough to believe that they can make war. I was en route for Sir Malcolm Locke's house, which is not five minutes' drive away, when I realised that a small Daimler was following me. I remembered, fortunately, that your flat was here, and trusted to luck that you would be at home. I worked an old trick. Fey, my man, slowed up around a corner just before the following car had turned it. I stepped out and cut through a mews. Fey drove on. But my two followers evidently detected the trick. I saw them coming back just before you opened the door! They know I am in one of two buildings. What I don't want them to know is where I am going. Hello—!"

The sound of a speeding automobile suddenly braked came up from Bayswater Road.

"Into the dining room!"

I dashed in behind Nayland Smith. We stared down. A police car stood outside. There were few pedestrians and there was comparatively little traffic. It was the lull before eleven o'clock, the lull which precedes the storm of returning theatre and picture goers. A queer scene was being enacted on the pavement almost directly below my windows.

Two men (except that they were dark fellows I could discern no more from my viewpoint) were struggling and protesting volubly amid a group of uniformed constables. Beyond, on the park side, I saw now a small car standing—it looked like a Daimler. A constable on patrol joined the party, and the police driver pointed in the direction of the Daimler. The expostulating prisoners were hustled in, the police car was driven off and the constable in the determined but leisurely way of his kind paced stolidly across the road.

"All clear!" said Nayland Smith. "Come along! I want you with me!"

"But, Sir Malcolm Locke? In what way can he be—?"

"He's the cousin of the home secretary. As a matter of fact, he's abroad. It isn't Locke I want to see, but a guest who is staying at his house. I must get to him, Kerrigan, without a moment's delay!"

"A guest?"

"Say, rather, someone who is hiding there."

"Hiding?"

16

"I can't mention his name—yet. But he returned secretly from Africa. He is the driving power behind one of Europe's dictators. By consent of the British Foreign Office, he came, also secretly, to London. Can you imagine why?"

"No."

"To see *me!*"

Sir Malcom's guest

Fey, that expressionless, leather-faced valet-chauffeur of Nayland Smith's, was standing at the door beside the Rolls, rug over arm, as though nothing unusual had occurred; and as we proceeded towards Sir Malcolm's house, Smith, smoking furiously, fell into a silence which I did not care to interrupt.

I count myself psychic, for this is a Celtic heritage, yet on this short journey nothing told me that, although as correspondent for the *Orbit* I had had a not uneventful life, I was about to become mixed up in a drama the outcome of which meant nothing less than the destruction of what we are pleased to call Civilisation. And in averting Armageddon, by the oddest paradox I was to find myself opposed to the one man who, alone, could save Europe from destruction.

Sir Malcolm Locke's house presented an unexpectedly festive appearance as we approached. Nearly every window in the large building was illuminated, a number of cars were drawn up and a considerable group of people had congregated outside the front door.

"Hello!" muttered Nayland Smith. He knocked out his pipe in the ash tray and dropped the briar into a pocket of his Burberry. "This is very odd."

Before Fey had pulled in Smith was out and dashing up the steps. I followed and reached him just as the door was opened by a butler. The man's face wore a horrified expression: a constable was hurrying up behind us.

"Sir Malcolm is not at home, sir."

"I am not here to see Sir Malcolm, but his guest. My name is Nayland Smith. My business is official."

"I'm sorry, sir," said the butler, with a swift change of manner. "I didn't recognise you."

The door opened straight into a lofty hallway, from the further end of which a crescent staircase led to upper floors. As the butler closed the door I immediately became conscious of a curiously vibrant atmosphere. I had experienced it before, in places taken by assault or bombed. It is caused, I think, by the vibrations of frightened minds. Several servants were peering down from a dark landing above but the hallway itself was brightly lighted. At this moment, a door on the right opened and a clean- shaven, heavily built man with jet-black, close-cropped hair came out. He glanced in our direction.

"Good evening, Inspector," said Nayland Smith. "What's this? What are *you* doing here?"

"Thank God you've arrived, sir!" The inspector stopped dead in his stride. "I was beginning to fear something was wrong."

"This is Mr Bart Kerrigan—Chief Inspector Leighton of the Special Branch."

Nayland Smith's loud, rather harsh tones evidently having penetrated to the room beyond, again the door opened, and I saw with astonishment Sir James Clare, the home secretary, come out.

"Here at last, Smith," was his greeting. "I heard your voice." Sir James spoke in a clear but nearly toneless manner which betrayed his legal training. "I don't know your friend"— staring at me through the thick pebbles of his spectacles. "This unhappy business, of course, is tremendously confidential."

Nayland Smith made a rapid introduction.

"Mr Kerrigan is acting for no newspaper or agency. You may take his discretion for granted. You say this unhappy business, Sir James? May I ask "

Sir James Clare raised his hand to check the speaker. He turned to Inspector Leighton.

"See if there is any news about the telephone call, Inspector," he directed, and as the inspector hurried away: "Suppose, gentlemen, you come in here for a moment."

We followed him back into the apartment from which he had come. It was a large library, a lofty room, every available foot of the wall occupied by bookcases. Beside a mahogany table upon which, also, were many books and a number of documents, he sat down in an armchair, indicating that we should sit in two others. Smith was far too restless for inaction, but grunting irritably he threw himself down into one of the padded chairs.

"Chief Inspector Leighton of the Special Branch," said Sir James, "is naturally acquainted with the identity of Sir Malcolm's guest. But no one else in the house has been informed, with the exception of Mr Bascombe, Sir Malcolm's private secretary. In the circumstances I think perhaps we had better talk in here. Am I to take it that you are unaware of what occurred tonight?"

"On your instructions," said Smith, speaking with a sort of smothered irritability, "I flew from Berlin this evening. I was on my way here, and I can only suppose that the purpose of my return was known. A deliberate attempt was made tonight to wreck my car as I crossed Bond Street, by the driver of a lorry. Only Fey's skill and the fact that at so late an hour there were no pedestrians averted disaster. He drove right on to the pavement and along it for some little distance."

"Did you apprehend the driver of this lorry?"

"I did not stop to do so, although I recognised the fact that it was a planned attack. Then, when we reached Marble Arch, I realised that two men were following in a Daimler. I managed to throw them off the track, with Mr Kerrigan's assistance—and here I am. What has happened?"

"General Quinto is dead!"

The green death

This news, coupled with the identity of the hidden guest, shocked me inexpressibly. General Quinto! Chief of Staff to Signor Monaghani; one of the most formidable figures in political Europe! The man who would command Monaghani's forces in the event of war; the first soldier in his country, almost certain successor to the dictator! But if I was shocked, the effect upon Nayland Smith was electrical.

He sprang up with clenched fists and glared at Sir James Clare.

"Good God, Sir James! You are not telling me that he has been—"

The home secretary shook his head. His legal calm remained unruffled.

"That question, Smith, I am not yet in a position to answer. But you know now why I am here; why Inspector Leighton is here." He stood up. "I shall be glad, gentlemen, if you will follow me to the study which had been placed at the disposal of the general, and in which he died."

A door at the further end of the library was thrown open and I entered a small study, intimately furnished. There was a writing desk near a curtained window, which showed evidence of someone's recent activities. But my attention was immediately focussed upon a settee in an arched recess upon which lay the body of a man. One glance was sufficient—for I had seen him many times in Africa.

It was General Quinto. But his normally sallow aquiline features displayed an agonised surprise and had acquired a sort of ghastly greenish hue. I cannot better describe what I mean than by likening the effect to that produced by green limelight.

A man whose features I could not distinguish was kneeling beside the body, which he appeared to be closely examining. A second man looked down at him, and as we entered the first stood up and turned.

It was Lord Moreton, the king's physician.

Introductions revealed that the other was Dr Sims, the divisional police surgeon.

"This is a very strange business," said the famous consultant, removing his spectacles and placing them in a pocket of his dress waistcoat. "Do you know"—he looked from face to face, with a sort of naïve astonishment—"I have no idea what killed this man!"

"This is really terrible," declared Sir James Clare. "Personal considerations apart, his death here in London under such circumstances cannot fail to set ugly rumours afloat. I take it that you mean, Lord Moreton, that you are not prepared to give a certificate of death from natural causes?"

"Honestly," the physician replied, staring intently at him, "I am not. I am by no means satisfied that he did die from natural causes."

"I am perfectly sure that he didn't," the police surgeon declared.

Nayland Smith, who had been staring down at the body of the dead soldier, now began sniffing the air suspiciously.

"I observe, Sir Denis," said Lord Moreton, "that you have detected a faint but peculiar odour in the atmosphere?"

"I have. Had you noticed it?"

"At the very moment that I entered the room. I cannot identify it; it is something outside my experience. It grows less perceptible—or I am becoming used to it."

I, too, had detected this strange but not unpleasant odour. Now, apparently guided by his sense of smell, Nayland Smith began to approach the writing desk. Here he paused, sniffing vigorously. At this moment the door opened and Inspector Leighton came in.

"I see you are trying to trace the smell, sir. I thought it was stronger by the writing desk than elsewhere, but I could find nothing to account for it."

"You have searched thoroughly?" Smith snapped.

"Absolutely, sir. I think I may say I have searched every inch of the room."

Nayland Smith stood by the desk tugging at the lobe of his ear, a mannerism which indicated perplexity, as I knew; then:

"Do these gentlemen know the identity of the victim?" he asked the minister.

"Yes."

"In that case, who actually saw General Quinto last alive?"

"Mr Bascombe, Sir Malcolm's private secretary."

"Very well. I have reasons for wishing that Mr Kerrigan should be in a position to confirm anything that I may discover in this matter. Where was the body found?"

"Where it lies now."

"By whom?"

"By Mr Bascombe. He phoned the news to me."

Smith glanced at Inspector Leighton.

"The body has been disturbed in no way, Inspector?"

"In no way."

"In that case I should like a private interview with Mr Bascombe. I wish Mr Kerrigan to remain. Perhaps, Lord Moreton and Doctor Sims, you would be good enough to wait in the library with Sir James and the Inspector . . ."

Mr Bascombe was a tall fair man, approaching middle age. He carried himself with a slight stoop, although I learned that he was a Cambridge rowing Blue. His manner was gentle to the point of diffidence. As he entered the study he glanced in a horrified way at the body on the settee.

"Good evening, Mr Bascombe," said Nayland Smith, who was standing before the writing table, "I thought it better that I should see you privately. I gather from Inspector Leighton that General Quinto, who arrived here yesterday morning at eleven o'clock, was to all intents and purposes hiding in these rooms."

"That is so, Sir Denis. The door behind you, there, opens into a bedroom, and a bathroom adjoins it. Sir Malcolm, who is a very late worker, sometimes slept there in order to avoid disturbing Lady Locke."

"And since his arrival, the general has never left those apartments?"

"No."

"He was a very old friend of Sir Malcolm's?"

"Yes, a lifelong friend, I understand. He and Lady Locke are in the south of France, but are expected back tomorrow morning."

"No member of the staff is aware of the identity of the visitor?"

"No. He had never stayed here during the time of Greaves, the butler—that is, during the last three years—and he was a stranger to all the other servants."

"By what name was he known here?"

"Mr Victor."

"Who looked after him?"

"Greaves."

"No one else?"

"No one, except myself and Greaves, entered these rooms."

"The general expected me tonight, of course?"

"Yes. He was very excited when you did not appear."

"How has he occupied himself since his arrival?"

"Writing almost continuously, when he was not pacing up and down the library, or glancing out of the windows into the square."

"What was he writing?"

"I don't know. He tore up every shred of it. Late this evening he had a fire lighted in the library and burnt up everything."

"Extraordinary! Did he seem very apprehensive?"

"Very. Had I not known his reputation, I should have said, in fact, that he was panic-stricken. This frame of mind seemed to date from his receipt of a letter delivered by a district messenger at noon yesterday."

"Where is this letter?"

"I have reason to believe that the general locked it in a dispatch box which he brought with him."

"Did he comment upon the letter?"

"No."

"In what name was it addressed?"

"Mr Victor."

Nayland Smith began to pace the carpet, and every time he passed the settee where that grim body lay, the right arm hanging down so that half-closed fingers touched the floor, his shadow, moving across the ghastly, greenish face, created an impression that the features worked and twitched and became still again.

"Did he make many telephone calls?"

"Quite a number."

"From the instrument on the desk there?"

"Yes—it is an extension from the hallway."

"Have you a record of those whom he called?"

24

"Of some. Inspector Leighton has already made that inquiry. There were two long conversations with Rome, several calls to Sir James Clare and some talks with his own embassy."

"But others you have been unable to check?"

"The inspector is at work on that now, I understand, Sir Denis. There was—er—a lady."

"Indeed? Any incoming calls?"

"Very few."

"I remember—the inspector told me he was trying to trace them. Any visitors?"

"Sir James Clare yesterday morning, Count Bruzzi at noon today—and, oh yes, a lady last night."

"What! A lady?"

"Yes."

"What was her name?"

"I have no idea, Sir Denis. She came just after dusk in a car which waited outside, and sent a sealed note in by Greaves. I may say that at the request of the general I was almost continuously at work in the library, so that no one could gain access without my permission. This note was handed to me."

"Was anything written on the envelope?"

"Yes: 'Personal—for Mr Victor.' I took it to him. He was then seated at the desk writing. He seemed delighted. He evidently recognised the handwriting. Having read the message, he instructed me to admit the visitor."

"Describe her," said Nayland Smith.

"Tall and slender, with fine eyes, very long and narrow—definitely not an Englishwoman. She had graceful and languid manners, and remarkable composure. Her hair was jet black and closely waved to her head. She wore jade earrings and was wrapped up in what I assumed to be a very expensive fur coat."

"H'm!" murmured Nayland Smith, "can't place her, unless" – and a startled expression momentarily crossed his brown features – "the dead are living again!"

"She remained in the study with the general for close upon an hour. Their voices sounded animated, but of course I actually overheard nothing of their words. Then the door was opened and they both came out. I rang for Greaves, the general conducted his visitor as far as the end of the library and Greaves saw her down to her car."

"What occurred then? Did the general seem to be disturbed in any way? Unusually happy or unusually sad?"

"He was smiling when he returned to the study, which he did immediately, going in and closing the door."

"And today, Count Bruzzi?"

"Count Bruzzi lunched with him. There have been no other visitors."

"Phone calls?"

"One at half past seven. It was immediately after this that General Quinto came out and told me that you were expected, Sir Denis, between ten and eleven, and were to be shown immediately into the study."

"Yes. I was recalled from Berlin for this interview which now cannot take place. This brings us, Mr Bascombe, to the ghastly business of tonight."

"The general and I dined alone in the library, Greaves waiting."

"Did you both eat the same dishes and drink the same wine?"

"We did. Your suspicions are natural, Sir Denis, but such a solution of the mystery is impossible. It was a plain and typically English dinner—a shoulder of lamb with mint sauce, peas and new potatoes. Greaves carved and served. Followed by apple tart and cream of which we both partook, then cheese and young radishes. We shared a bottle of claret. That was our simple meal."

Nayland Smith had begun to walk up and down again. Mr Bascombe continued:

"I went out for an hour after dinner. During my absence General Quinto received a telephone call and afterwards complained to Greaves that there was something wrong with the extension to the study—that he had found difficulty in making himself audible. Greaves informed him that the post office was aware of this defect and that an engineer was actually coming along at the moment to endeavour to rectify it. As a matter of fact the man was here when I returned."

"Where was the general?"

"Reading in the library, outside. The man assured me that the instrument was now in order, made a test call and General Quinto returned to the study and closed the door. I remained in the library."

"What time was this?"

"As nearly as I can remember, a quarter to ten."

"Yes, go on."

"I sat at the library table writing personal letters, when I heard Greaves in the hall outside putting a call through to the general in the study. I heard General Quinto answer it, dimly at first, then more clearly. He seemed to be shouting into the receiver. Presently he came out in a state of some excitement—he was, I may add, a very irascible man. He said: 'That fool has made the instrument worse. The lady to whom I was speaking could not hear a word.'

"Realising that it was too late to expect the post office to send anyone again tonight, I went into the study and tested the instrument myself."

"But," snapped Nayland Smith, "did you observe anything unusual in the atmosphere of the room?"

"Yes—a curious odour, which still lingers here as a matter of fact."

"Good! Go on."

"I put a call through to a friend in Chelsea and was unable to detect anything the matter with the line."

"It was perfectly clear?"

"Perfectly. I suggested to the general that possibly the fault was with his friend's instrument and not with ours. I then returned to the library. He was in an extraordinarily excited condition—kept glancing at his watch and inquiring why *you* had not arrived. Some ten minutes later he threw the door open and came out again. He said: 'Listen!'

"I stood up and we both remained quite silent for a moment.

"'Did you hear it?' he asked.

"'Hear what, General?' I replied.

"'Someone beating a drum!'"

"Stop!" snapped Smith. "Those were his exact words?"

"His exact words . . . 'Surely you can hear it?' he said. 'An Arab drum—what they call a darabukkeh. Listen again.'

"I listened, but on my word of honour could hear nothing whatever. I assured the general of this. His face was inflamed and he

27

remained very excited. He went in and slammed the door—but I had scarcely seated myself before he was out again.

"'Mr Bascombe' he shouted (as you probably know he spoke perfect English), 'someone is trying to frighten me! But by heavens they won't! Come into the study. Perhaps you will hear it there!'

"I went into the study with him, now seriously concerned. He grasped my arm—his hand was trembling. 'Listen!' he said, 'it's coming nearer—the beating of a drum—'

"Again I listened for some time. Finally: 'I'm sorry, General,' I had to say, 'but I can hear nothing whatever beyond the usual sounds of distant traffic.'

"The incident had greatly disturbed me. I didn't like the look of the general. This talk of drums was unpleasant and uncanny. He asked again what on earth had happened to you, Sir Denis, but declined my suggestion of a game of cards, so that again I left him and returned to the library. I heard him walking about for a time and then his footsteps ceased. Once I heard him cry out: 'Stop those drums!' Then I heard no more."

"Had he referred to the curious odour?"

"He said: 'Someone wearing a filthy perfume has been in this room.' At about twenty to eleven, as he had become quite silent, I rapped on the door, opened it and went in." He turned shudderingly in the direction of the settee: "I found him as you see him."

"Was he dead?"

"So far as I was able to judge, he was.'

28

The girl outside

To that expression of agonised surprise upon the dead man's face was now added, almost momentarily, a deepening of the greenish tinge. A fingerprint expert and a photographer from Scotland Yard had come and gone. After a longish interview, Nayland Smith had released Lord Moreton and Dr Sims. He put a call through on the desk telephone which General Quinto had found defective. Smith found it in perfect order. He examined the adjoining bedroom and the bathroom beyond and pointed out that it was just possible, although there was no evidence to confirm the theory, that someone might have entered through the bathroom window during the time that the general was alone in the study.

"I don't think that's how it was done," he said, "but it is a possibility. This dispatch box must be opened, and if Mr Bascombe can't find the key we must force it. In the meantime, Kerrigan, you have a nose for news. I have observed that quite a number of people remain outside the house. Slip out the back way, go around and join the crowd. Ask stupid questions and study every one of them. It would not surprise me to learn that there is someone there waiting to hear of the success or failure of tonight's plot."

'Then you are satisfied that General Quinto was—murdered?"

"Entirely satisfied, Kerrigan."

When presently I came out into the square I found that Lord Moreton's car had gone. Smith's, that of the home secretary and a Yard car were still standing there. Ten or twelve people were hanging about, attracted by that almost psychic awareness of tragedy which ahead of radio or newspaper in some mysterious way creeps through.

I examined them all carefully and selected several for conversation. Apart from the fact that they had heard that "something had happened," I gathered little news of value.

Then standing apart from the main group, I saw a girl.

This was a dark night but suddenly the house door was opened to admit someone who had driven up in a taxi. In the light from the doorway, I had a glimpse of her face. She was dressed like a working girl, wearing a light raincoat which, however, did not disguise the lines of her slim, trim figure. She wore a brown beret. But her face, as the light shone fully upon it, was so really lovely—a word which rarely can be applied—that I was astonished. In the shadows she looked like a brunette; in the swift light I saw red glints in her tightly waved hair beneath the beret, exquisitely modelled features, lips parted in what I can only describe as an expectant smile. She turned and stared at the departing taxi as I strolled in her direction.

"Any idea what's going on here?" I asked casually.

She raised her eyes in a startled way (they were wonderful eyes of a most unusual colour; they set me thinking of amethysts) keeping her hands tucked in the pockets of her coat.

"Someone told me"—she spoke broken English—"that something terrible had happened in this house."

"Really! I couldn't make out what the crowd was about. So that's it! Who's the owner of the house? Do you know?"

"Someone told me Sir Malcolm Locke."

"Oh yes—he writes books, doesn't he?"

"I don't know. They told me Sir Malcolm Locke."

She glanced up again and smiled. She had a most adorable, provocative smile. I could not place her, but I thought that with that face and figure she might be a mannequin or perhaps a show girl in a cabaret.

"Do you know Sir Malcolm Locke?" she asked, suddenly growing serious.

"No"—her change of manner had quite startled me—"except by name."

"May I speak truly to you? You look"—she hesitated—"sensible." There was a caressing note in her voice. "I know someone who is in that house. Do you understand?"

Nayland Smith had made the right move. Here was a spy of the enemy. Whatever my personal predilection, this charming young lady should be in the hands of Detective Inspector Leighton without delay.

"That's very interesting. Who is it?"

"Just someone I know. You see"—she laid her hand on my arm, and inclined ever so slightly towards me—"I saw you come out of the side entrance! You know—and so, if you please, tell me. What has happened in that house?"

Satisfied that I should not let her out of my sight:

"A gentleman known as Mr Victor has died."

"He is dead?"

"Yes."

Her slim fingers closed on my arm with a surprisingly strong grip.

"Thank you." Dark lashes were raised; she flashed up at me an enigmatical glance. "Good night!"

"Just a moment!" I grasped her wrist. "Please don't run away so quickly."

At which she lifted her voice:

"Let me go! How dare you! Let me go!"

Two men detached themselves from the group of loiterers and dashed in our direction. But the behaviour of my beautiful captive, who was struggling violently, was certainly remarkable. Pressing her lips very close to my ear:

"Please let me go!" she whispered. "They will kill you. Let me go! It's no use!"

I released her and turned to meet the attack of two of the most ferocious-looking ruffians I had ever encountered. They were of Mongolian type with an incredible shoulder span in proportion to their height. I had noticed them in the group about the door but had not seen their faces. Viewed from the rear with their glossy black hair they might have been a pair of waiters from some neighbouring hotel. Seen face to face they were altogether more formidable.

The first on the scene feinted and then by a trick, which fortunately I knew, tried to kick me off my feet. I stepped back. The second was upon me. Other loiterers were surrounding us now and I knew that I was on the unpopular side. But I threw discretion to the winds. Until I could turn my face from these two enemies I had no means of knowing what had become of the girl. I led off with a straight left against my second opponent.

He ducked it perfectly. The first sprang behind me and seized my ankles. The house door was thrown open and Inspector Leighton raced down the steps. Fey came up at the double, so did the driver of the police car. The attack ceased. I spun around, and saw the black-haired men sprinting for the corner.

"After that pair," cried Leighton gruffly. "Don't lose 'em!"

The police driver and Fey set out.

"'E was maulin' 'er about!" growled one of the loiterers. "They was in the right. I 'eard 'er cry out."

But the girl with the amethyst eyes had vanished. . .

Three notices

"She has got clear away," said Nayland Smith, "thanks to her bodyguard."

We stood in the library, Smith, myself, Mr Bascombe and Inspector Leighton. Sir James Clare was seated in an armchair watching us. Now he spoke:

"I understand, Smith, why General Quinto came from Africa to the house of his old friend, secretly, and asked me to recall you for a conference. This is a very deep-laid scheme. You are the only man who might have saved him—"

"But I failed."

Nayland Smith spoke bitterly. He turned and stared at me.

"It appears, Kerrigan, that your charming acquaintance who so unfortunately has escaped—I am not blaming you—differs in certain details from Mr Bascombe's recollections of the general's visitor. However, it remains to be seen if they are one and the same."

"You see," the judicial voice of the home secretary broke in, "it is obviously impossible to hush this thing up. A postmortem examination is unavoidable. We don't know what it will reveal. The fact that a very distinguished man, of totally different political ideas from our own, dies here in London under such circumstances is calculated to produce international results. It's deplorable—it's horrible. I cannot see my course clearly."

"Your course, Sir James," snapped Nayland Smith, "is to go home. I will call you early in the morning." He turned. "Mr Bascombe, decline all information to the press."

"What about the dead man, sir?" Inspector Leighton interpolated.

"Remove the body when the loiterers have dispersed. Report to me in the morning, Inspector."

It was long past midnight when I found myself in Sir Denis' rooms in Whitehall. I had not been there for some time, and from my chair I stared across at an unusually elaborate radio set with a television equipment.

"Haven't much leisure for amusement, myself," said Smith, noting the direction of my glance. "Television I had installed purely to amuse Fey! He is a pearl above price, and owing to my mode of life is often alone here for days and nights."

Standing up, I began to examine the instrument. At which moment Fey came in.

"Excuse me, sir," he said, "electrician from firm requests no one touch until calls again, sir."

Fey's telegraphic speech had always amused me. I nodded and sat down, watching him prepare drinks. When he went out:

"Our return journey was quite uneventful," I remarked. "Why?"

"Perfectly simple," Smith replied, sipping his whisky and soda and beginning to load his pipe. "My presence tonight threatened to interfere with the plot, Kerrigan. The plot succeeded. I am no longer of immediate interest."

"I don't understand in the least, Smith. Have you any theory as to what caused General Quinto's death?"

"At the moment, quite frankly, not the slightest. That indefinable perfume is of course a clue, but at present a useless clue. The autopsy may reveal something more. I await the result with interest."

"Assuming it to be murder, what baffles me is the purpose of the thing. The general's idea that he could hear drums rather suggests a guilty conscience in connection with some action of his in Africa—a private feud of some kind."

"Reasonable," snapped Smith, lighting his pipe and smiling grimly. "Nevertheless, wrong."

"You mean"—I stared at him—"that although you don't know *how*—you do know *why* General Quinto was murdered?"

He nodded, dropping the match in an ash tray.

"You know of course, Kerrigan, that Quinto was the right-hand man of Pietro Monaghani. His counsels might have meant an international war."

"It hangs on a hair I agree, and I suppose that Quinto, as Monaghani's chief adviser, might have precipitated a war—"

"Yes—undoubtedly. But what you don't know (nor did I until tonight) is this: General Quinto had left Africa on a mission to

34

Spain. If he had gone I doubt if any power on earth could have preserved international peace! One man intervened."

"What man?"

"If you can imagine Satan incarnate—a deathless spirit of evil dwelling in an ageless body—a cold intelligence armed with knowledge so far undreamed of by science—you have a slight picture of Doctor Fu Manchu."

In my ignorance I think I laughed.

"A name to me—a bogey to scare children. I had never supposed such a person to exist."

"Scotland Yard held the same opinion at one time, Kerrigan. But you will remember the recent suicide of a distinguished Japanese diplomat. The sudden death of Germany's foremost chemist, Erich Schaffer, was front-page news a week ago. Now—General Quinto."

"Surely you don't mean—"

"Yes, Kerrigan, the work of one man! Others thought him dead, but I have evidence to show that he is still alive. If I had lacked such evidence—I should have it now. I forced the general's dispatch box, we failed to find the key. It contained three sheets of note paper— nothing else. Here they are." He handed them to me. "Read them in the order in which I have given them to you."

I looked at the top sheet. It was embossed with a hieroglyphic which I took to be Chinese. The letter, which was undated, was not typed, but written in a squat, square hand. This was the letter:

First notice

The Council of Seven of the Si-Fan has decided that at all costs another international war must be averted. There are only fifteen men in the world who could bring it about. You are one of them. Therefore, these are the Council's instructions: You will not enter Spain but will resign your commission immediately, and retire to your villa in Capri.

PRESIDENT OF THE SEVEN

I looked up.

"What ever does this mean?"

"I take it to mean," Smith replied, "that the first notice which you have read was received by General Quinto in Africa. I knew him,

35

and he knew—as every man called upon to administer African or Asiatic people knows—that the Si-Fan cannot be ignored. The Chinese Tongs are powerful, and there is a widespread belief in the influence of the Jesuits; but the Si-Fan is the most formidable secret society in the world: fully twenty-five per cent of the coloured races belong to it. However, he did not resign his commission. He secured leave of absence and proceeded to London to consult *me.* Somewhere on the way he received the second notice. Read it, Kerrigan."

I turned to the second page which bore the same hieroglyphic and a message in that heavy, definite handwriting. This was the message:

Second notice
The Council of Seven of the Si-Fan would draw your attention to the fact that you have not resigned your commission. Failing your doing so, a third and final notice will be sent to you.
PRESIDENT OF THE SEVEN

I turned to the last page; it was headed *Third Notice* and read as follows:

You have twenty-four hours.
PRESIDENT OF THE SEVEN

"You see, Kerrigan," said Nayland Smith, "it was this third notice"—which must have reached him by district messenger at Sir Malcolm's house—"which produced that state of panic to which Bascombe referred. The Council of Seven have determined to avert war. Their aim must enlist the sympathy of any sane man. But there are fourteen other men now living, perhaps misguided, whose lives are in danger. I have made a list of some of those whose removal in my opinion would bring at least temporary peace to the world. But it's my job at the moment to protect them!"

"Have you any idea of the identity of this Council of Seven?"

"The members are changed from time to time."

"But the president?"

"The president is Doctor Fu Manchu! I would give much to know where Doctor Fu Manchu is tonight—"

And almost before the last syllable was spoken a voice replied:

"No doubt you would like a word with me, Sir Denis . . ."

For once in all the years that I knew him, Smith's iron self-possession broke down. It was then he came to his feet as though a pistol shot and not a human voice had sounded. A touch of pallor showed under the prominent cheekbones. Fists clenched, a man amazed beyond reason, he stared around.

I, too, was staring—at the television screen.

It had become illuminated. It was occupied by an immobile face—a wonderful face—a face that might have served as model for that of the fallen angel. Long, narrow eyes seemed to be watching me. They held my gaze hypnotically.

A murmur, wholly unlike Smith's normal tones, reached my ears . . . it seemed to come from a great distance.

"Good God! *Fu Manchu*!"

Satan incarnate

I can never forget those moments of silence which followed the appearance of that wonderful evil face upon the screen.

The utterly mysterious nature of the happening had me by the throat, transcending as it did anything which I could have imagined. I was prepared to believe Dr Fu Manchu a wizard—a reincarnation of some ancient sorcerer; Apollonius of Tyana reborn with the fires of hell in his eyes.

"If you will be so good, Sir Denis"—the voice was sibilant, unemotional, the thin lips barely moved—"as to switch your lights off, you will find it easier to follow me. Just touch the red button on the right of the screen and I shall know that you have complied."

That Nayland Smith did so was a fact merely divined from an added clarity in that image of the Chinese doctor, for I was unaware of any movement, indeed, of any presence other than that of Fu Manchu.

The image moved back, and I saw now that the speaker was seated in a carved chair.

"This interesting device," the precise, slightly hissing voice continued, "is yet in its infancy. If I intruded at a fortunate moment, this was an accident—for I am unable to hear you. Credit for this small contribution belongs to one of the few first-class mechanical brains which the West has produced in recent years."

I felt a grip upon my shoulders. Nayland Smith stood beside me.

"He was at work upon the principle at the time of his reported death! . . . He has since improved upon it in my laboratories."

Only by a tightening of Smith's grip did I realize the fact that this, to me, incomprehensible statement held a hidden meaning.

"I find it useful as a means of communication with my associates, Sir Denis. I hope to perfect it. Do not waste your time trying to trace the mechanic who installed it. My purpose in speaking to you was this: You have recently learned the distressing details concerning the death of General Quinto. Probably you know that he complained of a sound of drums just before the end—a characteristic symptom . . ."

The uncanny speaker paused—bent forward—I lost consciousness of everything save of his eyes and of his voice.

"My drums, Sir Denis, will call to others before I shall have satisfied the fools in power today that I, Fu Manchu and I alone, hold the scales in my hand. I ask you to join me now—for my enemies are your enemies. Consider my words—consider them deeply."

Smith did not stir, but I could hear his rapid breathing.

"You would not wish to see the purposeless slaughter in Spain, in China, carried into England? Think of that bloody farce called the Great War!" A vibrating guttural note had entered into the unforgettable voice. "I, who have had some opportunities of seeing you in action, Sir Denis, know that you understand the rules of boxing. Your objectives are the heart and the point of the jaw: you strike to paralyse brain and blood supply. That is how *I* fight. I strike at those who cause, at those who direct, at those who aid war—at the brain and at the heart, not at the arms, the shoulders—the deluded masses who suffer and die in order that arrogant fools may be gratified, that profiteers may grow fat. Consider my words . . ."

Dr Fu Manchu's eyes now were opened widely. They beckoned, they called to me . . .

"Steady, Kerrigan."

Darkness. The screen was blank.

A long time seemed to elapse before Nayland Smith spoke, before he stirred, then:

"I have seen that man being swept to the verge of Niagara Falls!" he said, speaking hoarsely out of the darkness. " I prayed that he had met a just fate. The body of his companion—a maddened slave of his will—was found."

"But not Fu Manchu! How could he have escaped?"

Smith moved—switched up the light. I saw how the incident had affected him, and it gave me courage; for the magnetism of those eyes, of that voice, had made me feel a weakling.

"One day, Kerrigan, perhaps I shall know."

He pressed a bell. Fey came in.

"This television apparatus is not to be used, not to be touched by anyone, Fey."

Fey went out.

I took up my glass, which remained half filled.

"This has staggered me," I confessed. "The man is more than human. But one thing I *must* know: what did he mean when he spoke of someone—I can guess to whom he referred—who died recently but who, since his death, has been at work in Fu Manchu's laboratories?"

Smith turned on his way to the buffet; his eyes glittered like steel.

"Were you ever in Haiti?"

"No."

"Then possibly you have never come across the ghastly tradition of the *zombie*?"

"Never."

"A human corpse, Kerrigan, taken from the grave and by means of sorcery set to work in the cane fields. Perhaps a Negro superstition, but Doctor Fu Manchu has put it into practice."

"What!"

"I have seen men long dead and buried labouring in his workshops!"

He squirted soda water into a tumbler.

"You were moved, naturally, by the words and by the manner of, intellectually, the greatest man alive. But forget his sophistry, forget his voice—above all, forget his eyes. Doctor Fu Manchu is Satan incarnate."

"Inspector Gallaho reports"

In the days that followed I thought many times about those words, and one night I dreamed of beating drums and woke in a nameless panic. The morning that followed was lowering and gloomy. A fine drizzling rain made London wretched.

When I stood up and looked out of the window across Hyde Park I found the prospect in keeping with my reflections. I had been working on the extraordinary facts in connection with the death of General Quinto and trying to make credible reading of the occurrence in Nayland Smith's apartment later the same night. All that I had ever heard or imagined about Dr Fu Manchu had been brought into sharp focus. I had sometimes laughed at the Germanic idea of a superman, now I knew that such a demigod, and a demigod of evil, actually lived.

I read over what I had written. It appeared to me as a critic that I had laid undue stress upon the haunting figure of the girl with the amethyst eyes. But whenever my thoughts turned, and they turned often enough, to the episodes of that night those wonderful eyes somehow came to the front of the picture.

London and the Home Counties were being combed by the police for the mysterious broadcasting station controlled by Dr Fu Manchu. A post-mortem examination of the general's body had added little to our knowledge of the cause of death. Inquiries had failed also to establish the identity of the general's woman friend who had called upon him on the preceding day.

The figure of this unknown woman tortured my imagination. Could it be, could it possibly be the girl to whom I had spoken out in the square?

I ordered coffee, and when it came I was too restless to sit down. I walked about the room carrying the cup in my hand. Then I heard the doorbell and heard Mrs Merton, my daily help, going down. Two minutes later Nayland Smith came in, his lean features wearing that expression of eagerness which charac-

41

terised him when he was hot on a trail, his grey eyes very bright. He nodded, and before I could speak:

"Thanks! A cup of coffee would be just the thing," he said.

Peeling off his damp raincoat and dropping it on the floor, he threw his hat on top of it, stepped to my desk and began to read through my manuscript. Mrs Merton bringing another cup, I poured his coffee out and set it on the desk. He looked up.

"Perhaps a little undue emphasis on amethyst eyes," he said slyly.

I felt myself flushing.

"You may be right, Smith," I admitted. "In fact I thought the same myself. But you see, you haven't met her—I have. I may as well be honest. Yes! She did make a deep impression upon me."

"I am only joking, Kerrigan. I have even known the symptoms." He spoke those words rather wistfully. "But this is very sudden!"

"I agree!" and I laughed. "I know what you think, but truly, there was some irresistible appeal about her."

"If, as I suspect, she is a servant of Doctor Fu Manchu, there would be. He rarely makes mistakes."

I crossed to the window.

"Somehow I can't believe it."

"You mean you don't want to?" As I turned he dropped the manuscript on the desk. "Well, Kerrigan, one thing life has taught me—never to interfere in such matters. You must deal with it in your own way."

"Is there any news?"

He snapped his fingers irritably.

"None. The man who came to Sir Malcolm Locke's house to adjust the telephone did not come from the post office, but unfortunately he can't be traced. The fellow who came to my flat to fix the television set did not come from the firm who supplied it—but he also cannot be traced! And so, you see—"

He paused suddenly as my phone bell began to ring. I took up the receiver.

"Hello—yes? . . . He is here." I turned to Smith. "Inspector Gallaho wants you."

He stepped eagerly forward.

"Hello! Gallaho? Yes—I told Fey to tell you I was coming on here.

What's that!—What?" His voice rose on a high note of excitement. "Good God! What do you say? Yes—details when I see you. What time does the train leave? Good! Coming now."

He replaced the receiver and turned. His face had grown very stern. Here was a sudden change of mood.

"What is it?"

"Fu Manchu has struck again. We have just twenty minutes to catch the train. Come on!"

"But where are we going?"

"To a remote corner of the Essex marshes."

In the Essex marshes

A depressing drizzle was still falling when amid semi-gloom I found myself stepping out of a train at a station on one of those branch lines which intersect the map of Essex. A densely wooded slope arose on the north. It seemed in some way to bear down oppressively on the little station, as though at any moment it might slip forward and crush it.

"Gallaho is a good man to have in charge," said Nayland Smith. "A stoat on a scent and every whit as tenacious."

The chief detective inspector was there awaiting us—a thickset, clean-shaven man of florid colouring and truculent expression, buttoned up in a blue overcoat and having a rather wide-brimmed bowler hat, very wet, jammed tightly upon his head. With him was a uniformed officer who was introduced as Inspector Derbyshire of the Essex Constabulary. Greetings over: "This is an ugly business," said Gallaho, speaking through clenched teeth.

"So I gather," said Nayland Smith rapidly. "We can talk on the way. I'm afraid you'll have to ride in front with the driver, Kerrigan."

Gallaho nodded and presently, in a police car which stood outside the station, we were on our way. It was a longish drive, mostly through narrow, muddy lanes. At last, on the outskirts of a village through which ran a little stream, we pulled up. A constable was standing outside a barnlike structure, separated by a small meadow, from the nearest cottage. He was a sinister-looking man who harmonised with his surroundings and whose jet-black eyebrows joined in the middle to form one continuous whole. He saluted as we stepped down, unlocked the barn door and led the way in. In spite of the disheartening weather a group of idlers hung about staring vacantly at the gloomy building.

"Not a pleasant sight, sir," Inspector Derbyshire warned us as he removed a sheet from something which lay upon a trestle table.

It was the body of a man wearing a tweed jacket and open-neck shirt, flannel trousers and thick-soled shoes: the equipment, I thought, of a hiker. All his garments—from which water dripped—were horribly stained with blood, and his face was characterised by an unnatural pallor.

I checked an exclamation of horror when I realised that he had died of a wound which appeared nearly to have severed his head from his body!

"Right across the jugular," Gallaho muttered, staring down savagely at the victim of this outrage.

He began to chew vigorously, although as I learned later he used no gum; it was merely an unusual ruminatory habit.

"Good God!" Nayland Smith whispered. "Good God! No doubt of the cause of death here! Thank you, Inspector. Cover the poor fellow up. The surgeon has seen him, of course?"

"Yes. He estimated that he had been dead for six or seven hours. But I left him just as we found him for you to see."

"He was hauled out of the river, I'm told?"

"Yes—half a mile from here. The body was jammed in under the branches of an overhanging willow."

"Who found it?"

"A gipsy called Barnett who was gathering rushes. He and his family are basket makers."

"When was that?"

"Ten-thirty, sir," Inspector Derbyshire replied. "I got straight through to Inspector Gallaho; he arrived an hour later. Doctor Bridges saw the body at eleven."

"Why did you call Scotland Yard?"

"I recognised him at once. He had reported to me yesterday morning—"

"As I told you, sir," Gallaho's growling voice broke in, "he was a bit after your time at the Yard. But Detective Sergeant Hythe was one of my most promising juniors. He was working under me. He was down here looking for the secret radio station. B.B.C. engineers had noticed interference from time to time and they finally narrowed it down to this end of Essex."

We came out of the barn and the constable locked the door behind us. Smith turned and stared at Gallaho.

"It looks," Gallaho added, "as though poor Hythe had got too near to the heart of the mystery."

"If you'll just step across to the constable's cottage, sir, I want you to see the few things that were found on the dead man," said Inspector Derbyshire.

As we walked along the narrow village street to the modest police headquarters the group of locals detached themselves from the barn and followed us at a discreet distance. Nayland Smith glanced back over his shoulder.

"No one of interest there, Kerrigan!" he snapped.

Laid out upon a table in the sitting room I saw a Colt automatic, an electric flashlamp and a Yale key.

"There wasn't another thing on him!" said Inspector Derbyshire. "Yet I know for a fact that he carried a knapsack and a stick. He was smoking a pipe, too; and he asked me for the name of a cottage where he could spend a night, quiet-like, in the neighbourhood."

Smith was staring at the exhibits.

"This key," he remarked, "is the most significant item."

"I spotted that," growled Gallaho. "It's the key of an A.A. call box—and the nearest is at the crossroads by Woldham Forges, a mile or so from here."

"Smart work," snapped Smith. "What did this important discovery suggest to you?"

"It's plain enough. He had been watching during the night (if the doctor's right, he was murdered between four and five) and he'd found out something so important that he was making for the nearest phone to get assistance."

"Anything else?"

"That the phone nearest to whatever he'd discovered was at Woldham Forges—and that he was working from some base where he must have left his other belongings."

"What did you do?"

"We've made a house-to-house search, sir," Inspector Derbyshire replied. "It isn't very difficult about here. But we can't find where he spent the night."

Nayland Smith gazed out of the window. Several loiterers were hanging about, but the arrival of the constable now released from his duty as keeper of the morgue dispersed them.

"I shall want a big-scale map of the district," said Smith.

"At your service, sir!"

We all turned and stared. The sinister-looking constable was the speaker. But he was sinister no more. His remarkable eyebrows were raised in what I assumed to be an expression of enthusiasm. He was opening the drawer of a bureau.

"Constable Weldon," explained Inspector Derbyshire, "is an authority on this area. . ."

The hut by the creek

Ten minutes later I set out along a road running south by east. Nayland Smith had split up the available searchers in such a way that, the police station as centre, our lines of inquiry formed a rough star.

Sergeant Hythe's equipment certainly suggested that if he had come upon a clue and had decided to work from some point near by while covering it, an uninhabited building, any old barn or hut, might prove to be the base selected.

Nayland Smith had some theory regarding the spot at which Hythe had been attacked and accordingly had set out for Woldham Forges.

My own instructions, based upon the encyclopaedic knowledge of the neighbourhood possessed by Constable Weldon, were simple enough. My first point was a timbered ruin, once the gatehouse of a considerable monastery long ago demolished. Half a mile beyond was an unoccupied cottage ("Haunted," Constable Weldon had said) in some state of dilapidation, but entrance could be effected through one of the broken windows. Finally, crossing a wooden bridge and bearing straight on, there was an old barn.

We had lunched hastily upon bread and cheese and onions and uncommonly flat beer . . .

The drizzling rain had ceased, giving place to a sort of Dutch mist which was even more unpleasant. I could see no further than five paces. My orders were so explicit, however, that I anticipated no difficulty; furthermore, I was provided with a flashlamp.

In the reedy marshes about me, wild fowl gave their queer calls. I heard a variety of notes, some of them unfamiliar, which told me that this was a bird sanctuary undisturbed for generations. Once a mallard flew croaking and flapping across my path and made me jump. The strange quality of some of those cries sounded eerily through the mist.

From a long way off, borne on a faint southerly breeze, came the sound of a steamer's whistle. I met never a soul, nor heard a sound of human presence up to the time that the ruined gatehouse loomed up in the gloom.

It was a relic of those days when great forests had stretched almost unbroken from the coast up to the portals of London, enshrined now in a perfect wilderness of shrubbery. I had no difficulty in obtaining entrance—the place was wide open. Decaying timbers supported a skeleton roof: here was poor shelter; and a brief but careful examination convinced me that no one had recently occupied it.

I stood for a moment in the gathering darkness listening to the notes of wild fowl. Once I caught myself listening for something else: the beating of a drum . . .

Then again I set out. I followed a narrow lane for the best part of half a mile. Ruts, but not recent ruts, combined to turn its surface into a series of muddy streamlets. At length, just ahead, I saw the cottage of ghostly reputation.

Mist was growing unpleasantly like certifiable fog, but I found the broken window and scrambled in. There was no evidence that anyone had entered the building for a year or more. It was a depressing place as I saw it by the light of the flashlamp. Some biblical texts were decaying upon one wall and in another room, among a lot of litter, I found a headless doll.

I was glad to get out of that cottage.

Greater darkness had come by the time I had regained the lane, and I paused in the porch to relight my pipe, mentally reviewing the map and the sergeant's instructions. Satisfied that the way was clear in my mind, I moved on.

Very soon I found myself upon a muddy path following the banks of a stream. I was unable to tell how much water the stream held, for it was thick with rushes and weeds. But presently as I tramped along I could see that it widened out into a series of reedy pools—and right ahead of me, as though the path had led to it, I saw a wooden hut.

I paused. This was not in accordance with the plan. I had made a mistake and lost my way. However, the place in front of me was apparently an uninhabited building, and pushing on I examined it with curiosity.

It was a roughly constructed hut, and I saw that it possessed a sort of crude landing stage overhanging the stream. The only visible entrance from the bank was a door secured by a padlock. The padlock proved to be unfastened. Some recollection of this part of Essex provided by the garrulous sergeant flashed through my mind. At one time these shallow streams running out into the wider estuary had been celebrated for the quality of the eels which came there in certain seasons. As I opened the door I knew that this was a former eel fisher's hut.

I shone a beam of light into the interior.

At first glance the place appeared to be empty, then I saw something . . . A recently opened sardine tin lay upon a ledge. Near it was a bottle bearing the label of a local brewer. And as I stepped forward and so obtained a better view I discovered in an alcove on the right of the ledge part of a loaf and a packet of butter.

My heart beat faster. By sheer accident I had found what I sought, for it seemed highly improbable from the appearance of the hut that this evidence had been left by anyone but Sergeant Hythe!

And now I made another discovery.

At one end of the place was what looked like a deep cupboard. Setting my lamp on the ledge I opened the cupboard— and what I saw clinched the matter.

There was a shelf about a foot up from the floor, and on it lay an open knapsack! I saw a clasp knife, a box of bar chocolate, a small tin of biscuits and a number of odds and ends which I was too excited to notice at the time—for, most extraordinary discovery of all, I saw a queer-looking hat surmounted by a coral bead.

At this I stared fascinatedly, and then taking it up, carried it nearer to the light. Its character was unmistakable.

It was a mandarin's cap!

And as I stared all but incredulously at this thing which I had found in a deserted hut on an Essex marsh, a faint movement made me acutely, coldly alert.

Someone was walking very quietly along the path outside . . .

What sounded like the booming call of a bittern came from over the marshes. The footsteps drew nearer. I stood still in an agony of indecision. Like a revelation the truth had come to me: We were searching for the base used by the murdered man. *Others* were searching, too. And this astounding piece of evidence which I held in my hand—this was the object of their search!

I knew from the nearness of the footsteps that retreat was impossible. Already I had selected my hiding place. What to do with the mandarin's cap was the only questionable point. I solved it quickly. I placed the cap upon the ledge littered with the remains of what had probably been poor Hythe's last meal, extinguished my flashlamp, crept into the cupboard and nearly closed the door...

The mandarin's cap

Through the chink of the opening I stared out. I wondered if the fact that I had left the door open would warn whoever approached that someone was inside. However, he might not be aware that it was ordinarily fastened. Closer and closer drew the footsteps on the muddy path; then the sound gave place to the swishing of long, wet grass, and I knew that the intruder was actually at the door.

What had seemed at first to be impenetrable darkness proved now to allow of some limited vision. Framed in the grey oblong of the doorway I saw a motionless figure.

So still it was in that small building that I wondered if the sound of my breathing might be audible. The booming cry sounded again from near at hand, and I questioned it, listening intently, wondering if it might have been simulated—a signal from some watcher covering the motionless figure framed in the doorway.

During the few seconds that elapsed in this way I managed to make out certain details. The new arrival wore a long raincoat and what looked like a black cap; also I saw leggings or riding boots. So much I had discovered, peering cautiously out, when a beam from an electric torch shot through the darkness, directed straight into the hut. Its light fell upon the mandarin's cap.

"*Ah!*" I heard.

That one exclamation revealed an astounding fact: the intruder was a girl!

She stepped in and crossed to the ledge. My heart began to beat irregularly. A queer mingling of fear and hope which had claimed me at the sound of her voice now became focussed in one huge indescribable emotion as I saw that pure profile, the clinging curls under the black cap, the outline, I thought, of a Greek goddess.

52

As I quietly slipped across to the open door and stood with my back to it, the girl turned in a flash—and I found myself looking into those magnificent eyes which had so strangely and persistently haunted me from the hour of that first brief meeting.

Their expression now in the light reflected from the ray of the torch, which moved unsteadily in her grasp, was compounded of fear and defiance. She was breathing rapidly, and I saw the glitter of white teeth through slightly parted lips.

Quite suddenly, it seemed, she recognised me. As I wore a soft-brimmed hat, perhaps my features were partly indistinguishable.

"You!" she whispered, "*you* again!"

"Yes," I said shortly. Now, although it had cost me an effort, I had fully mastered myself. "I again. May I ask what you are doing here?"

A hardness crept over her features; her lips set firmly. She put the torch down on the ledge beside her while I watched her intently, then:

"I might quite well ask you the same question," she replied, and her enchanting accent gave the words the value of music, I laughed, standing squarely in the doorway and watching her.

Wisps of fog floated between us.

"I am here because a man was brutally murdered last night— and here, on the ledge beside you, is the clue to his murderer."

"What are you talking about?" she asked quietly.

"Only about what I know."

"Suppose what you say is true, what has it to do with you?"

"It is every man's business to run down a murderer."

Her wonderful eyes opened more widely; she stared at me like a bewildered child—a pose, I told myself, perfectly acted.

"But I mean—what brings you here, to this place? You are not of the police."

"No, I am not 'of the police.' My name is Bart Kerrigan; I am a journalist by profession. Now I am going to ask you what brings *you* here to this place. What is your name?"

Her expression changed again; she lowered her lashes disdainfully.

"You could never understand and it does not matter. My name—

my name—would mean nothing to you. It is a name you have never heard before."

"All the more reason why I should hear it now."

Unwittingly I said the words softly, for as she stood there wrapped in that soiled raincoat, her little feet in muddy riding boots, I thought there could be no more desirable woman in the world.

"My name is Ardatha," she replied in a low voice.

"Ardatha! A charming name, but as you say one I have never heard before. To what country does it belong?"

Suddenly she opened her eyes widely.

"Why do you keep me here talking to you?" she flashed, and clenched her hand. "I will tell you nothing. I have as much right to be here as you. Please stand away from that door and let me go."

The demand was made imperiously, but unless my vanity invented a paradox her eyes were denying the urgency of her words.

"It is the duty of every decent Christian," I said, reluctantly forcing myself to face facts, "to detain any man or any woman belonging to the black organisation of which you are a member."

"Every Christian!" she flashed back. "I am a Christian. I was educated in Cairo."

"Coptic?"

"Yes, Coptic."

"But you are not a Copt!"

"Did I say I was a Copt?"

"You belong to the Si-Fan."

"You don't know what you are talking about. Even if I did, what then?"

I was drifting again and I knew it. The words came almost against my will:

"Do you understand what this society stands for? Do you know that they employ stranglers, garroters, poisoners, cutthroats, that they trade in assassination?"

"Is that so?" She was watching me closely and now spoke in a quiet voice. "And your Christian rulers, your rulers of the West—yes? What do *they* do? If the Si-Fan kills a man, that man is an active enemy. But when your Western murderers kill they kill men, women and children—hundreds—thousands who never harmed them—who never sought to harm anybody. My whole family—do you hear me?—my whole family, was wiped from life in one bombing raid. I alone escaped. General Quinto ordered that raid. You have seen what became of General Quinto . . ."

I felt the platform of my argument slipping from beneath my feet. This was the sophistry of Fu Manchu! Yet I hadn't the wit to answer her. The stern face of Nayland Smith seemed to rise up before me; I read reproach in the grey eyes.

"I think we've talked long enough," I said. "If you will walk out in front of me, we will go and discuss the matter with those able to decide between us."

She was silent for a moment, seeming to be studying my considerable bulk, firmly planted between herself and freedom.

"Very well." I saw the gleam of little white teeth as she bit her lip. "I am not afraid. What I have done I am proud to have done. In any case I don't matter. But bring the notebook it might help me if I am to be arrested."

"The notebook?"

She pointed to the open cupboard out of which I had stepped. I turned and saw in the dim light among the other objects which I have mentioned what certainly looked like a small notebook. Three steps and I had it in my hand.

But those three steps were fatal.

From behind me came a sound which I can only describe as a rush. I turned and sprang to the doorway. She was through—she must have reached it in one bound! The door was slammed in my face, dealing me a staggering blow on the forehead. I took a step back to hurl myself against it and heard the click of the padlock.

Undeterred, I dashed my weight against the closed door; but although old it was solid. The padlock held.

"Don't try to follow me!" I heard. "They will kill you if you try to follow me!"

I stood still, listening, but not the faintest sound reached my ears to inform me in which direction Ardatha had gone. Switching on my lamp I stared about the hut.

Yes, she had taken the mandarin's cap! I had shown less resource than a schoolboy! I had been tricked, outwitted by a girl not yet out of her teens, I judged. I grew hot with humiliation. How could I ever tell such a story to Nayland Smith?

The mood passed. I became cool again and began to search for some means of getting out. Barely glancing at the notebook, I thrust it into my pocket. That the girl had deliberately drawn my attention to it I did not believe. She had had no more idea than I what it was, but its presence had served her purpose. I could find nothing else of importance.

And now I set to work on the small shuttered window at the back of the ledge upon which those fragments of food remained. I soon had the shutter open, and as I had hoped, the window was unglazed. I climbed through on to a rickety landing stage and from there made my way around to the path. Here I stood stock still, listening.

One mournful boom of that strange solitary bird disturbed the oppressive silence, this and the whispering of reeds in a faint breeze. I could not recall ever to have found myself in a more desolate spot.

Fog was rapidly growing impenetrable.

At the Monks' Arms

I found myself mentally reviewing the ordnance map I had seen at the policeman's cottage, listening to the discursive instructions of the sinister but well-informed Constable Weldon.

"After you leave the cottage where old Mother Abel hanged herself"—a stubby finger moved over the map—"there's a path along beside a little stream. You don't take that"—I had —"you go straight on. This other road, bearin' left, would bring you to the Monks' Arms, one of the oldest pubs in Essex. Since the by-pass was made I don't know what trade is done there. It's kept by an old prize fighter, a Jerseyman, or claims to be; Jim Pallant they call him—a mighty tough customer; Seaman Pallant was his fightin' name. The revenue officers have been watchin' him for years, but he's too clever for 'em. We've checked up on him, of course. He seems to have a clean slate in this business . . ."

Visualising the map, I decided that the route back via the Monks' Arms was no longer than the other, and I determined to revive my drooping spirits before facing Nayland Smith. Licensed hours did not apply in my case for I was a "bonafide traveller" within the meaning of the act.

I set out on my return journey.

At one time I thought I had lost my way again, until presently through the gloom I saw a signboard projecting above a hedge, and found myself before one of those timbered hostelries of which once there were so many in their neighbourhood, but of which few remain today! I saw that the Monks' Arms stood on the bank of a stream.

I stepped into a stuffy bar. Low, age-blackened beams supported the ceiling; there were some prints of dogs and prize fighters; a full- rigged ship in a glass case. The place might have stood there when all but unbroken forest covered Essex. As a matter of fact though not so old as this, part of it actually dated back to the time of Henry VII.

There was no one in the barroom, dimly lighted by two paper-shaded lamps. In the bar I saw bottle-laden shelves, rows of mugs, beer engines. Beyond was an opening in which hung a curtain composed of strings of coloured rushes. Since no one appeared I banged upon the counter. This produced a sound of footsteps; the rush curtain was parted, and Pallant, the landlord, came out.

He was as fine a specimen of a retired prize fighter as one could hope to find, with short thick nose, slightly out of true, deep-set eyes and several battle scars. His rolled-up shirt sleeves revealed muscular forearms and he had all the appearance of being, as Constable Weldon had said, "a tough customer."

I called for a double scotch and soda.

"Traveller?"

"Yes. London."

He stared at me with his curiously unblinking deep-set brown eyes, then turned, tipped out two measures from an inverted bottle, squirted soda into the glass and set it before me. I paid, and he banged down my change on the counter. A cigarette drooping from his thick underlip he stood, arms folded, just in front of the rush curtain, watching me with that unmoving stare. I sipped my drink, and:

"Weather bad for trade?" I suggested.

He nodded but did not speak.

"I found you almost by accident. Lost my way. How far is it to the station?"

"What station?"

This was rather a poser, but:

"The nearest, of course," I replied.

"Mile and a half, straight along the lane from my door."

"Thanks." I glanced at my watch. "What time does the next train leave?"

"Where for?"

"London."

"Six-eleven."

I lingered over my drink and knocking out my pipe began to refill it. The unmoving stare of those wicked little eyes was vaguely disconcerting, and as I stood there stuffing tobacco into the hot bowl, a possible explanation occurred to me: Perhaps Pallant mistook me for a revenue officer!

"Is the fishing good about here?" I asked.

"No."

"You don't cater for fishermen then?"

"I don't."

Then with a final penetrating stare he turned, swept the rush curtain aside and went out. I heard his curiously light retreating footsteps.

As I had paid for my drink he evidently took it for granted that I should depart now, and clearly was not interested in the possibility that I might order another. However, I sat for a while on a stool, lighted my pipe and finished my whisky and soda at leisure. A moment later no doubt I should have left, but a slight, a very slight movement beyond the curtain drew my glance in that direction.

Through the strings of rushes, almost invisible, except that dim light from the bar shone upon her eyes, I saw a girl watching me. Nor was it humanly possible to mistake those eyes!

The formidable Jim Pallant was forgotten—everything was forgotten. Raising a flap in one end of the counter I stepped into the bar, crossed it and just as she turned to run along a narrow passage beyond, threw my arms around Ardatha!

"Let me go!" She struggled violently. "Let me go! I warned you, and you are mad—mad, to come here. For God's sake if you value your life, or mine, let me go!"

But I pulled her through the curtain into the dingy bar and held her firmly.

"Ardatha!" I spoke in a guarded, low voice. "God knows why you can't see what it means to be mixed up with these people, but I can, and I can't bear it. Listen! You have nothing, nothing in the world to fear. Come away! My friend who is in charge of the case will absolutely guarantee your safety. But please, please, come away with me now!"

She wore a silk pullover, riding breeches and the muddy boots which I remembered. Her slender body writhed in my grasp with all the agility of a captured eel.

One swift upward glance she gave me, a glance I was to remember many, many times, waking and sleeping. Then with a sudden unexpected movement she buried her wicked little teeth in my hand!

Pained and startled I momentarily released her. The reed curtain crackled as she turned and ran. I heard her pattering footsteps on an uncarpeted stair.

Clenching my fist I stood there undetermined what to do—until, realising that an uncommonly dangerous man for whom I might not prove to be a match was somewhere in the house, for once I chose discretion.

I was crossing to the barroom door when, heralded only by a crash of the curtain and a dull thud, Pallant vaulted *over* the counter behind me, twisted my right arm into the small of my back and locked the other in a hold which I knew myself powerless to break!

"I know your sort!" he growled in my ear. "Anyone that tries games with my guests goes the same way!"

"Don't be a fool!" I cried angrily as he hustled me out of the building. "I have met her before—"

"Well—she don't want to meet you again, and she ain't likely to!"

Down the three worn steps he ran me, and across the misty courtyard to the gate. He was heavier and undoubtedly more powerful than I, and ignominiously I was rushed into the lane.

"I've broke a man's neck for less," Pallant remarked.

I said nothing. The tone was very menacing.

"For two pins," he continued, "I'd chuck you in the river."

However, the gateway reached, he suddenly released his hold. Seizing me from behind by both shoulders, he gave me a shove which sent me reeling for three or four yards.

"Get to hell out of here!" he roared.

At the end of that tottering run I pulled myself up. What prompted the lunacy I really cannot say, except perhaps that a Rugby Blue doesn't enjoy being hustled out of the game in just that way.

I came about in one jump, ran in and tackled him low!

It was on any count a mad thing to do, but he wasn't expecting it. He went down beautifully, I half on top of him—but I was first up. As I stood there breathing heavily I was weighing my chances. And looking at the bull neck and span of shoulders, an uncomfortable conviction came that if Seaman Pallant decided to fight it out I was probably booked for a first-class hiding.

However, he did not move.

I watched him second after second, standing poised with clenched fists; I thought it was a trick. Still he did not move. Very cautiously, for I knew the man to be old in ringcraft, I approached and bent over him. And then I saw why he lay there.

A pool of blood was forming under his head. He had pitched on to the jagged edge of the gatepost—and was quite insensible!

For a long minute I waited, trying to find out if accidentally I had killed him. But satisfied that he was merely stunned, those counsels of insanity which I count to be hereditary, which are responsible for some of the tightest corners in which I have ever found myself, now prevailed.

Ardatha's dangerous bodyguard was out of the way. I might as well take advantage of the fact.

Turning, I ran back into the barroom, raised the flap, crossed the bar, and gently moving the rush curtain, stood again in the narrow passage. On my extreme right was a closed door; on the left, lighted by another of the paper-covered hanging lamps, I saw an uncarpeted staircase. I had heard Ardatha's footsteps going up those stairs, and now, treading softly, I began to mount.

That reek of stale spirits and tobacco smoke which characterised the bar was equally perceptible here. Two doors opened on a landing. I judged that on my left to communicate with a room overlooking the front of the Monks' Arms, and I recalled that as I returned from my encounter with Pallant I had seen no light in any of the windows on this side of the house. Therefore, creeping forward on tiptoe, I tried the handle of the other door.

It turned quite easily and a dim light shone out as I pushed the door open.

The room was scantily furnished: an ancient mahogany chest of drawers faced me as I entered and I saw some chairs of the same wood upholstered with horsehair. A lamp on an oval table afforded the only light, and at the far end of the room, which had a sloping ceiling, there was a couch or divan set under a curtained window.

Upon this a man was reclining, propped upon one elbow and watching me as I stood in the doorway ...

He wore a long black overcoat having an astrakhan collar, and upon his head a Russian cap, also of astrakhan. One slender hand

61

with extraordinarily long fingernails rested upon an outstretched knee; his chin was cupped in the other. He did not stir a muscle as I entered, but simply lay there watching me.

A physical chill of a kind which sometimes precedes an attack of malaria rose from the base of my spine and stole upwards. I seemed to become incapable of movement. That majestic, evil face fascinated me in a way I cannot hope to make clear. Those long, narrow, emerald-green eyes commanded, claimed, absorbed me. I had never experienced a sensation in my life resembling that which held me nailed to the floor as I watched the man who reclined upon the divan.

For this was the substance of that dreadful shadow I had seen on the screen in Nayland Smith's room . . . it was Dr Fu Manchu!

Dr Fu Manchu's bodyguard

Motionless I stood there staring at the most dangerous man in the world.

In that moment of realisation it was a strange fact that no idea of attacking him, of attempting to arrest him, crossed my mind. The complete unexpectedness of his appearance, a *danse macabre* which even in that sordid little room seemed to move behind him like a diabolical ballet devised by an insane artist, stupefied me.

The windows were closed and there was no sound, for how many seconds I cannot say. I believe that during those seconds my sensations were akin to the visions of a drowning man; I must in some way have accepted this as death.

I seemed to see and to hear Nayland Smith seeking for me, urgently calling my name. The whole pageant of my history joined and intermingled with a phantom army, invisible but menacing, which was the aura of Dr Fu Manchu. Dominating all was the taunting face of Ardatha, an unspoken appeal upon her lips; and the thought, like a stab of the spirit, that unquestionably Ardatha was the woman associated with the assassination of General Quinto, the willing accomplice of this Chinese monster, and a party to the murder of Sergeant Hythe.

Dr Fu Manchu did not move; the gaze of his unnatural green eyes never left my face. That bony hand with its long, highly polished nails lay so motionless upon the pile of the black coat that it might have been an ivory carving.

Then after those moments of stupefaction the spell broke. My duty was plain, my duty to Nayland Smith, to humanity at large. As quick resolve claimed my mind Dr Fu Manchu spoke:

"Useless, Mr Kerrigan." His thin lips barely parted. "I am well protected; in fact I was expecting you."

He bluffed wonderfully, I told myself; I plunged for my automatic.

"Stand still!" he hissed; "don't stir, you fool!"

And so tremendous was the authority in that sibilant voice, in the swiftly opened magnetic eyes, that even as my hand closed upon the weapon I hesitated.

"Now, slowly—very slowly, I beg of you, Mr Kerrigan— move your head to the left. You will see from what I have saved you!"

Strange it may sound, strange it appears to me now, but I obeyed, moving my head inch by inch. In that position, glancing out of the corner of my eye, I became again stricken motionless.

The blade of a huge curved knife resembling a sickle was being held motionless by someone who stood behind me, a hair's breadth removed from my neck! I could see the thumb and two fingers of a muscular brown hand which clutched the hilt. One backward sweep of such a blade would all but sever a man's head from his body. In that instant I knew how Sergeant Hythe had died.

"Yes"—Dr Fu Manchu's voice was soft again; and slowly, inch by inch, I turned as he began to speak—"that was how he died, Mr Kerrigan: your doubts are set at rest."

Even before the astounding fact that he had replied to an unspoken thought had properly penetrated, he continued:

"I regret the episode. It has seriously disarranged my plans: it was unnecessary and clumsily done—due to overzealousness on the part of one of my bodyguards. These fellows are difficult to handle. They are *Thugs*, members of a religious brotherhood specialising in murder—but long ago stamped out by the British authorities as any textbook will tell you. Nevertheless I find them useful."

I was breathing hard and holding myself so tensely that every muscle in my body seemed to be quivering. Dr Fu Manchu did not stir, his eyes were half closed again, but their contemplative gaze was terrifying.

"I can only suppose," I said, and the sound of my own voice muffled in the little room quite startled me, "that much learning has made you mad. What have you or your cause—if you have a cause—to gain by this indiscriminate murder? Let me draw your attention to the state of China, to which country I believe you belong. There is room there for your particular kind of activity."

This speech had enabled me somewhat to regain control of myself, but in the silence that followed I wondered how it would be accepted.

"My particular activities, Mr. Kerrigan, are at the moment directed to the correction of certain undesirable menaces to China. You are thinking of the armies who clash and vainly stagger to and fro in my country. I assure you that the real danger to China lies not within her borders, but outside. The surgeon seeks below the surface. Muscles are useless without nerves and brain. My concern is with nerves and brain. However, these details cannot interest you, as I fear you will not be in a position to impart them to Sir Denis Nayland Smith. Had your talents been outstanding I might have employed you—but they are not; therefore I have no use for you."

Following those softly spoken words came a high, guttural order.

A cloth was whipped over my mouth and secured before I fully realised what had happened. In less time than it takes to write of it I was lashed wrist and ankle by some invisible expert stationed behind me! The curved blade of the knife I could see out of the corner of my left eye.

Dr Fu Manchu never stirred a muscle.

I longed to cry out but could not. Another guttural order— and the blade disappeared. He who had held the knife stepped forward, and I saw a thick-set, yellow-faced man dressed in an ill-fitting blue suit. Immediately I recognised him for one of the pair who had attacked me on the night that I first saw and spoke to Ardatha. Although short of stature he was immensely powerful, and without ceremony he stooped, hoisted me upon his shoulder and carried me like a sack from the room!

My last impression was one of that dreadful, motionless figure upon the settee . . .

Down the stairs I was borne, helpless as a trussed chicken. Considering my weight it was an astonishing feat on the part of the man who performed it. Past the rush curtain of the bar we went and along the passage. Dread of my impending death was almost swamped by loathing of the blood-lustful creature who carried me. Another of Dr Fu Manchu's evil-faced thugs held a door open, and a damp smell, the ringing sound of footsteps on stone paving, told me that I was being taken down into the cellars. Something like a scream arose to my lips—but I stifled it, for I knew, not for the first time since I had met the Chinese doctor, stark terror's icy hand.

From those cellars I should never come out alive.

In the wine cellars

The cellars of the Monks' Arms were surprisingly equipped. They reminded me of those of a well-known speak-easy in New York which I had once explored. Beyond the cellar proper, the contents of which looked innocent enough, other cellars, altogether more extensive, lay concealed. By means of manipulating hidden locks seemingly solid walls could be opened.

In the light of a hurricane lamp carried by one of the Thugs, I saw casks of brandy and bins of French wines which certainly were never intended for the clièntele of the Monks' Arms. As Sergeant Weldon had more than hinted, this ancient inn was a smugglers' base. Its subterranean ramifications suggested that at some time the building above had been larger.

At what I judged to be the end of the labyrinth, I was carried up several well-worn steps into a long, rectangular room. I noticed a stout door set in the thickness of the wall, and then I was dumped unceremoniously upon the paving stones. The place contained nothing but lumber: broken fishing tackle, nets, empty casks, old furniture and similar odds and ends. Among these was the dismantled frame of a heavy iron bedstead. Hauling out what had been the headpiece—it had cross bars strong enough for a prison window—the two yellow men laid it on the floor and stretched me upon it.

From first to last they worked in silence.

Deftly they lashed me to the rusty bars until even slight movement became almost impossible and the pain was all I could endure. At first their purpose remained mysterious, then with a new pang of terror I recognised it . . .

Dr Fu Manchu was determined that a second body should not be found in the neighbourhood of the Monks' Arms. Secured to the heavy iron framework I was to be taken out and thrown into the river!

66

When at last the two had completed their task and one, standing up, raised the lantern from the floor, the horror of the fate which I felt was upon me reached such a climax that again I stifled a desire to scream for help. A sound, faint but just discernible, which came through a grating up in one corner of the wall, told me that the stream beside which the inn was built passed directly outside the door.

Perhaps I had little cause for it, but when the yellow men turned, and he carrying the lantern leading, went back by the way they had come, I experienced such a revulsion from despair to almost exultant optimism that I cannot hope to describe it.

I was still alive! My absence could not fail to result in a search party being sent out. My chances might be poor but my position was no longer desperate!

Why had I been left there?

Dr Fu Manchu's words allowed no room for doubt regarding his intention. Why then this delay? And—an even greater mystery— what had brought him to the Monks' Arms and why did he linger? Overriding my own peril, topping everything, was the maddening knowledge that if I could only communicate what I knew to Nayland Smith, it might alter the immediate history of the world.

Audacity is an outstanding characteristic of all great criminals, and that Dr Fu Manchu should calmly recline in that room upstairs while the district all about him was being combed for the murderer of Sergeant Hythe, illustrated the fact that he possessed it in full measure. The clue was perhaps to be found in his words that something had seriously disarranged his plans. I wondered feverishly if happy chance would lead Nayland Smith to the inn. Even so, and the thought made me groan, he would probably go away again never suspecting what the place contained!

Now came an answer to one of my questions—an answer which sent a new chill through my veins.

Dimly I heard the sound of oars. I knew that a boat was being pulled along the creek in the direction of the oak door close to which my head rested.

Of course I was to be transported to some spot where the water was deep, and thrown in there!

I listened eagerly, fearfully, to the creak of the nearing oars; and when I knew that the invisible boat had reached those steps which I divined to be beyond the door, I gave myself up for lost. But my calculations were at fault.

The boat passed on.

I could tell from the sound that an oar had been reversed and was being used as a punt pole. The swish of the rushes against the side of the craft was clearly discernible. I doubted if the little stream was navigable far above that point, but as those ominous sounds died away I knew at least that I had had a second reprieve.

Breathing was difficult because of the bandage over my mouth, and my heart was beating madly. Through the grating a sound reached me—that bumping and scraping which tells of someone entering or leaving a boat. Then I knew that poling had recommenced, but never once did I hear a human voice.

The boat was coming back. I heard the faint rattle of an oar set in a rowlock, the drip of water from the blade; but until the rower had crept past outside the oak door I doubt if I breathed again.

What did it all mean?

Someone, I reasoned, had been brought from the inn and was being rowed downstream to the larger river of which it was a tributary.

Dr Fu Manchu!

Yes, it must be. The monstrous Chinaman, having lain within the grasp of the law, almost under the very nose of Nayland Smith, was escaping!

I tugged impotently at my lashings, but the pain I suffered soon checked my struggles. In fact this, with the damp silence of the cellar and the difficulty which I experienced in breathing, now threatened to overcome me. Clenching my teeth, I fought against the weakness and lay still.

How long I lay it is impossible to say. Those moments of mental and physical agony seemed to stretch out each into an eternity, and then . . . .

I heard the boat returning.

This time there could be no doubt. Dr Fu Manchu had been smuggled away—doubtless to some larger craft which awaited him—and they were returning to deal with *me*.

Yes, I was right. I heard the boat grating against the stone steps, a stumbling movement and a key being inserted in the lock above and behind me. The door, which opened outward, was flung back. A draught of keen air swept into the cellar.

Shadowy, looking like great apes, the yellow men entered. One at my head and one at my feet, they lifted the iron framework to which I was lashed. I have an idea that I muttered a sort of prayer, but of this I cannot be certain, for there came an interruption so unexpected, so overwhelming, that I must have given way to my mental and physical agony. I remember little more.

A series of loud splashes, as though a number of swimmers had plunged into the water—the bumping and rolling of a boat—a rush of footsteps—a glare of light . . .

Finally, a voice—the voice of Nayland Smith:

"In you go, Gallaho! Don't hesitate to shoot!"

The Monks' Arms (concluded)

"All right, Kerrigan? Feeling better?"

I stared around me. I was lying on a sofa in a stuffy little sitting room which a smell of stale beer and tobacco smoke told me to be somewhere at the back of the bar of the Monks' Arms. I sat up and finished what remained of a glass of brandy which Smith was holding to my lips.

"Gad!" I muttered, "every muscle in my body will be stiff for twenty-four hours. It was mostly the pain that did it, Smith."

"Don't apologise," he returned drily, and looking at his blanched face as he stood beside me, I could read a deep anger in his eyes. "We were only just in time."

"Doctor Fu Manchu?"

He snapped his fingers irritably.

"A motor launch had crept up in the mist and his yellow demons got him aboard, only a matter of minutes before our arrival. Take it easy, Kerrigan; you can tell us your story later. I found this in your pocket, so I gather that you had succeeded where we failed." He held up the little notebook which I had found in the eel fisher's hut. "It tells the story of poor Hythe's last hours. It was traces of oil on the water that gave him the clue. He selected a hiding place which evidently you found, and watched from some point near by. He saw the motor craft arrive. It was met by a boat which belongs to the inn. Someone was rowed ashore. He seems to have waded or swum out to the deserted motor launch, and apparently he made a curious discovery—"

"He did." I stood up gingerly, to test my leg muscles. "He found a mandarin's cap."

"Good for you, Kerrigan. So he reports in his notes. He took this back to his hiding place as some evidence in case his quarry should escape him. His last entry says that the boat could only have been making for the Monks' Arms. The rest we have to surmise, but I think it is fairly easy."

He dropped the notebook back into his pocket.

"I assume that he crept up to the inn to learn the identity of the new arrival or arrivals. Having satisfied himself in some way, he then set out across country for the A.A. call box. Unfortunately he had been seen—and someone was following him. At a stone bridge which spans the stream the follower overtook him. Yes—I have found the bloodstains. As he received the fatal stroke he toppled over the parapet. A slow current carried his body down to the point at which it was found."

He ceased speaking and stood staring at me in a curious way. I was seated on the sofa, rubbing my aching leg muscles.

"There's one thing, Smith," I said, "for which I owe thanks to heaven. Whatever brought you to my rescue in the nick of time?"

"I was about to mention that," he snapped. "Someone called up the police (I had just returned from my visit to the scene of the crime) begging us to set out without a moment's delay—not for the inn itself, but for a stone boathouse which lies twenty yards further down the creek. We had come provided to break the door in, but as luck would have it, Constable Weldon, who was leading us, detected the sound made by those Thugs in the boat. You know the rest."

He continued to stare at me and I at him.

"Was it a man's voice?"

"No: a woman—a young woman."

A medley of emotions had me silent for a moment, and then:

"Did you find anyone here?"

"My party, with Gallaho, found the pair of Thugs, as you know. Inspector Derbyshire, who entered from the front, discovered the man Pallant bathing a deep cut in his forehead. There's a fellow who combines the duties of stablelad and bartender, but he's off duty . . . There was no one else."

"I am glad—although perhaps I shouldn't be."

After ten minutes' rest I was fit to move again.

Apart from the fact that the secret cellars were packed with contraband, nothing of value bearing upon the matter which had brought the police there was discovered in the Monks' Arms. Both yellow men remained imperturbably dumb. The ex-pugilist, under a gruelling examination by Chief Detective Inspector Gallaho, pleaded guilty to smuggling but denied all knowledge of the identity or activities of his Chinese guest. He said that from time to time this person whom he knew as Mr Chang, stayed at the inn, usually accompanied by two coloured servants, and sometimes by a lady. He flatly denied all knowledge of the tragedy, and finally:

"Take him away," Gallaho growled, "we'll find enough evidence later. Book him in on a charge of smuggling."

The Si-Fan

Many hours had elapsed, hours of bitter disappointment, before Nayland Smith and I found ourselves at his flat in Whitehall.

Fey had nothing to report. Smith glanced significantly at the television set which in some unaccountable manner Dr Fu Manchu had converted to his private uses.

"No sir." Fey shook his head.

When he had gone out:

"It seems almost incredible," said Smith, beginning to pace up and down the carpet, "that this man whom I held in the hollow of my hand has slipped away! Every point of egress was watched, every officer afloat and ashore notified for miles around."

"Perhaps he doubled back?"

Nayland Smith began to tug at the lobe of his left ear.

"Impossible to predict his movements. I am beginning to wonder if it is time I retired from the unequal contest. It is many years since Doctor Fu Manchu first crossed my path. It was in a swampy district of Burma and I was nearly counted out in the first round." He suddenly pulled up his sleeve and rolled back his shirt cuff, revealing a wicked-looking wound upon the forearm. "A primitive weapon, but a deadly one. An arrow, steeped in snake's venom."

He rolled his sleeve down again.

"You should never be alone, Smith. You need a bodyguard."

"I assure you I rarely go about alone. Why do you suppose I drag six feet of newspaper correspondent about with me? You are my bodyguard, Kerrigan! But Fu Manchu's methods are of a kind from which no bodyguard could protect me. I am saved by my utter futility. I believe he is laughing at me."

"He has small cause for laughter. Although you have failed to destroy him you have foiled him all along."

Nayland Smith's grim face relaxed in a smile.

"Then I can't account for it. He must enjoy the sport, or I should-n't be alive!"

"Do you think he was making for the open sea?"

"I have a strong suspicion that he was. It has occurred to me that this mysterious radio plant which he controls may be on some vessel."

"Such a vessel would require a pretty tall mast."

"Not at all. Fu Manchu is probably half a century ahead of what we call modern radio. However, I can do no more. We can hang the Thugs, no doubt, but like Fu Manchu, what we want to do is to strike at the 'nerves and brain.'"

He dropped into an armchair and began to load his pipe; then, looking up, he stared across at me.

"Judging from what you told me in the train," he said, "I gather that your feelings about this girl Ardatha remain the same. Am I right?"

I felt acutely uncomfortable under that piercing scrutiny, but I replied:

"Yes, I am afraid you are, Smith. You see, although a criminal, she doesn't realise that she is a criminal. In any case she has certainly saved my life. No one else could have given the warning."

Nayland Smith nodded, proceeded with the filling of his pipe and lighted it carefully.

"A cunning scheme," he muttered, standing up and walking about again. "Dictatorships with their ruthless methods have brought in crowds of willing recruits. Don't you see it, Kerrigan? There are thousands! perhaps hundreds of thousands, living today, embittered by injustice, willing, eager, to enter into a blood feud against those who have destroyed husbands, children, families, wrecked their homes. The Si-Fan, always powerful, working for a dimly seen end, an end never appreciated by the West, today has become a mighty instrument of vengeance – and that flaming sword, Kerrigan, is firmly held by Doctor Fu Manchu."

He stared from the window awhile, and I watched the grim out-line of his features.

"One thing, and it looks as though the clue had eluded me," he said suddenly, "is this: What was Fu Manchu doing in Essex? Assuming, as the radio experts believe, that this mysterious interference came from somewhere in that area, even that it came from a vessel lying off the Essex shore—we still come back to the same point. What was Fu Manchu doing there?"

He turned and stared at me fixedly.

"That problem is worrying me badly," he added.

Frankly, it had not occurred to me before, but so stated I saw the significance of the thing. I was considering it while Nayland Smith resumed his restless promenade, when, preceded by a gentle rap, Fey opened the door and entered.

"Chief Detective Inspector Gallaho."

Hot on the words came Gallaho, wrenching his tightly fitting bowler from his close-cropped skull and leaving a mark like a scar around his brow.

"Yes?" snapped Smith and took a step forward. "What is it? You have news!"

"News, yes!" the detective answered bitterly—"but has it come too late?"

He pulled out his pocket case and withdrew a slip of paper which he tossed on to the desk in front of Smith. As Smith picked it up I sprang to my feet and hurried forward. Over his shoulder I read—it was written in pencil, in plain block letters—the following:

Final notice

The Council of Seven of the Si-Fan grants you twelve hours in which to carry out its orders.

PRESIDENT OF THE COUNCIL

Nayland Smith's expression had something wild in it as he turned to Gallaho.

"To whom was this sent?" he snapped

"Doctor Martin Jasper."

Smith's expression changed; his face became almost blank.

"Who the devil is Doctor Martin Jasper?"

"I have looked him up, sir. He has a row of degrees; he's a research man and for some time was technical director of the great Caxton armament factory up in the north."

"Armament factory? I begin to understand. Where does he live?"

"That's the significant thing, sir. It may account for the presence of Doctor Fu Manchu where we found him—or rather, where we lost him. This Doctor Martin Jasper lives at a house called Great Oaks just on the Suffolk border, not ten miles, as the crow flies, from the Monks' Arms."

Great oaks

It was a cross-country journey and the night was misty and moonless; but although unknown to us by name clearly enough Dr Martin Jasper was someone of importance in the eyes of the Si-Fan.

Smith attacked the matter with feverish energy.

A special train was chartered. The railway officials were given twenty-five minutes in which to clear the line. Arrangements were made for a car to meet us at our journey's end. And at about that hour when after-theatre throngs are congesting the West End thoroughfares, we set out in the big Rolls, Fey at the wheel.

Nayland Smith's special powers (which enabled him to ignore traffic regulations) and the wizard driving of Fey, resulted in a dash through London's crowded streets which even I, who had known so many thrills, found exciting.

Smith uttered scarcely a word either to myself or to Gallaho, until arriving at the terminus he was assured by a flustered stationmaster that the special was ready to start. Once on board and whirling through that dark night, he turned to the inspector.

"Now, Gallaho, the full facts!"

"Well sir"—Gallaho steadied himself against the arm rest, for the solitary coach was rocking madly—"I have very little to add." He pulled out his notebook. "This is what I jotted down during the telephone conversation."

"The local police are not in charge then?" Smith snapped.

"No sir, and I took the step of requesting that they shouldn't be notified."

"Good."

"It was a Mr Bailey, the doctor's private secretary, who called up the Yard."

"When?"

"At ten-seventeen—so we've wasted no time! This was what he told me." He consulted his notes. "The doctor, who is engaged upon experiments of great importance in his private laboratory, had alarmed his secretary by his behaviour—that is in the last week or so. He seemed to be in deadly fear of something or someone, so Mr Bailey told me. But whatever was bothering him he kept it to himself. It came to a head though last Wednesday. Something reduced Doctor Jasper to such a state of utter panic that he abandoned work in his laboratory and for hours walked up and down his study. Today he was even worse. In fact Mr Bailey said he looked positively ill. But somewhere around noon as the result, it seems, of a long telephone conversation—"

"With whom?"

"Mr Bailey didn't know—but as a result, the doctor resumed work, although apparently on the verge of a nervous breakdown. He worked right on up till tonight, refusing to break off for dinner. His behaviour so alarmed his secretary that Mr Bailey took the liberty of searching the study to see if he could find any evidence pointing to the cause of it."

"And he found "

"The original of the message I showed you."

"No other message?"

"No other."

"Anything else?"

"Nothing that he could in any way connect with the remarkable behaviour of his employer. He went to the laboratory, which is separate from the house, but Doctor Jasper refused to unlock the door and said that on no account was he to be disturbed. Very wisely, Mr Bailey called up Scotland Yard, and that's about all I know."

Onward we raced through the black night, at one point passing very near to the scene of my last meeting with Ardatha. Within me I fought desperately to solve the mystery of those enigmatic eyes. Even when she looked at me with scorn, mocked me, fought with me, they seemed to mirror a second Ardatha, submerged, all but hidden perhaps from herself—a frightened soul who appealed, appealed for help—protection.

The whistle shrieked wildly. We went through stations at nightmare speed. Once we roared past a sidetracked express. I had a fleeting glimpse of lighted windows, staring faces.

A useful-looking Daimler met us at the station where we were received with some ceremony by the stationmaster. But brushing all inquiries aside, Smith climbed into the car followed by myself and Gallaho, and we set out for Great Oaks. Once on the way Smith glanced at his watch.

"I take it you don't know, Gallaho, at what time the original of this message was received?"

"No, Mr Bailey couldn't tell me."

Then having followed a high and badly kept yew hedge for some distance, the car was turned in between twin stone pillars and began to mount a drive which ascended slightly through a grove of magnificent oaks. I saw the house ahead. A low-pitched, irregular building, the characteristics of Great Oaks were difficult to discern, but the place was evidently of considerable age.

"Hullo!" muttered Smith; "what's this? Some new development?"

Light streamed out into the porch and I could see that the front door was open.

As our car swung around and was pulled up before the steps two men ran down. They evidently had been awaiting us.

Smith sprang out to meet them. Gallaho and I followed. One of the pair was plainly a butler; the other, a youngish, dark-haired man with a short military moustache, whom I assumed normally to be of healthy colouring but who looked pale in the reflected light, stepped forward and introduced himself.

"My name is Horace Bailey," he said in an agitated voice. "Do you come from Scotland Yard?"

"We do," said Gallaho. "I'm Detective Inspector Gallaho—this is Sir Denis Nayland Smith, and Mr Kerrigan."

"Thank God you're here!" cried Bailey, and glanced aside at the butler, who nodded sympathetically.

Both faces, I saw as we all entered Great Oaks, were stamped by an expression of horrified amazement.

"I have a foreboding," said Smith, glancing about the entrance hall in which we found ourselves, "that I come too late."

Mr Bailey slowly inclined his head and something like a groan came from the butler.

"Good God, Kerrigan! A second score to the enemy!"

He dropped down on a leather-covered couch set in a recess over which hung a trophy of antlers. For a moment his amazing vitality, his electrical energy, seemed to have deserted him, and I saw a man totally overcome. As I stepped towards him he looked up haggardly.

"The facts, Mr Bailey, if you please." He spoke more slowly than I remembered ever to have heard him speak. "When did it happen? Where? How?"

"I discovered the tragedy not five minutes ago." Bailey spoke and looked as a man distraught. "You must understand that Doctor Jasper has been locked in his laboratory since noon and at last I determined to face any rebuff in order to induce him to rest. I beg, gentlemen, that you will return there with me now! Hale, the chauffeur, and Bordon, the doctor's mechanic, are trying to cut out the lock of the door!"

"What do you mean?" I asked.

The overstrung man, waving us to follow, already was leading the way along a passage communicating with the rear of the house.

"When I reached the laboratory," he cried back, now beginning to run, "through the grille in the door I saw the doctor lying face downwards . . . I immediately returned for assistance . . . It was hearing the approach of your car that brought me to the porch to meet you."

A somewhat straggling party, we followed the hurrying figure through a dim garden and along a path which zigzagged, sloping slightly upwards to a coppice of beech trees. He knew the way, but we did not. Inspector Gallaho, stumbling and growling, produced a flashlamp for our guidance.

The laboratory was some two hundred yards removed from the house, a squat brick building with a number of high-set windows, screened and iron-barred. The entrance was on the further side, and as we approached I heard a sound of hammering and wrenching. Onto a gravel path and around the corner we ran, and there, where light shone out through a grille in a heavy door, I saw two men at work with chisels, hammers and crowbars.

"Are you nearly through?" Bailey panted.

"Another two minutes should do it, sir."

"Surely there is more than one key!" Smith snapped.

"I regret to say there is only one. Doctor Jasper always held it."

We crowded together to look through the thick glass behind the grille.

I saw a long, narrow workroom, well lighted. It resembled less a laboratory than a machine shop, but I noticed chemical impedimenta, mostly unfamiliar. That which claimed and held my attention was the figure of a short, thick-set man wearing a white linen coat. He lay face downward, arms outstretched, some two paces from the door. Owing to his position, it was impossible to obtain more than a glimpse of the back of his head. But there was something grimly significant in the slump of the body.

The workmen carried on unceasingly. I thought I had heard few more mournful sounds than those of the blows of the hammer and splintering of stout wood as they struggled to force a way into the locked laboratory.

"This is ghastly," Smith muttered, "ghastly! He may not be dead. Have you sent for a doctor?"

"I am myself a qualified physician," Bailey replied, "and following Inspector Gallaho's advice, I have not notified the local police."

"Good," said Gallaho.

"I am still far from understanding the circumstances," snapped Nayland Smith, with the irritability of frustration. "You say that Doctor Jasper has been locked in his laboratory all day?"

"Yes. His ways have become increasingly strange for some time past. Something—I can only guess what—evidently occurred which threw him into a state of nervous tension some ten days or a fortnight ago. Then again, last Wednesday to be exact, he seemed to grow worse. I have come to the conclusion, Sir Denis, that he had received two of these notices. The third—I dictated its contents to the inspector over the telephone—must actually have come by the second post this morning."

"Are you certain of this?"

"All his mail passes through my hands, and I now recall that there was one letter marked 'Personal & Private' which naturally I did not open, delivered at eleven forty-five this morning."

"Eleven forty-five?"

"Yes."

I saw Smith raise his wrist watch to the light shining out from the grille.

"Two minutes short of midnight," he murmured. "The message gave him twelve hours. We are thirteen minutes too late."

"But do you realise, Sir Denis," the secretary cried, "that he is alone, and locked in? This door is of two-inch teak set in an iron frame. To batter it down would be impossible—hence this damnable delay! How can the question of foul play arise?"

"I fear it does," Smith returned sternly. "From what you have told me I am disposed to believe that the ultimate result of these threats was to inspire Doctor Jasper to complete his experiments within the period granted him."

"Good heavens!" I murmured, "you are right, Smith!"

The chauffeur and the mechanic laboured on the door feverishly, their hammer blows and the splintering of tough wood punctuating our conversation.

"He doesn't move," muttered Gallaho, looking through the grille.

"Might I ask, Mr Bailey," Smith went on, "if you assisted Doctor Jasper in his experiments?"

"Sometimes, Sir Denis, in certain phases."

"What was the nature of the present experiment?"

There was a perceptible pause before the secretary replied.

"To the best of my belief—for I was not fully informed in the matter—it was a modified method of charging rifles—"

"Or, one presumes, machine guns?"

"Or machine guns, as you say. An entirely new principle which he termed 'the vacuum charger.'"

"Which increased the velocity of the bullet?"

"Enormously."

"And, in consequence, increased the range?"

"Certainly. My employer, of course, is not a medical man, but a doctor of physics."

"Quite," snapped Smith. "Were the doctor's experiments subsidised by the British government?"

"No. He was working independently."

"For whom?"

"I fear, in the circumstances, the question is rather an awkward one."

"Yet I must request an answer."

"Well—a gentleman known to us as Mr Osaki."

"Osaki?"

"Yes."

"You see, Kerrigan"—Smith turned to me—"here comes the Asiatic element! No description of Mr Osaki (an assumed name) is necessary. Descriptions of any one of Osaki's countrymen sound identical. This Asiatic gentleman was a frequent visitor, Mr Bailey?"

"Oh yes."

"Was he a technician?"

"Undoubtedly. He sometimes lunched with the doctor and spent many hours with him in the laboratory. But I know for a fact that at other times he would visit the laboratory without coming through the house."

"What do you mean exactly?"

"There is a lane some twenty yards beyond here and a gate. Osaki sometimes visited the doctor when he was working, entering by way of the gate. I have seen him in the laboratory, so this I can state with certainty."

"When was he here last?"

"To the best of my knowledge, yesterday evening. He spent near-ly two hours with Doctor Jasper."

"Trying, no doubt, to set his mind at rest about the second notice from the Si-Fan. Then this morning the third and final notice arrives. But Mr Osaki, anxious about results, phones at noon—"

"Binns, the butler, thinks the caller this morning was Osaki—"

"Undoubtedly urging him to new efforts," jerked Smith. "You understand, Kerrigan?"

"For heaven's sake are you nearly through?" cried Bailey to the workmen.

"Very nearly, sir. It's a mighty tough job," the chauffeur replied.

To the accompaniment of renewed hammering and wrenching:

"There are two other points," said Bailey, his voice shaking nerv-ously, "which I should mention, as they may have a bearing on the tragedy. First, at approximately half past eleven, Binns, who was in his pantry at the back of the house, came to me and reported that he had heard the sound of three shots, apparently coming from the lane. I attached little importance to the matter at the time, being pre-occupied about the doctor, and assuming that poachers were at work. The second incident, which points to the fact that Doctor Jasper was alive after eleven-thirty, is this:

"A phone call came which Binns answered. The speaker was a woman "

"Ah!" Smith murmured.

"She declined to give her name but said that the matter was urgent and requested to be put through to the laboratory. Binns called the doctor, asking if the line should be connected. He was told, yes, and the call was put through. Shortly afterwards, determined at all costs to induce the doctor to return to the house, I came here and found him as you see him."

A splintering crash announced that the end of the task of forcing the door was drawing near.

"Had the doctor any other regular visitors?" jerked Smith.

"None. There was one lady whom I gathered to be a friend although he had never spoken of her—Mrs. Milton. She lunched here three days ago and was shown over the laboratory."

"Describe Mrs Milton."

"It would be difficult to describe her, Sir Denis. A woman of great beauty of an exotic type, tall and slender, with raven black hair—"

"Ivory skin," Smith went on rapidly, "notably long slender hands, and unmistakable eyes, of a quite unusual colour, nearly jade green—"

"Good heavens!" cried Bailey, "you know her?"

"I begin to believe," said Nayland Smith, and there was a curious change of quality in his voice, "that I *do* know her. Kerrigan"—he turned to me—"we have heard of this lady before?"

"You mean the woman who visited General Quinto?"

"Not a doubt about it! I absolve Ardatha: this is a *zombie*—a corpse moving among the living! This woman is a harbinger of death and we must find her."

"You don't suggest," cried Bailey, "that Mrs Milton is in any way associated—"

"I suggest nothing," snapped Smith.

A resounding crash and a wrenching of metal told us that the lock had been driven through. A moment later and the door was flung open.

I clenched my fists and for a moment stood stock still.

84

An unforgettable, unmistakable, but wholly indescribable odour crept to my nostrils.

"Kerrigan!" cried Smith in a stifled voice and sprang into the laboratory—"you smell it, Kerrigan? He's gone the same way!"

Bailey had hurried forward and now was bending over the prone body. In the stuffy atmosphere of this place where many queer smells mingled, that of the strange deathly odour which I must always associate with the murder of General Quinto predominated to an appalling degree.

"Get those blinds up! Throw the windows open!"

Hale, the chauffeur, ran in and began to carry out the order, as Smith and Bailey bent and turned the body over . . .

Then I saw Bailey spring swiftly upright. I saw him stare around him like a man stricken with sudden madness. In a voice that sounded like a smothered scream:

"This isn't Doctor Jasper," he cried; "it's *Osaki!*"

In the laboratory

"The green death! The green death again!" said Nayland Smith.

"Whatever is it?" There was awe in my voice. "It's ghastly! In heaven's name what is it?"

We had laid the dead man on a sort of day bed with which the laboratory was equipped, and under the dark Asiatic skin already that ghastly greenish tinge was beginning to manifest itself.

The place was very quiet. In spite of the fact of all windows being opened that indescribable sweetish smell—a smell, strange though it may sound, of which I had dreamed, and which to the end of my life I must always associate with the assassination of General Quinto—hung heavily in the air.

Somewhere in a dark background beyond the shattered door the chauffeur and mechanic were talking in low voices.

Mr Bailey had gone back to the house with Inspector Gallaho. There was hope that the phone call which had immediately preceded the death of Osaki might yet be traced.

The extension to the laboratory proved to be in perfect order, but the butler was in so nervous a condition that Gallaho had lost patience and had gone to the main instrument.

"This," said Smith, turning aside and staring down at a row of objects which lay upon a small table, "is in many ways the most mysterious feature."

The things lying there were those which had been in the dead man's possession. There was a notebook containing a number of notes in code which it would probably take some time to decipher, a wad of paper money, a cigarette case, a railway ticket, a watch, an ivory amulet and a bunch of keys on a chain.

But (and this it was to which Nayland Smith referred) there were two keys—Yales—unattached, which had been found in the pocket of the white coat which Osaki had been wearing.

"We know," Smith continued, "that both these keys are keys of the laboratory, and Mr Bailey was quite emphatic on the point that Doctor Jasper possessed only one. What is the inference, Kerrigan?"

I sniffed the air suspiciously and then stared at the speaker.

"I assume the inference to be that the dead man also possessed a key of the laboratory."

"Exactly."

"This being the case, why should *two* be found in his possession?"

"My theory is this: Doctor Jasper, for some reason which we have yet to learn, hurried out of the laboratory just before Osaki's appearance, and—a point which I think indicates great nervous disturbance—left his key in the door. Osaki, approaching, duplicate key in hand, discovered this. Finding the laboratory to be empty, he put on a white jacket—intending to work, presumably—and dropped the key in the pocket in order to draw Doctor Jasper's attention to this carelessness when the doctor returned."

"No doubt you are right, Smith!"

"You are possibly wondering, Kerrigan, why Osaki, finding himself being overcome by the symptoms of the Green Death, of which we know one to be an impression of beating drums, did not run out and hurry to the house."

"I confess the point had occurred to me."

"Here, I think, is the answer. We know from the case of General Quinto that the impression of beating drums is very real. May we not assume that Osaki, knowing as he certainly did know that imminent danger overhung Doctor Jasper and himself, believed the menace to come from the outside—believed the drumming to be real and deliberately remained in this place?"

"The theory certainly covers the facts, but always it brings us back to—"

"What?"

"The mystery of how a man . . ."

"A man locked in alone," Smith snapped, "can nevertheless be murdered and no clue left to show what means has been employed! Yes!" the word sounded almost like a groan. "The second mystery, of course, is the extraordinary behaviour of Doctor Jasper . . ."

He paused.

From somewhere outside came the sound of running footsteps, a sudden murmur of voices, then—I thought Hale, the chauffeur, was the speaker:

"Thank God, you're alive, sir!"

A man burst into the laboratory, a short, thick-set, dark man, hair dishevelled and his face showing every evidence of the fact that he had not shaved for some time. His eyes were wild—his lips were twitching, he stood with clenched hands looking about him. Then his pale face seemed to grow a shade paler. Those staring eyes became focused upon the body lying on the sofa.

"Good God!" he muttered, and then addressing Smith:

"Who are you? What has happened?"

"Doctor Martin Jasper, I presume?"

"Yes, yes! But who are you? What does this mean?"

"My name is Nayland Smith; this is Mr Bart Kerrigan. What it means, Doctor Jasper, is that your associate Mr Osaki has died in your place!"

Dr Martin Jasper

"You are indeed a fortunate man to be alive." Nayland Smith gazed sternly at the physicist. "You have been preparing a deadly weapon of warfare—not for the protection of your own country, but for the use of a belligerent nation."

"I am entitled," said Dr Jasper, shakily wiping his wet brow, "to act independently if I choose to do so."

"You see the consequences. As he lies so you might be lying. No, Doctor Jasper. You had received three notices, I believe, from the Si-Fan."

Dr Jasper's twitching nervousness became even more manifest.

"I had—but how do you know?"

"It happens to be my business to know. The Si-Fan, sir, cannot be ignored."

"I know! I know!"

The doctor suddenly dropped on to a chair beside one of the benches and buried his dishevelled head in his hands.

"I have been playing with fire, but Osaki, who urged me to it, is the sufferer!"

He was very near to the end of his resources; this was plain enough, but:

"I am going to suggest," said Nayland Smith, speaking in a quiet voice, "that you retire and sleep, for if ever a man needed rest, you do. But first I regret duty demands that I ask a few questions."

Dr Jasper, save for the twitching of his hands, did not stir.

"What were the Si-Fan's orders?"

"That I deliver to them the completed plans and a model of my vacuum charger."

"This invention, I take it, gives a great advantage to those employing it?"

"Yes." His voice was little more than a whisper. "It increases the present range of a rifle rather more than fifty per cent."

'To whom were you to deliver these plans and model?"

"To a woman who would be waiting in a car by the R.A.C call box at the corner of the London Road."

"A woman!"

"Yes. A time was stated at which the woman would be waiting at this point. Failing my compliance, I was told that on receipt of a third and final notice at any hour during the twelve which would be allotted to me, if I cared to go to this call box, I should be met there by a representative."

"Yes?" Smith urged gently. "Go on."

The speaker's voice grew lower and lower.

"I showed these notes to Osaki."

"Where are they now?"

"He took them all. He urged me, always he urged me, to ignore them. By tonight I thought that my experiments would be completed, that I should have revolutionised the subject. He was to meet me here in the laboratory, and we both fully anticipated that the charger would be an accomplished fact."

"He had a key of the laboratory?"

"Yes."

Nayland Smith nodded to me.

"Just before half past eleven an awful dread possessed me. I thought that the price which I should receive for this invention would be useless to a dead man. Just before Osaki was due I took my plans, my model—everything, slipped on a light coat, in the pockets of which I placed all the fruits of my experiments, and ran—I do not exaggerate—ran to the appointed spot."

"What did you find? By whom were you met?" Smith snapped.

'There was a car drawn up on the north side of the road. A woman was just stepping into it—"

"Describe her."

"She is beautiful—dark—slender. I know her as Mrs Milton. I know now she is a spy!"

"Quite enough. What happened?"

"She seemed to be much disturbed as I hurried up. Her eyes— she has remarkable eyes—opened almost with a look of horror."

"What did she do—what did she say?"

"She said: 'Doctor Jasper, are you here to meet me?' I was utterly dumbfounded. I knew in that awful moment what a fool I had been! But I replied that I was."

"What did she say then?"

"She enumerated the items which I had been ordered to deliver up – took them from me one by one . . . and returned to the car. Her parting words were, 'You have been wise.'"

Then your invention, complete and practical, is now in the hands of the Si-Fan?"

"It is!" groaned Dr Jasper.

"Some deadly thing," said Nayland Smith bitterly, "was placed in the laboratory during the time that your key remained in the door— for in your nervous state you forgot to remove it. A few moments later Osaki entered. Someone who was watching mistook Osaki for you. The shots heard by the butler were a signal to that call box. The phone call is the clue! It was Osaki who took it . . ."

Inspector Gallaho dashed into the laboratory.

"I have traced the call," he said huskily—"the local police are of some use after all! It's a box about half a mile from here, on the London Road."

"I know," said Smith wearily.

"You know, sir!" growled Gallaho, then suddenly noticing Dr Martin Jasper: "Who the devil have we here?"

The doctor raised his haggard face from his hands.

"Someone who has no right to be alive," he replied.

Gallaho began chewing phantom gum.

"I said the local police were of some use," he went on truculently, staring at Nayland Smith. "What I mean is this: They have the woman who made the call."

"What!"

Smith became electrified; his entire expression changed.

"Yes. I roused everybody, had every car challenged, and luckily got a description of the one we wanted from a passing A.A. scout who had seen it standing near the box. The village constable at Greystones very cleverly spotted the right one. The woman is now at police headquarters there, sir! I suggest we proceed to Greystones at once."

91

Constable Isles's statement

When presently Smith, Gallaho and I set out in the police car for Greystones, we had succeeded in learning a little more about the mysterious Mrs Milton. A police inspector and the police surgeon we had left behind at Great Oaks; but as Nayland Smith said, what expert opinion had failed to learn in regard to the death of General Quinto local talent could not hope to find out.

Mrs Milton, Dr Jasper had told us before he finally collapsed (for the ordeal through which he had passed had entirely sapped his nervous energy), was a chance acquaintance. The doctor, during one of his rare constitutionals in the neighbouring lanes, had found her beside a broken-down car and had succeeded in restarting the engine. Quite obviously he had been attracted. They had exchanged cards and he had invited her to lunch and to look over his laboratory.

His description of Mrs Milton tallied exactly with that of the woman who had visited General Quinto on the night before his murder!

My excitement as we sped towards Greystones grew ever greater. With my own eyes I was about to see this harbinger of death employed by Dr Fu Manchu, finally to convince myself that she was not Ardatha. But indeed little doubt on this point remained.

"Unless I am greatly mistaken," said Nayland Smith, "you are going to meet for the first time, Kerrigan, an example of a dead woman moving among the living, influencing, fascinating them. I won't tell you, Inspector Gallaho"—he turned to the Scotland Yard officer—"whom I suspect this woman to be. But she is someone you have met before."

"Now that I know Doctor Fu Manchu is concerned in this case," the inspector growled in his husky voice, "nothing would surprise me."

We passed along the main street of a visage in which all the houses and cottages were in darkness and pulled up before one over which, dimly, I could see a tablet which indicated that this was the local police headquarters. As we stepped out:

"Strange," murmured Nayland Smith, looking about him—"there's no car here and only one light upstairs."

"I don't like this," said Gallaho savagely, marching up the path and pressing a bell beside the door.

There was some delay which we all suffered badly. Then a window opened above and I saw a woman looking out.

"What do you want?" she called: it was a meek voice.

"I want Constable Isles," said Gallaho violently. "This Is Detective Inspector Gallaho of Scotland Yard. I spoke to the constable twenty minutes ago, and now I'm here to see him."

"Oh!" said the owner of the meek voice, "I'll come down."

A minute later she opened the door. I saw that she wore a dressing gown and looked much disturbed.

"Where's the woman," snapped Nayland Smith, "whom the constable was detaining?"

"She's gone, sir."

"What!"

"Yes. I suppose he must have been satisfied to have let her go. My husband has had a very hard day, and he's fast asleep in the parlour. I didn't like to disturb him."

"What is the meaning of this?"

Nayland Smith spoke as angrily as he ever spoke to a woman. Accompanied by the hastily attired Mrs Isles, we stood in a little sitting room. A heavily built man who wore a tweed suit was lying on a couch, apparently plunged in deep sleep. Chief Detective Inspector Gallaho chewed ominously and glared at the woman.

"I think it's just that he's overtired, sir," she said. She was a plump, dark-eyed, hesitant sort of a creature, and our invasion seemed to have terrified her. "He has had a very heavy day."

"That is not the point," said Smith rapidly. "Inspector Gallaho here sent out a description of a car seen by an A.A. man near a call box on the London Road. All officers, on or off duty, were notified to look out for it and to stop it if sighted. Your husband telephoned to

93

Great Oaks twenty minutes ago saying that he had intercepted this car and that the driver, a woman, was here in his custody. Where is she? What has occurred?"

"I don't really know, sir. He was just going to bed when the phone rang, and then he got up, dressed, and went out. I heard a car stop outside, and then I heard him bring someone in. When the car drove away again and he didn't come up I went to look for him and found him asleep here. When he's like that I never disturb him, because he's a bad sleeper."

"He's drugged," snapped Smith irritably.

"Oh no!" the woman whispered.

Drugged he was, for it took us nearly ten minutes to revive him. When ultimately Constable Isles sat up and stared about I thought that I had rarely seen a more bewildered man. Smith had been sniffing suspiciously and had examined the stubs of two cigarettes in an ash tray.

"Hello, Constable," he said, "what's the meaning of this? Asleep on duty, I'm afraid."

Constable Isles sat up, then stood up, clenched his fists and stared at all of us like a man demented.

"I don't know what's happened," he muttered thickly. "I don't know!"

He looked again from face to face.

"I'm Chief Detective Inspector Gallaho. Perhaps you know what's happened *now*! You reported to me less than half an hour ago. Where's the car? Where's the prisoner?"

The wretched man steadied himself, outstretched hand against a wall.

"By God, sir!" he said, and made a visible attempt to pull himself together. "A terrible thing has happened to me!"

"You mean a terrible thing is going to happen to you," growled Gallaho.

"Leave this to me." Nayland Smith rested his hand on Isles's shoulder and gently forced him down on to the couch again. "Don't bother about it too much. I think I know what occurred, and it has occurred to others before. When the general order came you dressed and went out to watch the road. Is that so?"

"Yes sir."

94

"You saw what looked like the car described, coming along this way. You stopped it. How did you stop it?"

"I stood in the road and signalled to the driver to pull up."

"I see. Describe the driver."

"A woman, sir, young—" The speaker clutched his head. Obviously he was in a state of mental confusion. "A very dark young woman; she was angry at first and glared at me as though she was in half a mind to drive on."

"Do you remember her eyes?"

"I'm not likely to forget them, sir—they were bright green. She almost frightened me. But I told her I was a police officer and that there was a query about her car. She took it quietly after that, left the car at the gate out there and came in. That was when I telephoned to the number I had been given and reported that I had found the wanted car."

"What happened after that?"

"Well sir, I could see she was a foreigner, good looking in her way, although"—glancing at his buxom wife—"a bit on the thin side from my point of view. And she was so nice and seemed so anxious not to want to wake the missus, that I felt half sorry for her."

"What did she say to you? What did she talk about?"

"To tell you the truth, sir," he stared pathetically at Nayland Smith, "I can't really remember. But while we were waiting she asked me to have a cigarette."

"Did you do so?"

"Yes. I lighted it and one for her at the same time, and we went on talking. The reason I remember her eyes, is because that's the last thing I do remember—" He swallowed noisily. "Although there was nothing, I give you my word, there was nothing to give me the tip in time, I know now that that cigarette was drugged. I hope, sir"—turning to Gallaho—"that I haven't failed in my duty."

"Forget it," snapped Nayland Smith. "Men far senior to you have failed in the same way where this particular woman has been concerned."

A modern vampire

"There are certain features about this case, Kerrigan," said Nayland Smith, "which I have so far hesitated to mention to you."

Alone in the police car we were returning to London. The night remained mistily gloomy, and I was concerned with my own private thoughts.

"You mean perhaps in regard to the woman known as Mrs Milton?"

"Yes!" He pulled out his pipe and began to load it. "She is a phenomenon."

"You referred to her, I remember, as a *zombie.*"

"I did. A dead woman moving among the living. Yes, unless I am greatly mistaken, Kerrigan, Mrs Milton is a modern example of the vampire."

"Ghastly idea!"

"Ghastly, if you like. But there is very little doubt in my mind that Mrs Milton is the woman who was concerned—although as it seemed at the time, remotely—in the death of General Quinto. Those descriptions which we have had unmistakably tally. Stress this point in your notes, Kerrigan. For there is a bridge here between life and death."

Tucked into one corner of the car as it raced through the night, I turned and stared at my companion.

"You think you know her?"

"There is little room for error in the matter. The facts we learned from Constable Isles go to confirm my opinion. That so simple a character should fall victim to this woman is not surprising. She is as dangerous to humanity at large as Ardatha is dangerous to you."

I did not reply, for he seemed to have divined that indeed I had been thinking about Ardatha. Of one thing I was sure: Ardatha was not the harbinger of death employed by Dr. Fu Manchu in the assassination of General Quinto and in that of Osaki.

Chief Detective Inspector Gallaho had been left in charge of the inquiry in Suffolk. Among his duties was that of obtaining a statement from Dr Martin Jasper regarding the exact character of the vacuum charger and the identity of the man known as Osaki. That he, with local assistance, would come upon a clue to the mystery of the Green Death was unlikely, since London experts had failed in an earlier case.

Nayland Smith had worked himself to a standstill in the laboratory. The mystery of why Osaki, locked in there alone, should have died remained a mystery. I began to feel drowsy but became widely awake again when Nayland Smith, striking a match to light his pipe, spoke again.

"Whoever was watching that laboratory, Kerrigan, must have been prepared with some second means of dealing with Doctor Jasper."

"Why?"

"Well, they could not have known that he would open the door. They must have assumed when he *did* open the door that he was returning to the house and would come back."

"Why should they suppose that he would come back?"

"Obviously they knew of his appointment with Osaki."

"Why not have just removed the model and the plans?"

"They knew that neither model nor plans were of any avail if their inventor still defied the Si-Fan. Doctor Fu Manchu's object, Kerrigan, was not to steal the plans of the vacuum charger, but to prevent those plans falling into the hands of the Power represented by Mr Osaki. I am convinced that Osaki's death was an accident, but it probably suited the Si-Fan."

In the bumping of the car over a badly paved road I seemed to hear the beating of drums.

The red button

"Sir Denis evidently detained, sir. Expect any moment."

It was the evening of the following day and I had called at Smith's flat in Whitehall by appointment. I looked at the expressionless face of the speaker.

"That's all right, Fey. I'll come in and wait."

As I crossed the lobby and entered the sitting room which contained the big radio and that television set upon which miraculously once Dr Fu Manchu had manifested himself I heard the phone ringing. Staring at the apparatus, I took out a cigarette. I could detect Fey's monosyllables in the lobby. A few moments later he entered.

"Going out, sir," he reported. "Whisky-soda? Buffet at disposal. Sir Denis at Yard with Inspector Gallaho. Will be here inside ten minutes."

He prepared a drink for me and went out.

I sipped my whisky and soda and inspected some of the pictures and photographs which the room contained. The pictures were landscapes, almost exclusively Oriental. A fine photograph of a handsome grey-haired man I was able to identify as that of Dr Petrie, Nayland Smith's old friend who had been associated with him in those early phases of his battle with Fu Manchu, of which I knew so little. Another, a grimly humorous, square-jawed, moustached face, I was unable to place, but I learned later that it represented Superintendent Weymouth, once of the Criminal Investigation Department, but now attached to the Cairo police.

There were others, not so characteristic. And on a small easel on top of a bookcase I came across a water color of an ethereally beautiful woman. Upon it was written:

"To our best and dearest friend from Karamaneh."

I stared out of a window across the embankment to where old

Father Thames moved timelessly on. A reluctant moon, veiled from moment to moment, sometimes gleamed upon the water. For many years, as Nayland Smith had told me, the Thames had been Dr Fu Manchu's highway. His earliest base had been at Limehouse in the Chinese quarter. London River had served his purpose well.

Nothing passed along the stream as I watched and my thoughts wandered to that Essex creek on the banks of which stood the Monks' Arms. How hopelessly they wandered there!

Ardatha!—a strange name and a strange character. To me, lover of freedom, it was appalling to think that in those enigmatical amethyst eyes I had lost myself—had seen my philosophy crumble, had read the doom of many a cherished principle. Almost certainly she was evil; for how, otherwise, could she be a member of so evil a thing as the Si-Fan?

I tried to cease contemplating that bewitching image. Crossing to an armchair, I was about to sit down when I heard the phone bell in the lobby. I set my glass on a table and went out to answer the call.

"Hello," said a voice, "can I speak to Sir Denis Nayland Smith?"

"Sir Denis is out. But can I take a message?"

The speaker was a man who used good but not perfect English—a foreigner of some kind.

"Thank you. I will call again."

I returned to the armchair and lighted a cigarette.

What was the mystery of the Green Death? Where medical analysis had failed, where Nayland Smith had failed, what hope had I of solving it? It was an appalling exhibition of that power possessed by the awful man I had met out on the Essex marshes. A monster had been reborn—and I had stood face to face with him.

Closing my eyes I lay back in the chair . . .

"If you will be good enough to lower the light, Mr Kerrigan"—the voice was unmistakable—"and sit closer to the screen. There is something important to yourself and to Sir Denis which I have to communicate."

I sprang up—I could not have sprung up more suddenly if a bomb had exploded at my feet. The screen was illuminated, as once before I had seen it illuminated . . . And there looking out at me was Dr Fu Manchu!

Perhaps for a decimal moment I doubted what course to take;

and then (I think almost anyone would have done the same) I extinguished the light.

The switches were remote from the television screen; and I confess, as I turned and stood in darkness before that wonderful evil face which apparently regarded me, I was touched by swift fear. In fact I had to tell myself that this was not the *real* Dr Fu Manchu but merely his image before I summoned up courage enough to approach and to watch.

"Will you please touch the red button on the right of the screen," the sibilant voice went on, "merely to indicate that you have observed my wishes."

I touched the red button. My heart was beating much too rapidly; but sitting down on an ottoman, I compelled myself to study that wonderful face.

It might have been the face of an emperor. I found myself thinking of Zenghis Khan. Intellectually, the brow was phenomenal, the dignity of the lined features might have belonged to a Pharaoh, but the soul of the great Chinese doctor lay in his eyes. Never had I seen before, and never have I seen since, such power in a man's eyes as lay in those of Dr Fu Manchu.

Then he spoke, and his voice, too, was unforgettable. One hearing its alternate sibilants and gutturals must have remembered every intonation to the end of his days.

"I regret, Mr Kerrigan," he said, "that you are still alive. Your rescue meant that an old and useful base is now destroyed. I suspect that some member of the Si-Fan has failed me in this matter. If so, there will be retribution."

His words chilled me coldly.

Ardatha!

She had defied me, jeered at me, fought with me, but in the end she had saved me. It was a strange romance but I knew that on my side it was real. Ardatha was my woman, and if I lost her I should have lost all that made life worth-while. I think, except for that unreadable expression which seemed to tell me that her words did not mean all they conveyed, I had had but little hope, in spite of my masculine vanity, until I had realised that she had risked everything to rescue me from the cellars of the Monks' Arms.

I was watching the image of those strange eyes as this thought flashed through my mind.

Good Good! Did he suspect Ardatha?

"In the absence of Sir Denis"—the words seemed to reach me indistinctly—"I must request *you*, Mr Kerrigan, to take my message. It is very simple. It is this: Sir Denis has fought with me for many years. I have come to respect him as one respects an honourable enemy, but forces difficult to control now demand that I should act swiftly. Listen, and I will explain what I mean to do."

That forceful voice died away unaccountably. My brain suggested that the instrument, operated by an unknown principle, had failed. But then conscious thought petered out altogether, I suppose. The eyes regarding me from the screen, although the image was colourless, seemed, aided by memory, to become *green* . . . Then they merged together and became one contemplative eye. That eye grew enormous—it dominated the picture—it became a green lake—and a remorseless urge impelled me to plunge into its depths . . .

I stood up, or so I thought, from the ottoman on which I had been seated and walked forward into the lake.

Miraculously I did not sink. Stepping across a glittering green expanse, I found myself upon solid land. Here I paused, and the voice of Dr Fu Manchu spoke:

"Look!—this is China."

I saw a swamp, a vast morass wherein no human thing could dwell, a limitless and vile corruption . . . I saw guns buried in the mud; in pools I saw floating corpses: the foetid air was full of carrion, and all about me I heard wailing and lamentations. So desolate was the scene that I turned my head aside until the Voice spoke again:

"Look! It is Spain."

I saw a waste which once had been a beautiful village: the shell of an old church; ruins of a house upon whose scarred walls bougainvillea bloomed gaily. People, among them women and children, were searching in the ruins. I wondered for what they were searching. But out of the darkness the Voice came again:

"Look! This is London."

From my magic carpet I looked down upon Whitehall. Almost that spectacle conquered the magic of the Voice. I fought against mirage, but the mood of rebellion passed . . . I saw the cenotaph partly demolished. I heard crashes all around me, muted but awful. Where I thought familiar buildings should be there were gaping caverns. Strange figures, antlike as I looked down upon them, ran in all directions.

"*Your* world!" said the Voice. "Come, now, into mine . . ."

And Ardatha was beside me!

It was a rose garden, the scent of the flowers intoxicating. Below where the roses grew I saw steps leading down to a marble pool upon the cool surface of which lotus blossoms floated. Bees droned amid the roses, and gaily plumaged birds darted from tree to tree. An exquisite sense of well being overcame me. I turned to Ardatha—and her lips were irresistible.

"Why did you ever doubt what I told you?" she whispered.

"Only because I was a fool."

I lost myself in a kiss which realised all the raptures of which I had ever dreamed . . .

Ardatha melted from my arms . . . I sought her, called her name— "Ardatha! Ardatha!" But the rose garden had vanished: I was in darkness—alone, helpless, though none constrained me . . .

Flat on the carpet of Nayland Smith's apartment, as I had fallen back from the ottoman, I lay!—fully alive to my environment, but unable to speak—to move!

Living death

The screen, the magical screen, was black. Faint light came through the windows. Something—some damnable thing—had happened. I had gone mad—or been bewitched. That power, suspected but now experienced, of the dreadful Chinese doctor had swept me up.

With what purpose?

There seemed to be nothing different about the room—but how long had I been unaware of what was going on? Most accursed thing of all, I could think, but I couldn't move! I lay there flat on my back, helpless as one dead. My keen mental activity in this condition was a double agony.

As I lay I could see right into the lobby—and now I became aware of the fact that I was not alone!

A small, dark man had opened the outer door quietly, glanced in my direction, and then set down a small handbag which he had seemed to carry with great care. He wore thick-rimmed glasses. He opened the bag, and I saw him doing something to the telephone.

I tried to command nerve and muscle—I tried to move. It was futile.

My body was dead: my brain alone lived . . .

I saw the man go. Even in that moment of mental torment I must watch passively, for I could not close my eyes!

Here I lay at the point from which my journeys to China to Spain, to an enchanted rose garden had begun, and so lying, unable to move a muscle, again I heard a key inserted in the door . . . The door opened and Nayland Smith dashed into the room. He looked down at me.

"Good God!" he exclaimed, and bent over me.

My eyes remained fixed: they continued to stare towards the lobby.

"Kerrigan! Kerrigan! Speak, old man! What happened?"

103

Speak! I could not stir . . .

He placed his ear to my chest, tested my pulse, stood up and seemed to hesitate for a moment. I heard and partly saw him going from room to room, searching. Then he came back and again fully into view. He stared down at me critically. He had switched up all the lights as he had entered. He walked across to the lobby, and I knew that he was about to take up the telephone!

His intentions were obvious. He was going to call a doctor.

A scream of the spirit implored me to awake, to warn him not to touch that telephone. This was the supreme moment of torture . . .

I heard the faint tinkling of the bell as Nayland Smith raised the receiver.

I became obsessed with the horrible idea that Dr Fu Manchu had in some way induced a state of catalepsy! I should be buried alive! But not even the terror caused by this ghastly possibility would make me forget that small, sinister figure engaged in doing something to the telephone.

That it was something which meant death, every instinct told me.

Yet I lay there, myself already in a state of living death!

Smith stood, the receiver in his hand, and I could see and hear him dialling a number.

But it was not to be . . .

A crashing explosion shook the entire building! It shattered several panes of glass in one window, and it accomplished that which my own brain had failed to accomplish. It provided a shock against which the will of Dr Fu Manchu was powerless.

I experienced a sensation exactly as that of some tiny but tough thread which had held the cells of my brain immured in inertia being snapped. It was a terrifying sensation—but its terrors were forgotten in the instant when I realised that I was my own master again!

"Smith!" I cried and my voice had a queer, hysterical ring— "Smith! *Don't touch that telephone!*"

Perhaps the warning was unnecessary. He had replaced the receiver on the hook and was staring blankly across the apartment in the direction of the shattered window.

"Kerrigan!"

He sprang forward as I scrambled to my feet.

"I can't explain yet," I muttered (the back of my head began to ache madly) "except that you must not touch that telephone."

He grabbed me by the shoulders, stared into my eyes.

"Thank God you're all right, Kerrigan! I can't tell you what I feared—but will tell you later. Somewhere down the river there has been a catastrophe."

"It has saved us from a catastrophe far greater."

Smith turned, threw a window open (I saw now that he had been deeply moved) and craned out. Away downstream black smoke was rising over a sullen red glow.

Police whistles shrieked and I heard the distant clangour of a fire engine . . . Later we learned—and the tragedy was front-page news in the morning—of that disastrous explosion on a munition barge in which twelve lives were lost. At the moment, I remember, we were less concerned with the cause of the explosion than with its effect.

Smith turned from the window and stared at me fixedly.

"How did you get in, Kerrigan? Where is Fey?"

"Fey let me in, then he was called up by Inspector Gallaho from Scotland Yard to meet you there."

"I have not been there—and I have reason to know that Gallaho is not in London. However, go on."

"Fey evidently had no doubt that Gallaho was the speaker. He gave me a drink, told me that you would return directly he, Fey, reached Scotland Yard, and went out."

"What happened then?"

"Then the incredible happened."

"You are sure that you feel perfectly restored?"

"Certain."

Smith pushed me down into an armchair and crossed to the buffet.

"Go on," he said quietly.

"The television screen lighted up. Doctor Fu Manchu appeared."

"What!"

He turned, his hand on a syphon and his expression very grim.

"Yes! You wondered for what purpose he had caused the thing to be installed here, Smith. I can give you an example of *one* use he made of it! Perhaps I am particularly susceptible to the influence of this man. I think you believe I am, for you observed on a former occasion that I was behaving strangely as I watched those awful eyes. Well this time I succumbed altogether. I had a series of extraordinary visions, almost certainly emanations from the brain of Doctor Fu Manchu. And then I became fully conscious but quite incapable of movement!"

"That was your condition when I returned," Smith snapped. He crossed to me with a tumbler in his hand.

"I had been in that condition for some time before your return. A man admitted himself to the lobby with a key."

"Describe him."

"A small man with straight black hair, who wore what seemed to be powerful spectacles. He carried a bag which he handled with great care. He proceeded to make some adjustment to the mouthpiece of the telephone, and then with a glance in my direction—I was lying on the floor as you found me—he went out again as quietly as he had come."

"Clearly," said Smith, staring into the lobby, "your unexpected appearance presented a problem. They did not know you were coming. It had been arranged for Fey to be lured away by this unknown mimic who can evidently imitate Gallaho's voice; but you, the unexpected intruder, had to be dealt with in a different manner. I am wondering about two things now, Kerrigan. Do you feel fit to investigate?"

"Perfectly."

"First: how long you would have remained in that state in which I found you, failing the unforeseen explosion which shocked you into consciousness; and second: what the small man with the black hair did to the telephone."

"For heaven's sake be careful!"

He crossed to the lobby and very gently raised the instrument. I stood beside him. Apart from a splitting headache I felt perfectly normal. He tipped up the mouthpiece and stared curiously into it.

"You are sure it was the mouthpiece that he adjusted?"

"Quite sure."

And now he turned it round to the light which was streaming through the doorway of the sitting room.

We both saw something.

A bead, quite colorless and no larger than a small pea, adhered to the instrument just below the point where a speaker's lips would come . . .

"Good God!" Nayland Smith whispered. "Kerrigan! You understand!"

I nodded. I could not find my voice—for the appalling truth had come to me.

"Anyone speaking loudly would burst this bubble and inhale its contents! God knows what it contains—but we know at last how General Quinto and Osaki died!"

"The Green Death!"

"Undoubtedly. It was a subtle brain, Kerrigan, which foresaw that finding you unconscious, I should immediately call a doctor, that my voice would be agitated. The usual routine, as you must see now, was for someone to call the victim and complain that his voice was not audible, thus causing him to speak close to the receiver and to speak loudly."

Very gently he replaced the instrument.

At this moment the door was partly opened and Fey came in. He glanced from face to face.

"Glad, sir! Frightened! Something funny going on!"

"Very funny, Fey. I suppose when you got to the Yard you found that the summons did not come from there?"

"Yes sir."

The phone bell rang. Fey stepped forward.

"Stop! On no account are you to touch the telephone, Fey, until further orders."

"Very good, sir."

107

Tremors under Europe

"Doctor Fu Manchu evidently is losing his sense of humour," said Nayland Smith with a smile.

It was noon of the following day, and he stood in my room. He was seated at the desk and was reading my notes. Now he laid them down and began to fill his pipe.

"What do you mean, Smith?"

"I mean that two things—your unexpected appearance, and that explosion on the powder barge—together saved my life. By the way, here is an addition to your notes."

"What is it?"

"The home office analyst's report. You know the difficulty we had to remove the mouthpiece of the telephone without breaking the bubble. However, it was done, and you will see what Doctor O'Donnell says."

I took up the report from the home office consultant. It was not his official report but one he had sent privately to Nayland Smith.

"The construction of the small globe or bubble," I read, "is peculiarly delicate. Examination of the fragments suggests that it is composed of some kind of glass and is probably blown by an instrument which at the same time fills the interior with gas. The effect of breaking the bubble, however, is to leave no trace whatever, apart from a fragment of powder which normally would be indiscernible. It was attached to the mouthpiece by a minute speck of gum, and I should imagine the operation required great dexterity. As to its contents:

"My full report may be consulted, but briefly I may say that the composition of the gas which this bubble contained is unknown to me. It belongs to none of the groups with which I am familiar. It is the most concentrated poison in gaseous form which I have ever encountered. In addition to the other experiments (see report) I smelled this gas—but for a moment. The result was extraordinary. It induced a violent increase of blood pressure, followed by a drumming in my ears which created such an illusion of being external that for a time I was persuaded someone was beating a drum in the neighbourhood . . ."

As I laid the letter on the table:

"Have you considered," Nayland Smith asked, "what revolutionary contributions Doctor Fu Manchu could make to science, particularly to medicine, if he worked for heaven and not for hell?"

"Yes, it's a damnable thought."

"The greatest genius living—perhaps as great as has ever been born—toiling for the destruction of humanity!"

"Yet, at the moment, he seems to be working for its preservation."

"But only *seems*, Kerrigan. Its preservation for his own purposes—yes! I strongly suspect, however, that his recent attempt upon me was dictated by an uncanny knowledge of my movements."

"What do you mean?"

"I am being shadowed day and night. There have been other episodes which I have not even bothered to mention."

"You alarm me!"

"Fortunately for myself, the doctor has his hands full in other directions. If he once concentrated upon me I believe I should give up hope. You see, he knows that I am watching his next move, and with devilish cunning, so far, he has headed me off."

"His next move . . ." I stared questioningly.

"Yes. In his war against dictators. At the moment it is concentrated upon one of them—and the greatest."

"You don't mean—"

"I mean Rudolf Adlon! In view of the way in which he is guarded and of the many attempts by enemies to reach him which have failed, it seems perhaps absurd that I should be anxious because one more man has entered the lists."

"But that man is Doctor Fu Manchu!"

"Not a doubt about it, Kerrigan. Yet, officially, my hands are tied."

"Why?"

"Adlon has refused to see me, and I cannot very well force myself upon him."

"Have you definite evidence that Adlon has been threatened?"

Nayland Smith lighted his pipe and nodded shortly.

"I am in the difficult position of having to keep an eye on a number of notable people—many of them, quite frankly, not friends of Great Britain. With a view to doing my best to protect them, the legitimate functions of the secret service up to a certain extent have been switched into this channel, and I had information three days ago that Adlon had received the first notice from the Si-Fan!"

"Good heavens! What did you do?"

"I immediately advised him that whatever he might think to the contrary, he was in imminent peril of his life. I suggested a conference."

"And he refused to see you?"

"Exactly. Whatever is pending—and rest assured it will affect the fate of the world—it is clearly a matter of some urgency for I am informed that a *second notice* has reached Adlon."

"What do you make of it? What is he planning?"

Nayland Smith stood up, irritably snapping his fingers.

"I don't know, nor can I find out. Furthermore, for any evidence to the contrary, there might be no such person as Doctor Fu Manchu in the world. Do you think it conceivable that such a personality is moving about among us—as undoubtedly he is—and yet not one clue fall into the hands of a veritable army of searchers?"

I watched him for some time as he paced nervously up and down the carpet, then:

"Having met Doctor Fu Manchu," I replied slowly, "I am prepared to believe anything about him. What is bothering me at the moment, Smith, is this: On your own admission he knows that you are trying to protect Adlon."

Nayland Smith sighed wearily.

"He knows every move I make, Kerrigan. Almost, I believe, those which I am likely to make but upon which I have not yet decided."

"In other words your own danger is as great, if not greater, than that of the chancellor."

He smiled wryly.

"Since one evening in Burma, many years ago—an evening of which I bear cherished memories, for it was then that I first set eyes on Doctor Fu Manchu—I have gone in hourly peril of assassination. Yet, here I am—thanks to the doctor's sense of humour! You see"— he began to walk up and down again—"I doubt if ever before have I had the entire power of the Si-Fan directed against me. And so this time, I am wondering . . ."

A car in Hyde Park

An unavoidable business appointment called me away that after-noon. My personal inclination was never to let Nayland Smith out of my sight although heaven knows what I thought I could do to protect him. But as he never went about alone and rarely failed to notify me of any move in the game in order that I might be present, we parted with an understanding to meet at dinner.

My business took me to Westminster. Fully an hour had passed, I suppose, when I began to drive back, and I found myself in the thick of the afternoon traffic. As I made to cross towards Hyde Park I was held up. Streams of vehicles coming from four different directions were heading for the gate. I resigned myself and lighted a cigarette.

Idly I inspected a quantity of luggage strapped on the rack of a big saloon car. It was proceeding very slowly out of the Park in that pent-up crawling line of traffic and had just passed my off-side window. There were new labels over many old ones, but from my position at the wheel I could read none of them, except that clearly enough this was the baggage of a world traveller, for I recognised the characteristic hotel designs of Mount Lavinia in Colombo, Shepheard's in Cairo and others East and West which I knew.

The constable on the gate had apparently become rooted just in front of me with outstretched arms. Curious for a glimpse of these travellers who were presumably bound for Victoria Station, I leaned back and stared out at the occupants of the car. A moment I glanced—and then turned swiftly away.

A chauffeur whose face I could not see was driving. There were two passengers. One was a darkly beautiful woman. She was smoking a cigarette, and I could not fail to note her long ivory hand, her slender, highly burnished fingernails. In fact, except for their smooth beauty, those hands reminded me of the hands of Dr Fu Manchu. But it was that one glimpse of her companion which had urged me to turn aside, praying that I had not been recognised . . .

It was Ardatha!

Useless to deny that my heart had leapt at sight of her. She wore a smart little hat crushed down on her coppery curls, and some kind of fur-collared coat. I had seen no more, had noticed no more. I had eyes for nothing but that bewitching face. And now, as I stared at the broad, immovable back of the constable, I was thinking rapidly and hoping that he would remain stationary long enough for me to rearrange my plans.

Somehow, I must follow that car!

Once at Victoria it should not be difficult for a man with newspaper training to learn the destination of the travelers. If I failed to do so I could never face Nayland Smith again with a clear conscience. But here was a problem. I must enter the Park now for I was jammed in the traffic stream, and the car which contained Ardatha was leaving or waiting to leave! It meant a detour and I had to plan quickly. I must bear left, leave by the next gate (I prayed I might not be held up there) and make my way to Victoria across Knightsbridge.

This plan was no sooner formed than the constable moved and waved me on.

I proceeded as fast as I dared in the direction of the next gate— and I was lucky. Oncoming traffic was being let out, that from the opposite direction being held.

Last but one, I got through.

I was lucky on the rest of the way, too, and having hastily disposed of my car I went racing into the station. I knew that (a) I must take care not to be seen; that (b) I must find out what trains were about to depart and swiftly make up my mind for which I wanted a platform ticket.

A Continental boat train was due to leave in five minutes.

This struck me as being quite the likeliest bet. The next departure, seven minutes later, was for Brighton, and somehow I felt disposed to wash this out as a possibility. Turning up the collar of my topcoat and pulling my hat well forward, I took a platform ticket and strolled among departing passengers and friends, porters, refreshment wagons and news vendors.

I glanced at the luggage van, but doubted if I should recognise the particular baggage I had seen upon the tail of the car. Then, time being short, I walked along the platform. I could see no sign of two women, and I began to wonder if I had made a mistake. I started back again, scrutinising all the compartments and staring into the Pullman cars.

But never a glimpse did I obtain of Ardatha or her companion. I was almost in despair and was standing looking right and left when a conversation taking place near by arrested my attention.

"I've got an old lady going through to Venice. I noticed you had a party of two for Venice, so I wondered if you could arrange to give them adjoining places in the car. They might strike up an acquaintance—see what I mean?"

"You mean the two good-lookers—the red head and the dark one—in D? Yes, they're booked for Venice but I don't know if they're going direct. Where's your passenger?"

"D. Number eleven. Do what you can, Jack."

"Right-o!"

I glanced quickly at the speakers. One was a Cook's man and the other the chief Pullman attendant. It was perhaps a forlorn hope, but I had known equally unlikely things to come off. I turned back and went to look at coach D.

One glance was enough!

Ardatha was seated in a corner reading. Her companion was standing up and placing something upon the rack, for I had a momentary impression of a tall, slender, almost serpentine figure. I turned away quickly and hurried back to the barrier.

The beautiful dark mystery was undoubtedly the woman associated with the death of General Quinto—with the death of Osaki! The woman who had drugged Constable Isles and who had escaped with the model and plans of the vacuum charger! Although perhaps not blood guilty, Ardatha was her accomplice. It was an unhappy, a wildly disturbing thought. Yet, I must confess, so profound was my dread of the Chinese doctor, that I rejoiced to know she lived! His words about retribution had haunted me . . . But one thing I must do and do quickly:

I must advise Nayland Smith.

Here were two known accomplices of Dr Fu Manchu. My duty to

113

my friend—to the world—demanded that steps should be taken to
apprehend them at Folkestone. There was no room for sentiment;
my conscience pointed the straight road to duty.

"The brain is Dr Fu Manchu"

"Dinner's off, Kerrigan! We shall have to get what we can on the way."

"What!"

"Accident has thrown the first clue of many weary days and nights in your way, Kerrigan, and you handled it very cleverly."

"Thank you."

"My latest information, just to hand, explains why Doctor Fu Manchu's attention has become directed upon Rudolf Adlon. Adlon is on his way to Venice for a secret meeting with his brother dictator, Monaghani!"

"But that's impossible, Smith!" I exclaimed. I was still figuratively breathless from my dash to Victoria. "It's in the evening papers than Adlon is reviewing troops tomorrow morning."

Smith was pacing up and down in an old silk dressing gown and smoking his pipe. He paused, turned, and stared at me with raised eyebrows. His glance was challenging.

"I thought it was common knowledge, Kerrigan," he said quietly, "that Adlon has a double."

"A double!"

"Certainly. I assumed you knew; almost everybody else knows. Stalin of Russia has three."

"Three doubles?"

"Three. He knows that he is likely to be assassinated at almost any moment and in this way the odds are three to one in his favour. On such occasions as that which you have mentioned, when the director of his country stands rigidly at the salute for forty minutes or so while troops march by with mechanical accuracy, it is not Rudolf Adlon the First who stands in that painful position. Oh no, Kerrigan: It is Rudolf Adlon the Second! The Second will be there tomorrow, but the First, the original, the real Rudolf Adlon, is already on his way to Venice."

"Then you think that the fact of these two women proceeding to Venice means—"

"It means that Doctor Fu Manchu is in Venice, or shortly will be! Throughout his career he has used the weapon of feminine beauty, and many times that weapon has proved to be double-edged. However, we know what to look for."

"Surely you will take steps to have them arrested at Folkestone?"

"Not at all."

"Why?"

He smiled, paused.

"Do you recall Fu Manchu's words on striking at the heart, the brain? Very well. The heart is the Council of Seven—the brain is Doctor Fu Manchu. It is at the brain I mean to strike, therefore we are leaving for Venice immediately."

He had pressed the bell and now the door opened and Fey came in.

"Advise Wing Commander Roxburgh that I shall want the plane to leave for Venice in an hour. He is to notify Paris and Rome and to arrange for a night landing."

"Very good, sir."

"Stand by with the car."

Fey went out.

"You are sure, Kerrigan, you are sure"—Nayland Smith spoke excitedly—"that you were not recognised?"

"Sure as it is possible to be. Ardatha was reading. I am practically certain that she could not have seen me. The other woman doesn't know me."

Nayland Smith laughed aloud and then stared in an amused way.

"You have much to learn yet," he said, "about Doctor Fu Manchu."

Venice

Of those peculiar powers possessed by Nayland Smith, I mean the facilities with which he was accredited, I had a glimpse on this journey. And if confirmation had been needed of the gravity of the menace represented by Dr Fu Manchu and the Council of Seven, I should have recognised from the way in which his lightest wishes were respected that this was a very grave menace indeed.

We had travelled by a Royal Air Force plane which had performed the journey in little more than half the time of the commercial service!

As we entered the sitting room allotted to us in the Venice hotel, we found Colonel Correnti, chief of police, waiting.

Smith, dismissing an obsequious manager with a smile and wave of the hand, turned to the police officer.

He presented me.

"You may speak with complete confidence in Mr Kerrigan's presence. Has Rudolf Adlon arrived?"

"Yes."

Smith dropped into an armchair. He had not yet removed hat or Burberry, and groping in a pocket of the latter he produced that dilapidated pouch in which normally he carried about half a pound of tobacco. He began to load his pipe.

"This is a great responsibility for you?"

"A dreadful responsibility!" the colonel nodded gloomily. "The greater because Signor Monaghani is expected on Tuesday morning."

"Also incognito?"

"Alas, yes! It is these visits of which so few are aware which make my life a misery. Our task is far heavier than that of Geneva. Venice is the favourite rendezvous of some of the greatest figures in European politics. Always they come incognito, but not always for political reason! Why should Venice be selected? Why should this dreadful onus be placed upon me?"

His Latin indignation was profound.

"Where is the chancellor staying?"

"At the Palazzo da Rosa, as guest of the baron. He has stayed there before. They are old friends."

"Are there any other of Herr Adlon's friends in Venice at present?"

"But yes! James Brownlow Wilton is here. He leases the Palazzo Brioni on the Grand Canal, at no great distance from this hotel. His yacht Silver Heels is in the lagoon."

"Will he be entertaining Herr Adlon?"

"I believe there is to be a small private luncheon party, either at the Palazzo or on board the yacht."

Nayland Smith crushed tobacco into the big cracked bowl of his pipe. Only once he glanced at me. But I knew what he had in mind and thrilled with anticipation, then:

"You have arranged to have agents on board, Colonel?"

"Certainly. This was my duty."

"I appreciate that. No doubt you can arrange for Mr Kerrigan and myself to be present?"

For a moment Colonel Correnti was taken aback. He looked from face to face in astonishment.

"Of course." He endeavoured to speak easily. "It could be arranged."

Nayland Smith stood up and smiled.

"Let it be arranged," he said. "I have an appointment to meet Sir George Herbert who is accompanying me to see Herr Adlon. I shall be free in an hour. If you will be good enough to return then we can make all necessary plans . . ."

During the next hour I was left to my own devices. That Dr Fu Manchu, if not there in person certainly had agents in Venice, had made me so intensely nervous that I only let Nayland Smith leave the hotel when I realised that a bodyguard in the form of two plain-clothes police accompanied him.

I tried to distract myself by strolling about those unique streets.

This was comparatively new territory. I had been there but once before and only for a few hours. Night had long fallen touching Venice with its magic. Lights glittered on the Grand Canal, shone from windows in those age-old palaces, and a quarter moon completed the picture.

Somewhere, I thought, as I peered into the faces of passers-by, Ardatha might be near to me. Smith was of opinion that they would have flown from Paris, avoiding Croydon as at Croydon they were likely to be recognized. Assuming a fast plane to have been awaiting them, they were probably in Venice now.

Automatically, it seemed, and in common with everyone else, I presently drifted towards St. Mark's. Despite the late hour it seemed that all Venice took the air. Had my mind been not a boiling cauldron but normally at peace I must have enjoyed the restfulness of my surroundings.

But feverishly I was thinking, "Ardatha is here! At any moment she may become involved in a world tragedy from which I shall be helpless to extricate her."

One who, whatever his faults, however right or wrong his policy, was yet the idol of a great country, stood in peril of sudden death. Perhaps only one man could save him—Nayland Smith! And upon that man's head, also, a price had been set by the dreadful Chinese doctor.

I found it impossible to relax. I recalled Smith's words:

"Do as you please, Kerrigan, but for heaven's sake don't show yourself."

It was impossible, this walking in shadow, distrusting the moonlight, avoiding all places where people congregated, and slinking about like a criminal who feared arrest. I went back to the hotel.

The lounge appeared to be deserted, but I glanced sharply about me before crossing it, making my way to the suite reserved for Smith and myself.

I found the sitting room in darkness, but an odour of tobacco smoke brought me up sharply as I was about to cross the threshold.

"Hello!" I called, "is anyone there?"

"I am here," came Smith's voice out of the darkness.

He stood up and switched on the light, and I saw that his pipe was between his teeth. Even before he spoke his grim expression told me all there was to know.

"Have you seen him?"

He nodded.

"What was his attitude?"

"His attitude, you will be able to judge for yourself when you see him on Silver Heels tomorrow. He has gone so far, has risen so high, that I fear he believes himself to be immortal!"

"Megalomania?"

"Hardly that perhaps, but he sets himself above counsel. He admitted reluctantly that he had received the Si-Fan notices—two at least. He merely shrugged his shoulders when I suggested that a third had come to hand."

He was walking up and down the room now tugging at the lobe of his left ear.

"If Adlon is to be saved, he must be saved against himself. If I had the power, Kerrigan, I would kidnap him and transport him from Venice tonight!"

"I count upon you, Colonel," said Nayland Smith as the chief of police rose to go. "My friend and I will be present on Silver Heels tomorrow. I must have an opportunity of inspecting Mr Brownlow Wilton's guests and of seeing in which of them Rudolf Adlon is interested."

When we were alone:

"Have the police obtained any clue?" I asked.

Smith shook his head irritably.

"Very rarely indeed does the doctor leave clues. And this is a major move in his game. I don't know if Monaghani is marked down, but Adlon admits that he is. We have yet to see if Monaghani arrives. But for tonight, I suppose my work is done. Have you any plans?"

"No."

"I wish I could find Ardatha for you," he said softly, and went out. "Good night."

As the door closed and I heard him walking along to his room I dropped down on to a settee and lighted a cigarette. How I wished that *I* could find her! I had never supposed love to come in this fashion. Quite easily I could count the minutes—had often done so—that I had been in Ardatha's company. Collectively they amounted to less than an hour. Yet of all the women I had known, she was the one to whom my thoughts persistently turned.

I tried to tell myself that this was an obsession born of the mystery in which I had met her—an infatuation which would pass—but always the effort failed. No, she haunted me. I knew every expression of her piquant face, every intonation of her voice; I heard her talking to me a thousand times during the day—I dreamed of her, I suspected, throughout the night.

That Nayland Smith was tired I could not doubt, I was tired myself. Yet, although it was long past midnight, any idea of sleep I knew to be out of the question. Outside, divided from the window only by a narrow quay, the Grand Canal lapped its ancient walls. Occasionally, anomalous motorboats passed; at other times I heard the drip of an oar as some ghostly gondola crept upon its way. Once the creaking of a boat, as a belated guest returned to the hotel, reminded me—terrifyingly—of the cellars under the Monks' Arms where I had so nearly come to an end.

I rang for a waiter and ordered a drink to be brought to my room; then, extinguishing the lights of the sitting room, I went along the corridor intending to turn in.

However, when my drink arrived and I had lighted another cigarette, I was overcome with recklessness. Crossing to the window I threw open the shutters and looked down upon the oily glittering waters of the canal.

Venice! The picture city, painted in blood and passion. In some way it seemed fitting that Fu Manchu should descend upon Venice; fitting, too, that Ardatha should be there. The moon had disappeared; mysterious lights danced far away upon the water, beckoning me back to the days of the doges.

From my window I looked down upon a shadowy courtyard, a corner of the platform upon which the hotel (itself an old palace) was built. It could be approached from the steps which led up to the main door, but so far as I could make out in the darkness it formed a sort of cul-de-sac. My window ledge was no more than four feet from the stone paving.

And now, in the shadows, I detected someone moving . . .

I drew back. My hand flew to a pocket in which, always, since I had met Dr Fu Manchu, an automatic rested. Then a voice spoke—a soft voice:

"Please help me up. I must talk to you."

It was Ardatha!

Ardatha

She sat in a deep, cushioned divan, a Renaissance reproduction, watching me with a half smile.

"You look frightened," she said. "Do I frighten you?"

"No, Ardatha, it isn't that you frighten me, although I admit your appearance was somewhat of a shock."

She wore a simple frock and a coat having a fur-trimmed collar, which I recognised as that which I had seen in the car near Hyde Park corner. She had a scarf tied over her hair, and I thought that her eyes were mocking me.

"I am mad to have done this," she went on, "and now I am wondering—"

I tried to conquer a thumping heart, to speak normally.

"You are wondering if I am worth it," I suggested, and forced myself to move in her direction.

Frankly, I was terrified as I never could have believed myself to be terrified of a woman. My own wild longing had awakened some sort of response in Ardatha! I had called to her and she had come! But as the lover of a girl so complex and mysterious I had little faith in Bart Kerrigan.

Tonight it was my part to claim her—or to lose her forever. Her eyes as well as her words told me that the choice was mine.

I offered her a cigarette and lighted it, then sat down beside her. My impulse was to grab her—hold her—never let her go again. But I took a firm grip upon these primitive urges, and then:

"I saw you at Victoria," she said.

"What! How could you have seen me?"

"I have eyes and I can see with them."

She lay back among the cushions, and turning, smiled up at me.

"I had no idea you had seen me."

"That is why I am here tonight." Suddenly, seriously: "You must go back! I tell you, you must go back. I came here tonight to tell you this."

"Is that all you came for, Ardatha?"

"Yes. Do not suppose it means what you are thinking. I like you very much, but do not make the mistake of believing that I love easily."

She spoke with a quiet imperiousness of manner which checked me. My emotions pulled me in various directions. In the first place, this beautiful girl of the amethyst eyes, who, whatever she did, whatever she said, allured, maddened me, was a criminal. In the second place, unless the glance of those eyes be wildly misleading, she wanted me to make love to her. But in the third place, although she said her nocturnal visit had been prompted by friendship, what was her real motive? I clasped my knees tightly and stared aside at her.

"I am glad you are a man who thinks," she said softly, "for between us there is much to think about."

"There is only one thing I am thinking about—that I want you. You are never out of my mind. Day and night I am unhappy because I know you are involved in a conspiracy of horror and murder in which you, the real you, have no part. If I thought lightly of you and merely desired you, then as you say I should not have thought. I should have my arms around you now, kissing you, as I want to kiss you. But you see, Ardatha, you mean a lot more than that. Although I know so little about you, yet—"

"Ssh!"

Swiftly she grasped my arm—and I seized her hand and held it. But the warning had been urgent, and I listened.

We both sat silent for a while. My gaze was set upon a strange ring which she wore. The clasp of her fingers gave me a thrill which passionate kisses of another woman could never have aroused.

Somewhere out there in the shadows I had detected the sound of a dull thud—of soft footsteps.

Releasing Ardatha's hand, I would have sprung up, but:

"Don't look out!" she whispered. "No! No! Don't look out!"

I hesitated. She held me tightly.

"Why?"

"Because it is just possible—I may have been followed. Please, don't look out!"

I heard the sound of a distant voice out over the canal; splashing of water . . . nothing more. I turned to Ardatha. There was no need for words.

She slipped almost imperceptibly into my arms, and raised her lips . . .

Nayland Smith's room

For a long time after Ardatha had gone—I don't know how long a time—I knelt there by my open window staring out over the canal. She had trusted herself to me. How could I detain her—how could I regard her as a criminal? Indeed I wondered if ever I should be able so to regard her again.

The fear now burning in my brain was fear solely for her safety.

Always I had found it painful to imagine her in association with the remorseless murder group controlled by Dr Fu Manchu, but now that idea was agony. I dared not imagine what would happen if her visit to me should be discovered, if the double part which she played came to the knowledge of the Chinese doctor . . . and I could not forget that queer sound down by the waterside, those soft footsteps.

Ardatha suspected that she might have been followed. Perhaps her suspicions were well founded!

I stared out intently into misty darkness. I listened but could hear nothing save the lapping of water. From where had she come—to where had she gone? I knew little more about her than I had ever known, except that she was anxious to save me from some dreadful fate which obviously she believed to be pending.

One thing I had learned: Ardatha was of mixed Oriental and European blood. On her father's side she descended from generations of Eastern rulers; petty chieftains from a Western standpoint, but potentates in their own land. Her murderous hatred of dictatorships was understandable. Practically the whole of her family had been wiped out by General Quinto's airmen . . .

Silence!—and in the silence another idea was born. The watcher in the night perhaps had a double purpose. Satisfied that I was fully preoccupied, he might have given some signal which meant that Nayland Smith was alone!

Most ghastly idea of all—this may have been the real purpose of Ardatha's visit!

I tried in retrospect to analyse every expression in the amethyst eyes; and I found it hard, in fact impossible, to believe treachery to be hidden there. I thought of her parting kiss. My heart even now beat faster when I recalled it. Surely it could not have been a Judas kiss?

No sound could I detect anywhere about me. The Grand Canal was deserted, the moon partly veiled; but my thoughts had me restlessly uneasy. I must make sure that Nayland Smith was safe.

Quietly opening my door I walked along and switched up the light in the sitting room.

It presented exactly the same appearance as when I had left it. I moved on to Smith's closed door. I listened intently but could hear nothing. However, he was a deep, silent sleeper, and I was not satisfied. Very gently I moved the handle. The door was unlocked. Inch by inch I opened it, until at last, having made hardly any sound, I could creep in.

The room was in darkness, save for a dim reflection through the slats of the shutters. Yet I was afraid to switch on the light, for I had no wish to disturb him. I crept slowly forward in the direction of the bed, and my eyes growing accustomed to the semidarkness, by the time that I reached it a startling fact had become evident:

The bed was empty! It had never been slept in!

I switched on the bedside lamp and stared about me distractedly.

He had not undressed!

I crossed to the shuttered window. The shutters were not fastened but just lightly closed. I pushed them open and stared out. I could see across to the landing stage. The ledge was not more than four feet above the pavement, as was the case in my own room. Why, I asked myself desperately, had he of all men, he, marked down as Enemy Number One by Dr Fu Manchu, exposed himself to such a risk?

And where was he?

I pressed the night porter's bell, crossed to the sitting room and threw the door open. In less than a minute, I suppose, the porter appeared.

"Can you tell me," I asked, "if Sir Denis Nayland Smith has gone out tonight?"

"No sir, he has not gone out."

The man looked surprised—in fact, startled.

"But I suppose he could have gone out without being seen?"

"No sir. After midnight, except on special occasions, the door is locked. I open it for anyone returning late."

"And do you remain in the lobby?"

"Yes sir."

"Did anyone return late tonight?"

"No sir. There are few people in the hotel at the moment and all were in before eleven o'clock."

"When you came on duty?"

"When I came on duty, yes sir."

"You mean that it is quite impossible for Sir Denis to have gone out without your seeing him?"

"Quite impossible, sir."

Although his room exhibited no evidence whatever of a struggle, one explanation, a ghastly one, alone presented itself to my mind.

He had been overcome, carried out by way of the window and so to the landing stage! Those movements in the night were explained. My lovely companion's coolness under circumstances calculated to terrify a normal girl assumed a different aspect . . .

My friend, the best friend I should ever have, had been fighting for his life while I clung to the lips of Ardatha!

Venice claims a victim

A police officer was an almost unendurably long time in reaching the hotel. When at last he arrived, a captain of Carabinieri, he brought two detectives with him. His English was defective but fortunately for me one of the men spoke it well.

When I had made the facts clear and a search of the room had taken place:

"I fear, sir," said the English-speaking detective, "that your suspicions are confirmed. I am satisfied that your friend did not leave by the front door of the hotel. As he evidently did not go to bed, however, there is a possibility, is there not, that he left of his own free will?"

"Yes." I grasped gladly at this straw. "There is! Why had I not thought of that?"

There was a brief conference in Italian between the three, and then:

"It has been suggested," the detective went on, "that if Sir Denis Nayland Smith, for whom a bodyguard had been arranged by order of Colonel Correnti, had decided to go out for any reason, he would probably have awakened you."

"I was not asleep," I said shortly.

Where did my duty lie? Should I confess that Ardatha had been with me?

"It makes it all the more strange. You were perhaps reading or writing?"

"No. I was thinking and staring out of the window."

"Did you hear any suspicious sounds?"

"Yes. What I took to be footsteps and a faint scuffling. But I heard no more."

"It is all the more curious," the man went on, "because we have two officers on duty, one in a gondola moored near the steps, and the other at the back of the hotel. Before coming here I personally interviewed both these officers and neither had seen anything suspicious."

The mystery grew deeper.

"My own room was lighted," I said. "Are my windows visible from the point of view of the man in the gondola?"

"We will go and see."

We moved along to my room. My feelings as I looked at the divan upon which Ardatha had lain in my arms I find myself unable to describe . . . One of the detectives glanced out of the window and reported that owing to the wall of that little courtyard to which I have referred, this window would be outside the viewpoint of the man in the gondola.

"But the window of Sir Denis' room—this he could see."

Another idea came.

"The sitting room!"

"It is possible. Let us look."

We looked—and solely because, I suppose, no one had attached any importance to the sitting room, it now immediately became evident that one shutter was open.

It had not been open when I had parted from Smith that night!

"You see!" exclaimed the detective, "here is the story: He was overcome, perhaps drugged, in his room, carried in here and lowered out through that window!"

"But"—I was thinking now of Ardatha—"how could the kidnappers have got him away without attracting the notice of one of your men?"

Another consultation took place. All three were becoming wildly excited.

"I must explain"—a half-dressed and bewildered manager had joined us—"that passing under the window of your own room, Mr. Kerrigan, it is possible—there is a gate there—to reach the bridge over the Rio Banieli—the small canal."

"But you say"—I turned to the detective—"that you had a man on duty at the rear of the hotel?"

"True, but here is dense shadow at this hour of the night. It would be possible—just possible—for one to reach and cross that bridge unnoticed."

In my mind I was reconstructing the tragedy of the night. I saw

Nayland Smith, drugged, helpless, being carried (probably on the shoulder of one of Dr Fu Manchu's Thugs) right below my window as I lay there intoxicated by the beauty of Ardatha. I felt myself choked with rage and mortification.

"But it is simply incredible," I cried, "that such a crime can be committed here in Venice! We must find Sir Denis! We must find him!"

"It is understood, sir, that we must find him. This is very bad for the Venice police, because you are under our special protection. The chief has been notified and will shortly be here. It is a tragedy—yes: I regret it deeply."

Overcome by a sense of the futility of it all, the hopelessness of outwitting that criminal genius who played with human lives as a chess player with pieces, I turned and walked back to the sitting room. I stared dumbly at the open window through which my poor friend had disappeared, probably forever.

The police left the suite, in deference, I think, to my evident sorrow, and I found myself alone.

The girl to whom I had lost my heart, my reason was a modern Delilah. Her part had been to lull my suspicions, to detain me there—if need be with kisses—while the dreadful master of the Si-Fan removed an enemy from his path.

My thoughts tortured me—I clenched my teeth; I felt my brain reeling. In every way that a man could fail, I had failed. I had succumbed to the wiles of a professional vampire and had given over my friend to death.

There were perhaps issues greater than my personal sorrow. The life of Rudolf Adlon hung upon a hair. Nayland Smith was gone!

Venice, the city of the doges, had claimed one more victim.

Dawn was creeping gloriously over the city when the first, the only clue, came to hand.

A Carabinieri patrol returning at four o'clock was subjected, in common with all others who had been on duty that night, to a close examination. He remembered (a fact which normally he would not have reported) that a girl, smartly dressed and wearing a scarf over her hair, had hurried past him at a point not far from the hotel. He had paid little attention to her, except that he remembered she was pretty, but his description of her dress strongly suggested Ardatha!

Twenty yards behind and, as he recalled, seeming deliberately to keep in the shadow, he had noticed a man: an Englishman, he was confident, tall, wearing a tweed suit and a soft-brimmed hat.

The time, as nearly as I could judge, would have corresponded to that at which I had parted from Ardatha . . .

The detective's theory had been the right one. Something had drawn Smith's attention to the presence of the girl. He had not been kidnapped—he had watched and followed her. To where? What had become of him?

That sense of guilt which weighed heavily upon me became heavier than ever. I was indeed directly responsible for whatever had befallen my friend.

I was already at police headquarters when this report came in. The man was sent for and through an interpreter I questioned him. Since I knew the two people concerned more intimately than anyone present his answers to my questions removed any possibility of doubt.

The girl described was Ardatha. Nayland Smith had been following her!

Even at this stage, frantic as I was with anxiety about Smith, almost automatically I compromised with my conscience when Colonel Correnti asked me:

"Do you think this girl is someone known to Sir Denis?"

"Possibly," I replied. "He may have thought he recognised an accomplice of Doctor Fu Manchu."

When I left police headquarters to walk back to the hotel, Venice was bathed in its morning glory. But I moved through the streets and across the canals of that fairy city in a state of such utter dejection that any I passed surely pitied me.

Of Smith's plans in regard to the luncheon party on Silver Heels I had very little idea, but I had been fully prepared to go with him. I was anxious to see Rudolf Adlon in person. It seemed to me to be pointless to go alone. What he had hoped to learn I could not imagine. James Brownlow Wilton, the New York newspaper magnate, would seem to have no place in this tangled skein. It was a baffling situation and I was hopelessly worn out.

I tried to snatch a few hours' sleep, but found sleep to be impossible. Sir George Herbert called at ten o'clock, an old young man with foreign office stamped indelibly upon him. His expression was grave.

"This is a great blow, Mr Kerrigan," he said. "I can see how it has affected you. To me, it is disastrous. These threats to Rudolf Adlon, who is here incognito, as you know, are backed by an organisation which does not threaten lightly. General Quinto has been assassinated—why not Rudolf Adlon?"

"I agree. But I know nothing of Smith's plans to protect him."

"Nor do I!" He made a gesture of despair. "It had been arranged for him to go on board Mr Wilton's yacht during today's luncheon, but what he hoped to accomplish I have no idea."

"Nor I."

I spoke the words groaningly, dropped on to a chair and stared I suppose rather wildly at Sir George.

"The Italian authorities are sparing no effort. Their responsibility is great, for more than the reputation of the chief of police is at stake. If any news should reach me I will advise you immediately, Mr Kerrigan. I think you would be wise to rest."

A woman drops a rose

The human constitution is a wonderfully adjusted instrument. I had no hope, indeed no intention, of sleeping. Venice, awakened, lived gaily about me. Yet, after partially undressing, within five minutes of Sir George's departure I was fast asleep.

I was awakened by Colonel Correnti. Those reflected rays through my shutters which I had not closed told me the truth.

It was sunset, I had slept for many hours.

"What news?"

Instantly I was wide awake, a cloak or sorrow already draped about me.

He shook his head.

"None, I fear."

"The luncheon party on the yacht took place, I suppose? Sir Denis feared that some attempt might be made there."

"Rudolf Adlon was present, yes. He is known on these occasions as Major Baden. My men report that nothing of an unusual nature took place. The dictator is safely back at the Palazzo da Rosa where he will be joined tomorrow by Pietro Monaghani. There is no evidence of any plot." He shrugged his shoulders. "What can I do? Officially, I am not supposed to know that the chancellor is here. Of Sir Denis no trace can be found. What can I do?"

His perplexity was no greater than mine. What, indeed, could any of us do?

I forced myself to eat a hasty meal. The solicitude of the management merely irritated me. I found myself constantly looking aside, constantly listening, for I could not believe it possible for a man so well known as Nayland Smith to vanish like a mirage.

Of Ardatha I dared not think bat all.

To remain there inert was impossible. I could do nothing useful, for I had no plan, but at least I could move, walk the streets, search the cafés, stare up at the windows. With no better object than this in view, I set out.

Before St Mark's I pulled up abruptly. The magic of sunset was draping the façade in wonderful purple shadows. I was torn between two courses. If I lost myself in this vain hunt through the streets of Venice, I might be absent when news came. In a state of indecision I stood there before the doors of that ornate, ancient church. What news could come? News that Smith was dead!

From these ideas I must run away, must keep moving. Indeed I found myself incapable of remaining still, and now a reasonable objective occurred to me. Since Rudolph Adlon was staying at the Palazzo da Rosa this certainly would be the focus of Dr Fu Manchu's attention. Actually, of course I was seeking some excuse for action, something to distract my mind from the ghastly contemplation of Nayland Smith's fate.

I hurried back to the hotel and learned from the hall porter that no message had been received for me. Thereupon I walked out and chartered a motorboat.

A gondola was too slow for my humour.

"Go along the Grand Canal," I directed, "and show me the Palazzo da Rosa."

We set out, and I endeavoured to compose myself and to submit without undue irritation to the informative remarks of the man who drove the motorboat. He wished to take me to the Rialto Bridge, to the villa where Richard Wagner had died, to the Palace of Gabriel d'Annunzio; but finally, with a great air of mystery, slowing his craft:

"Yonder," he said, "where I am pointing, is the Palazzo da Rosa. It is here, sir, that Signor Monaghani, himself, stays sometimes when he is in Venice. Also it is whispered, but I do not know, that the great Adlon is there."

"Stop awhile."

Dusk had fallen and light streamed from nearly all the windows of the palace. I observed much movement about the water gate, many gondolas crowded against the painted posts, there was a stir and bustle which told of some sort of entertainment taking place.

A closed motorboat, painted black, and apparently empty, passed almost silently between us and the steps.

"The police!"

We moved on . . .

Two seagoing yachts were at anchor, and out on the lagoon we met a freshening breeze. One of the yachts belonged to an English peer, the other, Silver Heels, was Brownlow Wilton's beautiful white cruiser, built on the lines of an ocean greyhound. All seemed to be quiet on board, and I wondered if the celebrated American was being entertained at the Palazzo da Rosa.

"Where to now, sir?"

"Anywhere you like," I answered wearily.

The man seemed to understand my mood. I believe he thought I was a dejected lover whose mistress had deserted him. Indeed, he was not far wrong.

We turned into a side canal where there were ancient windows, walls and trellises draped in clematis and passion flower, a spot, as I saw at a glance, perpetuated by many painters. In the dusk it had a ghostly beauty. Here the motorboat seemed a desecration, and I wished that I had chartered a gondola. Even as the thought crossed my mind, one of those swan-like crafts, carrying the bearings of some noble family, and propelled by a splendidly uniformed gondolier, swung silently around a corner, heralded only by the curious cry of the man at the oar.

My fellow checked his engine.

"From the Palazzo da Rosa!" he said and gazed back fascinatedly.

Idly, for I was not really interested, I turned and stared back also. There was but one passenger in the gondola . . .

It was Rudolf Adlon!

"Stop!" I ordered sharply as the man was about to restart his engine. "I want to watch."

For I had seen something else.

On the balcony of a crumbling old mansion, once no doubt the home of a merchant prince but now falling into ruin, a woman was standing. Some trick of reflected light from across the canal made her features clearly visible. She wore a gaily-coloured showl which left one arm and shoulder bare.

She was leaning on the rail of the balcony, staring down at the passing gondola—and as I watched, eagerly, almost breathlessly, I saw that the gondolier had checked his graceful boat with that easy, sweeping movement which is quite beyond the power of an ama-

135

teur oarsman. Rudolph Adlon was standing up, his eyes raised. As I watched, the woman dropped a rose to which, I was almost sure, a note was attached!

Adlon caught it deftly, kissed his fingers to the beauty on the balcony and resumed his seat. As the gondola swung on and was lost in deep shadows of a tall, old palace beyond:

"Ah!" sighed the motor launch driver—and he also kissed his fingers to the balcony—"a tryst—how beautiful!"

She who had made the assignation had disappeared. But there was no possibility of mistake. She was the woman I had seen with Ardatha—the woman whom Nayland Smith had described as "a corpse moving among the living—a harbinger of death!"

The chief of police hung up the telephone.

"Major Baden is in his private apartments," he said, "engaged on important official business. He has given orders that he is not to be disturbed. And so"—he shrugged his shoulders —"what can I do?"

I confess I was growing weary of those oft-repeated words.

"But I assure you," I cried excitedly, "that he is *not* in his private apartments! At least he was not there a quarter of an hour ago!"

"That is possible, Mr Kerrigan. I have said that some of the great men who visit Venice incognito have sometimes other affairs than affairs of State. But since, in the first place, I am not supposed to know that Rudolf Adlon is at the Palazzo at all what steps can I take? I have one of my best officers on duty there and this is his report. What more can I do?"

"Nothing!" I groaned!

"In regard to protecting this minister, nothing, I fear. But the other matter—yes! This woman whom you describe is known to be an accomplice of these people who seek the life of Rudolf Adlon?"

"She is."

"Then we shall set out to find her, Mr Kerrigan! I shall be ready in five minutes."

Complete darkness had come when we reached the canal in which I had passed the dictator, but the light of a quarter moon painted Venice with silver. I travelled now in one of those sinister-looking black boats to which my attention had been drawn earlier.

"There is the balcony," I said, "directly over us."

Colonel Correnti looked up and then stared at me quite blankly.

"I find it very difficult to believe, Mr Kerrigan," he said. "Do not misunderstand me—I am not doubting your word. I am only doubting if you have selected the right balcony."

"There is no doubt about it," I said irritably.

"Then the matter is certainly very strange."

He glanced at the two plain-clothes police officers who accompanied us. I had met them before, one, Stocco, was he who spoke good English.

"Why?"

"Because this is the back of the old Palazzo Mori. It is the property of the Mori family, but as you see it is in a state of dilapidation. It has not been occupied, I assure you, for many, many years. I know for a fact that it is unfurnished."

"This does not interest me," I replied, now getting angry. "What I have stated is fact. Great issues are at stake, and I suggest that we obtain a key and search this place."

He turned with a despairing gesture to his subordinates.

"Where are the keys of the Palazzo Mori?"

There was a consultation, in which the man who drove the motor launch took part.

"The Mori family, alas, is ruined," said Correnti, "and its remaining members are spread all over the world. I do not know where. The keys of the palazzo are with the lawyer Borgese, and it would be difficult, I fear, to find him tonight."

"Also a waste of time," I replied, for I knew what Nayland Smith would have done in the circumstances. "From the balustrade of the steps there to that lower iron balcony is an easy matter for an active man. We are all active men, I take it? Even from here one can see that the latchet of the window is broken. Here is our way in. Why do we hesitate?"

The chief of police seemed to have doubts, but recognising, I suppose, what a terrible responsibility rested upon his shoulders, finally, although reluctantly, he consented.

The police boat was drawn up beside the steps, and I, first in my eagerness, clambered on to the roof of the cabin, from there sprang to the decaying stonework of the balustrade and climbed to the top. Balancing somewhat hazardously and reaching up, I found that I could just grasp the ornamental ironwork which I had pointed out.

"Give me a lift," I directed Stocco, who stood beside me.

He did so. The boat rocked, but he succeeded in lifting me high enough to enable me to release my left hand and to grasp the upper railing. The rest was easy.

Colonel Correnti, as Stocco in turn was hoisted up beside me, cried out some order.

"We are to go," said the detective, "down to the main door, open it if possible and admit the chief."

I put my shoulder to the broken lattice, and it burst open immediately. Out of silvery moonlight I stepped into complete darkness. My companion produced a flashlamp.

I found myself in a room which at some time had been a bedroom. It was quite denuded of furniture, but here and there remained fragments of mouldy tapestry. And on the once-polished floor I detected marks to show where an old-fashioned four-poster bed had rested.

"Let us hope the doors are not locked," said Stocco.

However, this one at least was not.

"Upstairs first!" I said eagerly, as we stepped out on to the landing.

Looking over a heavily carved handrail, in the light of the flashlamp directed downwards I saw the sweep of a marble staircase lost in Gothic gloom. A great shadowy hall lay below, with ghostly pillars amid which our slightest movement echoed eerily. There was a damp musty smell in the place which I found unpleasantly tomb-like. But we paused here for scarcely a moment. We went hurrying upstairs, our footsteps rattling uncannily upon marble steps. Here for a moment we hesitated on a higher landing, flashing the light of the lamp about.

"This is the room," I said, and indicated a closed door.

Stocco tried the handle; the door opened. Right ahead of me across the room beyond I saw a half-opened lattice. A moment later I was on the balcony from which the mysterious woman had dropped a rose to Rudolf Adlon.

"This is where she stood!"

The detective shone a light all about us. The room was choicely

138

panelled in some light wood and possessed what had once been a painted ceiling, now no more than a series of damp blotches where minute fungus grew.

"Shine the light down here," I ordered excitedly.

On the heavy dust of a parquet floor were slight but unmistakable marks of high-heeled shoes!

"God's mercy, you were right!" Stocco exclaimed.

Yes, I was right. This house was a tomb. Rudolph Adlon had made an appointment with a creature of another world, a *zombie*, a human corpse brought to life! And here indeed was a fitting abode for such a creature!

No doubt the place was partly responsible, but as I stood there staring at my companion, and remembered how Nayland Smith had been smuggled out of life by the master magician called Dr Fu Manchu, I was prepared to believe that a dead woman moved among the living.

Palazzo Mori

We admitted the chief of police by the main door. It was heavily bolted but not locked. He was at least as nonplussed as I when the marks of little heels were pointed out to him in the room above.

"This," he said, "is supernatural."

Although disposed to agree with him I was determined to leave no stone unturned in my efforts to solve the mystery. Discounting her sorcerous origin for the moment and therefore her magical powers, how had Dr Fu Manchu's accomplice got into this place, and how had she got out?

"Merely supernormal perhaps," I suggested. "Everything has an explanation, after all." I was trying desperately to restore my own self- confidence. "You know the history of these old buildings better than I do. Have you any explanation to offer of how a person could enter and leave the Palazzo Mori as undoubtedly someone entered and left it tonight?"

"I have no explanation to offer, Mr Kerrigan," said Colonel Correnti. His expression was almost pathetic. "None whatever."

The second detective began to speak urgently and rapidly, and as a result:

"This officer tells me," the colonel continued, "that at one time, but very, very long ago, there was an entrance to this old palace from the other side of the canal—I mean the Rio Mori, from which we entered."

"I don't think I follow you."

"A passage—they were not uncommon in old days—under the Rio Mori, which of course is quite shallow. It seems that the boathouse of the family was on the opposite bank in those days, and for the convenience of the gondoliers this passage was made. It has been blocked up for at least a century."

"That hardly seems to help us!"

"No, not at all. I think I know the place—an old stone shed."

140

He spoke rapidly to his subordinate who replied with equal rapidity. "It was used, I am told, as a store by a house decorator for a time but is now empty again. No, my friend, this is useless. We must seek elsewhere for the solution of our mystery."

Of our search of the old palace it is unnecessary that I give any account. It yielded nothing. Apart from those footprints in the upper room there was no evidence whatever to show that anyone had entered the building for many years. Certainly below the grand salon, where patches on the walls from which paintings had been removed, pathetically told of decayed grandeur, there were locked rooms.

To these we were unable to gain access, and it seemed pointless to attempt it. Examination of the locks clearly indicated that they had not been recently used. At this stage of the search I had given up hope.

We returned to police headquarters. There was no news. I turned aside to hide my despair. An officer who had remained in constant touch with the detectives in the Palazzo da Rosa reported that "Major Baden" had joined the guests for half an hour and had then excused himself on the grounds of urgent business, and had retired again to his own apartment.

"You see?" Colonel Correnti shrugged his shoulders. "We can do nothing."

I tried to control my voice when I spoke:

"Do you really understand what is at stake? An ex-commissioner of Scotland Yard has been kidnapped, probably murdered. He is one of the highest officials of the British Secret Service. The most prominent figure in European politics, and I do not except Pietro Monaghani, is, beyond any shadow of doubt, in deadly peril. Are you sure, Colonel, that every available man is straining himself to the utmost, that every possible place has been searched, every suspect interrogated?"

"I assure you, Mr Kerrigan, that every available man in Venice is either searching or watching tonight. I can do no more . . ."

I think during the next hour I must have plumbed the uttermost deeps of despair. I wandered about the gay streets of Venice like a ghost at a banquet, staring at lighted windows, into the faces of the passers-by, until I began to feel that I was attracting public attention.

I returned to the hotel, went to my room and sat down on that settee where Ardatha had bewitched me with kisses.

How I cursed every moment of that stolen happiness! No contempt I had ever known for a fellow being could approach that which I had for myself. I conjured up a picture of Nayland Smith; almost in my state of distraction I seemed to hear his voice. He was trying to tell me something, trying to direct me, to awaken in my dull brain some spark of enlightenment.

Had our cases been reversed what would *he* have done?

This idea seemed to give me a new coolness. Yes! what would he have done? I sat there, head buried in my hands, striving to think calmly.

That the dark woman had entered and left that ruined palace was a fact. Whoever or whatever she might be, of her presence there we had unassailable evidence. Our search had revealed no explanation of the mystery. But there were doors we had failed to open.

This would not have been Nayland Smith's way!

He would never have been satisfied to leave the Palazzo Mori until those lower rooms had been examined. Nor would he have been content with the assertion of the chief of police that the ancient passage under the canal was blocked . . .

I sprang up.

This was the line of inquiry which Smith would have followed! I was sure of it. This should be my objective. A dishevelled figure (I had not been undressed for thirty-six hours), once more I set out.

The ancient house of the gondoliers was easy to locate. It was solidly built of stone with three windows on the land side and a heavy, padlocked door at the end. The narrow lane by which one approached it was dark and deserted. I had brought an electric torch, and I shot a beam through one of the broken windows. It showed a quantity of litter: fragments of wall paper, mortar boards and numerous empty paint cans. I inspected the padlock.

This bore evidence of use: it had recently been oiled!

But it was fast.

Greatly excited, I returned to the broken window and looked in again. The litter had not been disturbed, I could have sworn, for a considerable time—yet the door had recently been used.

My excitement grew. I thought that from some place, in this world or beyond, Nayland Smith had succeeded in inspiring me with something of his old genius for investigation. A great task lay to my hand. I determined to do it well.

I studied the padlock. I had no means of picking it, nor indeed any knowledge of that art. To crash a pane in one of the windows would have been useless, for they were of a kind not made to open, and the panes were too narrow to allow entrance had the glass been entirely removed. I walked around to the other side. Here was evidence of a landing stage long demolished. There were three windows and a walled-up door. Inspection was carried out from a narrow ledge which overhung the canal. Baffled again, I was about to return—when I heard footsteps coming down the lane!

I stayed where I was. Directly opposite, the narrow canal glittering between, rose a wall of the deserted Palazzo Mori. I could see that stone balustrade up which I had scrambled, the iron balcony to which I had clung. Nearer and nearer the footsteps approached, and now I heard a woman's voice:

"Wait, just a moment! . . . I have the key."

It was a soothing, caressing voice, and I longed for a glimpse of the speaker, but dared not move.

I heard the rattling of the padlock, opening of the door.

"Please wait! Not yet! We may be seen!"

Light suddenly illuminated the interior of the building. I crouched low, my heart beating fast, and cautiously from one corner of a window, peered in.

What I saw made my heart beat faster. It strengthened my resolution to do what Nayland Smith would have done . . .

Rudolf Adlon, wearing a half mask, and a cloak over his evening dress, stood hands clasped behind him, watching a woman who knelt in a corner of the floor!

His eyes were ardent; he tore the mask off—and I saw a man enslaved. The woman wore a loose fur wrap, her arms resembled dull ivory. She was slender, almost serpentine, jet-black hair lay close to her shapely head. And as I looked and recognised her, she stood upright.

A trap had been opened, a section of floor with its impedimenta of pots and litter had been slid aside! She turned—and for the first time I saw her eyes.

Her eyes—long, narrow, dark-lashed eyes—were emerald green! I had thought that there were no eyes in the world like these except the eyes of Dr Fu Manchu.

She made a gesture of triumph. She smiled as perhaps long ago Calypso smiled.

"Be patient! This is the only way—come!"

The words reached me clearly through the broken window. Pulling her wrap over her bare shoulders, she beckoned and began to descend steps below the trap. I saw that she carried a flashlamp.

Rudolf Adlon obeyed. The light below shone up into his dark, eager face as he stooped to follow.

And then came darkness.

144

The zombie

Rudolf Adlon, dictator of a great European nation, was going to his death!

I thought rapidly, trying to envisage the situation from what I believed would have been Nayland Smith's point of view.

Probably I could reach police headquarters in ten minutes. A call box was of no avail, owing to my ignorance of the language, so that this meant ten minutes wasted. Before the police arrived, Adlon might have disappeared as Nayland Smith had disappeared. That the passage led to the Palazzo Mori I had good reason to suppose. But unless it had been planned to assassinate the chancellor in that deserted building and hide his body, where were they going?

My experience of the methods of the Si-Fan inclined me to believe that Adlon would be given a final opportunity to accept the Council's orders. My decision was soon made. I would follow; and when I had found out where the woman was leading the dictator, return and bring a party large enough to surround the place.

The door I knew to be unfastened. I groped my way to where a dim oblong light indicated the position of the trap. I saw stone steps. I descended cautiously. The place in which I found myself had a foul reek; the filthy water of the Rio Mori dripped through its roof in places. It was an ancient stone passage, slimy and repellent. A vague moving light at the further end was that of the flashlamp carried by the woman.

Adlon's infatuation had blinded him to his danger. But putting myself in his place and substituting Ardatha for the woman of death, I knew that I, too, would have followed to the very gates of hell.

Fixing my eyes on that guiding light, I proceeded. The light disappeared, but I discovered ascending steps. A spear in the darkness led me up to a door ajar. I heard a voice and recognised it. It was the voice of Adlon.

"Where are you leading me, Mona Lisa?"

In the exquisite face of this ghoul who hunted human souls for Dr Fu Manchu he had discovered a resemblance to that famous painting. The resemblance was not perceptible to me . . .

Along an arched cellar, silhouettes against the light of the moving lamp which cast grotesque shadows, I saw the pair ahead: the slender figure of the woman, the cloaked form of the doomed man. There was a great squat pillar in this forgotten crypt and I crept behind it until they had come to the top of the open stair and vanished into a Gothic archway.

Complete darkness had come when I crept forward and followed, feeling my way to the foot of the stair.

The sound of footsteps ceased. I stood stockstill. I heard the woman's laughter, low-pitched, haunting. It ended abruptly. There came thickly muttered words in a man's voice. He had her in his arms . . . Then the footsteps continued.

A key was placed in a lock and I heard the creaking of a door. It echoed, phantomesque, as though in a cavern; it warned me of what I should find. I waited until those sounds, mockingly repeated by the ghosts of the place, grew faint. Advancing, I found myself in the tomblike entrance hall of the Palazzo Mori.

The light carried by the woman was now a mere speck. However, using extreme caution, I followed it. As I crossed that haunted place, the shades of men trapped, poisoned, murdered there, seemed to move around me in a satanic dance. Tortured spirits of mediaeval Venice formed up at my back, barring the road to safety. Yet I pressed on, for I knew that the great outer door was open, that even if my way through the foul tunnel be cut off, here was another sally port although it meant a plunge into the Grand Canal.

The light faded out entirely, but a hollow ringing of footsteps assured me that I had further to go. One of those doors which the police party had found closed, was open! (The ancient lock had been wedged. It was fitted with a new, hidden lock.) And beyond that door Rudolf Adlon went to destruction.

Down five steps I groped, and knew that I was below water level again.

Far along a tunnel similar to that which led under the Rio Mori, I saw the two figures. The man's arm was around the woman; his head was close to hers. I knew that I could never be detected in the darkness of this ancient catacomb unless my own movements betrayed me; and when the silhouettes became blurred and then disappeared altogether I divined the presence of ascending steps at the end of the passage.

One fact of importance I noted: this damp and noisome burrow ran parallel to the Grand Canal. I must be a long way from my starting point.

And now it had grown so black that I had no alternative but to use my torch. I used it cautiously, shining its ray directly before my feet. The floor was clammily repulsive, but I proceeded until I reached the steps. I switched off the torch.

A streak of light told me that a door had been left ajar at the top.

Gently I pushed it open and found myself in an empty wine cellar. One unshaded electric light swung from the vaulted roof. An open stone stair of four steps led up to an arch.

I questioned the wisdom of further advance. But I fear the spirit of Nayland Smith deserted me, that hereditary madness ruled my next move, for I crept up, found a massive, nail-studded door open, and peered out into a carpeted passage!

Emerging from that subterranean chill, the change of atmosphere was remarkable. Rudolf Adlon's voice reached me. He spoke happily, passionately. Then the speaker's tone rose to a high note—a cry . . . and ceased abruptly!

They had him—it was all over! Inspired by a furious indignation, I stole forward and peered around the edge of a half-opened door into a room beyond. It was a small room having parquet flooring of a peculiar pattern: a plain border of black wood some three feet wide, the center designed to represent a lotus in bloom. Its walls were panelled, and the place appeared to be empty until, venturing unwisely to protrude my head, I saw watching me with a cold smile the woman of death!

I suppose she was exceptionally beautiful, this creature who, according to Nayland Smith, should long since have been dust; but the aura surrounding her, my knowledge, now definite, of her murderous work, combined to make her a thing of horror.

She had discarded her wrap; it was draped over her arm. I saw a slenderly perfect figure, small delicately chiselled features. Hers was a beauty so imperious that it awakened a memory which presently came fully to life. She might have posed for that portrait of Queen Nefertiti found in the tomb of Tutankhamen. An Arab necklace of crudely stamped gold heightened the resemblance. I was to learn later of others who had detected this.

But it was her eyes, fixed immovably upon me, which awakened ancient superstitions. The strange word *zombie* throbbed in my brain; for those eyes, green as emeralds, were long and narrow, their gaze was hard to sustain . . . and they were like the eyes of Dr Fu Manchu!

"Well"—she spoke calmly—"who are you, and why have you followed me?"

Conscious of my dishevelled condition, of the fact that I had no backing, I hesitated.

"I followed you," I said at last, "because it was my duty to follow you."

"Your duty—why?"

She stood there, removed from me by the length of the room, and the regard of those strange, narrowed eyes never left my face.

"Because you had someone with you."

"You are wrong; I am alone."

I watched her, this suave, evil beauty. And for the first time I became aware of a heavy perfume resembling that of hawthorn.

"Where has he gone?"

"To whom do you refer?"

"To Rudolf Adlon."

She laughed. I saw her teeth gleam and thought of a vampire. It was the laugh I had heard down there in the cellars, deep, taunting.

"You dream, my friend—whoever you are—you dream."

"You know quite well who I am."

"Oh!" she raised delicate eyebrows mockingly. "You are famous then?"

What should I do? My instinct was to turn and run for it. Something told me that if I did so, I should be trapped.

"If you were advised by me you would go back. You trespass in someone's house—I do not advise you to be found here."

148

"You advise me to go back?"

"Yes. It is kind of me."

And now although common sense whispered that to go would mean ambush in that echoing tomb which was the Palazzo Mori, I was sorely tempted to chance it. There was something wildly disturbing in this woman's presence, in the steady glance of her luminous eyes. In short, I was afraid of her—afraid of the silent house about me, of the noisome passages below—of all the bloodthirsty pageant of mediaeval Venice to which her sheath frock, her ivory shoulders, seemed inevitably to belong.

But I wondered why she temporised, why she stood there watching me with that mocking smile. Although I could hear no sound surely it must be a matter of merely raising her voice to summon assistance.

Forcing down this insidious fear which threatened to betray me, I rapidly calculated my chances.

The room was no more than twelve feet long. I could be upon her in three bounds. Better still—why had I forgotten it? I suppose because she was a woman . . .

In a flash I had her covered with my automatic.

She did not stir. There was something uncanny in her coolness, something which again reminded me of the dreadful Dr Fu Manchu. Her lips alone quivered in that slight, contemptuous smile.

"Don't move your hands!" I said, and the urgency of my case put real menace into the words. "I know this is a desperate game—you know it too. Step forward. I will return as you suggest, but you will go ahead of me."

"And suppose I refuse to step forward?"

"I shall come and fetch you!"

Still there was no sound save that of our low-pitched voices, nothing to indicate the presence of another human being.

"You would be mad to attempt such a thing. My advice was sincere. You dare not shoot me unless also you propose to commit suicide, and I warn you that one step in my direction will mean your death."

I watched her intently—although now an attack from the rear was what I feared, having good reason to remember the efficiency of Fu Manchu's Thugs. Perhaps one of them was creeping up behind me. Yet I dared not glance aside.

"Go back! I shall not warn you again."

Whereupon, realising that now or never I must force the issue, I leapt forward . . . That heavy odour of hawthorn became suddenly acute—overpowering—and stifling a scream, I knew too late what had happened.

The woman stood upon the black border, where I, too, had been standing. The whole of the center of the floor was simply an inverted "star trap."

It opened silently as I stepped upon it, and I fell from life into a sickly void of hawthorn blossom and oblivion . . .

Ancient tortures

"Glad to see that you are feeling yourself again, Kerrigan."

I stared about me in stupefaction. This of course was a grotesque dream induced by the drug which had made me unconscious—the drug which smelled like hawthorn blossom. For (a curious fact which even at this moment I appreciated) my memories were sharp-cut, up to the very instant of my fall through that trap in the lotus floor. I knew that I had dropped into some place impregnated with poison gas of an unfamiliar kind. Now came this singularly vivid dream . . .

A dungeon with a low, arched roof: the only light that which came through a barred window in one of the stone walls; and in this place I sat upon a massive chair attached to the paved floor. My hands and arms were free, but my ankles were chained to the front legs of the chair by means of gyves evidently of great age and also of great strength. On my left was a squat pillar some four feet in diameter, and in the shadows behind it I discerned a number of strange and terrifying implements: braziers, tongs and other equipment of a torture chamber.

Almost directly facing me and close beside the barred window, attached to a similar chair, sat Nayland Smith!

This dream my conscious mind told me must be due to thoughts I had been thinking at the moment that unconsciousness came. I had imagined Smith in the power of the Chinese doctor; I had seemed to feel all about me uneasy spirits of men who had suffered and had died in those old palaces which lie along the Grand Canal.

There came a low moaning sound, which rose and fell—rose and fell—and faded away . . .

"I know you think you are dreaming, Kerrigan!" Smith's voice had lost none of its snap. "I thought so myself, until I found it impossible to wake up. But I assure you we are both here and both awake."

Tentatively I tried to move the chair. Stooping, I touched the iron bands about my ankles. Then I stared wanly across at my fellow captive . . . I knew I was awake.

"Thank God you're alive, Smith!"

"Alive, as you say, but not, I fear, for long!"

He laughed. It was not a mirthful laugh. The sound of our voices in that horrible musty place was muted, toneless, as the voices of those who speak in a crypt. I had never seen Smith otherwise than well groomed, but now, growing accustomed to the gloom, I saw that there was stubble on his chin. His hair was of that crisp, wavy sort which never seems to be disordered. But this growth of beard deepened the shadows beneath his cheekbones, and the quick gleam of his small even teeth as he laughed seemed to accentuate the haggardness of his appearance.

"I left in rather a hurry, Kerrigan; I forgot my pipe. It's been damnable here, waiting for . . . whatever he intends to do to me. You will find that the chains are long enough to enable you to reach that recess on your right, where, very courteously, the designer of this apartment has placed certain toilet facilities for the use of one confined here during any considerable time. I am similarly equipped. A Thug of hideous aspect, whom I recognise as an old servant of Doctor Fu Manchu, has waited upon me excellently."

He indicated the remains of a meal on a ledge in the niche beside him.

"Knowing the doctor's penchant for experiments in toxicology, frankly, my appetite has not been good."

I stood up and moved cautiously forward, dragging the chains behind me.

"No, no!" Smith smiled grimly. "It is well thought out, Kerrigan. We cannot get within six feet of one another."

I stood there at the full length of my tether watching him where he sat.

"What I was about to ask is: do you happen to have any cigarettes?"

I clapped a hand to my pocket. My automatic, my clasp knife, these were gone—but not my cigarettes!

"Yes, the case is full."

"Do you mind tossing one across to me? I have a lighter."

I did as he suggested, and he lighted a cigarette. Returning to the immovable chair I followed his example; and as I drew the smoke between my lips I asked myself the question: Am I sane? Is it a fact that I and Nayland Smith are confined in a cell belonging to the Middle Ages?

That gruesome moaning arose again—and died away.

"What is it, Smith?"

"I don't know. I have been wondering for some time."

"You don't think it's some wretched—"

"It isn't a human sound, Kerrigan. It seems to be growing louder . . . However—how did you fall into this?"

I told him—and I was perfectly frank. I told him of Ardatha's visit, of the sounds which I had heard out on the canal side, of all that had followed right to the time that I had fallen into the trap prepared for me.

"There would seem to be a point, Kerrigan, where courage becomes folly."

I laughed.

"What of yourself, Smith? I have yet to learn how you come to be here."

"Oddly enough, our stories are not dissimilar. As you know, I did not turn in when you left me, but I put out the lights and stared from the window. The room was not ideal in view of the peril in which I knew myself to be. But I noted with gratitude a moored gondola in which a stout policeman was seated, apparently watching my window. It occurred to me that the sitting-room windows were equally accessible and, quietly, for I assumed you had gone to bed, I went in to look.

"I found that one was wide open and as I moved across to close it, I heard voices in your room. My first instinct was to dash in, but I waited for a moment because I detected a woman's voice. Then I realised what had happened. Ardatha had paid you a secret visit!

"Knowing your sentiments about this girl, I was by no means easy in my mind. However, I determined not to disturb you or to bring you into the matter in any way. But here was a chance not to be missed.

"Dropping out of the sitting-room window (which the man in the gondola could not see) I tripped and fell. The sound of my fall must have attracted your attention. I discovered a half-gate which shut me off from the courtyard directly below your room. I tried it very gently. It was not locked. Knowing that Ardatha must have approached from the other end, I crept past your window and concealed myself in a patch of shadow near the small bridge which crosses the canal at that point.

"When Ardatha came out (I recognised her from your description) I followed; and my experiences from this point are uncommonly like your own. She entered the old stone storehouse facing the Palazzo Mori; and I, too, performed that clammy journey through the tunnels. I lost her at the top of the steps leading out of the wine cellar. But having learned all I hoped to learn I was about to return when something prompted me to look into the room with the lotus floor."

He paused.

"Now, I want to make it quite clear, Kerrigan: I have no evidence to show that Ardatha suspected she was being followed. The presence of the woman whom I found in that room may have been accidental, but as I looked in I saw her . . ."

"You saw whom?"

"The *zombie!*"

"Good God!"

"My theories regarding her identity were confirmed. I had been right. Failing the presence of Doctor Fu Manchu in the case, she could only be a spirit, a creature of another world. For myself, I had seen her consigned to a horrible death. But woman or spirit, I knew now that she had to be silenced. I sprang forward to seize her—"

"I know!" I groaned.

"At that moment, Kerrigan, my usefulness to the world ended."

He stared down at the smoke arising from the tip of his cigarette.

"You say you recognised her. Who is she?"

"She is Doctor Fu Manchu's daughter."

"What!"

"Unchanged from the first moment I set eyes upon her. She is a living miracle, a corpse moving among the living. But—here we are! And frankly, I confess here we deserve to be!"

He paused for a moment as if listening—perhaps for that awesome moaning. But I could detect no sound save a faint drip-drip of water.

"Of course you realise, Smith," I said in a dull voice, "that Rudolf Adlon is in the hands of Doctor Fu Manchu?"

"I realise it fully. I may add that I doubt if he is alive."

Why I should have felt so about one who was something of a storm centre in Europe I cannot say, but momentarily forgetting my own peril I was chilled by the thought that Rudolf Adlon no longer lived, that the power which swayed a nation had ceased to be. We were silent for a long time, sitting there smoking and staring vacantly at each other. At last:

"As I see it," said Nayland Smith, "we have just one chance."

"What is that?"

"Ardatha!"

"Why do you think so?"

"Now that I know her Oriental origin, which all along I had suspected, I think if she learns that you are here she will try to save you."

I shook my head.

"Even if you are right I doubt if she would have the power . . . and I am sorry to say that I believe her to be utterly evil."

"Let us pray that she is not. She risked perhaps more than you understand to save you once before. If she fails to try again . . ."

That unendurable moaning arose, as if to tell us that Ardatha would fail—that all would fail.

I don't know how long I had been sitting there in hopeless dejection when I heard a slow, soft footstep approaching. I glanced across at Nayland Smith. His face was set, expressionless.

A rattling of keys came, and the heavy door swung open. At the same moment a light set somewhere behind that squat pillar sprang up, and I saw as I had suspected a fully equipped torture chamber. Nocturnal insects rustled to cover.

Dr Fu Manchu came in . . .

He wore a plain yellow robe having long sleeves, and upon his feet I saw thick-soled slippers. His phenomenal skull was hidden by a mandarin's cap, perhaps that which I had found in a hut on the Essex marshes.

I am unable to record my emotions at this moment, for I cannot recall that I had any. When on a previous occasion I had found myself in the power of the Chinese doctor, I had been fortified by the knowledge that Nayland Smith was free, that there was a chance of his coming to my aid. Now we were fellow captives. I was numbly resigned to whatever was to be.

Seated on Dr Fu Manchu's left shoulder I saw a tiny, wizened marmoset. I thought that it peered at me inquisitively. Fu Manchu crossed nearly to the centre of the cell—he had a queer, catlike gait. There, standing midway between us, he looked long and searchingly, first at Nayland Smith and then at me. I tried to sustain the gaze of his half-closed eyes. I was mortified when I found that I could not do it.

"So you have decided to join me, Sir Denis?" He spoke softly and raising one hand caressed the marmoset. "At last the Si-Fan is to enjoy the benefit of your great ability."

Nayland Smith said nothing. He watched and listened.

"Later I shall make arrangements for your transport to my temporary headquarters. I shall employ you to save civilisation from the madmen who seek to ruin it."

The meaning of these strange words was not entirely clear to me, but I noted, and drew my own conclusions, that Dr Fu Manchu seemed to have forgotten my presence.

"Tonight, a man who threatens the peace of the world will make a far-reaching decision. To me his life or death are matters of no importance, but I am determined that there shall be peace; the assumption of the West that older races can benefit by your ridiculous culture must be corrected. Your culture!"

His voice sank contemptuously on a guttural note.

"What has it done? What have your aeroplanes—those toys of a childish people—accomplished? Beyond bringing every man's home into the firing line—nothing! Napoleon had no bombers, no high explosives, nor any other of your modern boons. He conquered a great part of Europe without them. Poor infants, who transfer your prayers from angels to aeroplanes!"

He ceased for a moment and the silence was uncanny. From my point of view in the low wooden chair, Dr Fu Manchu appeared abnormally tall. He possessed a physical repose which was terrifying, because in some way it made more manifest the volcanic activity of his brain. He was like a pylon supporting a blinding light.

The silence was broken by shrill chattering from the marmoset. With a tiny hand it patted the cheek of its master.

Dr Fu Manchu glanced aside at the wizened little creature.

"You have met my marmoset before, Sir Denis, and I think I have mentioned that he is of great age. I shall not tell you his age since you might be tempted to doubt my word, which I could not tolerate." There was mockery in his voice. "My earliest experiments in arresting senility were carried out on my faithful Peko. As you see, they were successful."

He removed the marmoset from his shoulder and couched it in a yellow fold covering his left arm. Nayland Smith's face remained completely expressionless. I counted the paces between the chair in which I sat and the spot upon which Dr Fu Manchu stood.

He was just beyond my reach.

"You have genius, Sir Denis, but it is marred by a streak of that bulldog breed of which the British are so proud. In striving to bolster up the ridiculous pretensions of those who misdirect the West, you have inevitably found yourself opposed to me. Consider what it is that you would preserve, what contentment it has brought in its train. Look around at the happy homes of Europe and America, the labourers singing in your vineyards, the peace and prosperity which your 'progress' has showered on mankind."

His voice rose. I detected a note of repressed but feverish excitement.

"But no matter. There will be ample time in future to direct your philosophy into more suitable channels. I will gratify your natural curiosity regarding my presence in the world, which continues even after my unpleasant experience at Niagara Falls . . ."

Nayland Smith's hands closed tightly.

"You recovered the body of that brilliant maniac, Professor Morgenstahl, I understand, and also the wreckage of the motorboat. One of my most devoted servants was driving the boat. He was not killed as you supposed and his body lost. He was temporarily stunned in the struggle with Morgenstahl—whom I overcame, however. He recovered in time to deal with the emergency. He succeeded in running the boat against a rock near the head of a rapid. In this he was aided by a Very light contributed by an airman flying over us. This fellow of mine—a sea Dyak—is a magnificent surf swimmer. Carrying a line he swam from point to point and finally reached the Canadian shore."

Dr Fu Manchu stroked the marmoset reflectively.

"Unaided by this line and the strength of my servant, I doubt if I could have crossed to the bank. The crossing seriously exhausted me—and the boat became dislodged no more than a few seconds after I had taken the plunge . . ."

Nayland Smith neither spoke nor moved. His hands remained clenched, his face expressionless.

"You have observed," Fu Manchu continued, "that my daughter is again acting in my interests. She is unaware, however, of her former identity: Fah lo Suee is dead. I have reincarnated her as Korêani, an Oriental dancer whose popularity is useful. This is her punishment . . ."

The marmoset uttered a whistling sound. It was uncannily derisive.

"Later you will experience this form of amnesia, yourself. The ordeal by fire to which I once submitted Korêani in your presence was salutary, but the furnace contained no fuel. It was one which I had prepared for *you*, Sir Denis. I had designed it as a gateway to your new life in China."

Mentally I seemed to remain numb. Some of the Chinese doctor's statements I failed to follow. Others were all too horribly clear. At times there came a note almost of exultation, severely repressed but perceptible, into the speaker's voice. He had the majesty which belongs to great genius, or, and there was a new horror in the afterthought, to insanity. He was perhaps a brilliant madman!

"I am satisfied to observe," he continued, "that my new aesthetic, a preparation of *crataegus*, the common hawthorn, serves its purpose so admirably. Anaesthesia is immediate and complete. There are no distressing after-symptoms. I foresee that it will supplant my mimosa mixture with which, Sir Denis, you have been familiar in the past."

Slowly he extended a gaunt hand in the direction of the torture room:

"Medieval devices designed to stimulate reluctant memories."

He stepped aside and took up a pair of long-handled tongs.

"Forceps used to tear sinews."

He spoke softly, then dropped those instruments of agony. The clang of their fall made my soul sick.

"Primitive and clumsy. China has done better. No doubt you recall the Seven Gates? However, these forms of questions are no longer necessary. I can learn all that I wish to know by the mere exercise of that neglected implement, the human will. I recently discovered in this way that Ardatha—hitherto a staunch ally—is not to be trusted where Mr Kerrigan is concerned."

I ceased to breathe as he spoke those words . . .

"Accordingly I have taken steps to ensure her noninterference . . . You are silent, Sir Denis?"

"Why should I speak?"' Smith's voice was flatly unemotional. "I allowed myself to fall into a trap which a schoolboy would have distrusted. I have nothing to say."

"You refer to the lotus floor no doubt? Yes, ingenious in its way. That room with others giving access to the cellars and dungeons had been walled up for several generations. I recently had them reopened, but confess I did not foresee it would be for the accommodation of so distinguished a guest. In a dungeon adjoining this I came across two skeletons those of a man and a woman. Irregularities in certain of the small bones suggested that they had not died happily—"

He turned as if to go.

"I look forward to further conversation in the future, Sir Denis, but now I must leave you. A matter of the gravest urgency demands my attention."

As he moved towards the door the marmoset sprang from his arm to his shoulder, and turning its tiny head, gibed at us . . . The light went out . . . I heard the key turned in the lock—I heard those padding, catlike steps receding in the stone-paved passage . . .

I was drenched in perspiration.

The tongs

The silence which followed Dr Fu Manchu's departure was broken by that awful moaning as of some lost soul who had died horribly in one of the dungeons. It rose and fell, rose and fell . . . and faded away.

"Kerrigan!" Smith snapped, and I admired the vigour of his manner. "Was the wind rising out there?"

"Yes, in gusts . . . What do you think he meant about "

"The wind was from the sea?"

"Yes. Oh my God! Is she alive?"

Again that awful moaning arose—and now to it was added a ghostly metallic clanking.

"What ever is it, Smith?"

"I have been wondering for some time . . . Yes, she's alive, Kerrigan, but we can't count on her! . . . Now that you tell me a breeze has risen, I know what it is. There's a window or a ventilator outside in the passage. What we hear is wind howling through a narrow opening."

"But that awful clanking!"

"Irritatingly significant."

"Why?"

"It was not there before the doctor's visit! It means that he has left the key in the lock with the other keys attached to it. The draught of air—I can feel it blowing on the top of my head now through these bars—is swinging the attached keys to and fro."

Across the darkened cell he watched me.

"Among those keys, Kerrigan, in all probability, are the keys to our manacles!"

I thought for some time. A tumult had arisen in my brain.

"Surely *he* was never guilty of carelessness. Why should he have left the key?"

"According to my experience"—Smith stared down at his wrist watch—"the yellow-faced horror who attends to my requirements is due in about five minutes. The key was left in the lock for his convenience no doubt. And although Ardatha is alive—oh! I have learned to read Fu Manchu's hidden meanings—she will not come to our aid tonight. Someone else is alive also!"

"Adlon!"

"But I fear that his hours are numbered."

He stood up on the seat of the massive chair and stared out through the bars. Over his shoulder:

"I have carefully examined this passage no less than six times," he said. "It is no more than three feet wide. The end from which a current of air blows is invisible from here. But that is where the ventilator must be situated. The light is away to my right, the direction from which visitors always approach."

He stepped down and stood staring at me. His eyes were feverishly bright.

"I was wondering," he mused. "Could you toss me another cigarette?"

He lighted it, and apparently unconscious of the length of chain attached to his ankles, began to pace up and down the narrow compass of floor allowed to him, drawing on the cigarette with the vigour of a pipe smoker, so that clouds issued from his lips.

Hope began to dawn in my hitherto hopeless mind.

"Oh for the brain of a Houdini!" he murmured. "The problem is this, Kerrigan: The keys are hanging less than a foot below this grating behind me, but two feet wide of it. If you will glance at the position of the door you will see that I am right. It is clearly impossible for me to reach them. By no possible contortion could I get within a foot of the keyhole from which they are hanging. You follow me?"

"Perfectly."

"Very well. What is urgently required—for my jailer will almost certainly take the keys away—is an idea, namely, how to reach those keys and detach them from the lock. There must be a way!"

Following a long silence interrupted only by the clanking of Nayland Smith's leg irons, periodical moaning of the wind through that unseen opening and the chink of the pendant keys:

"It is not only how to reach them," I said, "but how to turn the lock in order to detach them."

"I agree. Yet there *must* be a way."

161

He stood still—in fact, seemed almost to become rigid. I saw where his gaze was set.

The sinew-tearing pincers to which Dr Fu Manchu had drawn our attention lay not at the spot from which he had taken them up, but beside the pillar . . .

"Smith!" I whispered, "can you reach them?"

With never a word or glance he walked forward to the extreme limit of the chain, went down upon his hands and crept forward with a stoat-like movement. Fully extended, his right hand outstretched to the utmost, he was six inches short of his objective!

Even as I heard him utter a sound like a groan:

"Come back, Smith!"

My voice shook ridiculously. He got back onto his feet turned and looked at me.

Although robbed of my automatic, my clasp knife and anything else resembling a lethal weapon, a small piece of string no more than a foot long which I had carefully untied from some package recently received and, a habit, had neatly looped and placed in my pocket proved still to be there. I held it up triumphantly.

Nayland Smith's expression changed.

"May I inquire what earthly use you can suggest for a piece of string?"

"Tie one end to the handle of that metal pitcher on the ledge beside you, then crawl forward again and toss the pitcher into the open arms of the tongs. You can draw them across the floor."

For a moment Smith's stare was disconcerting, and then:

"Top marks, Kerrigan," he said quietly. "Toss the string across. . . "

Many attempts he made which were unsuccessful, but at last he lodged the pitcher between the iron arms of the pincers.

Breathlessly I watched him as he began to pull . . .

The pitcher toppled forward: the pincers did not move.

"We are done," he panted. "It isn't going to work!"

And at that moment—as though they had been treading on my heart—I heard footsteps approaching.

Korêani

Those soft footsteps halted outside the door. There followed a provocative rattle of keys, the sound of a lock being turned; then the door opened, light sprang up . . .

Dr Fu Manchu's daughter came in.

She was dressed as I remembered her in the room with the lotus floor. Her frock was a sheath, clinging to her lithe figure as perfectly as scales to a fish. She wore no jewelry save the Arab necklace. As she entered the cell and looked about her I grasped the fact immediately that she was looking not for me, but for Nayland Smith.

When her long, narrow eyes met my glance their expression conveyed no more than the slightest interest; but as, turning aside, she looked at Smith I saw them open widely. There was a new light in their depths. I thought that they glittered like emeralds.

She stood there watching him. There was something yearning in her expression, yet something almost hopeless. I remembered Dr Fu Manchu's words. I believed that this woman was struggling to revive a buried memory.

"So you are going to join us," she said.

Fu Manchu had used a similar expression. There was some mystery here which no doubt Smith would explain, for the devil doctor had said also, "Fah lo Suee is dead. I have reincarnated her as Korêani . . ."

The spoken English of Korêani was less perfect than that of Ardatha, but she had a medium note in her voice, a soft caressing note, which to my ears sounded menacing as the purr of one of the great cats—a puma or tigress.

There was no reply.

"I am glad—but please tell me something."

"What do you want me to tell you?" Nayland Smith's tones were coldly indifferent. "Of what interest can my life or death be to you?"

She moved more closely to his side, always watching him.

"There is something I must know. Do you remember me?"

"Perfectly."

"Where did we meet?"

Smith and I had stood up with that automatic courtesy which prompts a man when a woman enters a room. And now she was so near to him that easily he could have grasped her. Watching his grim face into which a new expression had come, I wondered what he contemplated.

"It was a long time ago," he replied quietly.

"But how could it be so long ago? If I remember you how can I have forgotten our meeting?"

"Perhaps you have forgotten your name?"

"That is stupid! My name is Korêani."

"No, no." He smiled and shook his head. "Your real name I never knew, but the name given to you in childhood, the name by which I did know you, was Fah lo Suee."

She drew down her brows in an effort of recollection.

"Fah lo Suee," she murmured. "But this is a silly name. It means a perfume, a sweet scent. It is childish!"

"You were a child when it was given to you."

"Ah!" She smiled—and her smile was so alluring that I knew how this woman must have played upon the emotions of those she had lured into the net of Dr Fu Manchu. "You have known me a long time? I thought so, but I cannot remember your name."

For Korêani I had no existence. She had forgotten my presence. I meant no more to her than one of the dreadful furnishings of the place.

"My name has always been Nayland Smith. How long it will remain so I don't know."

"What does a name matter when one belongs to the Si-Fan?"

"I don't want to forget as you have forgotten—Korêani."

"What have I forgotten?"

"You have forgotten Nayland Smith. Even now you do not recognise my name."

Again she frowned in that puzzled way and took a step nearer to the speaker.

"Perhaps you mean something which I do not understand.

164

Why are you afraid to forget? Has your life been so happy?"

"Perhaps," said Smith, "I don't want to forget you as you have forgotten me."

He extended his hands; she was standing directly before him. And as I watched, unable to believe what I saw, he unfastened the gold necklace, held it for a moment, and then dropped it into his pocket!

"Why do you do that?" She was very close to him now. "Do you think it will help you to remember?"

"Perhaps. May I keep it?"

"It is nothing—I give it to you." Her voice, every line of her swaying body, was an invitation. "It is the Takbîr, the Moslem prayer. It means there is no god but God."

"That is why I thank you for it, Korêani."

A long time she waited, watching him—watching him. But he did not stir. She moved slowly away.

"I must go. No one must find me here. But I had to come!" Still she hesitated. "I am glad I came."

"I am glad you came."

She turned, flashed a glance at me, and stepped to the open door. There she paused and glanced back over her shoulder.

"Soon we shall meet again."

She went out, closed the door and extinguished the light. I heard a jingle of keys, then the sound of her footsteps as she went along the passage.

"For God's sake, Smith," I said in a low voice, "what has come over you?"

He raised a warning finger.

As I watched uncomprehendingly, Nayland Smith held up the gold necklace. It was primitive bazaar work, tiny coins hanging from gold chains, each stamped with an Arab letter. I saw that it was secured by means of a ring and a clumsy gold hook. Quickly but coolly he removed the string from the handle of the pitcher and tied it to the ring.

Now I grasped the purpose of that strange episode which in its enactment had staggered me. Once more he dropped onto the stone floor and crept forward until he could throw the hook of the necklace into the angle of the pincers. Twice he failed to anchor the hook; the third time he succeeded.

Gently he drew the heavy iron implement towards him—until he could grasp it in his

"Kerrigan, if I never worked fast in my life before I must work fast now!"

His eyes shone feverishly. He rattled out the words in a series of staccato syllables. In a trice he was onto the chair and straining through the iron bars, the heavy instrument designed to tear human tendons held firmly in his hand. By the tenseness of his attitude, his quick, short breathing, I knew how difficult he found his task.

"Can you reach it, Smith?"

That mournful howling arose, followed by a faint metallic rattling . . . The rattling ceased.

"Yes, I have touched them! But getting the key out is the difficulty."

More rattling followed. I clenched my hands, held my breath. Smith now extended his left arm through the bars. Stooping down, he began slowly to withdraw his right. I was afraid to speak, until with more confidence he pulled the iron pincers back into the cell— and I saw that they gripped a bunch of keys!

He stepped down, dropped keys and forceps on the floor, and closing his eyes, sat still for a moment . . .

"Splendid!" I said. "One mistake would have been fatal."

"I know!" He looked up. "It was a hell of a strain, Kerrigan. But what helped me was—she had forgotten to lock the door. The key slipped out quite easily!"

That short interval over, he was coolly efficient again.

Picking up the bunch, he examined each key closely, presently selected one and tried it on the lock of the band encircling his left ankle.

"Wrong! "

He tried another. I heard a dull grating sound.

"Right!"

In a moment his legs were free.

"Quick, Kerrigan! Come right forward. I will slide them across the floor to you. The one I have separated fits my leg iron; it probably fits yours."

In a moment I had the bunch in my hand. Fifteen seconds later I, too, was free.

"Now the keys! Be quick!"

I tossed them back. He caught them, stood upon the chair, looked out through the iron grating . . . and threw them onto the floor of the passage!

"Smith! Smith!" I whispered.

He jumped down and turned to face me.

"What?"

"We were free! Why have you thrown the keys back?"

Silently he pointed to the door.

I stared. There was no keyhole!

"Even if we had the key it would be useless to us. There is no means of opening this door from the inside! We must wait. Tuck your feet and the manacles well under your chair. I shall do the same. Soon the yellow jailer will be here. If he crosses first to you I will spring on his back. If he comes to me you attack him."

"He may cry out."

Smith smiled grimly. He picked up the iron forceps.

"Will you have them, or shall I? It's a fifty-fifty chance."

"Keep them, Smith; you will get an opportunity in any event."

And scarcely had we disposed ourselves in a manner to suggest that the leg irons were still in place, when I heard quick footsteps approaching along the passage.

"Good! he's here. Remember the routine, Kerrigan."

There was a pause outside the door and I heard muttering. Then came a jangle as the man stooped to pick up the keys. Their having fallen from the lock clearly had made him suspicious. When presently he opened the door and stepped in he glanced from side to side, doubt written upon one of the most villainous faces I had ever beheld.

He wore a shirt with an open collar, grey flannel trousers, and those sort of corded sandals which are rarely seen in Europe. By reason of his build, his glossy black hair and the cast of his features, I knew him for one of Dr Fu Manchu's Thugs. Indeed, as I looked, I saw the brand of Kâli on his forehead. His yellow face was scarred in such a way that one eye remained permanently closed, and the effect of the wound which reached the upper lip was to produce a perpetual leer.

His doubts were not easily allayed, for he stood staring about him for some time, his poise giving me the impression of a boxer on tiptoes. He had replaced the key in the door with the pendant bunch and now going out again, he returned with a tray upon which was something under a cover, a bowl of fruit and a pitcher. For yet another long moment before he crossed towards Nayland Smith he hesitated and glanced aside at me.

Then, walking over to the alcove, he was about to set the tray upon the ledge when I sprang.

I caught him at a disadvantage, collared his legs and threw him forward, head first. The tray and its contents crashed to the floor. But even as he fell I recognised the type of character with whom I had to deal.

He twisted sideways, took the fall on his left shoulder, and lashing out with his feet, kicked my legs from under me! It was a marvellous trick, perfectly executed. I fell half on top of him, but reached for a hold as I did so.

It was unnecessary . . .

As the Thug forced his trunk upward on powerful arms Smith brought the forceps down upon the glossy skull! Against this second attack the yellow man had no defence. There was a sickening thud. He dropped flat on his face and lay still.

Behind the Arras

"We are safe for an hour," snapped Smith. "Come on!"

"Some sort of weapon would be a good idea," I said, bruised and still breathless from my fall.

"Quite useless! Brains, not brawn, alone can save us now."

As we stepped out into the passage came that ghastly moaning and a draught of cold air. It tricked me into a momentary panic, but Nayland Smith turned and examined a narrow grille set near the top of the end of the passage; for here was a cul-de-sac.

"There's an air shaft above that," he said. "Judging from the look of this place, we are down below water level. The fact that the actual ventilator above evidently faces towards the sea conveys nothing."

The passage was about thirty feet long. A bulkhead light was roughly attached to one of the stone walls. It was reflection from this which had shone through the iron bars of our prison. We hurried along. There were other doors with similar grilles on one side, doubtless indicating the presence of more cells. At the end was a heavy door, but it was open.

"Caution," said Smith.

A flight of stone steps confronted us. We mounted them, I close behind Smith. I saw ahead a continuation of the passage which we had just left, but one wall was wood panelled. This passage also was lighted by one dim lamp.

Creeping to the end, we found similar corridors opening right and left.

Speaking very close to my ear:

"Let's try right," Smith whispered.

We stole softly along. Here, again, there was one dim light to guide us, but we passed it without finding any way out of the place. We came to a second door which proved to be unlocked. Very cautiously Nayland Smith pushed it open.

We were in a maze . . . beyond stretched yet another passage! But peering ahead I observed a difference.

The floor was thickly carpeted with felt. There was no lamp, but points of light shone upon the ancient stonework of one wall, apparently coming from apertures in the panels which formed the other. Only by a grasp of his hand did Smith enjoin special caution as we pushed forward to a point where two of these openings appeared close together.

We looked through.

I recognized a remarkable fact. That rough and ancient wood-work which extended along the whole of the right-hand wall was no more than a framework or stretcher upon which tapestry was supported.

We were in a passage behind the arras of a large apartment.

Something seemed to obscure my vision. Presently I realised what it was: At certain points the tapestry had been cut away and replaced by gauze, painted on the outside, so that to those in the room the opening would be invisible.

I saw a chamber furnished with all the splendour of old Venice, but it was decaying splendour. The carved chairs richly upholstered in royal purple were damaged and faded; a mosaic-topped table was cracked; the patterned floor was filmed with ancient dust. Tapestry (through one section of which I peered) covered all the walls. Upon it were depicted scenes from the maritime history of the Queen of the Adriatic. But it was mouldy with age.

Four magnificent wrought-iron candelabra, each supporting six red candles, gave light, and a fine Persian carpet was spread before a sort of dais upon which was set a carven ebony chair resembling a throne. Dr Fu Manchu, yellow robed, the mandarin's cap upon his head, sat there—his long ivory hands gripping the arms of the chair, his face immobile, his eyes like polished jade.

Standing before him, one foot resting on the dais, was a defiant figure: a man wearing evening dress, a man whose straight black hair and black moustache, his pose, must have revealed his identity to almost anyone in the civilised world.

It was Rudolf Adlon!

There had been silence as we had crept along the felt-padded floor behind the tapestry; a false step would have betrayed us. This silence remained unbroken, but the clash of those two imperious characters stirred my spirit as no rhetoric could have stirred me—and my conception of the destiny of the world became changed . . .

Then Adlon spoke. He spoke in German. Although my Italian is negligible I have a fair knowledge of German. Therefore, I could follow the conversation.

"I have been tricked, trapped, drugged!" The suppressed violence in the orator's voice startled me. "I find myself here—I realise now that I am not dreaming—and I have listened (patiently, I think) to perhaps the most preposterous statements which any man has ever made. I have one thing to say, and one only: Instantly"—he beat a clenched fist into his palm—"I demand to be set free! Instantly! And I warn you—I will not temporise—that for this outrage you shall suffer!"

He glanced about him swiftly, and as his face which I had always thought to lack natural beauty was turned in my direction, something in those blazing eyes, in the defiant set of his chin, won an admiration which I believed I could never have felt for him.

But Dr Fu Manchu did not move. He might have been not a man, but a graven image. Then he spoke in German. I had not heard that language spoken so perfectly otherwise than by a native of Germany.

"Excellency is naturally annoyed. I have sought a personal interview for one reason only. I could have removed you from office and from life without so much formality. I wished to see you, to talk to you. I believe that as one used to giving but not to receiving orders, the instructions of the Council of Seven of the Si-Fan might have seemed to be inacceptable."

"Inacceptable?" Rudolf Adlon bent forward threateningly. "Inacceptable! You fool! The Si-Fan! I have had more than enough of this nonsense! My time is too valuable to be wasted upon Chinese conjurers. Let this farce end or I shall be reduced to the extremity of a personal attack."

Fists clenched, nostrils dilated, he seemed about to spring upon that impassive figure enthroned in the ebony chair. Knowing from my own experience what he must be suffering at this moment, of humiliation, ignorance of his whereabouts, a bewilderment complete as that which belongs to an evil dream, I thought that Rudolf Adlon was a very splendid figure.

And in that moment I understood why a great, intellectual nation had accepted him as its leader. Whatever his failings, this man was fearless.

But Dr Fu Manchu never stirred. The twenty-four red candles burned steadily. There was no breath of air in that decaying, deadly room. And the gaze of those still eyes checked the chancellor.

"Dictators"—the guttural voice compassed that germanic word perfectly—"hitherto have served their appointed purpose. Their schemes of expansion I have been called upon to check. The Si-Fan has intervened in Abyssinia. We are now turning our attention to Morocco and Syria. China, my China, can take care of herself. She will always absorb the fools who intrude upon her surface as the pitcher plant absorbs flies. To some small extent I have forwarded this process."

And Rudolf Adlon remained silent.

"I opened the floodgates of the Yellow River"—that note of exultation, of fanaticism, came now into the strange voice. "I called upon those elemental spirits in whom you do not believe to aid me. The children of China do not desire war. They are content to live on their peaceful rivers, in their rice fields, in those white valleys where the opium poppy grows. They are content to die . . . The people of *your* country do not desire war. "

And Adlon still remained silent, enthralled against his will . . .

"My agents inform me that a great majority desires peace. There are no more than twelve men living today who can cause war. You are one of them. Your ideals cross mine. You would dispense with Christ, with Mohammed, with Buddha, with Moses. But not one of these ancient trees shall be destroyed. They have a purpose: they are of use—to me. You have been ordered by the Council of Seven not to meet Pietro Monaghani—yet you are here!"

Some spiritual battle the dictator was fighting—a battle which I had fought and lost against the power in those wonderful, evil eyes . . .

"I forbid this meeting. I speak for the Council of which I am the president. A European conflict would be inimical to my plans. If any radical change take place in the world's map, my own draughtsmen will make it."

Adlon had won that inner conflict. In one bound he was upon the dais, looking down quiveringly upon the seated figure.

"I give you the time in which I can count ten! We are man to man. You are mad and I am sane. But I warn you—I am the stronger."

I was so tensed up, so fired to action, that I suppose some movement on my part warned Nayland Smith, for he set a sudden grip upon my wrist which made me wince: it brought me to my senses. I think I had contemplated tearing a way through the tapestry to take my place beside Rudolf Adlon.

"From several loopholes," Dr Fu Manchu continued, his voice now soft and sibilant, "you are covered by my servants. I have explained to you patiently and at some length that I could have brought about your assassination twenty times within the past three months. Because I recognise in your character much which is admirable I have adopted those means which have brought us face to face. You have received the final notice of the Council; you have one hour in which to choose. Leave Venice tonight within that hour and I guarantee your safety. Refuse, and the world will know you no more . . ."

The lotus floor

Nayland Smith was urging me back in the direction we had come. Having passed the door which we softly opened and closed:

"Why this way?" I whispered.

"You heard Fu Manchu's words. He was covered by his servants from several loopholes—"

"Probably a lie—he has nerves of steel"

"That he has nerves of steel, I agree, Kerrigan, but I have never known him to lie. No, this is our way."

We groped back along those dimly lighted passages until we came to the point at which of two ways we had selected that to the right. We now tried the left. And dimly in the darkness, for there was no light here, I saw a flight of wooden steps. Smith leading, we mounted to the top. Another door was there on the landing and it was ajar. Light shone through the opening.

"I expect this is the way my jailer came," whispered Smith.

Beyond, as we gently pushed the door open, was a narrow lobby. Complete silence reigned . . . But at the very moment of our entrance this silence was interrupted.

Unmistakable sounds of approaching footsteps came from beyond a curtained opening. The footsteps ceased. There came a faint shuffling, and then—unmistakably again—the sound of someone retreating.

"Run for it!" Smith snapped, "or we are trapped!"

Dashing blindly across, I pulled up sharply on the threshold of a room. It was, I think, a horribly familiar perfume which checked me—that of hawthorn blossom! I clutched at Nayland Smith, staring, staring at what I saw . . .

It was the room with the lotus floor!

We had entered it from the other side, and at that door through which I had stepped into oblivion, Ardatha stood, her eyes widely open, her face pale!

"Mercy of God!" she said, "but how did you get here? Don't move. Stay where you are."

No word came from Nayland Smith. For a moment I could hear his hard breathing, then:

"Go round it, Kerrigan," he said. "Stick to the black border. Don't be afraid, Ardatha, you had nothing to do with this."

As I reached the other side of the room and stood beside her:

"Ardatha!" I threw my arm about her shoulders. "Come with me! I can't bear it!"

"No!" She freed herself, her face remained very pale. "Not yet!"

"Go ahead, Kerrigan." Smith was making his way around the room. "Leave Ardatha to me; she's in safe hands."

With one last look into the amethyst eyes, I hurried on—but at the top of the steps which led to the wine cellar paused, stepped back and:

"It's unnecessary to go the whole way," I said. "The door of the Palazzo Mori is not locked. For God's sake, don't linger, Smith."

He was standing looking down at her; she made no attempt to retreat . . .

My flashlamp had gone the way of my automatic, but a box of matches for some obscure reason had been left in my pocket. With the aid of these I groped my way through to that noisome passage which led to the old palace. Along I went, moving very slowly and working my way match by match. I wondered why Smith delayed, what he had in mind. Some quibble of conscience, I thought, for clearly it was his duty to arrest Ardatha.

My plan was to learn if the exit by way of the water were still practicable. I knew it must be very late, and I wondered if it would be possible to attract the attention of a passing gondolier. Otherwise we should have to swim for it.

The door remained unfastened as the police had left it Outside the wind howled through a dark night. The surface of the Grand Canal was like a miniature ocean. I could see no sign of any craft.

I confess that that second tunnel which led under the canal presented terrors from which I shrank.

Propping the great door open so that some dim light penetrated to the tomb-like hall, I began to retrace my steps. Approaching me, a ghostly figure, I saw Nayland Smith groping his way by the aid of a tiny torch—none other than his lighter!

He was alone . . .

As we stood together on the steps, buffeted by that keen breeze, and still at the mercy of the enemy should we be attacked from the rear:

"Smith," I said, for the thought was uppermost in my mind, "what became of her?"

"She had a second set of keys—God knows where she had found them—and was on her way to release us . . . I hadn't the heart to arrest her."

We stood there in the stormy night for three, four, five minutes, but no sort of craft was abroad.

"Nothing else to it," snapped Smith. "We must go through the tunnel. To delay longer would be madness."

"But the door at this end may be locked!"

"It is—but I have the key."

"You got it from Ardatha?"

"Yes."

"What of the padlock at the other end?"

"That is unfastened."

"Which means—someone is expected to go out tonight?"

"Exactly. I leave the identity of that someone to your imagination."

We groped across the clammy, echoing hall. With the key Ardatha had given him, Smith opened the door to that last gruesome tunnel. He locked it behind him.

"That was stipulated," he explained drily. "It also protects us from the rear."

We hurried as fast as we could through the foetid passage and up the steps at the end. The trap was open.

As we came out into that black and narrow lane which led to freedom:

"You must be worn to death, Smith," I said.

"I confess to a certain weariness, Kerrigan. But since frankly I had accepted the fact that I must lose my identity and be transported to some point selected by Doctor Fu Manchu to carry out the duties of another life, this freedom is glorious! But remember: Rudolf Adlon!"

"He had an hour—"

"We have less . . . if we are to save him."

176

In the Palazzo Brioni

Colonel Correnti sprang up like a man who sees a ghost. Even the diplomatic poise of Sir George Herbert had deserted him. These were the small hours of the morning, but police headquarters hummed with the feverish activity of a hive disturbed.

"The good God be praised!" Correnti cried, and the points of his grey moustache seemed to quiver. "It is Sir Denis Nayland Smith and Mr Kerrigan!"

"Glad to see you, Smith," said Sir George drily.

"Quick!" Smith looked from face to face. "The latest news of Adlon?"

The chief of police dropped back into his chair and extended his palms eloquently.

"Tragedy!"

"What? Tell me quickly!"

"He disappeared from the suite allotted to him at the palace— it has a private exit—some time during the night. No one can say when. It was certainly a love tryst—for Mr Kerrigan saw the appointment made. But, he has not returned!"

"He will never return," said Nayland Smith grimly, "if we waste a moment. I want a party—at least twenty men."

"You know where he is?" Sir George Herbert was the speaker.

The chief of police sprang up, his eyes mad with excitement.

"I know where he *was*!"

"But where? Tell me!"

"In a room in the Palazzo Brioni—"

"But Palazzo Brioni belongs to Mr Brownlow Wilton, the American!"

"No matter. Rudolf Adlon was there less than half an hour ago."

As the necessary men were assembled Smith began to issue rapid orders. One party under a Carabinieri captain hurried off to the old stone boathouse. A second party proceeded to the water gate of the Palazzo Mori, a third covered both palaces from the land side. Ourselves, with the main party and the chief of police, set out for the Palazzo Brioni.

It was not clear to me how Smith had determined that this was the scene of our recent horrible adventure, but:

"I counted my paces as I went—and returned—along the passage," he explained. "There is no shadow of doubt. The room in which we saw Doctor Fu Manchu and Rudolf Adlon is in the Palazzo Brioni . . .

Against that keen breeze which shrieked eerily along the Grand Canal, the black police launch headed for the palace. As we slowed up against the water steps, no light showed anywhere; the great door was closed. Persistent ringing and knocking, however, presently resulted in a light springing up in the hallway.

When at last, preceded by the shooting of several bolts, the door opened, I saw a half-clad and very frightened manservant staring out.

"I represent the police," said Nayland Smith rapidly. "I must speak immediately to Mr James Brownlow Wilton. Be good enough to inform him."

We all crowded into the hallway, a beautiful old place in which I had glimpses of fine pictures, statuary and furniture, every item of which I recognised to be museum pieces. The man, pulling his dressing gown about him, stared pathetically from face to face.

"But, please, I don't understand," he said. He was Italian, but spoke fair English. "What is this? What has happened?"

In that dimly lighted hall as we stood about him, wind howling at the open door, I could well believe that his bewilderment was not assumed.

"First, who are you?" Smith demanded.

"I am the butler here, sir. My name is Paulo."

"Mr Wilton is your employer?"

"Yes sir. "

"Where is he?"

"He left tonight, sir."

"What! Left for where?"

"For his yacht Silver Heels in the lagoon."

"But what of his guests?"

"They have all gone too."

"You mean that the house is empty?"

"Except for myself and the staff, sir, yes."

One of the party said urgently to the chief of police:

"Silver Heels has sailed."

"Silver Heels must be overtaken!" snapped Smith. "Send someone to make the necessary arrangements. I leave it to you. But I must be one of the party."

A man, following rapid instructions from Colonel Correnti, went doubling off.

Turning again to the frightened butler:

"How long have you worked here?"

"Only for two weeks, sir. I was engaged by Mr Wilton's secretary. But I have worked here before for others who have leased the palace."

"Lead the way to the tapestry room lighted by four iron candelabra."

The man stared in almost a horrified manner.

"That room, sir, is part of what is called the Old Palace. It has long been locked up. I have no key."

"Nor to the room with the lotus floor?"

Nayland Smith was watching him keenly, his unshaven face very grim.

"The room with the lotus floor!" Paulo's expression grew even more wild. "I have heard of it, sir, but it is also part of the Old Palace. I have never seen it. Those rooms have a very unpleasant reputation, you understand. No one would lease the palace if they knew of them. The doors have not been unlocked for twenty years."

"Then one must be broken down. Do you know where they are?"

"I know of two."

"Go ahead."

As Paulo turned to obey I heard a sound of distant voices.

"What is that?" snapped Smith.

"Some of the other servants, sir, who have been aroused!" Smith glanced at Colonel Correnti.

"Have this looked into, Colonel," he said. "You, Paulo, lead on."

Our party was broken up again, Smith, myself, the chief of police, Detective Stocco and two Carabinieri following the butler. He led us to a doorway set in an arched recess. A magnificent cabinet—a rare piece of violet lacquer—stood in front of the arch.

"Behind here, sir, is one of the doors, but I have no key to open it."

"Get this thing out of the way."

In a few minutes the men had set the cabinet aside. Smith stepped forward and examined an ancient iron lock. He was soon satisfied. He turned and shook his head.

"This is not the door in use. You say you know of another?"

"Yes sir, if you will come this way."

Aside to me:

"The fellow is honest," Smith muttered. "This is a very deep plot." He glanced at his wrist watch as we crossed a deserted dining room. "Our chance of saving Adlon grows less and less, but there is someone else in danger."

"Who is that?"

"James Brownlow Wilton! He is notorious throughout the United States for his Nazi sympathies. The full extent of this scheme is only just beginning to dawn upon me, Kerrigan."

In a room overluxuriously furnished as a study, Paulo opened a satinwood door inlaid with ivory and mother-of-pearl to reveal an empty cupboard.

"At the back of this cupboard, sir," he said, "you see there are very ancient panels. I have always understood it is an entrance to the Old Palace . . ."

"This door has been used recently. . . It has a new lock!" Smith's eyes glittered feverishly.

"I don't think so, sir. Mr Wilton used the room, and I am sure he did not know of the door. I have always been careful to avoid mentioning to tenants who came anything about those locked rooms."

"Carbines!" Smith cried on a high note of excitement. "Those two men forward. Blow the lock out. The fate of a nation hangs on it!"

The sound of muffled shots reverberated insanely in that lavishly furnished study. I heard cries—racing footsteps. The other police party dashed to join us . . . The lock was shattered, the door flung open.

"Follow me, Kerrigan!"

Nayland Smith, shining a ray of light ahead, stepped into the dark cavity. I went next, Colonel Correnti close at my heels.

"You see, Kerrigan! You see!"

Descending four stone steps we found ourselves in one of those narrow passages which surrounded the rooms of the Old Palace. I took a rapid bearing.

"This way, Smith, I think!"

"You're right!" he cried. "Ah! what's this?"

A door was thrown open, we crowded in, and flashlamps flooded the tapestry room in which I had seen Rudolf Adlon confronting Dr Fu Manchu!

The red candles in the candelabra were extinguished, and in the light of our lamps I saw that the tapestry was so decayed as to be in places dropping from the wall. The ebony chair on the dais was there, but save for the extinguished candles, one of which Smith examined, there was nothing to show that this sinister apartment had been occupied for a generation.

During the next hour we explored some of the strangest rooms I had ever entered. We even penetrated to the cellar below the lotus floor. The place still reeked of hawthorn, but that unknown gas was no longer present in anesthetic quantity. A net was hung below the trap . . .

We had a glimpse in those evil catacombs of the Venice in which men had disappeared never to be heard of again.

But not a soul did we find anywhere!

None of the other police parties had anything to report. Rudolf Adlon, whose slightest words disturbed Europe, had vanished as completely as in the days of the doges when prominent citizens of Venice had vanished!

It was a fact so amazing that I found it hard to accept. No member of that household had ever entered these locked rooms and cellars. All that I had heard, all that I had seen there might have been figments of a dream! Saving the presence and the evidence of Nayland Smith I should have been tempted to suppose it so.

Yet again, like an evil cloud out of which lightning strikes destruction, Dr Fu Manchu had gone with the breeze, to leave no trace behind!

And Ardatha?

Silver Heels

"Are you ready, Kerrigan?"

Nayland Smith burst into my room at the hotel. A bath and a badly needed shave had renewed the man. He lived on his nerves. To me he was a constant source of amazement.

"Yes, Smith, I'm ready. Is there any more news?"

He dropped down on the side of my bed and began to fill his pipe. Wind howled through the shutters, and this was the darkest hour of the night.

"Silver Heels has answered the radio and is waiting for us."

"What do you think it all means, Smith? To me it still seems like a dream that you and I were confined there in that vile place. Granting Paulo's statement to be true, that Brownlow Wilton and his guests had left before my arrival, it's still incredible. That scene between Fu Manchu and Rudolf Adlon . . . Now at this moment I cannot believe it ever happened!"

"Think," snapped Smith. "The Palazzo Brioni was leased on behalf of Brownlow Wilton by his secretary and a staff assembled. Neither the secretary, one assumes, nor Brownlow Wilton, had the remotest idea of the history of the place. It contained a series of rooms belonging to what is known apparently as the Old Palace which, for good reasons, were shut off—never entered."

"So far, I agree."

His pipe satisfactorily filled, Nayland Smith struck a match. While he lighted the tobacco, he continued:

"Only one member of the household, Paulo, the butler who has served there before, knows anything about those hidden rooms. Very well. A genius of evil who *does* know about them, seizes this opportunity. Wilton, who has upheld to his peril the Nazi banner in the United States, is in a position to entertain Rudolf Adlon. Fu Manchu knows that Rudolf Adlon is coming incognito to Venice. An invitation to a luncheon party on the millionaire's yacht is arranged. There are servants of Fu Manchu on board."

He paused, pushed down the smouldering tobacco with his thumb and lighted a second match.

"At that party, Rudolf Adlon meets the woman known as Korêani. He is attracted. She makes it her business to see that he *shall* be attracted; and of this art, Kerrigan, she is a past mistress. She promises him an appointment, but stresses the danger and difficulty in order to prepare Adlon for the journey through those filthy passages . . . No doubt she posed as an unhappily married woman."

"It's logical enough."

"Adlon, now enslaved, slips away from the Palazzo da Rosa and goes to the spot at which she has promised to confirm their meeting. In the interval she has consulted Doctor Fu Manchu and the nature of Adlon's reception has been arranged. Luckily, you saw the message delivered. Adlon keeps the appointment . . . We know what happened."

His pipe now well alight, he began to walk across and across the floor.

"But, Smith," I said, watching him fascinatedly, for his succinct summing up of the facts revealed again the clarity of his mind, "you mean that Brownlow Wilton has been ignorant of this from first to last?"

He paused for a moment, surrounding himself with clouds of smoke, and then:

"Hard to believe, I agree," he snapped, "but at the moment there is no other solution. Wilton, as you probably know, is an eccentric and a chronic invalid—in fact a dying man. Although he entertains lavishly, he often secludes himself from his guests. We have found out that his decision to leave for Villefranche was made suddenly, but the party was a small one. Two, I think, we have identified."

I nodded.

There was little doubt that Ardatha had been one of Brownlow Wilton's guests, according to the account of a police officer who had been on board. His description of the only other female member of the party made it clear that this was Korêani. Paulo's account of the women tallied.

"It had been most cunningly arranged," Smith went on, speaking rapidly and resuming his restless promenade. "No doubt Brownlow Wilton met them under circumstances which prompted the invitation. After all, they are both charming women!"

"You think they flew from Paris and joined the yacht party?"

"Undoubtedly. They were under Si-Fan orders, but Brownlow Wilton did not know it. Where he met them no doubt we shall learn. But the facts are obvious, I think."

"They cannot possibly have sailed in Silver Heels?"

"No—evidently Doctor Fu Manchu had other plans for them and for himself. But I know, in my very bones I know, that Wilton is in danger. He may even be running away from that danger now . . ."

The Adriatic was behaving badly from the point of view of a naval cutter, when presently we cleared the land and set out to overtake Silver Heels. I thought that the chief of police was not easy as our small craft rolled and pitched in a moderately heavy sea.

However, the storm was subsiding, and a coy moon began to peek through breaking clouds. For my own part I welcomed the storm, for neither the flashes of lightning nor rumbling of distant thunder were out of keeping with my mood.

Unknown to most of its inhabitants, Venice tonight was being combed for one of Europe's outstanding figures. Reserves of police had been called in from neighbouring towns. No representative of a great power was in his bed.

Rudolf Adlon had been smuggled out of life.

I think that high-speed dash through angry seas in some way calmed my spirit. Lightning flashed again, and:

"There she is!" came the hail of a lookout.

But from where we sat in the cabin, all of us, I suppose, had seen Silver Heels, bathed in that sudden radiance, a fairy ship, riding a sea bewitched, a white and beautiful thing.

A ladder was down when we drew alongside, but it was no easy matter to get aboard. At last, however, our party assembled on deck. We were received by Brownlow Wilton and the captain of the yacht.

My first glimpse of Brownlow Wilton provoked a vague memory to which I found myself unable to give definite shape.

He wore a beret and a blue rainproof overcoat with the collar turned up, a wizened little man as I saw him in the deck lights, with the sallow complexion of a southerner, peering at us through black-rimmed spectacles.

The captain, whose name was Farazan, had all the appearance of a Portuguese. He, too, was a sallow type; he wore oilskins. The astonishment of the American owner was manifest in his manner and in his eyes, magnified by the lenses of his spectacles.

"Although it is a very great pleasure to have you gentlemen aboard," he said in a weak, piping voice, "it is also a great surprise. I don't pretend that I have got the hang of it, but you are very welcome. Let's all step down to the saloon."

We descended to a spacious saloon to find a lighted table and a black-browed steward in attendance. I saw a cold buffet, the necks of wine bottles peeping from an ice bucket.

"I thought," said Wilton, peeling off his coat and his beret, "that on a night like this and at this hour, you might probably be feeling peckish. Just make yourselves comfortable, gentlemen. I was hauled out of bed myself by the radio message, and I guess a snack won't do any of us any harm."

Silver Heels was riding the swell with an easy and soothing movement, but the chief of police stared at the cold fare as a doomed man might stare at the black cap.

"I think, perhaps," he said, "that a brandy and soda might do me good."

The attendant steward quietly executed the order, and Brownlow Wilton, seated at the head of the table, dispensed an eager hospitality.

"It was all unexpected," he explained. "But I feel like a snack myself and I guess all of us could do no better than reinforce."

He had simple charm, I thought, this man who directed a great chain of newspapers and controlled the United States' biggest armament works. I had expected nothing so seemingly ingenuous. His reputation, his palace on the Grand Canal, his sea-going yacht, had prepared me, I confess, to meet someone quite different. Only in respect to his state of health did he conform to my expectations. He was a sick man. Despite his protestations, he ate nothing and merely sipped some beverage which looked like barley water.

"A little early in the morning," said Nayland Smith, "for

Kerrigan and myself"—when the efficient but saturnine steward proffered refreshments.

He glanced at me smilingly, but I read in his glance that he meant me to refuse.

"I turned in directly we sailed," said Wilton; "and when a man has just fallen asleep and then is called up suddenly, I always find it takes him a little while to readjust his poise. But now, Sir Denis Nayland Smith"—he peered across the table in his short-sighted way—"I can ask you a question: What is this all about?"

Nayland Smith glanced around the saloon, in shadow save for that lighted table at which we were seated.

"It is rather difficult," he replied, "to explain. But, to begin: where are your guests?"

"My guests!" Brownlow Wilton's magnified eyes opened widely. "I have no guests, sir."

"What!"

"Those I had staying on board—there were four only—returned by the late express to Paris. I was unexpectedly compelled to break up the party. I am alone with my crew."

The storm was dying away over the sea, but distant rumbles of thunder reached us from time to time.

"I understand," said Nayland Smith, "that your four guests were Count and Countess Boratov, Mr van Dee and Miss Murano."

"That's correct."

Wilton looked surprised.

"Who is Mr van Dee?"

"A well-known Philadelphia businessman. We have been friends for years."

"I see. And Miss Murano?"

"A schoolmate of Countess Boratov, very attractive and young. She has lived much in Africa where her family have met with serious misfortune. She has unusually beautiful titian hair."

I grew hotly unhappy, for I knew that he was describing Ardatha!

"And where did you make this lady's acquaintance?"

"In London four weeks back."

"Through the Boratovs I suppose?"

"Surely. I asked her to join us here (she was with the countess in London) and she consented."

"How long have you known the Boratovs, Mr Wilton?"

Brownlow Wilton's sallow face grew lined and stern. As he glanced at Colonel Correnti, that elfin memory peeped out, and then eluded me again. Silver Heels rolled uneasily. Dimly, I heard thunder.

"I appreciate the fact, gentlemen, that you are acting with full authority; but not knowing why I have been favoured with your company, perhaps I may ask in what way my friends are of interest?"

"No doubt I have been over-brusque, Mr Wilton," said Smith. "But your own future is at stake. A crime which may change the history of Europe was committed at the Palazzo Brioni earlier tonight—"

"What's that?"

Brownlow Wilton bent forward over the table.

"I have no time for details now. I merely ask for your cooperation. Where did you meet the Boratovs?"

"When they visited America, in the fall of last year."

"Could you describe the countess?"

"A very lovely woman, sir." A note of unmistakable admiration had entered the speaker's high-pitched voice. "Tall, slender, with fascinating eyes: they are brilliantly green—"

Nayland Smith nodded grimly.

"And the count?"

"A distinguished Russian aristocrat, once in the Imperial Guard."

"And they all left by the Paris express, you say?"

"All of them, yes."

"You remained alone for some time then at the palace?"

"No sir. We dined here on board. News from England had come which meant I had to get back. Captain Farazan got busy. He secured the necessary clearance papers and we sailed immediately. My guests made the train and are now on their way to Paris."

Nayland Smith stared hard at James Brownlow Wilton, and then:

"Excuse me," came a discreet voice.

The steward (his name was Lopez), who had gone out, stood now at Wilton's elbow, extending a message on a salver. Wilton took it, nodded his apologies, and read the message. The saturnine Lopez went out again.

"Ah!—a personal matter, gentlemen—of no importance."

But his expression belied his words. Nayland Smith's face offered me a perplexing study. As Wilton crumpled the scrap of paper in his hand:

"May I ask," said Smith, "if you used the small study in Palazzo Brioni? I refer to the one distinguished by a very beautiful figure of the Virgin."

Brownlow Wilton stared hard through his powerful spectacles. I thought he was striving for composure.

"I looked after all my correspondence there, sir. I have always been attracted to that room."

"Were you aware, or did the agent who negotiated the deal inform you, that there is a disused wing which has been locked for years?"

"I never heard that. This is news to me."

"I understand that you have a secretary who takes care of most of these details. I am told that he put Silver Heels into commission in Monaco and also came over to Venice to arrange a suitable household for your arrival. What is this gentleman's name?"

"You mean Hemsley? He has been with me for years. I sent him ahead to London. I am due back there myself, but I want to put the yacht into dry dock before I go. There's something radically wrong with her engines."

"He engaged the present crew, I believe?"

"He did—and by and large, very efficient they are."

"Have any of them worked for you before?"

"Not one. Hemsley believes in a clean slate. The same applies to the staff in Venice. Never saw one of them in my life before."

188

Silver Heels (continued)

Silver Heels rode the swell uneasily. The chief of police continued to look unhappy. He glanced at me from time to time. I could hear the tramping of feet on the deck above, and I knew that the police were going about their work inspecting the papers of the crew. Peering into the shadows at the darkened end of the saloon, I had a momentary impression that someone had been standing there . . . and had disappeared.

The creaking of the ship in a silence which had fallen became to my ears a sinister sound. Nayland Smith's eyes were fixed intently upon the face of the American owner. For some reason I was glad when he spoke:

"You entertained Rudolf Adlon to lunch on board?"

"I did. I had introductions to him from Pietro Monaghani with whom I am well acquainted."

"I suggest that Rudolf Adlon was much attracted by the countess?"

Brownlow Wilton smiled uneasily, then leaning forward selected a cigar from a box which lay upon the table. As he tore the label:

"Maybe you're right," he replied, "and I am not blaming him. But he is a man who makes no attempt to hide his feelings."

"Herr Adlon returned after luncheon to the Palazzo da Rosa?"

"Yes—and I won't say I was sorry."

"Did you go ashore to the palace during the afternoon?"

"No, I stayed on board, but most of the party went ashore. They had odd jobs to do, you understand, before leaving for Paris."

"Did you see them off?"

"No sir. They said good-bye on the yacht and went ashore in the launch. You see, I'm not as active as I used to be. I had a conference with the chief engineer. I wanted to find out if she could make Villefranche under her own steam."

"So that was the last you saw of your guests?"

"It was. But we are all meeting again in London in three days."

Again that uncomfortable silence fell, and then:

"You are quite sure, Mr Wilton, that your reason for breaking up the party was purely engine trouble? I mean you have not, by any chance, received a notice from the Si-Fan?"

At those words, Wilton's face changed completely. He laid down the cigar which he had just lighted, and the effect was as though he had discarded a mask. His large, dark eyes, magnified by spectacles, gleamed almost feverishly as he glared at Nayland Smith.

"How can you know that?" he asked and clutched the edge of the table. "How can you know that?"

"It may be my business to know, Mr Wilton."

"I had two! I got a third while Adlon was on board. Yes, I admit it. I was running away. Now you have the truth."

Nayland Smith nodded.

"I thought as much. You control a great American newspaper, Mr Wilton. Its sympathies are rather pointedly with Adlon and Monaghani. Am I right?"

"Maybe you are."

"Also, may I suggest that your armament works do a large trade with the governments represented by these gentlemen?"

"You seem to know a lot, sir. But, as you say, maybe it's your business."

"How long does the third notice give you?"

"Until noon tomorrow."

"What are you to do?"

"I was ordered to come here to Venice." His glance now as he looked about him was that of a hunted man. "And I was ordered to give that lunch on board to Adlon. Now I am told to beat it as fast as I can get away. This whole journey has been in obedience to those orders. I will admit it: I am a badly frightened man. I once spent some years in the Orient, and I know enough about the Si-Fan to have done what I have done."

Nayland Smith looked hard at me.

"You are noting these facts, no doubt, Kerrigan? You see how Mr Wilton has been used for a dreadful purpose, a purpose which I fear has succeeded."

For some time past, faintly, I had heard the crackling of radio, and now came hurrying footsteps. A police officer ran in carrying a message which he handed to the chief.

Colonel Correnti adjusted a powerful monocle and read it. Then he looked up, his hitherto pale face flushed with excitement.

"It is from headquarters," he exclaimed . . . "A body has been found in the canal!"

"What!"

Smith sprang to his feet.

"They cannot be certain but they think—"

"Merciful heaven! This is terrible! What does it mean?"

Wilton, also, had stood up and was staring at the colonel's pale face.

"It means, Mr Wilton," snapped Smith, "that something intended to avert war has happened tonight which, instead, may lead to it."

"Why should we be silent," the colonel cried, "about that which the world must know tomorrow! Mr Wilton, a terrible thing has happened in Venice. Rudolf Adlon, a short time after he left this yacht, disappeared completely!"

"What do you say?"

Wilton dropped back into his chair.

"Those are the facts," said Nayland Smith sternly. "You were used to bring together Adlon and the woman known to you as Countess Boratov under circumstances which would enable them to meet again secretly. This meeting took place—you have heard the result."

"But there may be a mistake! I find myself quite unable to believe it!"

"Catch him, Kerrigan—he has collapsed!"

Just as he stepped out onto the deck, we both saw Wilton stagger and clutch blindly for support . . . I caught him as he fell. In the deck light his face appeared ghastly.

"This murderous farce"—he spoke in a mere whisper—"has taken more out of me than I realised. Now I know why it was planned, the thing that has happened—I guess I'm through!"

Colonel Correnti was already on board the cutter, although it had proved no simple task to transfer his portly form from the moving ladder. I could see him staring up through a cabin window. We had all planned to return immediately, leaving the crew to bring Silver Heels back to port with two police on board.

Now I realised that our plans would have to be changed.

"My cabin is just forward," Brownlow Wilton muttered. "If I may lean on you I think I can make it."

Smith and I took him forward to his cabin. It was commodious, with up-to-date equipment, and having laid him on the bed:

"My small medical knowledge does not entitle me to prescribe," said Nayland Smith, "but would some stimulant—"

Lopez, the steward, appeared in the doorway. Behind him I saw the Carabinieri uniforms of the two men detailed to remain on board. In light shining out of the cabin, I disliked the steward's appearance more than ever.

"If you will leave Mr Wilton to me, gentlemen," he said, "I think I can take care of him."

Brownlow Wilton's face was now contorted; he appeared to be in agony.

"What is it?" I asked aside.

"Angina pectoris, sir. The excitement. I am afraid he is in for another attack. There are some tablets . . ."

"Good God! don't you travel with a doctor?"

"No sir. Mr Wilton has a regular physician in Venice, but I don't think he felt any symptoms of an attack until this present moment."

Nayland Smith was staring down at the sick man, and somehow from his expression I deduced what he was thinking. Dr Fu Manchu, he had told me on one occasion, could reproduce the symptoms of nearly every disease known to medical science . . .

"I will take no drugs—"

The sick man had forced himself upright—Smith sprang forward to assist him.

"Is this wise, Mr Wilton?"

"Be so good as to give me your arm—as far as that chair. Lopez! I have found that a small glass of old Bourbon whisky never does any harm at these times. If you abstemious gentlemen would join me, why that would hasten the cure!"

His pluck was so admirable that to refuse would have been

churlish. Lopez went to find the old Bourbon and Nayland Smith, going out on deck, hailed the cutter.

"Head for port! Don't delay. I am remaining on board. Silver Heels will put about and follow . . ."

At the small cabin table I presently found myself seated, the invalid on my left and Nayland Smith, too restless to relax, leaning against an elaborate washbowl with which the room was equipped. Behind me Lopez poured out the drinks.

"Pardon," Smith muttered, and turning, began to wash his hands. "Grimy from the journey."

When he turned to take the glass which Lopez handed to him, I had a glimpse of Smith's face in the mirror which positively startled me. His eyes shone like steel; his jaws were clenched. Almost, I doubted my senses—for as he fronted us again he was smiling!

Lopez withdrew quietly, leaving the cabin door open. I could hear the cutter moving off. There were shouted orders, and now I detected vibration. Silver Heels was being put about.

"To the future, gentlemen!"

Brownlow Wilton raised his glass, when:

"Good God! Look! *Doctor Fu Manchu!*"

Nayland Smith snapped out the words and glared across the cabin!

Brownlow Wilton, setting his glass unsteadily on the table (I had not touched mine), shot up from his chair with astounding agility and we both stared at the open door. I was up, too.

The deck outside was empty!

I turned with a feeling of dismay to Smith. He was draining his glass. He set it down.

"Forgive me, Mr Wilton"—he spoke with a nervousness I had never before detected in him—"that bogey is beginning to haunt me! It was only the shadow of a cloud."

"Well"—Wilton's high voice quavered—"you certainly startled me—although I don't know whom you thought you saw."

"Forget it, Mr Wilton. I'm afraid the strain is telling. But that whisky has done me good. Finish your drink, Kerrigan. Perhaps I might rest awhile, if there's an available cabin?"

"Why certainly!" Brownlow Wilton pressed a bell. "Your very good health, gentlemen!"

He drank his Bourbon like a man who needed it, and as Lopez came in silently I finished mine.

"Lopez—show Sir Denis Nayland Smith and Mr Kerrigan to cabin A. It is at your disposal, gentlemen. We have an hour's sailing ahead of . . ."

I glanced swiftly at Smith. The shock of his strange outcry had provoked another spasm of Wilton's dread ailment. His features were convulsed. He lay back limply in his chair!

"All right, sir!" said Lopez as I stooped and raised the frail body. "If he lies down I hope he will recover—"

I laid the sick man on his bed. His eyes were staring past me at Lopez. He tried to speak—but not a word came.

"Here's your next patient, Kerrigan," Nayland Smith spoke thickly . . . he was swaying!

I ran to him.

"This way, sir."

Lopez remained imperturbable. As I clutched Smith's arm and the steward led us along the deck, I cannot even attempt to depict my frame of mind. . .

What ailed Nayland Smith?

Lightning flickered far away over the sea; thunder sounded like rolling drums . . . The police cutter was already out of sight. Silver Heels swung slowly about.

As Smith reeled along the deserted deck:

"Take your cue from me!" he whispered in my ear. "When I lie on the bed drop down beside me in a chair—anywhere—but as near as you can! Begin to stagger . . ."

The steward opened a door and illuminated a commodious cabin, similar to that occupied by Brownlow Wilton.

"In here, sir."

"Always . . . poor sailor, I fear," Smith muttered thickly. "Lie down awhile . . ."

I assisted him on to one of the two beds, while Lopez removed the coverlet. He lay there with closed eyes, seeming to be trying to speak. An armchair stood near by, and distrusting my acting I slumped suddenly into it. I had ceased trying to think, but trusted Nayland Smith, for he could see where I was blind.

As the steward solicitously removed the coverlet from the neighbouring bed and spread it over me:

"Sorry . . . whacked!" I muttered and closed my eyes.

The steward went out and shut the cabin door.

"Don't speak—don't move!" It was a mere murmur. "Roll over so that you face me, and wait."

I rolled over on my side and lay still. Now I could see Smith clearly. His eyes, though half closed, were questing about the cabin, particularly watching the door and the two ports which gave upon the deck. Over the creaking and groaning of the ship I heard those distant drums. Something told me to lie still—that we were being watched.

"Speak softly," said Nayland Smith; "the man Lopez has gone to report. Do you realise what has happened?"

"Not in the least."

"We have fallen into a trap!"

"What!"

"Lie still. Someone else is probably watching us . . . I foresaw the danger but still walked into it. I suppose I had no right to bring you with me."

"I don't even know what you mean."

The manoeuvre of turning the ship about had been clumsily accomplished, and I realised that we were now headed back for Venice. There was less creaking and groaning and the sound of thunder drums grew fainter.

"I suspect Fu Manchu's plan to be that we shall never return."

"Good heavens!"

"Ssh! Quiet! Someone at the porthole."

I lay perfectly still; so did Nayland Smith. Only by the prompting of that extra sense which comes to us in hours of danger did I realise that someone was indeed peering into the cabin. My brain, tired by a whirl of grotesque experiences, obstinately refused to deal with this new problem. Why should we both be overcome? And what were we waiting for?

"All clear again," Smith reported in a low voice. "Even if the door is locked, which I doubt, those deck ports are wide enough to enable us to get out."

"But Smith, what do you suspect?"

"It isn't a suspicion, Kerrigan; it's a fact. This yacht is in the hands of servants of Doctor Fu Manchu from the commander downwards."

"Good God! Are you sure?"

"Quite sure."

"But Wilton . . ."

"In Europe our concern is concentrated upon kings and dictators, but Wilton in the United States wields almost as much power as, shall we say, Goebbels in Germany. His political sympathies are well known, his interests widespread."

"But Wilton is a dying man."

"I think you would be nearer the mark, Kerrigan, if you said 'Wilton is a dead man'!"

Only the sound of the propellers broke the silence now. I knew instinctively that Nayland Smith was thinking hard, and presently:

"Can you hear me, Kerrigan?" he asked in a low voice. "I dare not speak louder."

"Yes."

Those words "Wilton is a dead man" haunted me. I wondered what he meant.

"We should probably be well-advised to make a dash for it; grab those life belts and jump over the side. But there's a fairly heavy swell and I don't entirely fancy the prospect."

"I don't fancy it at all!"

"Perhaps we can afford to wait until we are rather nearer land. Our great risk at the moment is that they discover we are not insensible."

"Insensible! But why should we be insensible?"

Of all the strange and horrible memories which I have of this battle to prevent Dr Fu Manchu from readjusting the balance of world power, there is none more strange, I think than this muttered interlude, lying there in the cabin of Silver Heels.

"For the simple reason," the quiet, low voice continued, "that the drinks we shared with Wilton were drugged. Bourbon whisky was insisted upon for that reason: its marked flavour evidently conceals whatever drug was in it."

"But, Smith—"

"I switched them, Kerrigan, having created a brief distraction! My own, if you remember, I apparently drained at a draught. It went into the washbowl at my elbow."

"But mine?"

"There was no alternative in the time at my disposal. Wilton had yours—*you* had Wilton's."

"Good God! Do you mean you think he is lying dead there in his cabin?"

"Ssh! Remember we are through if they once suspect us. I mean that he is dead, yes—but not lying in his cabin . . ."

He lay silent for a while, and I divined the fact that he was listening. I listened also, puzzling my brain at the same time for a clue to the meaning of his words. Then:

"I am wondering why the two police have not—"

My sentence was cut short. I heard a sudden scuffling of feet, a wild cry—and then came silence again, except that very far away I detected a dull rumbling of thunder.

"Smith! Good God, can we do nothing!"

"The murderous swine! It's too late! I was playing for time—trying to make a plan"—there was an agony of remorse in his low-pitched voice. "Hello!"

The lights went out!

"Now we can move," snapped Smith, and as he spoke the engines ceased to move. Silver Heels lay rolling idly on the swell.

"This is where we jump to it! Quick, Kerrigan! Have your gun handy!"

I rolled off the bed and made for the door. I was nearer to it than Smith.

"Damnation!" I exclaimed.

The door was locked!

"I didn't note them do it."

Dimly I could see Smith trying one of the big rectangular ports which opened onto the starboard deck.

"Hullo! This is more serious than I thought! These are locked, too!"

We stood there for a moment listening to increasing sounds about us.

"They're getting the launch away," I muttered, for I had noted that the yacht carried a motor launch. "What does that mean?"

"It means they're going to sink Silver Heels—with ourselves on board!"

Silver Heels (concluded)

"Listen, Kerrigan, listen!"

To the sound of voices, running feet, creaking of davits and wheezy turning of chocks, a suggestive silence had succeeded, broken only by the cracking and groaning of the ship's fabric. If Nayland Smith's conclusions were true, and he was rarely wrong, we were trapped like rats, and like rats must drown.

I listened intently.

"You hear it, Kerrigan?"

"Yes. It's in some adjoining cabin."

It was a moaning sound; but unlike that which had horrified me in the cellars of Palazzo Brioni, this certainly was human. Even as I listened and wondered what I heard, Nayland Smith had a wardrobe door open. The wardrobe was empty, but in the dim light I saw that he had his ear pressed to the woodwork.

"It's behind here!" he said. "We daren't use a torch yet. Noise we must risk. The ship's noises may drown it, but this boarding has to be stripped. Hello!"

As I joined him I saw that there was a ventilator at the back of the wardrobe.

"No time and no means to unscrew it," he muttered, and I saw that he had succeeded in wedging his fingers between two of the bars. "Let's hope it doesn't make too much row!"

He wrenched it bodily from the light wood in which it was set. Speaking very close to the gap thus created:

"Anyone there?" he called softly.

A stifled muttering responded.

"Come on, Kerrigan! This is our only chance!"

So far as I could make out, every living soul on board, other than ourselves or whoever might be in the next cabin, had joined the launch. We attacked that job like demons, stripping three-ply woodwork from the back of the wardrobe. Every crack of the shattered fragments sounded in my ears like the shot of a pistol. We made a considerable gap—and no one hindered us.

"If anybody comes in," snapped Smith, "shoot him down."

There was a second partition behind, and now that stifled cry reached us more urgently.

"Stand behind me," said Smith.

He flashed a momentary beam upon this new obstacle.

"Matchboarding," I muttered. "These rooms once communicated."

Not awaiting his reply, I hurled myself against it.

I crashed through into a small cabin, as fitful moonlight from a porthole told me. On the floor the two men of the Carabinieri day bound—bandages tied over their mouths! One was struggling furiously; the other lay still.

"This one first."

Quickly we released the struggling man. He spoke a little English and the situation was soon explained. He had been struck down from behind as he patrolled the deck, and had recovered consciousness to find himself bound in the cabin. His opposite number, when we released him in turn, proved to be insensible, but alive.

"Now," snapped Smith. "Yes or no . . ."

The cabin was locked.

"This is awful!" I groaned. "But we could blow the lock out."

"Yes—fortunately we're armed, for these men's carbines have gone. But wait—"

He sprang to the porthole, worked feverishly for a few seconds and then:

"A different fitting," he gasped. "I have it open!"

I climbed through onto the deck . . . and the key was in the cabin door. We were on the starboard side of Silver Heels; the launch lay at the port ladder. And from the ladder-head at this moment sounds of disturbance arose. Facing us a small lifeboat hung at the davits; forward, just abaft the bridge, an alleyway connected the two decks.

"Do you know anything about boats?" Smith snapped.

"Not much."

"Do you?" to the police officer.

"Yes sir. I was at sea before I joined the Carabinieri."

"Right! Kerrigan, steal through that alleyway and watch what is going on. You"—to the ex-seaman—"lend a hand with your friend."

They began to haul the insensible man across the deck. I turned and crept along the alleyway. Soon I had a view of the ladder-head. The portside was in shadow, relieved only by the light of a solitary hurricane lantern.

One man stood there. He was tapping his foot impatiently upon the deck and watching a door which I thought led to the engine room. It was Lopez. Heralded by a rattling of feet on iron rungs, a man wearing dungarees burst into view.

"You have set it?"

"Yes."

"Down quickly!—not a moment to waste!"

"But Doctor Chang! Where is the doctor? I have not seen him."

"His orders were to join the launch immediately she was swung out."

"Doctor Chang is not on board," came a voice from the foot of the ladder.

"How long have we?"

"Three minutes."

Silver Heels, her wheel abandoned, creaked and groaned: it became difficult to hear the speakers.

"I shall not sacrifice myself for the doctor!" Lopez spoke furiously. "Already he has taxed my patience . . . Hoy!"— he hailed—"Doctor!"

"Doctor Chang!"

Other voices joined in the cry.

But Dr Chang—whoever Dr Chang may have been—did not appear.

At the head of the ladder the man in dungarees hesitated, looking back over his shoulder, whereupon:

"Down, I say!" cried Lopez, a note of cold authority in his voice. "Who is in charge here? Always the doctor was mad. If he wishes to be destroyed who cares? There is not a moment to spare! Everyone for himself!"

Nayland Smith and the police officer had succeeded in lowering away the ship's boat with the insensible Carabinieri on board, for when I got back to the starboard rail it was already riding an oil swell, fended off by the man in uniform. Smith, bathed in perspiration as I could see, was watching for my return.

"Well?"

"They've gone. The ship will blow up in two minutes! But Wilton—"

"Come on! The ladder is down."

"But—"

"There are no 'buts.' Come on!"

Although I have said that the swell was subsiding, boarding that boat was no easy matter. We accomplished it, however, so that I am in a position to testify to the fact that some prayers are answered.

As dimly we heard the launch racing away from Silver Heels, we began furiously to pull around the stern of the vessel. We rowed as though our lives depended upon our efforts.

And this indeed was the case.

I was too excited at the time, too exhausted, to be competent to say now how far from Silver Heels we lay when it happened . . . but the effect was as though a volcano had belched up from the sea.

A shattering explosion came—and the graceful yacht seemed to split in the middle. Minor explosions followed. Flames roared up as if to lick the clouds.

Her end, I think, was a matter of minutes . . .

I can hear myself now as that deafening explosion came, and Silver Heels disappeared below the waves, creating a maelstrom which wildly rocked the boat:

"Smith! I don't understand! . . . Why did we desert Brownlow Wilton? He died a terrible death, and we—"

"He deserved it. God knows how or when the *real* Wilton died! The staff engaged in Venice had never seen Wilton. It was a plot to trap Adlon. The man who died on Silver Heels was a double, a servant of Doctor Fu Manchu!"

"Good heavens, Smith! A memory has come back!"

"Dictators have no monopoly of doubles. Doctor Fu Manchu employs them with notable success."

"Those fellows were crying out for someone called Doctor Chang, who was missing—"

"Wilton's impersonator, no doubt! I suspected a Mongolian

streak. He lay drugged—by his own hand! I saw it all in the mirror, Kerrigan, hence my remarkable behaviour! The man, Lopez, was directing; he is senior to the other in the Si-Fan. But 'doctor' is significant. Probably Doctor Chang, apart from his resemblance to Brownlow Wilton, is a poison specialist—"

"I know he is, Smith—I know it! He is the man who came to your rooms and fixed the Green Death to the telephone!"

"Poor devil! You mean he *was* the man . . ."

203

The man in the park

The wheels seemed to turn very swiftly in those strange days and nights during which I found myself beside Nayland Smith in his battle to hold the world safe from Dr Fu Manchu.

Throughout the week that followed our escape from Silver Heels so many things happened that I find it difficult to select a point from which to carry on my story, since I realise that this story, almost against my will, from the first has wound itself insidiously about the figure of Ardatha.

First had come what Smith called "the great hush-up."

Since Rudolf Adlon's double had been reviewing troops at the time when the real Adlon had been at Palazzo da Rosa it was impossible for his government to divulge the fact that he had died (or disappeared) in Venice. When it became necessary to admit his death to a public which had looked up to him as to a god, they were told that he had died in his bed. The double, Rudolf Adlon No. 2, ceased to exist. It was done adroitly: the newspapers were muzzled. Patriotic physicians issued fictitious bulletins, then the final news for which a breathless Europe waited.

Mourning millions filed past a guarded dummy lying in state . . .

Next came the retirement from public life of the ruler of Turkey, "a bloodless victory for Fu Manchu" was Nayland Smith's comment. (Pietro Monaghani, I should mention had failed to keep the appointment with Adlon in Venice. He had accepted the orders of the Si-Fan.)

When an astonishing fact became undeniable—the fact that Fu Manchu with all his people, including Ardatha, had vanished from Venice as though they had never entered the City of the Lagoons, I remember that I advocated a secret departure to some base unsuspected by the Chinese doctor. "Will you never realise, Kerrigan," Nayland Smith had said, "that from the point of view of the organisation controlled by Fu Manchu, there is no such thing as a secret base. He knew that Adlon was going to be in Venice before the combined intelligence services of Europe knew it. He brought a crew of highly trained criminal specialists to deal with the situation and dispersed them into thin air when their work was done, as a conjurer vanishes a bowl of goldfish. And think of the pack of cutthroats who left Silver Heels in the murder launch. The explosion was heard for miles—we were picked up ten minutes later; but what of the launch? It hasn't been traced to this day, nor anybody on board!"

And so on one never-to-be-forgotten evening I found myself back at my flat in Bayswater Road.

I stared from my window across the park as dusk gathered and pedestrians moved in the direction of the gates. I had not seen Nayland Smith since the forenoon. At this time, frankly, I was terrified whenever he was out of my sight. That he continued to live while the awful hand of Fu Manchu was extended against him became every hour a miracle more worshipful.

Presently the behaviour of a man who had just reached the gate nearly opposite my window began to intrigue me.

He was a tall, rather shabby-looking man, bearded and bespectacled. His wide-brimmed hat suggested a colonial visitor, and he walked with a stoop, leaning heavily upon an ash stick. Under one arm he carried a bulky portfolio. He was accompanied by a park-keeper and a policeman who assisted his every step. But it was something else which had arrested my attention.

He was staring up intently at my window!

Now as I drew the curtain aside and peered out, he raised his stick and lowered it, pointing to the front door!

That he was directing me to go down and admit him was an unmistakable fact, for I saw during a halt in the traffic that he was being shepherded across. I delayed only long enough to slip an automatic into my pocket and then went out and began to descend.

Mrs Merton, my daily help, had gone, for I was not dining at home. As the flat below remained unoccupied and my upstairs neighbour was away, I confess that my steps to the front door were not unfearful. But I knew that this growing dread of the demoniac

Dr Fu Manchu was something I must combat with all my strength. Fear was his weapon.

I threw the door open and stood looking out at the man who waited there.

With a terse nod to his two supporters, he stepped in.

"Shut the door," he snapped.

It was Nayland Smith!

"Smith," I said reproachfully, "you promised you would never go about alone!"

"I was not alone!"

He removed the wide-brimmed hat, the glasses, and straightened bent shoulders.

"I cannot complete the transformation in the best stage tradition," he said, with a grim smile. "False whiskers, if they are to sustain close scrutiny, must be attached with some care."

"But Smith, I don't understand!"

"My dramatic appearance, Kerrigan, is easily explained. I was in a flying squad car with Gallaho. Nearly at the top of Sloane Street, just before one reaches Knightsbridge, there is a narrow turning on the right. Out of this at the very moment that we were about to pass, a lorry shot—I use the word advisedly—for the acceleration pointed to an amazing engine. It struck the bonnet of our car, turned us completely around. We capsized—and before the lorry driver could check his mad career, it resulted in the destruction of a taxicab, and, I fear, of the taximan!"

"But, Smith, do you mean—"

'That it was deliberate? Of course!" The pipe and pouch came from the pocket of his shabby coat. "Gallaho was knocked out, and I am afraid our driver was badly injured. As you see"—he indicated the side of his skull—"I did not escape entirely."

I saw a jagged gash which was still bleeding.

"Some iodine, Smith?"

"Later. A scratch."

"What happened then? How do you come to be here?"

"What happened was this: In spite of my disguise I had been recognised. This was a planned attempt to recover something which I had in my possession! In the tremendous disturbance which followed I climbed out of the window of the overturned car and lost myself in the crowd which began to collect. The casualties were receiving attention. My business was to slip away."

He paused, stuffing tobacco into the briar bowl and staring at me, familiar grey eyes in that unfamiliar bearded face leaving an odd impression.

"I always carry the badge of a king's messenger." He pulled back the lapel of his coat and I saw the silver greyhound. "It ensures prompt official assistance in an emergency without long explanations. I grabbed a constable, told him to come along, and made straight across the park. Here I roped in a parkkeeper. Even so, I kept as much as possible to open spaces and checked up on anybody walking in the same direction."

He stared through the window across to the darkening park.

"What should you have done if I had not been looking out or if I had not replied?"

"I should have been compelled to ring the bell, meaning delay—which I feared. But I knew you would be at home for I had promised to communicate."

As I crossed to the dining room for refreshments he dropped into an armchair and began to light his pipe. The big portfolio he set upon the floor beside him. On my return:

"The full facts of the Venice plot are now to hand," he said bitterly. "Our pursuit of Silver Heels may or may not have been foreseen, but in any event it is certain that they meant to destroy the vessel."

"Why?"

"The story of engine trouble had been circulated. She was as you know, a Diesel engine ship. By the simple device of blowing her up at sea, everybody on board having first slipped away on the motor launch, the death of James Brownlow Wilton would be satisfactorily explained. I think we may take it for granted that the launch did not make for land. I am postulating, though I may never be able to prove it, some other craft in the neighbourhood by which they were picked up."

"But . . . James Brownlow Wilton?"

"I have the facts—all of them, but the details are unimportant, Kerrigan. James Brownlow Wilton travelled by the Blue Train from London to Monte Carlo to join the yacht—I mean the *real* James

Brownlow Wilton. At some time during the night (the French police think at Avignon) he was smuggled off the train. His double took his place . . ."

"It's too appalling to think about!"

"His retiring habits made the job a comparatively easy one. He avoided—refused to see—those to whom the real Wilton was well known, and joining the yacht, sailed for Venice. The same procedure was followed there. Rudolf Adlon was dealt with, and saving our presence, the death of the millionaire at sea would have concluded the episode."

"That conclusion has been generally accepted, Smith. The newspapers are full of it."

"I know. Those who are aware of the real facts have been instructed to remain silent . . . as in the case of Rudolf Adlon."

"Good God! What a ghastly farce!"

He took the glass I handed to to him, and holding it up to the light, stared through it as though inspiration might reside in the bubbles.

"A farce indeed! But any government such as the Adlon government, which consistently hoodwinks the public, must be prepared to face such an emergency. One must admit that they have faced it well. General Diesler, Adlon's successor, acted with promptitude and vision. The figure lying in state was in the true tradition of Cesare Borgia. The bulletins of the medical men were worthy of Machiavelli. And now, today, an empty shell has reverently been set in place, and a monument will be raised above it!"

My phone rang.

"Careful, Kerrigan!" snapped Smith. "Remember that Doctor Fu Manchu employs mimics. Don't say I'm here unless you are absolutely sure to whom you are speaking. But it may be news of poor Gallaho."

I picked up the receiver.

"Hello," came a typically English voice. "Is that Mr Bart Kerrigan's flat?"

"Yes."

"I have been told by Sir Denis Nayland Smith's man that Sir Denis may be with you. This is Egerton of the Foreign Office speaking.

I turned to Smith, and without uttering the words, framed with my lips: "Egerton, F.O.!"

Close to my ear Smith whispered:

"Say you will communicate with me if he will give you Fey's number."

"If you will give me Fey's number," I said (wondering what Fey's number might be), "I will endeavour to communicate with Sir Denis."

"Seven six nine four," came the reply.

"Seven six nine four," I mouthed.

Nayland Smith took up the receiver.

"That you, Egerton? Yes . . . precautions are necessary I am afraid. We have had an unexpected scoop today. Be good enough to mention to *no one* that I am here . . . Yes . . . What's that? . . ."

He seemed to grow rigid. The grey eyes in that bearded face shone feverishly as he listened. Only once he interpolated a query:

"The mob killed him, you say? Is that certain?"

He listened again, nodding grimly. And at last:

"We knew he had had the notices," he said in a dull voice, "but he was even more obstinate than Adlon. In fact I am disposed to believe, Egerton, that he distrusted me. You know I was refused admission to the country?"

I heard the voice of the unseen Egerton talking for a while longer, and then:

"You may count upon me. I will communicate at once," said Smith and hung up the receiver.

He turned, and his expression warned me: Dr Fu Manchu had scored again.

"Yes," he nodded, "the work of the Si-Fan carries on."

"What has happened, Smith?"

"Something even more spectacular," he replied bitterly, "than the published facts relating to Rudolf Adlon. The newspapers and news bulletins will have it tonight. All the world must know, for this is something which cannot be suppressed, nor edited. Standing on a black-draped balcony before no less than two hundred thousand people, General Diesler was delivering a funeral oration over the draped shell which does *not* contain the body of Rudolf Adlon. He said, so Egerton informs me: 'We have all suf-

209

fered an irreparable loss. There is a fiendish enemy, by you unsuspected, an enemy in our very midst . . .' Those, roughly, were his words . . ."

"Well, what happened?"

"They were his last words, Kerrigan."

"What!"

"He stopped, clutched at his breast and fell. The sound of a distant, a very distant report, was heard. He had been shot through the heart."

"But, Smith, on such an occasion every place within range would have been emptied, held by the police or the military!"

"Every place within range—I agree, Kerrigan—that is, within ordinary range. This shot was fired from the top of the cathedral spire—thirty-five hundred yards away!"

"I don't understand!"

"A body of police who happened to be marching through the cathedral close by heard the report from the top of the steeple. They rushed in and caught a man who was hurrying down those hundreds of steps. It was none other than Baron Trenck, the millionaire publisher, ruined and exiled by Adlon, but acknowledged to be one of the three finest big-game shots in Europe!"

"But, Smith—"

"The rifle which he carried was fitted with telescopic sights . . . and a Jasper vacuum charger!"

"Good God!"

"You see, the doctor has already made use of that valuable invention, thanks to the work of his daughter, Korêani! In spite of the efforts of the police who endeavoured to escort the baron under arrest, fanatical Adlonites"—he paused for a moment—"I gather that he was practically torn to pieces."

"I am now going to make a curious request, Kerrigan."

"What is it?"

Let me confess that I had not yet recovered from the shock of that dreadful news.

"I am going to ask you to look out of the window while I select a hiding place somewhere in your rooms for this portfolio!"

"A hiding place?"

"Let me explain. It was to recover this portfolio which I was taking to Scotland Yard that that mad attack was made upon me in Sloane Street. A flying squad car will be here in a few minutes—I authorised the constable to phone for one— in which I propose to leave."

"And I to come with you."

"Not at all!"

"What!"

"Another attempt, although probably not of the same character, is to be expected. I shall be well guarded. Your presence could not save me. But this time the attempt might succeed. Therefore, I am going to hide this valuable thing in your rooms."

"Why hide it?"

"Because if you knew where to find it, Fu Manchu might discover a means of forcing you to tell him!"

"But why leave it here at all?"

"For a very good reason. Be so kind as to do as I ask, Kerrigan."

I stared out of the window, thinking into what a mad maze my footsteps had blundered since that first evening when Nayland Smith had rung my bell. I could hear him walking about in an adjoining room, and then he returned. I saw a police car pull up at the door. The bell rang.

"I shall be in good hands until I see you again," snapped Smith. "Later I will communicate when I have made arrangements for the safe transfer of the portfolio to a spot where I propose to place its contents before a committee which I must assemble for the purpose."

"But what is it, Smith?"

"Forgive me, Kerrigan, but I don't want to tell you. You will know in good time. One thing only I ask—and you will serve me best by doing exactly as I direct. Don't leave your flat tonight until you hear from me, and distrust visitors as I distrust every inch of my route from here to Scotland Yard!"

When he was gone (and I went down to the front door to satisfy myself that the car really belonged to the flying squad) I sat at my desk for some time endeavouring to get my notes in order, to transfer to paper something of the recent amazing developments in this campaign of the Si-Fan against dictatorship. It was a story hard to believe, harder to tell; yet one that some day must be told, and one well worth the telling.

A phone call interrupted me. It was from Scotland Yard, and I knew the speaker: Chief Inspector Leighton of the special branch. News of Gallaho. He had escaped with cuts and contusions. The doctors despaired of the life of the driver; and among other casualties great and small occasioned by the apparently insane behaviour of the truckman, was that of this person himself. His neck had been broken in the collision.

"He was some kind of Asiatic," said Inspector Leighton. "Sir Denis may be able to recognise him. The firm to whom the lorry belonged know nothing of the matter . . ."

I was still thinking over his words when again my phone rang. I took up the receiver.

"Hello!"

"Yes," said a voice, "is that Bart Kerrigan?"

The speaker was Ardatha!

My doorbell rings

By dint of a mighty effort I replied calmly:

"Yes, Ardatha. How did you find my number? It isn't in the book."

"You should know now"—how I loved her quaint accent—"that private numbers mean nothing to the people I belong to."

There was a moment of almost timorous hesitancy.

"I hate to hear you say that, Ardatha. I am desperately unhappy about you. Thank God you called me! Why did you call me?"

"Because I had to."

"What do you mean?"

"I cannot possibly speak to you long from here. I must see you tonight. This is urgent!"

I continued the effort to control my voice, to bid my thumping heart behave normally.

"Yes, Ardatha, you must know I am longing to see you. But—"

"But what?"

"I cannot go out tonight."

"I do not ask you to go out tonight. I will come to you."

"Oh, my dear, it's wonderful! But every time you take such risks for my sake—"

"This is a risk I must take, or there will be no you, no Nayland Smith!"

"When shall I expect you?"

"In five minutes. But, listen. I know the house where you live. You cannot believe how well I know it! Fasten open the catch of the front door, so that I do not have to wait out in the street. I will come up and ring your bell. Please do not look out of the window or do anything to show that you expect anyone. Will you promise?"

"Of course."

Silence.

I hung up the receiver as a man in a daze. Ardatha was real

after all. Nayland Smith was wiser than I, for always he had acted as her counsel when in my despair I had condemned her as a Delilah.

Then, as if to banish the wild happiness with which my spirit was intoxicated, came a logical thought . . .

That mysterious portfolio—so valuable that Smith had been afraid to take it with him even in a flying squad car! It was here . . . The Si-Fan knew. Ardatha was coming to find it!

My hand on the door, I paused, chilled, doubting, questioning.

Were my instincts betraying me? I could not recall that I had ever proved myself easily glamoured by that which was worthless. If the soul of Ardatha be not a brave and a splendid soul but a hollow, mocking thing, I told myself, then the years of my maturity have been wasted. I am indeed no philosopher.

In any event, now was the acid test. For if she came with a hidden purpose I should learn it. And whatever the wrench—it would be the finish.

For the rest I had nothing to fear unless I were overpowered and the flat ransacked. There was no information which I could give, even under torture, for I did not know where Nayland Smith had concealed the portfolio.

I went downstairs. The lights were on in the little glass arcade which led to the porch. I opened the door and fixed the catch so that a push from outside would give access; then, in that frame of mind which every man in such circumstances has shown, I returned to my flat.

The interval, though short, seemed interminable . . .

My doorbell rang. I walked from the study along the short passage. I was trying to frame words with which I should greet Ardatha, trying to school myself to control hot impulses, and yet not to seem too cold.

I opened the door . . . and there on the landing, wearing a French cape and a black soft-brimmed hat, stood Dr Fu Manchu!

Always I am just

When I say that horror, disillusionment, abject misery robbed me of speech, movement, almost of thought, I do not exaggerate the facts. My beliefs, my philosophy, my world, crumbled around me.

"Mr Kerrigan"—my dreadful visitor spoke softly—"do not hesitate to accept any order I may give."

His right elbow rested upon his hip, his long yellow fingers held an object which resembled a silver fountain pen. I wrenched my glance away from those baleful eyes and stared at this thing.

"Death in the form of disintegration I hold in my hand," he continued. "Step back. I will follow you."

The little silver tube he pointed in my direction. I walked slowly along to the study. I heard Dr Fu Manchu close the front door and follow me in. I stood in front of the table, and turning, faced him. I avoided his eyes, but watched the long silver object which he held in his hand.

I despised myself completely. This man—I judged him to be not less than seventy years of age—held no weapon other than a small tube, yet had me cowed. I was afraid to attack him, afraid to defend myself—for behind this thing which he held I saw all the deadly armament of his genius.

But my weakness of spirit was not due entirely to cowardice, to fear of the dreadful Chinese doctor. It was due in great part to sudden recognition of the frightful duplicity of Ardatha! She, she whom I longed to worship, she had tricked me into opening my door to this awful being!

"Do not misjudge Ardatha."

Those words had something of the effect of a flash of lightning. In the first place, they answered my unspoken thought (which alone was terrifying), and in the second place, they brought hope to a mind filled with black despair.

"Tonight," that strange impressive voice continued, "Ardatha

215

lives, or Ardatha dies. One of my purposes is to be present at your interview, for I know that this interview is to take place."

Love of a woman goes deep in a man as I learnt at that moment; for, clutching this slender thread of promise—a thread strengthened by Nayland Smith's assurance that Dr Fu Manchu never lied—I found a new strength and a new courage. I raised my eyes.

"Make no fatal mistake, Mr. Kerrigan," he said coldly, precisely. "You are weighing your weight against mine, youth against age. But consider this device which I hold in my hand. From a thing which once demanded heavy cables and arc lamps, it is now, as you see"—always pointing in my direction—"a small tube. I dislike that which is cumbersome. The apparatus with which I project those visible and audible images of which you have had experience can be contained in a suitcase. There are no masts, no busy engine rooms, no dynamos."

I watched him but did not move.

"This is Ericksen's Ray, in its infancy at the so-called death of its inventor, Doctor Sven Ericksen—rather before your time, I think—but now, perfected. Allow me to demonstrate its powers."

He pointed the thing, which I now decided resembled a hypodermic syringe, towards a vase which Mrs Merton had filled that morning with flowers.

"Do you value that vase, Mr Kerrigan?"

"Not particularly. Why?"

"Because I propose to use it as a demonstration. Watch."

He appeared to press a button at the end of the silver tube. There was no sound, no light, but where the vase of flowers had been there appeared a momentary cloud, a patch of darkness. I became aware of an acrid smell . . .

Vase and flowers had disappeared!

"Ericksen is a genius. You will observe that I say 'is.' For although dead to the world, he lives—to work for me. You will realise now why I said that I held death in my hands. Ardatha is coming to see you. She loves you: and when any of my women becomes thus infatuated with one who does not belong to me, I deal with her as I see fit. If she has betrayed me she shall die . . . Stand still! If she merely loves which is fallible but human, I may spare her. I am come in person, Mr Kerrigan, not for this purpose alone, but for that of recovering from you the letter of instruction signed by every member of the Council of Seven, which Sir Denis Nayland Smith—I have always recognised his qualities—secured this afternoon from a house in Surrey."

I did not speak; I continued to watch the tube.

"Love so transforms a woman that even my powers of plumbing human nature may be defeated. I am uncertain how low Ardatha has fallen in disloyalty to the Si-Fan where you have been concerned. I shall learn this tonight. But first, where is the document?"

I glanced into the brilliant green eyes and quickly glanced aside.

"I don't know."

He was silent. That deadly tube remained pointed directly at my breast.

"No. I recognise the truth. He brought it here but left without it. He has concealed it. He was afraid that my agents would intercept him on the way. He was afraid of *you*. No matter. Answer me. He left it here?"

I stared dazedly at the tube. The hand of Dr Fu Manchu might have been carved of ivory: it was motionless.

"Look at me—answer!"

I raised my eyes. Dr Fu Manchu spoke softly.

"He left it. I thought so. I shall find it."

My doorbell rang.

"This is Ardatha." The voice became guttural, a voice of doom. "You have a fine mushrabîyeh screen here, Mr Kerrigan, which I believe you brought from Arabia when you went there on behalf of your newspaper last autumn. I shall stand behind this screen, and you will admit Ardatha. She has been followed; she is covered. Any attempt to leave the building would be futile. Do not dare to warn her of my presence. Bring her into this room and let her say what she has come to say. I shall be listening. Upon her words rest life or death. Always I am just."

Fists clenched, bathed in clammy perspiration, I turned and walked to the door.

"No word, no hint of warning—or I shall not spare you!"

I opened the door. Ardatha stood on the landing.

"My dear!" I exclaimed.

God knows how I looked, how wild my eyes must have been, but she crept into my extended arms as into a haven.

"Darling! I cannot bear it any longer! I had to come to save you!"

I thought that our embrace would never end, except in death.

The mushrabîyeh screen

Ardatha, perhaps with the very next word which she uttered, was about to betray herself to the master of the Si-Fan!

My inclination was to take her up and race downstairs to the street. But Fu Manchu's servants were watching; he had said so, and he never lied. On the other hand, few human brains could hold a secret long from those blazing green eyes. If I tried to warn her, if I failed to return, I was convinced deep within me that it would be the end of us. I thought of that gleaming tube like a hypodermic syringe of which Dr Fu Manchu had said:

"I hold death in my hand."

No, I must return to the study, must allow Ardatha to say what she was there to say—and abide by the consequences.

Her manner was strangely disturbed: I had felt her trembling during those bitter-sweet moments when I had held her in my arms. Remembering her composure on the occasion of that secret visit in Venice, I knew that tonight marked some crisis in her affairs—in mine—perhaps in the history of the world.

I led her towards the study. At the doorway she looked up at me. I tried to tell her silently with my eyes (but knew how hopelessly I failed) that behind the mushrabîyeh screen Dr Fu Manchu was hidden.

"Sit down, dear, and let me get you a drink."

I forced myself to speak casually, but:

"No, no, please don't go!" she said. "I want nothing. I had to see you, but I have only a few moments in which to tell you—oh, so many things! Please listen." The amethyst eyes were wide open as she raised them to me. "Every second is of value. Just stay where you are and listen!"

Looking down at her, I stood there. She wore a very simple frock and her adorable creamy arms were bare. The red gleam of her wind-blown hair filled me with an insane longing to plunge my fingers in its living waves. I watched her. I tried to tell her . . .

"Although the affair of Venice was successful in its main purpose," she went on swiftly, "it failed in some other ways. High officials of the French police know that James Brownlow Wilton was stolen away from the Blue Train, that it was not James Brownlow Wilton who died on the yacht. Sir Denis—yes?—he knows all about it too. And Baron Trenck, who silenced General Diesler, he was not given safe protection . . . All these things are charged against the president."

She spoke those words with awe—the president! And watching her, watching her intently, I tried to say without moving my lips: "The president is here!"

But as a telepathist I found myself a failure, for she continued:

"I betray no Si-Fan secrets in what I tell you, because I tell you only what you know already. I am one of them—and all the wrong I have ever done has been to try to save you. Because I am a woman I cannot help myself. But now what I am here to say to you—and when I have said it I must go—is this: A new president is to be elected!"

"What!"

"By him all the power of the Si-Fan—you cannot even guess what that power is—will be turned upon Sir Denis and—you."

She clasped her hands and stood up.

"Please, please! if you value my happiness a little bit I beseech you from my soul, when that notice comes, make him obey it! Force him to obey it! Imprison him if you like!—for I tell you, if you fail in this, nothing, nothing on earth can save him—nor you! Come to the door with me, but no further. I must go."

"But not yet, Ardatha!"

Dr Fu Manchu stepped from behind the screen.

It was a situation so appalling that it seemed to dull my sensibilities. Such a weakling and traitor did I stand in my own regard that I would have welcomed complete oblivion.

Ardatha drew back from that tall cloaked figure—back and back—until she came to the wall behind her; and there, arms outstretched, she stood. The colour was draining from her cheeks, her expression was one of utter despair.

"Look at me, Ardatha"—Dr Fu Manchu spoke softly.

As she raised her eyes to the majestic evil of his face I thought of a hare and a cobra.

"I am satisfied"—his voice was little more than a whisper— "that your motives have been as you say, but I can no longer employ you in my personal service. Mr Kerrigan"—it was a harsh command. He raised the Ericksen tube—"be good enough to look out of your window and to report to me what you see."

Without hesitation I obeyed, stepping forward to the window so that Dr Fu Manchu stood behind me.

"Draw the curtain aside."

I did so. Immediately I recognised the fact that the house was invested by the forces of the Si-Fan!

Two men over by the closed park gate unmistakably were watching the windows. Two others lingered in conversation near the door below. A big car was drawn up on the corner, and another pair were engaged in peering under the bonnet.

"Be good enough, Mr Kerrigan, to raise your hand. The signal will be understood."

Automatically, I was about to obey . . . when a number of strange things happened.

A car coming from the direction of Marble Arch swung out sharply against oncoming traffic. It was pulled up by a skilful driver almost directly at my door. Another, approaching from the opposite direction, stopped with a great shrieking of brakes almost at the park gate. A third, which apparently had been following the first, checked dead on the corner of Porchester Terrace.

In a matter of seconds twelve or fifteen men were disgorged into Bayswater Road . . . Without a moment's hesitation they hurled themselves upon the loiterers!

My heart leapt madly. It was the flying squad!

One warning came; and one only—a weird, minor, wailing cry— but I knew that it was meant for Dr Fu Manchu. Its effect was immediate. From behind me he spoke in a changed voice, harsh, gutteral:

"What has occurred? Answer."

"The police, I think. Three cars."

"Stay were you are. Don't stir. Ardatha—with me."

I stood still, fists clenched, watching the mêlée below.

"Bart! Bart!" Ardatha cried my name despairingly.

"Be silent! Precede me."

I heard them hurrying along the passage. But he had said "Don't stir," and I did not stir. I made no move until the opening and closing of the door told me that they were gone. Then I sprang around.

Footsteps were bounding up the stairs. I could hear excited voices—and an amazing, an all but unbelievable fact dawned upon me:

Dr Fu Manchu was trapped!

Pursuing a shadow

"Kerrigan! Kerrigan!"

Nayland Smith was banging on the door.

I ran to open it. He sprang in, his eyes gleaming excitedly. He had removed the synthetic beard but still wore his shabby suit. Beside him was Inspector Gallaho, head bandaged beneath a soft hat which took the place of his usual tight-fitting bowler. Four or five plainclothes police came crowding up behind.

"Where is he?"

"Gone! He went at the moment that I heard you on the stair!"

"What!"

"That's not possible," growled Gallaho, staring at me in a questioning way. "No one passed us, that I'll swear."

"Lights on that upper stair!" snapped Smith. "Stay where you are, Gallaho—you men, also."

He examined me intently.

"I know what you're thinking, Smith," I said, "but I am quite myself. Ardatha and Fu Manchu were here two minutes ago. He held me up with a thing which disintegrates whatever it touches."

"Ericksen's Ray?"

"Yes. How did you know?"

"Good God! But it's a cumbersome affair!"

"No larger than a fountain pen, Smith! He has perfected it, so he says. But—where is he?"

Nayland Smith tugged at the lobe of his ear.

"You say the girl went with him?"

"Yes."

"Who lives above?"

"A young musician, Basil Acton—but he's abroad at present."

"Sure?"

He began to run upstairs, crying out over his shoulder:

"Gallaho and two men! The others stand by where they are."

We reached the top landing and paused before my neighbour's closed door.

Gallaho rang the bell, but there was no response.

"Hello!"

Smith stooped.

I had switched on the landing light, and now I saw what had attracted his attention. Also I became aware of a queer acrid smell.

Where a Yale lock had been there was nothing but a hole, some two inches in diameter, drilled clean through the door!

"It's bolted inside," said Gallaho.

"But they are trapped!" I cried excitedly. "There is no other way out!"

"Unfortunately," growled Gallaho, "there is no other way in. Down to the tool chest, somebody."

There came a rush of footsteps on the stair, an interval during which Gallaho tried to peer through the hole in the door and Nayland Smith, ear pressed to a panel, listened but evidently heard nothing. To the high landing window which overlooked Bayswater Road rose sounds of excited voices from the street below.

"Seven black beauties roped in there," said Gallaho grimly, "but it remains to be seen if we've got anything on them."

One of the flying squad men returning with the necessary implements, it was a matter of only a few minutes to break the door down. I had been in my neighbour's flat on one or two occasions, and when we entered I switched the lights up, for we found it in darkness.

"Is there anyone here?" called Gallaho.

There was no reply.

We entered the big, untidy apartment which, sometimes to my sorrow, I knew that Acton used as a music room. It had something of the appearance of a studio. Bundles of music were littered on chairs and settees. The grand piano was open. An atmosphere stale as that inside a pyramid told of closed windows. Knowing his careless ways, I doubted if Acton had made arrangements to have his flat cleaned or aired during his absence. There was no one there.

"How many rooms, Kerrigan?" Smith snapped.

"Four, and a kitchenette."

"Three men stay on the landing!" shouted Gallaho.

We explored every foot of the place, and the only evidence we found to show that Dr Fu Manchu and Ardatha had entered was the hole drilled through the front door, until:

"What's this?" cried one of the searchers.

We hurried into the kitchenette which bore traces of a meal prepared at some time but not cleared up. The man had opened a big cupboard in which I saw an ascending ladder.

"The cisterns are up there," I explained. "This is an old house converted."

"At last!" Smith's eyes glinted. "That's where he is hiding!"

Before I could restrain him he had darted up the ladder, shining the light of a flashlamp ahead. Gallaho followed and I came next.

We found ourselves under the sloping roof in an attic containing several large tanks, unventilated, and oppressively stuffy.

There was no one there.

"Doctor Fu Manchu is a man of genius," said Smith, "but not a spirit. He must be somewhere in this building."

"Not so certain, sir!" came a cry.

One of the Scotland Yard men was directing light upon lath and plaster at that side of the attic furthest from the door. It revealed a ragged hole—and now we all detected a smell of charred wood.

"What's beyond there?" Gallaho demanded.

"The adjoining house, at the moment in the hands of renovators. It is being converted into modern flats."

But already Smith, stooping, was making his way through the aperture—and we all followed.

We found ourselves in an attic similar to that which we had quitted. We crossed it and climbed down a ladder. At the bottom was a room smelling strongly of fresh paint, cluttered up with decorators' materials, in fact almost impassable. We forced a way through onto the landing, to discover planks stretched across a staircase, scaffolding, buckets of whitewash . . .

Nayland Smith ran down the stairs like a man demented, and even now in memory I can recapture the thud of our hammering feet as we followed him. It drummed around that empty, echoing house; the lights of our lamps danced weirdly on stripped walls, bare boards and half-painted woodwork. We came to the lobby. Smith flung open the front door.

It opened not on Bayswater Road as in the case of the adjoining house, but upon a side street, Porchester Terrace. He raced down three steps and stood there looking to right and to left.

Dr Fu Manchu had escaped . . .

'The biggest failure of my life, Kerrigan."

Nayland Smith was pacing up and down my study; he had even forgotten to light his pipe. His face was wan—lined.

"I don't think I follow, Smith. It's amazing that you arrived here in the nick of time. His escape is something no one could have anticipated. He has supernormal equipment. This disintegrating ray which he carried defeats locks, bolts and bars. How could any man have foreseen it?"

"Yet I *should* have foreseen it," he snapped angrily. "My arrival in the nick of time had been planned."

"What!"

"Oh, I didn't know Ardatha was coming. For this I had not provided. But my visit to you earlier in the evening, my leaving here, or pretending to leave, the most vital piece of evidence on which I have ever laid my hands, was a leaf torn from Doctor Fu Manchu's own book!"

"What do you mean?"

"I was laying a trail. I was doing what *he* has done so often. He knew that I had those incriminating signatures, he knew that failing their recovery, the break-up of the Council of Seven was at least in sight. You are aware of how closely I was covered, how narrowly I escaped death. What I didn't tell you at the time was this: In spite of my disguise, I had been followed from Sloane Street right to the door of your flat."

"Are you sure?"

"I made sure. I intended to be followed."

"Good heavens!"

"I had not hoped, I confess, for so big a fish as the doctor in person, but that you would be raided by important members of the Si-Fan shortly after my departure was moderately certain. They were watching. I saw them as I left in the Yard car. I gave them every opportunity to note that although I had arrived with a bulky portfolio, I was leaving without it!"

"But, Smith, you might have given me your confidence!"

Anger, mortification, both were in my tones, but instantly Nayland Smith had his hands on my shoulders. His steady eyes sobered me.

"Remember the Green Death, Kerrigan. Oh, I'm not reproaching you! But Doctor Fu Manchu can read a man's soul as you and I read a newspaper. I had men posted in the park (closed at that time), and I had a key of your front door—"

"Smith!"

"You were well protected. The arrival of Ardatha presented a new problem. I had not counted on Ardatha—"

"Nor had I!"

"But when no fewer than seven suspicious characters were massed in front of the house, and a tall thin man wearing a cloak was reported as having entered—(your front door, apparently being open)—I gave the signal. You know what followed."

"I understand now, Smith, how crushing the disappointment must be."

"Crushing indeed! I had King Shark in my net—and he bit his way out of it!"

"But the Ericksen Ray?"

"He has held the secret of the Ericksen Ray for many years. Doctor Ericksen, its inventor, died or is reported to have died in 1914. As a matter of fact, he (with God knows how many other men of genius) has been working in Doctor Fu Manchu's laboratories probably up to the present moment!"

"But this is incredible! You have hinted at it before, but I have never been able to follow your meaning."

Automatically Nayland Smith's hand went to the pocket of his dilapidated coat and out came the briar and the big pouch.

"He can induce synthetic catalepsy, Kerrigan. I was afraid when I found you in Whitehall the other day that for some reason he had practised this art upon you. Except in cases where I have been notified, these wretched victims have been buried alive."

"Good God!"

"Later, at leisure, his experts disinter them, and they are smuggled away to work for the Si-Fan!"

"And to where are they smuggled?"

"I have no idea. Once his base was in Honan. It is no longer there. He has had others, some as near home as the French Riviera. His present headquarters are unknown to me. His genius lies not only in his own phenomenal brain, but in his astonishing plan of accumulating great intellects and making them his slaves. This is the source of his power. He wastes nothing. You see already, as General Diesler's death proves, he is employing the Jasper vacuum charger. I think we both know the name of the man who invented the television apparatus which you have seen in action. But probably we don't want to talk about it . . ."

Up and down the carpet he paced, up and down, restless, overtensed, and stared out of the window.

"There lies London," he said, "in darkness, unsuspecting the presence in its midst of a man more than humanly equipped, a man who is almost a phantom—who is served by phantoms!"

A second later I sprang madly to his side.

Heralded by no other sound, there came a staccato crash of glass . . . then I was drenched in fragments of plaster!

A bullet had come through the window and had buried itself in the wall . . .

"Smith! Smith!"

He had not moved, but he turned now and looked at me. I saw blood and was overcome by a sudden, dreadful nausea. I suppose I grew pale, for he shook his head and grasped my shoulder.

"No, Kerrigan. It was the tip of my ear. Good shooting. The whizz of the bullet was deafening."

"But there was no sound of a shot!"

He moved away from the window.

"Diesler was killed at a range of three thousand odd yards," he said. "You remember we were talking about the Jasper vacuum charger?"

"I am disposed to believe that what Ardatha told you was true," said Nayland Smith.

He was standing staring down reflectively at something resting in his extended palm: the bullet which had made a hole in my wall. The cut in his ear had bled furiously, but now had succumbed to treatment and was decorated with a strip of surgical plaster.

"This attempt, for instance"—he held up the bullet—"somehow does not seem to be in the doctor's handwriting. In spite of its success I doubt if the 'silencing' of General Diesler was directed by Fu Manchu. If there is really trouble in the Council of Seven it may mean salvation. Assuming that I live to see it, I think I shall know, without other evidence, when Doctor Fu Manchu is deposed."

"In what way?" I asked curiously.

"Remind me to tell you if it occurs, Kerrigan. Ah! may I put the light out?"

"Certainly."

He did so, then glanced from my study window.

"Here are our escorting cars, I think. Yes! I can see Gallaho below."

He turned and began to reload his pipe.

'Tonight's near-triumph, Kerrigan, was made possible by the remarkable efficiency of Chief Detective Inspector Gallaho. Gallaho will go far. He obtained evidence to show that none other than Lord Weimer, the international banker, is a member of the Si-Fan . . ."

"What!"

I cried the word incredulously.

"Yes—astounding, I admit. In fact, it almost appears that his house in Surrey is the temporary headquarters of Si-Fan representatives at present in England. I obtained a search warrant, paid a surprise visit during Weimer's absence in the city, and went over the place with a microscope. I experienced little difficulty—such a violent procedure had not been foreseen. Nevertheless, although the staff was kept under observation, news of the raid reached Weimer . . . He has disappeared."

"But, Lord Weimer—a member of the Si-Fan!"

"He is. And a document involving even greater names was there as well. Even as I held it in my hand (I had time for no more than a glance) I wondered if I should ever get through alive with such evidence in my possession. I was not there in my proper person. You know what I looked like when I returned. The proceedings, officially, were in charge of Gallaho, but I adopted a precautionary measure."

His pipe filled, he now lighted it with care. I saw a grim smile upon his face:

"I sent Detective Sergeant Cromer back to Scotland Yard. He travelled in a Green Line bus, accompanied by one other police officer—and between them they carried evidence to upset the chancelleries of Europe! One idea led to another. I took it for granted that I should be followed, that attempts would be made to intercept me. I led the trail to your door, hoping for a big haul. I had one. But there was a hole in the net."

"What do we do now?"

"We are going to Number 10 Downing Street."

"What!"

"This discovery means an international situation. The Prime Minister has returned from Chequers and is meeting us there. The commissioner is bringing the documents from Scotland Yard, in person. Here is something for your notes, Kerrigan. I promised you a bigger story than any you had ever had. Come on!"

Indeed I had never expected to be one of such a gathering. There were three cars, one leading, then that in which I travelled with Nayland Smith, and a third bringing up the rear. The leading car, belonging to the flying squad, was driven at terrific speed through the streets. Under the circumstances I confess I was not surprised that we arrived at our destination without any attempt being made upon us. So vast were the issues at stake that even my fear for Ardatha was numbed.

Despairingly, I had come to the conclusion that I should never see her again . . .

In a room made familiar by many published photographs I found the Premier and some other members of the Cabinet. Sir James Clare, the home secretary whom I had met before, was there and two ambassadors representing foreign powers. An air of dreadful apprehension seemed common to all. Somewhat awed by the company, I looked at Nayland Smith.

He was pacing up and down in his usual restless manner, glancing at his wrist watch.

"Sir William Bard is late," murmured the Prime Minister.

Nayland Smith nodded. Sir William Bard, commissioner of metropolitan police, of all those summoned to this meeting was the only one who had not appeared.

"Until his arrival, sir," said Smith, "we can do nothing."

But even as he spoke came a rap on the door, and a voice announced:

"Sir William Bard."

What happened in Downing Street

"A trifle late, Sir William," said the Prime Minister genially.

"Yes sir—I must offer my apologies." The commissioner bowed perfunctorily to everyone present. "I think the circumstances will explain my delay."

A slightly built, alert man with a short jet-black moustache, he had a precision of manner and intonation which suggested, as was the fact, that his training, like that of the home secretary, had been for the legal profession. He laid a bulging portfolio upon the table. The Premier continued to watch him coldly but genially. Everyone else in the room became very restless, as Bard continued:

"Just as my car was about to turn out of Whitehall, a girl, a lady from her dress and bearing I judged, stepped out almost under my front wheel, and as my chauffeur braked furiously, sprang back again, but tripped and fell on the pavement."

"In these circumstances," said the home secretary, one eye on the rugged brow of the Prime Minister, "your delay is of course explained."

"Exactly," Sir William continued. "I pulled up, of course, and hurried back. Quite a crowd gathered, as always occurs, among them, fortunately, a doctor. The only injury was a sprained ankle. The lady, although one must confess it was her own fault, proved to live in Buckingham Gate, and naturally I gave her a lift home, Doctor Atkin accompanying her to that address. However, sir"—turning to the Prime Minister —"I trust I am excused?"

"Certainly, Bard, certainly. Anyone would have done the same."

Now quite restored, we sat down around the big table, the commissioner produced his keys and glanced at Nayland Smith.

"A strange attire for so formal an occasion, Smith!" he commented. "But it may be forgiven, I think, in view"—he tapped the portfolio—"of the information which is here. I had had time merely to glance over it, but I may say"—looking solemnly about him—"that in dealing with the facts revealed, the astonishingly unpleasant facts, our united efforts will be called for. And even when we have done our best . . ."

He shrugged his shoulders. He appeared to find some difficulty in fitting the key to the lock. We were all on tiptoes and all very impatient. I saw a sudden shadow creep over Sir William Bard's face as he glanced at his own initials stamped on the leather. He shrugged and persevered with the key.

There was no result.

"Might I suggest," snapped Nayland Smith, beginning to tug at his ear but desisting when he detected the presence of the plaster, "that you borrow a pair of stout scissors and force the catch, Sir William?"

"Always impatient, Smith!" The commissioner looked up, but his expression was not easy. "I don't understand this."

He tried again and then made an angry gesture.

"I locked it myself before I left Scotland Yard."

"Since time is our enemy," said the Prime Minister drily, "I think Sir Denis Nayland Smith's suggestion is a good one."

He rang a bell, and to a man who entered gave curt orders . . .

The lock proved to be more obstinate than we had anticipated, but with the aid of a pair of office scissors and the expenditure of considerable force, ultimately it was snapped open. The man withdrew. We were all standing up, surrounding the commissioner. He opened the portfolio.

I heard a loud cry. For a moment I could not believe Sir William Bard had uttered it. Yet indeed it was he who had cried out . . .

The portfolio was stuffed with neatly folded copies of *The Times!*

One by one with shaking fingers he drew them out and laid them upon the table. Last of all he discovered a square envelope, and from it he drew a single sheet of paper.

There had been such a silence during this time that I could hear nothing but the breathing of the man next to me, a portly representative of a friendly power.

Sir William Bard cast his glance over the sheet which the envelope had contained, and then, his face grown suddenly pallid, laid it before the Prime Minister.

I glanced swiftly at Nayland Smith, and found myself unable to read his expression.

The statesman, imperturbable even in face of this situation, adjusted his spectacles and read; then clearing his throat, he read again, this time aloud:

"The Council of Seven of the Si-Fan is determined to preserve peace in Europe. Some to whom this message is addressed share these views—some do not. The latter would be well advised to reconsider their policies, and to confine their attentions to their proper occasions.

PRESIDENT OF THE COUNCIL

"First notice"

"Smith! I am a ruined man!"

Sir William Bard sat in an armchair behind a huge desk laden with official documents, his head sunk in his hands. In that quiet room which was the heart of Scotland Yard, the menace represented by Dr Fu Manchu presented itself more urgently to my tired mind than had been possible in the official sanctum of the British government.

Out of the charivari which had arisen when we had realised that documents calculated to cast down those in high places had been stolen from none other than the commissioner of metropolitan police, only one phrase recurred to me: the Premier's inquiry:

"Do you consider, Sir Denis, that this is a personal threat?"

Nayland Smith stared at the commissioner, and then, jumping up from his chair: "I don't think," he said, "that I should take the thing so seriously. It may be mere arrogance on my part to say so, but with all my experience (and it has been a long one) the particular genius who tricked you tonight has tricked me many times."

Sir William Bard looked up.

"But how was it done? Who did it?"

"As to how it was done," Smith replied, "it was a fairly simple example of substitution. As to who did it—Doctor Fu Manchu!"

"I have accepted the existence of Doctor Fu Manchu with great reluctance, as you know, Smith—although I am aware that my immediate predecessor regarded this Chinese criminal with great respect. Are you sure that it was he who was responsible?"

"Perfectly sure," Smith snapped, then glanced swiftly at me.

"Describe the girl who was nearly run down by your car."

"I can do so quite easily, for she was a beauty. She had titian red hair and remarkable eyes of a pansy colour; a slender girl, not English, a fact I detected from her slight accent."

I did not groan audibly: it was my spirit that groaned.

235

"Quite sufficient!" Smith interrupted. "Kerrigan and I know this lady. And the doctor?"

"A tall man, grey-haired, of distinguished appearance, Doctor Maurice Atkin. I have his card here, and also Miss Pereira's."

"Neither card means anything," said Smith grimly. He turned to me. "This grey-haired aristocrat, Kerrigan, seems to play important parts in Fu Manchu's present drama. I detect a marked resemblance to that Count Boratov who was a guest of Brownlow Wilton, and of course you have recognised Miss Pereira?"

I nodded but did not speak.

"Don't make heavy weather of it, Kerrigan. Ardatha is in the toils—this task was her punishment."

He walked across to the wretched man sunk in the armchair and rested his hand upon his shoulder.

"May I take it that you usually carry the missing portfolio?"

The commissioner nodded.

"From my house to Scotland Yard every day, and to important conferences."

"The Si-Fan had noted this. After all, you are officially their chief enemy in London. I suggest that the duplicate portfolio has been in existence for some time. Tonight an occasion arose for its use. Judging from my own experience, farsighted plans of this character have been made with regard to many notable enemies of the Si-Fan."

Sir William was watching him almost hopefully.

'To illustrate my meaning," Smith went on, "they have duplicate keys of my flat!"

"What!"

"It's a fact," I interpolated; "I have seen the keys used myself."

"Exactly." Smith nodded. "They even succeeded in installing a special radio in my premises. It would not surprise me to learn that they have a key to Number 10 Downing Street. You must appreciate the fact, Bard, that this organisation, once confined to the East, now has its ramifications throughout the West. It is of old standing and has among its members, as the missing documents proved, prominent figures in Europe and the United States. Its financial backing is enormous. Its methods are ruthless. Your car, immediately following the pretended accident, was of course surrounded by a crowd."

"It was."

"Those members nearest to the door from which you jumped were servants of the Si-Fan and one of them carried the duplicate portfolio. He was no doubt an adept in his particular province. The substitution was not difficult. The address to which you took Miss Pereira was a block of flats?"

"Yes."

"Inquiry is useless. She does not live there."

"Smith!" Sir William Bard sprang up. "Your reconstruction of what took place is perfect—except in one particular. I recall the fact clearly now that Doctor Atkin carried a similar portfolio! The substitution was effected during the short drive to Buckingham Gate!"

"H'm!" Smith glanced at me. "Count Boratov would seem to be a distinct asset to the doctor's forces!"

"But what can we *do?*" groaned the commissioner. "Lacking the authority of those damning signatures, we dare not take action."

"I agree."

"We can watch these people whose names we have learnt, but it will be necessary to obtain new evidence against them before we can move a finger in such high places."

"Certainly. But at least we are warned . . . and I may not be too late to save their next victim. We cannot hope to win every point!"

We returned to Nayland Smith's flat in a flying squad car and two men were detailed to remain on duty in the lobby. Only by a perceptible tightening of Fey's lips did I recognise the mighty relief which he experienced when he saw us.

He had nothing to report. Smith laughed aloud when he saw me looking at a freshly painted patch on the front door.

"My new lock, Kerrigan!" The merriment in his eyes was good to see. Something of my own burden seemed to be lifted from my shoulders by it. "The lock was fitted under my own supervision, by a locksmith known to me personally. It's a nuisance to open, being somewhat complicated. But once I am in I think I'm safe!"

In the familiar room with photographs of his old friends about him, he relaxed at last, dropping down into an armchair with a sigh of contentment.

"If there is any place in the civilised world where you would really be safe, a month's rest would do you good, Smith."

He stared at me. Already he was groping for his pipe.

"Can any man rest till his task is finished?" he asked quietly. "I doubt it. Since Doctor Fu Manchu has tricked all the normal laws of life—will my task ever end?"

Fey served drinks and silently retired.

"I had a bad shock tonight, Smith," I said awkwardly. "Ardatha was instrumental in the theft of the commissioner's portfolio."

Smith nodded, busily filling his pipe.

"She had no choice," he snapped. "As I said at the time it was her punishment. At least she was not concerned in a murder, Kerrigan. Probably she had to succeed or die. I wonder if this really remarkable achievement has reinstated the doctor in the eyes of the Council."

"Is it a fact, Smith, that the names of the Council were actually in your possession?"

"Yes. Some I had suspected, nor would their identity convey anything to the public. But three of the Seven are as well known to the world as Bernard Shaw. Even to me those names came as a surprise. But lacking the written evidence, as the commissioner says, we dare not move. Ah well! the doctor has obtained a firm footing in the Western world since he first began operating from Limehouse."

He took up a bundle of letters which Fey had placed on a table near the armchair. He tossed them all aside until presently he came upon one at which he frowned queerly.

"Hello!" he murmured, "what's this?"

He examined the writing, the post office stamp—and finally tore open the envelope. He glanced at the single sheet of paper which it contained. His face remained quite motionless as he bent forward and passed it to me . . .

I stared, and my heart missed a beat as I read:

First notice

The Council of Seven of the Si-Fan has decided that you are an obstruction to its policy. Its present purpose being the peace of the world, a purpose to which no sane man can be opposed, you are given a choice of two courses. Remain in London tonight and the Council guarantees your safety and will communicate with you by telephone.

We are prepared for an honourable compromise. Leave, and you will receive a second notice.

PRESIDENT OF THE COUNCIL

I don't know why these words written in a square heavy hand, on thick paper embossed with a Chinese hieroglyphic, should so have chilled me, but they did. It was no novelty for Nayland Smith to go in peril of his life, but knowing its record, frankly the dictum of the Council of Seven touched me with an icy hand.

"What do they mean, Smith, about leaving London?" I asked in a hoarse voice. "I suspected some new move when you spoke to the commissioner about saving the next victim."

"Marcel Delibes, the French statesman, has received two warnings. Copies were among the papers I found in Lord Weimer's house!"

"Well?"

"You may also recall that I promised to tell you when Doctor Fu Manchu ceased to be president?"

"Yes."

"He has ceased to be president!"

"How can you possibly know?"

He held up the first notice.

"Doctor Fu Manchu's delicate sense of humour would never permit him to do such a thing! Surely you realise, Kerrigan, that this means I am safe until the second notice arrives?"

"And what are you going to do?"

"I have made arrangements to leave for Paris tonight. Gallaho is coming, and—"

"So am I!"

Blue carnations

"This is the sort of atmosphere in which Doctor Fu Manchu finds himself at home!"

We stood in the workroom of Marcel Delibes, the famous French statesman. He had been unavoidably detained but requested us to wait. Two windows opened onto a long balcony which I saw to be overgrown with clematis. It looked down on a pleasant and well-kept garden. Beyond one saw the Bois. The room, religiously neat as that of some Mother Superior, was brightened along its many bookshelves by those attractively light bindings affected by French publishers; and a further note of colour was added by the presence of bowls and vases of carnations.

The perfume of all these flowers was somewhat overpowering, so that the impression I derived during my stay in the apartment was of carnations and of photographs of beautiful women.

There was a nearly full moon; the windows were wide open; and with Smith I examined the balcony outside. Our translation in a Royal Air Force plane from London had been so rapid, so dreamlike, that I was still in a mood to ask myself: Is this really Paris?

Yes, that carnation-scented room, dimly lighted except for one green-shaded lamp upon the writing desk, with photographs peeking glamorously from its shadows was, as Nayland Smith had said, an ideal atmosphere for Dr Fu Manchu.

Gallaho was downstairs with Jussac of the Sûreté Générale, and I knew that the house was guarded like a fortress. Even at this hour messengers were coming and going, and a considerable crowd had collected in the Bois outside, invisible and inaudible from the house by reason of its embracing gardens.

That sort of rumour which electrifies a population was creeping about Paris. Delibes, the rumour ran, had planned a political coup which, if it failed in its purpose, would mean that before a new day dawned France would be plunged into war.

"The grounds may be guarded, Smith," I said, looking about me. "But Delibes takes no other precautions."

I indicated the widely opened windows.

Smith nodded grimly.

"We have here, Kerrigan," he replied, "another example of that foolhardy courage which has already brought so many distinguished heads under the axe of Doctor Fu Manchu." He took up the table telephone and examined it carefully, then shook his head.

"No! He has been warned of the Green Death, a fact of which the Si-Fan is undoubtedly aware. If only the fool would face facts—if only he would give me his confidence! He knows, he has been told, of the fate of his predecessors who have defied the Council of Seven! He is a gallant man in more senses than one"—Smith nodded in the direction of the many photographs. "I must know what he plans to do and I must know what time the Si-Fan has given him in which to change his mind."

"His peril is no greater than yours!"

"Perhaps not—but I don't happen to be the political master of France! You are thinking of the letter which awaited me at the hotel desk?"

"I am."

"Yes"—he nodded—"the second notice!"

"But, Smith—"

"About one thing I am determined, Kerrigan—and I come provided to see it through: M. Delibes must accept my advice. Another Si-Fan assassination would paralyse European statesmanship. It would mean submission to a reign of terror . . ."

Marcel Delibes came in, handsome, grey-haired; and I noted the dark eyebrows and moustache which had proved such a boon to French caricaturists. He wore a blue carnation in his buttonhole; he was charmingly apologetic.

"Gentlemen," he said, "you come at an hour so vital in the history of France that I think I may be forgiven."

"So I understand, sir," said Nayland Smith curtly. "But what I do not understand is your attitude in regard to the Si-Fan."

241

Delibes seated himself at his desk, assumed a well-known pose, and smiled.

"You are trying to frighten me, eh? Fortunately for France, I am not easily frightened. You are going to tell me that General Quinto, Rudolf Adlon, Diesler—oh, quite a number of others—died because they refused to accept the order of this secret society! You are going to say that Monaghani has accepted and this is why Monaghani lives! Pouf! a bogey, my friend! A cloud comes, the sky is darkened, when the end of a great life draws near. So much the Romans knew, and the Greeks before them. And this scum, this red-hand gang, which calls itself Si-Fan, obtains spectacular success by sending these absurd notices . . . But how many have they sent in vain?"

He pulled open a drawer of his desk and tossed three sheets of paper onto the blotting pad. Nayland Smith stepped forward and with no more than a nod of apology picked them up.

"Ah! The final notice!"

"Yes—the final notice!" Delibes had ceased to smile. "To *me*! Could anything be more impudent?"

"It gives you, I see, until half past eleven tonight."

"Exactly. How droll!"

"Yet, Lord Aylwin has seen you, and Railton was sent by the Foreign Office with the special purpose of impressing upon you the fact that the power of the Si-Fan is real. I see, sir, that you are required to lower and then to raise the lights in this room three times, indicating that you have destroyed an order to Marshal Brieux. That distinguished officer is now in your lobby. I had a few words with him as I came in. As a privileged visitor, may I ask you the exact nature of this order?"

"It is here, signed." Delibes opened a folder and drew out an official document. "The whole of France, you see, as these signatures testify, stands behind me in this step which I propose to take tonight. You may read it if you please, for it will be common property tomorrow."

With a courteous inclination of the head he handed the document to Nayland Smith.

Smith's steely eyes moved mechanically as he glanced down the several paragraphs, and then:

242

"Failing a message from Monaghani before eleven-fifteen," he said, "this document, I gather, will be handed to Marshal Brieux? It calls all Frenchmen to the Colours. This will be construed as an act of war."

"Not necessarily, sir." The Minister drew down his heavy brows. "It will be construed as evidence of the unity of France. It will check those who would become the aggressors. At three minutes before midnight, observe, Paris will be plunged into darkness—and we shall test our air defences under war conditions."

Smith began to pace up and down the thick Persian carpet.

"You are described in the first notice from the Si-Fan," he went on, "as one of seven men in the world in a position to plunge Europe into war. It may interest you to know, sir, that the first warning of this kind with which I became acquainted referred to fifteen men. This fact may be significant?"

Delibes shrugged his shoulders.

"In roulette the colour red may turn up eighteen times," he replied. "Why not a coincidence of eight?"

We were interrupted by the entrance of a secretary.

"No vulgar curiosity prompts my inquiry," said Nayland Smith, as the Minister stared angrily at him. "But you have two photographs in your charming collection of a lady well known to me.

"Indeed, sir?" Delibes stood up. "To which lady do you refer?"

Smith took the two photographs from their place and set them on the desk.

Both were of the woman called Korêani: one was a head and shoulders so fantastically like the bust of Nefertiti as to suggest that this had been one of her earlier incarnations; the other showed her in the revealing dress of a Korean dancer.

Delibes glanced at them and then stared under his brows at Nayland Smith.

"I trust, Sir Denis, that this friendship does not in any way intrude upon our affairs?"

"But certainly not—although I have been acquainted with this lady for some years."

"I met her during the time she was appearing here. She is not an

243

ordinary cabaret artiste, as you are aware. She belongs to an old Korean family and in performing the temple dances, has made herself an exile from her country."

"Indeed," Smith murmured. "Would it surprise you to know that she is also one of the most useful servants of the Si-Fan? . . . That she was personally concerned in the death of General Quinto, and in that of Rudolph Adlon?—to mention but two! Further, would it surprise you to know that she is the daughter of the president of the Council of Seven?"

Delibes sat down again, still staring at the speaker.

"I do not doubt your word—but are you sure of what you say?"

"Quite sure."

"Almost, you alarm me." He smiled again. "She is difficult this Korêani—but most, most attractive. I saw her only last night. Today, for she knows my penchant, she sent me blue carnations."

"Indeed! *Blue* carnations, you say? Most unusual."

He began looking all about the room.

"Yes, but beautiful—you see them in those three vases."

"I have counted thirty-five," snapped Smith.

"The other, I wear."

Smith sniffed at one cautiously.

"I assume that they came from some florist known to you?"

"But certainly, from Meurice frères."

Smith stood directly in front of the desk, staring down at Delibes, then:

"Regardless of your personal predilection, sir," he said, "I have special knowledge and special facilities. Since the peace of France, perhaps of the world is at stake, may I ask you when these carnations arrived?"

"At some time before I was awake this morning."

"In one box or in several?"

"To this I cannot reply, but I will make inquiries. Your interests are of an odd nature."

Nevertheless, I observed that Delibes was struggling to retain his self-assurance. As he bent aside to press a bell, surreptitiously he removed the blue carnation from his buttonhole and dropped it in a wastebasket . . .

Delibes' valet appeared: his name was Marbeuf.

"These blue carnations," said Nayland Smith, "you received them from the florist this morning?"

"Yes sir."

Marbeuf's manner was one of masked alarm.

"In one box or in a number of boxes?"

"In a number, sir."

"Have those boxes been destroyed?"

"I believe not, sir."

Smith turned to Delibes.

"I have a small inquiry to make," he said, "but I beg that you will spare me a few minutes when I return."

"As you wish, sir. You bring strange news, but my purpose remains undisturbed . . ."

We descended with the valet to the domestic quarters of the house. The lobby buzzed with officials; there was an atmosphere of pent-up excitement, but we slipped through unnoticed. I was studying Marbeuf, a blond, clean-shaven fellow with the bland hypocrisy which distinguishes some confidential manservants.

"There are four boxes here," said Smith rapidly and stared at Marbeuf. "You say you received them this morning?"

"Yes sir."

"Here, in this room?"

"Yes."

"What did you do?"

"I placed them on that table, sir, for such presents frequently arrive for Monsieur. Then I sent Jacqueline for vases, and I opened the boxes."

"Who is Jacqueline?"

"The parlourmaid."

"There were then nine carnations in each box?"

"No sir. Twelve in each box, but one box was empty."

"What!"

"I was surprised, also."

"Between the time that these boxes were received from the florist and placed on the table, and the time at which you began to open them, were you out of the room?"

"Yes. I was called to the telephone."

"Ah! By whom?"

245

"By a lady, but when I told her that Monsieur was still sleeping she refused to leave a message."

"How long were you away?"

"Perhaps, sir, two minutes."

"And then?"

"Then I returned and began to open the boxes."

"And of the four, one contained no carnations?"

"Exactly, sir; one was empty."

"What did you do?"

"I telephoned to Meurice frères, and they assured me that not three, but four dozen carnations had been been sent by the lady who ordered them."

Smith examined the four boxes with care but seemed to be dissatisfied. They were cardboard cartons about 18 inches long and 6 inches square, stoutly made and bearing the name of the well-known florist upon them. His expression, however, became very grave, and he did not speak again until we had returned to the study.

As Delibes stood up, concealing his impatience with a smile:

"The time specified for the reply from Monaghani has now elapsed," said Smith. "Am I to take it, sir, that you propose to hand that document to Marshal Brieux?"

"Such is my intention."

"The time allotted to you by the Si-Fan expires in fifteen minutes."

Delibes shrugged his shoulders.

"Forget the Si-Fan," he said. "I trust that your inquiries regarding Korêani's gift were satisfactory?"

"Not entirely. Would it be imposing on your hospitality to suggest that Mr Kerrigan and myself remain here with you until those fifteen minutes shall have expired?"

"Well"—the Minister stood up, frowned, then smiled. "Since you mention my hospitality, if you would drink a glass of wine with me, and then permit me to leave you for a few moments since I must see Marshal Brieux, it would of course be a pleasure to entertain you."

He was about to press a bell, but changed his mind and went out.

On the instant of his exit Smith did an extraordinary thing. Springing to the door, he depressed a switch—and all the lights went out!

"Smith!"

The lights sprang up again.

"Wanted to know where the switch was! No time to waste."

He began questing about the room like a hound on a strong scent. Recovering myself, I too began looking behind busts and photographs, but:

"Don't touch anything, Kerrigan!" he snapped. "Some new agent of death has been smuggled into this place by Fu Manchu! God knows what it is! I have no clue, but it's here. It's here!"

He had found nothing when Delibes returned . . .

The Minister was followed by Marbeuf. The valet carried an ice bucket which contained a bottle of champagne upon a tray with three glasses.

"You see, I know your English taste!" said Delibes. "We shall drink, if you please, to France—and to England."

"In that case," Nayland Smith replied, "if I may ask you to dismiss Marbeuf, I should esteem it a privilege to act as server—for this is a notable occasion."

At a nod from Delibes, Marbeuf, having unwired the bottle, went out. Smith removed the cork and filled three glasses to their brims. With a bow he handed one to the statesman, less ceremoniously a second to me, then, raising his own:

"We drink deep," he said—his eyes glittered strangely, and the words sounded oddly on his lips—"to the peace of France and of England—and so, to the peace of the world!"

He drank nearly the whole of the contents of his glass. Delibes, chivalrously, did the same. Never at home with champagne, I endeavoured to follow suit, but was checked—astounded—by the behaviour of Delibes.

Standing upright, a handsome military figure, he became, it seemed, suddenly rigid! His eyes opened widely as though they were starting from his head. His face changed colour. Naturally pallid, it grew grey. His wineglass fell upon the Persian carpet, the remainder of its contents spilling. He clutched his throat and pitched forward!

Nayland Smith sprang to his side and lowered him gently to the floor.

"Smith! Smith!" I gasped, "he's poisoned! They have got him!"

"Ssh!" Smith stood up. "Not a word, Kerrigan!"

Amazed beyond understanding, I watched. He crossed to the meticulously neat desk, took up the document with those imposing signatures which lay there, and tore it into fragments!

"Smith!"

"Quiet—or we're lost!"

Crossing to the switch beside the door, he put out all the lights. It is mortifying to remember now that at the time I doubted his sanity. He raised them again, put them out . . .

In the second darkness came comprehension:

He was obeying the order of the Si-Fan!

"Help me, Kerrigan. In here!"

A curtained alcove, luxuriously appointed as the bedroom of a screen star, adjoined the study. We laid Delibes upon a cushioned divan. And as we did so and I raised inquiring eyes, there came a sound from the room outside which made me catch my breath.

It resembled a guttural command, in a tongue unknown to me. It was followed by an odd scuffling, not unlike that of a rat . . . It seemed to flash a message to Nayland Smith's brain. With no glance at the insensible man upon the divan he dashed out.

I followed—and all I saw was this:

Some *thing*— I could not otherwise define it, nor can I say if it went on four or upon two legs—merged into the shadow on the balcony!

Smith pistol in hand, leapt out.

There was a rustling in the clematis below. The rustling ceased.

His face a grim mask in the light of the moon, Smith turned to me.

"There went death to Marcel Delibes!" he said, "but here"—he pointed to the torn-up document on the carpet—"went death to a million Frenchmen."

"But the voice, Smith, the voice! Someone spoke—and there's nobody here!"

"Yes—I heard it. The speaker must have been in the garden below."

"And in heaven's name what was the thing we saw?"

"That, Kerrigan, is beyond me. The garden must be searched, but I doubt if anything will be found."

"But . . ." I stared about me apprehensively. "We must *do* something! Delibes may be dead!"

Nayland Smith shook his head.

"He *would* have been dead if I had not saved him."

"I don't understand at all!"

"Another leaf from the book of Doctor Fu Manchu. Tonight I came prepared for the opposition of Delibes. I had previously wired to my old friend Doctor Petrie in Cairo. He is a modest genius. He cabled a prescription; Lord Moreton endorsed it; and it was made up by the best firm of druggists in London. A rapidly soluble tablet, Kerrigan. According to Petrie, Delibes will be insensible for eighteen hours but will suffer no unpleasant after-effects—nor will he recall exactly what occurred."

I could think of no reply.

"We will now ring for assistance," Smith continued, "report that the document was torn up in our presence, and express our proper regret for the sudden seizure of M. Delibes."

He poured water from the ice bucket into the glass used by Delibes, and emptied it over the balcony. He then partly refilled the glass.

"Having advised Marshal Brieux that Paris may sleep in peace, we can return to our hotel."

249

Ardatha's message

I think the bizarre drama of those last few minutes in the house of
Marcel Delibes did more than anything else I could have accomplished to dull the agony of bereavement which even amid the
turmoil of this secret world war shadowed every moment of my
life.

Ardatha was lost to me . . . She belonged to the Si-Fan.

Once too often she had risked everything in order to give me
warning. Her punishment was to work henceforth under the eye
of the dreadful Dr Fu Manchu. Perhaps, as Smith believed, he
was no longer president. But always while he lived I knew that he
must dominate any group of men with whom he might be associated.

Leaving no less than four helpless physicians around the bed
of the insensible Minister, we returned to our hotel. Gallaho was
with us, and Jussac of the French police. As in London one car
drove ahead and another followed.

As we entered the hotel lobby:

"This sudden illness of M. Delibes," said Jussac, "is a dreadful
thing. He would be a loss to France. But for myself"—he brushed
his short moustache reflectively—"since you tell me that before
his seizure he changed his mind, why, if this was due to a rising
temperature, I am not sorry!"

Smith was making for the lift, and I was following when something drew my attention to the behaviour of a girl who had been
talking to the reception clerk. She was hurrying away, and the
man's blank expression told me that she had abruptly broken off
the conversation.

Already she was disappearing across a large, partially lighted
lounge beyond which lay the entrance from the Rue de Rivoli.

Without a word to my companions I set off in pursuit. Seeing
me, she made as if to run out, but I leapt forward and threw my
arms around her.

"Not this time, Ardatha—darling!"

The amethyst eyes glanced swiftly right and left and then flamed into sudden revolt. But beyond the flame I read a paradox.

"Let me go!"

I did not obey the words, for her eyes were bidding me to hold her fast. I crushed her against me.

"Never again, Ardatha."

"Bart," she whispered close to my ear, "call to yourEnglish policeman . . . Someone is watching us—"

At that, she began to struggle furiously!

"Hullo, Kerrigan! A capture, I see—"

Nayland Smith stood at my elbow.

"Gallaho," he called, "a prisoner for you!"

I glared at him, but:

"Bart!"—I loved the quaint accent with which she pronounced my name—"he is right. I must be arrested—I *want* to be arrested!"

Gallaho hurried up. His brow remained decorated with plaster.

"Who's this?"

"She is known as Ardatha, Inspector," said Smith. "There are several questions which she may be able to answer."

"You are wanted by Scotland Yard"—said Gallaho formally, "to give information regarding certain inquiries. I must ask you to be good enough to come with me."

Smith glanced swiftly around. Jussac joined the party. Two men, their backs to us, stood talking just outside in Rue de Rivoli.

"I won't!" blazed Ardatha, "unless you force me to!"

Gallaho clearly was nonplussed. To Jussac:

"Grab that pair outside the door!" said Smith rapidly. "Lock them up for the night. If I'm wrong I'll face the consequences. Inspector, this lady is in your charge. Bring her upstairs . . ."

Jussac stepped outside and whistled. I did not wait to see what happened. Ardatha, between Inspector Gallaho and Nayland Smith, was walking towards the lift . . .

Having reached our apartment and switched all lights up:

"Inspector," said Smith, "examine the lobby and the smaller bedroom and bathroom. I will search the others."

In the sitting room he looked hard at Ardatha:

251

"I am going to have you locked in the end room," he remarked, "as soon as Inspector Gallaho reports that it is a safe place."

He went out. No sooner was the door closed than I had Ardatha in my arms.

She seemed to search me with her glance: it was the look which a woman gives a man before she stakes all upon her choice.

"I have run away, Bart—to you. I was followed, but they could do nothing while I stood there at the desk. Now they have seen me arrested, and if ever *he* gets me back, perhaps this may save me—"

"No one shall get you back!"

"You do not understand!" She clutched me convulsively. "Shall I never make you understand that unless we can get away from Paris, nothing can save us—*nothing!*" She clenched her hands and stared like a frightened hare as Nayland Smith came in. "It is the order of the Council. I do not know if there is anywhere in the world you can hide from them—but this place you must leave at once!"

"Listen to me, Ardatha," Smith grasped her shoulders. "Have you any knowledge, any whatever, of the Si-Fan plans for tonight?"

She faced him fearlessly; her hands remained clenched.

"If I had, I could not tell you. But I have no knowledge of these plans. As I hope for mercy, it is true. Only I know that you are to die."

"How do you know?"

Ardatha from her handbag took out a square envelope.

"I was ordered to leave this at the desk and not allow myself to be recognised. I waited until I *knew* . . . I had been recognised!"

Final notice

Lower and raise the lights in your sitting room slowly twice, to indicate that you are prepared to take instructions. You have until midnight.

PRESIDENT OF THE COUNCIL

252

The thing with red eyes

The apartments faced upon a courtyard. There were a number of police in the hotel under Jussac's orders, and the passports of all residents had been scrutinised. Some of the rooms around the courtyard were empty; the occupants of the others were supposedly above suspicion. But Ardatha's terror-stricken face haunted me. When she had realised that she was to be locked in the end room to await the hour of midnight, a fear so overwhelming had come upon her that my own courage was threatened.

Gallaho was in the lobby outside her door. And now I heard the clocks of Paris chiming . . .

It was a quarter to twelve.

We had curtained all the windows, although if one excepted opposite rooms, no point commanded them. The atmosphere was stale and oppressive. Paris vibrated with rumours and counterrumours. By some it was believed that France already was at war; another story ran that Delibes was dead. But to the quiet old courtyard none of this penetrated. Instead a more real, a more sinister menace was there. The shadaw of Fu Manchu lay upon us.

A hopeless fatalism began to claim me. Already I looked upon Nayland Smith as a dead man.

From Ardatha came no sound. Her eyes had been unnaturally bright when we had left her: I had seen that splendid composure, that proud fearless spirit, broken. I knew that if she prayed, she prayed for me; and I thought that now she would be in tears – tears of misery, despair—waiting, listening . . . for what?

"Have your gun ready, Kerrigan!"

"What are you going to do?"

"I am going to search every inch of this room."

"What for?"

"I don't know! But you remember the black streak that went over Delibes' balcony? That thing, or another, similar thing, is here!"

253

I took a grip of failing nerves and stepped up to a walnut cabinet containing many cupboards, but:

"Touch nothing!" Smith snapped. "Leave the search to me. Just stand by."

He began to walk from point to point about the room, sparsely furnished in the manner of a continental hotel. No drawer was left unopened, no nook or cranny unsearched.

But he found nothing.

The electric clock registered seven minutes to midnight. And now came a wild cry, for which I knew that subconsciously I had been waiting.

"Let me out! For God's sake—let me out! I want to be with you—I can't bear it!"

"Go and pacify her, Kerrigan. We dare not have her in here."

"I won't budge!"

"Let me out—let me out—I shall go mad!"

Smith threw the door open.

"Allow her to join you in the lobby, Gallaho. On no account is she to enter this room."

"Very good, Sir Denis."

As Smith released the door, I heard the sound of a lock turned. I heard Ardatha's running footsteps . . .

"Come out there! Dear God, I beg of you—come out!"

Gallaho's growing tones reached me as he strove to restrain her.

"If you are so sure, Smith"—my voice was not entirely under control—"that the danger is *here*, why should we stay?"

"I have asked you to leave," he replied coldly.

"Not without you."

"It happens to be my business, Kerrigan, to investigate the instruments of murder employed by Doctor Fu Manchu, but it is not yours. I believe some death agent to be concealed in this room, and I am determined to find out what it is."

"Smith! Smith!" I spoke in a hoarse whisper.

"What?"

"For heaven's sake don't move—but look where I am looking. There, under the cornice!"

The apartment had indirect lighting so that there was a sort of recess running around three of the walls directly below the ceiling.

From the darkness of a corner where there were no lamps, two tiny fiery eyes—they looked *red*—glared down at us.

"My God!"

"What is it, Smith? In heaven's name, what is it?"

Those malignant eyes remained immovable; they possessed a dreadful, evil intelligence. It might have been an imp of hell crouching there, watching . . . Raising my repeater, I fired, and . . . all the lights went out!

"Drop flat, Kerrigan!"

The urgency of Smith's order booked no denial. I threw myself prone on the carpet. I heard Smith fall near by . . .

There came a moaning cry, then a roar from Gallaho:

"What's this game? What's happened?"

The door behind me burst open. I became aware of a pungent odour.

"No lights, Gallaho – and don't come in! Make for the door, Kerrigan!"

I groped my way across the room. The awareness of that unknown thing somewhere in the darkness afforded one of the most terrifying sensations I had ever known. But I got to the door and into the lobby. Gallaho stretched out his hand and grasped my shoulder.

"Where's Sir Denis?"

"I am here."

There were sounds of movement all about, of voices.

"It's the big black-out," came Smith's voice incisively, "ordered by Delibes to take place tonight. Whoever is in charge of the air defences of Paris has received no orders to cancel it. This saved us— for I'm afraid you missed, Kerrigan!"

"Ardatha!" I said shakily, "Ardatha!"

"She fainted, Mr Kerrigan, when the shot came . . ."

The thing with red eyes (concluded)

"Open this door."

We stood before a door bearing the number 36. It was that of a room which adjoined our apartments. Lights had been restored. An alarmed manager obeyed.

"Stand by outside, Gallaho. Come on, Kerrigan."

I found myself in a single bedroom which did not appear to be occupied. There was an acrid smell, and the first object upon which my glance rested was a long, narrow cardboard box labelled: "Meurice frères."

I glanced at an attached tab and read:

Mme Hulbert:
To be placed in number 36 to await Mme Hulbert's arrival.

"Don't touch that thing!" snapped Smith. "I'm not sure, yet—Hullo!"

He was staring up at part of the wall above the wardrobe. There was a jagged hole, perhaps six inches in diameter, which I could only suppose to penetrate to the adjoining apartment.

Smith dragged a chair forward, stood on it and examined the top of the wardrobe.

"Apologise, Kerrigan! You didn't miss after all . . . There's blood here!"

Down he came and began questing all about the floor.

"Here's a fresh stain, Smith!"

"Ah! near the window! By gad! I believe it's escaped! I'm going to pull the curtains open. If you see anything move, don't hesitate—shoot!"

Colt in hand I watched him as he dragged the heavy curtains apart. The window was open about four inches at the bottom.

"Stains here, look!"

Standing beside him, I saw on the ledge bloodstains of so

strange a character that comment failed me. They were imprints of tiny hands!

"Singular!" murmured Smith

He stared out right and left and down into the courtyard. The building was faced with ornamental stone blocks.

"Smith—" I began.

"A thing as small as that could climb down such a wall," he rapped, "and into an open window—assuming its wound not to be serious."

"But, Smith—this is the print of a *human* hand!"

"I know!" He ran to the door. "Gallaho! Instruct Jussac to search all rooms opening on this courtyard and to make sure that nothing—not even a small parcel—leaves any of them. Come on, Kerrigan."

Picking up the florist's box, he returned to our locked apartments. Ardatha was in a room near by, in charge of a sympathetic housekeeper. As we entered the sitting room, I pulled up, staring . . .

At the moment of my firing at that thing up under the cornice, Smith, just behind me, had been standing in front of a walnut cabinet.

The top of the cabinet had disappeared!

"Merciful heaven!" I whispered, "you escaped death by a fraction of a second!"

"Yes! Ericksen's Ray! The thing with the red eyes has at least elementary intelligence to be entrusted with such a weapon. This creature, or one like it, had been smuggled into Delibes' house, but made its escape. In the present case the same device of the flower box was used, an adjoining room having been reserved by a mythical Mme Hulbert. During our absence this evening, by means of the ray, that hole was bored through the wall."

"But the box remains unopened!"

"So do the boxes, apparently, used by stage magicians. I think we may risk it now!"

"Is all well in there, Sir Denis?" came Gallaho's husky voice from the lobby.

"All's well, Inspector."

He cut the string and opened the box.

It was empty.

"Assuming a thinking creature small enough to get into such a box, for it to get out again would be a simple matter: merely necessary to draw these two end flaps and replace them without unfastening the string . . ."

I cannot say, I shall never know, what drew my attention away from the trick box, but I found myself staring fixedly into the shadows beneath the bureau. This bureau stood almost immediately below the hole high up under the cornice. Some dully shining object lay upon the carpet.

As I stepped forward to pick it up, indeed, all but had my hand upon it, I recognised it for what it was—just such a tube as I had seen in the possession of Dr Fu Manchu.

And as this recognition came I saw the thing with the red eyes!

"Quick! Grab it for your life, Kerrigan!"

Wounded, the creature had dropped the silver tube in that sudden darkness, had sought to escape, and then for some reason had returned for the day. It crouched now beside the bureau, a black dwarf no more than fifteen inches high, naked save for a loincloth also black: a perfectly formed human being!

Its features, which were Negroid, contorted in animal fury, its red eyes glaring like those of a rabid dog, it sprang up the tube.

But I snatched it in the nick of time . . .

That which happened next threatens to defeat my powers of description. Smith, who had been manoeuvring for a shot fired—but as I made that frenzied grab, stumbling onto my knees, my fingers closed upon a sort of trigger in the butt end of the tube.

Smith's bullet buried itself in the wall. I experienced a tingling sensation. The thing with the red eyes which crouched before me, disappeared!

My last recollection is that of the bureau crashing down upon my head.

"Bart, dearest, are you better?"

I lay propped on cushions. Ardatha's arms were around me. My head buzzed like a wasps' nest, and a man whom I took to be a surgeon was bathing a painful cut on my brow.

"Yes, he is better," said the surgeon, smiling. "No serious damage." He turned to Nayland Smith who stood watching. "It must have been a heavy blow, nevertheless."

"It was!" Smith assured him. "Fortunately, he has a thick skull."

When the medical man was gone and I felt capable of sitting up and observing my surroundings, I realised that I had been moved to another room.

"Explanation of what had occurred would have been too difficult," Smith declared. "So we brought you in here."

And now came the memory of the black dwarf who had disappeared . . .

"Smith—he was disintegrated!"

"So was a portion of the bureau," Smith replied, "hence your being knocked out. It toppled before I had a chance to get at it. I have the mysterious tube, Kerrigan, Exhibit A, which resolves matter into its particles; but I don't propose to experiment further. We should be grateful for the fact that it was not ourselves who were dispersed!"

Ardatha held my hand tightly, and a swift glad wave of happiness swept over me. The unbelievable had come true.

"I am by no means sure how long this peaceful interlude will last," Smith continued. "My taking forcible means to save Marcel Delibes may be construed, however, as a triumph for the Si-Fan. In this case our interests were identical. Possibly we shall be granted a reprieve!"

"We deserve one!" I was staring at something which lay upon a side table. It resembled a small watch but I knew that I had never seen it before. "What have you there, Smith?"

"Exhibit B!" He smiled. "It must have been in the possession of the dwarf—the smallest and also the most malignant human being I have ever come across. Gallaho found it in the cavity between the two rooms, so that I assume the dwarf intended to return, having recovered the silver tube, and to make his escape by way of the window of number 36. I suspect that this possibility had been provided for."

"But what is it?"

Ardatha's grasp on my hand tightened.

"It is a radiophone," she said. "Sometimes—not often—those

carrying out Si-Fan instructions are given one. In this way they are kept directly in contact with whoever is directing them."

I turned my aching head and looked into her eyes.

"Did *you* ever use one, Ardatha?"

"Yes," she answered simply, "when I was sent to get the portfolio of the police commissioner in London!"

"You understand now, Kerrigan," snapped Smith, "that voice which we both heard in the study of M. Delibes? I am going to ask you, Ardatha, to show me how to get 'directly in contact'!"

Ardatha released my hand and stood up. She was supremely graceful in all her movements. Her poise was perfect, and I knew now that that momentary despair had been for *me* . . .

"I will do so if you wish. Nothing may happen. You can only listen: you cannot reply."

She took the tiny instrument which Smith handed to her and made some adjustments. We both watched closely. Paris lay about us, not sleeping, but seething with rumours of war. But in that room was silence—silence in which we waited.

It was broken.

A guttural voice spoke rapidly in a tongue unknown to me. It ceased. Ardatha adjusted the instrument.

"To move it to there," she said—but her tones were not steady— "means 'I do not understand.'"

And now (I confess that my heart leapt uncomfortably) that guttural voice spoke in English . . . and I knew that the speaker was Dr Fu Manchu!

"Can it be Sir Denis who calls me?"

Ardatha's fingers moved.

"Indeed! I rejoice that you live, Sir Denis. I suspect that Ardatha is with you. Any information which she may be able to impart you will find of small value. I assume that one of my three Negritos pygmies is lost. But this is no more than just. Your work in regard to M. Delibes resulted in the cancelling of the grotesque order for your removal. I welcome your co-operation . . . I regret my dwarf. Such a specimen represents twenty years' culture. Destroy the Ericksen tube: it is dangerous. Those who use it do not live long. The radio-phone I commend to you. Waste no time seeking me . . ."

That unique voice faded away. Ardatha was trembling in my arms.

Emperor Fu Manchu

Chapter I

"Once you pass the Second Bamboo Curtain, McKay, unless my theories are all haywire, you'll be up against the greatest scientific criminal genius who has ever threatened the world."

Tony McKay met the fixed regard of cold grey eyes which seemed to be sizing him up from the soles of his shoes to the crown of his head. The terse words, rapid, clipped sentences, of the remarkable man he had come to meet penetrated his brain with a bullet-like force. They registered. He knocked ash from his cigarette. The sounds and cries of a busy Chinese street reached him through an open window.

"I didn't expect to be going to a cocktail party, Sir Denis."

Sir Denis Nayland Smith smiled; and the lean, tanned face, the keen eyes, momentarily became those of a boy.

"I think you're the bird I'm looking for. You served with distinction in the United States Army, and come to me highly recommended. May I suggest that you have some personal animus against the Communist regime in China?"

"You may. I have. They brought about my father's death and ruined our business."

Nayland Smith re-lighted his briar pipe. "An excellent incentive. But it's my duty to warn you of the kind of job you're taking on. Right from the moment you leave this office you're on your own. You're an under cover agent—a man alone. Neither London nor Washington knows you. But we shall be in constant touch. You'll be helping to save the world from slavery. And I know your heart's in the game."

Tony nodded; stubbed out his cigarette in an ash-tray.

"No man could be better equipped for what you have to do. You were born here, and you speak the language fluently. With your cast of features you can pass for Chinese. There's no Iron Curtain here. But there are two Bamboo Curtains. The first has plenty of holes in it; the second so far has proved impenetrable.

263

Oddly enough, it isn't in the Peiping area, but up near the Tibetan frontier. Have to know the identity of the big man it conceals. He's the real power behind the Communist règime."

"But he must come out sometimes," Tony protested.

"He does. He moves about like a shadow. All we can learn about him is that he's known and feared as 'The Master'. His base seems to be somewhere in the province of Szechuan—and this province is behind the Second Bamboo Curtain!"

"Is that where you want me to go, Sir Denis?"

"It is. You could get there through Burma—"

"I could get a long way from right here, with a British passport, as a representative of, say, Vickers. Then I could disappear and become a Chinese coolie from Hong Kong—that's safe for me—looking for a lost relative or girl friend, or somebody."

Make your choice, McKay. I'd love to go, myself, but I can't leave my base at the moment. I have a shrewd idea about the identity of The Master. That's why I'm here."

"You think you know who he is?"

"I think he is the president of the most dangerous secret society in the world, the Si-Fan—Dr. Fu Manchu."

"Dr. Fu Manchu!"

"I believe he's up to his old game, running with the hare and hunting with the hounds—"

There was a sound resembling the note of a tiny bell. Nayland Smith checked his words and adjusted what looked like an Air Force wrist watch. Raising his hand, he began to speak into it. Tony realized that it must be some kind of walkie-talkie. The conversation was unintelligible, but when it ended, Nayland Smith glanced at him in an odd way.

"One of my contacts in Szechuan," he explained drily. "Reports the appearance of another Cold Man in Chia-Ting. They're creating a panic."

"A Cold Man? I don't understand."

"Nor do I. But it'll be one of your jobs to find out. They are almost certainly monstrosities created by Dr. Fu Manchu. I know his methods. They seem to be Burmese or Tibetans. Orders are issued that anyone meeting a Cold Man must instantly report to the police; that on no account must the creature be *touched*."

264

"Why?"

"I can't say. But they *have* been touched—and although they're walking about, their bodies are said to be icily cold."

"Good God! *Zombies*—living dead men!"

"And they always appear in or near Chia-Ting. You should head for there."

"It sounds attractive!" Tony grinned.

"You'll have one of these." Nayland Smith tapped the instrument he wore on his wrist. "I may as well confess it's a device we pinched from Dr. Fu Manchu. Captured on a prisoner. Looks like a wrist watch. One of our research men broke down the formula and now a number of our agents are provided with them. You can call me here at any time, and I can call you. Whatever happens, don't lose it. Notify me regularly where you are—if anything goes wrong, get rid of it, fast."

"I'm all set to start."

"There's some number one top secret being hidden in Szechuan. Military Intelligence thinks it's a Soviet project. I believe it's a Fu Manchu project. He may be playing the Soviets at their own game. Dr. Fu Manchu has no more use for Communism than I have for Asiatic 'flu. But so far all attempts to solve the puzzle have come apart. Local agents have only limited use, but you may find them helpful and they'll be looking out for you. You'll have the sign and countersigns. Dine with me tonight and I'll give you a thorough briefing . . ."

Chapter II

There was a rat watching him. In the failing light he couldn't see the thing; but he could see its eyes. Waiting hungrily, no doubt, for any scraps of rice he might leave in the bowl. Well, the rat would be in luck. The rice was mouldy.

Tony McKay drank a little more tepid water and then lay back on his ticky mattress, his head against the wall, looking up at a small, square window. Iron bars criss-crossed the opening and now, as dusk fell, hardly any light came in. He could have dealt with the iron bars, in time, but the window was just out of reach—two inches out of reach.

It was another example of Chinese ingenuity, like the platter of ripe peaches his jailer had left in the dungeon one morning. By walking to the end of the chain clamped to his right ankle and lying flat, he could stretch his arm across the grimy floor—to within two inches of the fruit!

But none of their cunning tricks would pay off. Physically, he was getting below par, but his will remained strong as on the day he left Hong Kong, unless . . .

He dismissed the thought.

A dark shape crossed the pattern of the bars, became lost in shadows of a stone ledge which ran from the window around the angle to the grilled door. Two more wicked little eyes appeared beside the pair in the corner of his cell. The rat's mate had joined up.

He didn't mind them. In their repulsive way, they formed a sort of link with the free world outside. And he was sorry for any creature that was hungry, except the horrible small ones which inhabited his straw mattress and filled the night with misery.

He fell into a sort of dozing reverie. These reveries had saved his sanity, given him the strength to carry on.

It was hard to grasp the fact that only two weeks ago he had been in Hong Kong. Throughout the first week he had kept in close touch with Nayland Smith, and this awful sense of loneliness which weighed him down now had not swept over him. Once he had overcome his stage fright on first assuming the part of Chi Foh, a Hong Kong fisherman, he had begun to enjoy his mission . . .

There were faint movements in the corridor, but they ceased, and Tony returned again to the recent past which now seemed so distant . . .

Anyway, he had penetrated the Second Bamboo Curtain—was still behind it. Of the mystery brain which Sir Denis Nayland Smith believed to be that of the fabulous Dr. Fu Manchu he had learned less than nothing. But in one part of his mission he had succeeded. The discovery had been made because of the thoroughness with which he identified himself with his assumed part of a Hong Kong fisherman seeking a missing fiancée. He had selected a remote riverside village not far above Chia-Ting on the Ya Ho River as the place to which his mythical girl friend had been taken by her family.

Quite openly he canvassed the inhabitants, so that if questioned later he could call witnesses to support his story. And it was from a kindly old woman whose sympathy with his quest made him feel an awful hypocrite that he got the clue which led him to his goal.

She suggested that the missing girl might be employed in "the Russian camp". It appeared that a grand-daughter of hers had worked there for a time.

"Where is this camp?" he asked.

It was on the outskirts of the village.

"What are Russians doing here?" he wanted to know.

They were employed to guard the leprosy research centre. Even stray dogs who came too near to the enclosure were shot to avoid spreading infection. The research centre was a mile outside the village.

"When did your grand-daughter leave, and why?" he inquired.

To get married, the old woman told him. She left only a month ago. The wages were good and the work light. She and her husband now lived in the village.

Tony interviewed the girl, describing "Nan Cho", his missing fiancée, but was assured that she was not employed at the Russian camp. He gathered that there were not more than forty men there in charge of a junior officer and two sergeants . . .

How vividly he remembered his reconnaissance in the grey dawn next morning!

The camp was a mere group of hutments, with a cookhouse and an orderly room displaying the hammer and sickle flag. He estimated that even by Russian standards it couldn't accommodate more than forty men. From cover he studied it awhile, and when the sleeping camp came to life decided that it was the most slovenly outfit he had ever come across. The entire lack of discipline convinced him that the officer in charge must be a throw-out sent to this dismal post as useless elsewhere.

There was a new and badly-made road leading from the camp up into the hills which overlooked the river. He was still watching when a squad of seven men appeared high up the road, not in any kind of order but just trudging along as they pleased. The conclusion was obvious. The guard on the research centre had been relieved.

He made a wide detour. There was plenty of cover on both sides of the road, oaks and scrub, and not a patch of cultivation that he could see. It was a toilsome journey, for he was afraid to take to the winding road even when far out of sight of the camp below. This was fortunate; for suddenly, beyond another bend of the serpentine road, he came in sight of the research station.

It was unlike anything he had anticipated.

A ten-foot wire fence surrounded an area, or so he guessed, of some twelve acres. Roughly in the centre of the area, which had been mown clear of vegetation and looked like a huge sheet of brown paper, he saw a group of buildings roofed with corrugated iron. One of them had what he took to be a smokestack or ventilation shaft.

The road ended before a gate in the wire fence. There was a wooden hut beside the gate, and a Russian soldier stood there, his rifle resting against the hut. He was smoking a cigarette.

And presently another man appeared walking briskly along outside the wire. The smoker carefully stubbed out his cigarette, stuck it behind his ear, and shouldered his rifle. The other man stepped into the hut—evidently the corporal in charge; who had posted the remaining five men of his squad at points around the circumference of the fence.

The cunning of Soviet propaganda! Leprosy is a frightening word, although leprosy had rarely appeared in Szechuan. But the mere name was enough to keep all at a distance.

This was the germ factory . . .

Where had he gone wrong?

Chung Wa-Su? Was it possible that Chung had betrayed him? It would be in line with Chinese thinking (if he, Tony, had aroused suspicion) to plant a pretended helper in his path. Yet all that Chung Wa-Su had done was to admit that he worked for Free China and to give him directions how best to cross the Yangtsze into Szechuan without meeting with frontier guards.

It was hard to believe.

There was the man he knew simply as Li. Who was Li? True, Tony hadn't trusted him very far although he had given sign and countersign, but all the same it was Li who had put him in touch with Chung Wa-Su.

Had Li been seized, forced to speak? Or was it possible that a report of his, Tony's visit to Hua-Tzu had preceded him down the river? Questioned, he had spoken freely about the visit; for although he knew, now, what was hidden there, he couldn't go back on his original plan without destroying the carefully built-up evidence of the purpose of his long journey.

He fell into an uneasy doze. He could hear, and smell, the rats in his rice bowl. As he slipped into sleep, his mind carried him back to his last examination by the dreadful creature called Colonel Soong . . .

"If you searched this village you speak of, looking for some girl, you can tell me the name of the former mandarin who lives in the big house."

"There is no large house in Hua-Tzu."

"I mean the house in the hills."

"I saw no house in the hills."

His heart warmed again in his near-dream state. There were few Americans, or Europeans either, who could have sustained the character of a love-lorn fisherman from Hong Kong under the fire of those oblique, ferocious eyes.

Yes, Sir Denis Nayland Smith was a good picker. No man could be better fitted for the job than one born in China, whose maternal grandmother had belonged to an old Manchurian family . . .

In a small room, otherwise plainly furnished, a man sat in a massive, high-backed ebony chair behind a lacquer desk. The desk glistened in the light of a silk-shaded lantern which hung from the ceiling, so that golden dragons designed on the lacquer panels seemed to stir mysteriously.

The man seated there wore a loose yellow robe. His elbows rested on the desk, and his fingers—long, yellow fingers—were pressed together, so that he might have suggested to an observer the image of a praying mantis. He had the high brow of a philosopher and features indicating great intellectual power. This aura of mental force seemed to be projected by his eyes, which were of a singular green colour, and as he stared before him, as if at some distant vision, from time to time they filmed over in an extraordinary manner.

The room, in which there lingered a faint, sickly smell of opium, was completely silent.

And this silence was scarcely disturbed when a screen door opened and an old Chinese came in on slippered feet. His face, in which small, twinkling eyes looked out from an incredible map of wrinkles, was that of a man battered in a long life of action, but still unbowed, undaunted. He wore an embroidered robe and a black cap topped by a coral bead.

He dropped down on to cushions heaped on the rugs, tucking his hands into the loose sleeves of his robe, and remained there, still as a painted Buddha, watching the other man.

The silence was suddenly and harshly broken by the voice of the dreamer at the lacquer desk. It was a strange voice, stressing the many sibilants in the Chinese language and emphasizing the gutturals.

"And so, Tsung-Chao, I am back again in China—a fugitive from the West, but a power in the East. You, my old friend, are restored to favour. General Huan Tsung-Chao, a former officer of the Chinese Empire, now Communist governor of a province! A triumph for the Si-Fan. But similar phenomena have appeared in Soviet Russia. You have converted Szechuan into a fortress in which I am secure. You have done well."

"Praise from the Master warms my old heart."

"It is a stout heart—and not so old as mine."

"All that I have done has been under your direction."

"What of the reorganization of the People's Army? You are too

270

modest, Tsung-Chao. But between us we have gained the confidence of Peiping. I have unlimited authority, for Peiping remains curiously, but fortunately, ignorant of the power of the Si-Fan."

"I pray that their ignorance may continue."

"I have inspected many provinces, and have found our work progressing well. I detected several United States agents, and many of Free China. But Free China fights for the same goal as the Si-Fan."

"But not for the same leader, Master!"

Dr. Fu Manchu smiled. His smile was more terrifying than his frown.

"You mean for the same *Emperor!* We must be patient." His voice rose on a note of exaltation. "I shall restore this ancient Empire to more than its former glory! Communism, with its vulgarity, its glorification—and enslavement—of the workers, I shall sweep from the earth! What Bonaparte did I shall do, and as he did, I shall win control of the West as well as of the East!"

"I await the day, Master!"

"It will come. But if the United States, Britain, or particularly Soviet Russia, should unmask the world-wide conspiracy of the Si-Fan, all our plans would be laid in ashes! So, when I am in China, my China, I must travel incognito; I am a shadow."

The old general smiled; a wrinkled but humorous smile. "I can answer for most of our friends in Formosa. From the United States agents you have little to fear. None of them knows you by sight—only by repute. I have entertained several Soviet visitors—and your name stands high with the Kremlin. But news reached me yesterday that Nayland Smith has left England, and I believe is in Hong Kong."

"Tchee!" It was a hiss. "The old hound is hot on my trail! He will not be working alone. We must take precautions. He lacks genius. He is a product of the Scotland Yard tradition. But he has inexhaustible patience. Note this, Tsung-Chao: any suspect arrested by the blundering Communists in or near Szechuan must be reported to me at once. I shall interrogate such suspects, personally . . ."

Tony awoke with a start, shot upright in bed.

It wasn't the rats and it wasn't the lice. It was a woman's scream that had pierced his sleep like a hot blade.

Everything was silent again, the night hot and still. His cell stank foully. But he hadn't dreamed. He had heard a woman scream—a sudden, agonized scream. He clenched his fists. His palms were clammy. And he listened—listened.

He had no means of knowing what time it was, how long he had slept. The barred window resembled a black hole in the wall. It overlooked a small courtyard and he could barely see the sky.

Further sleep was out of the question. His brain was on fire. Somewhere, in this hell hole, they were persecuting a woman.

Footsteps and voices broke the silence. He recognized one voice. It was that of his jailer.

They were coming for him!

This would be the great test.

The heavy door was unlocked. Two armed men wearing the uniform of the Red Army held up lanterns. His thickset, leering jailer opened the padlock which confined McKay's ankle.

"This way, Chi Foh. They want to ask you something about fishing!"

He assumed that stony passivity which belonged to his part. Head held low, he went out between the two guards. Quite unnecessarily, they prodded him with their rifle butts to keep him moving. Strange how Soviet training dehumanized men!

Colonel Soong sat at a bamboo table in the lighted courtyard. The governor, an older man whom Tony could have respected, sat on the colonel's right. A junior officer who looked like a coolie in uniform was on his left. Two soldiers stood behind them.

"Stand him there," Colonel Soong commanded, pointing, "where he can see what we do with spies!"

The governor had put on heavy-rimmed spectacles, and was trying to read some document which lay before him—probably, the several examinations of Suspect Wu Chi Foh. The junior officer watched Tony with an expression a gourmet might assume before a choice meal.

"Those who admit their guilt, Chi Foh"—the colonel was addressing him—"die an easy death. I recommend an open confession. Bring in the prisoners."

Escorted by four soldiers, two men came into the courtyard, their hands tied behind their backs.

272

Tony saw the elderly Chung Wa-Su, and the younger Li. He had covered many hundreds of miles by road, river and canal since his dealings with them. Yet here they were to confront him, lined up no more than three paces away.

"Wu Chi Foh, do you know these men? Make them look up."

Guards prodded the prisoners. Both stared impassively at Tony.

"No, Excellency."

"You are a lying son of a pig! Again I ask you—and this is your last chance of an easy death—do you know these men?"

"No, Excellency."

Colonel Soong rapped out a harsh order. The official executioner came in, a stocky, muscular figure, stripped to the waist and showing a torso and arms like those of a gorilla. He carried a short, curved sword.

Neither of the prisoners displayed the slightest interest in the proceedings. . .

When, with an efficiency which commanded Tony's reluctant admiration, Chung Wa-Su and Li had been beheaded and their bodies hauled from the courtyard: "That is the easy death, Chi Foh," Colonel Soong told him. "I am returning you to your cell to consider this. Be prepared at any hour to buy the same painless end."

Tony was dragged back to the smelly dungeon which had confined him so long, and was thrown in with such sudden violence that he fell on his face. The chain was relocked to his ankle.

He dropped onto the bed and sank his head into his hands.

Even supposing that neither Chung Wa-Su nor Li had involved him in their confessions (and it was possible), he was marked for death. He could admit all he had learned (very little), and have his head neatly lopped off by an expert, or he could persist in his story that he was a harmless fisherman. Then he would be put in the stocks, and—

They had no evidence whatever to connect him with Sir Denis Nayland Smith. The wonderful little long-range walkie-talkie which Sir Denis had entrusted to him before he set out, he had, mercifully, managed to drop in the river when he saw them coming to arrest him.

He seemed to hear again that snappy voice: "If anything goes wrong—get rid of it, fast . . ." It had helped him in many emergencies, made him feel that he wasn't alone. Now—

He could, of course, reveal his true identity and challenge Soong to execute a United States officer. But there's a code in these affairs, and it is never broken, except by renegades.

This was the end . .

Something came through the window bars and fell right at his feet.

It made a dull thud, but there was a faint metallic jingle, too. Tony stooped eagerly and picked up a piece of thin paper wrapped around two keys and another metal object.

His hands shook as he unrolled the parcel. The third object was a cigarette-lighter!

He snapped it up and read on thin rice paper:

> From Nayland Smith.
>
> The smaller key frees your chain. The other opens the door. Leave before daylight. The guard on the gate is bribed. Your boat still lies where you left it. Money and some food aboard. Follow Min River left bank, down to any navigable creek, then use irrigation canals to Niu-fo-tu on Lu Ho River. Ask for the house of the Lama. He expects you. Memorize and swallow message.

His heart leapt madly. Thank God! Nayland Smith hadn't lost contact with him! His last message on the walkie-talkie had placed his location—and he was no longer alone.

Tony had little difficulty in memorizing the directions, for his journey up to Chia-Ting had made him familiar with the river and place-names. He masticated the piece of rice paper; then had to make a lightning decision about the keys. Footsteps sounded in the passage. Voices. They were coming back for him.

He thrust the keys and the lighter under his mattress.

But in his heart he knew help had come too late . . .

"Colonel Soong is asking for you, fisherman!"

His leering jailer threw open the cell door. Two men— the same as before—stood by while the chain was unfastened, banged his ribs with their rifle butts as he was marched along the passage and out again into the courtyard.

Many men have been condemned for cowardice in the face of the enemy. But, knowing what was in store for him, Tony wondered if Nayland Smith would understand (and sympathize) if he simply accepted "the easy death" and became another missing agent. For he couldn't hope to survive the ordeal ahead.

If he could, and did, stay silent, and they released him (which was unlikely), his sufferings would have made him useless, helpless; his memory would be gone. He would be a mere parody of a man . . .

"Have you anything more to say, Chi Foh?"

"No, Excellency."

Tony was forced onto his knees in front of the stocks, facing outward, and his feet were clamped in the openings provided. Then, wrists pinioned behind, his body was drawn as far back as it would go without something snapping and the rope was tied to a crossbeam.

The executioner, satisfied, awaited orders.

"For the last time, Wu Chi Foh, have you anything to say?"

"Nothing, Excellency."

Colonel Soong raised his hand . . .

(*"Your boat still lies where you left it . . ."*)

"Release the prisoner!"

Colonel Soong's hand remained raised. It was held in a vice-like grip by a Nubian of enormous physique, a man built like the executioner but on a much larger scale. This ebony giant had rested his free hand on the shoulder of the Chinese lieutenant, who was clearly unable to stir.

"I gave an order."

The mist was dispersing more and more. Now, half in the shadow of an archway behind the table, Tony could see a tall figure. The executioner became electrified. In a matter of seconds Tony found himself free, saw the executioner bowing humbly to the man who stood motionless in the archway.

Another crisp command, not spoken in Chinese, resulted in the Nubian's stepping back. Both officers sprang to their feet, spun around and stood at the salute.

"Colonel Soong"—the imperious tones carried clearly all over the courtyard—"it is contrary to my wishes that these primitive methods of questioning be employed. China will flower again as a land of beauty and of culture. If harsh means must be used to extract the truth, at least let them be refined. Brutality without purpose is neither enjoyable nor artistic. Remain in your quarters until I send for you."

Colonel Soong retired, followed by his lieutenant.

"I will interview the prisoner."

Chapter III

Tony, dazed, bewildered, but calm with the numb calm of utter desperation, found himself in an elaborately furnished room (probably the prison governor's study), facing a long desk, over-ornamented in the Burmese manner, behind which was placed a commodious chair. He was tinglingly conscious of the presence of the giant Nubian in the shadows at his elbow.

No one else was there—until the man who had ordered his release came in.

He came in from the other end of the room and walked to the desk. His movements had a catlike quality; his step was feline, silent. Tony couldn't mistake the tall, lean figure of which he had a glimpse in the courtyard. He recognized a sort of cavalry cloak in which the man with the imperious voice had been wrapped and which he now discarded and dropped on the rug beside the chair.

Tony saw that he wore a uniform resembling those which had once distinguished Prussian officers, with glossy top boots. And as he took his seat, resting his elbows on the desk and pressing his long, yellow fingertips together, Tony experienced a fluttering in the stomach.

He was looking at one of the most wonderful faces he had ever seen. The high forehead, the chiselled, aggressive nose, the thin lips, were those of an aristocrat, a thinker, and a devil. But the long, half closed eyes, eyes of a phenomenal green colour, completed the impression of *force* which radiated from this man's personality, as he sat there perfectly still.

Then suddenly he spoke.

"Well, my friend, I think the time has come to lay your cards on the table. Don't you agree with me?"

The last shadow of doubt was swept from Tony's mind. He recalled fragments of Nayland Smith's vivid word picture of the person he was seeking: "A brow like Shakespeare and a face like

Satan. Eyes of the true cat green . . . He speaks every civilized language with near-perfection, as well as countless dialects. He has the brains of any three men of genius embodied in one man . . ."

Tony found it impossible to sustain the stare of those hypnotic eyes. But he knew, and counted himself lost, that here was Number One, The Master, the driving power behind the Communist regime—for the words had been spoken in perfect English. He had succeeded—but too late.

This was Dr. Fu Manchu!

The shock of that question in English was so unexpected that he nearly betrayed himself by replying in the same language.

It was a crucial test. And he survived it.

"I don't understand, Excellency," he said in Chinese.

"Don't be a fool. You understand well enough."

Tony shook his head in a bewildered way. Meeting the intolerable stare of those green eyes, he became aware that, again, his life hung on a thread.

Silence. The negro behind him made no sound. He could hear the faint spluttering of perfume sticks set before a shrine at one end of the room. The air was oppressive. He was becoming dizzy. His appalling experience, his imprisonment, had stolen his stamina.

He was recalled by a brusque question in Chinese.

"Your name is Wu Chi Foh? You are accused of spying?"

He met the hypnotic stare.

"Yes, Excellency."

In that fleeting second he had discovered something. The disturbing quality of Fu Manchu's gaze was that he seemed to be looking not at him, but through him.

"Are you guilty?"

"No, Excellency."

"For a humble fisherman, you have a pure accent. You interest me. Take him back to his cell."

For once, Tony was glad to throw himself wearily on the filthy mattress, glad to find even brief sanctuary in his dungeon from those dreadful eyes.

("Leave before daylight . . .")

He jumped up and stared at the barred window. He could see the stars against a grey background. Dawn was breaking . . .

(". . . Your boat still lies where you left it . . .")

Had the arrival—clearly unexpected—of The Master, put the scheme out of gear? Had the guard on the gate been changed? Was the sampan still lying in the river?

Well, he could find out.

The key of the leg iron worked rather stiffly, gave him uneasy moments. But at last came a welcome click, and his leg was free. His heart pounded hard as he fitted the second key into the keyhole of the door. It turned without a hitch. He swung the heavy door open and looked out cautiously into the stone-paved passage.

There was no one there. The only light, a very faint one, came through a barred window at the end. He heard nothing; slipped out into the cool open air.

He clung close to the buildings. The courtyard was deserted. A shadow of the whipping-post lay like a band across the stone paving. No window showed any light. At last he got to the corridor which led to freedom. He peeped around an angle of the wall. This prison had been a fortress in feudal times, and just inside the great nail-studded gate there was a cramped guardroom.

A dim light, probably that of a lantern, shone out from the guard-room door.

And he had to pass that door.

He inhaled deeply, then went ahead. No one was to be seen inside, the lantern stood on a table. He passed, and came to the gate.

The bolts—they seemed to be well oiled—were already withdrawn from the sockets which secured the gate.

Inch by inch, Tony swung open the mass of teak and iron. When the gap was wide enough to slip through, he stepped out, paused for a moment, breathing hard, then gently reclosed the gate.

He set off at a good pace, but avoided running. His escape had been perfectly planned. The guard had only to shoot the bolts into place, employ his national talent for lying, and the prisoner's disappearance would look like magic, for Tony had taken the keys and the lighter with him. Sound staff work. But it must have cost a lot of money.

When he came to the river, there was his old sampan, tied up to a rickety stage.

Not pausing to examine the craft, he cast loose the mooring line and stepped on to the oarsman's platform, aft.

When day broke into full flame he was many miles south. He tied up in a cactus-lined backwater from which he could see no signs of a nearby road. Then he stooped under the strip of plaited roof and went in to find where the money was hidden and what provisions he had.

There was a Chinese girl asleep in the cabin.

She was curled up on a heap of matting, one arm half covering her face. Her clothes were at least as ragged and soiled as his own and her black hair was dishevelled. He could see that she had long dark lashes and there were tear tracks from her closed eyes cutting through the dirt on her cheeks.

How had she got on board, and when? She might have been there from the time he started, or she might have crept on later, during one of his several reconnaissance tours ashore.

However, here she was, and he had to make up his mind what he was going to do with her. An added problem, when he had far too many to cope with already. First and foremost stood the problem of Chien-Wei. Where was Chien-Wei? He had never heard of it. Such names cropped up like nettles all over the map of China. Was it a town or merely a village? This he must find out, and soon, for he might be getting farther away from the place instead of nearer.

Creeping quietly out to the stern, carrying soap and shaving material, he stripped, soaped himself all over and then dropped into the cool water. Climbing back, much refreshed, he towelled and, stifling his disgust, got into the filthy rags which were all he had. Then he lighted his galley fire (an iron bucket with holes punched in it) using dry wood gathered on the bank, and boiled a pannikin of water.

He was struggling through his first shave for more than two weeks when he saw the girl watching him. He paused, shaving brush in hand, and stared. He had expected coal-black eyes. But her eyes were dark blue. He remembered, though, that some of the up-country peasants had blue eyes. She looked like a very dirty Chinese doll.

"So you are awake at last?"

"Yes." She looked down and shuddered. "How long did I sleep?" She had a pretty, bell-like voice, but it shook nervously.

"I don't know." More to reassure her than for any other reason he went on shaving. "When did you come on board?"

"Some time last night," she answered.

Wiping his face, he began anxiously to forage in the locker. His own few pots and pans were there. He had jettisoned everything incriminating when he had realized they were coming to arrest him. He found a considerable sum of money, mostly in small currency, and there were cigarettes and a carton of canned meat, soup and other edibles. Sea toast and rice he found, too, and fresh fruit; soap, shaving kit, matches, a bottle of lime juice and a bottle of Scotch. And, last of all, a .38 and a box of shells.

Then, resoaping his chin, he went on shaving again. "You came on board at Chia-Ting?"

"Yes. Please don't throw me off. I don't know what I shall do if you won't let me stay."

At Chia-Ting! The ways of these people were strange and tortuous. Did they know more than he supposed? Was this little stowaway a spy? Perhaps it was a plot to learn where he was going, to identify his associates.

He finished shaving. The girl, her hands clasped, waited with entreaty in her eyes.

"What's your name?"

"Yueh Hua. I can cook, and fish, and manage a boat. I won't be any trouble!"

Yeuh Hua meant "Moon Flower". This poor little waif hardly looked the part.

"Where did you come from?"

"A small village ten miles from Chia-Ting. It is called Su-Chien."

"And what were you doing in Chia-Ting?"

"Running away from my stepfather." She spoke eagerly. "He had sold me to Fuen Chang, a horrible old man who would have beaten me. It is his only pleasure, beating girls."

"You had friends in Chia-Ting, I suppose?"

"Yes." Yueh Hua nodded. "My sister. But she had gone. There was nothing to do but try to get to my aunt. It is a long way."

Tony sponged his face, washed the shaving brush, and began, very thoughtfully, to clean the razor blade. If this girl was an agent of the Master she certainly knew her piece.

"Where does your aunt live?"

"In Lung Chang."

"Where is Lung Chang?"

"On the Lu Ho."

This startled him. He was far from sure of his route to the Lu Ho.

"Do you know the way to Lung Chang?"

"Of course!" There came a flash of white teeth in the grimy face. "I used to go there in my father's boat. I mean, my real father."

"I see." He replaced the razor in its box. "What I don't see is why you came on to my boat and fell asleep."

"I was tired and frightened. I had walked a long way. People were beginning to notice me—to follow me. I came on your boat to hide. I don't remember falling asleep. Are you angry with me?"

Chapter IV

Some hours before this interesting conversation took place, a less amiable conversation had been held in the office of the governor of the prison. Dr. Fu Manchu sat behind the desk. The old governor and Colonel Soong stood before him.

"I fear, Colonel Soong, that here is some serious breach of discipline. There would seem to be traitors among your men." He spoke softly, but there was menace in every syllable.

Colonel Soong's voice was unsteady when he replied, "I assure you, Most High, it is not so. This man's escape was magic."

The narrowed green eyes were turned in the old governor's direction.

"Who had charge of the keys?"

"The head jailer, Highness."

"Where are they now?"

"In their usual place where he placed them having re-locked the prisoner in his cell after his interview with Highness."

"Were they ever left unprotected?"

"Never. The head jailer and another were in the room up to the very moment that Highness ordered the prisoner to be brought here again."

"Unless both men are lying, duplicate keys were smuggled into the prisoner's cell. And what of the main gate?"

Colonel Soong broke in. "The main gate was found locked, Most High. The man on guard reports that no one passed, that the gate was never opened."

Dr. Fu Manchu took a pinch of snuff from a small silver box before him. "I shall interrogate these men later. I have means of learning the truth without resorting to your barbarous methods, Colonel Soong. The discipline of your men is disgraceful. Several patients undergoing special treatment in the clinic which I recently established have wandered from the compound and into the

283

town. Yet you have orders to patrol the area day and night. These patients are suffering from a dangerous infectious disease. How do you explain this laxity?"

Colonel Soong's yellow face had assumed a grey tinge. "Most High, my troops have orders not to touch them—although some have done so. They report that these people are not human. They are dead men who have escaped from their tombs!"

"Fools!" Dr. Fu Manchu's cold voice rose on a sudden note of frenzy. "I am doomed to be served by fools!" He clenched his hands, and by an obvious effort of will conquered his anger. "This man who calls himself Wu Chi Foh must be recaptured. You lost him. Find him. Colonel Soong—move. I shall accompany you . . .

Tony decided that his best course would be to pretend to believe Yueh Hua, so he asked, "Is Lung Chang far from Niu-fo-Tu?"

"About eight miles. We have to pass it. We used to come to this place sometimes, too. It is called Pool of Lily Dreams. Once it was part of the garden of a big house. But the house has gone. May I come and show you the way to Niu-fo-tu? I can row the boat when you want to rest."

Her eagerness was pathetic. He nodded, and smiled for the first time.

"All right, Yueh Hua. I'll take you to Lung Chang."

"Oh, thank you! You are very good." And he read deep gratitude in the blue eyes. "Please—" as he was about to replace his washing kit—"may I—"

Tony handed her soap and comb. "The towel's wet, but it's the only one."

Yeuh Hua grabbed them and jumped ashore. He saw her heading for a clump of alders where the bank sloped down to the pool.

He was hunting for some plausible explanation of how he had come by his canned provisions, when he heard her running back. Her hair was wet. And she was trying to fasten a ragged pyjama jacket, which, with baggy trousers, made up her costume.

"Quick! We must be quick!"

She jumped on board with the agility of a wild goat, throwing down soap and towel.

"What's the matter, Yueh Hua?"

284

"Coming along—now! A motor boat! It must be the police—for me! They think I stole your sampan!"

The widely opened eyes never wavered.

"Wait," Tony said. "Don't stir until I come back."

Yueh Hua was right.

An old fourteen-foot motor craft was coming down. Colonel Soong stood up in the stern, sweeping the banks on either side through field-glasses.

Tony raced back. When he reached the boat he pulled up, staring. Yeuh Hua had cast off and stood at the oar, ready to leave.

"Be quick! I know a hiding-place. These people are new here. They may not find us."

He climbed aboard and sat down watching her. He might as well let her have her way, for he had no plan of his own.

She swung the sampan about with an easy, deep sweep of the long oar. Then, using a minimum of effort, she headed straight across the pool, avoiding traps set by clumps of wild lilies, and drove straight in through a forest of rushes with a sudden powerful stroke. For a moment, he thought they were stranded. Then, using the oar like a punt pole, Yueh Hua got the boat free, and they were in a smaller pool, deep and clear, roofed over by the foliage of majestic old willows.

"That was very good, Yueh Hua."

"Did you see who it was?"

"Yes. An Army officer, with field-glasses."

"Not—a tall, thin man, wearing a long cloak?"

Tony was startled, but hid the fact. "No. Short, wearing uniform. Are you afraid of this tall man?"

"Yes . . . Ssh! Sounds carry over the pool. They had stopped, but they are just turning in."

And, as she spoke, the engine coughed into action again. Although he couldn't see, Tony knew that the motor boat had entered the narrow opening, that Colonel Soong would be inspecting the banks of the pool. They lay down side by side, peering through the rushes.

A sudden protective impulse made him put his arm around Yueh Hua's shoulders. He realized that she was still wet from her bath—hadn't had time to use a towel. And she was trembling.

At last came Colonel Soong's grating voice: "Nobody here. Back out."

The motor craft went coughing out astern.

As the sound of the engine died away, Tony stood up, helping Yueh Hua to her feet. It was dark under the willows and he could hardly see her face.

"Thank you, Yueh Hua," he said. "You are wet and will catch cold. Dry yourself. I won't look."

He ducked forward under the matting roof, turned his back, and lighted a cigarette.

His first ideas about Yueh Hua required an overhaul. Even Chinese duplicity couldn't account for what had happened. She was as scared of Colonel Soong as he was himself—and desperately afraid of Dr. Fu Manchu. Her explanation that she might be suspected of stealing his boat didn't add up, either. Agreed that she was running away, from *whom* was she running? Someone far more formidable than her stepfather. And there were other points . . .

"Please come out. I'm dry now."

The bell voice recalled him from speculation. He went out to the stern. Yueh Hua had tidied up considerably. But he knew her clothing must be damp. She was smiling shyly.

"Do I look any better?"

He thought she looked very well indeed. There were few Mongolian characteristics. Prominent cheekbones and very slightly slanting eyes—yes. But many Celts had these. Now that her face was clean, he saw that she had a fresh, healthy complexion. In fact, he decided that Yueh Hua was quite pretty in a quaint way.

He planned to remain hidden where they were until the searchers returned and passed on the way up to Chia-Ting. Yueh Hua shook her head.

"When they don't find the sampan anywhere we could have got to in this time, they will search again on the way back. Someone may tell them of this place. It was once used as duck decoy."

Tony thought viciously of his .38, and wondered how many of the crew, beginning with Colonel Soong, he could knock off as they came into the decoy. But he dismissed the idea quickly.

We shall have to cross the river before they come back and hide in a creek I know there," she continued.

"Is it used much?"

"No. It is too shallow."

This programme was a desperate venture. For, should the motor cruiser turn about sooner than anticipated, they could be trapped on the way over. He pointed out that Soong might search the creek.

"It is upstream. They will have searched it coming down."

Tony grasped the long sweep and began to pole along the bank, edging the boat toward the opening through the rushes.

"Nearer the middle," Yueh Hua directed. "Look—where the dragon-fly is."

He gave a powerful thrust. The bow of the sampan was driven in some three feet, then progress was checked.

"Another push from this side—hard."

He swung the oar over, found a firm spot, and thrust with all his weight. The boat glided along an unseen channel, and they were out again in the main part of the pool.

"Let me go ashore first and see if the river is clear," Yueh Hua said.

Tony rowed in to the spot against which he had first tied up, and she leaped ashore lightly and ran off through the cactus lining the bank. He waited, listening. And as he listened, he heard voices singing some monotonous song, and faintly, the sound of a reed pipe.

Yueh Hua came running back.

"A big raft coming down! They may have been told to look out for us. We must wait until they pass."

He nodded. But every minute's delay might mean capture.

The sounds drew nearer. The song was a bawdy ditty once popular on the Hong Kong Flower Boats. Tony glanced at Yueh Hua, but read only anxiety in her face. They stayed quite silent until the raft had gone by.

Then he swung the sampan through the opening. The stream was deserted. Piloted by Yueh Hua, they crossed; Tony found the narrow creek, rowed the boat into it until Yueh Hua called, "Stop here!"

There was a mat shed—a rough hut—under the trees. He turned to her in sudden doubt.

"Are there people here?"

"I hope not. It is used sometimes by fishers, but nobody lives in it."

In fact, the tumble-down place proved to be deserted. It was so far gone in decay that not even an eel fisher would have consented to live there. The palm roof was full of holes and the bamboo framework largely collapsed. When he had tied up the boat he secretly charged his .38 and slipped its comforting weight into a pouch inside his ragged pants.

"I must find my way along the bank to the end of the creek, Yueh Hua, and watch for the motor boat."

She touched his arm. "Please, let me come, too."

They set out together in blazing sunshine. There was a sort of path through thick undergrowth, but evidently it hadn't been used for a long time. Then came the bare banks lower down. There proved to be a wandering gully, though, which gave good cover and which led them to the river only some yards above the creek.

They had trudged along in silence. Now both looked upstream. The raft was no longer in sight. The river showed deserted. They sat down side by side among the rushes and wildgrass, watching a slow tide go whispering by. Tony felt that Yueh Hua was furtively studying him. He glanced at her.

She smiled. "What is your honourable name, if you please?"

"My family name is Wu. I am called Chi Foh."

"Mine is Kwee. You don't belong in this part of China?"

He looked at her searchingly. She was still smiling.

"No. My father—" (He hesitated. He had nearly said "was a merchant")—"is a storekeeper in Hong Kong. I was brought up there."

His father had been senior partner in the firm of McKay, Anderson and Furth, Incorporated, tea exporters.

"I suppose, Chi Foh, he was ruined by the war?"

But he didn't answer. He had heard the asthmatic coughing of Colonel Soong's motor craft. They were coming back, close to the right bank.

Yueh Hua grasped his hand. He saw that her lips trembled. "We must lie behind these rushes, Chi Foh. We can see from there, but they won't see us."

They crept back from the bank and lay down side by side. The old cruiser was very close now.

Almost unconsciously, he put his left arm around Yueh Hua's shoulders.

From where he lay, he couldn't see Soong in the stern. But he could see a man who stood up in the bows. It was the giant Nubian!

Then, came a voice, a clear, imperious voice. It sent a trickle of ice down Tony's spine.

"I fear, Colonel Soong, that you are wasting valuable time."

The motor boat had swung around slightly on the current. He saw Soong in the stern, field-glasses in hand—and he saw someone else, seated in the cabin behind the man at the wheel. A figure wrapped in a dark cloak.

Yueh Hua trembled so violently that he glanced at her anxiously. Every trace of colour had left her face.

"Don't be afraid," he whispered, and held her closely. "They can't see us."

But she didn't answer. Colonel Soong's harsh tones were raised unsteadily. "I assure you, Most High, it is not so. The escaped prisoner must certainly have come this way."

Most High! Nayland Smith hadn't over-estimated the power of The Master. The mysterious Dr. Fu Manchu seemed to be all set to take over the reins of government. British Secret Service wasn't far wrong in regarding him as a danger to the Western World.

"I regret that I cannot share your confidence." The words were spoken in sibilant, cultured Chinese. Then with a change of language to what Tony thought might be Arabic, a short sentence followed.

The Nubian spun around and stood at attention. He shook his head and answered briefly in the same guttural tongue.

"I was inclined—" Fu Manchu was addressing Soong— "to send Mahmûd ashore again to search the mat shed on the creek. But he assures me no one has been there. I believe him, for he has the instincts of a hunting leopard."

The motor cruiser had drifted now to within a few yards of the bank. It was plain enough that "Mahmûd" on his former visit must have followed the gully in which they lay, that if he did come ashore again he could hardly fail to stumble over them.

Tony fingered the useful weapon in his pocket. The big negro, if he came, might carry a gun; Soong was armed. There might be other arms on board. But there were only four men to deal with. Given luck, and surprise to help him, he thought he could deal with them.

Silence for a few seconds, and then, "Shall I go, myself, Highness?" Soong volunteered.

Tony was planning his tactics. If Soong came ashore, he would shoot the big negro first, then, before the colonel could grasp what had happened, he would shoot Soong.

"Proceed upstream," the imperious voice commanded. "We passed no other possible hiding-place on our way down. Therefore, we cannot have left the sampan behind . . ."

Late that evening, Dr. Fu Manchu sat at the lacquered desk, reading. Old General Huan, from his favourite seat on cushions, watched him.

"I observe that Andre Skobolov is expected here tomorrow. You have instructions from Peiping to entertain him. Why was the presence of this dangerous Soviet agent in China not reported to me?" Fu Manchu glanced up from the notes which lay before him on the desk. "It would seem that our intelligence service is sleeping."

General Huan Tsung-Chao slightly shook his head. "This man Skobolov travels almost as secretly as you do, Master."

Dr. Fu Manchu's eyes glittered wickedly from under half-lowered lids. "I have perhaps been misled in my belief that the elusive escaped prisoner was a British agent acting under Nayland Smith. His remarkable disappearance is more easily explained if he is a secret agent of the Soviet. They have facilities here which are denied to Nayland Smith."

"If that were so, why should he have been imprisoned?"

"Wake up, Tsung-Chao! The identity of such an agent would not be known to the blundering Colonel Soong, nor to the prison governor. It pains me to think that I may have saved the life of a Soviet spy!"

Old General Huan smiled a wry, wrinkled smile. "There is unfortunate news, Master, which may confirm your suspicions. But I am assured that Wu Chi Foh could not have had anything to do with the documents."

Fu Manchu's eyes became fully opened. They blazed. His

expression remained immobile as a mask. But when he spoke it was in tones very subdued, oddly sibilant.

"Unfortunate news? Documents? What have you to tell me?"

And, outwardly calm as always, Huan Tsung-Chao replied, "My house in Chengtu was entered last night and important papers stolen from my office. Amongst these documents—for no other valuables are missing—was the Si-Fan Register . . ."

Slowly, Dr. Fu Manchu stood up. His hands were clenched. Yet, when he spoke again, his tones remained unemotional.

"The register is in the Si-Fan cipher, which has never been broken."

"No cipher is unbreakable, Master."

"Spare me your platitudes. But whether the register has been stolen by British or Soviet agents, it cannot be deciphered except by an expert, either in London or in Moscow. Was your safe forced?"

"The register was not in my safe. I kept it in what I believed to be a secret hiding-place. Not even my steward, who sends me this bad news, knew of it."

"You mean," Fu Manchu suggested softly, "that some supernatural agency has been at work?"

Huan Tsung-Chao maintained his phenomenal calm. "I mean that some spy armed with powerful binoculars has watched me through my study window, from a tree in my garden possibly, and has seen me open the receptacle. Entrance was made through this window by someone who silently climbed the vine outside."

Dr. Fu Manchu slipped his hands into the loose sleeves of his robe and stared into space, standing perfectly still. There was a long, silent interval; then he spoke again.

"Why is Skobolov coming *here*?"

"Officially, as an attaché of the Soviet Embassy, to promote relations between Communist China and Soviet Russia. He wishes to meet prominent figures in the Chinese movement."

"But why *here* at your summer villa rather than at the official residence in Chengtu?"

"I frequently entertain here. It is more pleasant, except in winter."

"He is aware that I am here?"

Tsung-Chao smiled his wrinkled smile. "It is improbable—since even I did not know of your arrival in China until you stood at my door."

Fu Manchu remained motionless as a statue. "He has courage. It was he, or a professional thief in his employ, who stole the register. Whilst he is your guest he knows he is safe. We dare not make the attempt. But he will obey his orders and be here tomorrow. We cannot be sure that he has the register in his possession; but whether he has the register or is to meet the man who stole it, he is far too dangerous an enemy to be permitted to return to Moscow. For it is to the Kremlin he would report such a triumph, not to Peiping. André Skobolov must never reach Russia . . .""She has got clear away," said Nayland Smith, "thanks to her bodyguard."

We stood in the library, Smith, myself, Mr Bascombe and Inspector Leighton. Sir James Clare was seated in an armchair watching us. Now he spoke:

"I understand, Smith, why General Quinto came from Africa to the house of his old friend, secretly, and asked me to recall you for a conference. This is a very deep-laid scheme. You are the only man who might have saved him—"

"But I failed."

Nayland Smith spoke bitterly. He turned and stared at me.

"It appears, Kerrigan, that your charming acquaintance who so unfortunately has escaped—I am not blaming you—differs in certain details from Mr Bascombe's recollections of the general's visitor. However, it remains to be seen if they are one and the same."

"You see," the judicial voice of the home secretary broke in, "it is obviously impossible to hush this thing up. A postmortem examination is unavoidable. We don't know what it will reveal. The fact that a very distinguished man, of totally different political ideas from our own, dies here in London under such circumstances is calculated to produce international results. It's deplorable—it's horrible. I cannot see my course clearly."

"Your course, Sir James," snapped Nayland Smith, "is to go home. I will call you early in the morning." He turned. "Mr Bascombe, decline all information to the press."

"What about the dead man, sir?" Inspector Leighton interpolated.

"Remove the body when the loiterers have dispersed. Report to me in the morning, Inspector."

It was long past midnight when I found myself in Sir Denis' rooms in Whitehall. I had not been there for some time, and from my chair I stared across at an unusually elaborate radio set with a television equipment.

"Haven't much leisure for amusement, myself," said Smith, noting the direction of my glance. "Television I had installed purely to amuse Fey! He is a pearl above price, and owing to my mode of life is often alone here for days and nights."

Standing up, I began to examine the instrument. At which moment Fey came in.

"Excuse me, sir," he said, "electrician from firm requests no one touch until calls again, sir."

Fey's telegraphic speech had always amused me. I nodded and sat down, watching him prepare drinks. When he went out:

"Our return journey was quite uneventful," I remarked. "Why?"

"Perfectly simple," Smith replied, sipping his whisky and soda and beginning to load his pipe. "My presence tonight threatened to interfere with the plot, Kerrigan. The plot succeeded. I am no longer of immediate interest."

"I don't understand in the least, Smith. Have you any theory as to what caused General Quinto's death?"

"At the moment, quite frankly, not the slightest. That indefinable perfume is of course a clue, but at present a useless clue. The autopsy may reveal something more. I await the result with interest."

"Assuming it to be murder, what baffles me is the purpose of the thing. The general's idea that he could hear drums rather suggests a guilty conscience in connection with some action of his in Africa—a private feud of some kind."

"Reasonable," snapped Smith, lighting his pipe and smiling grimly. "Nevertheless, wrong."

"You mean"—I stared at him—"that although you don't know *how*—you do know *why* General Quinto was murdered?"

He nodded, dropping the match in an ash tray.

"You know of course, Kerrigan, that Quinto was the right-hand man of Pietro Monaghani. His counsels might have meant an international war."

"It hangs on a hair I agree, and I suppose that Quinto, as Monaghani's chief adviser, might have precipitated a war—"

"Yes—undoubtedly. But what you don't know (nor did I until tonight) is this: General Quinto had left Africa on a mission to Spain. If he had gone I doubt if any power on earth could have preserved international peace! One man intervened."

"What man?"

"If you can imagine Satan incarnate—a deathless spirit of evil dwelling in an ageless body—a cold intelligence armed with knowledge so far undreamed of by science—you have a slight picture of Doctor Fu Manchu."

In my ignorance I think I laughed.

"A name to me—a bogey to scare children. I had never supposed such a person to exist."

"Scotland Yard held the same opinion at one time, Kerrigan. But you will remember the recent suicide of a distinguished Japanese diplomat. The sudden death of Germany's foremost chemist, Erich Schaffer, was front-page news a week ago. Now—General Quinto."

"Surely you don't mean—"

"Yes, Kerrigan, the work of one man! Others thought him dead, but I have evidence to show that he is still alive. If I had lacked such evidence—I should have it now. I forced the general's dispatch box, we failed to find the key. It contained three sheets of note paper— nothing else. Here they are." He handed them to me. "Read them in the order in which I have given them to you."

I looked at the top sheet. It was embossed with a hieroglyphic which I took to be Chinese. The letter, which was undated, was not typed, but written in a squat, square hand. This was the letter:

First notice

The Council of Seven of the Si-Fan has decided that at all costs another international war must be averted. There are only fifteen men in the world who could bring it about. You are one of them. Therefore, these are the Council's instructions: You will not enter Spain but will resign your commission immediately, and retire to your villa in Capri.

PRESIDENT OF THE SEVEN

I looked up.

"What ever does this mean?"

"I take it to mean," Smith replied, "that the first notice which you have read was received by General Quinto in Africa. I knew him, and he knew—as every man called upon to administer African or Asiatic people knows—that the Si-Fan cannot be ignored. The Chinese Tongs are powerful, and there is a widespread belief in the influence of the Jesuits; but the Si-Fan is the most formidable secret society in the world: fully twenty-five per cent of the coloured races belong to it. However, he did not resign his commission. He secured leave of absence and proceeded to London to consult *me*. Somewhere on the way he received the second notice. Read it, Kerrigan."

I turned to the second page which bore the same hieroglyphic and a message in that heavy, definite handwriting. This was the message:

Second notice

The Council of Seven of the Si-Fan would draw your attention to the fact that you have not resigned your commission. Failing your doing so, a third and final notice will be sent to you.

PRESIDENT OF THE SEVEN

I turned to the last page; it was headed *Third Notice* and read as follows:

You have twenty-four hours.

PRESIDENT OF THE SEVEN

"You see, Kerrigan," said Nayland Smith, "it was this third notice"—which must have reached him by district messenger at Sir Malcolm's house—"which produced that state of panic to which Bascombe referred. The Council of Seven have determined to avert war. Their aim must enlist the sympathy of any sane man. But there are fourteen other men now living, perhaps misguided, whose lives are in danger. I have made a list of some of those whose removal in my opinion would bring at least temporary peace to the world. But it's my job at the moment to protect them!"

"Have you any idea of the identity of this Council of Seven?"

"The members are changed from time to time."

"But the president?"

"The president is Doctor Fu Manchu! I would give much to know where Doctor Fu Manchu is tonight—"

And almost before the last syllable was spoken a voice replied:

"No doubt you would like a word with me, Sir Denis . . ."

For once in all the years that I knew him, Smith's iron self-possession broke down. It was then he came to his feet as though a pistol shot and not a human voice had sounded. A touch of pallor showed under the prominent cheekbones. Fists clenched, a man amazed beyond reason, he stared around.

I, too, was staring—at the television screen.

It had become illuminated. It was occupied by an immobile face—a wonderful face—a face that might have served as model for that of the fallen angel. Long, narrow eyes seemed to be watching me. They held my gaze hypnotically.

A murmur, wholly unlike Smith's normal tones, reached my ears . . . it seemed to come from a great distance.

"Good God! *Fu Manchu!*"

296

Chapter V

Yueh Hua broke a long silence.

"Were you educated in Hong Kong, Chi Foh?"

"Yes. Why?"

"I knew you had more education than most fishermen. You are so kind to me."

"Aren't most fishermen kind?"

"Not just like you are."

Yes, he was hamming the part. He had shown her his small stock of un-Chinese provisions and told her that his father, the storekeeper, who knew he had acquired a taste for foreign delicacies, had packed a case for him when he left Hong Kong. She had laughed happily; clapped her hands. But he wondered if she had believed him. Except for the lime juice and the fresh fruit she seemed to prefer the national monotonous rice. But she went for the cigarettes. All the same, Yueh Hua's keen feminine instincts might have detected some chink in the façade. He decided to shift the focus of interest.

"Yueh Hua, there's something I've been wanting to ask you." She lay very still. "Why are you so afraid of the tall man who wears a long cloak, the man they call 'Most High'? Has he ever done you any harm?"

Yueh Hua was so long replying that he turned and looked at her.

"Shall I tell you, Chi Foh?" she asked softly.

"Of course. I want to know."

And as she stared up again at the broken roof of the mat shed, he knew in his bones that she had been trying to make up her mind how far she could trust him and that she had failed to reach a decision. He was sure that whatever she told him now wouldn't be the truth.

"Very well," She seemed to be thinking hard. "When I came away from the house where I thought I should find my sister, it

297

was dark. I didn't know what to do or where to go. I had no money. I was afraid to speak to anyone. And there were soldiers in the streets. I was hiding from two of them in the shadow of a big gateway, when the gate was opened."

She stared fixedly up at the tattered palm roof.

"A tall man came out. He wore a uniform—an officer. Four men came out behind him. One was a black man, very big. He carried a lantern. The light shone on the officer's face, and on his eyes, which were like pieces of green jade. You saw him in the boat. His eyes are like that."

"Yes, I suppose they are."

"I knew he could see me where I was trying to hide. I turned to run. But I was too late. He called me back. You have heard his voice. No one would ever think of disobeying him. He was very gentle when he asked me some questions; but I was shaking so much I could hardly stand. He told me to wait inside the courtyard until he returned."

"And did you wait, Yueh Hua?"

"No. When the porter had locked the gate and gone inside the house, I sat down on a bench and tried to think what to do. There was an old plum tree growing on one of the walls. It had very strong branches. I climbed up. Then I let myself drop on the other side. I tried twice to steal out of the town. But there were soldiers at both gates. Then I thought I would go down to the river and take a boat or try to swim across. Right at the end of the canal I found your sampan."

Tony considered this story with some care. It had at least one merit. It could be true. Yet he felt almost certain it wasn't.

"So you see," Yueh Hua said, "why I am afraid of him."

"Yes, of course." He tried to speak casually. "I suppose he is the Communist governor of the province?"

Yueh Hua shook her head. "No. I think he is something more than that. They treat him like the emperors used to be treated."

"Do you think he wanted you for himself?"

Yueh Hua shuddered visibly.

"I don't know, Chi Foh. But I should die if he even touched me."

Tony then began to realize, as they waited for sundown, that Yueh Hua knew the country well. This was another mark in her

298

favour, for he knew less than nothing at all. His route back was not of his own choosing. On his earlier trip, before he had been captured, he had lost his way a score of times, following promising creeks and canals the loneliness of which had attracted him, only to find himself nearer to the place from which he was coming away. Maps were unobtainable. Inquiries he had found to be both dangerous and useless.

But his big mistake had been in trying to slip past Chia-Ting on a moonlight night. How Nayland Smith had found out that he was in jail there, he had no idea.

"What sort of place is Lung Chang, Yueh Hua?" he asked.

"A small town, Chi Foh."

"Your aunt lives there, you told me?"

"Yes."

"She is married, I suppose?"

"She is a widow. I shall be safe with her."

"Have you other friends there?"

"I expect they have all gone, those I knew. Everything is changed."

After careful consideration, he said, "Lung Chang has gone over to the Communists, I suppose, Yueh Hua?"

"Yes." She passed him a tin cup. "They all had to."

"You mean, they didn't want to?"

"No. Lung Chang for ever so long has been the property of the great Lao clan. The people all belonged to the estate. They were content. Now, they are unhappy."

Yueh Hua was watching him and smiling. It would be unwise to probe deeper, he decided.

"I have to see a man in Niu-fo-Tu. Is it a small place, Yueh Hua?"

"Yes. But there is a market there. I think Niu-fo-Tu is dangerous for us, Chi Foh."

And instinctively he knew she was thinking of the officer with eyes "like pieces of green jade".

They set out towards sundown. By morning, Yueh Hua said, they could reach a canal which connected with a creek. It was rarely used and they could tie up there until it seemed safe to go on.

They sculled and rested in turn through the hours of the night. Sometimes Tony would lean on the long oar and bend forward, looking in to see if Yueh Hua was asleep. At a place where the bank he followed became low, he swung in to a point formed by several small creeks joining the river, forming a little delta carpeted with wild hyacinths.

Yueh Hua woke up as the regular sweep of the oar stopped.

"Is anything the matter, Chi Foh?"

"Yes. I'm thirsty!" he said quickly.

"Shall I make tea?"

"Not unless you want tea. Whisky will do for me. Would you like some?"

"No, thank you. But I should like some lime juice."

They sat and sipped their drinks, diluted with boiled water cooled in an old clay jar. This was a custom Tony followed throughout his journey. He used to do it in Burma and never had a trace of dysentery.

If Yueh Hua wondered about it, she never said so, and he knew that his use of chopsticks was faultless. Yet he often caught her watching him in a queer way.

He was sure of himself where passing acquaintances were concerned. But he hadn't counted on a close intimacy with any bred-in-the-bone Chinese. Almost hourly he found himself wondering if Yueh Hua suspected that he wasn't what he pretended to be . . .

It was a dim hour of the night, but old General Huan Tsung-Chao and Dr. Fu Manchu still remained in conference in the room with the lacquered desk. Apparently, they had conferred there since dusk. Piles of documents littered the desk. General Huan, wearing horn-rimmed spectacles, was reading one of them. He glanced up; began to speak. Dr. Fu Manchu, fingertips pressed together, sat with closed eyes and compressed lips.

"We can rely upon the armed forces in the four provinces adjoining Szechuan. Some seventy-five per cent have joined the Si-Fan. I have a report here from Peiping which states that agents of Free China are securing many recruits, and I have ordered those of these agents who already belong to our Order to make sure of these recruits."

Fu Manchu, still keeping his eyes closed, spoke softly.

"There is a *rapport* between the free Chinese and the Secret Service of which our old friend, Nayland Smith, is an active member. Great caution is necessary. We are not ready. And if our present standing with Peiping should be disturbed—if they lost their confidence in me—our strategy would be badly shaken." His voice sank yet lower. "This loss of the register alarms me. Such evidence, in the hands either of the Allies or of Russia, would destroy us.'

"It is certain that the register could not be in the possession of the man called Wu Chi Foh—and equally certain that he could not have stolen it. He was in prison at the time. I doubt if he is concerned in any way."

"Yet the affair, Tsung-Chao, was so cunningly contrived that some outside agency must have planned it. The escape was brilliantly managed, and the complete disappearance of the man and his boat is phenomenal. Some hiding place had been prepared for him."

General Huan smiled wrily. "This is possible. But he may yet be found. It is now nearing the time when I must prepare to entertain André Skobolov."

"I have already made my preparations." Fu Manchu's soft tones assumed that sibilant character which was something more than a hiss. "I have some choice glossina in my laboratory—a highly successful culture. I shall take steps to ensure his mental incapacity and ultimate death. The symptoms will develop some hours after he leaves here. I selected this method as the most suitable. Mahmûd and a selected party will cover his movements from the moment of his departure. They will take the first possible opportunity to seize any briefcase or other receptacle he may carry. If he has the register, we shall recover it, and if he has notified Moscow, his death, should the body be found, cannot be laid at your door. The trypanosomes which the insects will inject are so amplified that fatal conditions develop in twenty-four to thirty-six hours."

General Huan's wrinkled face, which was not unlike a map of Asia, assumed a troubled expression.

"I agree, although with reluctance, that this man's execution is necessary to our safety, but I do not understand how these insects to which you refer—I am a scientist only of war—are to be employed."

Dr. Fu Manchu opened his eyes, and smiled. It was a deathly smile. He dipped his long fingers in a silver snuff box.

"I, also, have studied the science of war. But my strategy is designed to prevent it—by removing those few who have power to loose upon the world forces of wholesale destruction. It is simple and it is just . . . I have ordered that one of my Cold Men be brought here. He will arrive about dawn. These living-dead, as the ignorant masses term them, are dispensable. And handling the glossina is very dangerous. I shall smoke awhile, Tsung-Chao, and repose; for I have much work to do. Be so good as to send Chung-Wa to prepare my pipe . . ."

Dawn was stealing shyly over the river when Yueh Hua piloted the sampan into the canal. They went up for a mile or more before coming to a place where a gnarled tree hung right over the water, forming a sort of green cover. They tied up under the tree.

It was as Tony was eating his unpalatable breakfast that a slight movement in a field of rape in full yellow bloom drew his attention to the bank. At first he thought he was mistaken. Then he knew he wasn't.

A pair of bright, beady black eyes peered out intently!

Tony stood up, staring under raised hands. And presently, in rapid flight along a path through the five-feet-high rape he saw a tiny boy, naked except for a loincloth.

"Why should he run away, Yueh Hua?"

He saw her face flush.

"He may have been watching us for all sorts of reasons. I suppose he thought you would beat him."

An old rush basket, water-logged and broken, was drifting toward them along the canal. He watched it until it had reached the sampan. Then he pulled it on board.

"If anyone comes to ask questions, Yueh Hua, I shall disappear. Say this is your boat, and say that there has been no one else with you."

"As you wish, Chi Foh. But how are you going to disappear?"

A flight of wild ducks passed overhead. It was the fact that this marshy land teemed with wild fowl which had given him the idea.

"It may not be necessary. If it is, I'll show you."

While Yueh Hua washed the rice bowls, he made a sounding

with the long sweep. He found more than five feet of water in the canal.

He had no sooner completed this than he saw that his disappearance was going to be necessary.

Far off across the fields, on the side to which they were tied up, a small figure, little more than a yellow dot in the distance, came running along an embankment. Two men in uniform followed!

"Yueh Hua!" He spoke quietly. She turned. "Yes, Chi Foh?"

"Remember what we arranged. That little devil of a boy is bringing two soldiers. It's your word against his."

He ducked into the low cabin and came out carrying the pistol. Yueh Hua had seemed alarmed the first time she saw it, but now she smiled bravely and nodded her approval.

Then he managed to pull away the heavy iron pin which did duty as a rowlock. He tied it to a line on which he knotted a loop and threw it overboard. Next, with a piece of string he fastened the automatic around his neck. Last, he went overboard himself, feet first, holding the ground line and the rush basket.

"Oh!" Yueh Hua's eyes danced joyously for one fleeting moment. "Like snaring wild duck."

He grinned cheerfully, although he felt far from cheerful, and hauled on the line until he could get one foot into the loop to steady him. Standing on the bed of the canal, he found that his shoulders were well above water. He waded several yards from the sampan, pulled the old rush basket over his head—and disappeared.

Through the basket's many holes he could see quite well. He unfastened his pistol and held it inside the basket clear of the water line.

If anything went wrong with Yueh Hua's story, he didn't mean to hesitate. There might have to be two casualties in the ranks of the People's Army . . .

The two men and the boy reached the canal bank. The boy was a grubby little cross-eyed specimen. The men were shoddily dressed irregulars of the peasant type. They carried old service revolvers.

"We want to see the man, not you," one of them said.

He seemed to be the senior. The other, deeply pockmarked, stared dumbly at Yueh Hua.

"There's some mistake!" Yueh Hua stood upright, open-eyed. "There's no man on my boat!"

"You are a liar!" the boy piped shrilly.

Tony held his breath.

"And you're an ugly little son of a sow!" Yueh Hua screamed at him. "What lies have you been telling about me? I'm an honest girl. My mother is sick in Chia-Ting and I'm going to nurse her. If my father heard you, he would cut your tongue out!"

"Chia-Ting! Who is your father?" the man asked.

"My father is head jailer at the prison. Only wait until he hears about this!"

This flight of fancy was sheer genius.

"If you're going to Chia-Ting," the boy piped, "what are you doing here?"

"Resting, you mangy little pig! I've come a long way."

She was a virago, a shrill-voiced river girl. Her blue eyes challenged them. But the man who did all the talking still hesitated.

"Ask her—" the boy began.

The man absently gave him a flip on the head which nearly knocked him over.

"We are doing our duty. What is your name?"

"Tsin Gum."

"There is a reward for a prisoner called Wu Chi Foh. He escaped from Chia-Ting."

Tony held his breath again.

"Oh!" Yueh Hua's entire manner changed magically. "My poor father! When anyone escapes he is always punished."

"It is a big reward. You have seen no one?"

"No one. How much is the reward?"

The man hesitated, glancing at his pock-marked companion. "Fifty dollars."

Tony made a rapid mental calculation. Fifty dollars (Chinese) added up to about two dollars and fifty cents American. Beyond doubt, his recapture was worth more than that.

"Fifty dollars? Ooh!" Yueh Hua clapped her hands. "And my father would be so glad. What does he look like, this prisoner?"

"He is rather tall, and pretends to be a fisherman. He is really a dangerous criminal. He is very ugly."

"I will look out for him all the way to Chia-Ting," Yueh Hua promised. "If I find him, will I get the reward there?"

"You haven't searched the cabin!" came the boy's shrill pipe. "And the reward isn't fifty dollars, it's—"

His second, unfinished remark had sealed his fate. He saw this just in time. Turning, he ran like the wind across the rape field.

"Look in the cabin," the senior man directed. Then, meeting a fiery glance from Yueh Hua: "He may have slipped on board," he added weakly.

His pockmarked assistant scrambled clumsily on to the sampan, one eye on Yueh Hua. He looked in under the low, plaited roof, then climbed quickly back to the bank.

"Nobody there."

They turned and walked off.

Yueh Hua rowed when Tony thought it safe to move, and nothing occurred on the way down the canal to suggest that they were watched. When they turned into the creek, Tony saw that the left bank was a mere bamboo jungle. But the right bank showed cultivated land away to the distant hills. It was a charming prospect; acres of poppies, the buds just bursting into dazzling whiteness; for opium cultivation had been renewed in a big way by the Communist government. Beyond, was a small orchard of peach trees lovely in a mantle of pink blossom.

"I'll take the oar, Yueh Hua."

"As you say, Chi Foh. But it is still dangerous."

He took the sweep, and made Yueh Hua rest. He would never be able to understand how those small hands could manage the long oar.

She lay down, and almost immediately fell asleep like a tired child.

Chapter VI

From a guest house in the extensive and beautiful grounds of General Huan's summer residence Dr. Fu Manchu in the grey of dawn watched the approach of two bearers with a stretcher along a winding flower- bordered path. A third man followed. The stretcher was occupied by a motionless figure covered from head to feet with a white sheet.

The young Japanese doctor who had followed, directed the men to a room where there was a rubber-covered couch and to lay the patient on it. This was done, and the bearers, who appeared to be shivering, went away.

And when the Japanese removed the sheet from the motionless body, the action seemed to excite a draft of cold air which sensibly affected the temperature of the room. The man on the stretcher apparently was a dead man. He might have been Burmese, but his normal complexion had become a sort of ghastly grey. The Japanese was feeling for his pulse when Dr. Fu Manchu came in.

"Have you selected a specimen in good condition, Matsukata?"

Matsukata bowed. "Perfect, Excellency. A former dacoit from the Shan hills who was drafted into the Cold Corps for insubordination. He can move as silently as a cat and climb better than any cat. He is one of three who escaped recently and reached the town, creating many undesirable rumours. I selected him for his qualities and have prepared him carefully as you see."

Fu Manchu examined the apparently frozen body, using a stethoscope. He lifted an eyelid and peered into the fishlike eye. He nodded.

"You have prepared him well. This one will serve." He stood upright, glancing at the Japanese. "You were studying the pupils of my own eyes through the powerful lenses of those glasses you wear."

"I feared, Excellency, that you had not slept."

"You are a brilliant diagnostician, Matsukata. *Chandu* is a treacherous friend. Sometimes it stimulates the subconscious memory but does not induce sleep. I smoked last night and lived through incidents as remote as my first meeting, in Burma, with Mr. Commissioner (now Sir Denis) Nayland Smith." He suddenly changed the topic. "You were expecting a report from the lodgemaster in Tokio concerning the progress of our Order in Japan?"

"It is not yet to hand, Excellency."

"No matter. Japan is safe. You may return to the clinic."

Matsukata bowed deeply and went out. . .

More than an hour after Yueh Hua had fallen asleep, Tony found a break in the bamboo wall bordering the creek. He had been hailed only twice from the other bank, and they were friendly hails to which he had replied cheerily. He had passed no other craft.

A narrow stream—little more than a brook—joined the creek, its surface choked with wild lilies. The bamboo jungle faded away inland. There was a sort of miniature bay. Farther up he saw banyan and cypress trees.

This looked the very place to hide the sampan until nightfall.

He swung in, tested the depth of the water and the strength of the lily stems, then pushed a way through. He found himself in a shaded pool, the water deep and crystal clear.

Yueh Hua woke up and prepared a meal, which included the inevitable rice, and tea. As he smoked a cigarette, Tony's eyes began to close.

"Now *you* must rest awhile," Yueh Hua insisted. "I will watch until you're ready to go on. There is an early moon tonight. It will help us to find the way."

And he fell fast asleep with the words, "It will help us to find the way", ringing in his ears like a peal of fairy bells . . .

He had no idea how long he slept, nor what wakened him. But he sat up with a start and looked around.

It was night. The moon hung like a great jewel over the bamboo jungle . . . and he couldn't see Yueh Hua!

He got to his feet, listening, staring to right and left about the pool. He could see no one, hear nothing.

A sense of utter desolation crept over him. He was just going to

307

call out her name. But he checked the cry in time. He crouched back under shelter of the plaited roof and stared, enthralled.

He had seen Yueh Hua.

She was swimming across the pool to a shallow bank on which they had cooked their dinner. Part of it was brightly and coldly lighted. The other part lay in shadow.

He saw her walk ashore and stand, wringing water from her dark hair. Then, she stretched her arms above her head and looked up at the sky as he had seen her do before. But that had been Yueh Hua, the river girl. This was Moon Flower, the goddess of night.

Her agility and grace he had noted. He had never suspected that she had so slimly beautiful a body, such smooth, ivory skin and perfect limbs.

He almost ceased to breathe.

When Yueh Hua came back to the sampan after her bath, he pretended to be asleep, and let her wake him.

But the light touch of her hand affected him strangely . . .

On the way to Niu-fo-Tu he tried to conquer a sense of awkward restraint which had come over him. He felt guilty. He rarely met Yueh Hua's glance, for he was afraid she would read his secret in his eyes.

Surely no river girl was ever shaped like that?

He rowed furiously, pushing the sampan ahead as if competing in a race.

The river, when he came to it, gleamed deserted in the moonlight. The current favoured him, and he made good going. He passed a tied-up junk but there seemed to be nobody on board, or nobody on watch. He couldn't see if Yueh was asleep, but she lay very still. A slight breeze rattled the junk's sails, making a sound like dry palm fronds in a high wind.

"Chi Foh!"

She was awake.

"Yes, Yueh Hua?"

"We have to look out for lights. Then we have to cross to the other bank and find the creek which will take us behind Niu-fo-Tu. We mustn't miss it."

Remembering his experience at Chia-Ting, Tony had no intention of missing it.

"Are there soldiers there, Yueh Hua?"

"No. At least, I don't think so."

"A jail?"

"No." She laughed, that musical laugh. "Criminals have to be sent up to Chia-Ting."

"And that, then, is where your father takes care of them?"

He rowed on. He knew Yueh Hua was watching him, and presently:

"Were you angry with me for being such a liar?" she asked.

"Don't be silly, Yueh Hua! I never admired you more."

"Oh."

He had said too much. Or said it the wrong way. She had spoken the "Oh" like a wondering sigh.

He decided on a policy of silence. And Yueh Hua didn't speak again. The river swept round in a long, flattened curve. Tony detected faintly a twinkling light ahead.

"Is that Niu-fo-Tu, Yueh Hua?"

"No." She hesitated. "I think it must be another junk."

So she had been awake all the time!

"I hope they are all asleep!"

"Let me row, Chi Foh. It is better. Don't risk being seen."

He wavered for a moment, then gave way and passed the oar over to her.

Navigation called for little but steering. The current carried them along. He crouched out of sight, watching Yueh Hua handle the long sweep with an easy grace he had never acquired. Beyond doubt, she had been born on the river.

She gave the junk as wide a berth as possible. If anybody was awake, it was someone who paid no attention. They passed unchallenged. Yueh Hua stayed at the oar, and Tony sat studying her, a silhouette against the moonlight, as she swayed rhythmically to and fro. They were silent for a long time, until she checked her rowing and stared intently ahead.

"Niu-fo-Tu!" she said. "Somewhere here we turn off."

General Huan personally conducted André Skobolov to the apartment in his country residence reserved for distinguished guests.

The Russian agent, a native of a Far Eastern province, had

marked Mongolian features and spoke almost flawless Chinese. He had requested his host to invite no other guests to meet him, as he wished to talk business and to avoid attention. He was travelling by unfrequented roads, he explained, as he had many contacts in out-of-the-way places.

He had been entertained in a manner which recalled the magnificence of pre-Communist days, a fact upon which he congratulated General Huan so warmly that that monument of cunning knew that Skobolov suspected his loyalty to the present régime.

The "business" which Skobolov discussed introduced the names of so many members of the Order of the Si-Fan that the old strategist began to wonder if Skobolov might be an expert cryptographer who had already broken the cipher in which the Si- Fan Register was written. He had carefully inspected the visitor's light baggage and had noted a large briefcase which Skobolov kept with him even during dinner. The Russian had apologized, explaining that it contained dispatches and must never be out of his sight.

General Huan bade André Skobolov good-night, regretting that some other method could not have been found to silence him; for he had a soldier's respect for brave men.

Skobolov, when the door had closed, placed the briefcase under his pillow and once more, as he had already done on his arrival, checked every item of his baggage, locked the door, examined the window which opened on a balcony overlooking the beautiful gardens, and reexamined every compartment of a large and priceless lacquered cabinet which was set against one wall.

He did this so carefully, with the aid of a flashlamp that Dr. Fu Manchu, who was watching his every movement through a spy-hole in a part of the cabinet which formed the back of a closet in an adjoining room, was compelled to close the aperture.

Such devices for ensuring the comfort of guests were known in China long before the days of the Borgias.

When Skobolov, who had dined and wined well, finally retired, the spacious double room became dark except for furtive moon-beams stealing through the windows.

There was a brief silence, presently broken by the snores of the sleeping man.

Fu Manchu flashed a signal from the next room and returned to his observation post at the back of the closet.

He had watched and listened no longer than half a minute when the shadow of a man swept down past the moonlighted window and temporarily vanished. A moment later, the shadow reappeared as the man outside stood slowly upright. He had dropped from the roof to the balcony silent as a panther.

A nearly soundless manipulation, and the window opened. Although the night was warm, this resulted in a draught of cold air penetrating the room, perceptible even at the spy-hole.

The ghostly figure of the Cold Man became visible briefly in moonlight. His body, as well as his face, had an unearthly grey tinge. He wore only a grey loincloth. His eyes were lifeless as the eyes of a dead fish. He carried what looked like a small cage covered with gauze. Gliding nearer to the sleeping Skobolov, he removed the gauze.

A high, dim buzzing sound became audible in the suddenly chilly room.

The Cold Man, carrying the cage, crept back to the window, climbed out, and closed it. The keen ears of Dr. Fu Manchu heard a dull thud far below. The Cold Man had dropped from the balcony to the garden—where the Japanese, Matsukata, awaited him.

Dr. Fu Manchu watched and listened.

The high-pitched droning ceased by degrees . . . and suddenly the sleeper awoke.

Came a torrent of Russian curses, a sound of slapping . . . Skobolov was out of bed, the ray of his flashlamp shining now right, now left, now down below. With a slipper he began to kill flies, of which there seemed to be a number in the room, chasing them wherever that faint, high note led him.

When, at last, he had killed all he could find, shuddering coldly, he opened a bag and took out a tube of ointment which he began to rub on to his face, neck and arms.

Dr. Fu Manchu closed the little trap, smiling his mirthless smile . .

311

Chapter VII

It was a long way up the creek to the canal behind Niu-fo-Tu. And having found it, Tony had to go on for another mile or more before finding a suitable mooring where they might safely tie up. Dawn was very near by the time they made fast.

After a scant breakfast, he made Yueh Hua promise not to leave the boat until he returned. Reluctantly, she did so, and Tony set out.

He found a road lined with cypress trees which evidently led to the town. Already the sun was very warm. It promised to be a hot day. Soon he found himself in the shadow of one of several memorial arches which spanned the road outside the gate. Not without misgivings, for he was a marked man, he pressed on.

Entering the town, he saw the market place directly on his right, and the stalls of dealers in everything from sugar cane, water chestnuts, pork and pumpkins to clothing and millet whisky.

As he turned in, for he expected to get information here, a rickshaw coolie came out and nearly knocked him down. A fat Chinese woman smoking a cigarette sat in the rickshaw. The wife of some sort of official, he judged.

"Why don't you look where you're going?" she snapped at him.

He lowered his head humbly and passed on.

An old woman selling preserved duck stuck on long sticks and other Chinese hors d'œuvres, gave him a toothless grin.

"There she goes! See what it is to be the wife of a jailer!"

"A jailer, Mother?"

"Don't you know her? Her husband is head jailer at Chia-Ting! Give me the old days!"

Head jailer at Chia-Ting! The leering brute who used to gloat over his misery! The man Yueh Hua had claimed as her father!

Yueh Hua's instincts hadn't misled her. Niu-fo-Tu was dangerous.

312

"Can you tell me the way to the house of the Lama?" he asked.

"You can't miss it, son. Straight up the main street. The second turning on the right, and his house faces you."

He bought two of her smelly delicacies and returned to the main street.

It was just possible to see part of the waterfront, sails and masts of junks. Then, he saw the fat woman in the rickshaw. She was talking to an excited boy who stood beside her.

This time, his heart really seemed to miss a beat.

It was the cross-eyed little monster Tony had thought, and prayed, they had shaken off!

Under other circumstances he might have admired the deductive powers of this young Chinese Sherlock. As things stood, he could cheerfully have strangled him.

He must make a decision—and swiftly.

The group was some distance away down the narrow, crowded street. But even so, he heard the shrill voice of the fat woman.

"Impudent liar! My daughter indeed! My husband will flog the skin off her back!"

Tony cast one swift, longing glance toward the gate, and as he did so, Mahmûd, Dr. Fu Manchu's giant bodyguard, came in!

Instinctively, Tony swung around, forced his way through a surge of people hurrying in the direction of the disturbance, and plunged into a narrow and odorous alley on the right which would lead him from the point of danger. Some heads craned from windows, but they were all turned in the direction of the main street.

He cursed the hour that he had entered Niu-fo-Tu . . . for now, from behind, he heard a renewed uproar and detected the words, "Escaped prisoner! Reward . . ."

Swift footsteps were following him. To run would be to betray himself. But he knew that his life hung in the balance. He went on walking fast. The following footsteps drew nearer still. A hand touched his shoulder.

"Have you seen a man with a crutch?" came a crisp inquiry.

The password! Gulping in his relief, Tony gave the countersign: "What is the name of his crutch?"

He twisted around. The speaker was a Buddhist lama, his head closely shaved; he wore horn-rimmed glasses. The proper reply was "Freedom". But the monk gave another.

"Nayland Smith!" he snapped and went on in English, "I wasn't sure, McKay, but, thank God! I was right. Your disguise is perfect. Keep calm, and keep walking. I came to look for you. Don't bother to say anything. Look! We're in another street. Walk on left two blocks and the lama's house is right opposite. Jump to it! It's urgent!"

Giving Tony's arm a reassuring squeeze, Nayland Smith turned and hurried back along the way they had come.

Tony gave a parting glance to the tall figure, then turned left and hurried along the narrow street. He passed the first alley he came to, reached the second and pulled up, staring anxiously at the house indicated.

It was an old house, the front quaintly decorated, and as he slipped into a small passage, immediately he noticed a smell of incense.

The passage was very dark. He began to walk quietly along. As his eyes became used to this gloom, he saw two doors ahead. The one directly before him was closed. The other, on the right, was open a few inches, and light showed through the cranny.

Walking on tiptoe, he reached it, hesitated . . .

"Please come in," a pleasant old voice invited, speaking a pure Chinese of a kind he rarely heard.

He pushed the door open.

He was in a room furnished as a library. Shelves were packed with scrolls of parchment and bound books. There was a shrine directly facing the door. Incense burned in a bronze bowl. And squatting behind a long, low table on which a yellow manuscript was spread, he saw a very old man who wore just such a lama robe as that which Nayland Smith had worn.

The old man removed his spectacles and looked up. Tony found himself being analysed by a pair of eyes which seemed—like the dreadful eyes of Fu Manchu—to read his thoughts. But these were kindly eyes.

There was a wooden stool near the door. He sat down, and listened for sounds from the street. He had to say something.

"Your door was open, Excellency—"

"My door is always open to those who may need me. Nor have I achieved excellency, my son."

Tony became tongue-tied.

"I perceive," the gentle voice went on, "that you are in some urgent danger. Give me the facts, and leave it to me to decide if I may justly help you."

"There are people out there who want to arrest me."

This confession was considered quietly.

"Have you committed any crime?"

"No, my father. My only crime is that I tried to help China, where I was born."

Then the lama smiled again and said an unexpected but welcome thing.

"Have you seen a man with a crutch?"

Tony jumped up in his glad excitement.

"What is the name of his crutch?" he asked hoarsely.

"Freedom, my son. You are welcome." He began to speak almost faultless English. "You are Captain McKay, for whom Sir Denis Nayland Smith is searching."

"By God's mercy, he found me out there and saved me from the mob!"

"He felt responsible for your safety. I hope he will join us shortly. No one saw you together?"

"I believe and hope not. A big Nubian, who is personal bodyguard of the man you call 'The Master' and who knows me, has just come into the town."

"Has he seen you?"

"Not to my knowledge. But there's a boy—"

He got no further. Splitting the perfumed quiet of the room, came uproar: "Escaped prisoner! . . . Search all the houses! . . . Reward for whoever . . ."

Tony felt the sharp pang of despair. A group had gathered just outside the house. The old lama raised his hand.

"Pray don't disturb yourself, my son."

He stood up. He proved to be much taller than Tony had judged. There was quiet dignity in his bearing. He went out, leaving the door ajar. Tony reached it in one stride and stood there, breathlessly listening.

Communist China might be irreligious, but the old beliefs still swayed the masses. On the babel outside fell sudden silence. It was broken by the gentle voice.

"What troubles you, my children?"

A chorus replied. There was a dangerous criminal hiding in the town. They were going to search all the houses.

"As you please. Search by all means—but not here. There is no criminal, dangerous or otherwise, in my house. And you are interrupting my studies."

Tony heard him coming back. He heard mutterings outside as well. But when the lama re-entered the room his calm remained unruffled.

"My door is still open. But no one will come in."

"You have great courage, father—and I thank you."

The priest returned to his place behind the low table.

"Courage is a myth. There are only faith and doubt. Nor have you cause to thank me. You owe me nothing. If what I do has merit then mine is the debt to you."

Tony dropped back on the stool, conscious of perspiration on his forehead. The noise of the crowd outside faded away. But, almost immediately, came a swift step along the passage and Nayland Smith walked in. He nodded to Tony and addressed the old lama in English.

"Dr. Li Wu Chang, you are a magician. I was on the fringe of the crowd outside and heard you dismiss them. Those people would eat out of your hand!"

"Because they know, Sir Denis, that I never told them a lie."

"Misdirection is an art." Nayland Smith grinned at Tony. "I prefer to call it magic!"

"Between you," Tony burst out, "you have surely saved my life. But what do I do now?"

"First," snapped Nayland Smith, "reverting to the last report I had before you were compelled to scrap your walkie-talkie. You explored some village on the pretext of looking for a mythical relative, or somebody. Sound strategy. Confirmation of your story, if questioned. You reported that you came across a large barbed-wire enclosure on the outskirts, with several buildings, resembling isolation hospital. Guards. You retired unobserved. Remember?"

"Clearly."

"What was the name of this village?"

Tony clutched his head, thought hard, and then: "Hua-Tzu," he said.

"Good," came the gentle voice of the lama. "As I suspected. That is the Soviet research plant!"

Nayland Smith, a strange figure with his shaven skull and monk's robe, clapped Tony on the shoulder. "Sound work! And have you fathomed the identity of the Master?"

"I have. He cross-examined me in jail! The Master is Dr. Fu Manchu!"

Half an hour later, wearing a new outfit and a bamboo hat, supplied by the lama, the size of a car tyre, and bending under a load of lumber, Tony set out along a narrow track formed by a dried-up ditch which ran at the foot of the lama's little garden. It joined the canal not far from the sampan.

He was sweating, his new suit soiled, when he broke out on to the bank above the boat.

"Yueh Hua! Yueh Hua!"

There was no reply.

"Yueh Hua!"

He couldn't keep a sudden terror out of his voice as he jumped on board.

Then he dropped down and buried his face in his hands.

He had saved himself.

They had caught Moon Flower.

That abominable boy must have seen the boat and raced into the town to report it.

A wave of madness swept over him. He heard again the shrill voice of the fat wife of the jailer. He knew what Yueh Hua's fate would be. And he had left her to it.

There was a mist before his eyes. He clenched his teeth, tried to think.

He leaped ashore like a madman and began to run. He had reached the road when he stopped running and dropped into a slow walk. Sanity, of sorts, was returning.

Why, as he still remained free, had no watch been posted over the sampan?

If only he could think clearly. He had avoided any reference to Yueh Hua during his interview with Nayland Smith and the lama. He was too sensitive on the subject to have faced the embarrassment of such an explanation, the quizzical smile of Sir Denis. So although he had another of the remarkable walkie-talkies and could easily get in touch with him in any emergency, the present emergency was one in which that resourceful man couldn't be consulted.

So he must handle this situation alone.

He kept on his way toward the town. His huge hat and new clothes altered his appearance, but he was sure, by now, that his enemies would be hard to deceive.

Along the road ahead, he began to count the trees: One-two-three, up to seven, then straining his eyes, looking for the little figure.

In his sorrow and fury, he had thought of a lone-hand rescue of Yueh Hua from wherever they had her locked up, saw himself shooting a way out in the best Western tradition. But, even had this wild plan succeeded, they were still many miles behind the second Bamboo Curtain. It was certain they would never get through alive.

Head down, he thought miserable thoughts as he walked past a bend in the tree-lined road. Then he looked up unhappily and began counting again—One-two-three- four-five . . .

He stood still, as if checked by a blow in the face.

A small figure was hurrying along ahead, making for the town!

As if the sound of his racing footsteps had been a dreaded warning, the figure suddenly turned aside, and disappeared among the banks of golden grain.

Wondering if he was going mad, if grief had led to illusion, he ran on until he came to the spot, as well as he could judge, where the disappearance had taken place, He stood, panting, and staring into a golden sea, billowing softly in a slight breeze.

He could find no track, see no broken stalks. Nothing stirred, except those gentle waves which passed over the sunny yellow sea.

"Yueh Hua!" he shouted hoarsely. "Yueh Hua! This is Chi Foh!"

And then the second illusion took place. Like a dark little Venus arising from golden foam, Yueh Hua stood up—not two yards from the road!

She stretched out her arms.

"Chi Foh! Chi Foh! I didn't know it was you . . . thought they . . . I was going to look for you . . ."

Trampling ripe grain under his feet, Tony ran to her. Tears were streaming down her face. Her eyes shone like blue jewels.

"Moon Flower! my Moon Flower!"

He swept her close. His cry of welcome was almost a sob. Her heart beat against him like a hammer as he began to kiss her. He kissed her until she lay breathless in his arms . . .

Chapter VIII

Dr. Fu Manchu moved a switch, and a spot of blue light disappeared from a small switchboard on the lacquered desk. He looked at General Huan, seated on a couch facing him across the room.

"Skobolov has reached Niu-fo-Tu," he said softly; "so Mahmûd reports. It is also suspected that the man Wu Chi Foh was seen there today. But this rumour is unconfirmed. It is possible—for we have no evidence to the contrary—that Wu Chi Foh has a rendezvous there with Skobolov, that, after all, Wu Chi Foh is a Communist agent."

Huan Tsung-Chao shook his head slightly. "This I doubt, Master, but I admit it may be so. As Skobolov is closely covered, should they meet, Mahmûd, who knows this man, will take suitable steps."

The conversation was interrupted.

Uttering a shrill whistling sound, a tiny marmoset which had been hiding on a high ledge sprang like a miniature acrobat from there to Fu Manchu's shoulder and began chattering angrily in his ear. The saturnine mask of that wonderful but evil face softened, melted into something almost human.

"Ah, Peko, my little friend! You are angry with me? Yet I have small sweet bananas flown all the way from Madeira for you. Is it a banana you want?"

Peko went on spitting and cursing in monkey language.

"Some nuts?"

Peko's language was dreadful.

"You are teasing him," General Huan smiled. "He is asking for his ration of my 1850 vintage rose wine which, ever since he tasted it, he has never forgotten."

Peko sprang from Fu Manchu's shoulder on to the rug-covered floor, from there on to the shoulder of Huan. The old soldier raised his gnarled hand to caress Peko, a strange creature which he knew to be of incalculable age.

Dr. Fu Manchu stood up, crossed to a cabinet, and took out a stoppered jar of old porcelain. With the steady hand of a pharmacist, he poured a few drops into a saucer; restoppered the jar. Peko rejoined him with a whistle not of anger, but of joy, grasped the saucer and drank deep.

Then, the uncanny little animal sprang on to the desk and began to toss manuscripts about in a joyous mood. Dr. Fu Manchu picked him up, gently, and put him on his shoulder.

"You are a toper, Peko. And I'm not sure that it is good for you. I am going to put you in your cage."

Peko escaped and leapt at one bound on to the high ledge.

"Such is the discipline," murmured Dr. Fu Manchu, "of one of my oldest servants. It was Peko to whom I first administered my elixir, the elixir to which he and I owe our presence amongst men today. Did you know this, my friend?"

"I did."

Fu Manchu studied Huan Tsung-Chao under lowered eyelids.

"Yet you have never asked me for this boon."

"I have never desired it, Master. Should you at any time observe some failure in my capacity to serve you, please tell me so. I belong to a long-lived family. My father married his sixth wife at the age of eighty."

Dr. Fu Manchu took a pinch of snuff from a box on the desk. He began to speak, slowly, incisively.

"I have learned since my return to China that Dr. von Wehrner is the chief research scientist employed here by the Soviet. I know his work. Within his limitations, it is brilliant. But the fools who employ him will destroy the world—and all my plans—unless I can unmask and foil their schemes. Von Wehrner is the acknowledged authority on pneumonic plague. This is dangerously easy to disseminate. Its use could nearly depopulate the globe. For instance, I have a perfected preparation in my laboratory now, a mere milligramme of which could end human life in Szechuan in a week."

"This is not war," General Huan said angrily. "It is mass assassination."

Fu Manchu made a slight gesture with one long, sensitive hand. "It must never be. For several years I have had an impalpable powder which can be spread in many ways—by the winds, by individ-

321

ual deposits. A single shell charged with it and exploded over an area hundreds of miles in extent, would bring to the whole of its human inhabitants nearly instant death."

"But you will never use it

"It would reduce the area to an uninhabitable desert. No living creature could exist there. What purpose would this serve? How could you, General, with all your military genius, occupy this territory?"

Huan Tsung-Chao spread his palms in a helpless gesture. "I have lived too long, Master. This is not a soldier's world. Let them close all their military academies. The future belongs to chemists."

Dr. Fu Manchu smiled his terrible smile.

"The experiments of those gropers who seek, not to improve man's welfare, but to blot out the human race, are primitive, barbaric, childish. I have obtained complete control of one of the most powerful forces in the universe. Sound. With sound I can throw an impenetrable net over a whole city, or, if I wish, over only a part of it. No known form of aerial attack could penetrate this net. With sound I could blot out every human being in Peiping, Moscow, London, Paris or Washington, or in selected areas of those cities. For there are sounds inaudible to human ears which can destroy. I have learned to produce these lethal sounds."

Old General Huan bowed his head. "I salute the world's master mind. I know of this discovery. Its merit lies in the simple fact that such an attack would be confined to the target area and would not create a plague to spread general disaster."

"Also," Dr. Fu Manchu added, "it would enable your troops to occupy the area immediately. So that Othello's occupation would not be gone . . ."

The sampan seemed like sanctuary when Tony and Yueh Hua reached it. But they knew that it wasn't.

"We dare not stay here until sunset, Chi Foh. They are almost sure to search the canal."

She lay beside him, her head nestled against his shoulder. He stroked her hair. Tony knew he had betrayed himself when he had called out in his mad happiness, "Moon Flower"—in *English*! But, if

Yueh Hua had noticed, she had given no sign. Perhaps, in her excitement, she had not heard the revealing words.

"I know," he said. "I expect they are looking for us now. But what can we do?"

"If we could reach Lung Chang we should be safe—" she spoke dreamily—"It is not far to Lung Chang."

He nodded. Oddly enough, Nayland Smith's instructions had been for him to abandon his boat and hurry overland to Lung Chang! He was to report there to a certain Lao Tse-Mung, a contact of Sir Denis's and a man of influence.

"What I think we should do, Chi Foh, is to go on up this canal and away from the river. They are not likely to search in that direction. If we can find a place to hide until nightfall, then we could start for Lung Chang, which is only a few miles inland."

Tony considered this programme. He laughed and kissed Yueh Hua. This new happiness, with fear of a dreadful death overhanging them, astonished him.

"What should I do without you, Yueh Hua?"

They started without delay. It was very hot, and Tony welcomed his large sun hat, gift of the lama. He worked hard, and Yueh Hua insisted upon taking her turn at the oar. There was no evidence of pursuit. The rich soil of this fertile plain, called "the Granary of Szechuan", was now largely given over to the cultivation of opium poppies, offering a prospect of dazzling white acres where formerly crops of grain had flourished.

Nothing but friendly greetings were offered by workers in the fields. Evidently the hue and cry for an escaped prisoner had not reached this agricultural area. In the late afternoon Yueh Hua found a perfect spot to tie up; a little willow-shadowed creek.

There was evidence, though, that they were near a village, for through the trees they could see a road along which workers were trudging homeward from the fields.

"It will do," Tony agreed, "for we shall never be noticed here. But presently I'm going to explore a little way to try to find out just where we are."

When they had moored the sampan they shared a scanty and dull meal, made more exciting by a seasoning of kisses, and Tony went ashore to take a look around.

He discovered that they lay not more than a few hundred yards from the village, which only a screen of bamboos concealed from them. It was an insignificant little group of dwellings, but it boasted an inn of sorts which spanned the road along which they had seen the peasants walking homeward. He returned and reported this to Yueh Hua.

"I think we should start for Lung Chang at once," she advised. "The fields are deserted now, and soon dusk will come. I believe I can find the way if we go back a mile or so nearer to Niu-fo-Tu."

Tony loved her more and more every hour they were together. Her keen intelligence made her a wonderful companion. Her beauty, which he had been so slow to recognise, had completely conquered him.

"Let's wait a little while longer, Yueh Hua," he said yearningly. "I want to tell you how much I love you." He took her in his arms. "Kiss me while I try . . ."

He tried so hard that dusk was very near when Yueh Hua sighed, "My dear one, it is time we left here!"

Tony reluctantly agreed. They pushed the boat out again to the canal and swung around to head back toward Niu-fo-Tu. He was so happy in this newly found delight whose name was Moon Flower that the dangers ahead seemed trivial.

Tony had dipped the blade of the oar and was about to begin work when he hesitated, lifted the long sweep, and listened.

Someone was running down to the canal, forcing a way through undergrowth, and at the same time uttering what sounded like breathless sobs! It was a man, clearly enough, and a man in a state of blind panic.

"Chi Foh!" Yueh Hua spoke urgently. "Be quick! We must get away! Do you hear it?"

"Yes. I hear it. But I don't understand."

A gasping cry came. The man evidently had sighted the boat. "Save me! Help, boatman!"

Then, Tony heard him fall, heard his groans. He swung the boat into the bank. "Take the oar, Yueh Hua, while I see what's wrong here."

Yueh Hua grasped him. "Chi Foh! You are mad! It may be a trap. We know we are followed—"

324

Gently, he broke away. "My dearest—give me my gun—you—you know where it is. If this man is in distress I'm not going to desert him."

From the locker Yueh Hua brought the automatic. She was trembling excitedly. Tony knew that it was for his safety, not for her own, that she trembled. He kissed her, took the pistol, and jumped ashore.

Groans, muffled hysterical words, led him to the spot. He found a semi-dressed figure writhing in a tangle of weeds two to three feet high, a short, thickset man of Slavonic type, and although not lacking in Mongolian characteristics, definitely not Chinese. He was clutching a bulging briefcase. He looked up.

"A hundred dollars to take me to Huang Ko-Shu!" he groaned. "Be quick!"

Tony dragged the man to his feet. He discovered that his hands were feverishly hot. "Come on board. I can take you part of the way."

He half carried the sufferer, still clutching his leather case, on to the sampan.

"Chi Foh, you are mad!" was Yueh Hua's greeting. "What are we to do with him?"

"Put him ashore somewhere near Niu-fo-Tu. He's very ill."

He dragged the unwanted passenger under the mat roof and took to the oar.

But, again, he hesitated—although only for a moment.

There were cries, running footsteps, swiftly approaching from the direction of the hidden village . . .

Chapter IX

Tony drove the sampan at racing speed. He could only hope that they had been out of sight before the party evidently in pursuit of their passenger had reached the canal.

The banks were deserted. Moonlight transformed poppy fields into seas of silver. When, drawing near to Niu-fo-Tu, grain succeeded poppy, the prospect became even more fairy-like. It was a phantom journey, never to be forgotten, through phantom landscapes. Willows bordering the canal were white ghosts on one bank, black ghosts on the other.

Yueh Hua crouched beside him. The man they had rescued had apparently gone mad. He struck out right and left in his delirium, slapping his face and hands as if tormented by a swarm of mosquitoes.

"Chi Foh," Yueh Hua whispered, "he is very ill. Could it be—" she hesitated—"that he has the *plague?*"

"No, no! don't think such things. He shows no signs of having the plague. Take the oar for a few minutes, my dearest. He must want water."

"Oh, Chi Foh!"

But Tony clasped her reassuringly and ducked in under the low roof. He was far from confident, himself, about what ailed the mystery passenger, but common humanity demanded that he should do his best for him.

The man sipped water eagerly; he was for ever trying to drive away imaginary flying things which persecuted him. His head rested on his bulky briefcase. His hectic mutterings were in a language which Tony didn't know. To questions in Chinese he made no reply. Once only he muttered, "Huang-ko-Shu."

Tony returned to Yueh Hua. "Tell me, where is Huang-ko-Shu?"

"It is on the Yangtse River—many miles below Niu-fo-Tu."

"I told him I would take him part of the way," Tony murmured. "We must put him ashore this side of Niu-fo-Tu."

"I wish we had never found him," Yueh Hua whispered, giving up the oar to Tony . . .

They retraced the route by which they had come. Tony insisted on doing most of the rowing, and was getting near to exhaustion.

The countryside showed deserted.

"Let me take the oar," Yueh Hua said gently, but insistently. "There is not far to go now and I can manage it easily. You must, Chi Foh."

He gave in. He watched Yueh Hua at the long sweep, swinging easily to its movement with the lithe grace of a ballerina. What a girl!

Tony found it hard to keep awake. The man they had rescued had stopped raving; become quite silent. The gentle movement of the boat, the rhythmic swish of the long oar, did their hypnotic work. He fell asleep . . .

"Chi Foh!" Yueh Hua's voice. "Wake up. I am afraid!"

Tony was wide-awake before she ceased speaking. He drew her down to him. She was trembling. "Where are we? What's happened?"

He looked around in the darkness. The boat was tied up in a silent backwater. Through the motionless leaves of an overhanging tree which looked like a tree carved in ebony, he could see the stars.

"We are just above the place where we tied up before, Chi Foh. You remember the footbridge over the canal? There's a path from the bridge which leads to a main road—the road to Lung Chang." Yueh Hua caught her breath. "But . . . the man is dead!"

Tony got to his feet. He had a flashlamp in the locker; groped his way to it, found it, and shone its light on to the man who lay there.

Beyond doubt, Yueh Hua was right. Their passenger was dead. Yueh Hua knew that Tony had an automatic pistol, but he had hidden the flashlamp. He wondered if she would say something about it, tried to think of an explanation. But she said nothing.

Tony searched the man's scanty clothing, but found no clue to his identity. In a body belt, which he unfastened, there was a considerable sum of money, but nothing else. The big portfolio was locked, and there was no key. So far he had gone when Yueh Hua called out:

"Throw him overboard, Chi Foh! He may have died of plague!"

But Tony, who had a smattering of medical knowledge, knew that he had not died of plague. Of what he had died he didn't know, but he did know that it wasn't of plague.

"Don't worry, Yueh Hua. I told you before, there's no question of plague. I must try to find out who he was."

He went to work on the lock of the briefcase and ultimately succeeded in breaking it. He found it stuffed with correspondence in Russian, a language of which he knew nothing, much of it from the Kremlin and some from the Peiping Embassy; this fact clearly indicated by the embossed headings of the stationery. The man was a Soviet agent!

There was also a bound book containing a number of manuscript pages in Chinese, which, although he knew written Chinese, Tony was unable to decipher.

He put the book and the correspondence back in the broken briefcase and dropped the briefcase in the locker.

His walkie-talkie was there, too, carefully wrapped up. This was an occasion on which he desperately wanted to ask for Nayland Smith's advice. If only he dared to take Yueh Hua into his confidence! He no longer doubted her loyalty. She had given him her love. But she was Chinese, and he hated the thought of breaking this idyll by confessing that he was an impostor, an American posing as one of her countrymen.

It was an impasse. He must rely upon his own common sense.

The body of the dead Russian must be disposed of. This was clear enough. When it was found (and eventually it would be found), the evidence must suggest that he had fallen into the hands of thieves who had taken whatever he had had in his possession. Therefore— the money belt must not be found on him.

Having come to these conclusions, Tony switched off the flash-lamp and rejoined Yueh Hua, who was watching him, wide-eyed.

"Is it a straight road to Lung Chang?"

"There are no straight roads in China."

He forced a laugh, and kissed her. "All the better for us. Somewhere near by, I am going to throw the dead man overboard."

"That is right," Yueh Hua agreed. "We need not carry much.

When we get to Lung Chang, my aunt will take care of us. But"—she drew back—"you will lose your boat!"

Tony was baffled. "I must take a chance. I have some money left . . . or I might steal another sampan, as you meant to steal mine!"

He pushed the boat out of the little backwater and on to the canal. Yueh Hua, he knew, was unusually highly strung. She watched him in a queer way he didn't like. Just by the bridge he stopped rowing.

"Look the other way, Yueh Hua. I'm going to dump him here."

Some hazy idea that prayers should be said at such a time flashed through his mind. He dismissed the idea. It was impracticable, in the first place. In the second, the dead man, as a Soviet Communist, was an atheist. He dragged the half-clad body out and dropped it in the canal.

"May God have mercy on your soul," he whispered.

Tony forced a laugh. "So this is where we say goodbye to our boat. It's too shallow to sink it here. We shall have to take a chance, and just leave it."

"Oh, Chi Foh, my dear!" She threw her arms around him. "Your poor little boat—and we have been so happy on it."

Tony loved her for the words, but immediately became practical again.

"We'll drop whatever we don't want overboard and pack up the rest. I can carry two bundles on this bamboo rod and you can carry what's left in the old basket . . ."

There were tears in Yueh Hua's eyes as she looked back at the deserted sampan. But she said nothing, and, Yueh Hua going ahead as arranged, and Tony following, still adorned with his huge bamboo hat, they started on the last leg of their journey to Lung Chang.

The road, when they came to it, didn't look particularly dangerous, except to motorists. One thing was certain. At that hour, it carried little traffic. On the straight stretches, Tony allowed Yueh Hua to go ahead as far as he could keep her in sight. At bends, she slowed down until he drew nearer.

He had plenty of opportunity for thinking. Yueh Hua, he knew, had become an indispensable part of his life. He didn't mean to lose her, whatever she was, where ever she came from.

Even if this added up to changing his career, he would marry her. He could live with Yueh Hua on a desert island, and be happy. She could be happy, too. She had proved it.

He heard an automobile coming swiftly from behind!

Stepping to the side of the neglected road, he let it go by. He was only just in time. It passed at racing speed—a new Buick. He never had a glimpse of the driver. Such speed, on such a road, betrayed urgency.

Yueh Hua was waiting for him by a bend ahead. He saw that she was frightened.

"In that car! . . . The man with green eyes! The big black was driving!"

This was staggering news.

It might mean, as he had feared, that Dr. Fu Manchu had learned of his contact in Lung Chang!

He longed to take Yueh Hua into his confidence. Her knowledge of the place, her acute intelligence, her intuition, would be invaluable now. But he was bound to silence.

The road here passed through an area of unreclaimed land where nature had taken over. They were in a jungle. They found their way to a spot where the fallen branch of a tree offered a seat. Dropping their loads, they sat down. He looked at Yueh Hua. There was no gladness in her eyes.

"Chi Foh, they know where we are going. *He* will be waiting for us in Lung Chang!"

But, as Tony watched her, the mystery of Yueh Hua was uppermost in his mind. It was hard to credit the idea that Fu Manchu could have conceived such a burning passion for the grubby little girl Yueh Hua had then appeared to be, as to drive him up to this frantic chase.

He dismissed the supposition. He himself was the quarry. Perhaps he had made some mistake. Perhaps those hypnotic eyes had read more than he suspected. Dr. Fu Manchu had planned to interview him again. Nayland Smith had saved him. But the reward for his capture, flashed to so many centres, indicated that Fu Manchu knew more than he had credited him with knowing.

Tony put his arm around the dejected little figure beside him:

"Tell me more about your friends in Lung Chang, Yueh Hua. If we can get to them, shall we be safe?"

"As safe as we can hope to be, Chi Foh. My aunt is an old, retired servant of the Lao family."

"Does your aunt live right in the town?"

"No. In a small house on the estate. It is a mile from from Lung Chang."

"This side, or beyond?"

"This side, Chi Foh."

"We have a chance—even if they have found the boat. They won't be watching your aunt's house. And we have to get there—fast..."

Chapter X

It became a forced march. Twice they took cover; once, while a bullock cart heavily loaded went lumbering by, and again when they were nearly overtaken by an old jeep in which four soldiers were travelling toward Lung Chang.

Tony was less concerned with traffic going the same way as themselves than with any approaching, or with enemy outposts watching the road. For this reason he had wanted to take the lead but had changed his mind when he realized that this would mean leaving Yueh Hua behind. Also, he had learned that she had the instincts of a trained scout.

But dawn was not far when, footsore in his straw sandals, they reached a point in a long, high wall which had bordered the road for over half a mile. Dimly, he saw Yueh Hua stand still and beckon to him. He hurried forward.

She stood before a heavy, ornamental gate through the bars of which he could see a large, rambling building partly masked in ornamental gardens—a typical Chinese mansion—on a slope beyond. The high wall evidently surrounded the property.

"My uncle was Lao Tse-Mung's gardener," Yueh Hua explained. "He and his wife always lived here, and my aunt is allowed to stay."

"Is that Lao Tse-Mung's house over there?"

"Yes, Chi Foh. Please wait a little while outside, where they can't see you, until I explain"—she hesitated for a second—"who you are."

Yueh Hua had led him to the very door of the man he had to see!

He saw her reach inside the gate. An interval, foot steps, then a woman's cry—a cry of almost hysterical gladness:

"My baby! My Yueh Hua!"

The gate was unlocked. The voice died away into unintelligible babbling as they went in.

This gave him something else to think about.

Evidently Yueh Hua had told him her real name. But, unless her aunt had brought her up from childhood, the old woman's emotion was difficult to explain. And why had Yueh Hua asked him to wait, and gone in first herself?

In any case, he didn't have to wait long. She came running back for him.

"I haven't told her, Chi Foh, about—us. But she knows how wonderful you have been to me."

This clearly was true. Tears were streaming down her aunt's face when Yueh Hua brought him into the little house, evidently a gate-lodge. She seemed to want to kneel at his feet. He wondered what the exact relationship could be between Yueh Hua and Mai Cha, for this was her aunt's name. Two people less similar in type it would have been hard to find than this broad-faced old peasant woman and Yueh Hua. But Mai Cha became Tony's friend on sight, for it was plain that she adored Yueh Hua.

She left them together while she went to prepare a meal. But Yueh Hua, who seemed to have become suddenly and unaccountably shy, went out to help her.

He walked quietly under the flowered porch and looked across to the big house in its setting of arches, bridges and formal gardens. He could be there in five minutes. A winding path, easy to follow in starlight, led up to the house.

Yueh Hua had reached sanctuary, but Tony's business was with Lao Tse-Mung. Exposure of his real identity to Yueh Hua he couldn't hope to avoid once he had reported to the friend of Nayland Smith. This he must face.

But, the major problem remained: where was Dr. Fu Manchu?

Had this man, who seemed to wield supreme power in the province, out-manœuvred Sir Denis? He could not expect the late gardener's widow to know anything of what had happened tonight in the big house.

He must watch his step.

There were several little bridges to cross and many steps to climb before he reached a terrace which ran the whole length of the house. Flowering vines draped a pergola. Some night-scented variety gave out a strong perfume. He wondered where the main entrance was located, and if he should try to find it.

He increased his caution; stood still for a moment, listening.

A murmur of conversation reached him. There were people in some nearby room.

Step by step, he crept closer, hugging shadowy patches where the vines grew thickly. Three paces more and he would be able to look in.

But he didn't take the three paces. He stopped dead. An icy trickle seemed to run down his spine.

He had heard a voice, pitched in a clear, imperious tone.

"We have no time to waste."

It was the voice of Dr. Fu *Manchu!*

He had walked into a trap!

Tony put out a big effort, checked a mad panorama racing across his brain. Nayland Smith would gain something after all. He fingered the automatic which he had kept handy in a waist belt and moved stealthily forward. Whatever his own end might be, he could at least remove the world menace of Dr. Fu Manchu.

He could see into the room now.

It was furnished in true Chinese fashion, but with great luxury. Almost directly facing him, on a divan backed by embroidered draperies, he saw a white-bearded figure wearing a black robe and with a beaded black cap on his head. A snuff bowl lay before him.

Facing the old mandarin so that his back was toward the terrace, someone sat in a dragon-legged armchair. His close-cropped hair showed the shape of a massive skull.

Dr. Fu Manchu . . .

The mandarin's eyes were half-closed, but suddenly he opened them. He looked fixedly toward the terrace—and straight at Tony!

Holding a pinch of snuff between finger and thumb and still looking directly at him, he waved his hand gracefully in a sweeping side gesture as he raised the snuff to his nostrils.

But Tony had translated the gesture.

It meant that he had moved too near. He could be seen from the room.

Quickly he stepped to the right. His life hung on a very thin thread. But a wave of confidence surged through him.

This was Lao Tse-Mung who sat watching him, who had known him instantly for what he was, who had warned him of his danger. A highly acute and unusual character.

Tony could still see him clearly, through a screen of leaves, but, himself, was invisible from the room.

The mandarin spoke in light, easy tones.

"This is the first time you have honoured my poor roof, Excellency, in many moons. To what do I owe so great a privilege? "

"I am rarely in Lung Chang," was the sibilant reply. "I see that it might have been wise to come more often."

"My poor hospitality is always at my friends' disposal."

"Doubtless." Fu Manchu's voice sank to a venomous whisper. "Your hospitality to members of the present régime is less certain."

Lao Tse-Mung smiled slightly, settling himself among his cushions. "I retired long since from the world of politics, Excellency. I give all my time to the cultivation of my vines."

"Some of them grow thorns, I believe?"

"Many of them."

"Myself, Lao Tse-Mung, I also cultivate vines. I seek to restore to the garden of China its old glory. And so I fertilize the human vines which are fruitful and tear out those which are parasites, destructive. Let us come to the point."

Lao Tse-Mung's far-seeing eyes sought among the shadows for Tony.

Tony understood. He was to listen closely.

"My undivided attention is at your disposal, Excellency."

"A man calling himself Wu Chi Foh, who is a dangerous spy, escaped from the jail at Chia-Ting and was later reported to be near Lung Chang. He may carry vital information dangerous to the Peiping regime." Fu Manchu's voice became a hiss. "I suggest that you may have news of Wu Chi Foh."

Lao Tse-Mung's expression remained bland, unmoved.

"I can only assure Excellency that I have no news concerning this Wu Chi Foh. Are you suggesting that I am acquainted with this man?"

Dr. Fu Manchu's voice rose on a note of anger. "Your record calls for investigation. As a former high official, you have been allowed privileges. I merely suggest that you have abused them."

"My attention remains undivided, Excellency. I beg you to make your meaning clearer."

Tony knew that his fate, and perhaps the fate of Lao Tse-Mung, hung in the balance. He knew, too, that he could never have fenced with such an adversary as Fu Manchu, under the X-ray scrutiny of those green eyes, with the imperturbable serenity of the old Mandarin.

"Subversive elements frequent your house."

"The news distresses me." Lao Tse-Mung took up a hammer which hung beside a small gong. "Permit me to assemble my household for your inspection."

"Wait." The word was spoken imperatively. "There are matters I have to discuss with *you*, personally. For example, you maintain a private airfield on your estate."

Lao Tse-Mung smiled. His smile was directed toward Tony, whom his keen eyes had detected through the cover of leaves.

"I am sufficiently old-fashioned to prefer the ways of life of my ancestors, but sufficiently up-to-date to appreciate the convenience of modern transport." Lao Tse-Mung calmly took another pinch of snuff, smiling his sly smile. "I may add that in addition to chairs and rickshaws, I have also several automobiles. We are a long way from the railhead, Excellency, and some of my guests come from distant provinces."

"I wish to inspect this airfield. Also, the garage."

"It will be an honour and a great joy to conduct you. Let us first visit the airstrip, which is some little distance from the house. Then, as you wish, we can visit the garage. Your own car is there at present. And, as the garage is near the entrance gate, and I know Excellency's time is valuable"—the shrewd old eyes were staring straight into Tony's through the darkness—"*there should be no unnecessary delay.*"

This statement was astonishing to Tony for several reasons. First, that its ingenuous simplicity would disarm any man, even Dr. Fu Manchu. Second, because it was a veiled suggestion that the visitor was not welcome. Third, because it was unmistakably a direct order to *himself.*

He accepted it.

Silently, he slipped away from the lighted window, back along the terrace, and then began to run headlong down the slope to the gate lodge.

Old Mai Cha was standing in her doorway.

"Quick, Mother! Get Yueh Hua! There's not a minute to spare—"

"She has already gone, Chi Foh."

"Gone!" He stood before her, stricken—unable to understand.

"Yes, Chi Foh. But she is safe. You will see her again very soon. She has taken all you brought with you in your bundles. You know they are in good keeping."

He grasped Mai Cha by the shoulders, drawing her close, peering into her face. Her love for Moon Flower he couldn't doubt. But what was she hiding?

"Is this true, Mai Cha?"

"I swear it, in the name of my father, Chi Foh. I can tell you no more, except that my orders are to lead you to the garage. A car is waiting. You must hurry—for Yueh Hua's sake—and for your own, Please follow me."

Even in that moment of danger, of doubt, he was struck by the fact that she showed no surprise, only a deep concern. She seemed to be expecting this to happen. She was no longer an emotional old woman. She was controlled, practical.

A long, gently sloping path, tree-shadowed, which he knew must run parallel to the wall beside nearly a mile of which he and Moon Flower had tramped before coming to the gate, led them to a tiled yard upon which a lighted garage opened. One car, a sleek Rolls, showing no lights, stood in the yard. He saw two other cars in the garage beyond.

Mai Cha opened a door of the Rolls, and Tony tumbled in. She kissed his hand as he closed the door. In light from the garage behind he saw the back of a driver, a broad-shouldered Chinese with a shaven skull. The car was started. Smoothly, they moved out of the paved yard.

"Thank God, you're safe, McKay," came a snappy voice.

The driver was Nayland Smith!

Chapter XI

"Don't worry about Lao Tse-Mung, McKay. He has the guile of the serpent and the heart of a great patriot. He could convince men like you and me that night is day, that a duck is a swan. He called me an hour ago, and all's well. This isn't his first brush with The Master, and my money was on Tse-Mung all along. By the way, what about another drink?"

Tony grinned feebly, watching Nayland Smith mix drinks. It was hard to relax, even now; to accept the fact that, temporarily, he was in safety. He glanced down at a clean linen suit which had taken the place of his Chinese costume and wondered afresh at the efficient underground network of which he had become a member.

This charming bungalow on a hill overlooking Chungking was the property of the great English drug house of Roberts & Benson and was reserved for the use of their chief buyer, Ray Jenkins, who operated from the firm's office in the town. As Nayland Smith handed him a glass:

"You'll like Jenkins," Sir Denis rapped in his staccato fashion. "Sound man. And what he doesn't know about opium, even Dr. Fu Manchu couldn't teach him. He buys only the best, and Chungking is the place to get it."

He dropped into a split-cane chair and began to fill his pipe. He wore a well-cut linen suit and would have looked his familiar self but for the shaven skull. Noting Tony's expression, he laughed his boyish laugh.

"I know I'm better dressed than you are, McKay, because this is my own suit. Yours is borrowed from Jenkins's wardrobe."

Tony laughed, too, and was glad that he could manage it; for, in spite of Mai Cha's assurance, he was desperately worried about Moon Flower. And inquiries were out of the question.

"I can only thank you again, Sir Denis, for all you have done."

"Forget it, McKay. The old lama is one of ours, and he had orders to look out for you. Your last message had warned me that you expected to be arrested and I notified him. Then, I put Lao Tse-Mung in charge until I arrived."

"This is amazing, Sir Denis. I begin to hope that China will shake off the Communists yet."

Nayland Smith nodded grimly; lighted his pipe. "From my point of view, there are certain advantages in our recognition of the Peiping crowd. For instance, I can travel openly in China—but I avoid Szechuan."

"How right you are!"

"Lao Tse-Mung, of course, is our key man in the province. Job calls for enormous courage, and something like genius. He has both. He master-minded the whole affair of getting you out of jail. The Lama, who has more degrees than you could count on all your fingers, gave you your instructions. He speaks and writes perfect English. Also, he has contacts inside the jail."

"That's what I call efficiency!"

"We're not washed up yet in the East, McKay."

"So it seems."

Nayland Smith tugged at the lobe of his ear, a trick Tony knew to indicate deep reflection. "If Fu Manchu can enlist the anti-Communist elements," he said, "the control of this vast country may pass into his hands. This would pose another problem . . . But let's cross that bridge when we come to it. This bungalow is one of our bases. It was here that I converted myself into a lama before proceeding farther. Jenkins provided me with a vintage Ford—a useful bus on Chinese roads. You see, McKay, there's constant coming and going of Buddhist priests across the Burma frontier, and if my Chinese is shaky, my Burmese is sound." He glanced at his watch. "Jenkins is late. Feeling hungry?"

"No." Tony shook his head. "After my first bath for weeks in a civilized bathroom, a change of clothes and a drink, I feel delightfully relaxed."

"Good for you. Jenkins has another guest who is probably revelling in a warm bath, too, after a long journey; Jeanie Cameron-Gordon. Her father, an old friend of mine, is the world-famous medical entomologist, Dr. Cameron-Gordon. His big work on sleeping sickness and the *tsetse* fly *is* the text book for all students of tropical medicine. Ran a medical mission. But more later."

"Whatever brings his daughter here?" Tony wanted to know.

Before Nayland Smith could reply, the stout, smiling and capable resident Chinese housekeeper, whom Tony had met already, came in. She was known simply as Mrs. Wing. She bowed.

"Miss Cameron-Gordon," she said, in her quaint English, "is dressed, and asks if she should join you, or if you are in a business conference."

Nayland Smith smiled broadly. "The conference is over, Mrs. Wing. Please ask Miss Jeanie to join us."

Mrs. Wing bowed again, went out, and a moment later Miss Cameron-Gordon came in, her face shaded by a wide-brimmed hat. She wore a tailored suit of cream shantung which perfectly fitted her perfect figure. Smart suede shoes. She had remarkable grace of movement.

For an interval that couldn't be measured in terms of time, Tony stood rigid. Then he sprang forward.

Miss Jeanie Cameron-Gordon found herself locked in his arms.

"Moon Flower! Moon Flower!"

"I had an idea," Nayland Smith said drily, "that you two might be acquainted. . .

Ray Jenkins joined them for lunch. He was evidently used to uninvited guests, for he expressed no surprise when Tony and Moon Flower were introduced. A thin man with large, wiry hands, gaunt features, Chinese yellow, and a marked Cockney accent, he had a humorous eye and the self-confidence of a dentist. Moon Flower was reserved and embarrassed, avoiding Tony's looks of admiration. He felt he was the cause of this and cursed the impulse which had prompted him to betray their intimacy. He didn't attempt to deny that he was in love with her, but gave a carefully edited account of their meeting and of how he had come to form a deep affection for his native helper.

"I never saw Jeanie in her other kit," Jenkins said nasally. He called one and all by their first names. "But, looking at her now, Tony, I should say you were nuts not to know she wasn't Chinese."

"But I am," Moon Flower told him, "on my mother's side."

340

Ray Jenkins regarded her for a long time; then: "God's truth!" he remarked. "Your mother must have been a stunner!"

Nayland Smith threw some light upon what had happened at Lao Tse-Mung's. He had arrived there several hours ahead of Tony, intending to proceed at speed to Chungking directly Tony showed up. He found the mandarin in an unhappy frame of mind. The daughter of his old friend, Dr. Cameron-Gordon, who had been staying at his house, had disappeared nearly a week before. He suspected that she had gone in search of information about her father, contrary to his, Lao Tse-Mung's, advice. He had used all the facilities (and they were many) at his disposal, but with no result.

"I'll leave it to Moon Flower, as you call Jeanie, to tell you the whole story, McKay," Sir Denis said, with one of his impish grins. "She will tell it better than I can."

Moon Flower gave him a reproachful, but half-playful glance.

"I was staggered," he went on. "I had heard in Hong Kong that her father had died in a fire which destroyed the medical mission building. But I supposed that Jeanie was still in England. Unfortunately, I didn't know that Cameron-Gordon had a married sister in Hong Kong, or I might have been better informed."

He paused to congratulate Mrs. Wing, who had just come in, upon her cooking, and when that lady, smiling happily, went out, he continued:

"I was discussing the problem of Jeanie's disappearance with Tse-Mung when his secretary ran in and announced, '*The Master is here!*'

"Snappy action was called for. Very cautiously I made my way back toward the entrance gate. From behind a bank of rhododendrons I had the pleasure of seeing my old friend Dr. Fu Manchu, wearing what looked like a Prussian uniform, striding up to the house. A big Nubian, whom I had seen somewhere before, followed him."

"You probably saw him in Niu-fo-Tu," Tony broke in. "I was running away from him when you spoke to me!"

"Possibly. Fu Manchu's car, a Buick, still hot, was in the garage. It was parked alongside a majestic Rolls belonging to Lao Tse-Mung. My old Ford stood ready in the yard. What to do next was a problem. I had to stand by until you arrived. But I had to keep out of the way of Fu Manchu, as well, I thought up several plans to intercept you, when suddenly they were all washed out."

"What happened?" Tony asked excitedly.

"My walkie-talkie came to life! Tse-Mung's secretary reported that Jeanie and a Chinese companion, Chi Foh, were in the gate-lodge! I had arranged with Tse-Mung, if I should miss you and you appeared at the house, to direct you to the garage. But I hadn't expected Jeanie."

"Heart failure," Ray Jenkins murmured nasally.

"What?" Nayland Smith demanded.

"I should have had heart failure."

"No, you wouldn't. I know you better. You'd have done some fast thinking, as I did. I told Sun Shao-Tung, the secretary, to send me a driver who knew the way to Chungking, to order the man to stand by the Ford in the garage. Then I headed for the gate lodge. Mai Cha, the gardener's widow, who lives there—we are old friends—after she recovered from her surprise, told me that Moon Flower (as she had always called Jeanie), was in the bedroom sorting out some clothes which she had left with Mai Cha to be cleaned and pressed . . . I had Moon Flower away with her bundle of dresses, inside five minutes. Am I right, Jeanie?"

"Yes," Moon Flower agreed, and her eyes told the story of her gratitude. "You certainly drove me remorselessly!"

"And so here you are! God knows where you'd be if Dr. Fu Manchu had found you. The driver was standing by, as ordered, and off you went in my Ford to Ray Jenkins, a harbour in any storm."

"Thanks a lot," Ray Jenkins said. "Drinks all round, if I may say so. Keep a pretty good cellar, Denis."

"Your absence, McKay," Sir Denis added, "was an unexpected headache. But you have told me how Tse-Mung handled a difficult situation. You took your cues perfectly. And so, for the moment, Dr. Fu Manchu is baffled . . ."

On the flower-covered porch of the bungalow, with a prospect of snowy poppy fields below extending to the distant foothills, Tony at last found himself alone with Moon Flower. She lay beside him, in a long cane chair, smoking a cigarette and no longer evading his looks of adoration.

"We're a pair of terrible liars, aren't we?" she said softly; and the sound of her musical voice speaking English made his heart glad.

"I'm still in a maze, Moon Flower. I seem to have come out of a wonderful dream. And I still don't know where the dream ends and real life begins. I know, of course, that you're not a Chinese girl and you know I'm not a fisherman from Hong Kong. I never suspected that you weren't what you pretended to be, but I often thought you had doubts about me."

"How right you were, Chi Foh. (I like Chi Foh better than Tony.) But it was a long time before doubts came. That part is all over now, and I think I'm sorry."

Tony reached across urgently: grasped her arm. "You don't regret an hour of it, Moon Flower? Tell me you don't."

"Not one minute," she whispered.

"You know I learned to adore you as Yueh Hua, don't you? I had planned to risk everything and to marry my little river girl. In my heart, anyway, I shall always call you Yueh Hua—"

"And to me, Tony, you will always be Chi Foh."

He longed to take her in his arms, but knew it was neither the time or place.

"I was just doing a job I had volunteered to do. And what a man to work under—Sir Denis! But your motive was a sad one—your father."

"Let me tell you about it in my own way, Chi Foh. It is sad, yes; but, now, there is hope. Shall I begin with what happened before I fell asleep on your sampan?"

"Begin where you like, dearest, but tell me."

Jeanie stubbed out her cigarette. "Lao Tse-Mung is my grand-uncle, by marriage. My father, Dr. Cameron-Gordon, married Lao Tse-Mung's niece, daughter of his only sister and her American husband. So, you see, I am really Chinese."

"No more than I am," Tony broke in. "My mother's mother was Chinese, too! That's why I can pass as Chinese, myself, for I have traces of the maternal side in my features."

"Very slight traces, Chi Foh, and I don't dislike them. My father, of course, had travelled all over the world and become famous for his work. Then, he came to China to study diseases here which he believed to be insect-borne. He met my mother. She was a very

343

beautiful woman, Chi Foh. He married her. For her sake, I believe, he accepted the post as director of the medical mission at Chien Wei. The mission used to stand by the Pool of Lily Dreams. Do you remember the Pool of Lily Dreams?"

"Can I ever forget it!"

"I was born there, Chi Foh. Mai Cha was my nurse, and I was allowed to play with her son, who is now living in the United States and has become very prosperous. He taught me to handle a sampan, and of course I picked up the local dialect. My mother taught me pure Chinese. She and my father often spoke it together. Everybody loved father. Lao Tse-Mung was one of his oldest friends. When I grew up, I was sent to school in England."

She stopped. Tony found her hand, and held it. "What then, Moon Flower?"

"My mother died. The news nearly killed me, too, for I worshipped her. I came back. Oh, Chi Foh, I found everything so changed! My poor father was still distracted by the loss of my mother, and the Communist authorities had begun to persecute him, because he openly defied their orders. A deeply religious Scotsman can never bow to Communism."

Moon Flower opened her cigarette case, but changed her mind and closed it again. "He wouldn't let me stay at the mission. He insisted that I return to my aunt in Hong Kong and wait there until he joined me. He knew the Communists meant to close the mission, but he wasn't ready to go."

"So you went back to Hong Kong?"

"Yes. We had two letters. Then—silence. We tried to find out what had happened. Our letters to Lao Tse-Mung were never answered. At last—and the shock nearly drove me mad—came news that the mission had been burned down, that my father was believed to have died in the fire. My aunt couldn't stop me. I started at once—"

Tony wanted to say, "How glad I am you did," but was afraid to break Moon Flower's train of thought, and so said nothing.

"I went to Lung Chang, to my uncle's house. I asked him why he had not answered my letters—and he told me. He had never received them! He tried to make me understand that China was now a police state, that no one's correspondence was safe. He confirmed the news that the mission had been burned. My father was too well loved by the people for such a thing to happen, but young fools from outlying districts who had submitted to injections of the Communist poison were called in to create a riot. What Lao Tse-Mung called 'the usual routine'. What had become of my father he didn't know. He believed he was alive, but under arrest."

Moon Flower, now, was what, in any other girl, he would have described as "wound up"—fired with enthusiasm and indignation.

"You see, Chi Foh, the Chinese farm worker will not submit to collective farming. My father knew that customs a thousand years old can't suddenly be changed by a Soviet-trained overlord. He helped them in their troubles, helped them to escape from this tyranny if they wanted to leave their farms, where they starved, and look for employment elsewhere. So—he was marked down."

She opened her cigarette case again, and this time took one out and allowed Tony to light it.

"My uncle Tse-Mung advised caution, and patience. But I wasn't in the mood for either. Wearing a suit of peasant clothes belonging to Mai Cha, but taking some money of my own, I slipped out early one morning and made my way, as a Chinese working girl, to what had been my home. Oh, Chi Foh!"

Moon Flower dropped her cigarette in a tray and lay back with closed eyes.

"I think I understand," he said—and it was said sincerely.

"Nothing was left, but ashes and broken lumber. All our furniture, everything we possessed, all the medical stores, had been burned, stolen, or destroyed. I was walking away from the ruins, when I had the good luck to see an old woman I remembered, one of my father's patients. I knew she was a friend; but I thought she was going to faint when she recognized me. She didn't, and she gave me news which saved me from complete collapse."

"What was it, Moon Flower?"

"My father had not died. He had been arrested as a spy and taken away! She advised me to try to get information at a summer villa not far from Chia-Ting, owned by Huan Tsung-Chao, Communist governor of the province. She said he was a good and just man. Her daughter, Shun-Hi, who had been a nurse in the mission hospital, was employed at the villa. I remembered Shun-Hi. And so, of course, I made my way up to Chia-Ting. But my money was running short. When at last I found the villa, a beautiful place surrounded by acres of gardens, I didn't quite know what to do."

Tony was learning more and more about the intrepid spirit of his little companion on the sampan with every word she spoke. She was a treasure above price, and he found it hard to believe that such a pearl had been placed in his keeping.

"There were many servants," Moon Flower went on, "and some of them didn't live in the villa. I watched near the gate by which these girls came out in the evening. And at last I saw Shun-Hi. She walked towards the town, and I followed her until I thought we were alone. Then, I spoke to her. She recognized me at once, began to cry, and nearly went down on her knees."

Moon Flower took her smouldering cigarette from the ash-tray and went on smoking.

"But I found out what I wanted to know. My father was alive! He was under house arrest and working in a laboratory attached to the villa. The Master was a guest of Huan Tsung-Chao! I had very little money left and nothing but my gratitude to offer Shun-Hi, but I begged her to try to let my father know that I was waiting for a message from him."

"Did she do it?"

"Yes, good soul, she did. I shared her room that night and wrote a letter to my father. And the next evening she smuggled a note out to me. It said, first, 'Burn this when you have read it, then go to Lao Tse-Mung who will get you to Hong Kong. Apply there to British authorities. Tell them the facts.' You see, Chi Foh, I have memorized it! My father wrote that he was in the hands of Dr. Fu Manchu, adding, 'Now known as *The Master.*' He told me that at all costs I must get away from, in his own words, 'that devil incarnate'. He warned me not to let anyone even suspect my identity."

"Moon Flower, my dearest, whatever did you do next?"

"I went down to the river to see if I could find someone to take me part of the way. I had had several free rides by land and water on my journey from Lung Chang, and I still had enough to pay something. But I had no luck at all . . . and the police began to watch me. Finally, I was arrested as a suspicious character and thrown into jail—"

"That awful jail!"

346

"Yes, Chi Foh. They wouldn't believe the story I told them. It was the same story that I told *you*! They punished me—"

"The swine!" Tony burst out. "It was Soong?"

"Yes. I screamed."

"I heard you."

The blue eyes were turned to him. "How could you hear me? Where were you?"

"I was a prisoner, too! And so I heard you scream in that ghastly place."

"So did Wu Chung-Lo, the prison governor, a friend of my father's. He came to see me. He released me. He could do no more. It was only just in time. As I was creeping away, a car passed close by me. The passenger was a man wearing a cloak and a military cap. In the moonlight his eyes shone like emeralds. They seemed to be turned in my direction, and I shuddered. I knew it was *The Master*— the man my father had called a devil incarnate. You know what happened after that, Chi Foh . . ."

"And I thank God it did happen, Moon Flower—but you're not really called Moon Flower, after all?"

Moon Flower drew nearer to him. "Don't look so sad, dearest, I am. I was born on the night of a new moon, and to please my mother, my father agreed to name me Jean Yueh Hua. Oddly enough, I love the moon."

"I know you do." An ivory vision arose in Tony's memory. "Will you marry me on the next day there's a new moon?"

Moon Flower took his hand in both her own.

"I'll marry you, Chi Foh—but on the first day my father is free again . . ."

Dr. Fu Manchu sat in his favourite chair behind the lacquer desk. It was early dawn. But only one lamp relieved the gloom: a green-shaded lamp on the desk. This cast a sort of phantom light over the yellow-robed figure. Fu Manchu lay back, his elbows resting on the arms of the chair, the tips of his bony fingers pressed together, his eyes half closed, but glinting like emeralds where the light touched them.

In the shadowy room, two paces from the desk, the gigantic figure of Mahmûd the Nubian stood motionless.

Fu Manchu took a pinch of snuff from the silver snuffbox. He spoke softly.

"Go to your quarters, Mahmûd, and remain there until further orders."

The big Nubian knelt on the rug, bent his head to the floor, stood up, made a deep *salaam,* and went out. He had a stealthy step, almost silent.

And, as he left by one door, another opened, and Huan Tsung-Chao came in. Fu Manchu lay back in his chair, with closed eyes. General Huan settled himself upon the divan facing the desk.

"The man is honest and devoted," he said. "I have heard his account of all that happened, as you wished."

Fu Manchu's eyes opened widely. They stared into the shadows from which Huan Tsung-Chao had spoken. "You heard how Skobolov, a dying man, tricked him in Niu-fo-Tu and fled to some obscure resthouse? You heard how the Russian escaped again, taking his papers with him?"

He almost hissed the words, stood up, a tall, menacing figure.

"I heard, Master. I heard, also, that the escaped prisoner, Wu Chi Foh, was seen in Niu-fo-Tu after Skobolov had arrived there."

"So that the Si-Fan register may now be on its way to Moscow!"

"Or to London," came placidly out of the shadows. "Sir Denis Nayland Smith is in China. A dying man is not hard to rob. And you suspected the prisoner called Wu Chi Foh to be working for British Intelligence in the first place."

Fu Manchu dropped back in his chair.

"Perhaps, Tsung-Chao, the weight of years bears me down. My powers may be failing me at last. You know of my visit to Lao Tse-Mung. His behaviour aroused deep suspicions. But he has the powers of a great diplomat. I have watched him for some years. Is he working with Nayland Smith? Is he opposed to Peiping? He remains impenetrable—and his estate is a fortress! To what party does he belong? These things we must find out, Tsung-Chao—or Lao Tse-Mung must be destroyed ...

348

Chapter XII

"This man, Skobolov," Nayland Smith snapped, "was one of the most trusted agents of the Kremlin." He raised his eyes from the documents found in the portfolio. "Top marks to you, Jeanie, for taking care of such valuable evidence. I know very little Russian, but enough to recognize his name as the person to whom these letters are addressed."

Tony nodded, smiling at Moon Flower.

"What I am anxious to know," Sir Denis added, "is what Skobolov was doing in Szechuan. Why was he sent here? It's a shot in the dark, but I venture to guess—for *this*."

He held up the bound manuscript that was written in Chinese.

"I agree with you, Sir Denis," Moon Flower said quietly, "I know written Chinese fairly well, but this is in cipher and quite beyond me. Why should it be in cipher if it weren't something very secret?"

"Quite obvious, Jeanie. It can't be a top secret dispatch from Peiping. In the first place, it couldn't be in Chinese; in the second, he would have headed for Russia and not come wandering around this remote province. Therefore, he must have acquired it in Szechuan." He dropped the manuscript on the table and pulled at the lobe of his ear. "There are three people known to me who might decipher it. Lao Tse-Mung—his secretary—or our friend the Lama in Niu-fo-Tu. What's more, all of them speak Russian, and this correspondence interests me."

"Let us go to my uncle's," Moon Flower said eagerly. "We shall at least be safe while we're there, and Lao Tse-Mung's secretary is very clever as you say, and knows many languages."

"You'd be still safer with your aunt in Hong Kong, young lady," Nayland Smith rapped.

Moon Flower smiled. "I shall never go back to Hong Kong until my father goes with me," she assured him. And there was a note of finality in the soft voice which carried conviction.

"You're going to be a big responsibility in the kind of work we have to do, Jeanie."

Moon Flower turned to Tony. "Was I a big responsibility to *you*, Chi Foh, in the kind of work we had to do?"

And honesty forced Tony to answer, "I couldn't have done it without you, Moon Flower."

Nayland Smith took his old briar pipe out of his pocket and began to fill the bowl with coarse-cut mixture. His expression was very grim, but a smile lurked in the grey eyes.

"If McKay's against me, too, I suppose I must compromise. From the moment we leave this house we all carry our lives in our hands. We don't know what this Chinese manuscript is, but your account, McKay, of Skobolov's behaviour and his strange death, tells us plainly that it's dynamite, and that *somebody* was following him to recover it. You agree?"

"I do, Sir Denis," Tony told him. "But if it was of such value to the Kremlin, it may be of equal value to us."

"If we can hang on to it," Nayland Smith snapped, "and not go the way of Skobolov!"

There was a brief silence while he dropped his pouch back in his pocket and lighted his pipe.

"You have some theory about Skobolov?" Tony suggested.

Nayland Smith nodded. "I have. He was poisoned. The purpose of the poisoner was to recover this manuscript. I can think of only one man who is not only an expert poisoner but also a danger to the Soviet empire."

"Dr. Fu Manchu!"

Nayland Smith blew out a cloud of tobacco smoke.

"If I'm right, and I think I am, we have here the most powerful weapon against Fu Manchu which I have ever held in my hands . . ."

Many hours later, the security police held up an old Ford car on a nearly impassible road some miles east of Lung Chang. The Chinese driver, whose shaved skull betrayed nothing but a stubble of hair, was a dull, taciturn fellow. His passengers were a lama, who wore glasses, and a Chinese boy.

The lama did the talking.

"Where did you come from and where are you going?" the man in charge wanted to know.

"From Yung Chuan," the Buddhist priest told him. "Are you a member of the faith, my son?"

"Never mind about that—"

"But it's more important than anything else."

"Who's the boy?"

"My pupil. I am returning to my monastery in Burma, and I am happy to say that I bring a young disciple with me."

The man, who evidently had special orders of some kind, looked from face to face.

"Who owns this car?"

"A good friend in Yung Chuan, and one of the faith. I have out-stayed my leave and am anxious to return."

"What's your friend's name?"

"Li Tao-shi. He has found the Path. Seek it, my son."

The man made a rude noise and waved the car on.

When they had gone a safe distance, the driver slowed down and turned a grinning face to his passengers.

"Good show, McKay!" he said. "You remembered your lines and never flunked once! I don't know why those fellows were so alert, but I was prepared for emergencies. It's just possible that The Master has sent out special orders. We're getting into the danger zone, now . . . Which way do we turn, Jeanie? Here's a crossroads. One leads to a marsh as far as I can make out!"

The "disciple" hesitated. "I'm not sure, Sir Denis. It's a long time since I came this way. But I think it's the road to the marsh! Except in rainy weather, it's quite passable. Then we should come to the main road to Lung Chang—if you think it's safe for us to use a main road?"

"I don't. But is there any other way?"

"Not for a car. By water, yes. Otherwise, we have to walk!"

"H'm!" Nayland Smith pulled reflectively at the lobe of his ear. "If we drive to the high road, how far is it from there to Lao Tse-Mung's house?"

"About five miles," Moon Flower told him.

"But from here, walking?"

"About the same, if I don't lose my way!"

"Then, as two experienced pedestrians, I think you and McKay must walk. If challenged again, you know the story, McKay. Stick to it. We must separate for safety."

He raised the wizard walkie-talkie to his ear, adjusted it and listened; then: "Hullo, is that Sun Shao-Tung?" he said. "Yes. Nayland Smith here. Tell Lao Tse-Mung I have Yueh Hua and McKay with me. We're about five miles from the house and they are proceeding on foot. First, I must know if my Ford was noted by The Master when he arrived at the garage . . . It was? And what explanation was offered for its disappearance?" He listened attentively . . . "Ford used for collecting gardening material? Good. Had been sent into Chungking for repairs? Would be returned later by mechanic? Excellent! We'll be on our way." He turned to Tony.

"Did you follow, McKay?" he rapped.

"Yes, I did. Fu Manchu has given orders for all ranks to look out for a Ford car. That's why we were held up. There must be more Fords in Szechuan than I suspected, or we shouldn't have slipped through so easily. You're right about breaking up the part, Sir Denis."

"I suspected this, McKay. I shall have to hang on to the briefcase. A missionary lama from Burma can't very well carry one! But, for safety, suppose you take the Chinese manuscript? If challenged, it's a religious treatise to be presented to your principal in Burma. No soldier or policeman will know any better. And lama priests still command some slight respect in this part of China."

The leather case was taken from its hiding-place in the car and the mysterious manuscript tucked into a capacious pocket inside Tony's ample garment, which resembled a long-sleeved bathrobe.

But when the parting took place, Moon Flower looked wistfully after the old Ford jolting away on the unpaved road. Tony knew what she was thinking, but it didn't hurt him. He shared her feeling. Nayland Smith was an oasis in a desert, a well of resource. He put his arm around a slim waist concealed by the baggy boy's clothes.

"Come on, my lad!" he said gaily, and kissed her. "We have faced worse things and survived."

Moon Flower clung to him, her blue eyes raised to his; and the blue eyes were sombre.

"I am not afraid for us, Chi Foh," she assured him. "I am thinking about my father."

"We'll get him out, dearest. Don't doubt it."

"I don't dare to doubt it. But I feel, and you must feel, too, that this awful man, Dr. Fu Manchu, is drawing a net around all of us. He has dreadful authority, and he has strange powers. I understand now that it was he who killed the Russian. But *how* did he kill him?"

"God knows! But it's pretty certain that his purpose was to get hold of this thing I have in my pocket. So we score over the great Fu Manchu!"

"Not we, Chi Foh. Fate stepped in. I have seen Dr. Fu Manchu. You have spoken to him. He holds my father, a clever man and a man of strong character, helpless in his hands. Dr. Fu Manchu is not an ordinary human being . . . He's a devil-inspired genius. Sir Denis is our only hope. And he has tried for years to conquer him. Alone, what could you and I do?"

Tony laughed, but not mirthfully. "Very little, I admit. Fu Manchu has a vast underground organization behind him, and, at present anyway, the support of the government of China. We have nothing but our wits."

Moon Flower forced a smile. "Don't let me make you gloomy, Chi Foh. You mustn't pay too much attention to my moods. I don't expect us to overthrow Dr. Fu Manchu. I only pray we may be able to get my father out of his clutches."

Tony hugged her affectionately, kissed her hair, which she had allowed Mrs. Wing, Ray Jenkins's housekeeper, to cut short when Nayland Smith had decided that a lama priest couldn't travel in the company of a girl. She turned her head aside, pursing her lips in a way which Tony found delicious.

"I don't like my hair so short, Chi Foh. Although, when I left England, it was quite fashionable to wear one's hair like a boy."

"I'm quite happy about it, Moon Flower. Anyway, it will soon grow again."

And they set out on the path to Lung Chang.

It was a crazy path, in places along embankments crossing flooded paddy fields, and sometimes wandering amongst acres of opium poppies which had become a major crop since all restrictions had been removed. The collective authorities reaped a rich harvest from the sale of opium; the growers struggled to live.

The few peasants they met paid little attention to the lama priest and the boy who trudged on their way, except for one or two who were Buddhists. These respectfully saluted Tony, and he gave them a sign of his hand which Nayland Smith had taught him.

After one such encounter, "I sincerely hope," he told Moon Flower, "that we don't meet a real lama! Sir Denis might have been up to it, but I'm not!"

They were in sight of a village which Moon Flower recognized, not more than a mile and a half from their destination, before anything disturbing happened. The day had been hot and they had pushed on at speed. They were tired. They had reached a point at which there was a choice of routes; the main road or a detour which would lengthen their journey.

"Dare we risk the main road?" Tony asked. "Is it much used?"

"No," Moon Flower admitted. "But we should have to pass through the village. I think this is a county line, and there may be a police post there."

"Then I think we must go the long way, Moon Flower. Where will that bring us out?"

"By a gate into part of Lao Tse-Mung's property, nearly half a mile from the house. It is locked. But there's a hidden bell-push which rings a bell in the house. We have to cross the main road at one point, but the path continues on the other side."

"Lead on!"

They resumed their tramp, Tony with his arm around Moon Flower, except where the path was so narrow and bramble bordered that they had to march in single file. At a point where the path threatened to lose itself amongst a plantation of young bamboo, their luck deserted them. The thicket proved to border the road and as there was no sound of traffic they stepped out from the path on to a narrow, unpaved highway. And Moon Flower grasped Tony's arm.

A dusty bicycle lay on a bank, and sitting beside the cycle, smoking a cigarette, they saw a man in khaki police uniform!

Moon Flower suppressed a gasp. The policeman, however, looked more startled than they were as he got to his feet, dropping his Chinese cigarette, which Tony knew from experience tasted like a firework. It was now growing dusk and their sudden appearance out of the shadow bordering the road clearly had frightened him. In consequence he was very angry. He picked up his cigarette.

"Where do you two think you're going?" he then demanded.

"We are trying to find our way to the river, which we have to cross. But we took the wrong path," Tony told him.

"And where are you going, then?"

"I have to return to my monastery in Burma. I am taking this young disciple with me."

"If you come from Burma, show me your papers—your permit to enter China."

Tony took himself in hand. The sudden appearance of the security officer had shaken him. But now he was his own man again. He fumbled inside the loose robe. It was the one that Nayland Smith had worn before him. In an interior pocket he had all the necessary credentials, equally applicable to Sir Denis or to himself. They had been sent at speed by Lao Tse-Mung to Chungking before the party set out; how obtained Tony could only guess. Lao Tse-Mung was a clever man.

He handed the little folder to the police officer, wondering if the man could read. Whether he could or not, evidently he recognized the official forms. They authorized the bearer to enter China and remain for thirty days. There was still a week to go. Tony wondered that the smoke of his cigarette, drooping from a corner of his coarse mouth, didn't suffocate him.

The man handed the passport back, clearly disappointed.

"Who is this boy?" he asked roughly. "Has he any official permit to travel?"

Thanks to Ray Jenkins, who had influential, and corruptible, friends in Chungking, "he" had. Tony produced a certificate for travel, signed by a member of the security bureau, authorising Lo Hung-Chang, aged 14, to leave his native town of Yung Chuan but to report to security police at the Burma frontier before leaving China.

The disappointed policeman returned the certificate. Evidently he could read, for:

"You have only seven days to reach the frontier," he growled. "If it takes you any longer, look out for trouble."

"If I have earned this trouble, brother," Tony told him piously, "undoubtedly it will come to me, for my benefit. Have you not sought the Path?"

"*Your* path is straight ahead," the surly officer declared, furious because he had found nothing wrong. "You'll have to walk to Lung Chang and then on to Niu-fo-Tu to reach the river." He dropped the last fragment of his odorous cigarette and put his foot on it as Tony fumbled to return the certificate to his inside pocket. "You seem to have a lot of things in that pouch of yours. I have heard of lama priests getting away with pounds of opium that never saw the Customs. Turn out all you have there!"

Tony's pulse galloped. He heard Moon Flower catch her breath. And he had to conquer a mad impulse to crash his fist into the face of this servant of Red China. As he had done in jail at Chia-Ting, he reflected that Communist doctrines seemed to turn men into sadists. He hesitated. But only for a decimal of a second. He had money in a body belt, but carried nothing else, except the official (and forged) papers, and—the mystery manuscript.

He turned the big pocket out, handed the Chinese manuscript to the policeman.

If he attempted to confiscate it, Tony knew that no choice would be left. He would have to knock the man out before he had time to reach for the revolver which he carried. He watched him thumbing over the pages in fading light, until:

"What is this?" he demanded.

Tony's breath returned to normal. He remembered Nayland Smith's advice.

"A religious writing in the hand of a great disciple of our Lord Buddha. A present from this inspired scholar to my principal. If you could understand it, brother, you would already be on the Path."

"Brother" threw the manuscript down contemptuously. "Move on!" he directed, and turned to his bicycle.

Moon Flower breathed a long sigh of relief as he rode off. "I wonder if you can imagine, Chi Foh," she said, "my feelings when you trusted that thing to him? I seemed to hear Sir Denis's words, 'the most powerful weapon against Fu Manchu which I ever held in my hands'. Did you realize, my dear, that he might have orders to look for it?"

"Yes. But the odds against it were heavy. And if he had tried anything, I was all set to make sure he didn't get away with it." The cyclist was nearly out of sight. Tony grasped Moon Flower and kissed her ardently. "I love the way you call me Chi Foh. It makes my heart jump, Yueh Hua!"

They reached their destination without further incident—to find Nayland Smith anxiously waiting for them . . .

357

Chapter XIII

For two days they remained in Lao Tse-Mung's house, apparently inactive, except that Nayland Smith spent hours alone, smoking pipe after pipe, deep in thought. Tony deduced that he was trying to discover a plan to rescue Dr. Cameron-Gordon and found it no easy thing to do.

With Moon Flower, Tony roamed about the beautiful gardens, so that this brief interlude of peace was a chapter in his life which he knew he would always remember with happiness. Lao Tse-Mung had warned them all that Fu Manchu was by no means satisfied with what he had seen and heard.

"My house will be watched. I shall be spied upon. If he discovers that you are here, none of us will any longer be safe. So never show yourselves at any point which is visible from the road. The entire property is walled, and the wall-tops are wired. But at places there are tall trees outside which overlook the walls—and these trees I cannot wire . . ."

Lao Tse-Mung's talented secretary, Sun Shao-Tung, had translated all the Russian letters in Skobolov's briefcase, and Nayland Smith had been lighted up on learning from the correspondence that the research scientist employed at the hidden Soviet plant was not a Russian, but a German, Dr. von Wehrner. But even more exciting was a pencilled note which Sir Denis deduced to be a translation of a code message:

"If hidden MS. as reported secure at any cost. Proceed as arranged to governor's villa to allay suspicion. Cancel further plans. Join plane at Huang Ko-Shu."

"I was right, McKay!" Nayland Smith declared. "This Chinese document is dynamite!"

Sun Shao-Tung had gone to work on the mysterious manuscript. He had worked far into the night, only to find himself baffled.

Nayland Smith asked him to make a careful copy in case the

358

original should be lost—or stolen. And it was late on the second night of their stay at Lao Tse-Mung's hospitable house that something happened.

The secretary worked in a top room, equipped as an up to date office, with typewriter, filing cabinets, book-cases and a large desk. This betrayed the modern side of the old mandarin, and was in keeping with his private plane, his cars, his electrical lighting plant and other equipment; a striking contrast to the Oriental character of the reception rooms below.

Tony occupied a room next to the office. Nayland Smith was lodged in one on the other side of the corridor. He was unaccountably restless. Lao Tse-Mung's guest-rooms had electric light and all the other facilities of a modern residence. It was very late when Tony switched off his bedside lamp and tried to sleep. But the night seemed to be haunted by strange sounds, furtive movements which he couldn't identify, or place.

The shadow of Fu Manchu was creeping over him. He began thinking, again, about the dead Russian, seeing in his imagination the man's ceaseless battle with clouds of invisible insects. Of course, it had been delirium. But what a queer kind of delirium. Skobolov had died at the hand of Dr. Fu Manchu. But of what had he died?

Tony found himself listening intently for a buzz of insects in the room.

He heard none. He tried to laugh at these phantom fears.

Then, he began to listen again.

There was a sound—a very faint sound. It was not a sound of insects, and it was not in his room. It came from the adjoining office.

He knew that Sun Shao-Tung had retired two hours before. He had heard him go . . . Yet, something or someone moved stealthily in the office!

Tony swung out of bed; stole to the door of his room; opened it cautiously.

Bare-footed, he crept along to the office door.

Silent, he stood listening.

Yes!—There was someone inside!

He began to turn the handle, gently open the door. And, as it opened, a draft of cold air swept into his face!

It brought with it a sense of horror. He shuddered—then fully opened the door.

The office was in darkness. But a beam of moonlight through the window, which he saw to be open, just brushed the top of the large desk. There was a dim figure in the shadow behind the desk—and two hands, which alone were in the moonlight, busily swept up a litter of papers lying there . . .

Perhaps the lighting created an illusion. But *they were grey hands!*

Tony clenched his fists, took a step forward—and a lean figure sprang over the desk, leapt upon him and had his throat in an icy grip!

He uttered a stifled shriek as that ghastly grip closed on him: it was a cry of loathing rather than of fear. But, in the face of what he knew to be deathly peril, his brain remained clear. He struck up, a right, a left, to the jaw of his antagonist. The blows registered. The grip on his throat relaxed. He struck again. But he was becoming dizzy.

Desperately, he threw himself on the vague figure which was strangling him. He touched a naked body—and this body was *cold* . . .

He was fighting with a living corpse!

Very near the end of his resources, he used his knee viciously. The Thing grunted, fell back, and sprang toward the open window.

Swaying like a drunken man, he saw dimly a grey figure sweep up something from the desk and leap to the window. Tony tottered—fell—threw out his arms to save himself and collapsed on the floor. His outstretched hands touched a heavy bronze bowl which the secretary used as a waste-basket.

Pain, anger, gave him a brief renewal of strength. He grasped the bowl, forced himself to his feet, and hurled the bowl at the head of the retreating Thing.

It reached its target. He heard the dull thud. It rebounded and crashed against the glass of the opened window.

But the living dead horror vanished . . .

Lights . . . voices . . . arms which lifted him . . . the tang of brandy. Tony came to life.

The lighted office looked red. His head swam. Through this red mist he saw Nayland Smith bending over him.

360

"A close call, McKay! Take it easy."

Tony found himself in a deep rest-chair. He had some difficulty in swallowing. He managed to sit up.

"It went through the window," he croaked hoarsely; "although . . . I hit it on the head with . . . that."

The bronze bowl lay amongst a litter of glass.

"I know," Sir Denis snapped. "It's phenomenal. We have search parties out."

"But—"

"Don't strain your throat, McKay. Yes. It has the cipher manuscript . . ."

In Lao Tse-Mung's library, surrounded by an imposing collection of books in many languages, four men assembled. A servant, awakened for the purpose, placed a variety of refreshments on a low table around which they sat, and was dismissed. The staff's quarters were separated from the house, and the disturbance in the office had not reached them. Mercifully, it had failed to arouse Moon Flower, whose apartment was in the west wing. So that the thing which had happened in the night was known only to these four who met in the library.

Lao Tse-Mung and his frightened secretary sipped tea. Tony and Nayland Smith drank Scotch and soda. Tony smoked a cigarette and Sir Denis smoked his pipe.

"My chief mechanic reports," their host stated in his calm voice and perfect English, "that the connections are undisturbed. Six men are now examining the possible points of entry, and if anything is discovered to account for the presence of this thief in my house, I shall be notified immediately."

"When it's daylight," Nayland Smith said, "I'll take a look, myself."

"Of course you understand, Sir Denis, what has happened? We have had a visit from a Cold Man. These creatures have been reported in the neighbourhood of Chia-Ting on more than one occasion, but never here. It is a punishable offence to touch them. If seen, the police must be informed. An ambulance from a hospital established recently in that area by the governor, Huan Tsung-Chao, is soon on the scene, I understand; the attendants seem to know how to deal with these ghastly phenomena. They are believed, by the ignorant people, to be vampires and are known as 'the living-dead'. "

"The ignorant people have my sympathy!" Tony declared hoarsely.

"Personally," Nayland Smith snapped, "I'm not surprised. That master of craft, Dr. Fu Manchu, has discovered that I am here. That it was he who murdered Skobolov in order to recover this manuscript is beyond dispute. But how he found out that it had fallen into my hands is a mystery."

"I warned you," Lao Tse-Mung pointed out in his quiet way, "that my house would be watched."

"You did," Nayland Smith agreed, bitterly. "But even so, how did the watcher discover the very room in which this manuscript lay? And, crowning mystery, how did the Cold Man get in to steal it? Damn the cunning devil! He has tricked me again!"

As he ceased speaking, the large room seemed to become eerily still. And this stillness was broken by a sound which sent a chill through Tony's nerves. Although a long way off, it was clearly audible, penetrating, and horrifying as the wail of a banshee.

A long minor cry, rising to a high final note on which it died away.

Even Lao Tse-Mung clutched the arms of his chair. Nayland Smith sprang up as if electrified.

"You heard it, McKay?"

"Of course I heard it. For God's sake, what was it?"

"A sound I hadn't heard for years and never expected to hear in China. It was the warning cry of a *dacoit*. Fu Manchu has always employed these Burmese robbers and assassins. Come on McKay! I have a revolver in my pocket. Are you armed?"

"No."

"Allow me to arm you," Lao Tse-Mung volunteered, entirely restored to his normal calm. From under his robe he produced a small but serviceable automatic. "It is fully charged. What do you propose to do, Sir Denis?"

"To try to find the spot from which that call came."

Nayland Smith was heading for the door when a faint bell note detained him.

"Wait," Lao Tse-Mung directed.

The old mandarin drew back the loose sleeve of his robe. Tony saw that he wore one of the phenomenal two-way radios on his wrist. He listened, spoke briefly, then disconnected.

"My chief mechanic reports, Sir Denis, that the cry we heard came from a point between the main gate and the drive-in to the garage. He is there now."

"Come on, McKay!" Nayland Smith repeated, and ran out, followed by Tony.

They headed for the main gate, a spot which Tony was never likely to forget, two figures grotesque in their pyjamas and robes. Sir Denis ran at a steady jog trot, harbouring his resources.

"These radios," Tony said as he ran, "are supernormal. On what frequency do they operate and where does the power come from?"

"We don't know !" Nayland Smith replied jerkily. "Our technicians worked for over a year on the only one we ever captured from a Fu Manchu agent. Gave up trying to find out. Concentrated on making an exact duplicate. At last, got contact between the two. Found it had an unlimited range. No blind spots. No interference."

"Not from Fu Manchu?"

"Nothing. Entirely new principle . . . Here we are!"

They slowed down as they reached the main gate, stood still, and listened. A sound of voices reached them from somewhere ahead.

And Tony found himself retracing that sloping path which, behind the high wall, led to the garage, the path along which Mai Cha had taken him on the memorable night he had escaped the Master.

The light of a flashlamp presently led them to Lao Tse-Mung's chief mechanic, who answered to the name of Wong. He had two other men with him. A tall ladder was propped against the wall, and another man could be seen on the top staring over. Sir Denis was expected, for Wong saluted and reported. He spoke Chinese with a Szechuan accent which seemed to puzzle Sir Denis but with which Tony's travels in the area had made him fairly familiar. Fortunately, he also spoke fairly good English.

He had been walking toward this point, scanning the parapet of the wall with his flashlamp, when that awful cry broke the silence, and died away. "It came from about here. I called out, and the nearest man of the search party ran to join me. My orders were not to open the gates and not to disconnect the wiring. The gardeners brought a ladder so that we could look into the road. It is set so that the rungs don't touch the wires. But the man up there can see nothing and I have ordered him to come down."

"You have heard no other sound?" Tony asked him.

"Not a movement," the man assured him. "Nothing stirred

When the gardener descended from the long ladder and was about to remove it:

"One moment," Nayland Smith rapped. "I want to take a look. This interests me."

"Be careful of the wiring!" Wong warned. "It carries a high voltage and a touch is enough!"

" *That* wouldn't interest you!" Tony called out as Nayland Smith started up the ladder.

"That's just what *does* interest me!" Sir Denis called back.

He mounted right to the top of the ladder. He didn't look out on to the road he looked fixedly at the parapet where the wires were stretched. Then he came down. From a pocket of his gown he took his pipe and his pouch.

"There are two other things I must know, McKay. For one of them we have to wait for daylight. The other it's just possible we might find tonight." He turned to Wong. "Take the ladder away. I'm glad you brought it."

He grasped Tony's arm. "I have a flashlamp in my pocket. Walk slowly back to the house—not by the route we came, but the nearest way to the windows of your room and the office."

And so they started, Nayland Smith, pipe in mouth, flashing light into shadowy shrubberies which bordered the path:

"I don't know what you're looking for," Tony declared.

"I may be wrong, McKay. It's no more than what you call a hunch. But I do know what I'm looking for. It's a hundred to one chance and if I'm wrong, I'll tell you. If I'm right, you'll see for yourself."

They walked slowly on. There was little breeze. Sometimes the flashlamp created queer rustling in the shrubberies as of sleeping creatures disturbed or nocturnal things scuffling to shelter. In the light of a declining moon, bats could be seen swooping, silent, overhead.

His gruesome experience with a Cold Man vividly in mind, Tony found himself threatened, as they moved slowly along, by a shapeless terror. Partly, it was a creation of the dark and the stillness, an upsurge of hereditary superstition. Things he couldn't explain had happened. At any moment, he thought, icy fingers might clutch his throat again. Of human enemies he had no fear. But what were these Cold Men? Were they human— or were they as some who had seen them believed, animated dead men, zombies?

His own encounter with a Cold Man suggested that they were not mortal.

But Nayland Smith worked diligently along, yard by yard.

He found nothing.

And Tony knew, by noting the furious way in which he puffed at his pipe, that he was disappointed

They had reached the gate lodge, which was in darkness, and had turned left, instead of to the right, which was the way they had come, before Sir Denis uttered a word. Then:

"Here's our last chance!" he said rapidly.

They were in a narrow path, little used, overgrown by wild flowers. It led to the east wing of the house but to no entrance. It would, though, as Tony realised, lead them to a point directly below the window of his own room and that of the office.

Tirelessly, Nayland Smith explored every shadow with his flashlamp, but found nothing, until, in a clump of tangled undergrowth surrounding a tall tulip tree, he pulled up.

"I was right!"

The ray of the lamp lighted a grisly spectacle.

A man lay there, a man whose body was grey, whose only clothing consisted of a loin cloth, and this was grey, and a tightly knotted grey turban. He lay in a contorted attitude, his head twisted half under his body.

"This is what I was looking for!" Nayland Smith rapped. "Look! His neck's broken!"

"Good God! Is this—"

"The Cold Man who attacked you? Yes. And you killed him! "

Tony stood, hands clenched, looking at the ghastly object under the tulip tree. Suddenly, in that warm night, he felt chilled.

"The first specimen," Nayland Smith stated grimly, "to fall into my hands. Rumour hasn't exaggerated. I can feel the chill even here." He stepped forward.

"Sir Denis!"

Nayland Smith turned. "The poor devil's harmless—now—McKay. He's out of the clutches of Dr. Fu Manchu at last. Some day, I hope, we shall know how these horrors are created. His skin is an unnatural grey, but I recognize the features. The man is Burmese." He stooped over the contorted body. "Hullo! Thank heaven, McKay, the hundred to one chance has come off!"

From the grey loin cloth he dragged out a bundle of papers, shone the ray of the lamp on to it—and sprang upright so unusually excited that he dropped his pipe.

"Sun Shao-Tung's notes—and *the Chinese manuscript*! Our luck's changed, McKay." He picked up his pipe. "Let me show you something." He stooped again, lighted the face of the Cold Man. "Contrary to official belief, *Dacoity* (said to be extinct) is a religious cult, like *Thuggee*. Look!"

He tore the grey turban from the dead man's head. Tony drew nearer.

"What, Sir Denis?"

The flashlamp was directed on the shaven head.

"The caste mark."

Tony looked closely. Just above the line of the turban he saw a curious mark, either tattooed or burnt on to the skin.

"A dacoit!" Nayland Smith told him.

"Then it was he who gave that awful cry?"

"No!" Sir Denis rapped. "That was my hunch! It was *another* dacoit who gave the cry . . ."

Chapter XIV

Three times Matsukata, the Japanese physician in charge of the neighbouring clinic, had come into a small room attached to Dr. Fu Manchu's laboratory in which the Doctor often rested, and sometimes, when he had worked late, in which he slept. It was very simply equipped, the chief item of furniture being a large, cushioned divan.

A green-shaded lamp stood on a table littered with papers and books, and its subdued light provided the sole illumination. The air was polluted with sickly fumes of opium.

Dr. Fu Manchu lay on the divan entirely without movement. Even his breathing was not perceptible. A case of beautifully fashioned opium pipes rested on a small table beside him, with a spirit lamp, a jar of the purest *chandu,* and several silver bodkins. In spirit Dr. Fu Manchu was far from the world of ordinary man, and his body rested; perhaps the only real rest he ever knew.

Matsukata stood there, silent, watching, listening. Then once more he withdrew.

Some few minutes had passed in the silent room, when Fu Manchu raised heavy lids and looked around. The green eyes were misty, the pupils mere pinpoints. But, as he sat up, by some supreme command of his will the mist cleared, the contracted pupils enlarged. He used opium as he used men, for his own purpose; but no man and no drug was his master.

It was his custom, in those periods of waiting for a fateful decision which the average man spends in pacing the floor, checking each passing minute, to smoke a pipe of *chandu* and so enter that enchanted realm to which opium holds the key.

He was instantly alert, in complete command of all his faculties. He struck a small gong on the table beside him.

Matsukata came in before the vibration of the gong had ceased.

"Well?" Fu Manchu demanded.

367

Matsukata bowed humbly. "I regret to report failure, Master."

Fu Manchu clenched his hands. "You mean that Singu failed?"

"Singu failed to return, Master."

"But Singu was a Cold Man, a mere automaton under your direction," Fu Manchu spoke softly. "If anything failed, Matsukata, it was your direction."

"That is not so, Master. Something unforeseen occurred. Where, I cannot tell. But when more than ten minutes over his allotted time had elapsed, Ok, who was watching from the point of entry, reported a man with a flashlamp approaching. I ordered Ok to give the warning to which Singu should have replied. There was no reply. I ordered Ok to remove evidence of our mode of entry. It was just in time. A party of men was searching the grounds."

Dr. Fu Manchu stood up slowly. He folded his arms.

"Is that all your news?" he asked in a sibilant whisper. "The Si-Fan register is lost?"

"That is all, Master."

"You may go. Await other orders."

Matsukata bowed deeply, and went out . . .

In Lao Tse-Mung's library, Nayland Smith was speaking. Grey ghostly daylight peered in at the windows.

"Dacoits never work alone. During my official years in Burma, I furnished reports to London which proved, conclusively, that Dacoity was not dead. I also discovered that, like *Thuggee*, it was not merely made up of individual gangs of hoodlums, but was a religious cult. Dr. Fu Manchu, many years ago, obtained absolute control of the dacoits and also of the thugs. He has a bodyguard of dacoits. Probably the Cold Man, who lies dead out there, was formerly one of them."

Lao Tse-Mung's alert, wrinkle-framed eyes were fixed upon Sir Denis. Tony chain-smoked.

"Of the powers of these creatures, called, locally, Cold Men, we know nothing. But we do know, now, that they are—or were—normal human beings. By some hellish means they have been converted to this form. But certainly their powers are supernormal, and the temperature of their bodies is phenomenal. I have never heard that the fabulous zombies of Haiti are cold as blocks of ice!"

Tony found himself shuddering. His first encounter with a Cold Man had made an impression that would last for ever.

"How you got on to the fact that he was lying somewhere on that path is beyond me," he declared.

"It was a theory, McKay, based on experience. Whenever I have heard that call it has always been a warning to one dacoit, who was operating, from another who was watching. As it's getting light, I hope to find out shortly how the Cold Man got into the grounds."

"But how did he get into the office?"

"That," Nayland Smith rapped, "is not so difficult. There is a tall tulip tree growing close to the house some twenty yards from the window. These Burmese experts often operate from the roof. Evidently, even when changed to Cold Men, they retain these acrobatic powers."

"Professional thieves in this Province," Lao Tse-Mung remarked, "use much the same methods. But how they do it, I have yet to learn."

"I hope I may be able to explain later," Nayland Smith told him. "So that although the Cold Man may have dropped from the office window, for dacoits are capable of performing astonishing falls, it's more likely that he returned to the roof. Your lucky shot with the metal bowl registered," he turned to Tony—"it would have killed a normal man. It only dazed the dacoit. He got back as far as the tall tulip tree, sprang to a high branch —and missed it."

He knocked ashes from his pipe and began to reload the charred bowl.

"Your analysis of the night's events," came Lao Tse-Mung's mellow voice, "is entirely credible. But there's one mystery which you have not cleared up. I refer to the fact that those who instructed this man (if he *is* a man) must have known that the document in cipher was here."

Nayland Smith paused in the act of pressing down tobacco in the bowl of his pipe.

"I don't think they *knew* it," he replied thoughtfully. "But as McKay was identified in Niu-fo-Tu as the escaped prisoner, and as the dying Skobolov was in the neighbourhood at the same time, Fu Manchu may have surmised that McKay had got possession of the document and brought it to me . . ."

In the early morning, a party of frightened and shivering men under Nayland Smith's direction carried a long, heavy wooden box out from the main gate and across the narrow road. In a cypress wood bordering the road they dug a deep grave, and buried the Cold Man.

The body remained supernaturally chilled.

Sir Denis, having dismissed the burial party, set off at a rapid pace in the direction of the gate lodge. A man now was in charge there, old Mai Cha having moved up to the big house to look after Moon Flower.

They passed the silent bungalow and went on to the spot where the gardeners had placed the ladder that night. Nayland Smith quickly identified it by marks on the soil where it had rested. Then, foot by foot, he examined every inch of ground under the wall for several yards east and west of it. And at last:

"Look!" he cried triumphantly and pointed down. "As I thought!"

Tony looked. He saw two narrow holes in the earth, as if made by the penetration of a walking stick.

"What does this mean?"

"It means what I expected, McKay. I have the key of the main gate. Here it is. Go out and walk back along the road. I'll sing out to guide you. When you get to the spot where I'm standing inside, look for similar marks, outside."

Tony took the key and ran to the gate. He unlocked it and began to do as Nayland Smith had directed. When he reached a point which he judged to be near that where Sir Denis waited, he called out.

"Three paces more," came crisply.

He took three paces. "Here I am."

"Search."

Tony found the job no easy one. Coarse grass and weeds grew beside the road close up to the wall. But, persevering, he noticed a patch which seemed to have been trodden down. He stooped, parted the tangled undergrowth with his fingers, and at last found what he was looking for:

Two identical holes in the earth!

"Found 'em?" Nayland Smith rapped from the other side of the wall.

370

"Yes, Sir Denis. They're here!"

"Come back, and relock the gate. It isn't supposed to be opened until the gate porter is on duty."

Tony obeyed; rejoined Nayland Smith. "What does all this mean?"

Sir Denis grinned impishly. "It means two light bamboo ladders, long enough to clear the wiring and meeting above it on top. It's as easy as that!"

Tony gaped for a moment; then he began to laugh.

"So much for Lao Tse-Mung's fortress!"

"Quite so." Nayland Smith spoke grimly. "It could be entered by an agile man using only *one* ladder. But he would have to stay inside until he found another way out. So that's that. Now, to find the last piece of evidence on which my analysis of this business rests. I have examined the wall below the office window, and no one could reach the window from the ground. Therefore, he reached it from the roof."

They returned to the house, where Wong was waiting for them.

"The trap to the roof," he reported, "is above the landing of the east wing. I have had a step-ladder put there and have unbolted the trap."

"Good." Nayland Smith lighted his pipe. "Lead the way."

The opening above the ladder gave access to a low, stuffy loft formed by the curved, tiled roof which projected over the house like an umbrella. Wong carried a flashlamp, directing its light on to the cross-beams and warning them to stoop. Four of the many ornamental brackets supporting the eaves—viewed from outside, a picturesque feature of Chinese architecture—masked traps by which it was possible to get on to the upturned lip of the curving roof, and so inspect or repair the tiles.

Lao Tse-Mung had gently grafted modern efficiency on to ancient feudalism.

"This is the nearest," Nayland Smith muttered, and turned to Wong. "Open this one up."

Wong ducked his head, stepped into the narrow, V-shaped closet, reached up and opened a trap. A shaft of daylight appeared in the opening.

"Wait until I'm up, McKay," Sir Denis directed. "Then follow on. Four eyes are better than two."

He raised his arms, wedged his foot on a projection, and was gone. Tony followed—to find himself lying at the base of the curved roof, and only prevented from falling off by the curl of the highly decorated edge. Nayland Smith, on all fours, was already crawling along the ledge. Tony glanced over the side, and saw at a glance that they were no more than a few yards from the office and his own room below.

As this fact dawned upon him, Nayland Smith turned his head, looked back.

"I was right!" he cried. "Here's what I was looking for!"

He held up a length of shiny, thin rope. One end apparently was fastened to an ornament on the curling lip of the roof.

Tony turned cautiously and crawled back. He decided that the profession of steeplejack was not for him. He noted, when Sir Denis joined him, that he carried the coil of rope. But it was not until they were in Tony's room that he explained what already was fairly clear. He held up the thin line.

"Note," he rapped, "that it's knotted at intervals. It's a silk rope and strong as a cable. You saw that it was fastened to one of the gargoyles decorating the edge of the roof. A dacoit's rope. I have seen many. At a pinch, it can serve the same purpose as a thug's cord. His weight, as he first swung down to the window and then hauled himself up again, so tightened the knot that he couldn't get it free. He dared not wait. He ran along the roof to the tulip tree—and broke his neck."

372

Chapter XV

That night a counsel of war was held.

"Whatever information he may have," Lao Tse-Mung stated, "The Master dare not take active steps against me. It is clear that we hold a document which is of vital import to him. This is my shield. Your presence, Sir Denis, requires no explanation, nor does that of Moon Flower. But you, Captain McKay, as a secret agent once under arrest, pose a problem."

"I quite agree, sir," Tony admitted.

"What are we going to do?" Moon Flower asked, her blue eyes anxious. "Even if Fu Manchu does not have you arrested, Sir Denis has told you that his awful servants, the Cold Men, can get in almost any night!"

Lao Tse-Mung smiled in his gentle way.

"For a few more nights, possibly, Moon Flower. And I have arranged a patrol of the walls which will make even this difficult. Then, advised by Sir Denis, and in conference with my engineers, I have prepared a surprise for invaders."

"It boils down to this," Nayland Smith rapped out: "We're all three going to move—tonight! We meet at the house of the lama, Dr. Li Wu Chang, in Niu-fo-Tu. I could discard disguise and travel openly, as I'm entitled to do, taking Jeanie with me. Fu Manchu knows I'm in Szechuan, although I'm uncertain how he found out. It's open warfare. But in view of all we have to do, this would be to play into Fu Manchu's hands. He must be made to believe that I have returned to Hong Kong—Our good friend, Lao Tse-Mung, has undertaken this part of the scheme, and his private plane will leave for Hong Kong tonight."

"But you won't be on board?" Tony suggested.

"I shall be on my way to Niu-fo-Tu. I shall take over the part of the Burmese monk retiring to his monastery with a young disciple. Our host has provided me with suitable papers. Hang on to those you have. You, also, must travel as a Buddhist priest. You know your own story, your name and the name of your monastery. The travel permit for disciple I must have."

"All clear."

"We'll set out together, in the old Ford, until I say 'Beat it!' Then you'll beat it, and be on your own!"

"Agreed," Tony said.

"Leave the details to me. Yours may be the harder part, McKay, but you're used to the hard way. Jeanie insists on joining us, so let it go at that. We start at nine sharp. . ."

On a long, cane settee, outside the library, where flowering vines laced the terrace, and the gardens under a crescent moon looked like fairyland, Tony and Moon Flower continued the conference.

"Yueh Hua," he whispered, "why must you come with us? God knows I always want you near me, but we're up against enemies who stick at nothing. Dr. Fu Manchu uses strange methods. These Cold Men! Couldn't you stay right here, where you're safe, until a better time comes to join me?"

He could feel her heart beating against his own when she answered.

"No, Chi Foh. I know Sir Denis has some plan to release my father, and I may be part of it. I can't be wrong, because otherwise I'm sure he would have told me to stay."

Tony held her close. "When Sir Denis needs you he will send for you."

"He needs me now, or he wouldn't take me. Don't worry about me, Chi Foh. It is you I'm worrying about! If we have to separate, and someone recognizes you as an escaped prisoner—"

"The odds are against it. I know enough about the game, now, to take care of myself. I have credentials, too, and I'll get by."

"Please heaven you do, my dearest."

The rest of the conference had no bearing on the problem . . .

There was a fairly good road, as Chinese roads go, to Niu-fo-Tu, as Tony remembered. And when they set out, Nayland Smith driving, Moon Flower beside him, and Tony in the back, moonlight was adequate to prevent a driver from coming to grief on the many obstacles met with.

Nayland Smith was an expert driver, but his speed, on this unpredictable surface, might have alarmed a nervous passenger. There was no great distance to go, and he took bends with a confidence which showed that he meant to get there in the shortest possible time.

"I'm afraid, Jeanie," Tony heard him say, "my many journeys in the old days with Scotland Yard's Flying Squad have taught me bad manners!"

His remarkable driving got them intact to within sight of dim lights which indicated the market town of Niu-fo-Tu—of unhappy memory.

And suddenly these dim lights were reinforced by a red light!

"Beat it, McKay!" Nayland Smith rapped and slowed down. "Make a detour. You know something of the lay of the land. Head for Li Wu Chang's back door. If picked up, do your stuff. Admit that's where you're going. You're fellow Buddhists."

Tony jumped out. He had a glimpse of Moon Flower looking back; then, he made his way to the roadside, tried to recall what he knew of the immediate neighbourhood to place himself, and groped a way through a bamboo jungle to a spot where he could sit down.

He had a packet of cigarettes and a lighter in the pocket of his ungainly robe. He took them out, lighted a cigarette, and sat down to consider his next move.

Which side was the river? If he could mentally locate the spot where the sampan had been tied up, he could work out his route to that path which would lead him to the back door of the lama's house.

From cover, he watched the Ford pass out of sight.

He was alone again. He must act alone.

A few minutes' reflection convinced him that the Lu Ho river lay on his left. Then he must follow the road as close as possible to the outskirts of the town. As the road ran roughly east and west, on this side of Niu-fo-Tu he must bear north- westerly, if he could find a path, and this would bring him to the open country behind the lama's house.

Without further delay, he returned to the road and started walking.

What was Nayland Smith's plan? That he had one seemed evident, as he was re-entering the danger zone. Tony's heart sank when he reflected that he had rescued Moon Flower from the clutches of Fu Manchu and that now she was venturing again into his reach. But how he loved her loyalty, her intrepid spirit, that glorious, fighting spirit, ready to defy even such an enemy as Dr. Fu Manchu.

He knew that heaven had been good to him, and strode along confidently until he had a distant view of the gate of the town—but not the gate by which he had entered on a previous occasion. He pulled up, made a swift mental calculation, and got his bearings.

As he stepped aside from the high road into a tangle of bushes, a heavy wagon of market produce lumbered along, and from cover he saw, again, the red light spring up ahead.

Evidently, there was a guard at the gate. What was the reason of these unusual precautions? . . . And how had Nayland Smith been received?

Anxiety surged up in him like a hot spring.

He peered out. The big cart was being detained. He saw a number of men around it. He moved on. Still keeping parallel with the road, he tried to find some sort of path leading in the direction he wanted to go.

And, soon, he found one.

It was a footpath from the highroad, bearing north-westerly, just such a path as he had hoped to find. He sighed with relief; began to trudge along.

But, fifty yards from the road, he stopped. His heart seemed to stop, too.

A Ford car (and he couldn't mistake it!) stood beside the narrow footpath!

He sprang forward. The car was empty. It had been deserted.

His brain began to behave like a windmill, and he broke into a run. What did it mean? What had happened? This was the car Nayland Smith had been driving. Where was Nayland Smith—and where was Moon Flower?

The path led into a patch of dense shadow, deserted by moonlight. He ran on.

A steely grasp on his ankle! He was thrown—pinned down!

Tony twisted, threw off his unseen enemy, nearly got on to his knees, when a strangle-hold ended the struggle.

"The light—quick!" came a snappy command.

A light flashed dazzlingly on to Tony's face.

"Chi Foh!" Moon Flower's voice!

"Damn it, McKay! I'm awfully sorry!"

He had been captured by Nayland Smith . . .

"I thought my manœuvre had been spotted," Sir Denis explained. "Hearing someone apparently in pursuit, I naturally acted promptly."

"You did!" Tony admitted. "I'm getting quite used to being strangled!"

"You see, McKay, in sight of the town gate, I saw a loaded cart being examined there; several lanterns were brought out. By great good luck, I recognized one of the searchers—the big Nubian! That settled it. I looked for an opening where I could turn in, scrapped the old Ford and went ahead on foot."

"I understand. I did the same thing; and I think, but I'm not sure, that you have picked the right path. If so, we haven't far to walk. But what's going on in Niu-fo-Tu? Is Fu Manchu expecting us?"

They were walking ahead cautiously, speaking in low tones.

"That's what bothers me," Nayland Smith confessed. "I don't understand it."

Moon Flower had said little for some time, but now she broke her silence. "As we have the mysterious manuscript, surely Fu Manchu would expect us to get away and not to come back here."

"I agree," Sir Denis said. "There may be some other reason for these strange precautions."

They came out from the shadow of trees. The path led sharply right, and silvered by moonlight, they saw the scattered houses of Niu-fo-Tu. The house of the Lama, Dr. Li Wu Chang, was easy to identify, and Tony recognized the door by which he had escaped.

"Is the Lama expecting us?" he asked Nayland Smith.

"Yes. He has been advised. Hurry! We can be seen from several points now."

In less than two minutes they were at the door. It was a teak door with a grille. It was locked.

Nayland Smith fumbled about urgently, and presently found what he was looking for. A faint bell note sounded inside the house.

"I think someone is coming along this way," Moon Flower whispered. "Perhaps we have been seen!"

The grille opened. There was an outline of a face behind the bars.

"Nayland Smith!" Sir Denis snapped.

The door was opened. They hurried in, and the old woman who had opened the door reclosed and barred it.

At that moment the lama came out of his study, hands extended.

"You are welcome. I was growing anxious. My sister, who looks after me, will take charge of Miss Cameron-Gordon, and presently we will all share a frugal supper . . ."

Later in the Lama's study, with its church-like smell, and refreshed by a bottle of excellent wine: "I have brought you a problem, Doctor," Nayland Smith said, "which I know will appeal to you. Guard it carefully—for its solution may determine the fate of China."

And he handed the Lama the Chinese manuscript.

The old Lama glanced over a few pages, smiled, looked up.

"It is unusual, Sir Denis, but I don't despair. No doubt you have a copy?"

Nayland Smith nodded. "I had one made at Lao Tse-Mung's."

"I received a message from him. He called to learn if you had arrived. It seems that a Cold Man entered his house to steal this document, but that the attempt was frustrated and the creature killed?"

"Correct," Nayland Smith agreed. "He was also buried."

"So I understand, Sir Denis. Lao Tse-Mung informs me that his chief mechanic, a very faithful and intelligent servant, reported to him shortly after you had departed that he had heard voices and strange sounds from the cypress grove in which the burial had taken place. He asked for permission to investigate. It was granted."

"Wong's a good man," Nayland Smith said, his grey eyes lighting up. "I don't know another of them all that would go near that grave at night. What did he find?"

"He found the grave reopened—and empty!"

A blue light went out in the small cabinet which faced Dr. Fu Manchu. He glanced across at General Huan who sat watching him.

"Mahmud reports that the consignment from Lung Chang has passed through Niu-fo-Tu. On the outskirts of the town it will be transferred to the motor wagon and should be here very shortly."

General Huan took a pinch of snuff. "In my ignorance, Master, it seems to me that to employ your great powers upon a matter which cannot advance our cause—"

Fu Manchu raised his hand, stood up slowly. His eyes became fixed in an almost maniacal stare, his fingers seemed to quiver.

"Cannot advance our cause?" The words were hissed. "How do you suppose, Tsung-Chao, that I have accomplished even so little? Is it because I am a master politician? No. Because I am a great soldier? No. Why do I stand before you, alive? Because I was chosen by the gods to outlive my normal span of years? No!"

His voice rose to a guttural cry. He clenched his hands.

"I regret my clumsy words, Master. I would have said—"

"You would have spoken folly. It is because I have explored more secrets of nature than any man living today. The fools who send rockets into space: what cause do these toys advance? I constructed a machine thirty years ago which defies the law of gravity. What of those who devise missiles with destructive warheads to reach distant targets? I could erase human life from the face of the earth without employing such a clumsy device."

Fu Manchu dropped back into his chair, breathing heavily.

"Forgive me. I had no wish to disturb you."

"I am not disturbed, Tsung-Chao. I am disappointed to find that our long association has not shown you that it is my supremacy as a scientist which alone can carry our projects to success. And what is my greatest achievement to this present hour? The creation of the Cold Men. You may not know, therefore I tell you, that the Cold Men are *dead men*."

Huan Tsung-Chao stirred uneasily, looked aside.

"You are startled! Matsukata alone knew the secret, which now you share. Every one of the Cold Men has died, or has been put to death, and from the cold ashes I have re-created the flame of life. None, save Singu, has ever been buried as dead. For a man once dead cannot die a second time!"

General Huan's mask-like features relaxed into an expression which almost resembled one of fear.

"I am appalled, Master. Forgive my ignorance—but Matsukata reported that Singu died of a broken neck."

Dr. Fu Manchu laughed harshly. "He reported that Singu had

suffered a dislocation of the anterior ligament as the result of a fall on his head. There were other injuries to the skull which may indicate the cause of this fall. The ligament I can repair; the other injury also."

"But—"

"But if I cannot restore Singu to life long years of research will have led me to a hollow fallacy. I believed the Cold Men to be indestructible except by total disintegration."

There was a faint sound, and Fu Manchu turned a switch. The voice of the Japanese physician, Matsukata, came faintly:

"I have the body in the clinic, Master."

"Do nothing until I join you."

Dr. Fu Manchu stood up. "Would you care to witness one of the most important experiments I have ever carried out, Tsung-Chao?"

"Thank you, no," the old soldier replied. "I fear no living man; but dead men who walk again turn my old blood to water. . .

Chapter XVI

Tony stared out of a window into one of the busiest streets of Chia-Ting. This was part of the city he had never previously visited. His knowledge of Chia-Ting was confined to the waterfront and the jail. Accompanied by the old Lama, whose credentials were above suspicion, they had made the thirty-odd miles journey without incident, as members of his family bound for Chengtu.

Nayland Smith and Tony had adopted the dress of members of the professional class, and Moon Flower was a girl again—Sir Denis's daughter. The house in Chia-Ting belonged to a cousin of the Lama, a prosperous physician and a fervent anti-Communist.

But, this evening, Tony was worried.

Nayland Smith and his "daughter" had traced, at last, the house in which Shun-Hi, former servant of Dr. Cameron-Gordon (now employed in the summer villa of the governor of the province) was living. Moon Flower's memory of its location was rather hazy. They had gone to interview Shun-Hi.

And, although dusk was near, they had not returned.

Sir Denis had insisted that, until the time for action came, Tony must not show himself unnecessarily in Chia-Ting. Too many people knew him, and the reward for his arrest would stimulate recognition. But he suffered agonies whenever Moon Flower was out on the search.

He still had little more than a vague idea of Nayland Smith's plan. That the girl, Shun-Hi, was a link with Moon Flower's father he saw clearly. But, regarding his release from Dr. Fu Manchu, he saw no prospect whatever. Only his faith in the chief who had employed him shone like a guiding star. If anyone could do it, Nayland Smith was the man.

Just before suspense became unendurable, Tony saw Moon Flower and Sir Denis making for the door below. They had a girl with them whom he guessed to be Shun-Hi, and a few moments later all three came into the room.

Nayland Smith looked elated. "Our luck holds, McKay! Here's a useful recruit. Sit down, Shun-Hi. We have a lot to talk about."

Shun-Hi, a good-looking working-class girl, smiled happily at Moon Flower and sat down. Moon Flower sat beside her, an encouraging arm thrown around Shun-Hi's shoulders, as Nayland Smith began to fill his pipe.

"Is your father well, Yueh-Hua?" Tony asked.

Moon Flower nodded. "Yes—but very unhappy."

"Shun-Hi," Sir Denis explained, "speaks remarkably good English. So now, Shun-Hi, I want to ask you some questions. Your old employer, the doctor, you tell me, works in a laboratory in the garden but sleeps in the house. How large is this laboratory?"

"It is—" Sun-Hi hesitated—"like four of this room in a row—so." She extended her hands.

"A long, low building. I see. And where's the door?"

"One at each end. From the door at the far end there is a path to a gate. But the gate is always locked."

"And inside?"

"No one is allowed inside. Sometimes, I carry a tray down for the doctor. His lunch. But I put it on the ledge of a window and he takes it in. This was how I got Miss Yueh-Hua's message to him and got his reply back."

"Does he work alone there?"

"Yes. Except when a Japanese from the hospital comes, or when The Master is here. The Master spends many hours inside this place."

"And when the window is opened, what can you see?"

"Only a very small room, with a table and some chairs."

"Does Dr. Cameron-Gordon work there late?"

"I don't know. He is always there when I leave in the evening."

"Does he never go outside the walls?"

"No."

"When he leaves the laboratory, what is to prevent him walking out by one of the gates?"

"They are always locked, except when visitors come. Then, a

382

gate porter opens them. There is a small door in the wall, used by the staff. It is opened for us when we arrive and again when we leave."

Moon Flower smiled. "That was the door, Shun-Hi, I watched until I saw you come out one evening. Do you remember?"

Shun-Hi turned her head and affectionately kissed the hand resting on her shoulder.

"Is Huan Tsung-Chao a good master?" Nayland Smith asked.

"Yes. He is kind to us all."

"But you would rather be with Dr. Cameron-Gordon again?"

"Oh, yes!"

"And The Master—do you have much to do with him when he is there?"

"No!" Shun-Hi spoke shudderingly. "I should be afraid to go near him!"

Nayland Smith had not lighted his pipe. He did so now; and as smoke rose from the bowl:

"Tell me, Shun-Hi," he rapped, "is any watch kept in the gardens at night?"

"I don't know. I am never there at night. But I don't think so. It is just a summer house where his Excellency comes for a rest."

Nayland Smith nodded. "Do you take a tray to Dr. Cameron-Gordon every day?"

"Oh, no. Some days one of the other girls is sent."

"And does the same girl bring it back?"

"As a rule, yes. The doctor leaves it on the ledge. But, the day I gave him the message, he waited until I came to return the tray and give me the reply."

Nayland Smith pulled at the lobe of his ear, thoughtfully. "So that if we gave you another message for Dr. Cameron-Gordon, it might be several days before you could deliver it?"

"Yes."

"H'm! That complicates matters."

Tony, who had listened to every word, broke in: "It only means, Sir Denis, a few days more delay."

"Perhaps. But Fu Manchu is merely a bird of passage in Szechuan. He may move on at any time. I haven't an idea in what way he's employing Cameron-Gordon's special knowledge. But as

383

it's obviously of some value to Fu Manchu, when one goes the other goes with him!"

Moon Flower's eyes opened widely. "Oh, I couldn't bear it! We are so near to him—and yet!"

"We have to face facts, Jeanie," Sir Denis said. "Even if we're given our chance, it may not come off. But I have a strong conviction that if we make no mistakes it will."

At a glass-topped table a man whose iron-grey hair, fresh complexion and a close-trimmed grey moustache leant him something of the look of a Scottish sergeant major bent over a powerful microscope. He wore the white linen jacket which is the scientist's field uniform. Whatever he was studying absorbed all his attention.

A faint sound made by an opening door failed to distract him.

The tall figure which had entered, that of a man also in white, stood silent, watching.

The student, without removing his eye from the instrument, scribbled something on a pad which lay near his hand. He looked a while longer, then standing up and completing the note he had made, sat down and turned to a globular lamp-glass, the top closed with cotton-wool, standing in a Petri dish. Several sheets of damp filter paper lay in the bottom. He took up a lens and stared intently into the glass globe.

"I see, Doctor," came a sibilant voice from the shadowed doorway, "you are studying my new sandflies."

"Yes." The man addressed didn't even glance aside.

"Are you satisfied?"

"Yes. But you won't be."

"Why?"

"They are not absorbing the virus."

"It is fed to them."

"It is here, on the filter-papers. But they reject it." He looked up for the first time. Light-blue eyes blazed under shaggy eyebrows. "For your own filthy purpose these new imports are useless."

Fu Manchu walked slowly into the room, stood over the seated man; smiling his icy smile.

"Your mulish obstinacy in ignoring my high purpose begins to annoy me." He spoke softly. "You are well aware of the fact that I do not strike at random. Only the guilty suffer. You persist in confusing my aims with those of the crazy Communist fools who wrecked your mission hospital. You presume to classify my work with that of the ignorant, power-drunk demagogues who have forced their way into the Kremlin."

"Your methods are much the same."

There was a moment of tense silence, broken only by a rhythmic throbbing in the adjoining room. Fu Manchu's clenched hands relaxed.

"You forget that I saved you from the mob who burned your home."

"By arresting me and making me a prisoner here. It was you who inspired the mob—for that purpose alone."

Fu Manchu's voice was coldly calm when he spoke again. "Dr. Cameron-Gordon, I respect your knowledge. I respect your courage. But I cannot respect your blindness to the fact that our ideals are identical. My methods in achieving them are beyond your understanding. Be good enough to leave your work for an hour. I wish to talk to you."

"When I undertake a thing, though I may loathe it, I carry it out. My work here is not finished."

"You are dedicated to your studies, Doctor. That is why I admire you. Please come with me."

Dr. Cameron-Gordon shrugged his shoulders and stood up. He followed the tall figure to the room at the end of the long, low building which Fu Manchu used as a rest room; sat down in a comfortable chair. Fu Manchu opened a closet.

"May I offer you a Scotch and soda, Doctor?"

"Thank you, no." Cameron-Gordon sniffed. "But I have no objection to your smoking a pipe of opium. If you smoke enough the world will soon be rid of you."

Dr. Fu Manchu smiled his mirthless smile. "If I told you for how many years I have used opium, you would not believe me. Opium will not rid the world of me."

He closed the closet, sat down on the couch.

"That's a pity," Cameron-Gordon commented drily.

Fu Manchu took a pinch of snuff, then pressed the tips of his fingers together. "I have tried many times, since you have been my

385

guest—" Cameron-Gordon made a snorting sound—"to enlighten you concerning the aims of the Si-Fan. I have told you of the many distinguished men who work for the Order—"

"You mean who are slaves of the Order!"

"I mean convinced and enthusiastic members. It is unavoidable, Doctor, if the present so-called civilization is not to perish, that some intellectual group, such as that which I mention, should put an end to the pretensions of the gang of impudent impostors who seek to create a Communist world. This done, the rest is easy. And the Si-Fan can do this."

"So you have told me. But your methods of doing it don't appeal. My experience of the Si-Fan isn't exactly encouraging!"

Fu Manchu continued calmly, "I have no desire to use coercion. Without difficulty, and by purely scientific means, I could exact your obedience."

"You mean, you could drug me?"

"It would be simple. But it is a method which, in the case of a delicately adjusted brain such as yours, might impair your work. As I wish you to continue your researches during my absence, I have been thinking that your daughter—"

Cameron-Gordon came to his feet at a bound, fists clenched, eleven stones of dangerous Scot's brawn fighting mad. In two strides he stood over Dr. Fu Manchu.

"By God! Speak another word of that threat and I'll strangle you with my bare hands!"

Fu Manchu did not stir. He remained perfectly still, the lids half lowered over his strange eyes.

"I spoke no threat," he said softly. "I was thinking that your daughter would be left unprovided for if any rash behaviour on your part should make her an orphan."

"In other words, unless I submit to you, I shall be liquidated."

"I did not say so. You can join the Si-Fan whenever you wish. You will enjoy complete freedom. You can practise any form of religion which may appeal to you. Your place of residence will be of your own choosing. Your daughter can live with you. All that I shall call upon you to do will be to carry out certain experiments. Their purpose will not concern you. My object is to crush Communism. You can help me to attain that goal."

Cameron-Gordon's clenched hands relaxed. Dr. Fu Manchu's sophistry had not deceived him, but it had made him reflect.

"Thanks for the explanation," he said dourly. "I'll be thinking it over. Maybe I could get back to my work now?"

"By all means, Doctor." Fu Manchu raised drooping lids and gave him a brief, piercing glance of his green eyes. "Return to your experiment . . ."

Chapter XVII

It was early next morning when Nayland Smith and Tony joined the stream of workers, many of them silk weavers, pouring through the narrow streets. Tony wore thick-rimmed glasses, a sufficient disguise. Shun-Hi hurried along ahead, and they kept her in sight.

On the outskirts of the town, she was joined by two companions, evidently fellow servants. And after passing a large factory in which the stream of workers were finally absorbed, they came to the country road leading to the summer villa of Huan Tsung-Chao. Sir Denis and Tony, and the three girls ahead, now alone remained of the former throng.

"Drop back a bit," Nayland Smith cautioned. "Those other girls might think we're following them from amorous motives." He grabbed Tony's arm. "In here!"

They stepped through an opening in a cactus hedge and found a path parallel to the road which bordered a large field of poppies.

"Gosh!" Tony exclaimed. "Here's a crop!"

"The Reds have certainly stepped up the opium trade," Nayland Smith rapped drily.

They went ahead, guided by the girls' voices, and when these grew faint in the distance came out again on to the road. Shun-Hi and her friends had turned into a side-path. Tony caught a glimpse of the three figures just before they were lost in the shadows of a cypress grove.

"We must chance it," Nayland Smith muttered. "Have to keep them in sight. I want a glimpse of this staff entrance Shun-Hi and Jeanie mentioned."

But they had gone all of another mile before theysaw the roof of a large house gleaming in the morning sun. It stood on a slight eminence in the middle of what was evidently a considerable estate, and the narrow lane along which, now, the girls were hurrying, was bordered by a high wall of similar construction to that which enclosed the property of Lao Tse-Mung.

They had drawn up closer to the three, and suddenly:

"There's the entrance!" Tony exclaimed. "They're just going in!

"So I see," Nayland Smith spoke quietly. "We must wait awhile, in case there are others to come. We might venture a little farther and then take cover. That stately banyan twenty yards ahead appeals to me."

And three minutes later, having forced a way through tangled undergrowth, they stood in the shade of the huge tree. The gate in the wall was clearly in view.

It was a metal-studded teak door, evidently of great strength; and at the moment it remained open.

"Someone else expected," Sir Denis muttered.

They waited. And Tony, watching the open door in the high wall, realized for the first time that the high wall alone separated two implacable enemies. The thought appalled him. He and Nayland Smith were alone. On the other side of the wall, in the person of the governor, all the strength of the Red Régime was entrenched.

"Hullo! What's this?"

Nayland Smith grabbed his arm.

Four bearers appeared from somewhere along the lane, carrying the Chinese equivalent of a sedan chair. It was a finely made chair, and the men wore some kind of uniform. They stopped before the open door; set the chair down.

A tall man, wearing a mandarin robe and a black cap with a coral beard, came out and stepped into the chair. The bearers took it up and passed so close to the banyan tree that Sir Denis dragged Tony down on to his knees. The chair went by. Nayland Smith, still grasping his arm, stared into Tony's eyes.

"Dr. Fu Manchu!"

Neither spoke during a long minute, then: "It's too optimistic to hope that he's leaving Szechuan," Tony said.

"I'm afraid so," Nayland Smith agreed. "But, having a revolver in my pocket, I'm wondering if I should have missed such an opportunity!"

Oddly enough, this aspect of the thing had never occurred to Tony. Only as Sir Denis spoke did he realize how deep was the impression which the personality of Fu Manchu had made upon him. The regal dignity and consciousness of power which surrounded the Chinese doctor like a halo seemed to set him above common men.

"I wonder, too."

"Don't fall for the spell he casts, McKay. I admit he's a genius. But—"

Tony looked hard at Nayland Smith. "Could you do it?"

"Once, I could have done it. Now, when I have learned to assess the phenomenal brilliance of that great brain—I doubt myself. My hand would falter. But we can at least carry out our investigations without meeting Fu Manchu! He, alone, would know me. You have no one to fear but the big Nubian."

They came out of cover. The chair with its four bearers had disappeared in the direction of the town. First, they walked to the door in the wall. Nayland Smith examined it carefully; turned away. "Pretty hopeless," he rapped.

The lane was deserted, and they followed the high wall for all of a quarter-mile without finding another entrance. Nayland Smith scanned it yard by yard, and at a point where the pink blossom of a peach tree evidently trained against the wall peeped over the top, he paused.

"Apparently an orchard. Do you think you could find the spot at night, McKay?"

"Quite sure."

"Good."

Tony asked no questions as they passed on. Another twenty yards and they came to a corner. The wall was continued at a right angle along an even narrower lane, a mere footpath choked with weeds. They forced a way through. This side of Huan Tsung-Chao's property was shorter than that on the south side, but Nayland Smith studied every yard of the wall with eager attention. It ended where they had a prospect of a river, and turned right again on a wider road.

This road was spanned by a graceful bridge from the grounds of the big house, and Tony saw a landing stage to which a motor cruiser was tied up.

"That river will be the Tung Ho, I suppose," Nayland Smith muttered; stared up at the bridge; "and this will be the governor's water-gate."

"He must be a wealthy man."

Sir Denis grinned. "Huan Tsung-Chao is a fabulously wealthy man. He's a survival of imperial days and God alone knows his age. How he came to hold his present position under the Peiping régime is a mystery."

"Why?"

"He is Dr. Fu Manchu's chief of staff! I met him once, and whatever else he may be, he is a gentleman, however misguided."

Tony was too much amazed to say anything. He saw, several hundred yards along, what was evidently the main entrance. A man in military uniform stood outside.

"What do we do now?" he asked.

"Turn back. I don't want that fellow to see us. Come on!"

They retired around the corner; and Nayland Smith pulled up.

"How high do you guess that bridge to be, McKay, at its lowest point where it crosses the wall?"

Tony thought for a moment, then, "About twelve feet," he answered.

Nayland Smith nodded. "I should judge it fourteen. In either case, too high.".

Before a gate in a barbed-wire fence, Dr. Fu Manchu stepped out of his chair. A soldier on duty there saluted The Master as he went in. There were flowering trees and shrubs in the enclosure surrounding a group of buildings evidently of recent construction. A path bordered by a cactus hedge led to the door of the largest of these.

The door was thrown open as Fu Manchu appeared, and the Burmese doorman bowed low. Fu Manchu ignored him and went on his way, walking slowly with his strange catlike step. The place unmistakably was a hospital, with clean, white-walled corridors, and before a door at the end of one of these corridors, above which a red light shone, Fu Manchu paused and pressed a button.

A trap masking a grille in the door slid aside and someone looked out. At almost the same moment the door was opened. Matsukata, the Japanese physician, stood inside.

"Your report," Fu Manchu demanded tersely.

"There is no change, Master."

Dr. Fu Manchu made a soft hissing sound, not unlike that of certain species of snakes.

"Show me the chart."

They went into a small dressing-room. Fu Manchu removed his robe and cap and put on a white jacket similar to that worn by the Japanese. Matsukata turned away, but was back again as Fu Manchu completed his change of dress.

"Here is the chart, Master."

It was snatched from his hand. Dr. Fu Manchu scanned it rapidly.

"You have checked everything—the temperature inside, the oxygen supply?"

"Everything."

Fu Manchu walked out of the room and into another, larger room equipped as a surgery. In addition to the operating table and other usual equipment, there were several quite unusual pieces of apparatus here and one feature which must have arrested the attention of any modern surgeon.

This was a glass case, not unlike one of those in which Egyptian mummies are exhibited, and the resemblance was heightened by the fact that it contained a lean, nude, motionless body. But here the resemblance ended.

The heavy case rested upon what were apparently finely adjusted scales. A dial with millesimal measurements recorded the weight of the case and its contents. A stethoscopic attachment to the body was wired to a kind of clock. There was an intake from a cylinder standing beside the case; a mechanism which showed the quality of the air inside; and two thermometers. The instrument (known by a sixteen-letter name) for checking blood pressure was strapped to an arm of the inert grey figure and communicated with a mercury manometer outside the case. There were also a number of electric wires in contact with the body.

Dr. Fu Manchu checked everything with care, comparing what he saw with what appeared on the chart.

He began to pace up and down the floor.

"Are you sure, Master," Matsukata ventured, "that in repairing the spinal fracture you did not injure the cord?"

Fu Manchu halted as suddenly as if he had walked into a brick wall. Then, he turned, and his eyes blazed murderously, madly.

"Are you presuming to question my surgery?" he shouted. "Am I, now, to return to Heidelberg, to the Sorbonne, to Edinburgh, and beg to be re-enrolled as a student—I, who took highest honours at all of them."

He was in the grip of one of those outbursts of maniacal frenzy which, years before, had led Nayland Smith, and others, to doubt his sanity.

Matsukata seemed to shrink physically. He became speechless.

Fu Manchu raised clenched hands above his head. "God of China!" he cried, "give me strength to conquer myself—or I shall kill this man!"

He dropped down on to a chair, sank his head in his hands. Matsukata began to steal away.

"Stand still!" Fu Manchu hissed softly.

Matsukata stood still.

There was complete silence for several minutes. Then, Dr. Fu Manchu stood up. He was calm; the frenzy had passed.

"Prepare the cold room," he ordered. "I must reexamine the patient . . ."

On his return from the early morning investigation, Nayland Smith's behaviour was peculiar. After a hasty meal, he appeared dressed as a working man. Grinning at Tony and Moon Flower:

"I'm off again!" he announced. "All I want you two to do is to stay indoors until I come back. Can you bear it?"

Tony and Moon Flower exchanged glances. Tony's inclinations and his sense of duty were at war. "Can't I be of any use, Sir Denis?" he asked.

"There's not a thing you could do, McKay, that I can't do better alone."

And off he went.

"Chi Foh—" Moon Flower spoke almost in a whisper —"it's wonderful for us to be together again. I know that Sir Denis is working to rescue father. But you must feel, as I do, that to stay inactive is dreadful."

Tony threw his arms around her. "You weren't inactive, Moon Flower, in finding Shun-Hi, and I don't think it will be long before we are active again. I'm learning a lot about Sir Denis. When he tells me to stay put, I stay put. He's a grand man, and I'm glad to take his orders . . ."

Their party occupied a floor of the house, and their landlord and host, the doctor, had his office and residence on the floor below. The lama had arranged everything. They enjoyed complete privacy. So that the interval of waiting, to these affianced lovers, was rapturous rather than boring. But, even with Moon Flower's arms around him, Tony had pangs of conscience. Nayland Smith was on the big job, and he was dallying.

And as the day wore on, and Sir Denis didn't return, this uneasiness became alarm.

Where had he gone? What was he doing?

With the coming of dusk, both were wildly uneasy. Tony's sight of Dr. Fu Manchu that morning had sharpened his dread of The Master. He was painfully aware of the fact that if anything happened to Nayland Smith they would be helpless; two wanderers lost behind the second Bamboo Curtain.

Tony paced the room. Moon Flower rarely stirred from the window.

"If I had any idea where he had gone . . ." Tony said desperately.

There sounded a crisp step on the landing. Nayland Smith walked in.

"Thank God!" Tony added.

Moon Flower turned in a flash. "I didn't see you on the street!"

"No, Jeanie. I came another way and entered by the back door. I had an uneasy feeling I was being followed."

"I hope you were wrong," Tony said.

"So do I," Sir Denis admitted, opening the closet where they kept a scanty stock of liquor. "A stiff Scotch and soda is clearly indicated."

"I had hoped to hear from Shun-Hi," Moon Flower began—

"No luck today," Nayland Smith rapped. "I have seen her. She'll try again to-morrow. By that time we'll be ready to go into action."

"Why tomorrow and not to-day?" Tony asked.

Sir Denis grinned in his impish way. "I had to clear the course," he stated cryptically, and began to fill his pipe . . .

Chapter XVIII

Tony woke early on the following morning. Looking across the room which he shared with Nayland Smith, he saw that the bed was empty. He thought little about it, for Sir Denis's hours of rising were unpredictable. He took a shower, went into the living-room and lighted a cigarette.

When the woman who looked after their apartment appeared, to lay the table for breakfast, he asked her in Chinese at what time Sir Denis had gone out. They always spoke Chinese in the presence of the servants. She looked surprised and told him that it must have been before six o'clock, as no one had gone out since.

Moon Flower joined him half an hour later. "Isn't Sir Denis up yet?" she asked in surprise.

"Very much up!" Tony told her. "He must have gone out around dawn!"

She stared at him in a puzzled way. "He's behaving very oddly, isn't he? Of course, I know it's all something to do with getting father free, but I wish he wouldn't scare us by these disappearances."

"Who's scaring you?" came a snappy voice from the direction of the doorway.

Tony turned—and there was Nayland Smith smiling at them. He wore his workman's clothes.

"Where on earth have you been?" Tony asked. "And at what time did you start?"

"I started some time before daylight, McKay. I didn't disturb you by taking a bath, so I'll take one now. As to where I have been, I have been finishing the job of clearing the course. All we're waiting for is word from Cameron-Gordon. Be with you in ten minutes."

And a moment later they heard the bath water turned on; for the house of the Lama's cousin, who had graduated in New York, boasted Western equipment.

During breakfast, in spite of Moon Flower's cross examination, Nayland Smith evaded any explanation of his plans. "I believe, Jeanie, I have done all that can be done so far. Our next move will be touch-and-go. And I don't want to raise false hopes."

He spent the forenoon smoking his pipe near the window, constantly watching the passers by. Once, he spoke to Tony, out of Moon Flower's hearing: "If they once suspected we were here, all my plans would be shattered."

Tony felt like a greyhound on the leash, and Moon Flower, reproachfully, retired to her own room.

During luncheon, Nayland Smith tried to divert their gloomy thoughts with memories of his many encounters with Dr. Fu Manchu, particularly those in which he had foiled the cunning Chinese scientist. "I'm only a moderately competent policeman. This man is a criminal genius. But I have had him on the mat more than once. Unfortunately, he always got up again . . ."

The afternoon was passed in the same way; and when evening drew near, Nayland Smith's imperturbable calm began to show signs of breaking down. Several times he looked at his watch, then out of the window again, until suddenly:

"Here she is!" he cried out, and sprang to the room door in his eagerness.

Shun-Hi, flushed and excited, came in. Moon Flower ran to meet her.

"Here it is, Miss Yueh Hua. The answer from your father!"

Moon Flower almost snatched a folded sheet of paper which Shun-Hi held in her hand.

"Quick, Jeanie—is it for to-night?" Nayland Smith snapped.

She read quickly, tears in her eyes, then looked up.

"Yes! To-night! Oh, Sir Denis, please God you succeed!"

In the dusk, Tony and Nayland Smith set out. They had weathered a bad storm with Moon Flower.

"I simply dare not take her, McKay," Sir Denis said. "I understand her anxiety to see her father; but if anything goes wrong tonight, we shall have walked into hell! Whatever happens to you and me, Jeanie will be safe, if she does as I told her to do. You heard my instructions to Lao Tse-Mung. If we get Cameron-Gordon clear, the plans are laid for Jeanie and her father to fly to Hong Kong. Your capture of the Chinese manuscript was a divine miracle. We may have Dr. Fu Manchu at our mercy. But Skobolov's correspondence has given me ideas about the Soviet research centre. We are going to take a look at the Soviet research centre, McKay ..."

They followed the route which they had taken before when Shun-Hi had led them to the staff entrance of General Huan's house. But tonight the streets were not thronged. In one quarter a fringe of which touched their route they could see in adjoining streets lighted lanterns, and hear barbaric music, but it was soon left behind.

Once clear of the outskirts of the town, two working men and their moon-shadows alone walked the highway.

There was something melancholy in the empty countryside, in the breathless silence, which bred in Tony's mind a sense of foreboding. In his long journey by land and water, before he had met Moon Flower, he had known many such lonely nights; but they had not created quite the same impression of impending harm. Nayland Smith had been silent for some time. Suddenly he spoke.

"Your automatic is ready, I take it, McKay?"

And the words suggested to Tony that Sir Denis was victim of a similar depression.

"Yes, sure."

"So's my revolver. Always want to be prepared."

Tony was possessed by an urgent desire to talk, and so, "You said you had cleared the course," he went on, trying to speak lightly. "To which part of the course did you refer?"

"The last hundred yards," Nayland Smith said, and fell silent again.

Twenty paces on, he stopped suddenly, grasped Tony's arm. "Listen!"

Tony stood stock-still, and listened. He could hear nothing.

"What did you think you heard?" he asked in a hushed voice.

"Someone behind us. But there's no one in sight."

But, as they resumed their march, Tony knew that the shadow which had fallen upon his spirits had also touched Nayland Smith.

They reached the point where they had turned into the poppy field, but now kept to the highroad. Soon, they were on the path into which Shun-Hi and her friends had gone, and deep in the shadow of the cypresses. Tony's spirits sank even lower in the darkness.

Nayland Smith pulled up, detained him with a touch.

A weird, plaintive wail rose on the night—died away.

"Stupid of me," Sir Denis rapped. "For one unpleasant moment I thought it was a dacoit. Night hawk!"

They came to the lane bordering the high wall. Nayland Smith looked swiftly to right and left before stepping out. That side on which they stood, opposite the wall, lay in shadow. "All clear. Come on!"

Almost silent in their straw sandals they moved on nearer to the door in the wall. In the shade of the banyan tree, Nayland Smith turned aside, plunging into undergrowth. Tony followed. He was completely at a loss until Sir Denis produced a flashlamp and shone a light on to the tangled roots of the great tree.

"Look!"

And Tony looked; was astounded by what he saw.

A long, slender bamboo ladder lay there!

"Always glad to learn from the enemy, McKay. This clears the course from here to the laboratory, where Cameron-Gordon is waiting for us!"

"You still have me guessing."

Nayland Smith laughed. "This ladder is light enough for a child to carry. It's long enough to reach the top of General Huan's wall. It's strong enough to support a man of reasonable weight. We're both lean specimens. All clear?"

"So far, all clear. But where did you get it?"

"I found a friendly carpenter. Told him I was a gardener employed in a place where there were tall trees to be pruned. He had the ladder ready by evening. I collected it, and carried it halfway to the governor's house, where I parked it in a clump of bamboos. Quite impossible to spot from the road. Early next morning, when no one was about, I carried it here."

He dragged the light ladder from the outflung roots of the tree.

"I get it!" Tony spoke excitedly.

"What a frozen dacoit can do, we can do!"

They returned to the lane, Tony carrying the ladder on his shoulder. "I have to look out for the peach tree?"

"Right. Go ahead. I want to keep an eye on the lane behind."

Tony tramped on. Promise of action blew aside the cloud of foreboding which had crept over him. And soon, against the bright sky, he saw peach blossom peeping over the wall, to awaken a memory of a Japanese water-colour painting.

"All clear," Nayland Smith rapped. "Set the ladder up, McKay."

Tony found a spot among the weeds at the foot of the wall where he could make the base of the ladder firm, and gingerly manœuvred its delicate frame into place.

"All ready."

"Stand by, McKay. I must make sure that the trellis is strong enough to be safe. We may want to retire in a hurry!"

Nayland Smith went up the ladder with an agility surprising in a man no longer young. Tony watched, breathless with excitement. Sir Denis climbed over the wall and began to climb down on the other side. When his head was level with the pink blossom:

"Follow on," he instructed. "Safe as an oak staircase!"

"Do I leave the ladder?"

"No choice, McKay. If it's moved, we'll have to drop from the wall."

Tony was up in a count of seconds; looked over the top. He saw a well-planted orchard, pear trees, plum, and other fruits. Nayland Smith stood below.

"A wire frame, clamped to the wall. Perpendicular but safe."

Tony swung his leg over, found a stout branch and scrambled down.

"What's our direction, Sir Denis?"

"Not quite sure. Must get my bearings."

Nayland Smith stood there, in the shadow of the wall, tugging at his ear.

"Shun-Hi tried to explain the location of the laboratory."

"She did. And it's clear in my mind, now. Follow on."

They had to make a wide detour around the house. The property was landscaped as a pleasure garden, with lily ponds and streams of running water; with miniature waterfalls amid a blaze of rockery flowers. In moonlight it was entrancing, but Tony felt more concern about sticking to the shadows than admiration of the many beauties of the garden.

The laboratory, when at last they sighted it, proved to be partly screened in a grove of orange trees. This was all to the good. It was an ugly building evidently of recent construction; a long, narrow hut, but much larger than Tony had visualized.

"We have to show ourselves in the moonlight to reach the orange trees, which frightens me," Nayland Smith said. "But at this point we're not in view from the house."

"There isn't a light in the house," Tony pointed out.

"That's what frightens me. Let's make a dash for it!"

They raced across the moon bright patch and into the shadow of the trees.

Two windows of the laboratory building were lighted; a small one near the door; a larger at the side of the hut. Tony pushed forward. But Nayland Smith stood still, looking back, listening. He said nothing, but joined Tony on a narrow path which led to the door.

He rapped on the panels. The light in the window disappeared. The door was opened, and a man in a white coat peered out.

"Smith!"

"Cameron-Gordon!"

"Quick! Come in! Who's with you?"

"Tony McKay, one of us."

They entered in darkness. The door was closed again and a light sprang up.

Tony saw a tiny room, with a table and two chairs, such as Shun-Hi had described. The man in the white coat spoke hoarsely:

"Thank God you found me, Smith! I didn't know you were in China. And God bless Jeanie for getting my message through! I didn't want to show a light when I opened the door. I never know when I'm watched."

"Nor do I," Nayland Smith rapped. "I suggest we start."

Cameron-Gordon had his hand in a fervent grip of greeting. "Wait just a few moments, Smith. I want you to see the kind of work I do." He transferred the handgrip to Tony. "You must be a sound man to be here, and I'm glad to meet you."

400

He opened a door, beckoned them to follow. They did so, reluctantly.

On the threshold they halted, both together. There was a muffled buzzing sound, and a strange, repulsive odour. The place was lined by glass cases, in which, as Cameron-Gordon switched light on, a feverish activity came to life. The cases were filled with insects, some with wings and some without; huge flies, bloated spiders, ants, centipedes, scorpions!

"My God!" Tony muttered.

"I have seen something like this before," Nayland Smith said; "in another of Fu Manchu's establishments."

"My dear Smith"—Cameron-Gordon was alight with the enthusiasm of the specialist—"he is doing work here which, if it were used for the good of humanity, would make his name immortal. His knowledge of entomology is stupendous."

"I have had some experience of it," Nayland Smith rapped drily. " 'My little allies', he once called these horrors."

Cameron-Gordon ignored the interruption. "His experiments, Smith, are daring beyond what is allowed to God-fearing men. He has bred hybrids of the insect world which never before existed except for sufferers from delirium tremens. I'll show you some. But he has also prepared drugs from these sources which, if made available to physicians, would almost certainly wipe out the ravages of many fatal diseases."

"Tell me, Doctor," Tony said faintly, "what is *that*?"

He was staring at a case which contained an enormous centipede of a dull red colour. It was fully a foot long and was moving around its glass prison with horrible, febrile activity.

"A Mexican specimen of the *morsitans* species. Twice its hitherto known largest size. From its toxin he hopes to prepare an inoculation giving immunity from cholera. One of my duties is to extract the toxin!"

"And what about this hideous spider?"

"Known in New Zealand as a *katipo*, but in this instance, crossed with a tarantula! Its sting is deadly. Dr. Fu Manchu has a poison made from that creature's toxin which, swallowed—and it's tasteless—would kill in five minutes; injected, kill instantly! Look at that colony of red ants! Another hybrid species. They multiply from

401

hundreds to millions in a short time. They eat anything. Set loose here in China, they would turn Asia into a desert from the sea to the Himalayas in a few months!"

Nayland Smith was glancing anxiously at his watch. But Cameron-Gordon remained in the grip of professional enthusiasm.

"These"—he pointed—"are plague fleas. They are reinforced with plague-cultures. One bite would mean the end—I have to feed them!"

Sir Denis broke in: "These cases filled with buzzing flies particularly interest me. What are they?"

" *Tsetse* flies," Cameron-Gordon told him, turning. "Each one of the cases is kept at a different temperature, which I regulate. The first, at which you are looking, is kept at tropical heat, the normal temperature for these insects. The second is sub-tropical. The third is temperate. And the fourth is arctic. So far, we have failed with the fourth. But some of the flies in there are still alive."

"So I see."

"They are fed on blood plasma, charged with the trypanosome of sleeping-sickness. They are so reinforced that their bite would induce a form of the disease which would pass through its entire course in a matter of days instead of months! They could operate anywhere short of the Arctic Circle. They are utterly damnable!"

Nayland Smith looked grimly at Tony. "Now we know how Skobolov died!"

And, as he spoke, the light went out.

"I fear," came a cold, sibilant voice, "that you know too much, Sir Denis. . ."

In complete darkness, Tony, his heart beating a tattoo, realized that he stood nearest to the door. He reached it—to find it unopenable.

"We're trapped, McKay!" Nayland Smith said. "What about—"

"What about the other door, you were thinking, Sir Denis?" came the mocking voice. "Unfortunately, as it belongs to my laboratory, I make a point of keeping it locked.

Tony, cool again after that first shock, began to peer through the darkness in the direction from which the voice came. His hand closed over the butt of his automatic. He had seen something.

High up at the end of this home of insect horrors, he saw a square patch of dim light. He raised his automatic and fired.

The odour of the discharge mingled with the other unpleasant smell which haunted the place. Vibration caused a rattle of glass, but it came from the surrounding cases. Then, the silence was complete again, except for faint buzzing of the *tsetse* flies and whispering sounds made by some of the other inhabitants of the cases.

"No good, McKay," Nayland Smith said sharply. "I saw that opening, too."

"It's over the door of my workroom," Cameron-Gordon whispered. "That's where he is."

His words were answered by a harsh laugh from Dr. Fu Manchu.

"Since the arrival of my old acquaintance, Sir Denis, in China, I have made it a practice to look in unobtrusively whenever you have remained late at work, Dr. Cameron-Gordon. To-night I seem to have disturbed you showing your friends around this small collection of rare specimens."

"Enough of idle chatter!" Nayland Smith cried angrily. "You have trapped us. Very well—come and take us!"

"Sir Denis, how strangely you misread my purpose. If I desired your death, it would be necessary only to shatter any one of the cases of specimens surrounding you —which I assure you I could do without exposing myself to your fire. Should you prefer the *tsetse* flies? This would be a lingering death. Or, perhaps, the fleas and the painful result of bubonic plague?"

"You're not a man, you're a demon!" Tony rasped.

"I have knowledge which few men possess, Mr. McKay—that, I understand, is your name. And as you are clearly a man of courage, possibly you would prefer to try to repel in the dark the attack of my *katipo* tarantula? He is a strangely active nocturnal creature."

"Stop talking!" Nayland Smith shouted. "Words don't frighten us. Smash everything in the place, if you like, but stop talking!"

"That is indeed the familiar language of the British policeman! But for your very stubbornness I admire you, Sir Denis. Dr. Cameron-Gordon is useful to me, and I believe I could use the qualities of Mr. McKay also."

"You never will!" Tony assured him.

"Let me explain myself," the cold, emotionless voice continued.

"There are more ways than the way of drugs, of physical pain, to enforce obedience. One of these means I hold in my hands. There is no place for heroics. Dismiss any plans you may have made. I assure you that you have no alternative other than acceptance of my terms—whatever they may be. . ."

Chapter XIX

Tony opened his eyes; looked around. He closed his eyes again. This was part of the dream. In the part which had passed earlier he had wandered in a strange paradise. There were trees laden with blossoms he had never seen before and the ground upon which he trod was carpeted with flowers. The air was filled with their intoxicating perfume.

Seated under one of the dream trees, from which in a gentle breeze fragrant petals dropped from time to time, a gracefully beautiful girl had joined him, seated herself beside him. She carried a flask of wine and two crystal glasses. She smiled, and her dark eyes challenged him, provocatively. She filled the glasses.

"You will drink with me?" she whispered, handing him one of them. "I belong to you, and so let us drink together."

Tony hesitated. She wore a gauzy robe through the mist of which every line of her shapely body was visible. She threw her arms around his neck. Her ripe lips were very near.

Some swift revulsion swept over him. He dashed his glass to the ground—and sudden darkness fell. . .

When the dark cloud passed, he found himself in another part of the garden. A sweet voice, a woman's voice, spoke from the shadows of a flowering bush near to which he lay.

"Why are you so sad?" the voice asked. "You are young and the world is before you. There is nothing to prevent a soldier trained in diplomacy from rising to the greatest heights. Your President is a soldier-diplomat. May I talk to you?"

"Yes," he remembered saying.

He was joined by a fair woman, neither so young nor so beautiful as the dark siren who had offered him wine, but all the same very attractive. She seated herself beside him on the mossy bank where he lay. She had strange violet eyes, alight with intelligence.

"Together," she said softly, "we could go far."

Tony looked into the violet eyes, and as he looked they seemed to turn green, the fair features to become yellow—and he found himself staring into the face of Dr. Fu Manchu!

So the dream had ended, and now, he thought, it was continuing.

He opened his eyes again.

The wonderful garden had gone. But he lay, not among flowers, but on a cushioned divan. Looking around, he still saw what he had seen before: a small room luxuriously furnished in the Oriental manner. The only light came from a shaded lantern hung from the ceiling. But there were rich rugs on the floor, lacquer-ware gleamed from the shadows. There was a faint odour of sandalwood.

He sat up, conscious of a swimmy feeling but with no trace of headache to explain what he supposed to have been delirium. He tried to stand up. He couldn't do so. Looking down, angrily, at his ankles, he saw that they were secured by a tiny cord of something that resembled catgut. He put his heels together and tried to snap it.

The effort was useless. The fastenings pierced his skin, and he knew that any further attempts would only cut the tendons.

And, in that moment of acute pain, real memory came, bridging the mirage which had clouded his mind. He remembered that last scene in the insect vivarium lined with cases of loathsome creatures, remembered the mocking words of Fu Manchu.

Then had come that perfumed cloud, oblivion. . .

A heavy curtain was silently drawn aside—and Dr. Fu Manchu came in.

He wore a yellow robe, and his nearly hairless head was bare. A sort of Satanic majesty seemed to radiate from the tall figure. Silent, he stood watching Tony. Then, at last, he spoke.

"Your impersonation of Chi Foh, the fisherman, was excellent. Almost you deceived me. I must congratulate you."

Tony said nothing.

"The gas which overcame you is a preparation perfected by me some years ago. If any of it had penetrated the cases, it would not have affected the creatures confined there."

It was hard to sit and listen to that cold voice. Dr. Fu Manchu spoke English with careful perfection and his manner was that of a professor addressing a class of students.

"What a pity!" Tony commented.

"I note that you are imitating the brand of repartee favoured by

Sir Denis Nayland Smith. It is usually prompted by bravado in moments of danger. I am completely acquainted with the psychological features of Sir Denis's character. I endeavoured to learn something of your own, particularly of one aspect, during the time that you remained under the influence of the drug. Its composition renders the subject peculiarly impressionable to what is sometimes termed hypnotic suggestion."

Tony began, now, to listen intently.

"I projected on to your brain images of two desirable women, who are members of my organization. There was no trace of sexual reaction. You rejected their overtures. In fact, you dispelled the second image, for I saw recognition of myself dawning in your eyes. But I had learned what I wanted to know. You are completely enslaved by one woman. And I think I know her name."

Tony found himself alone again. Dr. Fu Manchu had stepped silently to the draped opening, raised the curtain and silently disappeared.

He could detect no sound of any kind. Where was he? What place was this? And where were Nayland Smith and Cameron-Gordon? He stood up; and learned that by taking short, mincing steps he could walk; for there was about a foot of fine, unbreakable cord between his ankles.

First, he crossed to the curtain from behind which Fu Manchu had entered and retired. He raised the heavy brocade. He saw a blank wall. That it masked a door was perfectly obvious; but to find how to open it was another matter.

He hobbled right around the room, examining the wall foot by foot.

The room had no window, and no door!

For one horrifying moment panic touched him with its icy finger.

Except that it was exotically furnished, this place was no better than an *oubliette,* one of those dreadful mediaeval dungeons without exit other than an inaccessible trap, of which he had seen an example in an ancient French castle.

He returned to the settee and tried to recover composure, to get himself in hand.

That he might be left in this luxurious cell to starve to death was a nightmare he could safely dismiss. Dr. Fu Manchu had other plans for him; for he had spoken of terms, which "whatever they may be", he must accept.

He wanted to shout out curses on Fu Manchu, that cold-blooded villain who used human emotions as ingredients in a scientific formula. But he smothered the useless words, clutched his head and groaned.

How long a time had elapsed since that moment when, surrounded by obscene insects, they had heard the sardonic voice of Dr. Fu Manchu? He could have been unconscious for hours, days, weeks! The devilish genius who had them all in his power possessed medical knowledge which, as Cameron-Gordon had said, properly belonged to the future of science.

Tony groped in his Chinese garments. He was desperately thirsty, but a smoke might steady his nerves. His automatic was gone, but a packet of cigarettes and a lighter remained. He lighted a cigarette.

As he blew smoke from his lips he noted that it hung motionless in the stagnant air. There was little or no ventilation.

But sitting there, watching the smoke, trying to conquer useless anger and to think constructively, he became aware of two curious facts. The first: smoke clouds began to swirl; second, the air grew suddenly cold.

A premonition swept into his mind. He dropped the cigarette in a jade bowl which lay on a table near the divan, and stood up.

The curtain masking the hidden opening was moving!

It was swept aside.

The gaunt figure of a man wearing only a loin-cloth stood there, looking into the room . . .

His neck was fixed in a brace which seemed to make his head immovable, for he never turned it in the slightest degree. Ghastly grey features and fish-like eyes in that rigid head were indescribably revolting. There was a long scar over the creature's heart.

But, crowning terror, this apparition unmistakably was that of the Cold Man whom he had killed, whose body, with a broken neck, he had seen lying at the foot of a tree near the wall of Lao Tse-Mung's house!

Tony stifled a cry of horror. He became cold as though his spine had frozen; incapable of action.

The grey thing spoke. Its voice resembled one on a worn-out record.

"Follow!"

Very slowly, the grey figure turned, never moving the rigid neck. A black opening in the wall gaped behind him. The temperature of the room had perceptibly become lower. Tony, fists clenched convulsively, hesitated. Every human instinct prompted him to refuse to follow a thing which he could only believe to be of another world.

He overcame that helpless inertia, which had seized him; took a deep breath. Dead or alive, the creature which had said "Follow" offered a way out of the prison in which he was trapped . . . But perhaps this was another dream, a further example of Dr. Fu Manchu's psychological examinations—a test of his courage!

Tony followed; slowly, because of the fastenings around his ankles, fearfully because uncertain if he dreamed or was awake.

Ahead, silhouetted against a lighted opening, he could see the mummylike figure moving. He kept his distance. Even the narrow passage was chilled by the creature's presence. There was a short stair. He allowed the grey thing to reach the top before he followed, and found himself in a white-walled corridor, doors opening to right and left. The corridor was empty.

Before one of these doors, the grey figure paused, pressed a bell and went on, moving mechanically like an automaton. When Tony came to the door—it was a sliding door—he found it wide-open. He hesitated, glanced along the lighted passage. His phantom guide had disappeared.

He looked into a small room. The only illumination came from one wall of the room which appeared to be made of glass.

Three chairs were set facing the glass wall; and two of them were occupied.

"Hullo, McKay!" Nayland Smith's unmistakably snappy speech! "You're rather late. But the curtain hasn't gone up yet . . ."

As Tony stepped in, the sliding door closed noiselessly behind him.

He made his way to the vacant chair next to Nayland Smith; sat down. Dr. Cameron-Gordon, his head in his hands, occupied the third chair. Somewhere below Tony could see, through the glass wall, a large, dimly lighted place masked in vague shadows. Sir Denis grasped his hand.

"Keep smiling, McKay! I don't know what all this is about any more than you do. But we're still alive."

Came Cameron-Gordon's voice: "It's all over, Smith! What will become of Jeanie when we disappear for good?"

"Don't worry," Nayland Smith said. "We're in a tight corner, but I have got out of tighter ones."

Cameron-Gordon sighed and dropped his head into his hands again.

"I was led here by the dacoit we buried in the cypress grove!" Tony whispered to Sir Denis. "It's supernatural!"

"Nothing is supernatural where Dr. Fu Manchu is concerned. You may recall that the dacoit was dug up again?"

"What about it?"

"I have known of others buried as dead who have been disinterred by Fu Manchu and restored to life."

"But a man with a broken neck!"

"Clever surgeons have mended broken necks before now. And Dr. Fu Manchu is probably the greatest surgeon the world has ever known."

As Nayland Smith stopped speaking, Tony noted for the first time how completely silent the cabinet in which they were assembled seemed to be. Not a sound was audible from outside its walls . . . until suddenly the stillness was broken by a voice, apparently the voice of someone in the room. But no one else was in the room!

"I am instructed," this modulated voice said, "to explain the purpose of what you are about to see. This is a sound-proof observation room which both I and The Master use frequently. He is about to pay his daily visit to the *necropolites,* known locally as Cold Men—a duty which devolves on me when The Master is absent."

"Dr. Matsukata," Cameron-Gordon muttered, "Fu Manchu's chief technical assistant."

"Is that so?" Nayland Smith rapped. "Why don't you join us, Dr. Matsukata, instead of speaking on radio?"

"I am following my instructions. Be so good, Sir Denis, as to listen to what I am here to tell you."

"Seems we have no choice!" Tony commented.

The precise voice continued: "I believe you have already made the acquaintance of a *necropolite* and must have noted the unusual qualities which these creatures possess. In certain respects they resemble the Haitian *zombies,* whose existence has been disputed in some quarters. In fact, in certain respects, the process of reanimation is similar, but superior. They work as automata, being entirely under control of the power miscalled hypnotic suggestion. Otherwise than by complete disintegration, their faculties are indestructible. So that the *necropolite* is perfectly equipped to carry out dangerous missions."

"You're telling me nothing!" Tony broke in. "But there's one thing you might tell me—what a Japanese is doing in Fu Manchu's gang!"

"For a friend of Sir Denis Nayland Smith, you betray remarkable ignorance of the Order of the Si-Fan," Matsukata answered heatedly. "Its membership is not confined to China. It includes the whole of Asia, the Near East, many parts of Europe and America. Its secret power is at least equal to that of Communism . . ."

Light sprang up in the dim place below—and Tony found himself looking down upon a morgue!

Nearly a score of grey bodies lay there in two rows, one row on the right and one on the left. But here the resemblance to a morgue ended. They lay, not on stone slabs, but on neat hospital cots.

"The *necropolites,*" came Matsukata's voice. "This clinic was constructed for the purpose of creating and maintaining them. They represent The Master's supreme achievement; for they are dead men who live again at his command. The process of reducing their bodies to the low temperature at which alone reanimation can be brought about is too technical for description here. But I should be glad to discuss it, later, with Dr. Cameron-Gordon."

"Thank you, no," Cameron-Gordon muttered. "I want to keep what little sanity I have left."

"Be good enough to watch closely what now takes place. I must explain that a *necropolite* retains in his living-death whatever useful qualities were his in normal life—also his physical appetites or vices. Without occasional gratification of the latter, the creature's usefulness deteriorates. Watch carefully."

Tony was watching more than carefully. He was trying hard to convince himself that this thing was reality, that he wasn't lost again in a nightmare dream. Nayland Smith's crisp voice came to reassure him.

"I warned you, McKay, that if we made a mistake, we should walk into hell!"

Dr. Fu Manchu came into the ward below with its rows of grey corpses. He wore a white coat, and his manner was that of cool detachment which marks the specialist visiting a hospital ward. A white-coated orderly followed, pushing a glass-topped cabinet on rubber-tyred wheels. He was sallow-faced, but looked European.

Not a sound penetrated to the observation room, and Matsukata remained silent.

Dr. Fu Manchu stopped beside the first cadaver at the end of the row and made a swift, skilful examination. He spoke over his shoulder to the orderly. The man charged a hypodermic syringe; handed it to him. Fu Manchu gave an injection, not in the arm, but in the breast of the still body, and passed on to the next.

This singular proceeding continued until every cot had been visited. Two of the Cold Men received no injection.

And, as Fu Manchu walked out with his strange, feline step, followed by the orderly wheeling the glass trolley . . . three or four of those Cold Men first treated began to stir!

Tony found himself shivering.

"My God! It's unholy!" Cameron-Gordon whispered.

Matsukata spoke again. "The Master has detected signs in two of the *necropolites* which necessitate their removal to the surgery for further examination."

Almost as he ceased speaking, two stretchers were carried in and the two Cold Men placed on them and carried out.

"The most instructive feature of the treatment," the smooth Japanese voice went on, "will now begin. The Master will project to each creature the images appropriate to his particular appetite when a normal man. To one, the figure of his enemy; to another, a banquet of his favourite food; to a third, the image of a seductive woman—and so forth."

Now, the Cold Men were rising up, moving grey arms convulsively; and all seemed to be crying out.

"They are calling for *Looma*," Matsukata explained. "By this name they know a drink which transports them to a dream life where there is no satiety. One can kill his enemy a hundred times, another eat and drink without experiencing repletion, a third enjoy the pleasures of love indefinitely. Something like the promised paradise of Mohammed."

"Don't they murder one another?" Tony asked shakily.

"They cannot leave their cots. Their movements are restricted by a length of slender cord, such as that which is attached to your ankles. They are about to receive their instructions."

Dr. Fu Manchu returned, alone. He carried a lamp of unusual design. The light of this lamp was shone into the face of the Cold Man until his twitching and mouthing ceased. Then, Fu Manchu rested his long fingers on the creature's temples and stared into his eyes. This routine was continued until all had been dealt with.

"Now comes *Looma*, their wine of paradise," Matsukata said softly.

And, as Dr. Fu Manchu went out, a nurse in a trim white uniform came in, followed by the same orderly pushing the glass trolley. It carried, now, a large glass jug filled with some liquid of a colour resembling green Chartreuse, and a number of small glasses. The orderly filled the glasses and the nurse carried each to a Cold Man. In every case it was grasped avidly and swallowed in one eager draught.

But Tony scarcely followed what took place after the appearance of the nurse.

For the nurse was *Moon Flower* . . .

Chapter XX

Tony's impressions of the next few minutes were chaotic. The frantic behaviour of Cameron-Gordon, the crisp, soothing words of Nayland Smith, the tumult in his own mind, had built up a jungle of frustrated hopes, terror and abject misery in which the details of what actually occurred were lost.

He knew that the tiny but tough shackles which confined their ankles had been removed by a smiling Chinese mechanic, dexterously and swiftly. The man used an instrument resembling a small electric buzz-saw.

And now the three of them were assembled in a room which reminded him of that in which he had been confined, except that it was larger. There was a low, round table in the centre, and on it lay a note in small, legible characters which Nayland Smith picked up and read aloud:

"You may refresh yourselves as you please. I beg you to do so. Chinese hospitality forbids me to poison my guests. Sir Denis will assure you that my word is inviolable. Fu Manchu."

Nayland Smith had just finished reading the letter when the door opened and two Chinese servants came in carrying laden trays. They placed on the table a delicate meal of assorted dishes, also a variety of wines, a bottle of Napoleon brandy, Scotch whisky, a number of glasses and an English siphon of soda water. One of the servants uncorked all the bottles, placing the white wines in ice, and withdrew.

Nayland Smith grinned almost happily. "Let's make the best of it, and prepare for the worst!"

"We'll all be drugged!" Cameron-Gordon said.

Sir Denis held up the note. "This is the first example of Fu Manchu's handwriting which I have seen," he declared. "But it must obviously be genuine. I accept his word—for I have never known him to break it."

414

Cameron-Gordon groaned. "Right or wrong, a shot of brandy is what I need."

"It would do none of us any harm," Sir Denis agreed, and poured out three liberal tots. "A compromise is going to be offered. It will be one we can't accept. But let us all sharpen our wits, and have something to eat."

But Cameron-Gordon made a very poor attempt. "How did that cunning fiend get his hands on Jeanie?" he asked in a voice of despair.

"I suspect," Sir Denis told him, "owing to her own obstinacy."

"Meaning what?" Tony wanted to know.

"Meaning that I detected, or thought that I detected, the footsteps of someone following us. Jeanie is high-spirited, and as nearly fearless as any woman I ever met. My guess is that Jeanie was the follower. We have even to suppose that she climbed the bamboo ladder and was actually in the garden when Fu Manchu saw her."

"God help her!" Cameron-Gordon groaned; "for no one else can, now."

"I don't agree," Nayland Smith rapped in his sudden fashion. "There are weak spots in Fu Manchu's armour. I think I can find one. But leave the talking to me."

Nayland Smith, alone of the three, did justice to the *smorgasbord*. He particularly favoured, too, an excellent bottle of burgundy.

And presently the Chinese servants reappeared, cleared the table, leaving only the brandy, and served coffee. They also brought cigars and cigarettes, port and a number of liqueurs. When they went out:

"It's evidently dinner time," Sir Denis remarked. "I had an idea it might be luncheon."

"I have lost all track of time," Tony confessed. "My wrist watch is missing."

"All our watches are missing. We're not intended to know the time."

They had finished their coffee, and Cameron-Gordon sat deep in silent gloom, when the door opened again.

The huge Nubian stepped in. He wore some kind of uniform, had a revolver in a holster and a *tarbush* on his head.

"March out!" He had a deep, negroid voice. "One at a time. I will follow."

Nayland Smith glanced wrily at Tony, shrugged his shoulders. "You go first, McKay; then Cameron-Gordon. I'll bring up the rear."

The big coloured man stood stiffly beside the open door, his hand on the butt of his revolver, as they filed out. Tony was seized by sudden misgiving. To what ordeal were they being taken? He dared not allow himself to think of Moon Flower . . .

At the end of a short passage he came to a flight of stairs.

"Go down!" came the deep voice.

Tony went down. He was in one of the white-walled corridors which he had seen before. His fellow captives followed silently. He came to a cross-passage.

"Right turn!"

He obeyed. He was a cadet again, being ordered about by a drill-sergeant.

The cross-passage ended in what appeared to be a vestibule. It was well lighted. He could see a large double door which might be the main entrance to the building.

"Halt!"

The tone of command was unmistakable. This big African was an ex-soldier.

Tony halted, standing stiffly upright, then recovered himself, turned, looked back. Cameron-Gordon, grim and angry, growled, "Impudent swine!" Nayland Smith grinned reassuringly. The Nubian stepped forward and pointed to a long, wooden bench.

"Sit down."

They sat down. Tony was assessing their chances of overpowering the man by a simultaneous attack. But even assuming that the double-doors opened on freedom, how far could they go . . . and how would it help Moon Flower?

Nayland Smith seemed to read his thoughts, for he caught his eye and shook his head, as a side door opened and two stocky Burmese came out.

Tony submitted to having his eyes scientifically bandaged. He divined rather than knew that his companions were undergoing the same indignity. Next, he was raised to his feet and led out into the open air. He was helped into a vehicle which he judged to be a limousine. A slight odour of petrol told him that it was an automobile.

All three were packed into the back seat, the door was closed and the car started. The engine had the velvet action of a Rolls.

"No talking!" came the deep African voice.

The big Nubian was still with them!

A dreadful idea crossed Tony's mind. They were being taken to the jail at Chia-Ting! The thought seemed to chill his blood. Once inside that grim prison they would be lost to the world. Even Sir Denis, with all the power of Britain behind him, would merely be listed as missing!

But the horror was quickly dismissed. The car stopped long before they could have reached Chia-Ting, and he was hauled out. Unseen hands guided him through what he knew to be a garden; for a faint fragrance of flowers told him so.

He was led in on to a softly carpeted floor, led upstairs. He could hear the stumbling footsteps of his friends who followed. He was thrust down in a chair. And, last, the bandage was removed from his eyes.

Tony blinked, for a light shone directly on to his face. For awhile, he couldn't get accustomed to it after complete darkness. But at last he did . . .

He saw a luxuriously furnished room. There were rich Chinese rugs, cabinets in which rare porcelain vases gleamed, trophies of arms; openings veiled by silk curtains. The lighting was peculiar. It came from a shaded lamp, the shade so constructed that light shone fully on to his face and on to the faces of his two companions. This lamp stood on a long lacquer desk, its gleaming surface littered with a variety of objects: books, manuscripts, some curious antique figures on pedestals, a small gong, and several queer-looking objects of the nature or use of which he was ignorant.

But these things he saw clearly later. His first impression of them was a vague one. For his attention became focused upon the man who sat behind the lacquer desk, wearing a plain yellow robe, his long-fingered hands resting on the desk before him. Owing to the cunning construction of the lampshade, his face was in half-shadow.

417

His green eyes glinting under partly lowered lids, Dr. Fu Manchu sat passively regarding the three trapped men.

"It is a long time, Sir Denis," he said softly, "since I had the privilege of entertaining you. I trust you enjoyed your supper?"

"Oh! it was supper?—it was excellent."

"Prepared by a first-class French chef."

"Tell him if he cares to come to London I can find him better employment."

Dr. Fu Manchu took a pinch of snuff. "Incorrigible as always. In our many years' association I cannot recall that you ever admitted defeat."

Nayland Smith didn't reply. The green eyes were turned upon Tony, and he felt, again, the horrible sensation that they looked, not at him, but *through* him.

"You have proved yourself a nuisance, Captain McKay," the sibilant voice continued; "but not a serious menace. Suppose I offered you your freedom, on two conditions?"

"What conditions?"

"One that you married Miss Cameron-Gordon."

Tony's throat grew dry. "And the other?"

"That you both took the oath of allegiance to the Order of the Si-Fan."

Tony turned and met a glance from the haggard eyes of Cameron-Gordon as he cried out, "I don't understand. I didn't know you were even acquainted!"

"We were thrown together for a long time, sir. I love your daughter deeply, sincerely. And she has consented to marry me, with your approval. . . but not until you are free."

"I have already offered Dr. Cameron-Gordon his freedom." Fu Manchu murmured.

"On the same terms," Cameron-Gordon began, then stopped, sank his head in his hands.

Nayland Smith sat silent, looking neither right nor left, but straight ahead at Dr. Fu Manchu.

"Suppose I decline?" Tony asked hoarsely.

Fu Manchu struck the small gong. Draperies before one of the several doors were swept aside, and Moon Flower came in!

She wore the nurse's uniform in which Tony had recently seen her.

418

"Yueh Hua!" he gasped, half stood up.

"Jeanie, darling!" Cameron-Gordon's voice rose on a note of high emotion.

She ignored them. Her blue eyes were turned upon Dr. Fu Manchu. Without even glancing in her direction:

"You are happy in your new work?" he asked.

"I am happy, Master."

"You may go."

Moon Flower turned and walked out automatically through the opening by which she had come in.

Cameron-Gordon and Tony sprang simultaneously to their feet. Nayland Smith reached out right and left and grabbed an arm of each in a powerful grip.

"Sit down!" he snapped. "Don't act like bloody fools!"

Tony conquered the furious rage which had swept sanity aside, and sat down. Cameron-Gordon resisted awhile, but finally sank back in his chair. "You yellow blackguard!" he muttered. "Why didn't I strangle you long ago!"

Fu Manchu, who had remained impassive, replied in that sibilant undertone so like a snake's hiss, "Probably out of consideration for your daughter, Doctor. I am obliged to you, Sir Denis. If you will glance behind you, I think you must realize how childish any display of force would have been."

Tony turned in a flash.

Four stockily built Burmese, armed with long knives, stood behind their chairs!

"I knew they were there," Nayland Smith told him.

"You have the ears of a desert fox, Sir Denis," Fu Manchu said, "and a long experience of my methods."

He added three guttural words, not in English, and Tony knew, although he heard no sound, that the four body-guards had retired.

"Now let us hear—" Nayland Smith spoke crisply— "what plans for our welfare you may have in mind if your generous offer is declined."

His irony ruffled Dr. Fu Manchu no more than Cameron-Gordon's violence had done. Resting his elbows on the desk, he pressed the tips of his long fingers together. Moon Flower's evident submission to the will of the perverted genius had shaken Tony so badly that his brain seemed numbed.

Waiting for Fu Manchu's next words, he felt like a criminal awaiting sentence.

"There was a time, Sir Denis," he heard the sibilant, cool voice saying, "when I employed mediaeval methods. You may recall the Wire Jacket and the Seven Gates of Wisdom?"

Tony looked aside at Nayland Smith, noted a tightening of the jaw muscles, and knew that he had clenched his teeth; then:

"Quite clearly!" he rapped. "Hungry rats featured in the Seven Gates, I remember."

"I have abandoned such crudities. Doubtless they were appropriate in dealing with the river pirates, if only as a warning to other low-class criminals. But I recognized that they were useless to me. I had to deal with enemies on a higher social and intellectual plane. Therefore more subtle means were indicated—"

"Such as kidnapping and hypnotizing a man's daughter!" Cameron-Gordon burst out.

"You are misinformed, Doctor," the poisonously suave voice assured him. "It is not a case of kidnapping. On my way to visit you in the laboratory I found your daughter hiding on General Huan's property."

"Go on," Nayland Smith said irritably. "We are splitting hairs. The plain fact is that you have all four of us in your hands. What do you propose to do with us?"

"I hope to make you understand that it is my methods and not my ideals against which you have fought, without notable success, for many years. In England, I agree, those methods were unusual. In consequence, your Scotland Yard branded me as a common criminal. My political aims were described as 'The Yellow Peril'!"

Fu Manchu's strange voice had increased in volume, had become guttural. He had changed his passive pose. Lean hands lay clenched upon the desk before him.

"Was Scotland Yard wrong?" Nayland Smith asked, coolly.

Fu Manchu half stood; then dropped back in his chair. "Sometimes your persistent and insufferable misunderstanding rouses my anger. This is bad—for both. You are perfectly well aware that the Si-Fan is international. Ridding China of Communism is

420

one of its objectives—yes. But ridding *the world* of this Russian pestilence is its main purpose. In this purpose do we, or do we not, stand on common ground?"

Tony almost held his breath. He sensed a storm brewing between these two strong personalities, and—he was thinking solely of Moon Flower—if it broke, God help all of them!

"As I am still employed by the British government," he heard Nayland Smith answer calmly, "your question is one difficult for me to answer."

"The British government!" Fu Manchu hissed the words. "Why do they soil their hands by contact with the offal who pose as lords of China? Can you conceivably believe, knowing the history of my people, that these unclean creatures can retain their hold upon China, my China? Do you believe that the proud Poles, the hot-blooded Hungarians, the stiff-necked Germans, will bend the knee to the childish nonsense of Marx and Lenin? You asked me what I proposed to do with you. Here is my answer: Work with me, for we labour in a common cause, not against me."

There was an interruption; a faint bell note. Dr. Fu Manchu stooped to a cabinet beside him. A muffled voice spoke. The voice ceased. Fu Manchu pressed a switch and lay back in his chair; impassive again.

"Well, Sir Denis?" he prompted softly.

"Unofficially—" Nayland Smith spoke slowly, as if weighing every word—"there might be certain advantages. I should be glad to see China rid of the Communist yoke—"

"For which reason, perhaps—and unofficially—you had André Skobolov intercepted in Niu-fo-Tu?"

Tony suppressed a gulp. Fu Manchu knew, as Nayland Smith suspected, that he had been seen in Niu-fo-Tu!

"André Skobolov?" Nayland Smith murmured. "The name is familiar. A Kremlin agent? But I never met him, nor even saw him."

Fu Manchu bent forward. The hypnotic eyes were turned upon Tony.

"But you met him, Captain McKay, in Niu-fo-Tu!"

Tony thought hard, and quickly; tried to act on Nayland Smith's lead. "I was in Niu-fo-Tu for less than half an hour—on the run from jail. I certainly never saw the man you speak of there, and shouldn't have known him if I had."

"Then, for what other purpose were you in Szechuan?"

"For *my* purpose, Dr. Fu Manchu!" Nayland Smith rapped out fiercely. "His mission was to confirm my belief that the man known as The Master was yourself!"

The overpowering gaze of green eyes was transferred to Sir Denis. "Then your trusted agent, Sir Denis, who seems to have acquired what he would call 'a girl friend' on his way, safely reached the house of Lao Tse-Mung to report to you?"

"Lao Tse-Mung is an old and honoured acquaintance who has offered me hospitality on any occasion when my affairs brought me to this part of China."

"You mean he is an agent of British Intelligence?"

"I mean that he is a patriot, and a gentleman."

There was a brief silence.

"I, also, am a patriot, Sir Denis. What is more, I hope to save not only the Chinese but the peoples of every nation from obliteration. This will be their fate if the insane plans of the Soviet should ever be put into execution. Their latest instrument of destruction is so secret, and so dangerous, that research on it is being conducted in this remote area of China."

"We are aware of this."

"Indeed?" Fu Manchu's tones slightly changed. "We are on common ground again. You regard it with deep concern?"

"We do. If—accidentally—this research plant could be destroyed, its loss would be welcome. Germ warfare is too horrible to be permitted, and Dr. von Wehrner, their chief scientist, is the greatest living expert on the subject."

Fu Manchu's masklike features melted in a smile. But it was a chilling smile.

"You see, Sir Denis, we must work together. I was informed a few minutes ago that Dr. von Wehrner had been recalled to Moscow."

Nayland Smith started, then shook his head. "Collaboration, I fear, is impossible. So I ask you again—what do you propose to do with us?"

Fu Manchu lay back in the chair, so that his strange powerful features became half-masked in shadow. The long hands rested on the desk and a large emerald seal which he wore gleamed and seemed to shoot out sparks of green fire as pointed nails tapped the surface of the desk. He spoke in a low, sibilant voice.

"I anticipated your reply. Yet I never despair of convincing you one day that your government, and others, must accept me—as they have accepted the puppet régime at Peking. But my power in China hangs upon a silken thread. The Kremlin distrusts me. In spite of my acknowledged eminence in science, I have never been invited to inspect the Soviet research station. And I have not sought an invitation—for I intend to destroy it!"

"In that," snapped Nayland Smith, "you have my sympathy. But you have not answered my question."

The long fingers resting on the desk became intertwined in a serpentine fashion; and Tony experienced a sort of spiritual chill.

"I shall answer it, Sir Denis," the sibilant whisper went on, almost dreamily. "Your death could avail me nothing, and might one day be laid at my door with disastrous consequences; for you are no longer a mere Burmese police officer but an esteemed official of the British Secret Service."

"Therefore?" Nayland Smith prompted.

"Therefore, I shall see to it that you disappear for a time. Dr. Cameron-Gordon will resume his work in my laboratory here, or perhaps in another, elsewhere. His charming daughter I shall keep usefully employed. Concerning Captain McKay, I am undecided."

Tony had been struggling hard to bottle his rising anger, but as Fu Manchu's voice ceased the cork came out.

"Then I'll decide for you!" he shouted, and sprang to his feet.

Nayland Smith grabbed him and threw him back in his chair. "For the last time," he snapped, "shut up!"

"I am obliged to you, Sir Denis," Fu Manchu murmured. "I recall that you were one of the first Englishmen to master judo. With advancing years, and increasing perils, it is a desirable accomplishment."

"There is one objection to your plans, Dr. Fu Manchu," Nayland Smith said grimly.

"From your point of view, no doubt?"

"No. From yours."

"And what is this objection?"

Fu Manchu bent forward, fixing his strange gaze on Sir Denis's face.

"I will explain it only if you give me your word—which I respect—that should you decline to accept what I propose, no coercion of any kind be used upon any of us to force compliance and that I am not asked to identify others concerned. We should remain, as we are now, your prisoners."

Fu Manchu watched him in silence for some time, his fingers pressed together; then:

"I give you my word, Sir Denis," he said quietly.

Tony, fists clenched tightly, glanced at Nayland Smith. What was he going to say? What plan had flashed through that resourceful brain? And what was the word of this archcriminal worth?

"Good," Sir Denis said calmly. "I accept it. You suggested recently that I had attempted to intercept the man Skobolov. On the contrary, I was unaware that he was in China, nor did I know what I should have had to gain by such an attempt. But your evident interest in his movements suggest that it was something of great importance."

Dr. Fu Manchu did not stir; his face remained expressionless. Tony almost held his breath. He knew, now, what Nayland Smith was going to propose.

"By mere chance," Sir Denis went on, speaking calmly and unusually slowly, "a man unknown appealed to McKay to help him. He was very ill and apparently in danger. McKay took him on board his boat, and during that night the man died. His body was consigned to the canal. His sole baggage—a large briefcase—McKay brought with him to the meeting place I had appointed."

Fu Manchu's expression remained impassive. But his long fingers became intertwined again. He said nothing.

"From the correspondence in the briefcase, when translated, we learned that the man was André Skobolov. We also learned that he had something in his possession which was of vital interest to the Kremlin. This could only be a bound manuscript, written in Chinese."

And at last Fu Manchu spoke. "Which was also translated?"

"It could not be deciphered. May I suggest that this manuscript is the reason for your interest in André Skobolov?"

There was a brief silence. Cameron-Gordon had raised his bowed head and was watching Nayland Smith.

"If it were so," Fu Manchu said smoothly, "in what way could this be an objection to my plans?"

"At the moment, it could be none. In the event of my disappearance it might prove a source of annoyance. The manuscript is in safe keeping, but should I fail to reclaim it in the next few days, it will be dispatched to the British Foreign Office to be decoded. . ."

Chapter XXI

In his memories of his mission to Szechuan, memories both bitter and sweet, Tony found the electric silence which followed Nayland Smith's words one of the most poignant. That clash of mental swords, recognition of the fact that the fate of all of them rested upon the combat, had penetrated even Cameron-Gordon's lethargy of despair. There were beads of perspiration on his forehead as he watched Dr. Fu Manchu.

To Tony it appeared that they held all the cards—but only if Fu Manchu's word was worth a dime. No man—even Nayland Smith—could stand up to Chinese tortures. He was almost afraid to think about the copy of the cipher manuscript which was in the keeping of Lao Tse-Mung, for he believed that Fu Manchu could read men's minds. And he knew that Sir Denis, although a master of evasion, would never tell an outright lie. He knew that the original was safe with the lama at Niu-fo-Tu.

It was a masterly bluff. Clearly enough Nayland Smith had been right when he said, "The most powerful weapon against Fu Manchu which I ever held in my hands."

For Dr. Fu Manchu, eyes closed, sat deep in meditation for several agonizing minutes considering the matter.

What was the manuscript for which André Skobolov had given his life?

Tony, in his agitation, found himself grasping Nayland Smith's arm—when Dr. Fu Manchu spoke:

"Where is this cipher document" came in guttural tones.

"I have your word, Dr. Fu Manchu, that I am not to be asked to reveal the names of others concerned," Nayland Smith answered coldly.

Fu Manchu leaned forward, his green eyes staring venomously at Sir Denis.

"You have rejected my offer. You force me to accept yours."

426

His voice was lowered to the sibilant hiss. "Very well. My word is my bond. What are your conditions?"

"That we are all four free to leave, and will not be intercepted; that Jean Cameron-Gordon be released from the control you have laid upon her and returned to her father's care; that I be given an official travel permit to recover the document you want; that no attempt is made to trace my journey or destination."

Dr. Fu Manchu closed his eyes again. "These conditions I accept."

"Then I can start at once?"

"Directly your travel permit is ready, Sir Denis. Two must remain until the manuscript is in my hands. Whom do you wish to go with you."

Nayland Smith hesitated only a moment, then: "Captain McKay," he said. "But before we leave, Miss Cameron-Gordon must join her father."

"She shall do so. As my guests they shall be safe and comfortable until your return."

"I accept your terms. But you must allow me an hour to confer with my friends before I leave—in a room which is not *wired*."

"To this also I agree . . ."

"For mercy's sake, mix me a drink, McKay! Dr. Fu Manchu and I have struck a strange bargain. You may talk freely. We have his word for it there'll be no eavesdropping—and as I told you recently, I never knew him to lie. He's the blackest villain unhung, but his word is sacred."

"Okay," Tony said, and crossed to the buffet.

Cameron-Gordon growled something under his breath.

Although they were unaware of the fact, they had been conducted to the luxurious suite formerly occupied by André Skobolov.

"How I miss my pipe!" Nayland Smith muttered. "I see there are cigarettes. Toss a packet over. Here's the situation—Fu Manchu has his own plans for ruling China. He doesn't want those plans disturbed by a sudden, crazy use of germ weapons. As you know, McKay, I found the name of von Wehrner in the Russian correspondence."

He lighted a cigarette, took a sip from the glass which Tony handed to him.

"This was news for which Military Intelligence would have paid a foreign agent anything he asked. You see, von Wehrner was employed by the Nazis on similar research during the war. M.I. located the germ plant in occupied France. There was a Commando raid—German plant completely destroyed. Somehow or another they dragged von Wehrner out of the blazing building and brought him back with them. He was interned. And I had several long interviews with him. I found him to be a brilliantly clever man; and when he got to know me better he confided that although he had devoted his skill day and night to the secret researches, he abhorred the idea of germ warfare."

"He would have no choice," Cameron-Gordon declared. "I know the method!"

"Later on," Sir Denis added, "he confessed that he had repeatedly delayed results. And I think it's a logical deduction that he's doing the same again. Hence his recall!"

"But the situation is different," Cameron-Gordon objected. "Maybe he was never a Nazi. But now he's clearly a Communist."

"No more a Communist than you are!" Nayland Smith snapped. "I have great respect for von Wehrner. At the end of the war I secured his release and he went back to Germany. I heard from him from time to time; then his letters ceased. I had an inquiry started, and after a month or more got a report of the facts. Von Wehrner had been kidnapped one night and rushed over to East Berlin! Never a word since."

"You mean he's a prisoner of the Communists, just as I am?"

"The situation is almost identical—but I haven't been idle. In addition to making the plans which led to our present position, I got in touch with von Wehrner. I foresaw the possibility of things going wrong—heaven knows they did!—and realized that my cordial relations with von Wehrner might be useful."

"But how the devil did you get in touch with him?" Cameron-Gordon demanded.

"Through our talented friend the lama. He has a contact in the Russian camp, by whom one of the phantom radios was smuggled in to von Wehrner."

"And what is von Wehrner prepared to do?"

"This: If I can guarantee his escape from the Soviets, he will guarantee to destroy the plant!"

"But Fu Manchu intends to destroy it!"

"And to make a slave of von Wehrner! I mean to move first . . . "

Dr. Fu Manchu remained in his place behind the lacquer desk. Old General Huan faced him from his cushioned seat.

"The ancient gods of China are with us, Tsung-Chao." General Huan seemed to be pondering.

"You agree with me?" Fu Manchu said softly.

"That the Si-Fan Register should be returned to us by the hand of Nayland Smith certainly savours of a miracle, Master. It is a sword of Damocles removed. In possession of the men at the Kremlin, or the British Foreign Office, it would spell disaster."

Fu Manchu took a pinch of snuff from his silver box. "Its recovery sets me free to move against the Soviet research plant—a plague-spot in Szechuan."

General Huan fanned himself, for the night was warm.

"It is this project which alarms me," he stated placidly.

Fu Manchu's voice changed, became harsh. "I recall, when I communicated with you from England, that you advised against it, pointing out that it would result in a flock of Soviet investigators descending upon Szechuan and possibly finding evidence of your part in the disaster."

"I recall the correspondence very well. As a former officer of the old régime, I am not above suspicion. And having escaped one grave danger, it seems to me to be tempting Fate to plunge into another."

Fu Manchu hissed contemptuously. "Always we live on the edge of a volcano. We are accustomed to such conditions. Very well. Here is an opportunity to achieve one of my minor objectives without exposing you or myself to charges of complicity."

General Huan folded his fan. "Your plan, as I recall it, Master, involved the employment of a number of Cold Men?"

"It did."

"As it is well known that these ghastly creatures come from the clinic which you established and which I constructed, surely this fact would expose us both to a charge of complicity?"

Fu Manchu smiled his icy smile. "By whom will such a charge be made? At night the circumference of the plant is patrolled by a squad of Russian guards. They are easily disposed of. Members of the staff live in the neighbouring village. There is a Russian camp about a mile distant. The guard on the plant is relieved at regular intervals. The wire fence enclosing it is electrified."

"I have made it my business, Master, to acquaint myself with the Russian arrangements. I did so on receipt of your letter from London. It is true that only six men and a sergeant guard the place. The sergeant holds the key of the gate. There are telephone connections between a box at the gate and the Russian headquarters inside the camp. Reinforcements could be on hand very quickly."

"We should, first, cut this connection—then, overpower the sergeant."

General Huan bowed slightly. "Professionally, I should have planned the defence otherwise, although I admit that an attempt to seize the research station is not a likely contingency. It is believed, throughout the area, to be devoted to the study of leprosy."

Fu Manchu laughed. It was harsh, mocking laughter. "The affair will be over long before an alarm reaches the Russian camp. "

"And who will direct these Cold Men?"

"Matsukata. Or I may go, myself."

"Master! You would be running your head into a noose!"

"Why? The supply truck from the clinic will be standing by. The *necropolites* have rioted and escaped. This will be our story if our presence is detected. I am there to recapture them. I had anticipated a possible occasion when a number of these might be used, and so had instructed Matsukata to turn one at large from time to time in order to create popular terror of the creatures . . ."

"You believe that the operation can be carried through without sound of it reaching the Russian camp?"

"Certainly, if no one blunders. Long ladders will be taken, such as those we have used before, in case we fail to find the key of the gate. Dr. von Wehrner, who lives in the enclosure, will be seized first. He will have keys of the buildings, or know where to find them. . ."

And in their own luxurious quarters, Nayland Smith was outlining his own plans. "You see, the loss of our mystery radio sets ties me badly. I'm glad we left them behind of course. If found on us, I don't doubt that Fu Manchu would have put the system controlling them out of order."

"Tell me something," Tony interrupted: "How long have we been here?"

Nayland Smith smiled grimly. "I know how you feel. That filthy, sweet-smelling gas in the insect room! It might have happened a week ago. But it's my guess that it happened at approximately ten o'clock on Wednesday night. That would make the time, now, at about three a.m. on Thursday morning. Events have moved quickly, McKay."

"And now tell *me* just one thing," Cameron-Gordon broke in: "Where is Jeanie?"

But before Nayland Smith could reply, the door opened—and Moon Flower came in!

She wore the dress of a working girl with which Tony was familiar. Her father sprang up at a bound and had her in his arms.

"Jeanie, my Jeanie! I didn't think I should ever see you again!"

When at last, wet-eyed, she turned, "Chi Foh!" she whispered—"Sir Denis! I know what a fool I have been. I spoiled all your plans. Try to forgive me."

Nayland Smith grasped both her hands. "Jeanie, my dear, your devotion to your father and your courage outran discretion: But you have nothing to be ashamed about. Just sit down and tell us all that happened."

It was a simple story. She had followed them, as Sir Denis had suspected, had climbed the bamboo ladder and had tried to keep in sight when they crossed the garden. When she had a glimpse of her father opening the laboratory door, she hid in a clump of bushes to wait for them all to come out again.

A long time seemed to pass, and still the door remained closed. At which point:

"God forgive me, Jeanie! It was my fault," Cameron-Gordon moaned.

"Forget it!" Nayland Smith snapped. "I was equally to blame."

"Suddenly," Moon Flower went on, "I heard footsteps. I crouched down in the shrubbery. And I saw Dr. Fu Manchu walking towards the laboratory! I nearly screamed, but not quite. There was that huge African following behind him. And this horrible man—although honestly I don't think I made a sound—like a bloodhound, seemed to scent me. He sprang to the spot where I was hiding and swept me up into his arms, one big, black hand over my mouth—"

"If ever I have half a chance!" Tony whispered.

"Shut up!" Nayland Smith snapped.

"Then," Moon Flower said, "those awful green eyes of The Master were looking at me. I tried not to see them, but they compelled me to keep my own eyes open." She stopped, sighed, and clutched her father's arm. "I don't remember a thing that happened after that until I woke up in a room somewhere quite near this one. A kind old Chinese woman was telling me that I was all right and that my friends were waiting for me. She brought me to the door."

"Give Jeanie a drink, McKay," Nayland Smith said crisply. "She needs one. Here's our problem. Deprived of radio, I can get nothing through to the lama and nothing to Lao Tse-Mung. I don't know when von Wehrner is leaving. It's essential that he should have all his plans laid before I can help. This means that I have to get back to Chia-Ting."

"When do we start?" Tony asked.

"Directly transport and our travel permits are available. But Jeanie doesn't know what it's all about. I'm leaving it to you, McKay, to explain to her . . ."

Chapter XXII

It was not long after dawn when, Nayland Smith driving, the Buick—which Tony had seen before—entered the outskirts of Chia-Ting.

"Everybody will be asleep," he said. "How do we get in?"

For the hundredth time he glanced back. He couldn't believe that they weren't followed.

"We shall have to wake poor Mrs. Wu. I think that's her name. You do the talking, McKay. Your Chinese is better than mine. And don't waste your energy looking for a tail. Fu Manchu has at least one virtue. He keeps his word."

Nayland Smith parked near the house of the hospitable physician who had given them shelter. The normally busy street was deserted. They walked to the door; relentlessly pressed the bell. At last they heard movements, and the doctor's old housekeeper opened the door.

"We are very sorry to disturb you," Tony began. "But—"

The Chinese woman's expressionless features melted in a smile. "I am so glad to see you, Mr. Chi Foh! The doctor has been very anxious. Where is the dear young Miss?"

Tony assured her that the young Miss was very well, and they went in and up to their old quarters. Nayland Smith made a dash to the writing-desk in the living-room, took out the two radio equipments which they had left there. He strapped one to his wrist, adjusting the tiny dial.

"Calling the lama," he said; and a moment later, "Nayland Smith here. Regret disturbing you so early . . . Good . . . Yes, back at your cousin's house. Just one thing. It's urgent. What is the call number of the instrument you got through to von Wehrner?" He grabbed a pencil from the desk; listened and scribbled. "Good! Now I can move. See you later."

Tony had listened breathlessly. "These things are magic, Sir Denis!"

433

"Yes!" Nayland Smith smiled grimly. "We pinched the secret from Fu Manchu—and now it's working in his own interests! For mercy's sake get me a drink. There's still something in the locker."

He found his pipe and pouch where he had left them, filled and lighted his old briar. Tony opened the closet which they used as a wine cellar.

"Beer or whisky, Sir Denis? Beer a trifle warm."

"Beer. I'm thirsty." He drank a glass of frothy, imported beer, then: "Now for von Wehrner," he muttered.

Tony watched anxiously while Sir Denis twirled the tiny dial, the figures on which only a keen eye could distinguish. There was a nerve-racking interval . . . but no reply.

Nayland Smith's lean face assumed an expression Tony had never seen there before. "He can't surely have left already! " Sir Denis muttered.

Even as he spoke, came a faint voice.

"Von Wehrner?" Tony whispered.

Nayland Smith nodded, signalled him to come nearer to listen.

"Nayland Smith here! Your delay worried me."

"I keep my radio hidden." Von Wehrner spoke English with a German accent. "I was engaged, and so—"

"Everything is ready, von Wehrner. When do you leave?"

"My Russian successor is due tomorrow."

"Then we must act tonight!"

"I fear so. Is it possible?"

"Yes!" Nayland Smith rapped. "It has to be. How long will it take to make your arrangements?"

"I have already installed the necessary equipment in each of the buildings. No one can detect it. I have only to connect them with the power house and make contact and all will be over."

"From the time you make contact, how long will you have to get clear?"

"It is a simple device which controls the contact. I can set it for no longer than thirty minutes. But this should be enough."

"What time would suit you best? Give me as long as you can."

"Between fifteen minutes after midnight and one a.m. would be best."

"Good enough. Have your radio handy. We must keep in constant touch . . ."

Tony stared at Nayland Smith. "Does this mean that after getting the manuscript from the Lama we are not going to rush it to Fu Manchu?"

Nayland Smith relighted his pipe, which had gone out.

"It seems unavoidable to me, if I'm to carry out my promise to von Wehrner."

"But, Sir Denis!" Tony blazed, "what will become of Moon Flower and her father if things happen to go wrong?"

Nayland Smith smoked furiously. "That problem has been bothering me, McKay. But there's a way out. We must drop off here tonight when we return from Niu-fo-Tu and leave the thing in your charge. I'll go on to the research station and—"

"Stop! That's plain nonsense, Sir Denis. I won't do it!"

"I was afraid you wouldn't," Nayland Smith remarked drily. "There is another way: To leave the manuscript, packed and sealed, with our good friend the doctor. If we don't claim it before daylight tomorrow, he must undertake to have it delivered at once to General Huan."

Tony began to walk up and down in agitated thought, then: "I have another idea," he said. "If you think it's crazy, say so. We shall have to leave the Buick in some place well away from the germ plant. That's clear. Neither of us knows the route there. The doctor has a car, and a driver who possibly does know the way—"

"I rather warm to your idea," Nayland Smith rapped. "We take the manuscript with us? Having parked the car, we leave our driver with instructions to wait for us for an agreed time, and then to hurry back to the General's house and deliver the package. This means delaying here until our host is awake and his chauffeur reports for duty."

"I think it's worth it, Sir Denis, on both counts."

And, almost as he spoke, their host the doctor, whom they saw rarely, knocked on the door and came in. He wore a brown dressing robe over his pyjamas, an attire which increased his resemblance to his cousin the Lama. Like his cousin, he spoke perfect English.

"How glad I am to see you, Sir Denis—and you, Captain McKay! Your absence began to disturb me."

Nayland Smith apologized for arousing him so early, and then broached the subject of the driver for their midnight journey . . . "We should, of course, pay him handsomely for his services. He would be in no danger, and this will see the last of us; you can sleep in peace!"

"You may rest assured that Tung will be waiting for you, Sir Denis. He knows the road to Hua-Tzu perfectly. It is a difficult road at night. I formerly had a patient in that village . . ."

Half an hour later they were on their way to Niu-fo-Tu . . .

Nayland Smith knew this route well; so did Tony. They had travelled it recently with the Lama. They were stopped once only, at Jung. But their papers, issued by the governor of the province, produced polite bows and instant permission to proceed. Sir Denis drove the Buick as though competing in an overland race, and they reached Niu-fo-Tu in just under three hours.

He pulled up in sight of the gate.

"I have been thinking, McKay. Openly to visit the Lama might be dangerous—for the Lama. We still wear Chinese dress. But our visit, coming in an automobile, might reach the ears of Fu Manchu and result in inquiries. You know the way from here to the back entrance. Off you go! I'll call him to expect you."

"And what are *you* going to do?"

"Tinker with the engine until you come back!"

Tony grinned and set out at a steady trot for the path he remembered so well, the path on which he had found the abandoned Ford and been attacked in the dark by Nayland Smith who mistook him for an enemy. He found it easily enough and turned in off the road.

The Ford had disappeared, as he had expected. He passed the spot, and a run of a few hundred yards brought him out in sight of that stretch of wasteland upon which the rear windows of the Lama's house looked out. Although no one was in sight, he dropped to a walk as he crossed to the door. It was wide open, and he entered without hesitation and went on to the door of the Lama's study. That also was open.

"Come in, Captain McKay." Dr. Li Wu Chang, the Lama, stood up to greet him. "You are indeed welcome!"

"It's good to see you again. Sir Denis has told you what I've come for?"

The Lama held up a sealed package. "Here is the cipher manuscript. And here"—he indicated a long envelope which lay before him—"is the result of many hours of labour. I have held it deliberately until it was complete."

"What is it?" Tony wanted to know.

"I have broken the cipher, my son, and this is its translation in plain English!"

"Gosh!" Tony whispered. "That's genius!"

"Merely acquired knowledge and perseverance. There is no merit in a special talent unless its exercise is of use to others."

Tony dropped down on a stool and faced the Lama who had resumed his seat behind the low table. A faint smell of incense which pervaded the air carried him back to his first interview with Dr. Li Wong Chang.

"Certain perfumes stimulate the subconscious," the Lama said, as if reading his thoughts. "What troubles your mind?"

"Tell me, first, Doctor, what is this manuscript?"

"It is a Register of the Order of the Si-Fan—one of the most powerful secret societies in the world. It contains the names of every lodge-master in China, some of them men of great influence. It includes the name of the Grand Master . . . General Huan Tsung-Chao, governor of the province!"

Tony's brain was in a whirl.

"Confide your problem to me, Captain McKay," the gentle voice urged. "For I see you have one. It may be I can help you to solve it."

And Tony, without hesitation, told him of Nayland Smith's bargain with Dr. Fu Manchu . . . "Sir Denis has such a nice sense of honour," he explained finally, "that if he knows the cipher has been broken, having told Fu Manchu that it was undecipherable, I'm uncertain of his reaction."

The Lama closed his eyes for a few moments and evidently reflected deeply. Then, he spoke again.

"Sir Denis is a throwback to the age of chivalry. Your course is clear. Forget what I have told you. Take this decoding of the manuscript, but produce it only when you are all in safety. I set the overthrow of the archcriminal called Dr. Fu Manchu, obviously not his real name, above all subtleties of conscience. If I err, the error is mine. Go, Captain McKay, for I know time is of vital importance to you . . ."

Chapter XXIII

Tony was for ever looking at his watch. The hours of waiting in the doctor's house at Chia-Ting had been hours of torture. He was so near to Moon Flower, yet so far away; for not mileage but a touch-and-go midnight venture lay between them.

Nayland Smith had called von Wehrner on the secret radio soon after their arrival, but von Wehrner had explained, briefly, that while the technical staff remained he could not safely talk. Now, he was free to do so, and Sir Denis, notebook in hand, was riddling him with quick-fire questions and noting his replies.

They had met Tung, who had undertaken to drive them to their dangerous rendezvous. He was a competent-looking lad, not uneducated, although he had little English. He assured them that he knew the road to Hua-Tzu by day or night.

He was instructed to have the Buick in condition by ten o'clock.

Nayland Smith made a final note and turned to Tony.

"I have the essential facts, McKay. You're all strung up. Take a drink while I make a rough sketch. Might as well finish the bottle. We shan't be coming back!"

Tony mixed a drink, lighted a cigarette, and watched Sir Denis making a pencil sketch on a writing pad.

"I wonder what you're doing," he said, rather irritably.

Nayland Smith looked up, grinned. "You'll be with Jeanie in a few hours, McKay. The symptoms stick out like brass knobs. Simmer down. Come here and let me explain." Tony crossed and looked down at a crude plan. "This is the back of the enclosure you saw. Here is the bungalow where von Wehrner lives. Note that it's a long way from the only gate, but quite near the wire fence. Here, and here"—he indicated two crosses—"are the spots at which sentries are posted at night. They operate on a circulatory system. A moves around to B's post, B moves on, and so forth,

438

every hour. So that they report one by one to the sergeant at the gate. All clear?"

Tony, now absorbed in the job before them, nodded. "It's a routine we scrapped years ago."

"Suits us!" Nayland Smith rapped. "Have you noticed the weather? It's going to be a cloudy night. The fence, of course, is lethally electrified. But von Wehrner will switch the juice off. He'll join us here." He marked a point midway between the two crosses. "All clear?"

"Except the wire fence. Are we taking ladders?"

"Von Wehrner has made his own. He's an active ten-stone man. Cord, with bamboo rungs. Easily tossed over the fence. Any questions?"

"No—except where do we park the Buick? Beyond the village there's no road I know of. The Russian camp isn't far up the hill and there's a road from the camp to the research station. But even if we could reach it, we daren't use it."

"Too bad. We shall have to walk there and back!"

At ten o'clock they were on their way; Tung at the wheel, Sir Denis and Tony seated behind.

"We can't use our radio until this man's out of the way," Tony whispered.

"I don't intend to do so!" Nayland Smith rapped. "Have you noticed the weather?"

"Yes. There's a hell of a thunderstorm brewing. We'll probably be drenched."

Nayland Smith was silent; began to charge his pipe.

Tony thought hard. There were many snags to be looked for. If the storm broke, a flash of lightning might reveal them to the sentries. There were other unpleasant possibilities . . .

As though a dam had burst in the sky, rain crashed down on to the roof of the car. In a white blaze of lightning he saw the road ahead. It led up into the hills, was little more than a goat track which no reasonably sane motorist would have fancied even in ideal weather. Now, it had become a raging cataract.

A crash of thunder came like that of a mighty bomb. Tony glanced at Nayland Smith. He was lighting his pipe. And the Chinese driver held steadily on his course, axle deep in water.

"I presume that this car belongs to General Huan, but I don't want it to break down all the same," Sir Denis remarked in his dry way.

The deluge ceased as suddenly as it had begun. The next roar of phantom artillery was farther away, the lightning less blinding. The storm was passing eastward, They had crossed the crest of the rocky hill, and Tony, in a moment of illumination, saw a densely wooded valley below, oak, alder, and other varieties he hadn't time to identify.

They descended a road winding through trees, the driver picking his way by the aid of powerful headlights. This road brought them at last to the bank of a sullenly running stream, and here the driver suddenly slowed down.

"This is Hua-Tzu, sir. Do you wish me to drive through?"

Tony and Nayland Smith stepped out on the muddy track. "I think," Tony said, peering around in the gloom, "it might be wiser to park the car right here. The path to the Russian camp starts at the farther end of the village street, I remember."

"Good," Nayland Smith snapped, glanced at the illuminated dial of his wrist-watch and instructed Tony to switch off the headlights. "Park here somewhere"—he spoke Chinese—"near the roadside, and for your life don't be seen. Here is the parcel you have to deliver to General Huan. Does your watch keep good time?"

"Yes, sir."

"Then you understand—you wait for us until three o'clock. If we're not here by three, you start for the governor's house. For God's sake don't fall asleep!"

"I understand. I shall not fall asleep."

"Now let's find a spot to hide the car."

They explored back up the slope, and Tony presently found an opening in a plantation of alders wide enough to admit the Buick. Tung brought the car up and backed in.

"Smoke if you like," Sir Denis told him. "But stamp your cigarette out if anybody comes near."

"I understand."

And so they left Tung and moved on.

Not a light showed in the one straggling street of the riverside village. They reached the path which Tony remembered without meeting anything human or animal and began to climb the hill toward the Russian camp. Through a rift in the racing clouds the moon peeped out for a few seconds and Tony saw the group of huts just ahead.

"Here we take to the rough!" he said.

They turned left into a tangle of scrub and made a detour around the camp, in which, as in the village, no light was visible. Above the camp, Tony led the way back to the rough road which connected the camp with the research plant. They stayed on the road during darkness, but ducked into cover whenever the moon broke through; and presently:

"We must be near the gate now," Tony decided. "Better stick in the rough and work left."

In this way, in sudden moonlight, they had their first view of the wired enclosure and of the hut beside the gate. There was a light in the window of the hut. Beyond, they could see the group of buildings.

"I went no farther than this," Tony reported. "To get round to the other side we shall have to explore, keeping well out of sight."

"Good enough," Nayland Smith agreed. "Let's hope there's cover all the way."

There proved to be up to the time that they sighted the first sentry. He was squatting on the ground, smoking. Just beyond came a patch of coarse grass which offered no cover at all. They had to creep farther away from the fence before they found bushes. Kept on their circular course only by rare bursts of moonlight, they passed the third sentry, who was asleep, and Nayland Smith looked at his watch.

"We're there! And it's just twelve o'clock. We have to wait for the sentries to change over." He lay flat down.

"I welcome the rest!"

And, as they lay there, came the sound of a distant whistle from the direction of the gate. Soon they heard footsteps, voices. Then, one of the guards (presumably the one who had been asleep) tramped past and disappeared.

"I wonder if the sergeant ever does a round of inspection," Nayland Smith murmured. "Better wait and make sure. "

441

They waited for some time, but heard and saw nothing. During a longish spell of moonlight Tony had a clear view of the upper part of a hut nestling amid bamboos. It stood less than fifty yards from the wire fence.

"I suppose that's where von Wehrner lives, Sir Denis?"

"According to my notes, it is. He described it as roughly midway between two of the points where guards are posted. I'll try to get him, now. When we know he's starting, we must crawl over to the fence and lie in that tangle of long grass and weeds which borders the wire." He paused. "Come nearer to shield me from the guard to the south of us. I must have light to see the dial."

Tony did so, and Nayland Smith shone a momentary light from a flashlamp on to the dial of his wrist-radio, then switched it off. Tony crouched close beside him, listening intently.

And presently came the faint voice of Dr. von Wehrner. "I'm waiting in the power house, Sir Denis. If you're ready, I'll make the connection, run back to my bungalow and get what I want, then steal through the bamboos to join you."

"Wait until clouds cover the moon," Nayland Smith warned.

"Trust me to be careful!"

"Phew!" Nayland Smith breathed. "So far, all according to plan."

Tony experienced a sensation not unlike that he had known when awaiting the signal for a raid into the enemy lines; exultation and tingling apprehension. Storm clouds were sweeping the sky. "Shall we move over, Sir Denis?"

"Yes—crawl. And lie flat if the moon breaks through."

Their dingy-hued Chinese clothes were admirable camouflage, and they crept across into the tangle of undergrowth fringing the fence without difficulty.

They had no more than reached this cover when from the direction of the distant gate came the sound of a choking scream. It broke off suddenly, as if the one who screamed had been swiftly silenced.

"What the devil's that!" Nayland Smith growled.

Whatever it was it had alerted the sentries to their right and left. Two shouts came simultaneously. Then one of the voices shouted alone—and silence fell.

"I wish I knew Russian," Tony muttered.

"So do I," Nayland Smith rapped back. "But it doesn't matter.

The men aren't moving. We daren't use a light out here. So I can't call von Wehrner. We can only wait and hope for the best."

They lay there, waiting—and listening.

To Tony, strung up to a high pitch, it seemed that every passing minute was ten. And presently, to enhance the stress, he seemed to become conscious of a vague, muffled tumult somewhere inside the wired enclosure.

"You hear it?" Nayland Smith whispered. "God knows what's going on—but it's something we don't want!"

Through a break in the clouds moon rays peeped out for a few fleeting seconds. Tony stared anxiously into the bamboo plantation masking von Wehrner's bungalow; but saw nothing. The muted, indescribable disturbance continued.

Darkness again.

"Sir Denis!" It was a husky whisper.

"Von Wehrner!"

"Move a few yards to your left. I'm throwing a weighted line across. Be quick!"

Tony's heart leapt with excitement as they scuffled at speed toward where, now, a shadowy figure showed on the other side of the fence. When they reached the spot:

"Here's the line," von Wehrner's voice told them. "Catch it and pull!"

Some heavy object was thrown over the fence. It fell almost into Tony's hands. He grabbed it—a bronze paperweight—and pulled on the line to which it was tied. He had the end of a rope ladder in his hands when it stuck!

"Stop pulling," von Wehrner said hoarsely. He seemed to be in a state of panic. "You'll break the ladder. Hold it fast. I'm coming over."

"Hurry!" Nayland Smith rapped softly. "I think the moon's breaking through!"

He and Tony hung on to the end of the ladder as von Wehrner mounted on the other side. Astride the top of the fence, he tossed a briefcase into the tangled grass near Tony, turned and groped for a rung of the ladder. Faint moonlight through the tail of a racing cloud began to dilute the darkness.

"Stand clear!"

And as they released their hold, von Wehrner dropped beside them.

"Flat down!" Nayland Smith whispered. "We must chance the ladder."

They were none too soon, for the moon burst fully out from a patch of starry sky, and it seemed to Tony that the landscape was drenched in silvery light, that the ladder hanging from the fence must certainly be seen.

The next few minutes were amongst the most nerve-racking of the night. Von Wehrner was gasping. He began to speak in a low, breathless voice.

"I had made the connection in the power house . . . hurried back to the bungalow. I went in, using a flashlamp. On my desk I had left the ladder—carefully rolled, in a black canvas bag, and my briefcase . . . I heard padding footsteps behind me."

He stopped, listening. They were all listening. That indefinable disturbance continued, but no sound came from the sentries. The moon was becoming veiled again. Nayland Smith passed his flask to von Wehrner, who accepted it gratefully. And when it was returned:

"I had a dreadful sense of chill—physical. Something *cold* was behind me . . . You will think I am mad . . . I picked up an old lancet which lay there. I use it as a pencil sharpener . . . I turned, and the light of my lamp showed me a grey thing, nearly naked . . . Its eyes were a dead man's eyes . . .

"It sprang upon me. It was supernaturally cold. The mouth was open in a hideous grin. I was held in a grip of ice . . . I plunged the lancet into the grinning mouth and upward through the soft palate . . . The creature relaxed and fell at my feet. For heaven's sake, what was it?"

"I know what it was!" Nayland Smith rapped grimly. "And it means we have to move—fast! Dark enough now. Crawl after me, Doctor."

And as they crept across the open ground to the cover beyond, Tony knew, too, what it was . . . Fu Manchu had chosen that night to raid the research station. He understood, at last, the muffled disturbance which filled the night. The place had been taken over by Cold Men— *necropolites*!

444

And they had not long reached cover when there was evidence that they were outside as well as inside. A shriek, instantly stifled, came from the direction of the sentry on the south.

"Back the way we came!" Nayland Smith spoke between clenched teeth. "And God be with us!"

Then began the detour around the plant by which they had come. Von Wehrner had recovered from the horror of an encounter with a Cold Man and they made good going. Once Tony heard von Wehrner mutter, "There was no haemorrhage!" And he knew that he was still thinking about the *necropolite*.

But at last they reached the point where the road from the Russian camp ended before the gate of the enclosure.

"The gate's open!" Nayland Smith muttered. "They must have overpowered the sergeant, and he must have had the key."

Tony found it hard to credit what he saw. Just before a trailing cloud obscured the moon again, a company of grey phantoms became detached from the shadows like floating vapour or evil spirits materializing, and swept into the open gateway . . .

Chapter XXIV

"What's this?"

Nayland Smith's voice was grim. They had reached the foot of the path which came out at one end of the village street. The Russian camp lay behind them silent and evidently undisturbed. On a path of scrub near the river bank a truck was parked!

"It wasn't here before," Tony muttered.

"There's probably someone in the cab," Sir Denis muttered. "We shall have to find a way behind the houses. The truck must be waiting for the Cold Men."

There proved to be such a path, and they followed it to a point where a bend made it safe to return to the crooked street. They had just done so and were headed for the spot where they hoped Tung awaited them when something happened which brought them to a sudden halt.

A piercing scream came from the other end of the village:

"Mahmûd ! . . . Master! . . . Help ! help!"

The cry was checked in a significant way.

"It was the Japanese—Matsukata!" Tony spoke in a hushed voice. "What the devil does it mean?"

"It means," Nayland Smith explained savagely, "that hell's let loose. Matsukata has lost control of the Cold Men. No time to talk. Listen!"

They heard the grating roar of a heavy engine starting.

"It is the big truck," von Wehrner said hoarsely.

"Back into cover!" Sir Denis rapped. "There's just time

They ran back to the opening between two small houses from which they had just come out, as the heavy vehicle appeared along the street. Tony tried to see the man in the cab, but failed to identify him. And as the truck passed, from its interior came a sort of muffled chant: "*Looma! Looma . . .*"

Shocked into silence, they saw the vehicle, with its load of living-dead demons, speeding up the winding road!

446

All three were listening in tense suspense. But when the sound of the motor died away in the distance their tension relaxed.

"They have passed Tung." Sir Denis sighed with relief. "Come on! This place isn't healthy . . ."

Tung was waiting in the plantation of alders, and Tony felt so relieved that he wanted to cheer.

"A big truck," the man reported, "passed here soon after you left. It has just passed again. Soon after the first time, a small car also went by. It has not returned."

Tung drove the Buick on to the road, and in a minimum of time they were on their way. Their driver did his best on the gradient, for Tony had urged him to hurry. Nayland Smith consulted his watch.

"We made a record coming down, von Wehrner. Just twenty-seven minutes since we picked you up!"

"I was delayed joining you. I set the clock for thirty minutes. But those creatures who entered the plant may have . . ."

His words were drowned in a shattering explosion which shook the solid earth . . . All four wheels momentarily left the surface, then dropped back with a sickening thud. Storm clouds, still moving overhead, became ruddy as though a setting sun burned under them. And fiery fragments began to fall in the road and on the roof of the car.

"First-class show, von Wehrner." Nayland Smith grinned. "One big good deed to your credit!"

"Two things are worrying me," Tony broke in, staring back at the raging inferno which had been the Soviet research centre. "Why did Matsukata yell for Mahmûd and The Master? Was Mahmûd the driver of the car Tung saw? In that case, Dr. Fu Manchu was at the plant when we left! The other thing—who's driving the truck and where are they going?"

Sir Denis began to fill his pipe before replying. "That Fu Manchu may have followed on I think probable. These unhappy creatures he has created are very near to jungle beasts. And the jungle becomes strangely disturbed during an electric storm."

"You think," von Wehrner suggested, "that these living-dead have gone berserk and overcome their controllers?"

"I do. I think that Dr. Fu Manchu, tonight, has overreached him-

447

self. Hitherto, I judge, he has used these ghastly zombies for solo performances, such as the affair at Lao Tse-Mung's house, when it has been possible for Matsukata to maintain control. But a party of *necropolites* poses a different problem—particularly in a thunderstorm."

"Then you *do* believe," Tony asked eagerly, "that Fu Manchu was there tonight in person?"

"I have said that I think it probable. What is certain is that a party of Cold Men—we don't know how many—has taken charge of the truck and taken Matsukata along with them. I'm worried."

"Where are they going?" Tony asked, blankly.

"That's just what worries me . . ."

The drive back was all too long for Tony. Already he was living in the future, and paid little attention to a conversation, in low tones, between Sir Denis and von Wehrner. They had carried out their part of the bargain, for they had the cipher manuscript, and if Dr. Fu Manchu was the man of his word which Nayland Smith believed him to be—they were free!

They could all return to Hong Kong for his wedding to Moon Flower . . .

His pleasant musing had lasted a long time. Von Wehrner had become silent. Nayland Smith's pipe was smoked out. The storm clouds had quite disappeared, and in bright moonlight he saw that they had nearly reached the main gate of General Huan's house.

"I was afraid of this!" Sir Denis rapped. "Look!"

The long, grey truck stood before the gate . . .

"God's mercy!" Nayland Smith whispered. "Truly, hell's loose tonight!"

The truck driver lay slumped in his cab. He was dead.

"What's happened?" Tony cried out. "We must get into the house!"

"I fear the gate is locked." Von Wehrner spoke on a note of despair.

"Wait!"

Nayland Smith was opening the rear door of the truck.

Matsukata lay prone on the floor inside!

"Get him out!" Sir Denis called. "Lend a hand, McKay." And

together they got the limp body out. "Dr. von Wehrner, this is your job. Tell me—is he alive?"

The German biologist who was also a physician bent over the Japanese, examined him briefly, and nodded.

"Tough they are, these Japanese. It is extreme nervous exhaustion. Is your flask empty, Sir Denis?"

It wasn't. And the doctor went to work to revive Matsukata.

"McKay!" Nayland Smith said, supporting the inert body. "There must be some kind of bell, or something, to arouse the gate porter. Tung may know!"

But Tung knew of no bell, so he began to rattle the bars and shout.

"Open the gate! Open the gate!"

He was still shouting when a light sprang up in the lodge, a door was unlocked. An old man looked out, cautiously.

"Quick! Let us in!"

"It is Dr. Matsukata!" Tony called in Chinese. "We have business with his Excellency!"

The ancient porter came to the gate. "Gladly—for the place is taken over by demons! " He peered about, fearfully. "I saw them—leaping over the wall!"

He opened the heavy gate almost at the moment that Matsukata revived enough to speak.

"They meant to kill me," he whispered. "They forced the driver to take the truck to the clinic. I was helpless. They can communicate with one another in some way. I knew this. They acted together. I was forced to open the store of *Looma*. They drank it all. Then they forced the driver to come here. I do not know why they compelled me to come. Perhaps to torture me. From the roof of the truck they sprang over into the governor's garden—all of them; like apes. I know no more, except that the Master—"

Matsukata passed out again.

McKay and Tung carried him into the gate lodge. Then Tung drove the car in and the gate was relocked. Dr. von Wehrner volunteered to look after Matsukata, and Tony and Nayland Smith started off towards the house.

Tony saw that every window in the large building was lighted!

"What's this?" he muttered.

449

"My guess is that the Cold Men are inside—looting!" Nayland Smith told him rapidly. "By the way, hide your radio."

He began to run. So did Tony.

A gong hung on the flower-draped terrace before the main door. Nayland Smith struck it a blow with the butt of his revolver.

Before its vibration had died away, the big, heavy door was thrown open, and a terrifying figure stood before them, a lean, muscular figure of a man wearing a shirt of chain mail, baggy trousers and some kind of metal helmet. He held a heavy sword having a curved blade from which certain stains had been imperfectly removed!

"You are welcome, gentlemen."

It was General Huan Tsung-Chao!

As the door was reclosed, Tony glanced around the lighted lobby, its exquisite tapestries and trophies of arms—from one of which he guessed that General Huan had taken his queer equipment. Nayland Smith was staring at the general in an odd way.

"I can assure you, Sir Denis," the old soldier said in his excellent English, "that I have not taken leave of my senses. But my house was invaded some time ago by creatures not of this world. My steward, an excellent and faithful servant, detecting one of them entering through a window, shot him. The Thing ignored the wound, sprang on my steward and strangled him!"

"The Cold Men!" Nayland Smith rapped. "What did you do?"

"I ordered the resident staff to lock themselves in their quarters, and took the same precautions with my guests, Dr. Cameron-Gordon and his daughter. I locked the door of their apartment."

"Thank God for that!" Tony murmured.

"Some of the creatures," General Huan went on in unruffled calm, "had obtained knives. Hence this." He tapped the shirt of mail. "It was worn by an ancestor many centuries ago. I called for aid from Chia-Ting and was interrupted by one of the grey horrors, who attacked me with a dagger. Although apparently immune to bullets, I am a sabre expert, and I struck the things heads off without difficulty."

Tony gasped. He had seen such a feat performed by the executioner in the prison yard at Chia-Ting. But General Huan he judged to be all of seventy years old!

"Listen!" Nayland Smith snapped.

A faint sound of maniacal laughter sent an icy chill down Tony's spine.

"Some of them are upstairs," General Huan declared. "They move like shadows. I beheaded another in the wine cellar. The creature was pouring a rare Château Yquem down his throat. But there are more to be accounted for. This imbecile laughter—"

A stifled shriek checked him.

"Moon Flower!" Tony shouted. "Lead the way, sir! Where is she?"

But that strange figure of a mediaeval Chinese warrior already led the way. Before a door carved in fanciful geometrical designs he halted and took a key from a pocket in his baggy trousers; threw the door open. It was their former apartment.

The effect resembled that caused by opening a refrigerator. Through a window having a balcony outside Tony saw the starry sky, and knew immediately how the Cold Man had got in. The room showed a scene of crazy disorder. Dr. Cameron-Gordon lay face-down by the window. But he had no time to observe details . . .

A *necropolite*, a grey, corpselike figure, was forcing Moon Flower back on to a divan; his lean left arm locked around her. She was past speech, but her feeble moans stung Tony to fighting madness. With his right hand the Cold Man stripped the clothing from her shoulders, pressing his loathsome lips to the soft curves he found.

Tony leapt forward and pumped three bullets into the Cold Man's sinewy grey shoulder. The creature uttered no cry of pain; but its left arm relaxed and then fell limply. Moon Flower staggered back, collapsing on the cushioned divan.

As Nayland Smith sprang forward, the Cold Man turned, a murderous grin on his face.

"Oblige me by stepping aside, gentlemen," General Huan cried in a tone of command.

Both twisted around, astounded by the words and the manner.

General Huan thrust himself before them. The *necropolite* plucked a knife from his loincloth. And at that same moment the long, curved blade of the great sword whistled through the air—and the grinning head rolled on the rug-covered floor. The trunk collapsed slowly, then slumped.

"See!" General Huan held up the blade. "No more blood than if one carved a fish! The creatures are not human . . ."

Cameron-Gordon had been stunned by a blow on his skull, received as the Cold Man silently entered through the window. Or so Nayland Smith deduced when his old friend came to his senses and stared dazedly across the room to where Tony knelt beside the divan whispering soothing words to Moon Flower. Her experience with a necropolite had brought her to the verge of hysteria, a feminine weakness which she despised.

The icy remains of her attacker, in two parts, had been removed before she recovered from the swoon; and General Huan had gone to call those male members of his staff who slept in the servants' annexe to assist in the search for the Cold Men still at large.

Assured by Cameron-Gordon that he had suffered no physical injury, Nayland Smith jumped up and glanced quizzically at Tony.

"Come on, McKay!" he rapped. "Jeanie will be all right now with her father to look after her. We're wanted downstairs."

"Close those shutters," Tony called to Cameron-Gordon as he started, "and lock the door after us!"

Their assistance proved to be unnecessary, however. Matsukata, fully restored, and Dr. von Wehrner, on their way to the house, had almost stumbled over several Cold Men lying in a state of coma induced by a surfeit of looted food and wine. Another, making his exit in the same way, from an upstairs window, had fallen on his head and lay unconscious on a tiled path.

Matsukata's manner was furtive. From the way in which he glanced at von Wehrner, Tony knew that there were questions he wanted to ask, and from the way he avoided meeting Nayland Smith's eyes that there were inquiries he didn't want to answer. In fact, he seemed to be half-dazed.

In the light of early morning Nayland Smith and Tony sat in Huan Tsung-Chao's study, the room with the large lacquered desk. General Huan was seated behind the desk.

"Isn't it remarkable, General," Sir Denis asked, "that Dr. Fu Manchu should have chosen last night for an attempt on the Soviet station? I had supposed the return of the manuscript before you to be of paramount interest."

452

General Huan rested his hand on the parchment bound Si-Fan Register.

"It is of great interest to me, also, Sir Denis. But The Master accepted your word that it would be restored as you accepted his that you and your friends should be free to leave. His reason for moving last night was that he feared the replacement of Dr. von Wehrner might result in more stringent precautions being taken."

"You tell me you have no news of him. This I don't understand."

The lined, remarkable old face relaxed in a smile

"There are many things, Sir Denis, concerning your own part in the affair which I do not understand! The Cold Men, in three parties, were instructed, hypnotically, to obey Mahmûd—a former sergeant-major of French-Algerian infantry. Contrary to my advice, The Master—aware that these awful creatures are strangely affected by electric storms—set out shortly after Dr. Matsukata and Mahmûd to take personal charge."

He paused, and very deliberately took a pinch of snuff.

"Dr. Matsukata tells me that the third party, whom he held in reserve, revolted. You are aware of what occurred later. You have scrupulously carried out your undertaking, Sir Denis, and I have arranged suitable transport for all of you, as The Master authorized me to do. I have included Dr. von Wehrner, whose presence in your party is one of the things I do not understand." He smiled again, a sly smile. "If you should call at Lung Chang, please give my best wishes to a mutual friend there. You will be provided with papers ensuring your free passage . . ."

Many hours later, in Lao Tse-Mung's library, a setting sun gleamed on the many bound volumes, cabinets and rare porcelain. Moon Flower was curled up on a cushioned settee; Tony's glance lingered on her adoringly. Their courteous host had personally conducted his old friend, Cameron-Gordon, and the unexpected guest, von Wehrner, to their apartments, and Nayland Smith lay back in a big rest-chair, relighting his pipe and looking gloriously at ease.

"Is it possible, Sir Denis, that Dr. Fu Manchu is dead?" Tony asked suddenly.

Nayland Smith looked up at him, match in hand.

"Judging from a long experience, highly improbable!"

"Because, it would be rather a pity, in view of something I have here." He pulled out the long envelope containing the translation of the cipher manuscript.

"The Lama advised me not to show it to you until we were out of danger."

"What the devil is it?" Sir Denis rapped, and took the envelope from Tony.

"It's the Lama's deciphering of the manuscript!"

"*What!*" Nayland Smith blew the match out in the nick of time, leapt to his feet. "This is incredible—"

"A list, the Lama told me, of every Si-Fan lodge master in China—some of them prominent persons—including General Huan!"

Nayland Smith dropped back in his chair.

"I said, McKay, when you recovered the thing from André Skobolov, that I believed it to be the most powerful weapon against Fu Manchu, which I ever held in my hands. An understatement. It could shatter his dream empire!"

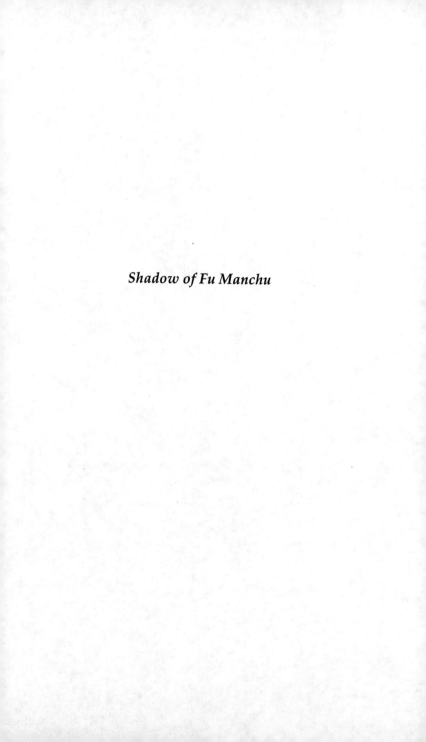

Shadow of Fu Manchu

Shadow of La Mancha

Chapter I

"Who's the redhead," snapped Nayland Smith, "lunching with that embassy attaché?"

"Which table?"

"Half-right. Where I'm looking."

Harkness, who had been briefed by Washington to meet the dynamic visitor, was already experiencing nerve strain. Sir Denis Nayland Smith, ex-chief of the Criminal Investigation Department of Scotland Yard, spoke in a Bren-gun manner, thought and moved so swiftly that his society, if stimulating, was exhausting.

Turning, when about to light a cigar, Harkness presently discovered the diplomat's table. The grill was fashionable for lunch, and full. But he knew the attaché by sight. He turned back again, dropping a match in a tray.

"Don't know. Never seen her before."

"Haven't you? I have!"

"Sorry, Sir Denis. Is she important?"

"A woman who looks like that is always important. Yes, I know her. But I haven't quite placed her."

Nayland Smith refilled his coffee cup, glanced reluctantly at a briar pipe which appeared to have been rescued from a blast furnace, and then put it back in his pocket. He selected a cigarette.

"You don't think she's a Russian?" Harkness suggested.

"I know she isn't."

Smith surveyed the crowded, panelled room. It buzzed like an aviary. Businessmen predominated. Deals of one sort or another hung in the smoke-laden air. Nearly all these men were talking about how to make money. And nearly all the women were talking about how to spend it.

But not the graceful girl with that glowing hair. He wondered what she was talking about. Her companion appeared to be absorbed, either in what she was saying or in the way she said it.

And while Nayland Smith studied many faces, Harkness studied Nayland Smith.

He had met him only once before, and the years had silvered his hair more than ever, but done nothing to disturb its crisp virility. The lean, brown face might be a trifle more lined. It was a grim face, a face which hid a secret, until Nayland Smith smiled. His smile told the secret.

He spoke suddenly.

"Strange to reflect," he said, "that these people, wrapped up, air tight, in their own trifling affairs, like cigarettes in cellophane, are sitting on top of a smouldering volcano."

"You really think so?"

"I know it. Why has a certain power sent all its star agents to the United States? What are they trying to find out?"

"Secret of the atom bomb?"

"Rot! There's no secret about it. You know that as well as I do. Once a weapon of war is given publicity, it loses its usefulness. I gain nothing by having a rock in my boxing-glove if the other fellow has one too. No. It's something else."

"England seems to be pretty busy?"

"England has lost two cabinet ministers, mysteriously, in the past few months." All the time Smith's glance had been straying in the direction of a certain party, and suddenly: "Right!" he rapped. "Thought I was. Now I'm sure! This is my lucky day."

"Sure of what?" Harkness was startled.

"Man at the next table. Our diplomatic acquaintance and his charming friend are being covered."

Harkness craned around again.

"You mean the sallow man?"

"Sallow? He's Burmese! They're not *all* Communists, you know."

Harkness stared at his cigar, as if seeking to concentrate.

"You're more than several steps beyond me. No doubt your information is away ahead of mine. But, quite honestly, I don't understand."

Nayland Smith met the glance of Harkness's frank hazel eyes, and nodded sympathetically.

"My fault. I think aloud. Bad habit. There's hardly time to explain, now. Look! They're going! Have the redhead covered.

458

Detail another man to keep the Burmese scout in sight. Report to me, here. Suite 1236."

The auburn-haired girl was walking towards the exit. She wore a plain suit and a simple hat. Her companion followed. As Harkness retired speedily, Nayland Smith dropped something which made it necessary for him to stoop when the attaché passed near his table.

Coming out onto Forty-sixth Street, Harkness exchanged a word with a man who was talking to a hotel porter. The man nodded and moved away.

Manhattan danced on. Well-fed males returned to their offices to consider further projects for making more dollars. Females headed for the glamorous shops on New York's Street-Called-Straight: Fifth Avenue, the great bazaar of the New World. Beauty specialists awaited them. Designers of Paris hats. Suave young ladies to display wondrous robes. Suave young gentlemen to seduce with glittering trinkets.

In certain capitals of the Old World, men and women looked, haggard-eyed, into empty shops and returned to empty larders.

Manhattan danced on.

Nayland Smith, watching a car move from the front of the hotel, closely followed by another, prayed that Manhattan's dance might not be a *danse macabre*.

When presently he stepped into a black sedan parked further along the street, in charge of a chauffeur who looked like a policeman (possibly because he was one), and had been driven a few blocks:

"Have we got a tail?" Smith snapped.

"Yes, sir," the driver reported. "Three cars behind us right now. Small delivery truck."

"Stop at the next drugstore. I'll check it."

When he got out and walked into the drugstore the following truck passed, and then pulled in higher up.

Nayland Smith came out again and resumed the journey. Two more blocks passed:

"Right behind us," the driver reported laconically.

Smith took up a phone installed in the sedan and gave brief directions. So that long before he had reached his destination the truck was still following the sedan, but two traffic police were following the truck. He had been no more than a few minutes in the deputy commissioner's office on Centre Street before a police sergeant came in with the wanted details.

The man had been pulled up on a technical offense and invited, firmly, to produce evidence of his identity. Smith glanced over the report.

"H'm. American citizen. Born in Athens." He looked up. "You're checking this story that he was taking the truck to be repaired?"

"Sure. Can't find anything wrong with it. Very powerful engine for such a light outfit."

"Would be," said Smith drily. "File all his contacts. He mustn't know. You have to find out who really employs him."

He spent a long time with the deputy commissioner, and gathered much useful data. He was in New York at the request of the Federal Bureau of Investigation, and had been given almost autocratic powers by Washington. When, finally, he left, he had two names pencilled in his notebook.

They were: Michael Frobisher, and Dr. Morris Craig, of the Huston Research Laboratory.

Michael Frobisher, seated in an alcove in the library of his club, was clearly ill at ease. A big-boned, fleshy man, Frobisher had a powerful physique, with a fighting jaw, heavy brows—coal-black in contrast to nearly white hair—and deep-set eyes which seemed to act independently of what Michael Frobisher happened to be doing.

There were only two other members in the library, but Frobisher's eyes, although he was apparently reading a newspaper, moved rapidly, as his glance switched from face to face in that oddly furtive manner.

Overhanging part of the room, one of the finest of its kind in the city, was a gallery giving access to more books ranged on shelves above. A club servant appeared in the gallery, moving very quietly—and Frobisher's glance shot upward like an anxious searchlight.

It was recalled to sea level by a voice.

"Hello, Frobisher! How's your wife getting along?"

Frobisher's florid face momentarily lost color. Then, looking up from where he sat in a deep, leather armchair, he saw that a third member had come in—Dr. Pardoe.

"Hello, Pardoe!" He had himself in hand again: the deep tone was normal. "Quite startled me."

"So I saw." Pardoe gave him a professional glance, and sat on the arm of a chair near Frobisher's. "Been overdoing it a bit, haven't you?"

"Oh, I don't say that, Doctor. Certainly been kept pretty busy. Thanks for the inquiry about Stella. She's greatly improved since she began the treatments you recommended."

"Good." Dr. Pardoe smiled—a dry smile: he was a sandy, dry man. "I'm not sure the professor isn't a quack, but he seems to be successful with certain types of neuroses."

"I assure you Stella is a hundred per cent improved."

"H'm. You might try him yourself."

"What are you talking about?" Frobisher growled. "There's nothing the matter with me."

"Isn't there?" The medical man looked him over coolly. "There will be if you don't watch your diet." Pardoe was a vegetarian. "Why, your heart missed a beat when I spoke to you."

Frobisher held himself tightly in hand. His wife's physician always got on his nerves. But, all the same, he wasn't standing for any nonsense.

"Let me tell you something." His deep voice, although subdued, rumbled around the now empty library. "This isn't nerves. It's cold feet. An organization like the Huston Electric has got rivals. And rivals can get dangerous if they're worsted. Someone's tracking me around. Someone broke into Falling Waters one night last week. Went through my papers. I've seen the man. I'd know him again. I was followed right here to the club today. That isn't nerves, Doctor. And it isn't eating too much red meat!"

"Hm." Irritating habit of Pardoe's, that introductory cough. "I don't dispute the fact of the burglary—"

"Thanks a lot. And let me remind you: Stella doesn't know, and doesn't have to know."

"Oh, I see. Then the attempt is known only—"

"Is known to my butler, Stein, and to me. It's not an illusion. I'm still sane, if I did have beefsteak at lunch!"

The physician raised his sandy brows.

"I don't doubt it, Frobisher. But had it occurred to you that your later impression of being followed—not an uncommon symptom—may derive from this single, concrete fact?"

Frobisher didn't reply, and Dr. Pardoe, who had been looking down at the carpet, now looked suddenly at Frobisher.

His gaze was fixed upward again. He was watching the gallery. He spoke in a whisper.

"Pardoe! Look where I'm looking. Is that a club member?"

Dr. Pardoe did as Frobisher requested. He saw a slight, black-clad figure in the gallery. The man had just replaced a vase on a shelf. Only the back of his head and shoulders could be seen. He moved away, his features still invisible.

"Not a member known to me, personally, Frobisher. But there are always new members, and guest members—"

But Frobisher was up, had bounded from his chair. Already, he was crossing the library.

"That's some kind of Asiatic. I saw his face!" Regardless of the rule, Silence, he shouted. "And I'm going to have a word with him!"

Dr. Pardoe shook his head, took up a medical journal which he had dropped on the chair, and made his way out.

He was already going down the steps when Michael Frobisher faced the club secretary, who had been sent for.

"May I ask," he growled, "since when Chinese have been admitted to membership?"

"You surprise me, Mr. Frobisher."

The secretary, a young-old man with a bald head and a Harvard accent, could be very patriarchal.

"Do I?"

"You do. Your complaint is before me. I have a note here. If you wish it to go before the committee, merely say the word. I can only assure you that not only have we no Asiatic members, honorary or otherwise, but no visitor such as you describe has been in the club. Furthermore, Mr. Frobisher, I am assured by the assistant librarian, who was last in the library gallery, that no one has been up there since."

Frobisher jumped to his feet.

"Get Dr. Pardoe!" he directed. "He was with me. Get Dr. Pardoe."

But Dr. Pardoe had left the club.

462

The research laboratory of the Huston Electric Corporation was on the thirty-sixth, and top floor of the Huston Building. Dr. Craig's office adjoined the laboratory proper, which he could enter up three steps leading to a steel door. This door was always kept locked.

Morris Craig, slight, clean-shaven, and very agile, a man in his early thirties, had discarded his coat, and worked in shirt-sleeves before a drawing desk. His dark-brown hair, which he wore rather long, was disposed to be rebellious, a forelock sometimes falling forward, so that brushing it back with his hand had become a mannerism.

He had just paused for this purpose, leaning away as if to get a long perspective of his work and at the same time fumbling for a packet of cigarettes, when the office door was thrown open and someone came in behind him.

So absorbed was Craig that he paid no attention at first, until the heavy breathing of whoever had come in prompted him to turn suddenly.

"Mr. Frobisher!"

Craig, who wore glasses when drawing or reading, but not otherwise, now removed them and jumped from his stool.

"It's all right, Craig." Frobisher raised his hand in protest. "Sit down."

"But if I may say so, you look uncommon fishy."

His way of speech had a quality peculiarly English, and he had a tendency to drawl. Nothing in his manner suggested that Morris Craig was one of the most brilliant physicists Oxford University had ever turned out. He retrieved the elusive cigarettes and lighted one.

Michael Frobisher remained where he had dropped down, on a chair just inside the door. But he was regaining color. Now he pulled a cigar from the breast pocket of his tweed jacket.

"The blasted doctors tell me I eat too much and smoke too much," he remarked. His voice always reminded Craig of old port. "But I wouldn't want to live if I couldn't do as I liked."

"Practical," said Craig, "if harsh. May I inquire what has upset you?"

"Come to that in a minute," growled Frobisher. "First—what news of the big job?"

"Getting hot. I think the end's in sight."

463

"Fine. I want to talk to you about it." He snipped the end of his cigar. "How's the new secretary making out?"

"A-I. Knows all the answers. Miss Lewis was a sad loss, but Miss Navarre is a glad find."

"Well—she's got a Paris degree, and had two years with Professor Jennings. Suits me if she suits you."

Craig's boyishly youthful face lighted up.

"Suits me to nine points of decimals. Works like a pack-mule. She ought to get out of town this week-end."

"Bring her along up to Falling Waters. Few days of fresh air do her no harm."

"No." Craig seemed to be hesitating. He returned to his desk. "But I shouldn't quit this job until it's finished."

He resumed his glasses and studied the remarkable diagram pinned to the drawing board. He seemed to be checking certain details with a mass of symbols and figures on a large ruled sheet beside the board.

"Of course," he murmured abstractedly, "I might easily finish at any time now."

The wonder of the thing he was doing, a sort of awe that he, the humble student of nature's secrets, should have been granted power to do it, claimed his mind. Here were mighty forces, hitherto no more than suspected, which controlled the world. Here, written in the indelible ink of mathematics, lay a description of the means whereby those forces might be harnessed.

He forgot Frobisher.

And Frobisher, lighting his cigar, began to pace the office floor, often glancing at the absorbed figure. Suddenly Craig turned, removing his glasses.

"Are you bothered about the cost of these experiments, Mr. Frobisher?"

Frobisher pulled up, staring.

"Cost? To hell with the cost! That's not worrying me. I don't know a lot about the scientific side, but I know a commercial proposition when I see one." He dropped down into an armchair. "What I don't know is this." He leaned forward, his heavy brows lowered: "Why is somebody tracking me around?"

"Tracking you around?"

"That's what I said. I'm being tailed around. I was followed to my club today. Followed here. There's somebody watching my home up in Connecticut. Who is he? What does he want?"

Morris Craig stood up and leaned back against the desk.

Behind him a deep violet sky made a back-cloth for silhouettes of buildings higher than the Huston. Some of the windows were coming to life, forming a glittering regalia, like jewels laid on velvet.

Dusk was falling over Manhattan.

"Astoundin' state of affairs," Craig declared—but his smile was quite disarming. "Tell me more. Anyone you suspect?"

Frobisher shook his head. "There's plenty to suspect if news of what's going on up here has leaked out. Suppose you're dead right—and I'm backing you to be—what'll this thing mean to Huston Electric?"

"Grateful thanks of the scientific world."

"Damn the scientific world! I'm thinking of Huston's."

Morris Craig, his mind wandering in immeasurable space, his spirit climbing the ladder of the stars toward higher and more remote secrets of a mysterious universe, answered vaguely.

"No idea. Can't see at the moment how it could be usefully applied."

"What are you talking about?" Michael Frobisher was quite his old roaring self again. "This job has cost half of a million dollars already. Are you telling me we get nothing back? Are we all bughouse around here?"

A door across the office opened, and a man came in, a short, thick-set man, slightly bandy, who walked with a rolling gait as if on the deck of a ship in dirty weather. He wore overalls, spectacles, and an eye-shade. He came in without any ceremony and approached Craig. The forbidding figure of Michael Frobisher disturbed him not at all.

"Say—have you got a bit of string?" he inquired.

"I have not got a bit of string. I have a small piece of gum, or two one-cent stamps. Would they do?"

The intruder chewed thoughtfully. "Guess not. Miss Navarre's typewriter's jammed up in there. But I got it figured a bit of string about so long"—he illustrated—"would fix things."

"Sorry, Sam, but I am devoid of string."

Sam chewed awhile, and then turned away.

"Guess I'll have to go look some other place."

As he went out:

"Listen," Frobisher said. "What does that moron do for his wages?"

"Sam?" Craig answered, smiling. "Oh, sort of handyman. Mostly helps Regan and Shaw in the laboratory."

"Be a big help to anybody, I'd say. What I'm driving at is this: We have to be mighty careful about who gets in here. There's been a bad leak. Somebody knows more than he ought to know."

Morris Craig, slowly, was getting back to that prosaic earth on which normal, flat-footed men spend their lives. It was beginning to dawn upon him that Michael Frobisher was badly frightened.

"I can't account for it. Shaw and Regan are beyond suspicion. So, I hope, am I. Miss Navarre came to us with the highest credentials. In any case, she could do little harm. But, of course, it's absurd to suspect her."

"What about the half-wit who just went out?"

"Knows nothing about the work. Apart from which, his refs are first-class, including one from the Fire Department."

"Looks like he'd been in a fire." Frobisher dropped a cone of cigar ash. "But facts are facts. Let me bring you up to date—but not a word to Mrs. F. You know how nervous she is. Some guy got into Falling Waters last Tuesday night and went through my papers with a fine-tooth comb!"

"You mean it?"

Craig's drawl had vanished. His eyes were very keen.

"I mean it. Nothing was taken—not a thing. But that's not all. I'd had more than a suspicion for quite a while someone was snooping around. So I laid for him, without saying a word to Mrs. F., and one night I saw him—"

"What did he look like?"

"Yellow."

"Indian?"

"No, sir. Some kind of Oriental. Then, only today, right in my own club, I caught another Asiatic watching me! It's a fact. Dr. Pardoe can confirm it. Now—what I'm asking is this: If it's what we're doing in the laboratory there that somebody's after, why am I followed around, and not you?"

"The answer is a discreet silence."

"Also I'd be glad to learn who this somebody is. I could think up plenty who'd like to know. But no one of 'em would be an Asiatic."

Morris Craig brushed his hair back with his hand.

"You're getting *me* jumpy, too," he declared, although his eager, juvenile smile belied the words. "This thing wants looking into."

"It's going to be looked into," Frobisher grimly assured him. "When you come up to Falling Waters you'll see I'm standing for no more monkey tricks around there, anyway." He stood up, glancing at the big clock over Craig's desk. "I'm picking up Mrs. F. at the Ritz. Don't have to be late. Expect you and Miss Navarre, lunch on Saturday."

Chapter II

Mrs. F., as it happened, was thoroughly enjoying herself. She lay naked, face downward, on a padded couch, whilst a white-clad nurse ran an apparatus which buzzed like a giant hornet from the back of her fluffy skull right down her spine and up again. This treatment made her purr like a contented kitten. It had been preceded by a terrific mauling at the hands of another, muscular, attendant, in the course of which Mrs. F. had been all but hanged, drawn, quartered, and, finally, stood on her head.

An aromatic bath completed the treatment. Mrs. F. was wrapped in a loose fleecy garment, stretched upon a couch in a small apartment decorated with Pompeian frescoes, and given an Egyptian cigarette and a cup of orange-scented China tea.

She lay there in delicious languor, when the draperies were drawn aside and Professor Hoffmeyer, the celebrated Viennese psychiatrist who conducted the establishment, entered gravely. She turned her head and smiled up at him.

"How do you do, Professor?"

He did not reply at once, but stood there looking at her. Even through the dark glasses he always wore, his regard never failed to make her shudder. But it was a pleasurable shudder.

Professor Hoffmeyer presented an impressive figure. His sufferings in Nazi prison camps had left indelible marks. The dark glasses protected eyes seared by merciless lights. The silk gloves which he never removed concealed hands from which the fingernails had been extracted. He stooped much, leaning upon a heavy ebony cane.

Now he advanced almost noiselessly and took Mrs. Frobisher's left wrist between a delicate thumb and forefinger, slightly inclining his head.

"It is not how do I do, dear lady," he said in Germanic gutturals, "but how do you do."

Mrs. Frobisher looked up at the massive brow bent over her,

468

and tried, not for the first time, to puzzle out the true color of the scanty hair which crowned it. She almost decided that it was color-less; entirely neutral.

Professor Hoffmeyer stood upright, or as nearly upright as she had ever seen him stand, and nodded.

"You shall come to see me on Wednesday, at three o'clock. Not for the treatment, no, but for the consultation. If some other engage-ment you have, cancel it. At three o'clock on Wednesday."

He bowed slightly and went out.

Professor Hoffmeyer ruled his wealthy clientele with a rod of iron. His reputation was enormous. His fees were phenomenal.

He proceeded, now, across a luxurious central salon where other patients waited, well-preserved women, some of them apparently out of the deep-freeze. He nodded to a chosen few as he passed, and entered an office marked "Private." Closing the door, he pulled out a drawer in the businesslike desk—and a bookcase filled with advanced medical works, largely German, swung open bodily.

The professor went into the opening. As the bookcase swung back into place, the drawer in the desk closed again.

Professor Hoffmeyer would see no more patients today.

The room in which the professor found himself was a study. But its appointments were far from conventional. It contained some very valuable old lacquer and was richly carpeted. The lighting (it had no visible windows) was subdued, and the peculiar character-istic of the place was its silence.

Open bookcases were filled with volumes, some of them bound manuscripts, many of great age and all of great rarity. They were in many languages, including Greek, Chinese, and Arabic.

Beside a cushioned divan stood an inlaid stool equipped with several opium pipes in a rack, gum, lamp, and bodkins.

A long, carved table of time-blackened oak served as a desk. A high-backed chair was set behind it. A faded volume lay open on the table, as well as a closely written manuscript. There were several other books there, and a number of curious objects difficult to iden-tify in the dim light.

The professor approached a painted screen placed before a recess and disappeared behind it. Not a sound broke the silence of the room until he returned.

He had removed the gloves and dark glasses, and for the black coat worn by Professor Hoffmeyer had substituted a yellow house robe. The eyes which the glasses had concealed were long, narrow, and emerald-green. The uncovered hands had pointed fingernails. This gaunt, upright, Chinese ascetic was taller by inches than Professor Hoffmeyer.

And his face might have inspired a painter seeking a model for the Fallen Angel.

This not because it was so evil but because of a majestic and remorseless power which it possessed—a power which resided in the eyes. They were not the eyes of a normal man, moved by the desires, the impulses shared in some part by us all. They were the eyes of one who has shaken off those inhibitions common to humanity, who is undisturbed by either love or hate, untouched by fear, unmoved by compassion.

Few such men occur in the long history of civilization, and none who has not helped to change it.

The impassive figure crossed, with a silent, catlike step, to the long table, and became seated there.

One of the curious objects on the table sprang to life, as if touched by sudden moonlight. It was a crystal globe resting on a metal base. Dimly at first, the outlines of a face materialized in the crystal, and then grew clear. They became the features of an old Chinese, white-moustached, wrinkled, benign.

"You called me, Doctor?"

The voice, though distant, was clear. A crinkled smile played over the parchment face in the crystal.

"You have all the reports?"

The second voice was harsh, at points sibilant, but charged with imperious authority. It bore no resemblance to that of Professor Hoffmeyer.

"The last is timed six-fifteen. Shall I give you a summary?"

"Proceed, Huan Tsung. I am listening."

And Huan Tsung, speaking in his quiet room above a shop in Pell Street, a room in which messages were received mysteriously, by day and by night, from all over Manhattan, closed his wise old eyes and opened the pages of an infallible memory.

This man whose ancestors had been cultured noblemen when

most of ours were living in caves, spoke calmly across a system of communication as yet unheard of by Western science . . .

"Excellency will wish to know that our Burmese agent was recognized by Nayland Smith in the grillroom and followed by two F.B.I. operatives. I gave instructions that he be transferred elsewhere. He reports that he has arrived safely. His notes of the conversation at the next table are before me." They contain nothing new. Shall I relate them?"

"No. I shall interview the woman personally. Proceed."

"Nayland Smith visited the deputy commissioner and has been alone with him more than two hours. Nature of conversation unknown. The Greek covering his movements was intercepted and questioned, but had nothing to disclose. He is clumsy, and I have had him removed."

"You did well Huan Tsung. Such bunglers breed danger."

"Mai Cha, delivering Chinese vase sent by club secretary for repair, attired herself in the black garment she carries and gained a gallery above the library where Michael Frobisher talked with a medical friend. She reports that Frobisher has had sight of our agent at Palling Waters. Therefore I have transferred this agent. Mai Cha retired, successfully, with price of repairs."

"Commend Mai Cha."

"I have done so, Excellency. She is on headquarters duty tonight. Excellency can commend her himself."

"The most recent movements of Frobisher, Nayland Smith, and Dr. Craig."

"Frobisher awaits his wife at the Ritz-Carlton. Nayland Smith is covered, but no later report has reached me. Dr. Craig is in his office."

"Frobisher has made no other contacts?"

"None, Excellency. The stream flows calmly. It is the hour for repose, when the wise man reflects."

"Wait and watch, Huan Tsung. I must think swiftly."

"Always I watch—and it is unavoidable that I wait until I am called away."

Moonlight in the crystal faded out, and with it the wrinkled features of the Mandarin Huan Tsung.

Complete silence claimed the dimly lighted room. The wearer of the yellow robe remained motionless for a long time. Then, he stood up and crossed to the divan, upon which he stretched his gaunt body. He struck a silver bell which hung in a frame beside the rack of opium pipes. The bell emitted a high, sweet note.

Whilst the voice of the bell still lingered, drowsily, on the air, draperies in a narrow, arched opening were drawn aside, and a Chinese girl came in.

She wore national costume. She was very graceful, and her large, dark eyes resembled the eyes of a doe. She knelt and touched the carpet with her forehead.

"You have done well, Mai Cha. I am pleased with you."

The girl rose, but stood, head lowered and hands clasped, before the reclining figure. A flush crept over her dusky cheeks.

"Prepare the jade pipe. I seek inspiration."

Mai Cha began quietly to light the little lamp on the stool.

Although no report had reached old Huan Tsung, nevertheless Nayland Smith had left police headquarters.

He was fully alive to the fact that every move he had made since entering New York City had been noted, that he never stirred far without a shadow.

This did not disturb him. Nayland Smith was used to it.

But he didn't wish his trackers to find out where he was going from Centre Street—until he had got there.

He favored, in cold weather, a fur-collared topcoat of military cut, which was almost as distinctive as his briar pipe. He had a dozen or more police officers paraded for his inspection, and select-ed one nearly enough of his own build, clean-shaven and brown-skinned. His name was Moreno, and he was of Italian descent.

This officer was given clear instructions, and the driver who had brought Nayland Smith to headquarters received his orders, also.

When a man wearing a light rainproof and a dark-blue felt hat (property of Detective Officer Moreno) left by a side entrance, walked along to Lafayette Street, and presently picked up a taxi, no one paid any attention to him. But, in order to make quite sure, Nayland Smith gave the address, Waldorf-Astoria, got out at that

472

hotel, walked through to the Park Avenue entrance, and proceeded to his real destination on foot.

He was satisfied that he had no shadow.

The office was empty, as Camille Navarre came out of her room and crossed to the long desk set before the windows. One end had been equipped for business purposes. There was a leather-covered chair and beside it a dictaphone. A cylinder remained on the machine, for Craig had been dictating when he was called to the laboratory. At the other end stood a draughtsman's stool and a quantity of pens, pencils, brushes, pans of colored ink, and similar paraphernalia. They lay beside a propped-up drawing board, illuminated by a tubular lamp.

Camille placed several typed letters on the desk, and then stood there studying the unfinished diagram pinned to the board.

She possessed a quiet composure which rarely deserted her. As Craig had once remarked, she was so restful about the place. Her plain suit did not unduly stress a slim figure, and her hair was swept back flatly to a knot at the nape of her neck. She wore black-rimmed glasses, and looked in every respect the perfect secretary for a scientist.

A slight sound, the click of a lock, betrayed the fact that Craig was about to come out. Camille returned to her room.

She had just gone in when the door of the laboratory opened, and Craig walked down the three steps. A man in a white coat, holding a pair of oddly shaped goggles in his hand, stood at the top. He showed outlined against greenish light. With the opening of the door, a curious vibration had become perceptible, a thing which might be sensed, rather than heard.

"In short, Doctor," he was saying, "we can focus, but we can't control the volume."

Craig spoke over his shoulder.

"When we can do both, Regan, we'll give an audition to the pundits that will turn their wool white."

Regan, a capable-looking technician, grey-haired and having a finely shaped mathematical head, smiled as he stepped back through the doorway.

"I doubt if Mr. Frobisher will want any 'auditions,' " he said drily.

473

As the door was closed, the vibrant sound ceased.

Craig stood for a moment studying the illuminated diagram as Camille had done. He lighted a cigarette, and then noticed the letters on his desk. He dropped into the chair, switching up a reading lamp, and put on his glasses.

A moment later he was afoot again, as the office door burst open and a man came in rapidly—closely followed by Sam.

"Wait a minute!" Sam was upset. "Listen. Wait a minute!"

Craig dropped his glasses on the desk, stared, and then advanced impulsively, hand outstretched.

"Nayland Smith! By all that's holy—Nayland Smith!" They exchanged grips, smiling happily. "Why, I thought you were in Ispahan, or Yucatán, or somewhere."

"Nearly right the first time. But it was Teheran. Flew from there three days ago. More urgent business here."

"Wait a minute," Sam muttered, his eye-shade thrust right to the back of his head.

Craig turned to him.

"It's all right, Sam. This is an old friend."

"Oh, is that so?"

"Yes—and I don't believe he has a bit of string."

Sam stared truculently from face to face, chewing in an ominous way, and then went out.

"Sit down, Smith. This is a great, glad surprise. But why the whirlwind business? And"—staring—"what the devil are you up to?"

Nayland Smith had walked straight across to the long windows which occupied nearly the whole of the west wall. He was examining a narrow terrace outside bordered by an ornamental parapet. He looked beyond, to where the hundred eyes of a towering building shone in the dusk. He turned.

"Anybody else got access to this floor?"

"Only the staff. Why?"

"What do you mean when you say the staff?"

"I mean the staff! Am I on the witness stand? Well, if you must know, the research staff consists of myself; Martin Shaw, my chief assistant, a Columbia graduate; John Regan second technician, who came to me from Vickers; and Miss Navarre, my secretary. She also

474

has scientific training. Except for Sam, the handyman, and Mr. Frobisher, nobody else has access to the laboratory. Do I make myself clear to your honor?"

Nayland Smith was staring towards the steel door and tugging at the lobe of his left ear, a mannerism which denoted intense concentration, and one with which Craig was familiar.

"You don't take proper precautions," he snapped. "*I* got in without any difficulty."

Morris Craig became vaguely conscious of danger. He recalled vividly the nervous but repressed excitement of Michael Frobisher. He could not ignore the tension now exhibited by Nayland Smith.

"Why these precautions, Smith? What have we to be afraid of?"

Smith swung around on him. His eyes were hard.

"Listen, Craig—we've known one another since you were at Oxford. There's no need to mince words. I don't know what you're working on up here—but I'm going to ask you to tell me. I know something else, though. Unless I have made the biggest mistake of my life, one of the few first-class brains in the world today has got you spotted."

"But, Smith, you're telling me nothing—"

"Haven't time. I baited a little trap as I came up. I'm going down to spring it."

"Spring it?"

"Exactly. Excuse me."

Smith moved to the door.

"The elevator man will be off duty—"

"He won't. I ordered him to stand by."

Nayland Smith went out as rapidly as he had come in.

Craig stood for a moment staring at the door which Smith had just closed. He had an awareness of some menace impending, creeping down upon him; a storm cloud. He scratched his chin reflectively and returned to the letters. He signed them, and pressed a button.

Camille Navarre entered quietly and came over to the desk. Craig took off his glasses and looked up—but Camille's eyes were fixed on the letters.

"Ah, Miss Navarre—here we are." He returned them to her. "And there's rather a long one, bit of a teaser, on this thing." He

475

pointed to the dictaphone. "Mind removing same and listening in to my rambling rot?"

Camille stooped and took the cylinder off the machine.

"Your dictation is very clear, Dr. Craig."

She spoke with a faint accent, more of intonation than pronunciation. It was a low-pitched, caressing voice. Craig never tired of it.

"Sweet words of flattery. I sound to myself like a half-strangled parrot. The way you construe is simply wizard."

Camille smiled. She had beautifully moulded, rather scornful lips.

"Thank you. But it isn't difficult."

She put the cylinder in its box and turned to go.

"By the way, you have an invitation from the boss. He bids you to Falling Waters for the week-end."

Camille paused, but didn't turn. If Craig could have seen her face, its expression might have puzzled him.

"Really?" she said. "That *is* sweet of Mr. Frobisher."

"Can you come? I'm going, too, so I'll drive you out."

"That would be very kind of you. Yes, I should love to come."

She turned, now, and her smile was radiant.

"Splendid. We'll hit the trail early. No office on Saturday."

There was happiness in Craig's tone, and in his glance. Camille drooped her eyes and moved away.

"Er—" he added, "is the typewriter in commission again?"

"Yes," Camille's lip twitched. "I managed to get it right."

"With a bit of string?"

"No." She laughed softly. "With a hairpin!"

As she went out, Craig returned to his drawing board. But he found it hard to concentrate. He kept thinking about that funny little *moue* peculiar to Camille, part of her. Whenever she was going to smile, one corner of her upper lip seemed to curl slightly like a rose petal. And he wondered if her eyes were really so beautiful, or if the lenses magnified them.

The office door burst open, and Nayland Smith came in again like a hot wind from the desert. He had discarded the rainproof in which he had first appeared, and now carried a fur-collared coat.

"Missed him, Craig," he rapped. "Slipped through my fingers— the swine!"

476

Craig turned half around, resting one shirt-sleeved elbow on a corner of the board.

"Of course," he said, "if you're training for the Olympic Games, or what-have-you, let me draw your attention to the wide-open spaces of Central Park. I *work* here—or try to."

He was silenced by the look in Nayland Smith's eyes. He stood up.

"Smith!—what is it?"

"Murder!" Nayland Smith rapped out the word like a rifle shot. "I have just sent a man to his death, Craig!"

"What on earth do you mean?"

"No more than I say."

It came to Morris Craig as a revelation that something had happened to crush, if only temporarily, the indomitable spirit he knew so well. He walked over and laid a hand on his friend's shoulder.

"I'm sorry, Smith. Forgive my silly levity. What's happened?"

Nayland Smith's face looked haggard, worn, as he returned Craig's earnest stare.

"I have been shadowed, Craig, ever since I reached New York. I left police headquarters a while ago, wearing a borrowed hat and topcoat. A man slightly resembling me had orders to come to the Huston Building in the car I have been using all day, wearing my own hat, and my own topcoat."

"Well?"

"He obeyed his orders. The driver, who is above suspicion, noticed nothing whatever unusual on the way. There was no evidence to suggest that they were being followed. I had assumed that they would be—and had laid my plans accordingly. I went down to see the tracker fall into my trap—"

"Go on, Smith! For God's sake, what happened?"

"This!"

Nayland Smith carefully removed a small, pointed object from its wrappings and laid it on the desk. Craig was about to pick it up, when:

"Don't touch it!" came sharply. "That is, except by the feathered end. Primitive, Craig, but deadly—and silent. Get your laboratory to analyze the stuff on the tip of the dart.

Curari is too commonplace for the man who inspired this thing."

"Smith! I'm appalled. What are you telling me?"

"It was flicked, or perhaps blown from a tube, into Moreno's face through the open window of the car. It stuck in his chin, and he pulled it out. But when the car got here, he was quite insensible, and—"

"You mean he's dead?"

"I had him rushed straight to hospital."

"They'll want this for analysis."

"There was another. The first must have missed."

Nayland Smith dropped limply into a chair, facing Craig. He pulled out his blackened briar and began to load it from an elderly pouch.

"Let's face the facts, Craig. I must make it clear to you that a mysterious Eastern epidemic is creeping West. I'm not in Manhattan for my health. I'm here to try to head it off."

He stuffed the pouch back into his pocket and lighted his pipe.

"I'm all attention, Smith. But for heaven's sake, what devil are you up against?"

"Listen. No less than six prominent members of the Soviet Government have either died suddenly or just disappeared—within the past few months."

"One of those purges? Very popular with dictators."

"A purge right enough. But not carried out by Kremlin orders. Josef Stalin is being guarded as even he was never guarded before."

Craig began groping behind him for the elusive packet of cigarettes.

"What's afoot, Smith? Is this anything to do with the news from London?"

"You mean the disappearance of two of the Socialist Cabinet? Undoubtedly. They have gone the same way."

"The same way?" Craig's search was rewarded. He lighted a cigarette. "*What* way?"

Nayland Smith took the fuming pipe from between his teeth, and fixed a steady look on Craig.

"Dr. Fu Manchu's way!"

"Dr. Fu Manchu! But—"

The door of Camille's room opened, and Camille came out. She held some typewritten sheets in her hand. There was much shadow

478

at that side of the office, for only the desk lights were on, so that as the two men turned and looked towards her, it was difficult to read her expression.

But she paused at sight of them, standing quite still.

"Oh, excuse me, Dr. Craig! I thought you were alone."

"It's all right," said Craig. "Don't—er—go, Miss Navarre. This is my friend, Sir Denis Nayland Smith. My new secretary, Smith—Miss Navarre."

Nayland Smith stared for a moment, then bowed, and walked to the window.

"What is it, Miss Navarre?" Craig asked.

"It's only that last cylinder, Dr. Craig. I wanted to make sure I had it right. I will wait until you are disengaged."

But Nayland Smith was looking out into the jewelled darkness, and seeing nothing of a towering building which rose like a lighted teocalli against the skyline. He saw, instead, a panelled grillroom where an attractive red-haired girl sat at a table with a man. He saw the dark-faced spy lunching alone near by.

The girl in the grillroom had not worn her hair pinned back in that prim way, nor had she worn glasses.

Nevertheless, the girl in the grillroom and Miss Navarre were one and the same!

Chapter III

In a little shop sandwiched in between more imposing Chinese establishments, a good-looking young Oriental sat behind the narrow counter writing by the light of a paper-shaded lamp. The place was a mere box, and he was entirely surrounded by mysterious sealed jars, packets of joss sticks wrapped up in pakapu papers, bronze bowls with perforated wooden lids, boxes of tea, boxes of snuff, bead necklaces, and other completely discordant items of an evidently varied stock. The shop smelled of incense.

A bell tinkled as the door was opened. A big man came in, so big that he seemed a crowd. He looked and was dressed like some kind of workman.

The young Oriental regarded him impassively.

"Mr. Huan Tsung?" the man asked.

"Mr. Huan Tsung not home. How many time you come before?"

"Seven."

The young man nodded. "Give me the message."

From some pocket inside his checked jacket the caller produced an envelope and passed it across the counter. It was acknowledged by another nod, dropped on a ledge, and the big messenger went out. The young Chinaman went on writing.

A minute or so later, a point of light glowed below the counter, where it would have remained invisible to a customer had one been in the shop.

The envelope was placed in a tiny cupboard and a stud was pressed. The light under the counter vanished, and the immobile shopman went on writing. He wrote with a brush, using India ink, in the beautiful, difficult idiograms of classic Chinese.

Upstairs, in a room the walls of which were decorated with panels of painted silk, old Huan Tsung sat on a divan. He resembled the traditional portrait of Confucius. From a cupboard at his elbow corresponding to that in the shop below, he took out the message, read it, and dropped message and envelope into a brazier of burning charcoal.

He replaced the mouthpiece of a long-stemmed pipe between his wrinkled lips.

On a low-set red lacquer stool beside the divan was a crystal globe, similar in appearance to that upon the long, narrow table in the study adjoining Professor Hoffmeyer's office.

Nothing occurred for some time. Huan Tsung smoked contentedly, reflection from the brazier lending a demoniac quality to his benign features.

Then the crystal globe came to life, like a minor moon emerging from a cloud. Within it materialized a gaunt, wonderful face, the brow of a philosopher, green, fanatical eyes in which slumbered the fires of an imperious will.

Below, in the shop, but inaudible in the silk-walled room above, a phone buzzed. The patient writer laid his brush aside, took up the instrument, and listened. He replaced it, scribbled a few pencilled lines, put the paper in the cupboard, and pressed the button.

Huan Tsung, with a movement of his hand, removed the message. He glanced at it—and dropped the sheet into the brazier. The face in the globe had fully materialized. Compelling eyes looked into his own. Huan Tsung spoke.

"You called me, Doctor?"

"No doubt you have later reports."

"The last one, Excellency, just to hand, is timed 7.26 P.M. Nayland Smith left Centre Street at seven twenty-three. Our agent, following, carried-out the operation successfully—"

"Successfully!" A note of anger became audible in the sibilant tones. "I may misunderstand you. What method was used?"

"B.W. 63, of which I have a little left, and the feathered darts. I instructed Sha Mu, who is expert, and he succeeded at the second attempt. He passed the police car undetected and retired in safety. Nayland Smith was taken, without being removed from the car, to the Rockefeller Institute."

Huan Tsung's eyes were closed. His features ware a mask of complacency. There was a brief silence.

"Open your eyes!" Huan Tsung did so, and shrank. "They think

481

Professor Lowe may save him. They are wrong. Your action was ill considered. Await instructions to establish contact."

"Excellency's order noted."

"Summarize any other reports."

"There are few of importance. The Emir Omar Khan died in Teheran this morning."

"That is well. Nayland Smith's visit to Teheran was wasted. Instruct Teheran."

"Excellency's order noted. There is no later report from Moscow and none from London."

Silence fell. The green eyes in the crystal mirror grew clouded, filmed over in an almost pathological way. The cloud passed. They blazed again like emeralds.

"You have destroyed that which might have been of use to us. Furthermore, you have aroused a nest of wasps. Our task was hard enough. You make it harder. A disappearance—yes. I had planned one. But this clumsy assassination—"

"I thought I had done well."

"A legitimate thought is the child of wisdom and experience. Thoughts, like children, may be bastards."

Light faded from the crystal. Old Huan Tsung smoked, considering the problem of human fallibility.

"This is stupendous!" Nayland Smith whispered

With Morris Craig, he stood under a dome which occupied one end of the Huston laboratory. It was opaque but contained four small openings. Set in it, rather as in an observatory, was an instrument closely resembling a huge telescope, except that it appeared to be composed of some dull black metal and had no lense.

Through the four openings, Nayland Smith could see the stars.

Like Craig, he wore green-tinted goggles.

That part of the instrument where, in a real telescope, the eye-piece would be, rested directly over a solid table topped with a six-inch-thick sheet of a grey mineral substance. A massive portcullis of the same material enclosed the whole. It had just been raised, An acrid smell filled the air.

"Some of the Manhattan rock below us is radioactive," Craig had explained. "So, in a certain degree, are the buildings. Until I found that out, I got no results."

Complex machinery mounted on a concrete platform, machinery which emitted a sort of radiance and created vibrations which seemed to penetrate one's spine, had been disconnected by Regan from its powerful motors.

In a dazzling, crackling flash, Nayland Smith had seen a lump of solid steel not melt, but disperse, disintegrate, vanish!

A pinch of greyish powder alone remained.

"Keep the goggles on for a minute," said Craig. "Of course, you understand that this is merely a model plant. I might explain that the final problem, which I think I have solved, is the transmuter."

"Nice word," snapped Smith. "What does it mean?"

"Well—it's more than somewhat difficult to define. Sort of ring-a-ring of neutrons, pocket full of plutrons. It's a method of controlling and directing the enormous power generated here."

Nayland Smith was silent for a moment. He was dazed by the thing he had seen, appalled by its implications.

"If I understand you, Craig," he said rapidly, "this device enables you to tap the great belt of ultraviolet rays which, you tell me, encloses the earth's atmosphere a hundred miles above the ionosphere—whatever that is."

"Roughly speaking—yes. The term, ultraviolet, is merely one of convenience. Like marmalade for a preparation containing no oranges."

"So far, so good. Now tell me—when your transmuter is completed, what can you *do* with this thing?"

"Well"—Craig removed his goggles and brushed his hair back—"I could probably prevent any kind of projectile, or plane, from entering the earth's atmosphere over a controlled area. That is, if I could direct my power upward and outward."

"Neutralizing the potential of atomic warfare?"

"I suppose it would."

"What about directed downward and inward?" rapped Smith.

"Well"—Craig smiled modestly—"that's all I *can* do at the moment. And you have seen one result."

Nayland Smith snatched the goggles from his eyes.

"Do you realize what this means?"

"Clearly. What?"

"It means that you're a focus of interest for God knows how many trained agents. I know now why New York has become a hotbed of spies. You don't appreciate your own danger."

Morris Craig began to feel bewildered.

"Do try to be lucid, Smith. *What* danger? Why should *I* be in danger?"

Nayland Smith's expression grew almost savage.

"Was *I* in danger today? Then tell me what became of Dr. Sven Helsen—inventor of the Helsen lamp?"

"That's easy. I don't know."

"And of Professor Chiozza, in his stratoplane, in which he went up to pass out of the earth's atmosphere?"

"Probably passed out of same—and stayed out."

"Not a bit of it. Dr. Fu Manchu *destroys* obstacles as we destroy flies. But he *collects* specialized brains as some men collect rare postage stamps. How do you get in and out of this place at night when the corporation offices are closed?"

"By special elevator from the thirty-second. There's a private door on the street, used by Mr. Frobisher, and a small elevator to his office on the thirty-second. Research staff have master keyes. All secure?"

"From ordinary intruders. But this thing is a hundred times bigger than I even suspected. If ever a man played with fire without knowing it, you are that man. Russia, I know, has an agent here."

"Present the moujik. I yearn to greet this comrade."

"I can't. I haven't spotted him yet. But I have reason to believe our own land of hope and glory is onto you as well."

Craig, in the act of opening the laboratory door, paused. He turned slowly.

"What on earth do you mean?"

"I mean that London can't afford to let this thing fall into the hands of Moscow—nor can Washington. And none of 'em would like Dr. Fu Manchu to get it."

"Dr. Fu Manchu? I imagined it to be a mere name to frighten children. If a real person, I thought he died long ago."

"You were wrong, Craig. He is here—in New York! He is like the phoenix. He arises from his own ashes."

A sense of unreality, not unmixed with foreboding, touched Morris Craig. He visualized vividly the fate of the man mistaken for Nayland Smith. But when he spoke, it was with deliberate flippancy.

"Describe this cremated character, so that if I meet him I can cut him dead."

But Nayland Smith shook his head impatiently.

"I pray you never do meet him, Craig."

Camille Navarre, seated in her room, had just put a call through. She watched the closed door all the time she was speaking.

"Yes . . . Nine-nine here . . . It has been impossible to call you before. Listen, please. I may have to hang up suddenly. Sir Denis Nayland Smith is in the laboratory. What are my instructions?"

She listened awhile, anxiously watching the door.

"I understand . . . the design for the transmuter is practically completed . . . Of course . . . I know the urgency . . . But it is terribly intricate . . . No—I have quite failed to identify the agent."

For some moments she listened again, tensely.

"Sir Denis must have told Dr. Craig . . . I heard the name Fu Manchu spoken here not an hour ago . . . Yes. But this is important: I am to go to Falling Waters for the week-end. What are my instructions?"

The door opened suddenly, and Sam came lurching in. Camille's face betrayed not the slightest change of expression. But she altered her tone.

"Thanks, dear," she said lightly. "I must hang up now. It was sweet of you to call me."

She replaced the receiver and smiled up at Sam.

"Happen to have a pair o' nail scissors, lady?" Sam inquired.

"Not with me, I'm afraid. What do you want them for?"

"Stubbed my toe back there, and broke the nail. See how I'm limpin'?"

"Oh, I'm so sorry." Camille's caressing voice conveyed real sympathy. "But I think there are some sharp scissors in Dr. Craig's desk. They might do."

"Sure. Let's go look."

They crossed the empty office outside now largely claimed by

485

shadows except where the desk lights dispersed them. Camille discovered the scissors, which Sam examined without enthusiasm but finally carried away and promised to return.

Camille lingered until the door had closed behind him, placing two newly typed letters on the desk. Then she took off her glasses and laid them beside the letters. Her ears alert for any warning sound from the laboratory, she bent over the diagram pinned to the board. She made rapid, pencilled notes, glancing down at them and back at the diagram.

She was about to add something more, when that familiar click of a lock warned her that someone was about to come out of the laboratory. Closing her notebook, she walked quickly back to her room.

Her door closed just as Nayland Smith and Craig came down the three steps.

"Does it begin to dawn on your mind, Craig, why the intelligence services of all the great powers are keenly interested in you?"

Morris Craig nodded.

"Which is bad enough," he said. "But the devil who tried to murder you today is a bigger danger than any."

"My dear Craig, *he* didn't try to murder me. If the man who did had been caught, he would never have heard of Dr. Fu Manchu."

"You mean he'd have said so?"

"I mean it would be true. Imagine a linquist who speaks any of the civilized languages, and a score of dialects, with perfect ease; an adept in many sciences; one with the brains of three men of genius. Such a master doesn't risk his neck in the hands of underlings. No. We have to deal with a detached intellect, with a personality scarcely human."

Nayland Smith fell silent—and Craig knew that he was thinking about Moreno, the man who had suffered in his place.

"Suppose, Smith," he said, "you give your problems a rest for a while and dine with me tonight?"

"I shall be glad, Craig. Let it be at my hotel. Join me there in, say, an hour from now. But let me point out it isn't my problem. It's yours! When you leave, get the man, Sam, to have a taxi waiting—and keep him with you. I take it he hasn't gone?"

"No. He's somewhere about. We're night birds here. But what good is Sam?"

"He's a *witness*. You're safe provided you're not alone."

"Safe from what?"

"Abduction! Being smuggled out by the mysterious subway which has swallowed up other men of use to Fu Manchu."

"Where do they go? What use can he have for them?"

"I don't know where they go," rapped Nayland Smith, "but I suspect. As for their use—the use that the ant has for the aphides. Except that Dr. Fu Manchu milks their *brains*."

Unnoticed by either, the door of Camille's room had been slowly and silently opening for some time.

"You're beginning to get me really jumpy, Smith. You don't intend to go out alone?"

Nayland Smith shook his head grimly, putting on the topcoat which had brought disaster to poor Moreno.

"I have a bodyguard waiting below—a thing I never dreamed *I'd* stoop to! But Dr. Fu Manchu doesn't want my brains. He wants my life!"

"For heaven's sake, be careful, Smith. The elevator man goes off at seven o'clock. I'll see you down to the street."

"Save yourself the trouble. You have work to do. I know the way. Lend me your master key. Whoever stays here on duty can do the same for you. And remember—stick by Sam until you get to my hotel."

The door of Camille's room began to close.

Chapter IV

And that night Manhattan danced on, merrily.

Restaurants were crowded with diners, later to proceed to equally crowded theatres, dance halls, bars. Broadway, a fantasy invented long ago by H.G. Wells, but one he never expected to come true, roared and glittered and threw up to the skies an angry glare visible for miles—as of Rome burning.

Whilst on top of a building taller than the towers of those early seekers, the priests of Bel, a modern wizard from Merton College, Oxford, trapped and sought to tame the savage powers which hold our tiny world in thrall. His spells were mathematical formulae, his magic circle rested on steel and concrete. Absorbed in contemplation of the purely scientific facets of his task, only now did it begin to creep upon his consciousness—an evil phantom, chilling, terrifying—that under his hand lay means whereby the city of New York might be reduced to "one with Nineveh and Tyre."

"But directed downward and inward?" Nayland Smith had asked. Morris Craig realized, in this moment of cold lucidity, that directed downward and *outward*, the secret plant so lovingly and secretly assembled in the Huston laboratory might well obliterate, utterly, a great part of Manhattan.

Manhattan danced on.

Craig studied his nearly finished diagram with new doubt — almost with distaste. In the blind race for domination, many governments, including, according to Nayland Smith, that of Great Britain, watched every step of his experiments. And Dr. Fu Manchu was watching.

The Huston Electric Corporation was not to be left in undisputed possession of this new source of power.

Assuming that these unknown watchers failed to solve the secret, and that Washington didn't intervene, what did Michael Frobisher intend to do with it?

For that matter, what did he, Morris Craig, intend to do with it?

He had to admit to himself that he had never, from the moment of inspiration which had led to these results right up to this present hour, given a thought to possible applications of the monstrous force he had harnessed.

Brushing back that obstinate forelock, he dismissed these ideas which were non-productive, merely disturbing, and sat down to read two letters which Camille Navarre had left to be signed. He possessed the capacity, indispensable to success in research, of banishing any train of thought not directly concerned with the problem before him.

But, even as he picked up the typed pages, another diversion intruded.

A pair of black-rimmed glasses lay on the desk. He knew they were Camille's, and he was surprised that she had not missed them.

He had often wondered what defect marred those beautiful eyes, and so he removed his own glasses and put hers on.

Craig's sight was good, and he aided it during prolonged work merely to combat a slight astigmatism of the left eye. His lenses magnified only very slightly.

But—Camille's didn't magnify at all!

He satisfied himself that they were, in fact, nothing but plain glass, before laying them down.

Having signed the letters, he pressed a button.

Camille entered composedly and crossed to the desk.

"It was so stupid of me, Dr. Craig," she said, "but I must have left my glasses here when I brought the letters in."

Craig looked up at her. Yes, she had glorious eyes. He thought they were very deep blue, but they seemed to change in sympathy with her thoughts or emotions. Their evasive color reminded him of the Mediterranean on a day when high clouds scudded across the sky.

She met his glance for a moment and then turned aside, taking up the typed pages and the black-rimmed glasses.

"That last cylinder was rather scratchy, and there are one or two words I'm uncertain about."

But Craig continued to look at her.

"Why wear those things at all?" he inquired. "You wouldn't miss 'em."

489

"What do you mean, Dr. Craig?"

"Well—they're plain glass, aren't they? Why wear two bits of windowpane—in such perfectly lovely optics?"

Camille hesitated. She had not been prepared for his making this discovery, and her heart was beating very fast.

"Really, I suppose it must seem strange. I know they don't magnify. But, somehow, they help me to concentrate."

"Avoid concentration," Craig advised earnestly. "I greatly prefer you when you're relaxin'. I have looked over the letter—"

"I did my best with it."

"Your best is perfection. Exactly what I said, and stickily technical." He looked up at her with frank admiration. "Your scientific equipment is A-l wizard. Full marks for the Sorbonne."

Camille veiled her eyes. She had long lashes which Craig felt sure were an act of God and not of Elizabeth Arden.

But all she said was, "Thank you, Dr. Craig," spoken in a tone oddly constrained.

Carrying the signed letters and her glasses, she moved away. Craig turned and looked after the trim figure.

"Slip out now," he advised, "for a plate of wholesome fodder. You stick it too closely. So long as you can give me an hour from ten onward, all's well in a beautiful world."

"Perhaps I may go out—although I'm really not hungry."

She went into her room and closed the door. For a long time she sat there, the useless glasses in her hand, staring straight before her . . . He was so kind, so delicately sympathetic. He almost apologized when he had to give orders, masking them under that affected form of speech which led many people to think him light-minded, but which had never deceived Camille.

Of course, he was brilliantly clever. One day the people of the world would wake up to find a new genius come among them.

He was so clever that she found it hard to believe he had really accepted her explanation. She had done her best on the urge of the moment, but it was only postponing the evil hour. Camille had never, before that day, met Sir Denis Nayland Smith, but his reputation made discovery certain. And he would tell Morris.

Or would he?

Meanwhile, Craig was tidying up prior to going out to join Nayland

Smith. He arranged pencils, bowls of ink, and like impedimenta in some sort of order. The board to which the plan was pinned he lifted from its place and carried across the office. Before a large safe he set it down, pulled out a key-ring, manipulated the dial, and unlocked the safe.

He placed the plan inside and relocked the steel door.

This done, he returned to his desk and pressed a button on the switchboard.

"Laboratory," said a tired voice. "Regan speaking."

"I'm cutting out for some dinner, Regan. Anything you want to see me about before I go?"

"Nothing, Doctor."

"Right. Back around ten."

He stood up—then remained standing, for a moment, quite still, and listening.

The sound of a short, harsh cough, more like that of a dog who has swallowed a fragment of bone than of a human being, had reached his ears.

Crossing, he opened the office door and looked out. The landing was empty.

"Sam!" he called.

Sam appeared from somewhere, chewing industriously.

"Yes, boss?"

"Did you cough?"

"Me? No, sir. Why?"

"Thought I heard someone coughing. Stand by. I want you to come along with me in a minute."

He returned took his jacket from a hook and put it on: then draped his topcoat over his arm. He was just reaching for his hat, when he remembered something. Dropping the coat over the back of a chair, he crossed to the door of Camille's room, rapped, and opened.

She looked up in a startled way, glancing at the glasses beside her.

"Sorry—er—Miss Navarre, but may I borrow your key? Lent mine to Nayland Smith."

Camille's eyes appeared to Craig to change color, but that faint twitch of the lip which heralded a smile reassured him.

"Certainly, Dr. Craig."

She pulled a ring out of her handbag and began to detach the key which opened both elevators and the street door. Craig watched her deft white fingers, noting with approval that she did not go in for the kind of nail varnish which suggests that its wearer has been disembowelling a pig.

And as he watched, the meaning of Camille's repressed smile suddenly came to him.

"I say!" he exclaimed. "Just a minute. Pause. Give me time to reflect."

Camille looked up.

"Yes. Dr. Craig?"

"How are you going to cut out for eats, as recommended, if I pinch your key?"

"Oh, it doesn't matter a little bit."

"Doesn't matter? It matters horribly. I'm not going to leave you locked up here in the ogre's tower with no means of escape. I firmly repeat—pause. I will borrow Regan's key."

"But —"

"There are no buts. I want you to nip out for a speck of nourishment, like a good girl."

He waved his hand and was gone

Camille sat looking towards the door for fully a minute after it had closed.

"It may be best," said Nayland Smith, "if we dine in the restaurant here. I expect calls, too."

"Must say I'll breathe more freely," Craig admitted. "I never expected to slink around New York as if crossing enemy territory. What news of Moreno?"

Smith knocked ash from his pipe with unusual care.

"Poor devil," he said softly.

"Like that, is it?"

Smith nodded. "I went there after leaving you. His wife had been sent for. Nice kid, little more than a child. Only married six months. Maddison Lowe is probably the ace man in his province, but he's beaten this time."

"Have they identified the stuff used?"

"No. It's nothing on the order of *curari*. And there are no tetanus

492

symptoms. He's just completely unconscious, and slowly dying. I suppose I should feel indebted to Dr. Fu Manchu. It's evidently a painless death."

"Good God, Smith! You make me shudder. What kind of man is this?"

"A genius, Craig. He is above ordinary emotions. Men and women are just pieces on the board. Any that become useless, or obstructive, he removes. It's quite logical."

"It may be. But it isn't human."

"You are not the first to doubt if Dr. Fu Manchu is human, in the generally accepted sense of the word. Certainly he has long outlived man's normal span. He claims to have mastered the secret of prolonging life."

"Do you believe it?"

"I can't doubt it. He was elderly from all accounts when I first set eyes on him, in a Burmese forest. He nearly did for me, then—using the same method—as he has done for poor Moreno, now. And that was more years ago than I care to count."

"Good heavens! How old is he?"

"God knows. Come on. Let's get some dinner. We have a lot to talk about."

As they entered the restaurant, to be greeted by a maître d'hôtel who knew Nayland Smith, Craig saw the steely eyes turning swiftly right and left. With the ease of one who has been a target for criminals all over the world, Smith was analyzing every face in the room.

"That table by the wall," he rapped, pointing.

"I am so sorry, Sir Denis. That table is reserved."

"Reserve another, and say you made a mistake."

A ten-dollar bill went far to clinch the matter. There was some running about by waiters, whispering and side glances, to which Nayland Smith paid no attention. As he and Craig sat down:

"You note," he explained tersely, "I can see the entrance from here. Adjoining table occupied. People harmless . . ."

Whilst Morris Craig attacked a honeydew melon, Smith covertly watched him. and then:

"Highly attractive girl, that secretary of yours," he jerked casually.

Craig looked up.

"Quite agree. Highly competent, too."

493

"Remarkable hair."

"Ah, you noticed it! Pity she hides it like that."

"Hides her eyes, too," said Smith drily.

But Craig did not reply. He had been tempted to do so, and then had changed his mind. Instead he studied a wine list which a waiter had just handed to him. As he ordered a bottle of Château Margaux, he was thinking, "Has Camille gone out? Where has she gone? Is she doing herself well?" Yes, Camille had remarkable hair, and her eyes— For some obscure reason he found himself wondering who could have coughed in the office just before he left, and wondering, too, in view of the fact that, failing Sam, it was quite unaccountable, why he had dismissed the incident so lightly.

"The devil of it is, Craig," Nayland Smith was saying, "that Fu Manchu, who has come dangerously near to upsetting the order of things more than once, is no common criminal."

"Evidently."

"He doesn't work for personal gain. He's a sort of cranky idealist. I said tonight that I prayed you might never meet him. The prayer was a sincere one. The force which Dr. Fu Manchu can project is as dangerous, in its way, as that which you have trapped in your laboratory. Five minutes in his company would convince you that you stood in the presence of a phenomenal character."

"I'm prepared to believe you. But I don't understand how such a modern Cesare Borgia can wander around New York and escape the police!"

Nayland Smith leaned across the table and fixed his steady gaze on Craig.

"Dr. Fu Manchu," he said deliberately, "will never be arrested by any ordinary policeman. In my opinion, the plant on top of the Huston Building should be smashed to smithereens." His speech became rapid, rattling. "It's scientific lunatics like you who make life perilous. Agents of three governments are watching you. I may manage the agents—but I won't make myself responsible for Dr. Fu Manchu."

Could Morris Craig have seen the face of the Chinese doctor at that moment, he might better have appreciated Nayland Smith's warning.

In his silk-lined apartment in Pell Street, old Huan Tsung was contemplating the crystal as a Tibetan devotee contemplates the Grand Lama. Mirrored within it was that wonderful face, dominated by the blazing green eyes.

"I am served," came sibilantly in Chinese, "by fools and knaves. We, of the Seven, are pledged to save the world from destruction by imbeciles. It seems that we are children, and blind ourselves."

Huan Tsung did not speak. The cold voice continued.

"We betray our presence, our purpose, and our methods, to the common man-hunters. Had this purpose been achieved, we should have been justified. We need so short a time. Interference, now, can be fatal. But the method employed was clumsy. This victim of your blundering must not die."

"Compassion, Excellency, is an attribute of the weak."

The compelling eyes remained fixed upon him.

"Rejoice, then, that I entertain it for you. Otherwise you would have joined your revered ancestors tonight. I am moved by expediency—which is an attribute of the wise. In the death of a police officer the seed of retribution is sown. I must remain here until my work is done. If he dies, I shall be troubled. If he survives, the affair becomes less serious. In one hour from now he will be dead—unless we act. I am preparing the antidote. It is for you to find means to administer it . . . Take instant steps."

The light in the crystal faded.

As a result of this conversation, just as Craig had begun on the sweet, Nayland Smith was called to the phone.

He was not away long. But when he came back, his face wore a curious expression. In part, it was an expression of relief—in part, of something else. As he sat down:

"A miracle has been performed in Manhattan," he said.

Craig stared. "What do you mean?"

"What! Professor Lowe has won, after all?"

Nayland Smith shook his head.

"No. Professor Lowe was beaten. But some obscure practitioner, instructed by Moreno's father, insisted upon seeing the patient. As the case was desperate, and the unknown doctor—who had practised in the tropics—claimed to recognize the symptoms, he was given permission to go ahead. Moreno would have died, anyway."

"But he didn't?"

"On the contrary. He recovered consciousness shortly after the injection which this obscure doctor administered. He is already off the danger list."

"This was a brilliant bird, Smith! He doesn't deserve to be obscure."

Nayland Smith tugged reflectively at the lobe of his left ear.

"He must remain so. The physician whose name he gave is absent in Philadelphia. Officer Moreno's father was not even aware of his son's illness."

Huan Tsung had taken instant steps. But Craig laid his spoon down in bewilderment.

"Then—I mean to say—if he was an impostor—what the devil's it all about?"

"Perfectly simple. For some deep reason we can't hope to fathom, Dr. Fu Manchu has decided that Moreno must live. I fear he has also decided that I must die. Granting equal efficiency, what are my chances?"

Chapter V

Sam was free until nine forty-five. He studied the menus displayed outside a number of restaurants suitable for one of limited resources, before making a selection. His needs were simple, it seemed, and having finished his dinner, he moved along to a bar, mounted a stool, and ordered himself a bourbon.

Seated there, in his short leather jacket, a cap with a very long peak pushed to the back of his bullet head, he surveyed the scene through his spectacles whilst lighting a cigarette.

"You're with the Huston Electric, aren't you?" said someone almost at his elbow.

Sam turned. A personable young man, of Latin appearance, had mounted the next stool and was smiling at him amiably. Sam stared.

"What about it?" he inquired.

"Oh, nothing. Just thought I'd seen you there."

"What *were* you doing there?"

"Newspaper story. I'm a reporter."

"Is that so?"

Sam eyed the reporter from head to heels, without favor.

"Sure. Laurillard's my name—Jed Laurillard. And I'm always out for a good story."

"Well, well," said Sam.

"Push that back and have the other half. Just going to order one myself."

"That's fine. My name's Sam."

"Sam *what*?"

"Sam."

"I mean, what's your other name?"

"Jim."

"Your name is Sam Jim?"

"You got it the wrong way around. Jim Sam."

"I never heard of it before. How do you spell it?"

497

"S-a-m. I got an uncle the same name."

For the decimal of a second, Laurillard's jaw hardened. Then the hard line relaxed. He slapped Sam on the back and laughed, signalling the barman.

"You're wasting your time," he declared. "You ought to be in show business."

Sam grinned, but made no reply. The second bourbon went the way of the first, apparently meeting with even less obstruction.

"This new thing Huston is bringing out," Laurillard went on. "Breaking into the news next week, isn't it?"

Sam held up his empty glass and appeared to be using it as a lens through which to count the bottles in the bar.

"Is it?" he said.

"You ought to know." Laurillard signalled the barman again. "If I could get the exact date it would be worth money to me."

"Would it? How much?"

"Well"—speculatively, he watched Sam considering his third drink—"enough to make it worth, say, fifty bucks to you."

Sam looked at Laurillard over the top of his spectacles and finished his drink. He made no other reply. Laurillard caught the barman's eye and glanced aside at Sam's glass. It was refilled.

For some time after the fourth, the barman, who was busy, lost count.

"You know what I'm talking about?" Laurillard presently inquired. "This new lighting system?"

"Sure."

"Some English scientist working on it."

"Sure."

"Well, when the story breaks it's going to be big. Science news is a dollar a word these days. Hurt nobody if I got it first. You're a live guy. I spotted you first time I was up there. Never miss one. It's my business—see?"

Sam emptied his glass and nodded.

"Suppose you made a few inquiries. No harm in that. I could meet you here tomorrow. Any time you say."

"What you wanna know, exac—'xac'ly?" Sam inquired.

His glance had become oblique. Laurillard signalled the barman and leaned forward confidentially.

"Get this." He lowered his voice. "I want to know when the job will be finished. That gives me a lead. It's easy enough."

A full glass was set before Sam.

"Goo' luck," he said, raising it.

"Same to you. What time tomorrow, here?"

"Same to you—mean, same time."

"Good enough. I must rush. Hard life, reporting."

Laurillard rushed. Outside, he looked in through the window and saw Sam raising the drink to his lips, sympathetically watched by the barman. What happened after that he didn't see. He was hurrying to the spot where his car was parked.

He had some distance to go, but less than twenty minutes later the doorbell jangled in that Chinatown shop where a good looking young Oriental labored tirelessly with India ink and brush. He laid his brush aside and looked up.

"Mr. Huan Tsung?" said Laurillard.

"Mr. Huan Tsung not in. You call before?"

Laurillard seemed to be consulting his memory, but, after a momentary pause, he replied.

"Yes."

"How many time?"

"Seven."

"Give me the message."

Laurillard leaned confidentially forward.

"The man from Huston Electric is taken care of. He's too drunk to go far. What's better, I've sounded him—and I think he'll play. That's why I came to see you."

"*I* think," was the cold reply, "that you are a fool." The young Oriental spoke now in perfect English. "You have exceeded your instructions. You are new to the work. You will never grow old in it."

"But —"

"I have no more to say. I will put in your report."

He scribbled a few lines in pencil, took up his brush, and went on writing.

Laurillard's jaw hardened, and he clenched his gloved hands.

"Good-bye," said the industrious scribe.

Laurillard went out.

499

In his report concerning Sam he had stated, quite honestly, what he believed to be true. But evidently he was mistaken.

Not three minutes had elapsed before the doorbell jangled again. A man came lurching in who walked as if on a moving deck. He wore a short leather jacket and a cap with a long peak. His eyes, seen through spectacles, were challenging. He chewed as he talked, using the gum as a sort of mute.

"Say—have you got a pipe-cleaner?" he inquired.

The young Oriental, without laying his brush down, slightly raised his eyes.

"No hab."

"What's the use of a joint like this that don't carry pipe-cleaners?" Sam demanded. He looked all around, truculently. "Happen to have a bit of string?"

"No string."

Sam chewed and glared down awhile at the glossy black head bent over the writing. Then, with a parting grunt, Sam went out.

The young Chinese student scribbled another note in pencil.

Camille sat quite still in her room for so long after Craig had gone that she lost all count of time.

He had not quite shut the door, and dimly she had become aware that he was calling Regan. She heard the sound of voices when Regan came out of the laboratory; then heard the laboratory door closed.

After which, silence fell.

The work she had come here to do grew harder every day, every hour. There were times when she rebelled inwardly against the obligations which bound her. There were other times when she fought against her heart. There was no time when her mind was otherwise than in a state of tumult.

It could not go on. But where did her plain duty lie?

The silence of the place oppressed her. Often, alone here at night—as she was, sometimes—she had experienced something almost like terror. True, always Shaw or Regan would be on duty in the laboratory, but a locked iron door set them apart. This terror was not quite a physical thing. Camille was fully alive to the fact that

500

spies watched Morris's work. But it wasn't any attempt from this quarter which dismayed her.

A deeper terror lay somewhere in the subconscious, a long way down.

Who was Dr. Fu Manchu?

She had heard that strange name spoken, for the first time, by Morris. He had been talking to Nayland Smith. Then—she had received a warning from another source.

But, transcending this shadowy menace, fearful as the unknown always must be, loomed something else—greater.

That part of Camille which was French, and therefore realist, challenged the wisdom of latter-day science, asked if greater and greater speed, more and more destructive power, were leading men to more and greater happiness. Her doubts were not new. They had come between her and the lecturers at the Sorbonne. She had confided them to a worthy priest of her acquaintance. But he, poor man, had been unable to give her guidance in this particular spiritual problem.

If God were a reality—and Camille, whilst not a communicant, was a Christian in her bones—surely such experiments as men of science were making today must anger Him?

In what degree did they differ from those which had called down a divine wrath on the Tower of Babel?

To what new catastrophe would this so-called Science lead the world? Morris Craig's enthusiasm for research she understood. It was this same eager curiosity which had driven her through the tedium of a science training. But did he appreciate that the world might be poisoned by the fruits of his creative genius?

Often it had come to her, in lonely, reflective moments, that the wonderful, weird thing which Morris had created might be a cause of laughter in Hell. . .

What was that?

Camille thought she had heard the sound of a harsh, barking cough.

Before her cool brain had entirely assumed command, before the subconscious, troubled self could be conquered, she was out of her room and staring all around an empty office.

Of course, it was empty.

Regan, she knew, stood watch in the laboratory. The plant ran day and night, and a record was kept of the alternations (so far inexplicable) of that cosmic force which had been tapped by the genius of Morris Craig. But no sound could penetrate from the laboratory.

She opened the office door and called:

"Sam!"

There was no reply. She remembered, now, hearing Morris instructing the handyman to go somewhere with him.

A great urge for human sympathy, for any kind of contact, overcame her. She glanced at the switchboard. She would call Regan. He was a cynical English northcountryman who had admired her predecessor, Miss Lewis, and who resented the newcomer. But he was better than nobody.

Then she thought of her phone call, which had been interrupted earlier in the evening. A swift recognition of what it had meant, of what it would mean to make the same call again, swept her into sudden desolation.

What was she going to do? Her plan, her design for life, had not worked out. Something had gone awry.

She must face facts. Morris Craig had crossed her path. She could not serve two masters. Which was it to be? Once again—where did her duty lie?

Listening tensely, her brain a battlefield of warring emotions, Camille turned and went back to her room. Seated at her desk, she dialled a number, and went on listening, not to a distant ring but to the silence beyond her open door. She waited anxiously, for she had come to a decision. But for a long time there was no reply.

The silent office outside was empty. So that there was no one to see a figure, a dark silhouette against the sky, against those unwatching eyes which still remained alive in one distant tower dominating the Huston Building. It was a hulking, clumsy figure, not unlike that of a great ape. It passed along the parapet outside the office windows . . .

"Yes?" Camille had got through. "Nine-nine here."

She had swung around in her chair, so that she no longer faced the open door.

"If you please."

She waited again.

Silently the door had been fully opened. The huge figure stood there. It was that of a man of formidably powerful physique. His monstrous shoulders, long arms, and large hands had something unnatural in their contours, as had his every movement, his behavior. He wore blue overalls. His swarthy features might have reminded a surgeon of a near successful grafting operation.

"Yes," Camille said urgently. "Can I see you, tonight—at once?"

The intruder took one silent step forward. Camille saw him.

She dropped the receiver, sprang up, and retreated, her hands outstretched to fend off horror. She gasped. To scream was impossible.

"My God!" (Unknown to herself, she whispered the words in French.) "Who are you? What do you want?"

"I—want"—it was a mechanical, toneless, grating voice—"you."

Chapter VI

When Morris Craig returned to his office, it remained as he had left it, illuminated only by two desk lights. He glanced automatically at the large electric clock on the wall above and saw that the hour was nine-fifty-five. He took off his topcoat and hung it up with his hat and jacket.

He was back on time.

What had Nayland Smith said?—"You're a pure fanatic. Some lunatic like you will blow the world to bits one of these days. You're science drunk. Even now, you're dancing to get away . . ."

Craig stared out of the window. Many rooms in that towering building which overtopped the Huston were dark now, so that he thought of a London coster dressed in "pearlies" from which most of the buttons had been torn off. Yes, he had felt eager to get back.

Was it the call of science—of that absorbing problem which engaged his mind? Or was it, in part at least, Camille?

If the latter, then it simply wouldn't do. In the life of a scientist steeped in an investigation which might well revolutionize human society there was no place for that sort of thing. When his work was finished—well, perhaps he might indulge in the luxury of thinking about an attractive woman.

Thus, silently, Dr. Morris Craig communed with himself—quite failing to appreciate the fact that he was thinking about an attractive woman all the time.

Nayland Smith suspected this interest. Hard to deceive Smith. And, somehow (Craig couldn't pin down the impression), he felt that Smith didn't approve. Of course, recognition had come to Craig, suddenly staggeringly, of the existence of danger he had never suspected.

He moved among shadowy menaces. Not all of them were intangible. He had seen the hand of Dr. Fu Manchu stretch out, fail in its grasp, and then bestow life upon one given up to death.

Dr. Fu Manchu . . . No, this was not the time to involve a girl in the affairs of a man marked down by Dr. Fu Manchu.

Craig glanced towards the door of Camille's room, then sat down resolutely and touched a control.

"Laboratory," came. "Regan here."

"Thought I'd let you know I'm back, Regan. How are the readings?"

"Particularly irregular, Doctor. You might like to see them?"

"I will, Regan, presently. Nothing else to report?"

"Nothing."

Craig stood up again, and crossed to the office door, which he opened

"Sam!"

"Hello, boss?"

Sam emerged from some cubbyhole which served as his headquarters. He had discarded the leather jacket and the cap with a long peak, and was resuming overalls and eye shade."

"Is there any need for you to hang around?"

"Sure—plenty. Mr. Regan he told me to report back. There's some job in the lab needs fixing up."

"I see." Craig smiled. "You're not just sort of killing time until I go home, so that you can dog my weary footsteps?"

Sam tried an expression of injured innocence. But it didn't suit him.

"Listen, Doctor —"

"Sir Denis tipped you to keep an eye on me until I was tucked up safely in my downy cot. Did he or didn't he?"

"Well, maybe he figures there's perils in this great city—"

"You mean, he did?"

"I guess that's right."

"I thought so. Just wanted to know." Craig took out his keys and turned. "I'm going into the lab now. Come on."

Followed by Sam, he crossed and went up the three steps to the metal door. As he unlocked it, eerie greenish-grey light shone out and a faint humming sound, as of a giant hornets' nest, crept around the office. A moment later, the door closed as they went in.

The office remained silent and empty whilst the minute hand of the clock swept the dial three times. There was an attachment which sounded the hours, and its single bell note had just rung out on the stroke of ten, when Camille came in.

She stood quite still for a moment one hand resting on the edge of the door, her slim fingers looking curiously listless. Then she came right inside and opened her handbag. Taking out the black-rimmed glasses, she stared at them as though they were unfamiliar in some way. Her glance wandered to the clock.

It would have seemed to one watching her that the clock had some special significance, some urgent message to impart; for Camille's expression changed. Almost, she might have been listening to explicit instructions. Her gaze grew alert.

She crossed to her room and went in, leaving the door half open.

Then, again, silence fell. By ones and twos, the gleaming buttons imagined by Craig disappeared from the pearly scheme which decorated a nocturne framed by long windows.

When Craig opened the laboratory door, he paused at the head of the steps.

"Be at ease, Sam. I will not stir a yard without my keeper."

He closed and locked the door, came down, and went straight across to the safe. Resolutely he avoided looking toward Camille's room to see if she had come back.

From his ring he selected the safe key, and spun the dial. Not until he took out his big drawing board, and turned, did he see Camille.

She stood right at his elbow, in shadows.

Craig was really startled.

"Good Lord, my dear!—I thought I'd seen a ghost!"

Camille's smile was vague. "Please forgive me. Didn't—you know—I was here?"

Craig laughed reassuringly.

"Forgive *me*. I shouldn't be such a jumping frog. When did you come in?"

"A few minutes ago." He saw now that she held a notebook in her hand. "There is this letter to Dr. White, at Harvard. I must have forgotten it."

Craig carried the board over to its place and fixed it up. Camille slowly followed. When he was satisfied, he suddenly grasped her shoulders and turned her around so that the reflected light from the drawing desk shone up onto her face.

506

"My dear—er—Miss Navarre, you have, beyond any shade of doubt, been overdoin' it. I warned you. The letter to Dr. White went off with the other mail. I distinctly recall signing same."

"Oh!" Camille looked down at her notebook.

Craig dropped his hands from her shoulders and settled himself on the stool. He drew a tray of pencils nearer.

"I quite understand," he said quietly. "Done the same thing myself, lots of times. Fact is, we're both overtired. I shan't be long on the job tonight. We have been at it very late here for weeks now. Leave me to it. I suggest you hit the hay good and early.'

"But—I am sorry"—her accent grew more marked, more fascinating—"if I seem distrait—"

"Did you cut out for eats, as prescribed?"

Craig didn't look around.

"No. I—just took a walk "

"Then take another one—straight home. Explore the icebox, refresh the tired frame, and seek repose. Expect you around ten in the morning. My fault, asking you to come back."

Camille sat on the studio couch in her small apartment, trying to reconstruct events of the night.

She couldn't.

It baffled her, and she was frightened.

There were incidents which were vague, and this was alarming enough. But there were whole hours which were entirely blank!

The vague incidents had occurred just before she left the Huston Building. Morris had been wonderfully sympathetic, and his kindness had made her desperately unhappy. Why had this been so? She found herself quite unable to account for it. Their entire relationship had assumed the character of an exquisite torture; but what had occurred on this particular occasion to make the torture so poignant?

What had she been doing just before that last interview!

She had only a hazy impression of writing something in a notebook, tearing the page off, and—then?

Camille stared dreamily at the telephone standing on her bureau. Had she made a call since her return? She moved over and took up the waste-basket. There were tiny fragments of ruled paper there. Evidently she had torn something up, with great care.

Her heart beginning to beat more swiftly, she stooped and examined the scraps of paper, no larger than confetti disks. Traces of writing appeared, but some short phrase, whatever it was, had been torn apart accurately, retorn, and so made utterly undecipherable.

Camille dropped down again on the divan and sat there staring straight before her with unseeing eyes.

Could it be that she had overtaxed her brain—that this was the beginning of a nervous collapse? For, apart from her inability to recall exactly what she had done before leaving the office, she had no recollection whatever, vague or other wise, of the two hours preceding her last interview with Morris!

Her memory was sharp, clear-cut, up to the moment she had lifted the phone on her own desk to make a certain call. This had been some time before eight. Whether she ever made that call, or not, she had no idea. Her memory held no record of the interval between then and Morris telling her she seemed tired and insisting that she go home.

But over two hours had elapsed—two lost hours!

Sleep was going to be difficult. She had an urge for coffee, but knew that it was the wrong thing in the circumstances. She went into the kitchenette and cut herself two sandwiches. She ate them standing there while she warmed some milk. This, and a little fruit, made up her supper.

When she had prepared the bed and undressed, she still felt wide-awake but had no inclination to read. Switching the lights off, she stood at the window looking down into the street. A number of darkened cars were parked on both sides, and while she stood there several taxis passed. There were few pedestrians.

All these things she noted in a subconscious way. They had no particular interest for her. She was trying all the time to recapture those lost hours. Never in her life before had such a thing happened to her. It was appalling . . .

At last, something taking place in the street below dragged her wandering mind back to the present, the actual.

A big man—abnormally big—stood almost opposite. He appeared to be looking up at her window. Something in his appearance, his hulking, apelike pose, struck a chord of memory, sharp, terrifying, but shapeless, unresolved.

Camille watched him. His presence might have nothing to do with her. He could be looking at some other window. But she felt sure he was looking at hers.

When, as she watched, he moved away, loose-armed and shambling, she stepped to the end of the bay and followed his ungainly figure with her eyes. From here, she could just see Central Park, and at the corner the man paused—seemed to be looking back.

Camille stole across her darkened room to the lobby, and bolted and chained the door.

A wave of unaccountable terror had swept over her.

Why?

She had never, to her knowledge, seen the man before. He was a dangerous-looking type, but her scanty possessions were unlikely to interest a housebreaker. Nevertheless, she dreaded the dark hours ahead and knew that hope of sleep had become even more remote.

Lowering the venetian blinds, she switched up her bedside lamp and toyed with a phial of sleeping tablets. She had known many restless nights of late, but dreaded becoming a drug addict. Finally, shrugging her shoulders, she swallowed one, got into bed, and sipped the rest of the warm milk.

She did not recall turning the light out. But, just as she was dozing off, a sound of heavy, but curiously furtive, footsteps on the stair aroused her. There was no elevator.

The sound died away—if she had really heard and not imagined it.

Sleep crept upon her unnoticed . . .

She dreamed that she stood in a dimly lighted, thickly carpeted room. It was peculiarly silent, and there was a sickly-sweet smell in the air, a smell which she seemed to recognize yet couldn't identify. She was conscious of one impulse only. To escape from this silent room.

But a man wearing a yellow robe sat behind a long, narrow table, watching her. And the regard of his glittering green eyes held her as if chained to the spot upon which she stood. He seemed to be draining her of all vitality, all power of resistance. She thought of the shell of a fly upon which a spider has feasted.

She knew in her dream, but couldn't remember a word that had passed, that this state of inertia was due to a pitiless cross-examination to which she had been subjected.

The examination was over, and now she was repeating orders already given. She knew herself powerless to disobey them.

"On the stroke of ten. Repeat the time."

"On the stroke of ten."

"Repeat what you have to write."

"The safe combination used by Dr. Craig."

"When are you to await a call in your apartment?"

"At eleven o'clock."

"Who will call you?"

"*You* will call me . . ."

She was exhausted, at the end of endurance. The dim, oriental room swam about her. The green eyes grew larger—dominated that yellow, passionless face—merged—became a still sea in which she was drowning.

Camille heard herself shriek as she fought her way back to consciousness. She sprang up, choked with the horror of her dreams; then:

"Did it really happen?" she moaned. "Oh, God! What did I do last night?"

Grey light was just beginning to outline the slats of the venetian blinds.

Manhattan was waking to a new day

Chapter VII

Nayland Smith crossed and threw his door open as the bell buzzed.

"Come in, Harkness."

There was an irritable note in his voice. This was his third day in New York, and he had made no progress worthy of record. Yet every hour counted.

They shook hands. Raymond Harkness was a highly improbable F.B.I. operative but a highly efficient one. His large hazel eyes were ingenuous, almost childish in expression, and he had a gentle voice which he rarely raised. Of less than medium height, as he stood there peeling a glove off delicate-looking fingers he might have been guessed a physician, or even a surgeon, but never a detective.

"Any news?" rapped Smith, dropping restlessly into an armchair and pointing to its twin.

"Yes." Harkness sat down, first placing his topcoat and hat neatly on a divan. "I think there is."

"Good. Let's have it."

Smith pushed a box of cigarettes across the table and began to charge his foul briar.

"Well"—Harkness lighted a cigarette—"Mrs. Frobisher had an appointment at three o'clock this afternoon with Professor Hoffmeyer, the Viennese psychiatrist who runs a business on the top floor of the Woolton Building."

"How did you know?"

"I'm having Falling Waters carefully covered. I want to find out who was responsible for the burglary there last week. Stein, the chauffeur-butler, drove Mrs. Frobisher into town, in their big Cadillac. When she had gone in, Stein's behaviour was just a bit curious."

"What did he do?"

"He parked the car, left his uniform cap inside, put on a light

511

topcoat and soft hat, and walked around to a bar on East Forty-eighth."

"What's curious about that?"

"Maybe not a lot. But when he got to the bar, he met another man who was evidently waiting for him. One of our boys who has ears like a desert rat was soon on a nearby stool."

"Hear anything?"

"Plenty. But it wasn't in English."

"Oh!" Nayland Smith lighted his pipe. "What was the lingo?"

"My man was counted out. He reports he doesn't know."

"Useful!"

"No, it isn't, Sir Denis. But Scarron—that's his name—had a bright thought when the party broke up. He didn't tail Stein. Knew he was going back to his car. He tailed Number Two."

"Good work. Where did the bird settle?"

And when Harkness, very quietly, told him, Nayland Smith suddenly stood up.

"Got something there, Harkness," he rapped. "The job at Falling Waters may have been Soviet-inspired, and not, as I supposed, a reconnaissance by Dr. Fu Manchu. What's Stein's background?"

"Man at work, right now, on it."

"Good. What about details of the bogus doctor who saved Moreno's life? To hand, yet?"

"Yes." Harkness took out a notebook and unhurriedly turned the pages. "It's a composite picture built up on the testimony of several witnesses. Here we are." He laid his cigarette carefully on the edge of an ash-tray. "Tall; well-built. Pale, clear-cut features. Slight black moustache, heavy brows; dark, piercing eyes."

"H'm," Smith muttered. "Typical villain of melodrama. Did he carry a riding whip?"

"Not reported!" Harkness smiled, returning the notebook to his pocket. "But there's one other item. Not so definite—but something I wish you could look into personally. It's your special province."

Nayland Smith, who had worn tracks in more carpets than any man in England, was pacing the room, now, followed by a wraith of tobacco smoke.

"Go ahead."

Harkness dusted ash into a tray and leaned back in his chair.

512

"For sometime before your arrival," he said, "but acting on your advice that Dr. Fu Manchu was probably in New York, we have been checking up on possible contacts in the Asiatic quarter."

"Maybe none. Fu Manchu's organization isn't primarily Chinese, or even Oriental. He's head of a group known as the Council of Seven. They have affiliations in every walk of society and in every country, as I believe. The Communists aren't the only plotters with far-flung cells."

"That may be so," Harkness went on patiently, "but as a matter of routine I had the possibility looked into. Broadly, we drew blank. But there's one old gentleman, highly respected in the Chinatown area, who seems to be a bit of a mystery."

"What's his name?"

"Huan Tsung."

"What does he look like?"

"He is tall, I am told, for a Chinese, but old and frail. I've never seen him personally."

"What!" Nayland Smith pulled up and stared. "Don't follow. Myth?"

"Oh, he exists. But he's hard to get at. Some sort of invalid, I believe. Easy enough to see him officially, but I don't want to do that. He has tremendous influence of some kind amongst the Asiatic population."

Nayland Smith tugged at the lobe of his ear reflectively.

"This aged, invisible character intrigues me," he said. "How long has he lived in New York?"

"According to police records, for many years."

"But his remarkable habits suggest that he might be absent for a long time without his absence being noticed?"

"That's true," Harkness admitted.

"For instance, you are really sure he's there now?"

"Practically certain. I have learned in the last few days, since I came up from Washington to meet you, that he has been seen going for a late drive—around eleven at night—in an old Ford which is kept in a shed not far from his shop."

"Where does he go?"

"I have no information. I have ordered an inquiry on that point. You see"—he spoke with added earnestness—"I have it on reliable

513

grounds that Huan Tsung is in the game against us. I don't know where he stands. But—"

"You want me to try to look him over?" Nayland Smith broke in. "I might recognize this hermit! I agree with you."

He began to walk about again in his restless way. His pipe had gone out, but he didn't appear to notice it.

"I could make the necessary arrangements, Sir Denis. You might try tonight, if you have no other plans."

"I have no other plans. At any hour, at any moment, Craig may complete his hell machine. In that hour, the enemy will strike—and I don't know where to look for the blow, how to cover up against it. Tell me"—Smith shot a swift glance at Harkness—"does Huan Tsung ever drive out at night *more than once*?"

Harkness frowned thoughtfully. "I should have to check on that. But may I suggest that, tonight—"

"No. Leave it to me. I'm tired of going around like an escorted tourist. I want my hands free. Leave it to me."

When Nayland Smith left police headquarters that night and set out to pick up Harkness, he might have been anything from a ship's carpenter to a bosun's mate ashore. His demands on the Bureau's fancy wardrobe had been simple, and no item of his make-up could fairly be described as a disguise.

Upon this, a sea-going walk, dirty hands, and a weird nasal accent which was one of his many accomplishments, Nayland Smith relied, as he had relied on former occasions.

He had started early, for he had it in mind to prospect the shop of Huan Tsung before joining Harkness at the agreed spot—a point from which that establishment could conveniently be kept in view.

Whilst still some distance from Chinatown proper, he found himself wondering if these streets were always so empty at this comparatively early hour. He saw parked vehicles, and some traffic, but few pedestrians.

The lights of the restaurant quarter were visible ahead, when this quietude was violently disturbed.

A woman screamed—the scream of deadly terror.

As if this had been a reveille, figures, hitherto unseen, began to materialize out of nowhere, and all of them running in the same direction. Nayland Smith ran, too.

A group of perhaps a dozen people, of various colors, surrounded a woman hysterically explaining that she had been knocked down and her handbag snatched by a man who sprang upon her from behind.

As Smith reached the outskirts of the group, pressing forward to get a glimpse of the woman's face, someone clapped a hand on his back and seemed to be trying to muscle past. His behavior was so violent that Smith turned savagely—at which moment he felt an acute stab in his neck as if a pin had been thrust in.

"Damn you!" he snapped. "What in hell are you up to?"

These words were the last he spoke.

Strong fingers were clasped over his mouth; a sinewy arm jerked his head back—and the stinging in his neck continued!

Nayland Smith believed (he was not in a condition to observe accurately) that the assaulted woman was giving particulars to a patrolman, that the group of onlookers was dispersing.

Making a sudden effort, he bent, twisted, and threw off his attacker.

Turning, fists clenched, he faced a tall man dimly seen in the darkness, for the scuffle had taken place at a badly lighted point. He registered a medium right on this man's chin and was about to follow it up when the man closed with him. He made no attempt to use his fists, he just threw himself upon Smith and twined powerful arms around his body, at the same time crying out:

"Officer! Come and lend me a hand!"

This colossal impudence had a curious effect.

It changed Nayland Smith's anger to something which he could only have described as cold hatred. By heavens! he would have a reckoning with this suave ruffian!

But he ceased to struggle.

Those onlookers who still remained, promptly deserted the robbed woman and surrounded this new center of interest. The officer, slipping his notebook into a tunic pocket, stepped forward, a big fellow marked by the traditional sangfroid of a New York policeman.

He shone a light onto the face of the tall man, who still had his arms around Nayland Smith, and Smith studied this face attentively.

He saw pale, clear-cut features, a shadowy moustache, heavy brows, and dark, penetrating eyes. The man wore a black overcoat, a white muffler, and a soft black hat. Smith noted with pleasure a thin trickle of blood on his heavy chin.

Then the light was turned upon himself, and:

"What goes on?" the patrolman asked.

"My patient grew fractious. Excitement has this effect. I think he's cooling down, though. Do you think you could lend me a hand as far as my car? I am Dr. Malcolm—Central Park South."

"Poor guy. Do what I can, Doctor."

But Nayland Smith smiled grimly. It was *his* turn.

"Listen, Officer," he said—or, more exactly, he framed his lips to say . . . for no sound issued from his mouth!

He tried again—and produced only a sort of horrible, gurgling laughter.

Then he understood.

He knew that he was in the hands of that same bogus physician who had visited Moreno—that the man was a servant of Dr. Fu Manchu.

And he knew that the stinging sensation had been caused by the point of a hypodermic syringe.

He was stricken *dumb* . . .

The only sound he could utter was that imbecile laugh!

"Poor guy," muttered the officer again.

"War veteran," Dr. Malcolm explained in a low voice. The onlookers murmured their sympathy. "Japanese prison camp. Escaped from my clinic yesterday. But we shall get him right—in time—with care."

During this astounding statement, Dr. Malcolm, overconfident, perhaps, in the presence of the burly patrolman, made the mistake of slightly relaxing his hold.

The temptation was too strong for Nayland Smith.

Tensing every relevant muscle in his body, he broke free. He had no foot room to haul off for a straight one, no time to manoeuvre, but he managed to register a really superior upper-cut on the point of Dr. Malcolm's prominent jaw. Dr. Malcolm tottered—and fell.

Then, turning, Smith ran for his life . . . He knew nothing less was at stake.

A whistle was blown. A girl screamed. Someone shouted, "Escaped madman! Stop him!" Runners were hot on his heels.

The hunt was up!

No nightmare of the past, in his long battle with Fu Manchu, approached in its terrors those which now hounded him on. Capture meant death—and what a death! For he could not doubt that Dr. Fu Manchu intended, first, to interrogate him.

And escape?

Escape meant the life of a dumb man . . .

He saw now, plainly enough, how he had held the game in his hands if only he had kept his poise. Many things that he might have done appeared to mock him.

And throughout this time, all about him, hunters multiplied. Voices cried, "Escaped madman—stop him!" Police whistles skirled; the night became a charivari of racing footsteps.

All New York pursued him.

He tried to think as he ran.

Instinctively he had turned back the way he had come. He had a faint hope that, contrary to his orders, a detective might have been assigned to follow him. How he regretted those orders! What madness to underestimate the profound cunning of Dr. Fu Manchu . . .

Suddenly someone stepped out upon him and tried a tackle. He missed. Smith tripped the tackler (he admired his pluck) and ran on.

"Escaped madman! Stop him!"

Those cries seemed to come from all around. Once he tried to shout also, wildly anxious to test again his power of speech. Only a guttural laugh rewarded him. After that he ran in silence, wondering how long he could hope to last at that pace.

Some swift runner was hot on his heels, having outdistanced all others. But Nayland Smith had recognized a warehouse just ahead, the yard gate open, which he had passed a few minutes earlier. If he could reach it first, he still had a chance. Desperation had prompted a plan.

Then, as he raced up to the gate, something happened which was not in the plan . . . A pair of stocky figures sprang out, one on either hand!

They had been posted to intercept him—the game was up!

The man on the left Smith accounted for—and he used his feet as well as his fists. The other threw him. He was a trained wrestler and gave not one opening. Then the pack came up. It was led by the big policeman who had muttered, "Poor guy." His were the footsteps which Smith had heard so close behind.

As he lay, face downward, in a stranglehold, this officer took charge, speaking breathlessly.

"Good work! Don't hurt him. The doctor's coming." Dimly Nayland Smith became aware of an increasing crowd. "Hand him over to me. I can manage him."

He was lifted upright and seized skillfully by the patrolman. The two thickset thugs vanished into darkness outside a ring of light cast by several flashlamps. Smith retained sufficient sanity to observe that one of them limped badly. He thought and hoped that his kick had put cancelled to his kneecap.

He opened his mouth to speak, remembered, and remained silent.

"Take it easy, brother," said the big officer sympathetically. He was still breathing hard from his run. "You're not in Japan now. I don't like holding you, but you surely can use 'em, and I'm not looking for a K.O." He steered Smith into the warehouse yard—that very haven he had prayed to reach!

"We'll wait here. Hi! you!"—to the audience—"shift!"

A car came along. It pulled up opposite the gateway in which they were standing . . . and Dr. Malcolm got out! A second patrolman was with him. Dr. Malcolm's voice sounded pleasantly shaky.

"Congratulations, Officer. I shall commend you for this."

"All in the day's work," replied the man who held Smith. "Glad to see you've snapped out of it. A nifty one, that was. Shall I get the wagon?"

"No, no." Dr. Malcolm stepped forward. "It would only excite him. Here is my chauffeur. He is used to—such cases. We can manage quite well between us. Just call me in about twenty minutes. Dr. Scott Malcolm, Circle 7-0300."

Whilst this conversation proceeded, Nayland Smith made up his mind to play the last card he held—the one he had planned to play if he could have gained temporary shelter. One arm being semi-free, although the other was pinioned behind him, he managed to pull his wallet out and to force it under the fingers of the man who held him.

That efficient officer grasped it, but did not relax his hold.

"Okay," he said in a low voice, like that of one soothing a child. "I've got it. Safe enough with me. Come along."

Smith was led to the car by Dr. Malcolm and a low-browed, grey-uniformed chauffeur, who had the face and the physique of a gorilla. Dr. Malcolm took the wheel; the chauffeur got in beside Smith.

And, as the car moved away and excited voices faded, Smith's brain seemed to become a phonograph which remorselessly repeated the words: "*Dr. Scott Malcolm . . . Circle Seven—0-3-0-0 . . . Dr. Scott Malcolm . . . Circle Seven . . . 0-3-0-0 . . .*

"*Dr. Scott Malcolm . . . Circle Seven—*"

Chapter VIII

It was on the following morning that Morris Craig arrived ahead of time to find Camille already there. He was just stripping his jacket off when he saw her at the door of her room.

"Hullo!" he called. "Why the wild enthusiasm for toil?"

She was immaculate as always, but he thought she looked pale. She did not wear her glasses.

"I couldn't sleep, Dr. Craig. When daylight broke at last I was glad to come. And there's always plenty to do."

"True. But I don't like the insomnia." He walked across to her. "You and I need a rest. When the job's finished, we're both going to have one. Shall I tell you something? I'm at it early myself because I mean to finish by Friday night so that we both have a carefree week-end."

He patted her shoulder and turned away. Pulling out a key ring, he went over to the big safe.

"Dr. Craig."

"Yes?" He glanced back.

"I suppose you will think it is none of my business, but I feel"—she hesitated—"there are . . . dangers."

Craig faced her. The boyish gaiety became disturbed.

"What sort of danger?"

Camille met his glance gravely, and he thought her eyes were glorious.

"You have invented something which many people—people capable of any outrage—want to steal from you. And sometimes I think you are very careless."

"In what way?"

"Well"—she lowered her eyes, for Craig's regard was becoming ardent—"I know Sir Denis Nayland Smith's reputation. I expect he came here to tell you the same thing."

"So what?"

"There are precautions which you neglect."

"Tell me one."

"The safe combination is one. Do you ever change it?"

Craig smiled. "No," he confessed. "Why should I? Nobody else knows it."

"How can you be sure?"

"Sam might have picked it up—so might you. But why worry?"

"I may be foolish. But even if only Sam and I knew it, in your place I should change it, Dr. Craig."

Craig stared. His expression conveyed nothing definite, but it embarrassed her.

"Not suggesting that Sam—"

"Of course not! I'm only suggesting that, for all our sakes, nobody but yourself should know that combination."

Craig brushed his hair back and began to grope in a pocket for cigarettes.

"Point begins to dawn, vaguely," he said. "Rather cloudy morning, but promise of a bright day. You mean that if something should be pinched therefrom, it must be clear that neither you nor Sam could possibly have known how to open the safe?"

"Yes," said Camille, "I suppose that is what I mean."

Craig stood there watching her door for some time after she had gone in and closed it. Then, he crossed, slowly, to the safe.

He had come to the conclusion that Camille was as clever as she was beautiful. He could not know that she had forced herself to this decision to warn him only after many sleepless hours.

Having arranged his work to his satisfaction, Craig took up the phone and dialled a number. When he got through:

"Please connect me with Sir Denis Nayland Smith," he said.

There was an interval, and then the girl at the hotel switchboard reported, "There's no reply from his apartment."

"Oh—well, would you give him a message to call Dr. Morris Craig when he comes in."

As he hung up he was thinking that Smith was early afoot. He had seen nothing of him since they had dined together, and was burning with anxiety on his behalf. The delicate instrument which Craig called a transmuter had already gone into construction. Shaw was working on a blueprint in the laboratory. It remained only for Craig to complete three details, and for tests to discover whether his plant could control the power he had invoked.

In view of what failure might mean, he had determined to insist that the entire equipment be moved, secretly, to a selected and guarded site in the open country for the carrying out of these tests.

He was beginning to realize that the transmuter might burst under the enormous load of energy it was designed to distribute. If it did, not only the Huston Building but also a great part of neighboring Manhattan could be dispersed like that lump of steel he had used in a demonstration for Nayland Smith.

Craig, in fact, was victim of an odd feeling of unrest. He continued to discount Smith's more dramatic warnings, and this inspite of the murderous attempt on Moreno, but he was unsure of the future. The feathered dart he had sent to Professor White at Harvard for examination, but so far had had no report.

He pressed a button, then sat on a corner of the desk, swinging one leg, as Sam came in, chewing industriously.

"Morning, boss."

"Good morning, Sam. What time do you turn up here as a rule?"

"Well"—Sam shook his head thoughtfully—"I'm mostly around by eight, on account of Mr. Shaw or Mr. Regan come off night watch then. I might easy be wanted—see?"

"Yes, I see. Reason I ask is I thought I saw you tailing me as I came along. If this impression was chimerical, correct me. But it isn't the first time I have had it."

Sam's eyes, behind his spectacles, betrayed childish wonder.

"Me tail you, Doctor! Listen. Wait a minute —"

"I am listening, and I am prepared to wait a minute. But I want an answer."

"Well"—Sam pulled his eye-shade lower—"sometimes it happens maybe I'm on an errand same time you happen to be going my way—"

"Enough! I understand. You are my Old Man of the Sea, kindly supplied by Nayland Smith. If Mr. Frobisher knew how you wasted time you owe to Huston Electric, he'd fire you. But I'll have it out with Smith, when I see him."

A curious expression crossed Sam's face as Craig spoke. but was gone so quickly that, turning away, he didn't detect it.

As Sam went out, Craig stood studying the detail on the drawing board, but found himself unable to conquer that spirit of unrest, an unhealthy sense of impending harm, which had descended upon him. Particularly, he was troubled by forebodings about Smith. And although Morris Craig would have rejected such a theory with scientific scorn, it is nevertheless possible that these were telepathic . . .

Less than nine hours before, police headquarters had become a Vesuvius.

Nayland Smith's wallet had been handed in by the frightened patrolman to whom he had passed it. He had given a detailed description of the man posing as "Dr. Malcolm." It was recognized, at Centre Street, to correspond to that of the bogus doctor who had saved the life of Officer Moreno!

Wires had hummed all night. The deputy commissioner had been called at his home. So had the district attorney. All cars in the suspected area were radioed. Senior police officers took charge of operations. What had been regarded, in certain quarters, as an outbreak of hysteria in the F.B.I. suddenly crystallized into a present menace, when the news broke that a celebrated London consultant had been swept off the map of Manhattan.

Prom the time that "Dr. Malcolm" had left with his supposed patient, nothing more was known of his movements. His identity remained a mystery. Feverish activity prevailed. But not a solitary clue came in.

An internationally famous criminal investigator had been spirited away under the very eyes of the police—and no one knew where to look for him!

But Manhattan danced on . .

Craig's uneasiness grew greater as the day grew older. It began seriously to interfere with concentration. His lunch consisted of a club sandwich and a bottle of beer sent up from the restaurant on the main floor, below. The nearer that Shaw's work came to completion in the laboratory, the further Craig seemed to be from contributing those final elements which would give it life. The more feverishly he toiled the less he accomplished.

Early in the afternoon he spoke to the manager of Nayland Smith's hotel.

He learned that Smith had gone out, the evening before, at what exact time the manager didn't know. He had not returned nor communicated. There had been many callers, and a quantity of messages, mail, and cables awaited him. The manager could give no further information.

Craig wondered if he should call police headquarters, but hesitated to make himself a nuisance. After all, the nature of Smith's business in New York would sufficiently account for long absences. But Craig recalled, unhappily, something he had said on the night they dined together: "I fear that he" (Dr. Fu Manchu) "has decided that I must die . . . What are my chances?"

He tried again to tackle his work, but found the problems which it presented so bewildering that he was not resentful, rather grateful, when Michael Frobisher burst into the office.

"Hullo, Mr. Frobisher!"

Craig swung around and faced his chief, who had dropped into one of the armchairs.

"Hello, Craig. Thought I'd just look in. Don't expect to be in town again this week. Picking up Mrs. F., who's having a treatment, and driving right out. How's the big job shaping?"

Frobisher pulled a cigar from his breast pocket, and Craig noted that his hand was unsteady. The florid coloring had undertones of grey. Sudden recognition came to him that Frobisher was either a sick man or a haunted one.

"Fairly bright," he replied in his most airy manner. "Time you saw the setup in the lab again."

"Yes—I must."

But Craig knew that he would avoid the visit, if possible. The throbbing monster which had its being in the laboratory frightened Michael Frobisher, a fact of which Craig was aware.

"Getting quite a big boy now."

Frobisher snipped off the end of his cigar. "What are the prospects of finishing by week-end?"

"Fair to medium. Mental functions disturbed by grave misgivings."

Frobisher glanced up sharply. His eyes, under drawn black brows, reminded Craig, for some reason, of smouldering fires in two deep caves.

"What misgivings?" he growled, and snapped up his lighter, which had a flame like a burning oil well.

Craig, facing Frobisher, dropped the stub of a cigarette and began to grope behind him for a packet which he had put somewhere on the desk.

"I'm a sort of modern Frankenstein," he explained. "Hadn't grasped it before, but see it now. In there"—he waved towards the laboratory door—"is a pup of a thing which, full grown, could eat up New York City at one gulp. This brute frightens me."

"Forget it." Frobisher lighted his cigar.

"Imposs. The thought hangs on like a bulldog. How this beast can be tamed to perform domestic duties escapes me at the moment. Like training a Bengal tiger to rock baby's cradle. Then, there's something else."

"Such as what?"

"My love child, the horror begotten in that laboratory, is coveted by the governments of the United States, of England, and of Russia."

Michael Frobisher stood up. His craggy brows struggled to meet over a deep vertical wrinkle.

"Who says so?"

"I say so. Agents of all those governments are watching every move we make here."

"I knew there was a leak! Do you know those agents?"

"Sir Denis Nayland Smith has arrived from London."

"Who in hell is Sir Denis Nayland Smith?"

"An old friend of mine. Formerly a commissioner of Scotland Yard. But I don't know the Washington agent and I don't know the Soviet agent. I only know they're here."

"Oh!" said Michael Frobisher, and sat down again. "Any more troubles?"

"Yes." Craig found his cigarettes and lighted one. "Dr. Fu Manchu."

Silence fell between them like a curtain. Craig had turned again to the desk. He swung back now, and glanced at Frobisher. His expression was complicated. But fear was in it. He looked up at Craig.

"You are sure there is such a person?"

"Yes—moderately sure."

For some reason this assurance seemed to bring relief to Frobisher. A moment later an explanation came.

"Then I'm not crazy—as that damned Pardoe thinks! Those Asiatic snoopers really exist. They seem to have quit tailing me around town, but queer things happen out at Falling Waters. Whoever went through my papers one night away back must have been working with inside help—"

"But I thought you told me that some yellow character—"

"He was outside. Saw him from my dressing-room window. No locks broken. Then, only last night, my private safe was opened!"

"What's that?"

"Plain fact. I was awake. Sleep badly. Guess I interrupted him. But the door of the safe was wide open when I got down!"

"See anybody?"

"Not a one. Nothing taken. Doors and windows secure. Craig"— Frobisher's deep voice faltered—"I was beginning to wonder—"

"If you walked in your sleep? Did these things yourself?"

"Well—"

"Quite understand, and sympathize."

Michael Frobisher executed a shaking movement with his head, rather like that of a big dog who has something in his ear.

"Listen—but not a word to Mrs. F. I have had a gadget fixed up to record any movement around the house, and show just where it's coming from. I want you to look it over this weekend."

"Delightful prospect. I am the gadget king. And this brings me to my main misgiving. You may recall the bother we had fitting up the plant in the lab?"

"Don't be funny! Didn't we import workmen from Europe to make it in sections—"

"We did. And I have been my own draughtsman."

"Then send 'em home again and assemble the sections ourselves?"

"'Ourselves' relating to Shaw, Regan and me? I fail to recall any instance when you put your Herculean but dignified shoulder to the wheel. Still, you were highly encouragin'. Yes—well—to be brief, we shall have to do likewise once more."

"What's that?"

"I cannot be responsible for tests carried out in the heart of New York City. Some of my experiments already are slightly alarming. But when I'm all set to tap the juice in quantities, I want to be where

I can do no harm." Craig was warming to his subject; the enthusiasm of the specialist fired his eyes. "You see, the energy lies in successive strata—like the skins of an onion. And you know what the middle of a raw onion's like!"

The tip of Frobisher's cigar glowed ominously.

"Conveying what?" he growled through closed lips.

"Conveying that a site must be picked for an experimental station. Somewhere in wide-open spaces, far from the madding crowd. Little by little and bit by bit we shall transfer our monster there."

"You told me you needed some high place."

"There are high places other than the top of the Huston Building. I wish to avoid repeating, in the Huston Building, the story of the Tower of Babel. It would be spectacular, but unpopular."

Michael Frobisher got up, crossed, removed the cigar from his lips, and stood right in front of Craig.

"Listen. You're not getting cold feet, are you?"

Craig smiled, that slightly mischievous, schoolboy smile which was so irresistibly charming.

"Yes," he said. "I am. What are you going to do about it?"

Michael Frobisher turned and picked up his hat, which he had dropped on the floor beside his chair.

"If *you* say so, I'll have to get busy." He glanced at his wrist watch. "Give me all the facts on Saturday."

When Frobisher opened the office door, he stood looking to right and left of the lobby for a moment before he went out.

Craig scratched his chin reflectively. What, exactly, was going on at Falling Waters? He felt peculiarly disinclined to work, considered ringing for Camille, not because he required her attendance, but for the pure pleasure of looking at her, then resolutely put on his glasses and settled down before the problem symbolized by that unfinished diagram.

He was destined, however, to be interrupted again.

The office door behind him opened very quietly, and Mrs. Frobisher peeped in. Craig remained unaware of her presence.

"Do I intrude?" she asked coyly.

Craig, conscious of shirt-sleeves, took off his glasses, jumped from the stool, and turned.

"Why—Mrs. Frobisher!" He swept back the drooping forelock. "I say—excuse my exposed laundry."

Stella Frobisher extended her hand graciously. She didn't offer it; she extended it. She was an Englishwoman and her pattern of life appeared to be modelled upon customs embalmed in old volumes of *Punch*. Her hair had been blond, and would always remain so. She had canary-like manners. She fluttered.

"I was waiting until Mike had gone. He mustn't know I have been here."

Craig pulled a chair forward, and Stella Frobisher's high heels clicked like castanets on the parquet as she crossed and sat down. She was correctly dressed in full mink uniform and wore a bird of paradise for a hat.

"Highly compromising. When did your heart first awaken to my charms?" said Craig as he put his coat on.

He had learned that airy badinage was the only possible kind of conversation with Mrs. Frobisher, who was some years younger than her husband and liked to think he had many rivals.

"Oh, you *do* say the queerest things!" Stella's reputation for vivacity rested largely upon her habit of stressing words at random. "I have been having a *treatment* at Professor Hoffmeyer's."

"Am I acquainted with the lad?"

"Oh, *everybody* knows him. He's *simply* too wonderful. He has made a new woman of me."

"Yes. You look quite new."

"Oh, now you think I'm being silly, Dr. Craig. But truly my *nerves* had quite gone. You see, there's something *very* queer going on."

"Queer goings on, eh?" Craig murmured, hunting for his cigarettes.

"*Most* peculiar. I know you're *laughing* at me. But truly I'm terrified. There have been the most uncanny people prowling about Falling Waters recently." She accepted a cigarette and Craig lighted it for her. "I simply *dare* not *speak* to Mike about it. You know how nervous he is. But I have ordered a pack of Alsatians from Wanamaker's or *somewhere* and insisted that they *must* be ferocious."

"A pack, you say?"

"A pack," Stella repeated firmly. "I don't know how many *dogs* there are in a pack, but I *suppose* fifty-two."

"Expect the pack this week-end?"

"I *hope* so. Of course, I have engaged a *special* man to look after them."

"Of course. Lion tamer, or some such character."

"I have had barbed *wire* installed, and I shall *loose* the dogs at night."

"Sounds uncommonly attractive. Lovers' paradise."

"I wanted to *warn* you, because now I must be *off*. If I'm late at the Ritz, Mike will think I've been *up* to something—"

Craig escorted her down to the street and was rewarded with an arch smile. Stella's smile was an heirloom which had probably belonged to her mother.

Chapter IX

Nayland Smith came to the surface from depths of an unfathomable purple lake. A voice, unpleasantly familiar, matter-of-fact, reached his ears through violet haze which overhung the lake.

"I trust you find yourself quite restored, Sir Denis?"

Smith strove to identify the speaker; to determine his true environment; to find himself.

"And don't hesitate to reply. You are no longer dumb. The discomfort was temporary."

The speaker was identified. He was Dr. Malcolm!

"I—I—why . . . thank God! I can *speak*!"

Nayland Smith's voice rose higher on every word.

"So I observe. You are an expert boxer, Sir Denis, for a man of your years a remarkable one. Myself, although trained in several types of wrestling, unfortunately I know little of boxing."

Dr. Malcolm wore a long white coat. He was regarding Smith with professional interest.

"Too bad. You'll miss it when I get loose!" Smith rapped.

But Dr. Malcolm retained his suavity.

"Pugnacity highly developed. You appear to feel no gratitude for your restored power of speech?"

He poured a vivid blue liquid from a beaker into a phial. The phial he placed in a leather case.

"No. I'm waiting for the later symptoms to develop."

Dr. Malcolm reclosed his case.

"You will wait in vain. The first injection I administered was intended merely to paralyze the muscles of articulation."

"Thanks. It did."

"A second counteracted it."

"Truly ingenious."

"But," Dr. Malcolm went on, "my duties in your case were not nearly so dangerous as in the case of the policeman, Moreno. I was subject to exposure throughout the time I remained in the hospital."

"So I gather," said Smith.

This man's cool audacity fascinated him.

"Of course"—Dr. Malcolm locked his leather case—"Circle 7-0300 is the number of a well-known hotel. I don't live there." He showed strong white teeth in a smile. "Mai Cha was most convincing as the girl who had been robbed, I thought?"

"I thought so too."

Nayland Smith glanced about him. The place proved to be more extensive than he had supposed at that strange awakening. It was a big cellar. Much of it was unlighted—a dim background of mystery.

"We had several key men in the crowd, of course. The police officer was an intruder. But I did my best with him."

("So did I!" Nayland Smith was thinking.)

"When you succeeded in knocking me out, I was indebted to this officer—and to a pair of our people placed to cover such a possibility—for your recapture."

"Yes, you were," said Smith conversationally. "All the luck lay with you." As Dr. Malcolm picked up his case: "Must you be going?"

"Yes. I am leaving you now. I regret the incivility of putting you under constraint. You will have noted, since you are fully restored, that your arms are lightly attached to the bench upon which you sit. These thin lines, however, are quite unbreakable, except by a wire-cutter. A preparation invented by my principal. I bid you good night, Sir Denis. It is improbable that we meet again."

"Highly improbable," Smith murmured. "But lucky, once more, for you! By the way, how long have I been here?"

Dr. Malcolm paused.

"Nearly twenty-four hours—"

"*What!*"

"Not actually in this cellar, but under my care, elsewhere. You have been suitably nourished, and I assure you there will be no ill effects."

Dr. Malcolm merged into the background. His white coat, ghostlike, marked his progress for a while and then became swallowed up. An evidently heavy door was opened—and closed.

Twenty-four hours!

Nayland Smith satisfied himself that he was indeed helpless. The slender, flexible threads, like strands of silk, which confined his arms were steel-tough. The bench was clamped to the floor. He peered into surrounding gloom. One light on the wall behind him afforded sole illumination. Outside its radius lay shadows ever increasing to complete blackness.

Somewhere in this blackness, almost defying scrutiny, objects were stacked against a further wall. Specks of color became discernible, vague forms.

Intently Smith stared into the darkness, picking out shapes, dim lines.

At last he understood.

He was looking at a pile of Chinese coffins . . .

The sound made by a heavy, unseen door warned him of the fact that someone had entered the cellar.

Long before a tall figure came silently out of the shadows, Nayland Smith knew who had entered. The quality of the atmosphere had changed, become charged with new portent.

Wearing a dark, fur-collared topcoat and carrying a black hat in one long, yellow hand, Nayland Smith's ancient adversary faced him.

A tense, silent moment passed.

"I confess that I had not expected to meet you, Sir Denis."

The words were spoken softly, the sibilants marked.

Nayland Smith met the regard of half-closed eyes.

"I, on the contrary, had hoped to meet *you*, Dr. Fu Manchu."

"Your star above mine. The meeting has taken place. If it is not as you had foreseen it, blame only that blind Fate which disturbs our foolish plans. Because our destinies were woven on the same loom, perhaps I should have known that you would be here—to obstruct me when the survival of mankind is at stake."

He stepped aside, and brought a rough wooden box. Upon this he sat down.

"You are compelled to remain seated," he explained. "Courtesy forbids me to stand."

And those words were a key to open memory's door. Nayland Smith, in one magical glimpse, lived again through a hundred meetings with Dr. Fu Manchu, through years in which he had labored to rid the world of this insane genius. He saw him as an assassin, as a torturer, as the most dangerous criminal the law had ever known; but always as an aristocrat.

"You honor me," he said drily. "How am I to die?"

Dr. Fu Manchu fully opened his strange eyes and fixed a gaze upon Smith which few men could have hoped to sustain.

"That rests with you, Sir Denis," he replied, and spoke even more softly than he had spoken before.

It is at least possible that the disappearance of Nayland Smith might have gone onto the unsolved list if any detective officer other than George Moreno (already back on duty) had been assigned to a certain post that night.

The shop of Huan Tsung, for which Smith had set out the night before, was being kept under routine observation. And at ten o'clock Moreno relieved a man who had been on duty since six. Chinatown was Moreno's special stamping-ground, and his orders were to make a record of all visitors and to note particularly any movements of the the mysterious proprietor.

The small and stuffy room from which he operated put up a blend of odors uniquely sick-making. It was one of several in the house commanding an excellent view of part of the Asiatic quarter, and this was not the first time it had been used for police surveillance. But the dangerous days of tong wars seemed to be over. Chinatown was as gently mannered as Park Avenue.

He had been there for a long time when old Huan Tsung's antique Ford was brought around to the front of the shop. Assisted by a yellow-complexioned driver of ambiguous nationality, and a spruce young shopman, the aged figure came out and entered the car. Huan Tsung wore a heavy, dark topcoat with a fur collar; the wide brim of a soft black hat half concealed his features. His eyes were protected by owlish spectacles.

The Ford was driven off. The shopman returned to the shop

Moreno knew that the journey would be kept under observation. But he doubted if any evidence of value would result. In all likelihood these drives were purely constitutional. The old man believed in the merit of night air.

After his departure, little more occurred for some time. Chinatown displayed a deadly respectability. Moreno, who had a pair of powerful glasses, began to grow restive. He learned that he could read even the smaller lettering on shop signs across the street. Faces of passers-by might be inspected minutely. But no one of particular interest came within range of the Zeiss lenses.

There were callers at Huan Tsung's, Asiatic and Occidental, some, at least, legitimate customers; but none to excite suspicion . . .

A small truck drew up before the shop. The young Oriental opened a cellar trap and assisted a truckman to lower a big packing-case covered with Chinese lettering into the basement.

Evidently a consignment of goods of some kind. Moreno wondered vaguely what kind. Something uncommonly heavy.

The trap was reclosed. The truck went away.

Moreno, in the airless room, began to grow sleepy. Then, in a flash, he was wide awake.

A tall man had just come out of Huan Tsung's. He wore a dark topcoat, a white scarf, and a neat black hat. He carried a leather case. Moreno, in the first place, hadn't seen this man go in, therefore he instantly focussed the glasses on his face. And, as he did so, his hands shook slightly.

It was the first face he had seen when he had opened his eyes in the hospital.

The man was "Dr. Malcolm"!

Moreno was hurrying downstairs when Huan Tsung's time-honored Ford returned, and the shopman came out to aid a darkcoated figure to alight. It had been driven away before Moreno reached the street—and Dr. Malcolm had disappeared.

"My mission," said Fu Manchu, "is to save the world from the leprosy of Communism. Only I can do this. And I do it, not because of any love I have for the American people, but because if the United States fall, the whole world falls. In this task, Sir Denis, I shall brook no interference."

Nayland Smith made no reply. He was listening, not only to the sibilant, incisive voice, but also to certain vague sounds which penetrated the cellar. He was trying to work out where the place was located.

534

"Morris Craig, a physicist touched with genius, is perfecting a device which, in the hands of warmongers, would wreck those fragments of civilization which survive the maniac, Hitler. News of this pending disaster brought me here. I am inadequately served. There has been no time to organize a suitable staff. My aims you know."

Nayland Smith nodded. From faint sounds detected, he had deduced the fact that the cellar lay near a busy street.

"I appreciate your aims. I don't like your methods."

"We shall not discuss them. They are effective. Your recent visit to Teheran (I regret that I missed you there) failed to save Omar Khan. He was the principal Soviet agent in that area. Power is strong wine even for men of culture. When it touches the lips of those unaccustomed to it, power drives them mad. Such a group of power-drunk fools threatens today the future of man. One of its agents is watching Craig's experiments. He must be silenced."

"Why don't you silence him?"

The brilliant green eyes almost closed, so that they became mere slits in an ivory mask. It is possible that Nayland Smith was the only man of his acquaintance who assumed, although he didn't feel, complete indifference in the presence of Dr. Fu Manchu.

"I have always respected your character, Sir Denis." The words were no more than whispered. "It has that mulish stupidity which won the Battle of Britain. The incompetents who serve me have failed, so far, to identify this agent. I still believe that if you could appreciate my purpose, you would become of real use to a world hurtling headlong to disaster. I repeat—I respect your character."

"It was this respect, no doubt, which prompted you to attempt my murder?"

"The attempt was clumsy. It was undertaken contrary to my wishes. You can be of greater use to me alive than dead." And those softly spoken words were more terrifying to Nayland Smith than any threat.

Had Fu Manchu decided to smuggle him into his far eastern base, by that mysterious subway which so far had defied all inquiry?

As the dreadful prospect flashed to his mind, Fu Manchu exercised one of his many uncanny gifts, that of answering an unspoken question.

"Yes—such is my present intention, Sir Denis. I have work for you to do. This cellar is shared by several Asiatic tradesmen, one of whom is an importer of Chinese coffins. A death has occurred in the district, and the deceased—a man of means—expressed a wish to be buried in his birthplace. When his coffin is sent there, via Hong Kong—he will not be in it . . ."

There was an interruption.

Heralded by the sound of an opening door, two stockily built, swarthy figures entered. One of them limped badly. Between them they carried an ornate coffin. This they set down on the concrete floor, and saluted Dr. Fu Manchu profoundly.

Nayland Smith clenched his fists, straining briefly but uselessly, at the slender, remorseless strands which held him. The men were Burmese ruffians of the dacoit class from which Fu Manchu had formerly recruited his bodyguard. One of them—the one who limped and who had a vicious cast in his right eye—spoke rapidly.

Fu Manchu silenced him with a gesture. But Nayland Smith had heard—and understood. His heart leapt. Hope was reborn. But Fu Manchu remained unmoved. He spoke calmly.

"The preparation for your long journey," he said, "is one calling for time and care. It must be postponed. In the past, I believe, you have had opportunities to study examples of that synthetic death (a form of catalepsy) which I can induce. I hope to operate in the morning. This"—he emended a long-nailed forefinger in the direction of the coffin—"will be your *wagon-lit*. You will require no passport . . ."

Nayland Smith detected signs of uneasiness in the two Burmese. The one who limped and squinted was watching him murderously—for this was the man upon whom he had registered a kick the night before. Faintly he could hear sounds of passing traffic, but nothing else. The odds against his survival were high.

Dr. Fu Manchu signalled again—and the two Burmese stepped forward to where the helpless prisoner sat watching them . . . .

The life of Chinatown apparently pursued its normal midnight course. Smartly dressed Orientals, inscrutably reserved, passed along the streets, as well as less smartly dressed Westerners. Some of the shops and restaurants continued to do business. Others were closing. There was nothing to indicate that Chinatown was covered, that every man and woman leaving it did so under expert scrutiny.

"If Nayland Smith's here," said the grim deputy commissioner, who had arrived to direct operations in person, "they won't get him out—alive or dead."

He spoke with the full knowledge which experience had given him, that practically every inhabitant knew that a cordon had been thrown around the whole area.

When Police Captain Rafferty walked into Huan Tsung's shop, he found a young Oriental there, writing by the poor light of a paper-shaded lamp. He glanced up at Rafferty without apparent interest.

"Where's Huan Tsung?'

"Not home."

"Where's he gone?"

"Don't know."

"When did he go?"

"Ten minute—quarter hour."

This confirmed reports. The Ford exhibit had appeared again. Old Huan Tsung had sallied forth a second time.

"When's he coming back?"

"Don't know."

"Suppose you try a guess, Charlie. Expect him tonight?"

"Sure."

The shopman resumed his writing.

"While we're waiting," said Police Captain Rafferty, "we'll take a look around. Lead the way upstairs. You can finish that ballad when we come down."

The young shopman offered no protest. He put his brush away and stood up.

"If you please," he said, and opened a narrow door at the back of the counter.

At about the time that Rafferty started upstairs, a radio message came through to the car which served the deputy commissioner as mobile headquarters. It stated that Huan Tsung's vintage Ford was parked on lower Fifty Avenue just above Washington Square.

Inquiries brought to light the fact that it stood before an old brick house. The officer reporting didn't know who occupied this house.

Huan Tsung had called there earlier that night and had returned to Pell Street. He was now presumably there again.

"Do I go in and get him?" the officer inquired.

"No. But keep him covered when he comes out."

This order of the deputy commissioner's was one of those strategic blunders which have sometimes lost wars . . .

Police Captain Rafferty found little of note in the rooms above the shop. They resembled hundreds of such apartments to be seen in that neighborhood. The sanctum of Huan Tsung, with its silk-covered walls and charcoal brazier, arrested his attention for a while. At the crystal globe he stared with particular interest, then glanced at his guide, whose name (or so he said) was Lao Tail.

"Fortuneteller work here?"

Lao Tai shook his head.

"Here Huan Tsung meditate. Huan Tsung great thinker."

"He'll have to think fast tonight. You have a cellar down below. Show me the way in."

Lao Tai obeyed, leading Rafferty through to the back of the shop where a narrow wooden stair was almost hidden behind piles of merchandise. He switched up a light at the bottom of the stair and Rafferty went clattering down.

He found himself in a cellar not much greater in area than the shop above. A chute communicated with a trap in the sidewalk overhead. Cartons and crates bearing Chinese labels and lettering nearly filled the place. It smelled strongly of spice and rotten fish.

One long, narrow packing-case seemed to have been recently opened. Rafferty examined it with some care, then turned to Lao Tai, who watched him disinterestedly.

"When did this thing come?"

"Come tonight."

Rafferty was beginning to wonder. All this man's answers added up correctly—for he knew that such a crate had been delivered earlier that night.

"What was in it?"

"This and that."

Lao Tai vaguely indicated the litter around.

"Well, show me some 'this.' Then we can take a look at any 'that' you've got handy."

538

Lao Tai touched a chest of tea with a glossily disdainful shoe, and pointed to a number of bronze bowls stacked up on a rough wooden bench. His slightly slanting eyes held no message but one of a boredom too deep for expression. And it was while Police Captain Rafferty was wondering what lay hidden under this crust and how to break through to it, that Huan Tsung's remarkable chariot returned to Pell Street and the old man was helped out.

He expressed neither surprise nor interest at finding police on the premises. He bowed courteously when Raymond Harkness stated that he had some questions to put to him, and, leaning on the arm of his Mongolian driver, led the way upstairs. Seating himself on the cushioned divan in the silk-lined room, he dismissed the driver, offered cigarettes, and suggested tea.

"Thanks—no," said Harkness in his quiet way. "Just a few questions. You are acquainted with a doctor; a European, I believe. He is tall, dark, and wears a slight moustache. He called here tonight. I should be glad of his address."

Huan Tsung began to fill a long-stemmed pipe. He had extraordinarily slender, adroit fingers.

"I fear I cannot help you," he replied in his courteous, exact English. "A European physician, you say?" He shook his head. "It is possible, if he came here, that he came only to make a purchase. Have you questioned my assistant?"

"I haven't. The man I mean is employed by Dr. Fu Manchu."

Not one of Huan Tsung's thousand wrinkles stirred. His benevolent gaze became fixed upon Harkness.

"A strange name," he murmured. "No doubt a *nom de guerre*. Tell me more of this strangely named doctor, if I am to help you."

"It's for you to tell *me* more. Will you tell me now, or will you come along and tell the boys at Centre Street?"

"Why, may I ask, should I drag my old bones to Centre Street?"

"It won't be necessary, if you care to talk. You are an educated man, and I'm prepared to treat you that way if you behave sensibly."

Huan Tsung went on filling his pipe. The illegible parchment of his features became creased by what might have been a smile.

"It is true. I formerly administered a large province of China, probably with justice, and certainly with success. Events, however, necessitated my departure without avoidable delay."

"Did you know Dr. Fu Manchu in China?"

Huan Tsung ignited a paper spill in the brazier and began to light his pipe.

"I regret deeply that your question is a foolish one. I thought I had made it clear that I am unacquainted with this person."

"Pity your memory's getting so unreliable," said Harkness.

"Alas, after seventy, each succeeding year robs us of a hundred delights."

Heavy footsteps sounded on the stairs and Captain Rafferty came in.

"Listen—there's a door down in the basement leading to some other place—another cellar, I guess. Let's have the key, or shall I break it open?"

Huan Tsung regarded the intruder mildly.

"I fear you have no choice," he said. "The door leads, as you say, into the storeroom of my neighbor, Kwee Long, whose premises are on the adjoining street. He will have gone, no doubt. The door is locked from the other side. I possess no key to this door."

"Sure of that, Huan Tsung?" Harkness asked quietly.

"Unless my failing memory betrays me."

The door in the cellar was forced. It proved no easy job: it was a strong, heavy door. The police found themselves in a much larger cellar, which evidently ran under several stores and was of irregular shape. Part of it seemed to be used by a caterer, for there were numerous cases of imported delicacies. They could find no switches and worked by the light of their lamps.

Then they came to the part where Chinese coffins were stacked.

This place struck a chill—to the spirit as well as to the body. The deputy commissioner had just joined the party. Their only clues, so far, led to Huan Tsung's. Hope rested on the report of Officer Moreno, that the pseudo-doctor had been seen leaving there that night.

"No evidence anybody's been around here," Rafferty declared. "See any more doors any place?"

"There's one over here, Captain," came a muffled voice.

All flocked in that direction. Sure enough, there was, at the back of a deep alcove. The man who had found it tried to open it. He had no success.

"Smash it!" the deputy commissioner ordered.

540

And they had just gone to work with that enthusiasm which such an order always inspires, when Rafferty held his hand up.

"Quiet, everybody!"

Nervous silence succeeded clamor.

"What did you think you heard?" a hoarse whisper came from the deputy commissioner.

"Sort of tapping, sir."

A silent interval of listening in semidarkness; then another whisper:

"Where from?"

"The coffins ... Ssh! There it is again!"

Another pause for listening followed, in which the ray of more than one flashlamp moved unsteadily.

"Maybe there's a rat in there."

"Quiet! Listen!"

A faint, irregular knocking sound became audible. It was followed by one which resembled a stifled moan.

"Quick! This way! Open all those things. Down with the lot!"

A rush back to the coffin cellar took place. They pulled down five or six, and found them empty. Rafferty held up his hand.

"Stop the clatter. Listen."

All became quiet. And from somewhere near the base of another pile not yet attacked they heard it again, more clearly ... tapping and a stifled groan.

"It's that thing with all the gilt! Last but one from the floor!"

They went to work with a will. To move the empty coffins on top was a business of minutes. And in the most ornate specimen of all, they found Nayland Smith.

His wrists and ankles were lashed up with what looked like sewing silk. But clasp-knives failed to cut it. A piece of surgical strapping was fastened across his mouth. When this had been removed:

"Thank God you heard me," he croaked. "I could just move one foot. Don't blunt your knives on this stuff. Get a wire-cutter. Lift me out."

Two men lifted him out, and supported him to a bench set before the opposite wall. He smiled grimly as he sat there. The deputy commissioner produced a flask.

"Thank God indeed, Sir Denis. It's a miracle you weren't suffocated."

"Air holes bored in coffin. Never mind *me*. What of Dr. Fu Manchu?"

"Not a sign of him."

Nayland Smith sighed, and took a drink.

"Yet he left here little more than half an hour ago."

"*What*! But it's impossible! No one has left this area during that time who wasn't known to be a regular resident."

Smith shot him a steely glance.

"What about Huan Tsung? Doesn't he wear a wide-brimmed hat and a heavy, fur-lined coat?"

The deputy commissioner and Captain Rafferty exchanged worried looks.

"He does, and he certainly went out again," said Rafferty. "He went twice to a house on lower Fifth. But he's back."

"He may be," Smith rapped. "But he only went there once. It was Dr. Fu Manchu, dressed like him, who came back and Dr. Fu Manchu who has just slipped through your fingers again! Have this Fifth Avenue place raided—*now* . . . But already it's too late."

Chapter X

Manhattan danced on tirelessly; a city of a thousand jewelled minarets, and not one mueddin to call Manhattan to prayer.

An enemy, one who aspired to nothing less than dictatorship of the United States, was within the gates, watching Morris Craig's revolutionary experiments. London, knowing the hazard, watched also. Washington, alive to the menace, had instructed the F.B.I. And the F.B.I., smelling out the presence of a further danger, in the formidable person of Dr. Fu Manchu, had sent for Nayland Smith.

But no hint of the desperate battle waging in their midst was permitted to reach the ears of those whose fate hung in the balance. That hapless unit, the Man in the Street, went about his affairs never suspecting that a third world war raged on his doorstep.

Nayland Smith called up Craig the next morning.

"Thought you might be worried," he said. "Had a bit of a brush with the enemy, but no bones broken. Watch your step, Craig. This thing is coming to a head. Hope to look in later . . ."

The mantle of gloom which had enveloped Craig dropped from his shoulders. His problems no longer seemed insuperable. Clearly enough, opposition more dangerous than that of commercial rivalry was in the field against Huston Electric. His science-trained brain, which demanded tangible evidence before granting even trivial surmises, had fought against acceptance, not merely of the presence, but of the existence, of Dr. Fu Manchu.

Now he was converted.

Ignorant, yet, of what had happened to Nayland Smith, he must regard the attempt on Moreno as the work of some enemy unusually equipped. The mode of attack certainly suggested oriental influence.

If, then, Dr. Fu Manchu, what of the Soviet agent?

543

He might reasonably suppose, although Smith had never even hinted it, that Smith acted for the British government. Very well. Who was acting for the Kremlin?

Certainly, his discovery (for which, in his modest way, Craig claimed no personal credit) had called down the lightning. But, in his new mood, there was no place for misgiving. On the contrary, he was exultant, for by that night, he believed, his task would be completed.

When Camille came in, he turned to her with a happy smile.

"Just heard from Nayland Smith. Thank heaven the old lad's okay."

"I am glad," said Camille, and Craig listened to the harp notes in her fascinating voice. "I know you were worried."

"I'm worried about you, too."

She started; her eyes seemed to assume a deeper shade.

"Why—Dr. Craig?"

"You're overdoin' it, my dear. It simply won't work, you know. Because I'm sure you're not getting enough sleep."

"Do I look such a wreck?" she smiled.

"You always look lovely," he replied impulsively, and then regretted the words, for a faint flush tinged Camille's cheeks, and so he added, "when you don't wear those damned glasses."

"Oh!" said Camille—and he watched for, and saw, that adorable little *moue*, like a suppressed dimple, appear on her lip. "As you told me you didn't like them, I only wear them, now, when I am working."

"I didn't say anything of the kind. I said I preferred your eyes in the nude, so to speak. There's only one other thing you might do to add to my joy."

"What is that, Dr. Craig?"

"Well—must you hide the most wonderful hair that ever escaped captivity in Hollywood by pinning it behind your ears as if you wanted to forget it?"

Then Camille laughed, and her laughter rang true.

"Really, you *are* ridiculous! But very complimentary. You see, I know my hair is rather—well—flamboyant. It waves quite obstinately, and I don't feel—"

"It's a display entirely in order for the office of a stuffy physicist? Well—I'll let you off. But there's a proviso."

544

"What is the proviso, Dr. Craig?"

"That you unloose the latent fires as from tomorrow, when we disport ourselves at Falling Waters."

"Oh," said Camille demurely. "Am I allowed to think it over?"

"Yes. But make up your mind by the morning."

Camille crossed toward the door of her room, then paused, and turned.

"I'm sorry. But I'm afraid I quite forgot to mention what I really came to ask you, Dr. Craig."

"Remembered now?"

"Yes. Mrs. Frobisher was speaking to me on the phone yesterday, and we discovered we both suffered from insomnia. She called me this morning to tell me she had arranged an appointment with Professor Hoffmeyer. Of course, I should never have dreamed of such a thing. But—"

"You can't duck it as the boss's wife has fixed it? Quite agree. He'll probably prescribe six weeks at Palm Beach. But pay no attention."

"What I wanted to ask you was if it would be all right for me to go along there at eight tonight?"

"Eight?"

"Yes. An unusual hour for a consultant. I suppose he is fitting me in when he has no other appointments."

"Between the cocktails and the soup, I should guess. Certainly, Miss Navarre. Why ask?"

"Well"—Camille hesitated—"I know you plan to work late tonight, and I'm often wanted to take notes—"

"Forget it. Proceed from the learned professor's straight to your sleeping-sack. We make an early start tomorrow morning."

"That's very kind of you, Dr. Craig, and I am grateful But when I took this appointment I knew what the hours would be. I shall certainly come back."

Camille went into her room, quietly closing the door. All her movements were marked by a graceful composure.

At a quarter to eight, when Camille set out, Craig was crouched over his work, a formula like a Picasso landscape pinned to a corner of the board and a pen in his mouth.

"I expect to return in an hour, Dr. Craig."

Craig raised his hand in a gesture of dismissal and said something that might have been "Go to bed."

Camille pressed the button of the private elevator, and when it arrived, opened the door with her pass-key and went down to the thirty-second floor. She closed the door there—they were all self-locking—and crossed the big office, in which a light was always left on, to a similar door on the other side. She knew the second elevator would be below, for Regan had gone down at four o'clock, when Mr. Shaw had relieved him.

She pressed the button, and when the signal light glowed, unlocked the door and descended to the main floor. There was a small, dark lobby which opened directly onto the street, a means of private entry and exit used only by the laboratory and Michael Frobisher. At the moment that Camille stepped out of the elevator and as the door closed behind her, she knew that someone was in this lobby.

She stood quite still.

"Who's there?" she asked in a low voice

"Don't be alarmed." A flashlamp came to life. "It's only me—or I, if you're a purist!"

"Oh!" Camille whispered. "Sir Denis Nayland Smith—"

She could see his face now, framed in the upturned collar of a fur-lined coat. It was a very grim face.

"Wondering how I got in? Well, I'll explain the great illusion. I have a duplicate key! Craig up there?"

"Yes, Sir Denis—and very busy."

"Are you off for the night?"

"Not at all. I hope to be back in an hour."

"Good girl!" That revealing smile swept grimness from his face as swiftly as a mask removed. "I have excellent reports of your keenness and efficiency."

He patted her shoulder, passed her, and put his key in the elevator door.

Camille found herself standing on the street without quite knowing how she got there. Two men who gave her searching glances were lounging immediately outside, but, although her heart was racing, she preserved her admirable poise, waiting with apparent calm until a cruising taxi came along.

She gave the address, Woolton Building, and then tried to carry out advice printed on a card before her, "Sit back and relax."

Useless to ignore the fact that she had reached a climax in her affairs. The tangled threads of her existence had tripped her at almost every turn. True, she had snapped one. But Camille found herself thinking of Omar's words, "The Moving Finger writes; and, having writ—"

Morris must be told. She had made up her mind to tell him tomorrow. Her crowning dread was that he would find out from someone else. She wanted him to learn the truth from her own lips . . .

Only one elevator remained in service at the Woolton Building. Most of the office staffs had left. Camille told the bored operator, "Professor Hoffmeyer."

"Hoffmeyer? Top."

She stepped out on an empty corridor. Directly facing her was a door marked, "Professor Hoffmeyer. Inquiries."

It proved to be a well-appointed reception office.

No one was there.

Camille sat down on a cushioned divan. A clock above the desk told her that she was three minutes ahead of time. Morris's words flashed through her mind, "Between the cocktails and the soup."

On the stroke of eight, a Chinese girl came in through a doorway facing that by which visitors entered. She wore national dress and had a grace of movement which reminded Camille of a gazelle. Clasping her hands on her breast, she bowed.

"If you will be pleased to follow me," she said.

Camille followed her, across a large salon decorated with miniature reproductions of classic statuary and paintings of flawless nudity. There were richly cushioned settees, desks provided with the latest periodicals, softly shaded lamps. She began to understand that Professor Hoffmeyer was a luxury reserved for the wives and concubines of commercial sultans, and to wonder if Mrs. Frobisher had any idea of her salary.

From here they passed along a tiled corridor between cubicles resembling those in a Pompeian bath. There were medical odors mingling with all those perfumes peculiar to a beauty parlor.

There had been no one in the salon, and there was no one in any of the cubicles.

The journey ended in an office which, unlike the other apartments, conformed with Camille's idea of what a consultant's establishment should be. There was a large, neat desk. One of the drawers was open, as if someone had been seated there only a moment before. A number of scientific books filled a heavy mahogany case. On the right of this was an opening which evidently communicated with another room.

Camille's Chinese guide clasped her hands on her breast, bowed, and retired.

The place possessed a faint, sweetish smell. It awakened some dormant memory. Then a voice spoke, the voice of someone in the dimly lighted room beyond.

"Be so good as to enter."

Camille's mind, her spirit, rose in revolt. Suddenly she was fired by one impulse only—to escape. But she seemed to be incapable of attempting escape. Those words were a command she found herself helpless to disobey.

Slowly, with lagging steps, she walked in. Her movements made no sound on a thick carpet. It was an apartment Orientally furnished. There were arched openings in which lanterns hung. She saw painted screens, lacquer. But these were sketchy, a pencilled background for a figure seated behind a long, narrow table.

He wore a yellow robe; his chin rested on his hands, his elbows on the table. And his glittering green eyes claimed and owned her.

Camille stifled a scream, turned—and the opening through which she had come in was no longer there; only a beautifully wrought lacquer panel. She twisted back, fighting down hysteria. Her glance took in the whole room.

"Yes," the sibilant voice assured her, "you are not mistaken, Miss Navarre . . . you have been here before."

548

Chapter XI

"The greatest compliment ever paid to me," said Nayland Smith grimly. "Dr. Fu Manchu considers I am more useful alive than dead!"

Morris Craig, seated, back to the desk, watched that lean, restless figure parading the office. Smith's hat and topcoat lay on the settee, his pipe bubbled between his small, even teeth. He looked gaunt, but his steps were springy, his eyes clear.

"I can only repeat—it's a miracle you're alive."

"I suppose it is. Mysterious news of the pending raid on Huan Tsung's led to a postponement of the treatment prescribed. Otherwise, I should have been found, certifiably dead, in that ghastly coffin. Failing the raid, I should by now be on my way to China."

"Do you think the headquarters of this thing are in China?"

"No," rapped Smith. "In Tibet. In a completely inaccessible spot. Lhasa is not the only secret city in Asia—nor Everest the highest mountain. But leave that. I want certain facts."

Craig lighted a cigarette which he had been holding for some time between his fingers.

"You shall have them. But there are certain facts I want, too. I'm not immune from human curiosity, even if I have harnessed a force new to physics. When the police found you last night, what about this fellow, Huan Tsung?"

Nayland Smith smiled. It was a smile of pure enjoyment. He pulled up, facing Craig.

"Huan Tsung, ex-governor of a Chinese province , and a prominent member of the Council of Seven, I had met before. He blandly denied any recollection of the meeting. As I had clearly been delivered at his shop during the evening in a crate, and taken into an adjoining cellar, Harkness and the commissioner proposed to arrest him."

"I should have proposed ditto."

"On what charge?" rapped Smith. "There are witnesses—including a police officer—to testify that he was not at home during the time I was being interviewed by Dr. Fu Manchu—"

"But you tell me he doubled with Fu Manchu—"

"Undoubtedly he did. But how can we prove it? A scholarly, elderly gentleman who claims to be French Canadian occupies the apartment on lower Fifth Avenue which Huan Tsung visited last night. They are old friends, it seems. They were discussing the political situation in China, and Huan Tsung returned to Pell Street for some correspondence bearing on the subject."

"But Smith—you were found in his cellar!"

"It isn't his cellar, Craig. Remember, the police *broke* into it. And the man to whom it really belongs is out of town! Lastly, the shopman, a cultured liar, produced an invoice for the contents of the crate in which I was brought there from wherever I had been before!"

"But you say you recognized Huan Tsung?"

"Certainly. But he blandly assures me I am mistaken. He had the impudence to point out that to the Western eye, Chinese faces look much alike. Had he had the privilege of meeting me before, he said, such an honor couldn't possibly have escaped his memory!"

"Do you mean to say he's going to get away with it?"

"For the time being, I'm afraid he is. Mr. La Fosse of lower Fifth Avenue, who is undoubtedly in Fu Manchu's employ, declares that he never even heard of such a person. Of course, the police will watch them closely, as astronomers watch a new comet. Their lines are tapped already."

"And what about those damned injections? Do you feel no ill effects?"

"None whatever. You must accept the fact, Craig, that Dr. Fu Manchu has a knowledge of medicine which is generations ahead of anything known to Western science. And now, waste no more of my time. Listen—"

The big clock above the desk sounded its single note. Eight o'clock. The office door opened and Regan came in. His dour face wore an odd expression.

"I may be mistaken," he said, "but I fancy I saw a pair of tough-looking lads loafing outside the private door, downstairs."

Nayland Smith laughed. "Part of my bodyguard!"

"Oh," said Regan. "That's it, is it?"

"We are invested," murmured Craig. "A beleaguered garrison. Look well to your armour, gentlemen, and let your swords be bright."

Regan nodded unhumorously, and going up the steps, unlocked the laboratory door. Eerie vibrations invaded the office. His figure showed outlined for a moment against green light. Then the door was closed as he went in.

"I want to know," rapped Nayland Smith, "when you will be finished."

"Tonight."

"Sure?"

"Perfectly sure."

"I thought as much. Even allowing an hour for dinner?" Craig brushed his hair back, staring.

"I'm stopping for no dinner."

Nayland Smith smiled again.

"Craig, I begin to agree with Dr. Fu Manchu, who informed me that you are what he described as 'touched with genius.' I don't want you to confirm his diagnosis by dying young. I have booked a table at a quiet restaurant. Until you are dragged away from that desk, your abstraction is deplorable. And there are many important things I want to tell you."

"Won't they keep?"

"No. And by the way, I miss the invaluable Sam."

"The said Invaluable has twenty-four hours' leave. His mother is ill in Philadelphia. Result, that for the first time in days I can go out for a drink without being tailed by a shadow in a peaked cap!"

"Oh!" rapped Smith, and gave Craig a steely glance. "Sorry to hear it."

The laboratory yawned again, and Shaw stepped out. He stood at the top of the steps for a moment, looking down. The chief technician had the heavy frame of an open-air man who has come indoors, a mass of unruly blond hair, and a merry eye. "Just off, Shaw?" Craig called. "You don't know my masterful friend, Sir Denis Nayland Smith? On my right, Masterful Smith; on my left, Martin Shaw."

Shaw came down and shook hands.

"Free man until midnight," he said. "Then back to the bloody Juggernaut that lives in there!" He turned to Craig. "If you had that valve detail ready tonight, I believe I could fit up the transmuter in time for tests on, say, Monday."

"Do you?" Craig replied, and grinned like a schoolboy. "Has no thought crossed the massive brain to file a will before that date?"

Shaw nodded. "It has, Doctor. Rests with you. But if we can keep the cork in when we really fill the bottle, well—"

He went out, giving an imitation of a man under heavy fire. As the office door closed:

"Our convoy awaits!" said Nayland Smith. "Let's move."

"Stop ordering me about," Craig exclaimed in mock severity. "Oh, I give up the unequal contest."

He called the laboratory.

"Regan here."

"I regret to state, Regan, that I am being forcibly removed to some restaurant to dine—"

"Good thing, too."

"Repeat."

"I didn't say anything."

"Oh, Well, I shall be back at nine. Want to see me before I go?"

"No, Doctor. Enjoy your dinner."

Craig carried his drawing board, and his notes, across to the safe. When they were locked away, he glanced towards the door of Camille's room.

"She's out," said Smith drily. "I passed her as I came in."

They were already speeding along in a police car, two F.B.I. men following in another, when Camille faced Dr. Fu Manchu across the bizarre study.

"You have been here before," the harsh voice had said. And, in a moment of cold horror, which seemed to check her heartbeats, Camille knew this to be true. Her dream had haunted her so persistently that she had spoken to Morris, warned him to change the safe combination, for in her wastebasket she had found those fragments of a torn-up note. And although she had spent hours trying to piece

552

the fragments together, and had failed, she knew that the paper on which the note was written came from the Huston Electric office.

Now—the man, the inscrutable, dreadful face of the man, every detail surrounding him, told her that the dream had been no dream, but a memory recaptured in sleep.

She had come to the appointment with Professor Hoffmeyer wearing her dark-rimmed glasses. At this moment the incongruity of her appearance in such an environment struck her forcibly.

One angle of the room was occupied by shelves filled with volumes, some of them large and faded leather bindings. Then came the lacquer panel. This, she knew, masked an opening through which she had entered. Beyond it a curtain partly concealed a recess. There was an arched doorway in which a silkshaded lantern hung.

A cushioned divan rose like an island in a sea of rugs. There were two strangely shaped mediaeval chairs.

A long black table bore books, open manuscripts, jars which apparently contained specimens of some kind, and a mummied head mounted on a wooden base. The dim light of a green lamp just outlined a crystal globe eclipsed in shadow.

And behind the table, hands with attenuated nails crossed under his chin, was the *Man* . . .

"Please sit down."

His half-closed eyes glanced sideways in the direction of the divan. He did not stir, otherwise.

Camille, fighting a desperate battle for calmness, for sanity, remained standing. She stared challengingly at the motionless figure. Her throat was dry, but when she spoke, her soft voice did not betray her.

"I came to consult Professor Hoffmeyer. Who are *you*?"

He remained immobile. When he replied, Camille could not see that the thin lips moved.

"I am accustomed to asking questions, Miss Navarre, not to answering them. But I must make a concession in the case of a fellow scientist—and one whose courage I respect. I am known as Dr. Fu Manchu."

"Dr. Fu Manchu!" she whispered.

"I believe you have been warned against me. I regret that, like the straying husbands, I should be so misunderstood, that the world should think badly of me."

"But what are you doing here? If Mrs. Frobisher knew—"

"If Mrs. Frobisher knew what? That Professor Hoffmeyer is Dr. Fu Manchu, or that Camille Navarre is employed by the intelligence service of an alien government? To which eventuality do you refer?"

"What do you say? What are you suggesting?"

"I suggest nothing. I ask a question. Mrs. Frobisher made the appointment for tonight because I told her to do so—"

"You meant—that Mrs. Frobisher knows—?"

"Mrs. Frobisher does not know anything. Few women do. But I believe that her husband might react unfavorably if he knew you to be an agent of Great Britain."

Camille's heart was throbbing wildly, but she had been trained to face the worst.

"Why do you say that?"

"Because it is true." Slowly Dr. Fu Manchu stood up. "Your employers are within their rights in seeking to learn the nature of those experiments being carried out in the Huston laboratory. We live in a dangerous age. I admire them for their ingenious removal to a better post of Dr. Craig's former assistant, and for providing you with the necessary credentials to take her place."

He was walking around the corner of the long, narrow table, and coming nearer. He had a catlike step.

"My credentials are my own."

"Indeed. And where did you acquire them?"

"Is that your business?"

Fear (the tall, yellow-robed figure was very close now) made her defiant.

"And where did you acquire them?" he repeated in a low, sibilant tone.

"I graduated at the Sorbonne."

"I congratulate you. These are details I had no time to gather at our former interview. And did you carry out intelligence work during the war?"

"I worked with the Resistance." Camille spoke faintly. "In Grenoble."

Dr. Fu Manchu returned to his seat behind the long table.

"Again, accept my congratulations. You speak perfect English."

"My mother was English."

Camille sank down on the divan. She was terrified, but her brain remained cool. One thing was clear. During that hiatus which had cost her so many sleepless nights, she must have been here. How had she got here? And why, except in a dream, had she completely forgotten all that happened?

Above all, what *had* happened? . . .

Camille clutched the cushions convulsively.

A quivering, metallic sound, like that of a distant sistrum, stirred the silence.

The crystal was coming to life. A radiance as of moonlight glowed and grew within it. For a moment it seemed cloudy, resembling a huge opal. Then the clouds dispersed, and a face materialized.

Camille thought, at first, that it was the living face of the Egyptian whose mummied head stood on the table, so yellow and wrinkled were its lineaments. But it soon declared itself as that of a very old Chinese.

"I have the report, Excellency."

The voice was clear, but seemed to come from a long way off.

"Repeat it."

Dr. Fu Manchu was watching the face in the crystal. A sudden urge to run flamed up in Camille's mind. She glanced swiftly right and left, and then:

"Remain where you are," came a harsh command. "There are no means of leaving this room without my permission. Continue, Huan Tsung."

"Nayland Smith and Dr. Craig are in the restaurant. Contact is impossible. There is an F.B.I. bodyguard at the doors. All my incoming messages are overheard. Therefore this was sent to me in the Shan dialect."

There came a momentary silence, in which Camille realized that she was not witnessing a supernatural phenomenon, but some hitherto unknown form of television; and then:

"I have one hour," said Dr. Fu Manchu, "in which to make the first move."

The face in the crystal faded slowly, like a mirage. The moonlight died away. As Dr. Fu Manchu turned his intolerable regard upon her again, Camille stood up.

"I want to know," she said, "why I have been trapped into coming here. Perhaps you think you can force me to betray Dr. Craig's secrets to you?"

"Were you not prepared to betray them to the British government?" he asked softly.

"Perhaps I was. But from a motive *you* could never understand. In the hope of preserving the peace of the world—if that is possible."

"Do you regard Great Britain as holding a monopoly in peaceful intentions? Do you suppose that Dr. Craig would welcome the knowledge that you worked with him only to betray him?"

Camille tried to meet the gaze of those half-closed eyes. "I—I—did not think of it as betrayal. Only as a duty; a duty for which I must be prepared to sacrifice—everything."

"Such as the respect of Dr. Craig—or possibly something more precious?"

Camille lowered her eyes and dropped back on the divan. Dr. Fu Manchu stood up and walked towards her. He carried a small volume.

"I will never reveal one of Dr. Craig's secrets to you," she said on a note of desperation.

"My dear Miss Navarre—you have already revealed them all, or all that you knew at the time. Let you and me be sensible. Communist criminals aspire to rule man by fear. Nations no longer have the right to choose their rulers. As a result, the market is glutted with politicians, but statesmen are in short supply. Man wants nothing but happiness. What Russian yearns to spread the disease from which he himself is suffering?"

He stood right before her now.

"You see this book? It is a complete list of the megalomaniacs who are threatening the world with a third, and final, war. Power-drunk fools. They could all, quite easily, be assembled in this room. The unhappy peoples they claim to speak for are only the fuel to be thrown into the furnace of their mad lust. Advance guards of these ignorant ruffians already knock at the door—and one man holds in his hands a weapon which may decide the issue.'

"You mean—Dr. Craig?"

"I referred to him—yes."

Camille, with desperate courage, stood up and faced Fu Manchu.

"And you think I would put that weapon into *your* hands—even if I could? I should prefer to die—and leave the law to deal with *you!*"

But Dr. Fu Manchu remained unmoved.

"One who hopes to save civilization cannot afford to respect the law. You are that rare freak of the gods, a personable woman with a brain. Yet, womanlike, you permit emotion to rule you. Why do you wear those pieces of plain glass?"

He fully opened his strange eyes, raised one long-nailed hand, and pointed at her.

Camille ceased to possess any individual existence. She found herself in that trancelike condition which had made her dreams so terrible.

"Take them off."

Automatically she obeyed. Something within rose in fierce, angry revolt. But Camille herself was helpless.

"Shake your hair down."

She released her wonderful hair. It cascaded, a fiery torrent, onto her shoulders. Mechanically Camille arranged it with her fingers.

"Kneel."

She knelt at Fu Manchu's feet.

"Bow your head . . . Sleep."

She bowed her head, a beautiful, submissive slave awaiting punishment.

Dr. Fu Manchu struck a silver bell which hung on a table beside the divan. Camille did not hear its sweet, lingering note. She was lost in a silent world from which only one sound could recall her— the voice of Fu Manchu.

A man entered through the archway. He never even glanced at the motionless, kneeling figure. He bowed, briefly but respectfully, to Fu Manchu. He was short, dark, and thickset, with a Teutonic skull. He wore a long, white-linen coat, like that of a surgeon.

Dr. Fu Manchu crossed and seated himself at the table.

"Koenig—tonight you will go to the Huston Building. The dupli-

557

cate key you made after Miss Navarre's last visit opens the private door and also that of the elevator to the thirty-second floor. On the thirty-second floor there is another elevator. The key opens this also. Any questions?"

"No."

"It will take you to the thirty-sixth, where you will enter the office of Dr. Craig. The laboratory adjoins the office. The communicating door is locked. A man called Regan will be on duty in the laboratory. He must be induced to come out. Any questions?"

"No."

"M'goyna will be with you—if this alarms you, say so. Very well. Regan must be overpowered and taken back to the laboratory. M'goyna will then remain there with him. You will make it clear to Regan that should M'goyna be found there, he, Regan, will be strangled. Regan must speak on intercommunication should Dr. Craig call him. Any questions?

"No."

Dr. Fu Manchu clapped his hands sharply.

"M'goyna!"

The embroidered curtain which partly concealed a recess in the wall was drawn aside. A gigantic figure appeared. The shoulders of an Atlas, long arms, grotesquely large hands, and a face so scarred as to be incomparable with anything human. A red tarboosh crowned these dreadful features, and the figure wore white Arab dress, a scarlet sash, and Turkish slippers.

Slowly M'goyna came forward. Every movement was unnatural, like that of an automaton. The huge hands hung limp, insensate— the hands of a gorilla. Like a gorilla, too, he coughed hollowly as he entered.

Koenig clenched his fists, but stood still. Camille remained kneeling. M'goyna crossed to the long table and came to rest there facing Dr. Fu Manchu, who addressed him in Turkish.

"Change to street clothes. You go with Koenig to the Huston Building."

"With Koenig to the Huston Building," M'goyna intoned in a rasping voice.

"You will be shown a man. You must seize him."

"Shown a man. I seize him."

"You must not kill him."

M'goyna slowly revealed irregular, fanglike teeth and then closed his lips again. He coughed.

"Must not kill him."

"You are under Koenig's orders. Salute Koenig."

M'goyna touched his brow, his mouth, and his breast and inclined his head.

"You will do as he tells you. At ten o'clock I shall come for you. Repeat the time."

"Ten o'clock—you come for me?"

"At ten o'clock." Dr. Fu Manchu turned to Koenig and spoke one word in English. "Proceed."

Morris Craig's office was empty. Night had dropped a velvet curtain outside the windows, irregularly embroidered with a black pattern where the darkened building opposite challenged a moonless sky.

Only the tubular desk lamp was alight, as Craig had left it.

So still was the place that when the elevator came up and stopped at the lobby, its nearly silent ascent made quite a disturbance. Then no movement was audible for fully a minute—when the office door opened inch by inch, and Koenig looked in. Satisfied with what he saw, he entered and crossed straight to Camille's room. This he inspected by the light of a flashlamp.

Noiseless in rubber soles, he moved to the laboratory door and shone a light onto the steps leading up to it. He examined the safe and went across to the long windows, staring out onto the terrace.

Then, turning his head, he spoke softly.

"M'goyna—"

M'goyna lumbered in. He wore brown overalls and a workman's cap. That huge frame, the undersized skull, were terrible portents. He stood just inside the door, motionless, a parody of Humanity.

"Close the door."

M'goyna did so, and resumed his pose.

"The man will come out from there." Koenig pointed towards the laboratory. "Seize him."

M'goyna nodded his small head.

"Choke him enough but not too much—and then carry him back. You understand me?"

559

"Yes. Must not kill him."

"Hide here, between the couch and the steps. When he comes out, do as I have ordered. Remember—you must not kill him."

M'goyna nodded, and coughed.

"Are you ready?"

"Yes."

Koenig switched off the desk lamp. Now it was possible to see that the night curtain beyond the windows was studded with jewels twinkling in a cloudless heaven. Koenig shone the light of his lamp onto a recess between the leather-covered couch and the three steps.

"Here. Crouch down."

M'goyna walked across as if motivated by hidden levers and squatted there.

Koenig switched his lamp off. He paused for a moment to get accustomed to the darkness, then went up the three steps and beat upon the door with clenched fists.

"Regan!" he shouted. "Regan . . . *Regan!* . . ."

He ran down and threw himself onto the couch beside which M'goyna waited.

Followed an interval of several seconds—ten—twenty—thirty.

Then came a faint sound. The steel door was opened. Green light poured out, such a light as divers see below the surface of the ocean; rays giving no true illumination. The office became vibrant with unseen force.

Regan stood at the top of the steps, peering down.

"Dr. Craig! Are you there?"

He began to descend, picking his way.

And, as his foot touched the bottom step M'goyna hurled himself upon him, snarling like a wild animal.

"My God!"

The words were choked out of Regan. They faded into a gurgle, into nothing.

"Not too much! *Remember!*"

M'goyna grunted. One huge hand clasping Regan's throat, he lifted him with his free arm and carried him, like a bundle, up the steps.

Koenig followed.

The door remained open. Green light permeated the office filled with pulsations of invisible power. Then Koenig reappeared.

560

"You understand—he must answer calls. If Dr. Craig, or anyone else, comes in . . . you have your orders."

He closed the door behind him, so that silence, falling again, became a thing notable, almost audible. He stood still for a moment, taking his bearings, then crossed and switched up the desk lamp.

Noiselessly he went out.

The elevator descended.

Chapter XII

"Wake!"

Camille opened her eyes, rose from her knees, and although her limbs felt heavy, cramped, sprang upright. She stared wildly at Dr. Fu Manchu, lifting one hand to her disarranged hair.

"What—what am I doing here?"

"You are kneeling to me as if I were the Buddha."

A wave of true terror swept over her. Almost, for the first time, she lost control.

"You. . . Oh, my God! What happened to me?"

She retreated from the tall, yellow-robed figure, back and back until her calves came in contact with the divan. Dr. Fu Manchu watched her.

"Compose yourself. Your chastity is safe with me. I wished to see you without your disguise."

"There was—someone else here—a dreadful man . . ."

"M'goyna? You were conscious of his presence? That is informative. I regret that I cannot give you an opportunity to examine M'goyna. As a fellow scientist, you would be interested. M'goyna carried my first invitation to you, although I thought you had forgotten."

"I had forgotten," Camille whispered. She was trembling.

"He can climb like an ape. He climbed from the fire ladders along the coping of the Huston Building in order to present my compliments. You spoke of 'a dreadful man.' But M'goyna is not a man. In Haiti he would be called a zombie. He illustrates the possibilities of vivisection. His frame is that of a Turkish criminal executed for strangling women. I recovered the body before rigor mortis had set in."

"You are trying to frighten me. Why?"

"Truth never frightened the scientific mind. M'goyna was created in my Cairo laboratory. I supplied him with an elementary brain—a trifle superior to that of a seal. Little more than a receiving set for my orders. He remains imperfect, however. I have been unable to rid my semihuman of that curious cough. Some day I must try again."

And, as the cold, supercilious voice continued, Camille began to regain her composure; for Dr. Fu Manchu had been unable wholly to conceal a note of triumph. He was a dangerous genius, probably a madman, but he was not immune from every human frailty . . . He was proud of his own fantastic achievements.

She dropped down onto the settee as he crossed, moving with that lithe, feline tread, and resumed his place behind the black table. When he spoke again he seemed to be thinking aloud . . .

"There are only a certain number of nature's secrets which man is permitted to learn. A number sufficient for his own destruction."

A high, wailing sound came from somewhere beyond the room. It rose, and fell, rose, and fell—and died away. But for Camille it was almost the last straw.

Clasping her hands, she sprang up, threatened now by hysteria.

"My God! What was it?"

Dr. Fu Manchu rested his chin on interlaced fingers.

"It was Bast—my pet cheetah. She thinks I have forgotten her supper. These hunting cats are so voracious."

"I don't believe you . . . It sounded like . . ."

"My dear Miss Navarre, I resent the implication. Sir Denis Nayland Smith would assure you that lying is not one of my vices."

Delicately he took a pinch of snuff from a silver box. Camille sat down again, struggling to recover her lost poise. She forced herself to meet his fixed regard.

"What is it you want? Why do you look at me like that?"

"I am admiring your beautiful courage. To destroy that which is beautiful is an evil thing." He stood up. "You wish for the peace of the world. You have said so. You fear cruelty. You flinched when you heard the cry of a cheetah. You have known cruelty— for there is no cruelty like the cruelty of war. If your wish was sincere, only I can hope to bring it true. Will you work *with* me, or *against* me?"

"How can I believe—"

"In Dr. Fu Manchu? In an international criminal? No—perhaps it is asking too much, in the time at my disposal—and the very minutes grow precious." He opened his eyes widely. "Stand up, Camille Navarre. What is your real name?"

And Camille became swept again at command of the master hypnotist into that grey and dreadful half-world where there was no one but Dr. Fu Manchu.

"Camille Mirabeau," she answered mechanically—and stood up. "Navarre was the name by which I was known to the Maquis."

The green eyes were very close to hers.

"Why were you employed by Britain?"

"Because of my success in smuggling Air Force personnel out of the German zone. And because I speak several languages and have had science training."

"Were you ever married?"

"No."

"How many lovers have you had?"

"One."

"How long did this affair last?"

"For three months. Until he was killed by the Gestapo."

"Have you ceased to regret?"

"Yes."

"Does Morris Craig attract you?"

"Yes."

"He will be your next lover. You understand?"

"I understand."

"You will make him take you away from the Huston Building not later than half past nine. He must not return to his office tonight. You understand?"

"I understand."

"Does he find you attractive?"

"Yes."

The insistent voice was beating on her brain like a hammer. But she was powerless to check its beats, powerless to resist its promptings; compelled to answer—truthfully. Her brain, her heart, lay on Dr. Fu Manchu's merciless dissecting table.

"Has he expressed admiration?"

"Yes."

"In what way?"

"He has asked me not to wear glasses, and not to brush my hair back as I do."

"And you love him?"

Camille's proud spirit rose strong in revolt. She remained silent.

"You love him?"

It was useless. "Yes," she whispered.

"Tonight you will seduce him with your hair. The rest I shall leave to Morris Craig. I will give you your instructions before you leave. Sleep . . ."

There came an agonized interval, in which Camille lay helpless in invisible chains, and then the Voice again.

"I have forgotten all that happened since I left my office in the Huston Building. Repeat."

"I have forgotten all that happened since I left my office in the Huston Building."

"When I return I shall remember only what I have to do at nine-fifteen—nine-fifteen by the office clock."

"When I return I shall remember only what I have to do at nine-fifteen, by the office clock."

"At nine-thirty Dr. Fu Manchu will call me: repeat the time."

"Nine-thirty."

"The fate of the world rests in my hands."

Camille raised her arms, clutched her head. She moaned . . . "Oh! . . . I . . . cannot bear this—"

"Repeat my words."

"The fate . . . of the world . . . rests . . . in . . . my hands . . ."

565

Chapter XIII

Morris Craig came back, "under convoy" from Nayland Smith's "quiet restaurant." Standing before the private door:

"Your restaurant was certainly quiet," he said. "But the check was a loud, sad cry. Come up if you like, Smith. But I have a demon night ahead of me. I must be through by tomorrow. Thanks for a truly edible dinner. Most acceptable to my British constitution. The wine was an answer to this pagan's prayer."

Nayland Smith gave him a long, steely-hard look.

"Have I succeeded in making it quite clear to you, Craig, that the danger is *now*, tonight, and for the next twenty-four hours?"

"Septically clear. Already I have symptoms of indigestion. But if I work on into the grey dawn I'm going to get the job finished, because I am bidden to spend the week-end with the big chief in the caves and jungles of Connecticut."

Nayland Smith, a lean figure in a well-worn tweed suit, for he had left his topcoat in the car, hesitated for a moment; then he grasped Craig firmly by the arm.

"I won't make myself a nuisance," he said. "But I want to see you right back on the job before I leave you. The fact is—I have a queer, uneasy feeling tonight. We must neglect no precaution."

And so they went up to the office together, and found it just as they had left it. Craig hung up hat and coat, grinning at Smith, who was lighting his pipe.

"Don't mind me. Carry on as if you were in your own abode. I'll carry on as if I were in mine."

He crossed to unlock the safe, when:

"Wait a minute," came sharply. "I'm going to make myself a nuisance after all."

Craig turned. "How come?"

"The duplicate key is in my topcoat! You will have to let me out."

"Blessings and peace," murmured Craig. "But I promise not to go beyond the street door. There will thus be no excuse for my being escorted upstairs again. Before we start, better let Regan know I'm back."

He called the laboratory, and waited.

"H'm. Silence. He surely can't have gone to sleep . . . Try again."

And now came Regan's voice, oddly strained.

"Laboratory . . . Regan here."

"That's all right, Regan. Just wanted to say I'm back. Everything in order?"

"Yes . . . everything."

Craig glanced at Nayland Smith

"Sounded very cross, didn't he?"

"Don't wonder. Is *he* expected to work all night too?

"No. Shaw relieves him at twelve o'clock."

"Come on, then. I won't detain you any longer."

They went out.

That faint sound made by the elevator had just died away, when there came the muffled thud of two shots . . . The laboratory door was flung open—and Regan hurled himself down the steps. He held an automatic in his hand, as he raced towards the lobby.

"Dr. Craig! . . . Help! . . . *Dr. Craig!*"

Making a series of bounds incredible in a creature ordinarily so slow and clumsy of movement, M'goyna followed. His teeth were exposed like the fangs of a wild animal. He uttered a snarl of rage.

Regan twisted around and fired again.

Instant upon the crack of his shot, M'goyna dashed the weapon from Regan's grasp and swept him into a bear hug. Power of speech was crushed out of his body. He gave one gasping, despairing cry, and was silent. M'goyna lifted him onto a huge shoulder and carried him back up the steps.

Only a groan came from the laboratory when the semiman ran down again to recover Regan's pistol.

He coughed as he reclosed the steel door . . .

The office remained empty for another two minutes. Then Craig returned, swinging his keys on their chain. He went straight to the safe, paused—and stood sniffing. He had detected a faint but unaccountable smell. He glanced all about him, until suddenly the boyish smile replaced a puzzled frown.

"Smith's pipe!" he muttered.

Dismissing the matter lightly, as he always brushed aside—or tried to brush aside—anything which interfered with the job in hand, he had soon unlocked the safe and set up his materials. He was so deeply absorbed in his work that when Camille came in, he failed to notice even *her* presence.

She stood in the open doorway for a moment, staring vaguely about the office. Then she looked down at her handbag, and finally up at the clock above the desk. But not until she began to cross to her own room did Craig know she was there.

He spun around in a flash.

"Shades of evenin'! Don't play bogey man with me. My nerves are not what they were in my misspent youth."

Camille did not smile. She glanced at him and then, again, at the clock. She was not wearing her black-rimmed glasses, but her hair was tightly pinned back as usual. Craig wondered if something had disturbed her.

"I—I am sorry."

"Nothing to be sorry about. How's Professor What's-his-name? Full of beans and ballyhoo?"

"I—really don't know."

She moved away in the direction of her open door. Her manner was so strange that he could no longer ignore it. Insomnia, he knew, could play havoc with the nervous system. And Camille was behaving like one walking in her sleep. But when he spoke he retained the light note.

"What's the prescription—Palm Beach, or a round trip in the *Queen Elizabeth*?"

Camille paused, but didn't look back.

"I'm afraid—I have forgotten," she replied.

She went into her room.

Craig scratched his chin, looking at her closed door. Certainly something was quite wrong. Could he have offended her? Was she laboring under a sense of grievance? Or was she really ill?

He took out a crushed packet of cigarettes from his hip pocket, smoothed one into roughly cylindrical form and lighted it; all the while staring at that closed door.

Very slowly, resuming his glasses, he returned to his work. But an

568

image of Camille, wide-eyed, distrait, persistently intruded. He recalled that she had been in such a mood once before, and that he had made her go home. On the former occasion, too, she had been out but gave no account of where she had gone.

Something resembling a physical chill crept around his heart.

There was a man in her life. And he must have let her down . . .

Craig picked up a scribbling block and wrote a note in pencil. He was surprised, and angry, to find how shaky his hand had become. He must know the truth. But he would give her time. With a little tact, perhaps Camille could be induced to tell him.

He had never kissed her fingers, much less her lips, yet the thought of her in another man's arms drove him mad. He remembered that he had recently considered her place in the scheme of things, and had decided to dismiss such considerations until his work was completed.

Now he was almost afraid to press the button which would call her.

But he did.

He was back at his drawing board when he heard her come in. She moved so quietly that he sensed, rather than knew, when she stood behind him. He tore off the top sheet and held it over his shoulder.

"Just type this out for me, d'you mind? It's a note for Regan. He can't read my writing."

"Of course, Dr. Craig."

Her soft voice soothed him, as always. How he loved it! He had just a peep of her delicate fingers as she took the page.

Then she was gone again.

Craig crushed out his cigarette in an ash-tray and sat staring at the complicated formula pinned to his drawing board. Of course, it probably meant something—something very important. It might even mean, as Nayland Smith seemed to think, a new era in the troubled history of man.

But why should he care *what* it meant if he must loose Camille?

He could hear her machine tapping . . .

Very soon, her door opened, and Camille came out. She carried a typed page and duplicates. The pencilled note was clipped to them. Craig didn't look up when she laid them beside the drawing board, and Camille turned to go. At the same moment, she glanced up at the clock.

Nine-fifteen . . .

Could Morris Craig have seen, he would have witnessed an eerie thing.

Camille's vacant expression became effaced; instantly, magically. She clenched her hands, fixing her eyes upward, upon the clock. For a moment she stood so, as if transfixed, as if listening intently. She symbolized vital awareness.

She relaxed, and, looking down, rested her left hand on the desk beside Craig. She spoke slowly.

"I am sorry—if I have made any mistakes. Please tell me if this is correct."

Craig, who was not wearing his glasses, glanced over the typed page. He was trying desperately to think of some excuse to detain her.

"There was one word," the musical voice continued.

Camille raised her hands, and deliberately released her hair so that it swept down, a fiery, a molten torrent, brushing Craig's cheek as he pretended to read the message.

"Oh! Forgive me!"

She was bending over him when Craig twisted about and looked up into her eyes. Meeting his glance, she straightened and began to rearrange her hair.

He stood up.

"No—don't! Don't bother to do that."

He spoke breathlessly.

Camille, hands still lifted, paused, watching him. They were very close.

"But—"

"Your hair is—so wonderful." He clasped her wrists to restrain her. "It's a crime to hide it."

"I am glad you think so," she said rather tremulously.

He was holding her hands now. "Camille—would you think me a really fearful cad if I told you you are completely lovely?"

His heart seemed to falter when he saw that tiny curl of Camille's lip—like the stirring of a rose petal, he thought of it—heralding a smile. It was a new smile, a smile he had never seen before. She raised her lashes and looked into his eyes . . .

When he released her: "Camille," he whispered, "How *very* lovely you are!"

"Morris!"

He kissed her again.

"You darling! I suppose I have been waiting for this moment ever since you first walked into the office."

"Have you?"

This was a different woman he held in his arms—a woman who had disguised herself; this was the hidden, the secret Camille, seductive, wildly desirable—and his!

"Yes. Did you know?"

"Perhaps I did," she whispered.

Presently she disengaged herself and stood back, smiling provocatively.

"Camille—"

"Shall I take the message to Mr. Regan?"

Morris Craig inhaled deeply, and turned away. He was delirious with happiness, knew it, yet (such is the scientific mind) resented it. Camille had swept solid earth from beneath his feet. He was in the grip of a power which he couldn't analyze, a power not reducible to equations, inexpressible in a diagram. He had, perhaps, probed the secret of perpetual motion, exalting himself to a throne not far below the knees of the gods—but he had met a goddess in whose slender hands he was a thing of clay.

"D'you know," he said, glancing aside at her, "I think it might be a good idea if you did."

She detached the top copy of the note and walked across to the laboratory steps.

"Will you open the door for me?"

Craig pulled out the bunch of keys and went to join her where she stood—one foot on the first step, her frock defining the lines of her slim body, reflected light touching rich waves of her hair to an incredible glory. Over her shoulder she watched him.

The keys rattled as he dropped the chain . . .

"Morris—please!"

He took the paper from her hand and tore it up.

"Never mind. Work is out of the question, now."

"Oh, I'm so sorry!"

571

"You adorable little witch, you're not sorry at all! I thought I was a hard-boiled scientific egg until I met you."

"I'm afraid," said Camille, demurely, and her soft voice reminded him again of the notes of a harp, "I have spoiled your plans for the evening."

"To the devil with plans! This is a night of nights. Let's follow it through."

He put his arm around her waist and dragged her from the steps.

"Very well, Morris. Whatever you say."

"I say we're young only once." He pulled her close. "At least, so far as we know. So I say let's be young together."

He gave her a kiss which lasted almost too long . . .

"Morris!"

"I could positively eat you alive!"

"But—your work—"

"Work is for slaves. Love is for free men. Where shall we go?"

"Anywhere you like, if you really mean it. But—"

"It doesn't matter. There are lots of spots. I feel that I want somewhere different, some place where I can get used to the idea that *you*—that there *is* a you, and that I have found you . . . I'm talkin' rot! Better let Regan know he's in sole charge again."

His keys still hung down on the chain as he had dropped them. He swung the bunch into his hand and crossed toward the steel door. At the foot of the steps, he hesitated. No need to go in. It would be difficult to prevent Regan from drawing inferences. Shrewd fellow, Regan. Craig returned to his desk and called the laboratory.

As if from far away a reply came:

"Regan here."

Craig cleared his throat guiltily.

"Listen, Regan. I shan't be staying late tonight after all." (He felt like a criminal.) "Pushing off. Anything I should attend to before Shaw comes on duty?"

There was a silent interval. Camille was standing behind Craig, clutching her head, staring at him in a dazed way . . .

"Can you hear, Regan? I say, do you want to see me before I leave?"

Then came the halting words. "No . . . Doctor . . . there's nothing . . . to see you about . . ."

Craig thought the sentence was punctured by a stifled cough.

A moment later he had Camille in his arms again.

"Camille—I realize that I have never been really alive before."

But she was pressing her hands frantically against him, straining back, wild-eyed, trying to break away from his caresses. He released her. She stared up at the clock then back to Craig.

"My God! Morris! . . . Dr. Craig—"

"What is it, Camille? What is it?"

He stepped forward, but she shrank away.

"I don't know. I'm frightened. When—when did I come in? What have I been doing?"

His deep concern, the intense sincerity of his manner, seemed to reach her. When, gently, he held her and looked into her eyes, she lowered her head until it lay upon his shoulder, intoxicating him with the fragrance of her hair.

"Camille," he whispered, tenderly. (He could feel her heart beating.) "Tell me—what is it?"

"I don't know—I don't know what has happened. Please—please take care of me."

"Do you mean you have made a mistake? It was an impulse? You are sorry for it?"

"Sorry for what?" she murmured against his shoulder.

"For letting me make love to you."

"No—I'm not sorry if—if I did that."

He kissed her hair, very lightly, just brushing it with his lips.

"Darling! Whatever came over you? What frightened you?"

Camille looked up at him under her long lashes.

"I don't know." She lowered her eyes. "How long have I been here?"

"How long? What in heaven's name d'you mean, Camille? Are you terribly unhappy? I don't understand at all."

"No. I am not unhappy—but—everything is so strange."

"Strange? In what way?"

The phone rang in Camille's office. She started—stepped back, a sudden, alert look in her eyes.

"Don't trouble, Camille. I'll answer."

"No, no. It's quite all right."

Camille crossed to her room, and took up the phone. She knew it to be unavoidable that she should do this, but had no idea why. Some ten seconds later she had returned to the half-world controlled by the voice of Dr. Fu Manchu . . .

When she came out of her room again, she was smiling radiantly.

"It is the message I have waited for so long—to tell me that my mother, who was desperately ill, is no longer in danger."

Even as he took her in his arms, Craig was thinking that there seemed to be an epidemic of sick mothers, but he dismissed the thought as cynical and unworthy. And when she gave him her lips he forgot everything else. Her distrait manner was explained. The world was full of roses.

They were ready to set out before he fully came to his senses. Camille had combed her hair in a way which did justice to its beauty. She looked, as she was, an extremely attractive woman.

He stood in the lobby, his arm around her waist, preparing to open the elevator door, when sanity returned. Perhaps it was the sight of his keys which brought this about.

"By gad!" he exclaimed. "I *have* got it badly! Can you imagine—I was pushing off, and leaving the detail of the transmuter valve pinned to the board on my desk!"

He turned and ran back.

Chapter XIV

Somewhere in Chinatown a girl was singing.

Chinese vocalism is not everybody's box of candy, but the singer had at least one enthusiastic listener. She sang in an apartment adjoining the shop of Huan Tsung, and the good looking shopman, who called himself Lao Tai, wrote at speed, in a kind of shorthand, all that she sang. From time to time he put a page of this writing into the little cupboard behind him and pressed a button.

The F.B.I. man on duty in a room across the street caught fragments of this wailing as they were carried to him on a slight breeze, and wondered how anyone who had ever heard Bing Crosby could endure such stuff.

But upstairs, in the quiet, silk-lined room, old Huan Tsung scanned page after page, destroying each one in the charcoal fire, and presently the globe beside his couch awoke to life and the face of Dr. Fu Manchu challenged him from its mysterious depths.

"The latest report to hand, Excellency."

"Repeat it."

Huan Tsung leaned back against cushions and closed his wrinkled eyelids.

"I have installed the 'bazaar' system. My house is watched and my telephone is tapped. Therefore, news is brought to Mai Cha and she sings the news to Lao Tai."

"Spare me these details. The report."

"Reprimand noted. Dr. Craig and Camille Navarre left the Huston Building, according to Excellency's plan, at nine thirty-seven. One of the two detectives posted at the private entrance followed them. The other remains. No report yet to hand as to where Craig and the woman have gone."

"Nayland Smith?"

"Nothing later than former report. Raymond Harkness still acting as liaison officer in this area."

The widely opened green eyes were not focussed upon Huan Tsung. A physician might have suspected the pinpoint pupils to indicate that Dr. Fu Manchu had been seeking inspiration in the black smoke. But presently he spoke, incisive, masterful as ever.

"Mount a diversion at four minutes to ten o'clock. Note the time. My entrance must be masked. Whoever is on duty—remove. But no assassinations. I may be there for an hour or more. Cover my retirement. My security is your charge. Proceed."

Light in the crystal died.

At a few minutes before ten o'clock, a man was standing at a bus stop twenty paces from the private entrance to the Huston laboratory. No bus that had pulled up there during the past hour had seemed to be the bus he was waiting for; and now he waited alone. An uncanny quietude descends upon these office areas after dusk. During the day they remind one of some vast anthill. Big-business ants, conscious of their fat dividends, neat little secretary ants, conscious of their slim ankles, run to and fro, to and fro, in the restless, formless, meaningless dance of Manhattan.

Smart cabs and dowdy cabs, gay young cabs and sad old cabs, trucks, cars, busses, bicycles, pile themselves up in tidal waves behind that impassable barrier, the red light. And over in front of the suspended torrent scurry the big ants and the little ants. But at night, red and green lights become formalities. The ants have retired from the stage, but the lights shine on. Perhaps to guide phantom ants, shades of former Manhattan dancers now resting.

So that when a boy peddling a delivery bike came out of a street beside the Huston Building, it is possible that the driver of a covered truck proceeding at speed along the avenue failed to note the light.

However this may have been, he collided with the boy, who was hurled from his bicycle. The truckman pulled up with an ear-torturing screech of brakes. The boy—apparently unhurt—jumped to his feet and put up a barrage of abuse embellished with some of the most staggering invective which the man waiting for a bus had ever heard.

The truckman, a tough-looking bruiser, jumped from his seat, lifted the blasphemous but justly indignant youth by the collar of his jacket, and proceeded to punish him brutally.

This was too much for the man waiting for a bus. He ran to the rescue. The boy, now, was howling curses in a voice audible for several blocks. Spectators appeared—as they do—from nowhere. In a matter of seconds the rescuer, the rescued, and the attacker were hemmed in by an excited group.

And at just this moment, two figures alighted from the rear of the temporarily deserted truck, walked quietly to the private door of the Huston Building, opened it, and went in. Later, Raymond Harkness would have something to say to the man waiting for a bus—whose name was Detective Officer Beaker.

Huan Tsung had mounted a diversion . . .

The telephone in Camille's room was buzzing persistently—had been buzzing for a long time.

Craig had left the desk light burning; but most of the office lay in shadow, so that when someone switched on a flashlamp in the lobby, a widening, fading blade of light swept across the parquet floor. Then the door was fully opened.

Koenig stepped in, looking cautiously about him. He carried a heavy leather case, which he set down by the safe.

And, as he stood upright again, a tall figure, draped in a black topcoat, the fur collar turned up, came in silently and joined him. Dr. Fu Manchu wore the tinted Hoffmeyer glasses, gloves, and carried a black hat. He looked in the direction of that persistent buzzing.

"Miss Navarre's office," said Koenig uneasily.

Dr. Fu Manchu indicated the safe, merely extending a gloved hand. Koenig nodded, knelt, and opened the leather case. Taking out a bunch of keys, he busied himself with the lock, working by the light of his flashlamp. Presently he paused. He turned.

"Combination has been changed!"

The tall figure standing behind him remained motionless. The buzzing in Camille's room ceased.

"You came prepared for such a possibility?"

"Yes—but it may take a long time now."

"You have nearly two hours. But no more."

The clock over Craig's desk struck its single note . . . ten o'clock.

Dr. Fu Manchu crossed and walked up the three steps. He beat upon the steel door.

"M'goyna!"

577

The door swung open. M'goyna's huge frame showed silhouetted against a quivering green background.

Dr. Fu Manchu entered the laboratory.

At half-past eleven, the man waiting for a bus was relieved by another detective. The avenue, now, was as completely deserted as any Manhattan avenue ever can be.

"Hello, Holland," he said. "You're welcome to this job! Like being the doorman of a vacant night club."

"What are we supposed to be doing, Beaker, anyway?"

"Search me! Stop anybody going in, I suppose. We had orders to tail Dr. Craig if ever *he* came out, and Stoddart went after him two hours ago when he took his secretary off to make whoopee. A redhead straight from heaven."

"Nothing else happened?"

"Bit of a scrap about ten o'clock. Big heel driving a truck knocked a boy off his bike. Nothing else . . . Goodnight."

"Goodnight."

Holland lighted a cigarette, looking left and right along the avenue and wondering what had originally attracted him to police work. Beaker was making for a subway station and Holland followed the retreating figure with his eyes for several blocks. He settled down to a monotony broken only by an occasional bus halting at the nearby stop. The night was unseasonably warm.

At a quarter to twelve, a remarkable incident occurred.

It had been preceded by another curious occurrence, invisible to Holland, however. A red light had been flashed several times from the high parapet of the Huston Building, immediately outside Craig's office . . .

Bearing down upon Holland at speed from the other end of the block, he saw a hatless young man in evening dress, who *screamed* as he ran!

"You won't get me! You devils! You won't get me!"

In spite of the emptiness of the streets, these outcries had had some effect. Two men were following, but maintaining a discreet distance from the screaming man. Keeping up that extraordinary pace, he drew nearer and nearer to Holland.

"Out of my way! They're after me!"

Holland sized up the situation. The runner was of medium build, dark, and not bad-looking in a Latin fashion. Clearly Holland decided, he's drunk, and a guy in that state is doubly strong. But I guess I'll have to hold him. He may do damage.

An experienced manhandler, Holland stepped forward. But the runner kept on running.

"Out of my way!" he screamed. "I'll kill you if you try to stop me!"

Holland stooped for a tackle, saw the gleam of a weapon, and side-stepped in a flash.

"They won't get me!" yelled the demented man, and went racing around the corner.

Had the missing Sam been present, he would have recognized the lunatic as that Jed Laurillard who had once talked to him in a bar. In fact, this disciple had been given a particularly difficult assignment, one certain to land him in jail, as a chance to redeem his former mistake. He had, furthermore, been given a shot of hashish to lend color to the performance.

Holland clapped a whistle to his lips, and blew a shrill blast. Drawing his own automatic, he went tearing around the corner after the still screaming madman . . .

During a general mix-up which took place there, a big sedan drew in before the private door of the Huston Building, and three men came out and entered it. One of them carried a heavy roll of office carpet on his shoulder.

Huan Tsung had successfully covered the retirement of Dr. Fu Manchu.

When Martin Shaw stepped from a taxi, paid the driver, and saw the yellow cab driven away, he unbuttoned his topcoat to find his key. Someone was walking rapidly towards him; the only figure in sight. It was midnight.

Holland, whilst still some distance away, recognized the chief technician, and moderated his pace. The screaming alcoholic had just been removed in charge of two patrolmen, and would, no doubt, receive his appropriate medicine in the morning. By the time Holland reached the door, Shaw had already gone in, and was on his way up.

Shaw half expected that Dr. Craig would be still at work, and even when he didn't see him at his desk, was prepared to find him in the laboratory. Then he noted that the drawing board was missing and the safe unlocked. Evidently, Craig had gone.

Whoever took the next (four-to-eight) duty usually slept on a couch in the office. But Regan seemed to have made no preparations.

Shaw went up the three steps and unlocked the steel door.

"Here we are, Regan!" he called in his breezy way. "Get to hell out of it, man!"

There was no reply. Everything seemed to be in order. But where was Regan?

Then, pinned to the logbook lying on a glass-topped table, Shaw saw a sheet of ruled paper. He crossed and bent over it.

A message, written shakily in Regan's hand, appeared there. It said:

Mr. Shaw—

Had a slight accident. Compelled to go for medical treatment. Don't be alarmed. Will report at 4 A.M. for duty.

J. J. REGAN

"Slight accident?" Shaw muttered.

He looked keenly about him. What could have happened? There was nothing wrong with any of the experimental plant. He quickly satisfied himself on that score. So unlike Regan not to have timed the message. He wondered how long he had been gone. The last entry in the log (almost illegible) was timed eleven-fifteen.

He was hanging his coat up when he noticed the bloodstains.

They were very few—specks on white woodwork. But, stooping, he came to the conclusion that others had been wiped from the tiled floor below.

Regan, then, must have cut himself in some way, been unable to staunch the bleeding, and gone to find a surgeon. Shaw decided that he had better notify Dr. Craig. The laboratory phone was an extension from the secretary's office. He reopened the door, went down the steps, and dialled from Camille's room.

There was no answer to his call.

Shaw growled, but accepted the fact philosophically. He would repeat the call later. He went back to his working-bench in the laboratory and was soon absorbed in adjusting an intricate piece of mechanism in course of construction there. He walked in an atmosphere vibrant with a force new to science. His large hands were delicate as those of a violinist . . .

He called Craig's number again at one o'clock, but there was no reply. He tried Regan's, with a similar result. Perhaps the injury was more serious than Regan had supposed. He might have been detained for hospital treatment.

Shaw tried both numbers again at two and then at three o'clock. No answers.

He began to feel seriously worried about Regan; nor could he entirely understand the absence of Craig. He knew how determined Craig had been to complete the valve detail that night, he knew he was spending the week-end away; and he felt sure that Morris Craig wasn't the man to waste precious hours in night spots.

In this, Shaw misjudged Craig—for once. At almost exactly three o'clock, that is, whilst Shaw was vainly calling his number, Morris Craig leaned on a small table, feasting his eyes on Camille, who sat facing him.

"Say you are happy," he whispered.

That she was happy, that this new wonderland was real and not a mirage, seemed to him, at the moment, the only thing that mattered—the one possible excuse for his otherwise inexcusable behavior.

Camille smiled, and then lowered her eyes. She knew that she had been dancing—dancing for hours, it seemed to her. Even now, a band played softly, somewhere on the other side of a discreetly dim floor. Yes—she was happy. She was in love with Morris, and they were together. But how could she surrender herself to all that such an evening should mean, when she had no idea how she came to be there?

She knew that she had set out to keep an appointment made for her by Mrs. Frobisher. Had she kept it? Apart from a vague recollection of talking to Morris in the office—of some sudden terror—the rest of the night remained a blank up to the moment when she had found herself here, in his arms, dancing . . .

"Yes—I am happy, Morris, very happy. But I think I must go home now."

It was nearly half past three when they left.

In the little lobby of her apartment house, between swing doors and the house door, Craig held her so long that she thought he would never let her go. Every time she went to put her key in the lock, he pulled her back and held her again. At last:

"I shall be here for you at nine in the morning," he said.

"All right. Good night, Morris."

She opened the door, and was gone. He watched her, through glass panels, as she hurried upstairs. Then he went out, crossed the street, and waited to see a light spring up in her room. When one did, he still waited—and waited.

At last she came to the window, pulled a drape aside, and waved him good night.

He had dismissed the taxi. He wanted to walk, to be alone with this night, to relive every hour of the wonder that had come into his life with Camille's first kiss.

When, at Central Park West, he decided to walk across the Park, two tired and bored detectives who had been keeping the pair in sight ever since they had left the night club, exhaled selfpitying sighs . . .

Chapter XV

At ten past four, Martin Shaw dialled Regan's number. No reply. Then he tried Craig's. No reply. Following a momentary hesitation, he called police headquarters.

He had no more than begun to explain what had happened when he heard the clang of the elevator door as someone slammed it shut. Laying the phone down on Camille's desk, he ran out into Craig's office. He arrived just as Nayland Smith burst in.

"Sir Denis! What's this?"

Nayland Smith was darting urgent glances right and left.

"Where's Regan?" he rapped.

"Hasn't shown up—"

"What!"

"Had an accident some time before I returned. Left a note."

Nayland Smith's challenging stare was almost frightening.

"You mean the place was empty when you arrived at twelve?"

"Just that."

"And you did nothing about it?"

"Why should I?" Shaw demanded. "But when he didn't appear at four o'clock, it was different. I have police headquarters on the line right now "

"Tell them I'm here. Then hang up."

Shaw, upon whom this visitor had swept as a typhoon, went back and did so.

"I know," a voice replied. "We're on the job. Stand by."

When Shaw rejoined him:

"Your handyman, Sam, was got away by a ruse," said Smith. "He wisely called the police, too—from Philadelphia. I came straight along. Someone wanted this place vacated tonight—and Craig played right into the enemy's hands—"

"But where is the Doctor? I have been calling him—"

"You'd be surprised!" Smith snapped savagely. "At the present moment, he's wandering about Central Park, moon-struck! One of two men looking after him got to a phone ten minutes ago."

Shaw looked thunderstruck.

"Has he gone mad?"

"Yes. He's in love. Show me this note left by Regan."

He went racing up the steps. Shaw had left the laboratory door open.

"There—on the table."

Nayland Smith bent over Regan's strange message. He turned.

"Sure it's his writing?"

"Looks like it—allowing for a shaky hand. He'd evidently cut himself. See—there are specks of blood here." Shaw pointed. "And I think blood has been wiped from the floor just below."

Nayland Smith pulled at the lobe of his ear. His brown face looked drawn, weary, but his eyes shone like steel. The green twilight of this place, the eerie throbbing which seemed to penetrate his frame, he disliked, but knew he must ignore. A moment he stood so, then turned and ran back to the phone. He called police headquarters, gave particulars of what had happened, and:

"Check all night taxis," he directed rapidly, "operating in this area. All clinics and hospitals in the neighborhood. Recall Detectives Beaker and Holland, on duty at the door here between eight and four. Order them to report to Raymond Harkness."

He hung up, called another number, and presently got Harkness.

"I'm afraid we lose, Harkness," he said. "I'm at the Huston Building. Something very serious has occurred tonight. I fear the worst. The two men posted below must have tripped up, somewhere. They will report to you. Make each take oath and swear he never left the door for a moment. Then call me. I shall be here . . ."

In the throbbing laboratory, Martin Shaw was making entries in the log. He looked up as Nayland Smith came in.

"Of course," he said, "I can see something has happened to poor Regan. But it's not clear to me that there's anything else to it."

"Not clear?" rapped Smith. "Why should a man who generally hangs around the place at all hours—Sam—receive a faked call to get him to Philadelphia? Is it a mere coincidence that Regan deserts his post the same night? For some time before twelve o'clock—we don't know for how long—no one was on duty here."

"There's an entry in the book timed eleven-fifteen."

"Very shaky one. Still leaving a gap of forty-five minutes."

"If you mean some foreign agent got in, how did he get in?"

"He probably had a duplicate key, as I have. The F.B.I. got mine from the locksmith who made the originals. Couldn't someone else have done the same thing? Or borrowed, and copied, an existing key?"

"But nothing has been disturbed. There's no evidence that any-one has been here."

"There wouldn't be!" said Smith grimly. "Dangerous criminals leave no clues. The visitor I suspect would only want a short time to examine the plant—and to borrow Craig's figure of the transmuter valve—"

"That would mean opening the safe."

"Exactly what *we* have to do—open the safe."

"No one but Dr. Craig has a key—or knows the combination."

"There are other methods," said Nayland Smith drily. "I am now going out to examine the safe."

He proceeded to do so, and made a thorough job of it. Shaw came down and joined him.

"Nothing to show it's been tampered with," Smith muttered . . . "Hullo! who comes?"

He had detected that faint sound made by the private elevator. He turned to face the lobby; so did Shaw.

The elevator ascended, stopped. A door banged. And Morris Craig ran in.

"Smith!" he exclaimed—and both men saw that he was deathly pale. "What's this? What has happened? I was brought here by two detectives—"

"Serves you right!" rapped Nayland Smith. "Don't talk. Act. Be good enough to open this safe."

"But "

"Open it."

Craig, his hand none too steady, pulled out his keys, twirled the dial, and opened the safe. Nayland Smith and Martin Shaw bent over his shoulders.

They saw a number of papers, and Craig's large drawing board.

But there was nothing on the board!

A moment of silence followed—ominous silence.

Then Nayland Smith faced Craig.

"I don't know," he said, and spoke with unusual deliberation, "what lunacy led you to desert your job tonight. But I am anxious to learn"—he pointed—"what has become of the vital drawing and the notes, upon which you were working."

Morris Craig forced a smile. It was an elder brother of the one he usually employed. Some vast, inexpressible relief apparently had brought peace to his troubled mind.

"If that's all," he replied, "the answer's easy. I had a horrible idea that—something had happened—to Camille."

Nayland Smith exchanged a glance with Shaw.

"Ignoring the Venusburg music for a moment"—the words were rapped out in his usual staccato manner—"where is the diagram?"

Morris Craig smiled again—and the junior smile was back on duty. He removed his topcoat, stripped his jacket off, and groped up under his shirt. From this cache he produced a large, folded sheet of paper and another, smaller sheet—the one decorated with a formula like a Picasso painting.

"In spite of admittedly high temperature at time of departure, I remembered that I was leaving town in the morning. I decided to take the job with me. If"—he glanced from face to face—"you suspect some attempt on the safe, all the burglar found was—Old Mother Hubbard. I carry peace to Falling Waters."

586

Chapter XVI

The library at Falling Waters was a pleasant room. It was panelled in English oak imported by Stella Frobisher. An open staircase led up to a landing which led, in turn, to rooms beyond.
There were recessed bookcases. French windows gave upon a
paved terrace overlooking an Italian garden. Sets of Dickens,
Thackeray, Punch, and Country Life bulked large on the shelves.

There was a handsome walnut desk, upon which a telephone
stood, backed by a screen of stamped Spanish leather. Leather-
covered armchairs and settees invited meditation. The eye was
attracted (or repelled) by fine old sporting prints. Good Chinese
rugs were spread on a well-waxed floor.

Conspicuous above a bookcase, and so unlike Stella's taste,
one saw a large, glazed cabinet containing a colored plan of the
grounds surrounding Falling Waters. It seemed so out of place.

On occasional tables, new novels invited dipping. Silver caskets and jade caskets and cloisonné caskets contained cigarettes
to suit every palate. There were discreet ornaments. A good
reproduction of Queen Nefertiti's beautiful, commercialized
head above a set of Balzac, in French, which no member of this
household could read. A bust of Shakespeare. A copy of the
Discus Thrower apparently engaged in throwing his discus at a
bust by Epstein on the other side of the library.

A pleasant room, as sunshine poured in to bring its lifeless
beauties to life, to regild rich bindings, on this morning following
those strange occurrences in the Huston research laboratory.

Michael Frobisher was seated at the walnut desk, the phone to
his ear. Stein, his butler-chauffeur, stood at his elbow. Michael
Frobisher was never wholly at ease in his own home. He
remained acutely conscious of the culture with which Stella had
surrounded him. This morning, his unrest was pathetic.

'"But this thing's just incredible! . . . What d'you say? You're
certain of your facts, Craig? Regan never left a note like that

before? . . . What d'you mean, he hasn't come back? He must be in some clinic . . . The police say he isn't? To hell with the police! I don't want police in the Huston laboratory . . . You did a wise thing there, but I guess it was an accident . . . Bring the notes and drawing right down here. For God's sake, bring 'em right down here! How do we know somebody hasn't explored the plant? Listen! how do we know?"

He himself listened awhile, and then:

"To hell with Nayland Smith!" he growled. "Huston Electric doesn't spend half a million dollars to tip the beans into *his* pocket. He's a British agent. He'll sell us out! Are you crazy? . . . He *may* be backed by Washington. What's good that comes to us from Washington, anyway?"

He listened again, and suddenly:

"Had it occurred to you," he asked on a note of tension, "that *Regan* could be the British agent? He joined us from Vickers . . ."

When at last he hung up:

"Is there anything you want me to do?" Stein asked.

Stein was a man who, seated, would have looked like a big man, for he had a thick neck, deep chest, and powerful shoulders. But, standing, he resembled Gog, or Magog, guardian deities of London's Guildhall; a heavy, squat figure, with heavy, squat features. Stein wore his reddish hair cut close as a Prussian officer's. He had a crushed appearance, as though someone had sat on his head.

Frobisher spun around. "Did you get it?"

"Yes. It is serious." (Stein furthermore had a heavy, squat accent.) "But not so serious as if they have found the detail of the transmuter."

"What are you talking about?" Frobisher stood up. "There's enough in the lab to give away the whole principle to an expert."

That grey undertone beneath his florid coloring was marked.

"This may be true—"

"And Regan's disappeared!"

"I gathered so."

"Then—hell!"

"You are too soon alarmed," said Stein coolly. "Let us wait until we have all the facts."

"How'll we ever have all the facts?" Frobisher demanded. "What are the facts about things that happen right here? Who walks around this house at night like a ghost? Who combed my desk papers? Who opened my safe? And who out of hell went through *your* room the other evening while you were asleep? Tell me *who*, and then tell me *why*!"

But before Stein had time to answer these reasonable inquiries, Stella Frobisher fluttered into the library. She wore a Hollywood pinafore over her frock, her hands were buried in gauntlet gloves, and she carried a pair of large scissors. Her blond hair was dressed as immaculately as that of a movie star just rescued from a sinking ship.

"I *know* I look a *fright*, dear," she assured Frobisher. "I have been out in the garden, *cutting* early spring flowers."

She emphasized "cutting" as if her more usual method was to knock their heads off with a niblick.

"Allow me to bring these in for you, madame," said Stein.

His respectful manner was in odd contrast to that with which he addressed Frobisher.

"Thank you, Stein. Lucille has the *basket* on the *back* porch."

She did not mention the fact that Lucille had also cut the flowers.

"Very good, madame."

As Stein walked towards the door:

"Oh, Stein—there will be *seven* to luncheon. Dr. and *Mrs.* Pardoe are coming."

Stein bowed and went out.

"Who's the old man?" growled Frobisher, opening a box of cigars which lay on the desk.

"Professor Hoffmeyer. Isn't it *splendid* that I got *him* to come?"

"Don't know till I see him."

"He's simply *wonderful*. He will *amaze* you, Mike."

"Don't care for amazement at mealtimes."

"You will fall *completely* under his *spell*, dear," Stella declared, and went fluttering out again. "I must go and *assemble* my flowers."

At about this time, Morris Craig was putting a suitcase into the back of his car. As he locked the boot he looked up.

"You know, Smith," he said, "I'm profoundly conscious of the gravity of this thing—but I begin to feel like a ticket-of-leave man.

589

There's a car packed with police on the other side of the street. Do they track me to Falling Waters?"

"They do!" Nayland Smith replied. "As I understand it, you are now going to pick up Miss Navarre?"

"That is the program." Craig smiled rather unhappily. "I feel a bit cheap leaving Shaw alone, in the circumstances. But—"

"Shaw won't be alone" Smith rapped irritably. "I think—or, rather, fear—the danger at the laboratory is past. But, to make sure, two carefully selected men will be on duty in your office day and night until you return. Plus two outside."

"Why not Sam? He's back."

"You will need Sam to lend a hand with this radio burglar alarm you tell me about "

"*I* shall?"

"You will. I can see you're dying to push off. So—push! I trust you have a happy week-end."

And when Craig turned into West Seventy-fifth Street, the first thing that really claimed his attention was the presence of a car which had followed him all the way. The second was a figure standing before the door of an apartment house—a door he could never forget.

This figure wore spectacles, a light fawn topcoat, a cerise muffler, and a slate-grey hat with the brim turned up not at the back, but in front . . .

"Morning, boss," said Sam, opening the door. "Happen to have—"

"I have nothing but a stern demand. It's this: What the devil are you doing *here*?"

"Well"—Sam shook his head solemnly—"it's like this. Seems you're carrying valuables, and Sir Denis, he thinks—"

"He thinks what?"

"He thinks somebody ought to come along—see? Just in case."

Craig stepped out.

"Tell me: Are you employed by Huston Electric or by Nayland Smith?"

Sam tipped his hat further back. He chewed thoughtfully.

"It's kind of complicated, Doctor. Sir Denis has it figured I'm doing my best for Huston's if I come along and lend a hand. He figures there may be trouble up there. And you never know."

590

Visions of a morning drive alone with Camille vanished.

"All right," said Craig resignedly. "Sit at the back."

In a very short time he had hurried in. But it was a long time before he came out.

Camille looked flushed, but delightfully pretty, when she arrived at Falling Waters. Her hair was tastefully dressed, and she carried the black-rimmed glasses in her hand. Stella was there to greet her guests.

"My *dear* Miss Navarre! It's so *nice* to have you *here* at last! Dr. Craig, you have kept her in *hiding* too long."

"Not my fault, Mrs. Frobisher. She's a self-effacing type." Then, as Frobisher appeared: "Hail, chief! Grim work at——"

Frobisher pointed covertly to Stella, making vigorous negative signs with his head. "Glad to see you, Craig," he rumbled, shaking hands with both arrivals.

"You have a charming house, Mrs. Frobisher," said Camille. "It was sweet of you to ask me to come."

"I'm so *glad* you like it!" Stella replied. "Because you must have seen such *lovely* homes in France and in England."

"Yes," Camille smiled sadly. "Some of them *were* lovely."

"But let me take you along to your *room*. This is your *first* visit, but I do hope it will be the first of *many*."

She led Camille away, leaving Frobisher and Craig standing in the lobby—panelled in Spanish mahogany from the old Cunard liner, *Mauretania*. And at that moment Frobisher's eye rested upon Sam, engaged in taking Craig's suitcase from the boot, whilst Stein stood by.

"What's that half-wit doing down here?" Frobisher inquired politely.

"D'you mean Sam? Oh, he's going to—er—lend me a hand overhauling your burglar system."

"Probably make a good job of it, between you," Frobisher commented drily. "When you've combed your hair, Craig, come along to my study. We have a lot to talk about. Where's the plan?"

Craig tapped his chest. He was in a mood of high exaltation.

"On our person, good sir. Only over our dead body could caitiffs win to the treasure."

And in a room all daintily chintz, with delicate water colors and lots of daffodils, Camille was looking out of an opened window, at an old English garden, and wondering if her happiness could last.

Stein tapped at the door, placed Camille's bag inside, and retired.

"Don't *bother* to unpack, my dear," said Stella. "Flora, my maid, is *superlative*."

Camille turned to her, impulsively.

"You are very kind, Mrs. Frobisher. And it was so good of you to make that appointment for me with Professor Hoffmeyer."

"With Professor Hoffmeyer? Oh! my dear! *Did* I, really? Of course"—seeing Camille's strange expression—"I *must* have done. It's queer and it's absurd, but, do you know, I'm *addicted* to the oddest *lapses* of memory."

"*You* are?" Camille exclaimed; then, as it sounded so rude, she added, "I mean *I* am, too."

"*You* are?" Stella exclaimed in turn, and seized both her hands. "Oh, my dear, I'm *so* glad! I mean, I know I *sound* silly, and a bit *horrid*. What I *wanted* to say was, it's such a *relief* to meet somebody *else* who suffers in that *way*. Someone who has no possible *reason* for going funny in the head. But *tell* me—what did you *think* of him?"

Camille looked earnestly into the childish but kindly eyes.

"I must tell you, Mrs. Frobisher—impossible though it sounds—that I have no recollection whatever of going there!"

"My dear!" Stella squeezed her hands encouragingly. "I *quite* understand. Whatever do you *suppose* is the matter with us?"

"I'm afraid I can't even imagine."

"*Could* it be some new kind of *epidemic*?"

Camille's heart was beating rapidly, her expression was introspective; for she was, as Dr. Fu Manchu had told her (but she had forgotten), a personable woman with a brain.

"I don't know. Suppose we compare notes—"

Michael Frobisher's study, the window of which offered a prospect of such woodland as Fenimore Cooper wrote about, was eminently that of a man of business. The books were reference books, the desk had nothing on it but a phone, a blotting-pad, pen, ink, a lamp, an almanac, and a photograph of Stella. The safe was built into the wall. No unnecessary litter.

"There's the safe I told you about," he was saying. "There's the key—and the combination is right here." He touched his rugged forehead. "Yet—I found the damned thing wide open! My papers"—he pulled out a drawer—"were sorted like a teller sorts checks. *I* know. I always have my papers in order. Then—somebody goes through my butler's room." He banged his big fist on the desk. "And not a bolt drawn, not a window opened!"

"Passing strange," Craig murmured. He glanced at the folded diagram. "Hardly seems worthwhile to lock it up."

Michael Frobisher stared at the end of his half-smoked cigar, twirling it between strong fingers.

"There's been nothing since I installed the alarm system. But I don't trust anybody. I want you to test it. Meanwhile"—he laid his hand on the paper—"how long will it take you to finish this thing?"

"Speaking optimistically, two hours."

"You mean, in two hours it will be possible to say we're finished?"

"Hardly. Shaw has to make the valves. Wonderful fellow, Shaw. Then we have to test the brute in action. When that bright day dawns, it may be the right time to say we're finished!"

Frobisher put his cigar back in his hard mouth, and stared at Craig.

"You're a funny guy," he said. "It took a man like me to know you had the brains of an Einstein. I might have regretted the investment if Martin Shaw hadn't backed you—and Regan. I'm doubtful of Regan—now. But he knows the game. Then—you've shown me things."

"A privilege, Mr. Frobisher."

Frobisher stood up.

"Don't go all Oxford on me. Listen. When this detail here is finished, you say we shall be in a position to tap a source of inexhaustible energy which completely tops atomic power?"

"I say so firmly. Whether we can control the monster depends entirely upon—that."

"The transmuter valve?"

"Exactly. It's only a small gadget. Shaw could make all three of 'em in a few hours. But if it works, Mr. Frobisher, and I *know* it will, we shall have at our command a force, cheaply obtained, which could (a) blow our world to bits, or (b) enable us to dispense with costly things like coal, oil, enormous atomic plants, and the like, forever. I am beginning to see tremendous possibilities."

"Fine."

Michael Frobisher was staring out of the window. His heavy face was transfigured. He, too, the man of commerce, the opportunist, could see those tremendous possibilities. No doubt he saw possibilities which had never crossed the purely scientific mind of Morris Craig.

"So," said Craig, picking up the diagram and the notes, "I propose that I retire to my cubicle and busy myself until cocktails are served. Agreed?"

"Agreed. Remember—not a word to Mrs. F."

When Craig left the study, Frobisher stood there for a long time, staring out of the window.

But Morris Craig's route to his "cubicle" had been beset by an obstacle—Mrs. F. As he crossed the library towards the stair, she came in by another door. She glanced at the folded diagram.

"My *dear* Dr. Craig! Surely you haven't come *here* to work?"

Craig pulled up, and smiled. Stella had always liked his smile; it was so English.

"Afraid, yes. But not for too long, I hope. If you'll excuse me, I'll nip up and get going right away."

"But it's too *bad*. How soon will you be *ready* to nip *down* again?"

"Just give me the tip when the bar opens."

"Of *course* I will. But, you know, I have been talking to Camille. She is *truly* a dear girl. I *don't* mean expensive. I *mean* charming."

Craig's attention was claimed, magically, by his hostess's words.

"So glad you think so. She certainly is—brilliant."

Stella Frobisher smiled her hereditary smile. She was quite without sex malice, and she had discovered a close link to bind her to Camille.

"Why don't you *forget* work? Why don't you two *scientific* people go for a walk in the *sunshine*? After all, that's what you're *here* for."

And Morris Craig was sorely tempted. Yes, that was what he was here for. But—

"You see, Mrs. Frobisher," he said, "I rather jibbed the toil last night. Camille—er—Miss Navarre, has been working like a pack-mule for weeks past. Tends to neglect her fodder. So I asked her to step out for a plate of diet and a bottle of vintage "

"That was *so* like you, Dr. Craig."

"Yes—I'm like that. We sort of banished dull care for an hour or two, and as a matter of fact, carried on pretty late. The chief is anxious about the job. He has more or less given me a deadline. I'm only making up for lost time. And so, please excuse me. Sound the trumpets, beat the drum when cocktails are served."

He grinned boyishly and went upstairs. Stella went to look for Camille. She had discovered, in this young product of the Old World, something that the New World had been unable to give her. Stella Frobisher was often desperately lonely. She had never loved her husband passionately. Passion had passed her by.

In the study, Michael Frobisher had been talking on the phone. He had just hung up when Stein came in.

"Listen," he said. "What's this man, Sam, doing here?"

Stein's heavy features registered nothing.

"I don't know."

"Talk to him. Find out. I trust nobody. l never employed that moron. Somebody has split us wide open. It isn't just a leak. Somebody was in the Huston Building last night that had no right to be there. This man was supposed to be in Philadelphia. Who *knows* he was in Philadelphia? Check him up, Stein. It's vital."

"I can try to do. But his talk is so foolish I cannot believe he means it. He walks into my room, just now, and asks if I happen to have an old razor blade."

"What for?"

"He says, to scrape his pipe bowl."

Michael Frobisher glared ferociously.

"Ask him to have a drink. Give him plenty. Then talk to him."

"I can try it."

"Go and try it."

Stein stolidly departed on this errand. There were those who could have warned him that it was a useless one.

Upstairs, in his room, Morris Craig had taken from his bag ink, pencils, brushes, and all the other implements of a craftsman's craft. He had borrowed a large blotting-pad from the library to do service in lieu of a drawing board.

Stella and Camille had gone out into the garden.

The sun was shining.

And over this seemingly peaceful scene there hung a menace, an invisible cloud. The fate of nations was suspended on a hair above their heads. Of all those in Falling Waters that morning, probably Michael Frobisher was the most deeply disturbed. He paced up and down the restricted floor space of his study, black brows drawn together over a deep wrinkle, his eyes haunted.

When Stein came in without knocking, Frobisher jumped around like a stag at bay. He collected himself.

"Well—what now?"

Stein, expressionless, offered a card on a salver. He spoke tonelessly.

"Sir Denis Nayland Smith is here."

Chapter XVII

"I can tell you, broadly, what happened last night," said Nayland Smith. "It was an attempt to steal the final plans assumed to be locked in Craig's safe."

"I guessed as much," Michael Frobisher replied.

Under drawn brows, he was studying the restless figure pacing to and fro in his study, fouling the air with fumes from a briar pipe which, apparently, Smith had neglected to clean since the day he bought it. Frobisher secretly resented this appropriation of his own parade ground, but recognized that he was powerless to do anything about it.

"The safe was opened."

"You're sure of that?"

"Quite!" Smith rapped, glancing aside at Frobisher. "It was the work of an expert. Dr. Fu Manchu employs none but experts."

"Dr. Fu Manchu! Then it wasn't—"

Smith pulled up right in front of Frobisher, as he sat there behind his desk.

"Well—go on. Whom did you suspect?"

Frobisher twisted a half-smoked cigar between his lips.

"Come to think, I don't know."

"But you do know that when a project with such vast implications nears maturity, big interests become involved. Agents of several governments are watching every move in your dangerous game. And there's another agent who represents no government, but who acts for a powerful and well organized group."

"Are you talking about Vickers?" Frobisher growled.

"No. Absurd! This isn't a commercial group. It's an organization controlled by Dr. Fu Manchu. In all probability, Dr Fu Manchu was in Craig's office last night."

"But—"

"The only other possibility is that the attempt was made by a Soviet spy. Have you reason to suspect any member of your staff?"

"I doubt that any Russian has access to the office."

"Why a Russian?" Nayland Smith asked. "Men of influence and good standing in other countries have worked for Communism. It offers glittering prizes. Why not a citizen of the United States?"

Frobisher watched him covertly. "True enough."

"Put me clear on one point. Because a false move, now, might be fatal. You have employed no private investigator?"

"No, sir. Don't trust my affairs to strangers."

"Where are Craig's original plans?"

Michael Frobisher glanced up uneasily.

"In my New York bank."

In this, Michael Frobisher was slightly misinformed. His wife, presenting an order typed on Huston Electric notepaper and apparently signed by her husband, had withdrawn the plans two days before, on her way from an appointment with Professor Hoffmeyer.

"Complete blueprints—where?"

"Right here in the house."

"Were they in the safe that was opened the other night?"

"No, sir—they were not."

"Whoever inspected the plant in the laboratory would be a trained observer. Would it, in your opinion, be possible to reconstruct the equipment after such an examination?"

Michael Frobisher frowned darkly.

"I want you to know that I'm not a physicist," he answered. "I'm not even an engineer. I'm a man of business. But in my opinion, no—it wouldn't. He would have had to dismantle it. Craig and Shaw report it hadn't been touched. Then, without the transmuter, that plant is plain dynamite."

Nayland Smith crossed and stared out at the woods beyond the window.

"I understand that this instrument—whatever it may be—is already under construction. Only certain valves are lacking. Craig will probably complete his work today. Mr. Frobisher"—he turned, and his glance was hard—"your estate is a lonely one."

Frobisher's uneasiness grew. He stood up.

"You think I shouldn't have had Craig out here, with that work?"

"I think," said Smith, "that whilst it would be fairly easy to protect the Huston laboratory, now that we know what we're up

598

against, this house surrounded by sixty acres, largely woodland, is a colt of a different color. By tonight, there will be inflammable material here. Do you realize that if Fu Manchu—or the Kremlin— first sets up a full-scale Craig plant, Fu Manchu—or the Kremlin— will be master of the world?"

"You're sure, dead sure, that they're *both* out to get it?"

Frobisher's voice was more than usually hoarse.

"I have said so. One of the two has a flying start. I want to see your radar alarm system and I want to inspect your armory. I'm returning to New York. Two inquiries should have given results. One leading to the hideout of Dr. Fu Manchu, the other to the identity of the Soviet agent."

Camille and Stella Frobisher came in from the garden.

"You know," Stella was saying, "I believe we have discovered something."

"All we seem to have discovered," Camille replied, "is that there are strange gaps in your memory, and strange gaps in mine. The trouble in your case seems to have begun after you consulted Professor Hoffmeyer about your nerves."

"Yes, dear, it *did*. You see, I had *been* so *worried* about Mike. I thought he was *working* too hard. In his way, dear, he's *rather* a treasure. Dr. Pardoe, who is a *neighbor* of ours, suggested, almost *playfully*, that I consult the professor."

"And your nerves improved?"

"*Enormously*. I began to *sleep* again. But these *queer* lapses came on. I *told* him. He *reassured* me. I'm not at *all* certain, dear, that we have *discovered* anything after all. *Your* lapses began before you had *ever* seen him."

"Yes." Camille was thinking hard. "The trouble doesn't seem to be with the professor's treatment, after all. Quite apart from which, I have no idea if I ever consulted him at all."

"No, dear—I quite *understand*." Stella squeezed her hand, sympathetically. "You have no *idea* how *completely* I understand."

They were crossing the library, together, when there came a sudden, tremendous storm of barking. It swept in upon the peace of Falling Waters, a hurricane of sound.

"Whatever is it?" Camille whispered.

As if in answer to her question, Sam entered through open french windows. He had removed his topcoat, his cerise scarf, and his slate-grey hat. He wore the sort of checked suit for which otherwise innocent men have been lynched. He grinned happily at Camille.

"Morning, lady."

"Good morning, Sam. I didn't expect to see you."

"Pleasant surprise, eh? Same with me." The barking continued; became a tornado. "There's a guy outside says he's brought some dogs."

"*Oh*!" Stella's face lighted up. "*Now* we shall be *safe*! How splendid. Have they sent *all* the dogs?"

"Sounds to me like they sent all they had."

"And a *kennelman*?"

Stella hadn't the slightest idea who Sam was, but she accepted his striking presence without hesitation.

"Sure. He's a busy guy, too."

"I must go and *see* them at once!" She put her arm around Camille. "Do *come* with me, dear!"

Camille smiled at Sam.

"I should love to."

"The guy is down there by the barbed-wire entanglements." Sam stood in the window, pointing. "You can't miss him. He's right beside a truckload of maybe a couple hundred dogs."

Camille and Stella hurried out, Stella almost dancing with excitement.

Their voices—particularly Stella's—were still audible even above the barrage of barking, when Nayland Smith and Michael Frobisher came into the library.

"You have a fair assortment of sporting guns and an automatic or two," Smith was saying. "But you're low on ammunition."

"Do you expect a siege?"

"Not exactly. But I expect developments."

Nayland Smith crossed to the glazed cabinet and stood before it, pulling at the lobe of his ear. Then he tilted his head sideways, listening.

"Dogs," he rapped. "Why all the dogs?"

Frobisher met his glance almost apologetically.

"It's Mrs. F.'s idea. I do try to keep all this bother from her, but she seems to have got onto it. She ordered a damned pack of these

600

German police dogs from some place. There's a collection of kennels down there like a Kaffir village. She's had men at work for a week fixing barbed wire. Falling Waters is a prison camp!"

"Not a bad idea. I have known dogs to succeed where men and machines failed. But, tell me"—he pointed to the cabinet—"how does this thing work?"

"Well—it's simple enough in principle. *How* it works I don't know. Ground plan of the property. Anyone moving around, when it's connected up, marks his trail on the scoreboard."

"I see."

"I'm having Craig overhaul it, when he has time. If you'll step into my study again for just a minute, I'll get the chart of the layout, which will make the thing more clear."

Nayland Smith glanced at his wrist-watch.

"I can give you just ten minutes, Mr. Frobisher."

They returned to Frobisher's study.

Sunshine poured into the empty library. A beautiful Italian casket, silver studded with semi-precious stones, glowed as though lighted by inner fires, or become transparent. The pure lines of the Discus Thrower were sharply emphasized. Barking receded as the pack was removed to the "Kaffir village" erected at Mrs. Frobisher's command.

Then Michael Frobisher came back. Crossing to the desk, he sat down and unlocked a drawer. He took out a chart in a folder, a chart which indicated points of contact surrounding the house as well as free zones. He pressed a bell button and waited, glancing about him.

Stein came in and Frobisher turned.

"Take this to Sir Denis in the study. Tell him I'll be right along in two minutes."

Stein nodded and went out with the folder.

Frobisher dialed a number, and presently:

"Yes—Frobisher," he said nervously. "Sir Denis Nayland Smith is here . . . They're onto us . . . Looks like all that money has been poured down the sewers . . . Huston Electric doesn't have a chance . . .'

He became silent, listening intently to someone on the other end of the line. His eyes kept darting right and left, furtively. Then:

601

"Got 'em all here, back of the drawer in this desk," he said, evidently in reply to a question . . . "That's none too easy . . . Yes, I'll have it in my hands by tonight, but . . . All right, give me the times.'

Frobisher pulled an envelope from a rack and picked up a pencil.

"It mayn't be possible," he said, writing rapidly. "Remember that . . . Nayland Smith is only *one* danger—"

He broke off. "Have to hang up. Call you later."

Stein, standing in the arched opening, was urgently pointing in the direction of the study. Frobisher nodded irritably and passed him on his way to rejoin Nayland Smith.

And, as Stein in turn retired, Sam stepped out from behind that Spanish screen which formed so artistic a background for the big walnut desk.

Without waste of time, he opened the drawer which Frobisher had just closed.

Chewing industriously, he studied the scribbled lines. Apparently they conveyed little or nothing to his mind for he was about to replace the envelope, and no doubt to explore further, when a dull, heavy voice spoke right behind him.

"Put up your hands. I have been watching you."

Stein had re-entered quite silently, and now had Sam covered by an automatic!

Sam dropped the envelope, and slowly raised his hands.

"Listen!—happen to have a postage stamp? That's what I was looking for."

Stein's reply was to step closer and run his hands expertly over Sam's person. Having relieved him of a heavy revolver and a flash-lamp, he raised his voice to a hoarse shout:

"Mr. Frobisher! Dr. Craig!"

"Listen. Wait a minute—"

There came the sound of a door thrown open. Michael Frobisher and Nayland Smith ran in. Frobisher's florid coloring changed a half tone.

"What's this, Stein? What goes on?"

"This man searches your desk, Mr. Frobisher. I catch him doing it."

As he spoke, he glanced significantly down at the envelope which Sam had dropped. Nayland Smith saw a look of consternation cross Frobisher's face, as he stooped, snatched it up, and slipped it into his pocket. But there was plenty of thunder in his voice when he spoke.

"I thought so! I thought so right along!"

"Suppose," rapped Smith, "we get the facts."

"The facts are plain! This man"—he pointed a quivering finger at Sam—"was going through my private papers! You took that gun off him?"

"Yes, sir."

"What's he doing armed in my house?" Frobisher roared.

"Part of the mystery is solved, anyway—"

A rataplan of footsteps on the stair heralded Morris Craig, in shirt-sleeves, and carrying his reading glasses. He came bounding down.

"Did I hear someone bawling my number?" he pulled up, considered the group, then stared from face to face. "What the devil's all this?"

Michael Frobisher turned now empurpled features in his direction.

"It's what I suspected, Craig. I told you I didn't like the looks of him. There stands the man who broke into the Huston office last night! There stands the man who broke into this house last week. Caught redhanded!"

Sam had dropped his hands, and now, ignoring Stein, he faced his accuser.

"Listen! Wait a minute! I needed a postage stamp. Any harm needing a postage stamp? I just pull a drawer open, just kind of casual, and look in the first thing I see there—"

Craig brushed his forelock back and stared very hard.

"But, I say, Sam—seriously—can you explain this?"

"Sure. I am explaining it!"

Nayland Smith had become silent, but now:

"Does the envelope happen to contain stamps, Mr. Frobisher?" he jerked.

"No, sir." Michael Frobisher glared at him. "It doesn't. That inquiry is beside the point. As I understand you represent law and order in this house, I'm sorry—but will you arrange for the arrest of that man."

His accusing finger was directed again at Sam.

"I mean to say," Craig broke in, "I may have missed something. But this certainly seems to me—"

"It's just plain silly," said Sam. "People getting so het up."

Came another rush, of lighter footsteps. Camille and Mrs. Frobisher ran in. They halted, thunderstruck by what they saw.

"*Whatever* is going on?" Stella demanded.

"Sam!" Camille whispered—and crossing to his side, laid her hand on his shoulder. "What has happened?"

Sam stopped chewing, and patted the encouraging hand. His upraised spectacles were eloquent.

"Thanks for the inquiry," he said. "I'm in trouble."

"You *are*!" Frobisher assured him. "Sir Denis! This is either a common thief or a foreign spy. In either case, I want him jailed."

Nayland Smith, glancing from Sam to Frobisher, snapped his fingers irritably.

"It is absurd," said Camille in a quiet voice.

"Listen!" Sam patted her hand again and turned to Smith. "I'm sorry. I took chances. The pot's on the boil, and I thought maybe Mr. Frobisher, even right now, might be thinking more about Huston Electric than about bigger things. I guess I was wrong. But acted for the best."

Michael Frobisher made a choking sound, like that of a faulty radiator.

"You see, Mr. Frobisher," said Nayland Smith, "whatever their faults, your police department is very thorough. James Sampson, an operative of the F.B.I., whom you know as Sam, was placed in the Huston research laboratory by his chief, Raymond Harkness, a long time before I was called in. I regret that this has occurred. But he is working entirely in your interests . . ."

Chapter XVIII

Luncheon at Falling Waters was not an unqualified success. Both in the physical and psychical sense, a shadow overhung the feast.

Promise of the morning had not been fulfilled. Young spring shrank away before returning winter; clouds drew a dull curtain over the happy landscape, blotting out gay skies. And with the arrival of Professor Hoffmeyer, a spiritual chill touched at least two of the company.

Camille experienced terror when the stooped figure appeared. His old-fashioned morning coat, his tinted glasses and black gloves, the ebony stick, rang a loud note of alarm within. But the moment he spoke, her terror left her.

"So this," said the professor in his guttural German-English, "is the little patient who comes to see me not—ha?"

Camille felt helpless. She could think of nothing to say, for she didn't know if she had ever seen him before.

"Never mind. Some other time. I shall send you no account."

Michael Frobisher hated the man on sight. His nerves had remained badly on edge since the incident with Sam. He gave the professor a grip of his powerful fingers calculated to hurt.

"Ach! not so hard! not so hard! These"—Hoffmeyer raised gloved hands—"and these"—touching the dark glasses—"and this"—tapping his ebony stick on the fioor—"are proofs that in war men become beasts. I ask you to remember that nails were torn from fingers, and eyes exposed to white heat, in some of those Nazi concentration camps. These things, Mr. Frobisher, could be again . . . While we may, let us be gentle."

Dr. Pardoe treated the professor in a detached way, avoiding technical topics, and rather conveying that he doubted his ability. But not so Mrs. Pardoe. She unbent to the celebrated consultant in a highly gracious manner. A tall, square woman, who always wore black, the sad and sandy Pardoe was not for her first love. There had been two former husbands. Nobody knew why. There

605

was something ominous about the angular frame. She resembled a draped gallows . . .

Professor Hoffmeyer addressed much of his conversation to Craig; and Mrs. Pardoe hung on his every word.

"You are that Morris Craig," he said, during luncheon, "who reads a paper on the direction of neutrons, at Oxford, two years ago—ha?"

"The same, Professor. Amazing memory. I am that identical egg in the old shell. Rather stupid paper. Learned better since."

"Modesty is a poor cloak for a man of genius to wear. Discard it, Dr. Craig. It would make me very happy to believe that your work shall be for the good of humanity. This world of ours is spinning—spinning on, to disaster. We are a ship which nears the rocks, with fools at the prow and fanatics at the helm."

"But is there no way to prevent such a disaster?" Mrs. Pardoe asked, in a voice which seemed to come from a condemned cell.

"But most certainly. There could be a committee of men of high intelligence. To serve this committee would be a group of the first scientific brains in the world—such as that of Dr. Craig." For some reason, Camille shuddered at those words. "These would have power to enforce their decisions. If some political maniac threatens to use violence, he will be warned. If he neglects this warning—"

Professor Hoffmeyer helped himself to more fried oysters offered by Stein.

"You believe, then, there'll be another war?" grumbled Frobisher.

"How, otherwise, shall enslavement to Communism be avoided—ha?"

"Unless I misunderstood you," Dr. Pardoe interjected sandily, "your concept of good government approaches very closely to that of an intelligent Communist."

"An intelligent Communist is an impossibility. We have only to separate the rogues from the fools. Yes, Mr. Frobisher, there is danger of another war—from the same quarter as before. Those subhumans of the German General Staff who escaped justice. Those fellows with the traditions of the stockyard and the mentalities of adding machines. Those ghouls in uniform smell blood again. The Kremlin is feeding them meat."

"You mean," Camille asked softly, "that the Soviet Government is employing German ex-officers to prepare another war?"

The secret agent within was stirring. She wondered why this man knew.

"But of course. You are of France, and France has a long memory. Very well. Let France remember. If it shall come another war, those ignorant buffoons will destroy all, including themselves. This would not matter much if selected communities could be immunized. For almost complete destruction of human life on the planet is now a scientific possibility. It is also desirable. But indiscriminate slaughter—no. The new race must start better equipped than Noah."

When, luncheon over, the professor refused coffee and prepared to take his leave, there was no one present upon whom, in one way or another, he had failed to impress his singular personality. Stella Frobisher flutteringly begged a brief consultation before he left, and was granted one. Mrs. Pardoe made an appointment for the following Friday.

"There is nothing the matter with you," Professor Hoffmeyer told her, "which your husband cannot cure. But come if you so want. You all eat too much. See to it that you permit not here prohibitions, rationings, coupons. Communism knows no boxing laws. Communism strikes at the stomach, first. To this you could never stand up."

A car, in charge of a saturnine chauffeur who had declined to lunch in the kitchen, declined a drink, and spent his leisure wandering about the property, awaited him. As the professor was driven away, drops of rain began to patter on the terrace.

Night crept unnoticed upon Falling Waters.

Rain descended steadily, and a slight, easterly wind stole, eerie, through the trees. Stella did not merely *ask*, she extended an invitation to Dr. and Mrs. Pardoe to remain to dinner. But Mrs. Pardoe, already enveloped in a cloak like a velvet pall, reminded her husband that a patient was expected at eight-thirty. Stella saw them off.

"Oh, I'm so *nervous*. It's getting so *dark*. I shan't feel really *safe* until everything is bolted and *barred* . . ."

Coming out of her room, later, having changed to a dinner frock so simple that it must have been made in Paris, Camille almost ran into Sam on the corridor.

"Gee, Miss Navarre! You look like something wonderful!"

"That's very sweet of you, Sam! I had a dreadful shock—yes, truly—when you were discovered today."

"Sure. Shock to me! Ham performance. Must try to make up for it."

"Sam—you don't mind if I still call you Sam?'

"Love it. Sounds better your way."

"Now I know what you are really doing here, I can talk to you—well, sensibly. Dr. Craig thinks, and so, I know, does Sir Denis, that we haven't only to deal with this dreadful Fu Manchu." She paused for a moment after speaking the name. "That there is a Soviet agent watching us, too. Have you any ideas about him?"

Sam nodded. He had given up chewing and abandoned his spectacles. Presumably they had been part of a disguise.

"Working on it right now—and I think we're getting some place."

"Oh! I'm so glad."

"Sure. I got a nose for foreign agents. Smell 'em a mile off."

"Really?"

"Sure." He grinned happily. "You look a hundred per cent Caesar. Excuse my bad spelling!"

He went off along the corridor.

When Camille came down, she found Michael Frobisher busily bolting and barring the French windows.

"Mrs. F.'s got the jumps tonight," he explained. "I have to fix all the catches, myself, to reassure her. Just making the rounds." He gave Camille an admiring smile. "Hope all today's hokum, and the alarm back at the office, hasn't upset you?"

"It's kind of you, Mr. Frobisher, but although, naturally, I am disturbed about it, all the same I am most happy to be here."

"Good girl. Craig has finished his job, and the new diagram and notes are in my safe. That's where they stay. They are the property of Huston Electric, and the property of nobody else!"

As he went out, Morris Craig came downstairs, slim and boyish in his tuxedo. Without a word, he took Camille in his arms.

"Darling! I thought we were never going to be alone again!"

608

When he released her:

"Are you sure, Morris?" she whispered.

"Sure? Sure of what?"

"Sure that you really meant all you said last night?"

He answered her silently, and at great length.

"Camille! I only wish—"

"Yes?"

"Camille"—he lingered over her name—"I adore you. But I wish you weren't going to stay here tonight—"

"What? Whatever do you mean?"

She leaned back from him. Her eyes suddenly seemed to become of a darker shade of blue.

"I mean that, at last, it has dawned on this defective brain of mine that I have done something which may upset the world again—that other people know about it—that almost anything may happen."

"But Morris—surely nothing can happen *here*?"

"Can't it? Why is old Frobisher in such a panic? Why all the dogs and the burglar alarms? The devil of it is, we don't know our enemies. There might be a Russian spy hiding out there in the shrubbery. There might be a British agent—not that that would bother me—somewhere in this very house."

"Yes," said Camille quietly. "I suppose there might be."

"Above all," Craig went on presently, "there's this really frightful menace—Dr. Fu Manchu. Smith is more scared of him than of all the others rolled into a bundle."

"So am I . . . Listen for a moment, Morris. Sometimes I think I have seen him in a dream. Oh! It sounds ridiculous, and I can't quite explain what I mean. But I have a vague impression of a tall, gaunt figure in a yellow robe, with most wonderful hands, long finger-nails, and"—she paused momentarily—"most dreadful eyes. Something, today, brought the impression back to my mind—just as Professor Hoffmeyer came in."

Craig gently stroked her hair. He knew it would be a penal offense to disarrange it.

"Don't get jumpy again, darling. I gather that, in one of your fey moods, you wandered the highways and byways of Manhattan last night instead of keeping your date with the professor. But, certainly, the old lad is a rather alarming personality—although he bears no

609

resemblance to your yellow-robed mandarin. I'm sorry for him, and, of course, his Germanic discourse simply sparkles. But—"

"I didn't mean that the professor reminded me of the man I had dreamed about. It was—something different."

"Whatever it was, forget it." He held her very close; he whispered in her ear: "Camille! The moment we get back to New York, will you marry me?"

But Camille shrank away. The dark eyes looked startled—almost panic-stricken.

"Morris! Morris! No! No!"

He dropped his arms, stared at her. He felt that he had grown pale.

"No? Do you mean it?"

"I mean—oh, Morris, I don't quite know *what* I mean! Perhaps—that you startled me."

"How did I startle you?" he asked on a level, calm note.

"You—know so little about me."

"I know enough to know I love you."

"I should be very, very happy for us to go on—as we are. But, marriage—"

"What's wrong with marriage?"

Camille turned aside. A shaded lamp transformed her hair, where it swept down over her neck, to a torrent of molten copper. Craig put his hands hesitantly on her shoulders, and turned her about. He looked steadily into her eyes.

"Camille—you're not trying to tell me, by any chance, that you're married already?"

"A door banged upstairs. Stella's voice was heard.

"And *do* make quite sure, Stein—quite *sure*—that there isn't a *window* open." She appeared at the stairhead. "Even with everything *locked*, and the *dogs* loose, I know I shall never *sleep* a wink." She saw Camille below. "Shall *you*, dear?"

"I'm not at all sure that I shall," Camille smiled. "Except that I can see no reason why anything should happen tonight more than any other."

"I must really get *Stein* to *draw* those curtains," Stella declared. "I keep on imagining *eyes* looking in out of the *darkness*. And now, for *goodness* sake, let's all have a *drink*."

Stein had wheeled in trays of refreshments some time earlier, but had been called away by Mrs. Frobisher in order to bolt a trap leading to a loft over the house.

"May I help?" Camille asked.

And presently they were surrounding the mobile buffet.

Michael Frobisher joined them.

"If you take my advice, my dear," he said to Stella, "you and Miss Navarre will have a good stiff one each after dinner, and turn in early. Think no more about it. Agree with me, Craig?"

Morris Craig stopped looking at Camille long enough to reply:

"Quite. But, if I may say so, somebody should more or less hang about to keep an eye on this thing." He indicated the cabinet above the bookcase. "I have looked over the works and pass same as okay. By the way, Mrs. Frobisher, will the wolf pack be at large tonight?"

"Of course!" Stella assured him. "I have given *explicit* instructions to the *man*. Such a *gentle* character."

"I was wondering," Craig went on, "if the dogs mightn't set the gadget going?"

"Oh, I don't *think* so. They have a *track* of their *own*. *Right* around the *place*—if you *see* what I mean."

"Yes. I have observed the same—from without. Certain hounds of threatening aspect were roaming around within."

"If you remember the layout I showed you," said Frobisher, "showed Nayland Smith, too, there are three gates which would register here"—he crossed and rested a finger on the plan—"if they were opened. Whoever opened one would have Mrs. F.'s dogs on him, I guess. But the dogs can't reach the house."

"Most blessed dispensation," Craig murmured to him. "Although I confess the brutes are rather a comfort, with Dr. Fu Manchu and a set of thugs, plus the Soviet agent assisted by sundry moujiks and other comrades, lined up outside."

Camille was watching Craig in an almost pleading way. Frobisher took his arm, and growled in his ear:

"We'll split up into watches when the women turn in. As you say, somebody ought to be on the lookout right along tonight. Stein can stand watch until twelve. Then I'll take over—"

"No," said Craig firmly, and caught Camille's glance. "I am a party to this disorder, and I'm going to do my bit. After all, I'm accustomed to late hours . . ."

Manhattan danced on, perhaps a slightly more hectic dance, for this was Saturday night, and Saturday night is Broadway night. Rain, although still falling farther north, had ceased in the city. But a tent of sepia cloud stretched over New York, so that eternal fires, burning before the altars of those gods whose temples line the Street of a Million Lights, cast their glow up onto this sepia canopy and it was cast down again, as if rejected.

Two bored police officers smoked and played crap in Morris Craig's office on top of the Huston Building. And behind the steel door, in an atmosphere vibrant with repressed energy, Martin Shaw worked calmly, and skillfully, to complete the instrument known as a transmuter. The gods of Broadway were false gods. The god enshrined behind the steel door was a god of power.

But the two policemen went on playing crap

Chinatown was busy, also. Country innocents gaped at the Chinese façades, the Chinese signs, and felt that they were seeing sights worth coming to Babylon-on-Hudson to see. Town innocents, impressing their girls friends, ate Chinese food in the restaurants and pretended to know as much about it as Walter Winchell knows about everything.

Mai Cha had just ceased to sing in an apartment near the shop of Huan Tsung. Lao Tai had put his last message in the little cupboard.

And upstairs, Huan Tsung reclined against cushions, his eyes closed. The head of Dr. Fu Manchu looked out from the crystal. It might have reminded an Egyptologist of the majestic, embalmed head of Seti, that Pharaoh whose body lies in a Cairo museum.

"To destroy the plant alone is useless, Huan Tsung," came in coldly sibilant words. "I have dealt with this. Otherwise, I should not have risked a personal visit to the laboratory. I sprayed the essential elements with F.SO5. The action is deferred. No—it is necessary also to destroy the inventor—or to transfer him to other employment."

"This may be difficult," murmured Huan Tsung. "Time is the enemy of human perfection, Excellency."

"We shall see. Craig's original drawings were obtained for me by

612

Mrs. Frobisher. Only two blueprints of the transmuter exist. One is in the hands of the chief technician, who is working from it. The other is with a complete set in possession of Michael Frobisher. Drawings of the valves alone remain to be accounted for."

"But Excellency informs me that they, too, are finished."

"They are finished. Give me the latest reports. I will then give you final instructions."

"I shall summarize. Excellency's personal possessions have been removed from the Woolton Building as ordered. They are already shipped. Raymond Harkness has posted federal agents at all points covering Falling Waters—except one; the path through the woods from the highway remains open. Lao Tai will proceed to this point at the time selected. But the dogs—"

"I have provided for the dogs. Continue."

"Provision noted. It is believed but not confirmed that the Kremlin, recognizing the actual plant no longer to be available, hopes to obtain the set of blueprints and the final drawings from Falling Waters before it is too late."

"Upon what does this 'belief' rest?"

"Upon the fact, Excellency, that Sokolov has ordered his car to be ready at ten o'clock tonight—and is taking a bodyguard."

So long a silence followed that Huan Tsung raised his wrinkled lids and looked at the crystal.

The eyes of Dr. Fu Manchu were filmed over, a phenomenon with which Huan Tsung was familiar. The brilliant brain encased in that high, massive skull, was concentrated on a problem. When the film cleared, a decision would have been made. And, as he watched, in a flash the long, narrow eyes became emerald-bright.

"Use the Russian party as a diversion, Huan Tsung. No contact must be made. Koenig has acquainted himself with the zones controlled by the alarm system, and M'goyna is already placed and fully instructed. Mrs. Frobisher has her instructions, also. Use all your resources. This is an emergency. At any moment, now, Nayland Smith will have the evidence he is seeking. Win or lose, I must leave New York before daybreak. Proceed . . ."

Chapter XIX

Morris Craig sat smoking in a deep leathern armchair. The darkened library seemed almost uncannily silent. Rain had ceased. But dimly he could hear water dripping on the terrace outside.

It was at about this moment that the two crap players in his office were jerked violently out of their complacent boredom.

Three muffled crashes in the laboratory brought them swiftly to their feet. There came a loud cry—a cry of terror. Another crash. The steel door burst open, and Martin Shaw, white as a dead man, tottered down the steps!

They ran to him. He collapsed on the sofa, feebly waving them away. A series of rending, tearing sounds was followed by a cloud of nearly vaporous dust which came pouring out of the laboratory in grey waves.

"Stand back!"

"We must close the door!"

One of the men raced up, and managed to close the door. He came down again, suffocating, fighting for breath. A crash louder than any before shook the office.

"What is it?" gasped the choking man. "Is there going to be an explosion? For God's sake"—he clutched his throat—"what's happening?"

"Disintegration," muttered Shaw wildly. "Disintegration. The plant is crumbling to . . . powder."

Pandemonium in the Huston Building. Fruits of long labor falling from the branches. A god of power reduced to a god of clay. But not a sound to disturb the silence of Falling Waters; a silence awesome, a silence in which many mysteries lay hidden. Yet it was at least conducive to thought.

And Morris Craig had many things to think about He would have more before the night ended.

In the first place, he couldn't understand why Michael Frobisher had been so damnably terse when he had insisted on

614

standing the twelve to four watch. At four, Sam was taking over. Sam had backed him up in this arrangement. Craig had had one or two things to say, privately, to Sam, concerning the deception practiced on him; and would have others to mention to Nayland Smith, when he saw Smith again. But Sam, personally, was a sound enough egg.

So Morris Craig mused, in the silent library.

What was that?

He stood up, and remained standing, motionless, intent.

Dimly he had heard, or thought he had heard, the sound of a hollow cough.

He experienced that impression, common to all or most of us, that an identical incident had happened to him before. But when—where?

There was no repetition of the cough—no sound; yet a sense of furtive movement. Guiding himself by a sparing use of a flashlamp, he crossed to the foot of the stair. He shone a beam upward.

"Is that you, Camille?" he called softly.

There was no reply. Craig returned to his chair . . .

What was old Frobisher up to, exactly? Why had he so completely lost his balance about the envelope business? Of course, Stein had dramatized it absurdly. Queer fish, Stein. Not a fellow he, personally, could ever take to. Barbarous accent. Clearly, it had forced Nayland Smith's hand. But what had Smith's idea been? Was there someone in the household he didn't trust?. . . Probably Stein.

No doubt the true explanation lay in the fact that Frobisher, having sunk well over half a million dollars in his invention, now saw it slipping through his fingers. It might not be the sort of thing to trust to development by a commercial corporation, but still—rough luck for Frobisher . . .

Then Craig was up again

This time, that hollow cough seemed to come from the front of the house.

He dropped his cigarette and went over to the arched opening which gave access to Frobisher's study, and, beyond, to the cedar-wood dining room. He directed a light along a dark passage. It was empty. He crossed the library again and opened a door on the other side. There was no one there.

Was he imagining things?

This frame of mind was entirely due to the existence of a shadowy horror known as Dr. Fu Manchu. He didn't give a hoot for the Soviet agent, whom- or whatever he might be. Nobody took those fellows seriously. The British agent he discounted entirely. If there had been one, Smith would have known him.

The idea of watching in the dark had been Sam's. As an F.B.I. operative, he had carried the point. Naturally enough, he wanted to get his man. It was a ghostly game, nevertheless. That drip-drip-drip of water outside was getting on Craig's nerves.

Incidentally, where *was* Sam? Unlikely that he had turned in.

But, above all, where was Camille? There had been no chance to make it definite; but he had read the message in her eyes as she went upstairs with Stella Frobisher to mean, "I shall come down again."

Frobisher had retired shortly after the women. "I'm going to sleep—and the hell with it all!"

A faint rustling sound on the stairs—and Craig was up as if on springs.

The ray of his lamp shone on Camille, a dressing gown worn over a night robe that he didn't permit himself to look at. Her bare ankles gleamed like ivory.

"Camille!—darling! At last!"

He trembled as he took her in his arms. She was so softly alluring. He released her and led her to the deep leathern settee, forcing a light note, as he extinguished the lamp.

"Forgive the blackout. Captain's orders."

"I know," she whispered.

He found her hand in his, and kissed her fingers silently. Then, as a mask for his excited emotions:

"I have a bone to pick with you," he said in his most flippant manner. "What did you mean by turning down my offer to make an honest woman of you? Explain this to me, briefly, and in well-chosen words."

Camille crept closer to him in the dark.

"I mean to explain." Her soft voice was unsteady. "I came to explain to you—now."

He longed to put his arms around her. But some queer sense of restraint checked him.

616

"I'm waiting, darling."

"You may not know—I don't believe you do, even yet— that for a long time, ever so long"—how he loved the Gallic intonations which came when she was deeply moved!—"your work has been watched. At least, you know now, when it is finished, that they will—stick at nothing."

"Who are 'they'? You mean the Kremlin and Dr. Fu Manchu?"

"Yes. These are the only two you have to be afraid of . . . But there is also a—British agent."

"Doubtful about that, myself. How d'you know there's a British agent?"

"Because I am the British agent."

There were some tense moments, during which neither spoke. It might almost have seemed that neither breathed. They sat there, side by side, in darkness, each wondering what the other was thinking. *Drip-drip-drip* went the rainwater . . . Then Craig directed the light of his lamp onto Camille's face. She turned swiftly away, raised her hands:

"Don't! Don't!"

"Camille!" Craig switched the light off . . . "Good God!"

"Don't look at me!" Camille went on. "I don't want you to see me! I had made up my mind to tell you tonight, and I am going to be quite honest about it. I didn't think, and I don't think now, that the work I undertook was wrong. Although, of course, when I started, I had never met you."

Craig said nothing . . .

"If I have been disloyal to anyone, it is to Mr. Frobisher. For you must realize, Morris, the dreadful use which could be made of such a thing. You must realize that it might wreck the world. No government could be blind to that."

Subtly, in the darkness, Morris Craig had drawn nearer. Now, suddenly, he had his arm around her shoulders.

"No, Morris! Don't! Don't! Not until I have told you everything." He felt her grow suddenly rigid. "What was that?"

It was the sound of a hollow cough, in the distance.

Craig sprang up.

"I don't know. But I have heard it before. Is it inside the house, or out?"

Switching on the lamp, he ran in turn to each of the doors. and stood listening. But Falling Waters remained still. Then he directed the light onto Camille—and away again, quickly. In a moment he was beside her.

"Morris!"

"Let me say something "

"But, Morris, do you truly understand that I have been reporting your work, step by step, to the best of my ability? Because I never quite understood it. I have been spying on you, all through . . . At last, I couldn't bear it any longer. When Sir Denis came on the scene, l thought I was justified in asking for my release . . ."

Morris's kiss silenced her. She clung to him, trembling. Her heart fluttered like a captive bird released, and at last:

"You see now, Morris, why I felt it was well enough for us to be— lovers. But how could I marry you, when—"

"You were milking my brains?" he whispered in her ear. But it was a gay whisper. "You little redheaded devil! This gives me another bone to pick with Smith. Why didn't he tell me?"

"I was afraid he would! Then I remembered he couldn't . . . Morris! I shall be all bruises! There are traditions in the Secret Service."

At which moment, amid a subdued buzzing sound like that of a fly trapped in a glass, the cabinet over the bookcase came to life!

Camille grasped Craig's hand as he leapt upright, and clung to it obstinately. A rectangle in the library darkness, every detail of the grounds surrounding Falling Waters showed as if touched with phosphorescence.

"We're off!" Craig muttered. "Look!"

A shadow moved slowly across the chart.

"That's the back porch!" Camille whispered. "Someone right outside."

"Don't panic, darling. Wait."

The faint shadow moved on to where a door was marked. It stopped. The buzzing ceased. The chart faded.

"Someone came into the kitchen!"

"Run back and hide on the stair."

"But—"

"Please do as I say, Camille."

Camille released his hand, and he stood, automatic ready, facing that doorway which led to the back premises.

He saw nothing. But he was aware that the door had been opened. Then:

"Don't shoot me, Craig," rapped a familiar voice, "and don't make a sound."

A flashlamp momentarily lighted the library. Nayland Smith stood there watching him—hatless, the fur collar of his old trench coat turned up about his ears. Then Smith's gaze flickered for a second. There came a faint rustling from the direction of the stairs—and silence.

Sam appeared just behind Smith. The lamp was switched off.

"Smith!—How did you get in?"

"Not so loud. I have been standing by outside for some time."

"I let him in, doc," Sam explained.

"There's some kind of thing slinking around out there," Nayland Smith went on, an odd note in his voice, "which isn't human—"

"What on earth do you mean?"

"Just that. It isn't a baboon, and it isn't a man. Normally, I should form a party and hunt it down. I have a strong suspicion it is some specimen out of Fu Manchu's museum of horrors. But"—Craig, dimly, could hear Smith moving in the dark—"just shine a light onto this."

Craig snapped his lamp up. Nayland Smith stood right beside him, holding out an enlargement of a snapshot. Sam stood at Smith's elbow. Upstairs, a door closed softly.

The picture was that of a stout, bearded man crowned with a mane of white hair; he had small, round, inquisitive eyes.

"Lights out," Smith directed. "I waited at police headquarters for that to arrive. Recognize him?"

"Never saw him in my life."

"Correct. Following his release from a Nazi prison camp, he disappeared. I think I know where he went. But it's of no immediate importance. That is the once celebrated Viennese psychiatrist, Doctor Carl Hoffmeyer!"

"What do you say?"

"Smart, ain't it?" Sam murmured.

"The man New York knew as Professor Hoffmeyer was Dr. *Fu Manchu!*"

"Good God! But he was here today!"

"I know. A great commander must be prepared to take all the risks he imposes on others."

"But he speaks English with a heavy German accent! And—"

"Dr. Fu Manchu speaks every civilized language with perfect facility—with or without an accent! Lacking this evidence, I could do nothing. But I made one big mistake—"

"We all made it," said Sam. "You're no more to blame than the rest."

"Thanks," rapped Smith. "But the blame is mine. I had the Hoffmeyer clinic covered, and I thought he was trapped."

"Well?" Craig asked eagerly.

"He didn't go back there!"

"Listen!" Sam broke in again. "We had three good men on his tail, but he tricked 'em!"

There was something increasingly eerie about this conversation in the dark.

"The clinic remains untouched," Nayland Smith continued. "But Fu Manchu's private quarters, which patients never saw, have been stripped. Police raided hours ago."

"Then where has he gone?"

"I don't know." Nayland Smith's voice had a groan in it.

"But all that remains for him to do, in order to complete his work, is here, in this house!"

"Shouldn't we rouse up Frobisher?" Craig asked excitedly

"No. There are certain things—I don't want Mr. Frobisher to know yet."

"Such as, for instance?"

"Such as—this is going to hit you where it hurts—that your entire plant in the Huston laboratory was destroyed tonight—"

"*What!*"

"Quiet, man!" Nayland Smith grasped Craig's arm in the darkness. "I warned you it would hurt. The Fire Department has the job in hand. It isn't their proper province. The thing is just crumbling away, breaking like chocolate. Last report to reach the radio car, that huge telescope affair—I don't know it's name—has crashed onto the floor."

"But, Smith! . . ."

"I know. It's bad."

"Thank heaven! My original plans are safe in a New York City bank vault!"

Silence fell again, broken only by a dry cough from Sam, until:

"They are not," Nayland Smith said evenly. "They were taken out two days ago."

"Taken out? By whom?"

"In person, by Mrs. Frobisher. In fact, by Dr. Fu Manchu. Frobisher doesn't know—but the only records of your invention which remain, Craig, are the blueprints hidden somewhere in this house!"

"They were in back of the desk there," Sam mumbled. "But they've vanished."

"You're not suggesting"—Craig heard the note of horrified incredulity in his own voice—"that Mrs. Frobisher—"

"Mrs. Frobisher," said Nayland Smith, "is as innocent in this matter as Miss Navarre. But—we are dealing with Dr. Fu Manchu!"

"Why are we staying in the dark? What happens next?"

"What happens next I don't know. We are staying in the dark because a man called Dimitri Sokolov, a Soviet official in whom Ray Harkness is interested, has a crew of armed thugs down by the lower gate . . . Sokolov seems to be expecting someone."

621

Chapter XX

In the stillness which followed, Morris Craig tried, despairfully, to get used to the idea that the product of months, many weary months, of unremitting labor, had been wiped out . . . How? By whom? He felt stunned. Could it be that Shaw, in a moment of madness, had attempted a test?

"Is poor old Shaw—" he began.

"Shaw is safe," Smith interrupted. "But badly shaken. He has no idea what occurred. Quite unable to account for it—as I am unable to account for what's going on here. I'm not referring to the presence of someone, or some *thing*, stalking just outside the area controlled by the alarms, but to a thing that isn't stalking."

"*What*?" Sam asked.

"The pack of dogs! Listen. Not a sound—but the drip of water. What has become of the dogs?"

"Gee!" Sam muttered. "I keep thinking how dead quiet everything is outside, and kind of wondering why I expect it to be different. Funny I never came to it there was no dogs!"

They all stood motionless for a few moments. That ceaseless drip-drip-drip alone broke the silence of Falling Waters—a haunting signature tune.

"Where is this kennelman quartered?" Nayland Smith asked jerkily.

He was unable to hide the fact that his nerves were strung to concert-violin pitch.

"Middle gate-cottage," came promptly from Sam. "I'll go call him. Name of Kelly. I can get the extension from out here."

"Speak quietly," Smith warned. "Order him to loose the dogs."

Sam's flashlamp operated for a moment. It cast fantastic moving shadows on the library walls, showed Nayland Smith gaunt, tense; painted Craig's pale face as a mask of tragedy. Then—Sam was gone.

622

Craig could hear Nayland Smith moving, restless, in darkness. Obscurely Sam's mumbling reached them. He had left the communicating doors open . . . Then, before words which might have relieved the tension came to either, the alarm cabinet glowed into greenish-blue life, muted buzzing began.

"What's this?"

A shadow moved across the plan. It was followed by a second shadow.

"Someone crossing the tennis court!" Craig's voice sounded hushed, unfamiliar. "Running!"

"Someone hot on his heels!"

"Into the rose garden now!"

"Second shadow gaining! First shadow doubling back!"

"That's the path through the apple orchard. Leads to a stile on the lane—"

"But," said Nayland Smith, "if my memory serves me, the dog track crosses before the stile?"

"Yes. One of the gates in the wire is there."

And, as Craig spoke, came a remote baying.

The dogs were out.

"Listen." Sam had joined them . . . "Say! What's this?"

"Action!" rapped Smith. "Was Kelly awake?"

"Sure. But listen. *Mrs. Frobisher* called him some time tonight, and ordered him to see the dogs *weren't loosed*! Can you beat it? But wait a minute. *Mr.* Frobisher gives him the same order half an hour earlier! . . . Oh, hell! Did you hear that?"

"He's through the gate," said Nayland Smith . . .

The first shadow showed on the chart at a point where a gate in the wire was marked. The second shadow moved swiftly back. A dim blur swept along the track. Baying increased in volume . . . A shot—a second. And then came a frenzied scream, all the more appalling because muted by distance.

"Merciful God!" Craig whispered. "The dogs have got him!

Nayland Smith already had the french windows open. A sting of damp, cold air pierced the library. There came another, faint scream. Baying merged into a dreadful growling . . .

"Lights!" Smith cried. "Where's the man, Stein?"

As Sam switched the lights up, Stein was revealed standing in the arched opening which led to Michael Frobisher's study. He was fully dressed, and chalky white.

"Here I am, sir."

A sound of faraway shouting became audible. Stella Frobisher ran out onto the stairhead, a robe thrown over her nightdress.

"*Please*—oh, *please* tell me what has *happened*? That *ghastly* screaming! And *where* is Mike?"

She had begun to come down, when Camille appeared behind her. Camille had changed and wore a tweed suit.

"Mrs. Frobisher!" Craig looked up. "Isn't the chief in his room?"

"No, he isn't!"

Camille's arm was around Stella's shoulders now.

"Don't go down, Mrs. Frobisher. Let's go back. I think it would be better if you dressed."

She spoke calmly. Camille had lived through other crises.

"Miss Navarre!" Nayland Smith called sharply.

"Yes, Sir Denis?"

"Go with Mrs. Frobisher to her room, and both of you stay there with the door locked. Understand?"

Camille hesitated for a moment, then: "Yes, Sir Denis," she answered. "Please come along, Mrs. Frobisher."

"But I want to *know* where Mike is—"

Her voice faded away, as Camille very gently steered her back to her room.

Nayland Smith faced Stein.

"Mr. Frobisher is not in his study?"

"No, sir."

"How do you know?"

"I do not retire tonight. I am anxious. Just now, I am in there to look."

"Was the window open?"

Stein's crushed features became blank.

"Was the window open?" Nayland Smith repeated harshly.

"Yes. I closed it."

"Come on, Craig! Sampson—follow!"

"Okay, chief."

Craig and Nayland Smith ran out, Sam behind them.

Stein stood by the opening, and listened. Somewhere out in the misty night, an automatic spat angrily. There was a dim background of barking dogs, shouting men. He turned, in swift decision, and went back through that doorway which led to the kitchen quarters.

He took up the phone there, dialled a number, waited, and then began to speak rapidly—but not in English. He spoke in a language which evidently enlarged his vocabulary. His pallid features twitched as he poured out a torrent of passionate words . . .

Something hard was jammed into the ribs of his stocky body.

"Drop that phone, Feodor Stenovicz. I have a gun in your back and your family history in my pocket. Too late to tip off Sokolov. He's in the bag. Put your hands right behind you. No, not up—behind!"

Stein dropped the receiver and put his hands back. There was sweat on his low forehead. Steel cuffs were snapped over his wrists.

"Now that's settled, we can get together."

Stein turned—and looked into the barrel of a heavy-calibre revolver which Sam favored. Sam's grinning face was somewhere behind it, in a red cloud.

"Suppose," Sam suggested, "we step into your room and sample some more of the boss's bourbon? What you gave me this morning tasted good."

They had gone when Camille came running along the corridor to the stairhead. And there was no one in the library.

"Please stay where you are." she called back. "I will find out."

A muffled cry came from Stella Frobisher: "Open the *door*! I can't stay *here*!"

Camille raced downstairs, wilfully deaf to a wild beating on wood panels.

"Let me *out*!"

But Camille ran on to the open windows.

"Morris! Morris! Where are you?"

She stood there clutching the wet frame, peering into chilly darkness. Cries reached her—the vicious yap of a revolver —the barking of dogs.

"Morris!"

She ran out onto the terrace. A long way off she could see moving lights.

Camille had already disappeared when Sam entered the library, having locked Stein in the wine cellar. Switching on his flash, he began hurrying in the direction of that distant mêlée.

The library remained empty for some time. With the exception of Stein, all the servants slept out. So that despairing calls of "Unlock the door, Mike! Mike!" won no response. And presently they ceased.

Then, subdued voices and a shuffling of feet on wet gravel heralded the entrance of an ominous cortege. Upon an extemporized stretcher carried by a half-dressed gardener and Kelly, the grizzled kennelman, Michael Frobisher was brought in. Sam came first, to hold the windows wide and to allow of its entrance. Nayland Smith followed. There were other men outside, but they remained there.

"Get a doctor," Smith directed. "He's in a bad way."

They lifted Frobisher onto the settee. He still wore his dinner clothes, but they were torn to tatters. His face and his hands were bloody, his complexion was greyish-purple. He groaned and opened his eyes when they laid him down. But he seemed to be no more than semi-conscious, and almost immediately relapsed.

Kelly went out again, with the empty stretcher. A murmur of voices met him.

"I know Dr. Pardoe's number," said the gardener, a youthful veteran whose frightened blond hair had never lain down since the Normandy landing. "Shall I call him?"

His voice quavered.

"Yes," rapped Smith. "Tell him it's urgent."

As the man hurried away to the phone in the back premises:

"Nothing on him?" Sam asked.

"Not a thing! Yet he was alone—with the dogs, God help him! I believe he was running for his life. Perhaps from that monstrosity I had a glimpse of when I first arrived."

"That's when he lost the plans!" said Sam excitedly. "He must have broken away from—whatever it was, and tried to cross the track. Lord knows what was after him, but I guess he was crazy with fright. Anyway, he figured the dogs were locked up—"

"When, in fact, they were right on top of him! Failing Kelly's arrival, I could have done nothing. Rouse somebody up. Get hot water, lint, iodine. Rush."

As Sam ran to obey, Raymond Harkness stepped in through the open window. He wore a blue rainproof, a striped muffler, and a brown hat. He was peeling off a pair of light suede gloves. He looked like an accountant who had called to advise winding up the company.

"It's not clear to me, Sir Denis, just what happened out there tonight—I mean what happened to Frobisher."

"You can see what happened to him!" said Smith drily.

"Yes—but how? Sokolov was waiting to meet him, but he never got there—"

"Somebody else met him first!"

"Sokolov's thugs made the mistake of opening fire on our party." Harkness put his gloves in his pockets.

"Otherwise I'm not sure we should have had anything on Sokolov—"

The wounded man groaned, momentarily opened his eyes, clenched his injured hands. He had heard the sound of someone beating on a door, heard Stella's moaning cry:

"Let me out! Mike!"

"Don't," Frobisher whispered . . . "allow her . . . to see me."

As if galvanized, Nayland Smith turned, exchanged a glance with Harkness, and went racing upstairs.

"Mrs. Frobisher!" he called. "Mrs. Frobisher—where are you?"

"I'm *here*!" came pitifully.

Smith found the locked door. The key was in the lock! He turned it, and threw the door open.

Stella Frobisher, on the verge of nervous collapse, crouched on a chair, just inside.

"Mrs. Frobisher! What does this mean?"

"She—Camille—*locked* me in! Oh, for *heaven's* sake, *tell* me: *What* has *happened*?"

"Hang on to yourself, Mrs. Frobisher. It's bad, but might be worse. Please stay where you are for a few minutes longer. Then I am going to ask you to lend us a hand. Will you promise? It's for the good of everybody."

"Oh, *must* I? If *you* say so, I suppose—"

"Just for another five minutes."

Smith ran out again, and down to the library. His face was

627

drawn, haggard. In the battle to save Frobisher from the dogs, with the added distraction of a fracas between F.B.I. men and Sokolov's bodyguard at the lower gate, he had lost sight of Craig! Camille he had never seen, had never suspected that she would leave Mrs. Frobisher's room. Standing at the foot of the stair:

"Harkness," he said. "Send out a general alert. Dr. Fu Manchu not only has the plans. He has Camille Navarre and the inventor, also . . . "

The police car raced towards New York, casting a sword of light far ahead. Against its white glare, the driver and a man beside him, his outline distorted by the radio headpiece, were silhouettes which reminded Nayland Smith of figures of two Egyptian effigies. The glass partition cut them off completely from those in the rear. It was a special control car, normally sacred to the deputy commissioner . . .

"We know many things when it's too late," Nayland Smith answered. "I knew, when I got back tonight, that Michael Frobisher was an agent of the Soviet, knew the Kremlin had backed those experiments. I knew Sokolov was waiting for him.

His crisp voice trailed off into silence.

Visibility in the rear was poor. So dense had the fog become, created by Smith's pipe, that Harkness experienced a certain difficulty in breathing. Motorcycle patrolmen passed and repassed, examining occupants of all vehicles on the road.

"That broken-down truck wasn't reported earlier," Harkness went on, "because it stood so far away from any gate to Falling Waters. What's more, it hadn't been there long."

"But the path through the woods has been there since Indian times," Smith rapped. "And the truck was drawn up right at the point where it reaches a highway. How did your team come to overlook such an approach?"

"I don't know," Harkness admitted. "It seems Frobisher didn't think it likely to be used, either. It doesn't figure in the alarm plan."

"But it figured in Fu Manchu's plan! We don't know—and we're never likely to know—the strength of the party operating from that truck. But those who actually approached the house stuck closely to neutral zones! His visit today—a piece of dazzling audacity—wasn't wasted."

628

Traffic was sparse at that hour. Points far ahead had been notified. Even now, hope was not lost that the truck might be intercepted. Both men were thinking about this. Nayland Smith first put doubt into words.

"A side road, Harkness," he said suddenly. "Another car waiting. Huan Tsung is the doctor's chief of staff—or used to be, formerly. He's a first-class tactician. One of the finest soldiers of the old régime."

"I wish we could pin something on him."

"I doubt if you ever will. He has courage and cunning second only to those of his distinguished chief."

"There's that impudent young liar who sits in the shop, too. And I have reports of a pretty girl of similar type who's been seen around there."

"Probably Huan Tsung's children.

"His *children*!" Even the gently spoken Harkness was surprised into vehemence. "But—how old is he?"

"Nearing eighty-five, I should judge. But the fecundity of a Chinese aristocrat is proverbial . . . Hullo! what's this?"

The radio operator had buzzed to come through.

"Yes?" said Harkness.

"Headquarters, sir. I think it may be important."

"What is it?" Nayland Smith asked rapidly.

"Well, sir, it comes from a point on the East River. A young officer from a ship tied up there seems to have been saying good night to a girl, by some deserted building. They heard tapping from inside a metal pipe on the wall, right where they stood. He spotted it was *Morse*—"

"Yes, yes—the message?"

"The message—it's just reached headquarters—says: '*J. J. Regan here. Call police . . .*' There's a party setting out right now—"

"Regan? *Regan*? Recall them!" snapped Smith. "Quickly!"

Startled, the man gave the order, and then looked back. "Well, sir?"

"The place to be covered, but by men who know their job. Anyone who comes out to be kept in view. Anyone going in to be allowed to do so. No suspicion must be aroused."

The second order was given.

"Anything more?"

"No." Nayland Smith was staring right ahead along the beam of light. "I am trying to imagine, Harkness, how many times the poor devil may have tapped out that message . . ."

Chapter XXI

Camille's impressions of the sortie from the house were brief, but terrifying.

That tragedy, swift, mysterious, had swept down on Falling Waters, she had known even before she ran from her room to prevent Stella Frobisher going downstairs. The arrival of Nayland Smith had struck a note of urgency absent before. Up to this moment, she had counted her confession to Morris the supreme ordeal which she must brave that night.

But, when she returned upstairs (and she knew Sir Denis had seen her), apprehension grew. She had dressed quickly. She realized that something was going to happen. Just what, she didn't know.

Then she heard someone running across the rose garden which her window overlooked. She laid down the cigarette she was smoking, went and looked out. She saw nothing. But it was a dark night. She wondered if it would be wise to report the occurrence. But before decision was reached had come that awful cry—shots—the baying of dogs.

Stella Frobisher, evidently wide awake, had come out of her room. Camille had heard her hurrying along the corridor, had run out after her . . .

It had been difficult, inducing Stella to return. Camille had succeeded, at last.

But to remain locked in, whilst Morris was exposed to some mysterious but very real peril—this was a trial to which Camille was unable to submit. It was alien to all her instincts.

She felt mean for locking Stella into her own apartment, but common sense told her that Mrs. Frobisher could be only a nuisance in an emergency.

Then had come that stumbling rush in cold, clammy darkness towards the spot where, instinctively, she knew Morris to be—in danger. Whilst still a long way off, she had seen that horrifying mix-up of dogs and men. Morris was there.

631

Almost unconsciously she had cried his name: "Morris! Morris!"

By means of what miracle Morris heard her voice above the tumult Camille would never know—unless her heart told her; for a second disturbance had broken out not far away: shots, shouting.

But he did.

He turned. Camille saw someone else, probably the kennelman, joining in the mêlée. Perhaps she was outlined against lights from the house; but Morris saw her, began to run towards her. He seemed to be shouting. His behavior was wild.

Something—it felt like a damp, evil-smelling towel—was dropped suddenly over her head . . .

And now?

Now she lay on a heap of coarse canvas piled up in a corner of what seemed to be a large, and was unmistakably a dilapidated, warehouse: difficult to assess its extent for the reason that the only light was that of a storm-lamp which stood on the roughly paved floor close to where Camille lay.

Another piece of this evidently abundant sacking had been draped over one side of the lantern, so that no light at all reached a great part of the place. There was a smell of dampness and decay with an overtone which might have been tea. It was very still, except that at the moment when she became conscious of her surroundings, Camille thought she had heard the deep, warning note of a steamer's whistle.

The impression was correct. The S.S. *Campus Rex* had just pulled out from a neighboring berth, bound for the River Plate. Her third officer was wishing he knew the result of his message to the police and wishing he could have spent one more night with his girl friend . . .

A scuffling sound brought Camille to her feet at a bound.

There were rats around her in the darkness!

She had physical courage such as, perhaps, few women possess. But the presence of rats had always set her heart beating faster. They terrified her.

Swaying slightly, she became aware of a nausea not due merely to fright. There was an unpleasant taste on her palate. A sickly sweet odor lingered, too, in her disordered hair. Of course, she might have expected it. The towel, or whatever had been thrown over her head, must have been saturated with an anaesthetic.

She stood quite still for a moment, trying to conquer her weakness. The scuffling sound had ceased. In fact, she could detect no sound whatever, so that it might have been some extra sense which prompted her to turn swiftly.

Half in the light from the storm-lamp and half in shadow a tall man stood watching her.

Camille stifled a cry almost uttered, and was silent.

The man who stood there wore a long, loose coat with a deep astrakhan collar. A round cap, of Russian type, and of the same close black fur, was on his head. His arms were folded, but the fingers of his left hand remained visible. They were yellow, slender fingers, prolonged by pointed fingernails meticulously manicured.

His features, lean, ascetic, and unmistakably Chinese, were wholly dominated by his eyes. In the lantern light they gleamed like green jade.

"Your sense of hearing is acute," he said, his harsh voice subdued. "I thought I moved quite noiselessly."

And, as he spoke, Camille knew that this was the man who had haunted her dreams.

"Who are you?" She spoke huskily. "What am I doing here?"

"You asked me a similar question not long ago. But you have forgotten."

"I have never seen you in my life before—as you are now. But I *know* you! You are Dr. Fu Manchu!"

"Your data are inaccurate. But your inference is correct. What are you doing here, you say? You are suffering the inconvenience of one who interferes with my plans. I regret the crude measures used by Koenig to prevent this interference. But his promptitude saved the situation."

"Where is Dr. Craig?" Camille demanded breathlessly "What have you done to him?"

He watched her through narrowed eyes and unfolded his clasped arms before he replied:

"I am glad your first, your only, concern is for Dr. Craig."

"Why?"

"Presently, you shall know."

And something in that expression, "You shall know," brought sudden revelation to Camille.

"You are the man who called himself Professor Hoffmeyer!"

"I congratulate you. I had imagined my German-English to be above reproach. I begin to wonder if you cannot be of use to me. As Professor Hoffmeyer, I have been observing the life of Manhattan. I have seen that Manhattan is Babylon reborn—that Manhattan, failing a spiritual revolution, must fall as Babylon fell."

"Where is Dr. Craig?" Camille repeated, mechanically, desperately. "Why have I been brought *here*?"

"Because there was no other place to which they could bring you. It surprises me, I confess, that a woman of such keen perceptions failed to learn the fact that Michael Frobisher was a Communist."

"A Communist? Mr. Frobisher? Oh, no—he is a Socialist—"

"Socialism is Communism's timid sister. Michael Frobisher is an active agent of the Soviet Union. Before his marriage, he spent many years in Moscow. Dr. Craig's invention was financed by the Kremlin. Had Frobisher secured it for them, he was promised a post which would have made him virtual dictator of the United States."

Even in her desolation, despair, this astounding fact penetrated to Camille's mind.

"Then he was clever," she murmured.

"Communism *is* clever. It is indeed clever to force the world's workers to toil and sweat in order that their masters may live in oriental luxury."

"Why do you tell me all this? Why do you talk to me, torture me, but never answer my question?"

"Because, even now, at this eleventh hour, I hope to convert you. You heard me, as Professor Hoffmeyer (the professor, himself, is at work in one of our research centers), outline a design for world harmony. To the perfecting of this design I have given the labor of a long life."

He paused. A soft, weired cry came from somewhere near. Its effect upon Camille was to shatter her returning composure. To her it portended a threat of death. Had Nayland Smith heard it, he would have recognized the peculiar call of a dacoit, one of that fraternity of Burmese brigands over whom Dr. Fu Manchu exercised a control hitherto unexplained.

"What was it?"

Camille breathed, rather than spoke, the words.

"A warning. Do not allow it to disturb you. My plans are complete. But my time is limited. You are anxious concerning Dr. Craig. I, too, am anxious. For this reason alone I have talked to you so long. I hope you can induce him to accept the truth. You may succeed where I have failed."

He turned and walked away. Camille heard the creak of an opening door.

The warning which Camille had construed as a message of evil omen had been prompted by something occurring on the nearby river front.

To any place, the wide world over, where men go down to the sea in ships, night brings no repose. So that, even at this hour, Manhattan danced on. Winches squealed. Anchor chains rattled. Sea boots clattered along decks. Lights moved hither and thither. Hoarse orders were shouted. Tugboats churned the muddy river. And the outgoing tide sang its eternal song of the ocean, from which it had come, to which it returned.

But no one had time to pay attention to a drunken sailor who came reeling along past deserted dock buildings, blacked-out warehouses, stumbling often, rebuking himself in an alcoholic monotone. He steadied up every once in a while against a friendly doorway, a lamp standard, or a stout pipe.

One such pipe seemed to give him particular satisfaction. Perhaps because it ran down the wall of a building marked for demolition upon the doors of which might still be read the words: "Shen Yan Tea Company."

This pipe he positively embraced, and, embracing it, sank ungracefully to the sidewalk, and apparently fell asleep.

A few minutes later he had established contact with Regan. He, too, was a Morse expert.

"Yes. John Regan here. Huston Electric. Who are you?"

"Brandt. Police officer. Where are you?"

"Old strong room. Basement. Don't know what building."

"Shout. I may hear you."

"Dumb."

This message shook Brandt.

635

"How come?"

"Injection. Attacked in lab Friday night. Get me out."

"Starving?"

"No. But food and water finished."

"Any movement overhead right now?"

"Yes. Someone up there."

"Hang on. Help coming."

The drunken sailor woke up suddenly. He began to strike matches and to try to light a cigarette. He remained seated beside the pipe. These matches attracted the attention of a patrolman (who had been waiting for this signal) and who now appeared from somewhere, and approached, swinging his club.

But the matches had also attracted the attention of another, highly skilled observer. So that, as the police officer hauled the drunk to his feet and led him off, the call of a dacoit was heard in the empty warehouse.

"This was formerly the office of a firm of importers known as the Shen Yan Tea Company," said Dr. Fu Manchu. "An old friend of mine had an interest in that business."

Morris Craig swallowed—with difficulty. He had by no means recovered from the strangling grip of those unseen fingers. He would have liked to massage his bruised throat. But his wrists were secured by metal clamps to the arms of his chair, a remarkable piece of furniture, evidently of great age; it had a curious, domed canopy which at some time might have been gilded. He was helpless, mad with anxiety about Camille, but undaunted.

"Strange coincidence," he replied huskily. "No doubt this attractive and comfortable rest-chair has quite a history, too?"

"A long one, Dr. Craig. I came across it in Seville. It dates from the days of the Spanish Inquisition, when it was known as the Chair of Conversion. I regret that of all those treasured possessions formerly in the Woolton Building, this one must be left behind."

"Seems a great pity. Cozy little piece."

Fu Manchu stood watching him, his long narrow eyes nearly closed, his expression indecipherable. There was that about the tall, fur-capped figure which radiated power. Craig's nonchalance in the presence of this formidable and wholly unpredictable man demanded an immense nervous effort.

"It may be no more than a national trait, Dr. Craig, but your imperturbable façade reminds me of Sir Denis."

"You flatter me."

"You may not know, but it will interest you to learn, that your capture, some hours ago, was largely an accident."

"Clearly not my lucky day."

"I doubt if the opportunity would have arisen but for the unforeseen appearance of Miss Navarre. In running to join her, you ran, almost literally, into the arms of two of my servants who were concerned only in retiring undetected."

"Practically left the poor fellows no choice?"

"Therefore they brought you along with them."

"Friendly thought."

Dr. Fu Manchu turned slowly and crossed the office. Like the adjoining warehouse, it was lighted only by a partly draped lantern which stood on a box beside the Spanish chair. The floor, in which were many yawning gaps, was littered with rubbish. A boarded-up window probably overlooked a passage, for there was no sound to suggest that a thoroughfare lay beyond.

Directly facing Craig, a long, high desk was built against the cracked and blackened wall. In this wall were two other windows, level with the top of the desk, and closed by sliding shutters. And on the desk Craig saw a metal-bound teak chest.

Very deliberately Dr. Fu Manchu lifted this chest, came back, and set it on the box beside the lantern. His nearness produced a tingling nervous tension, as if a hidden cobra had reared its threatening hood.

"Amongst those curious possessions to which I referred," he continued in his cold, conversational manner (he was unlocking the chest), "is the mummied head of Queen Taia known to the Egyptians as the 'witch queen.' Her skull posesses uncommon characteristics. And certain experiments I am carrying out with it would interest you."

"Not a doubt of it. My mother gave me a mummy's head to play with when I was only four."

"The crystal sets we use in our system of private communication also accompany me to headquarters. This"—he opened the chest—"which I borrowed from there, must never leave my personal possession until I return it."

Morris Craig's hands—for only his wrists were constrained—became slowly clenched. Here, he felt, came the final test; this might well be the end.

What he expected to happen, what he expected to see, he could not have put into words. What he did see was an exquisitely fashioned model of just such an equipment as that which had been destroyed in the Huston Building!

The top, front, and sides of the chest were hinged, so that the miniature plant, mounted on its polished teak-base, lay fully open to inspection. Wonder reduced Morris Craig to an awed silence. Apart from the fact that there were certain differences (differences which had instantly inflamed his scientific curiosity), to have constructed this model must have called for the labor of months, perhaps of years.

"I don't understand." His voice sounded unfamiliar to him.

"I don't understand at all!"

"Only because," came in cold, incisive tones, "you remain obsessed with the idea that you *invented* this method of harnessing primeval energy. The model before you was made by a Buddhist monk, in Burma. I had been to inspect it at the time that I first encountered Sir Denis Nayland Smith. Detailed formulae for its employment are in my possession. You, again, after a lapse of years, have solved this problem. My congratulations. Such men were meant to reshape the world—not to destroy it."

Dr. Fu Manchu began to reclose the chest.

"I don't understand," Craig repeated. "If the principle was known to you, as well as the method of applying it—and I can't dispute that it was—"

"Why did I permit you to complete your experiments? The explanation is simple. I wanted to know if you *could* complete them. On my arrival, the main plant had already been set up in the Huston laboratory. I was anxious to learn if the final problem would baffle you. It did not. Such a man is a man to watch."

Dr. Fu Manchu locked the teak chest.

"Then it was *you* who destroyed my work?"

"I had no choice, Dr. Craig. Your work was destined for the use of the Kremlin. I have also your original plans, and every formula. The only blueprints existing I secured tonight. One danger, only, remains."

"What's that?"

638

"Yourself."

And the word was spoken in a voice which made it a sentence of death.

Dr. Fu Manchu carried the chest across the littered room, and opened what looked like a deep cupboard. He placed the chest inside, and turned again to Craig.

"You will have noted that I am dressed for travel, Dr. Craig. My time is limited. Otherwise, I should employ less mediaeval methods to incline your mind to reason. You seem to have failed to recognize me as Professor Hoffmeyer, but a committee such as I spoke of when we met already exists. It is called the Council of Seven. In our service we have some of the best brains of every continent. We have wealth. We are not criminals. We are idealists—"

A second of those wailing cries, the first of which had terrified Camille, checked his words. Craig started.

"I may delay no longer. You have it in your power, while you live, to destroy all our plans. Therefore, Dr. Craig—I speak with sincere regret—either you must consent to place your undoubted genius at my disposal—or you must die."

"The choice is made."

"I trust not, yet."

Dr. Fu Manchu opened one of the sliding shutters over the long desk. It disclosed an iron grille through which crept a glimmer of light.

"Miss Navarre!" There was no slightest change of tone, of inflection, in his strange voice. "You were anxious about Dr. Craig. Here he is—perfectly well, as you may judge for yourself."

And Morris Craig saw Camille's pale face, her eyes wide with terror, her hair disordered, staring at him through the bars!

A torrent of words, frenzied, scathing, useless words, flooded his brain. But he choked them back—rejected them; and when he spoke, in a whisper, he said simply:

"*Camille!*"

"When we move"—Nayland Smith's expression was very grim—"we must be sure the net has no holes in it. We have Regan's evidence that there are people in that building. We know who put Regan there. So we know what to expect. Is our cordon wide enough?"

"Hard to make it wider," Harkness assured him. "But these old places are honeycombs. There are sixty men on the job. I have sent for the keys of all the adjoining buildings."

"We daren't wait!" Smith said savagely. "Fu Manchu has destroyed the last possibility of Craig's invention being used—except Craig . . . We daren't wait."

"Report coming through," said Harkness.

The report was one which might have meant next to nothing. A cry had been heard, more than once, in the neighborhood of the closely covered building, which at first hearing had been mistaken for the cry of a cat. Repeated, however, doubt had arisen on this point.

"That settles the matter!" rapped Smith. "It was the call of one of his Burmese bodyguard! Fu Manchu is there."

"There was a pleasant simplicity," Dr. Fu Manchu was saying, "in the character of the unknown designer of this chair. I fear I must start its elementary mechanism. The device bears some resemblance to a type of orange-squeezer used in this country."

He stood behind Craig for a moment; and Craig became aware of a regular, ticking sound, of vibrations in the framework of the chair: he clenched his teeth.

"I am going to ask Miss Navarre to add her powers of persuasion to mine. If you prefer to live—in her company—to devote yourself to the most worthy task of all, the salvation of men from slavery or from destruction, I welcome you—gladly. You are a man of honor. Your word is enough. It is a bond neither you nor I could ever break. Do you accept these terms?"

"Suppose I don't?"

Morris Craig had grown desperately white.

"I should lock the control, which, you may have noted, lies under your right hand: an embossed gold crown. I should prefer to leave it free. You have only to depress it, and the descent will be arrested. Choose—quickly."

"Whichever you please. The result will be the same."

"Words worthy of Molotov! The time for evasion is past. I offer you life—a life of usefulness. I await your promise that, if you accept, you will press the control. Your doing so will mean, on the word of an English gentleman, that you agree to join the Council of Seven. Quickly. Speak!"

"I give you my word"—Morris Craig's eyes were closed; he spoke all but tonelessly—"that if I press the control it will mean that I accept your offer."

Dr. Fu Manchu crossed to the door behind which he had placed the teak chest. As he passed the grilled window:

"The issue, Miss Navarre," he said, "rests with you."

He went out, closing the door.

"No! No! Come back!" Camille clutched the iron bars, shook them frantically. "Come back! . . . No! *No*! Merciful God! stop him! Morris! Agree! Agree to anything! I—I can't bear it . . . "

The domed canopy, its gilding barely touched by upcast lantern light, was descending slowly.

"Don't look at me. I shall—weaken—if you look at me . . ."

"Weaken Morris, darling, listen to me! Dr. Fu Manchu is a *madman*! There can be no obligation to a madman . . . I tell you he's mad! Press the control! Do it! *Do* it!"

The canopy continued to descend, moving in tiny jerks which corresponded to audible ticks of some hidden clockwork mechanism. It was evidently controlled by counterweights, for Craig found the chair to be immovably heavy.

He closed his eyes. He couldn't endure the sight of Camille's chalk-white, frenzied face staring at him through those bars. A parade of heretics who had rejected conversion passed before him in the darkness, attired in the silk and velvet, the rags and tatters, of Old Seville. Their heads lolled on their shoulders. Their skulls were crushed.

"Morris! Have you no pity for me? Is this your love . . . "

He must *think*. "A bond neither you nor I could ever break." Those had been the words. That had been the bargain. If he chose life, Dr. Fu Manchu would claim his services.

"Camille, my dearest, you have faced worse things than this—"

"I tell you he is mad!"

"Unfortunately, I think he's particularly sane. I even think, in a way he has the right idea."

Tick-tick . . . Tick-tick . . . Tick-tick. In fractions of an inch, the canopy crept lower.

641

"I shall lose my reason! O God in heaven, hear me!"

Camille dropped to her knees, hands clasped in passionate supplication. Kneeling, she could no longer see Morris. But, soon, she must look again.

Meaningless incidents from the past, childish memories, trivial things, submerged dreams of a future that was never to be; Morris's closed eyes; the open, dreadful eyes of Dr. Fu Manchu: all these images moved, in a mocking dance, through her prayers . . .

A whistle skirled—a long way off. It was answered by another, nearer.

Camille sprang up, clutched the bars.

The canopy almost touched Morris's head. His eyes remained closed.

She began to scream wildly:

"*Help*! *Help*! Be quick! Oh, be quick!" She clenched her hand so tightly that her nails bit into the palms, and spoke again, a low, quivering whisper: "Morris! He may be right, as you think. Morris! for my sake, believe it. There is—just time."

Craig's hand twitched, where it rested over the gilded crown of life which meant . . . He did not open his eyes.

There came a wild tide of rushing footsteps, a charivari of shouting, crash of axes on woodwork . . .

"This way! This—way!"

Camille's attempted cry was only a strangled murmur. She supported herself by clinging with all but nerveless fingers to the grille.

"Alight in here!" came a breathless shout.

The blade of an axe split through woodwork covering the only exterior window in the office. A second blow—a third. The planking was wrenched away. Outside lay a stone-paved passage crowded with men.

"Good God! Look! Here's Dr. Craig, sir!"

"Be quick!" Camille murmured, and fought to check insane laughter which bubbled to her lips. "Under his hand . . . that knob . . . *press* it . . ."

Nayland Smith, his dark complexion oddly blanched, forced his way through. The canopy just touched the top of Craig's head. A wave of strength, sanity, the last, swept over Camille.

"Sir Denis! That—gold crown—on the arm of the chair . . . Press it."

Nayland Smith glanced swiftly towards the grille, then sprang to the chair, groped for and found a crown-shaped knob under Craig's listless fingers, and pressed it, pressed it madly.

The clockwork sound ceased. He dropped to one knee.

"Craig! Craig!"

Beads of sweat trickled from a limp forelock down an ivory face' but there was no reply.

Morris Craig had fainted.

"This is the way she pointed, but maybe it didn't mean anything." Sam had joined the party. "Gee! Those two must have gone through hell!"

"Fortunately," said Nayland Smith, "they have youth on their side. But the ordeal was—ghastly. It is characteristic of Fu Manchu's unusual sense of humor that the canopy is made so that it cannot descend any further. Craig was in no danger! Hullo! what's this?"

They had reached the foot of a short flight of stone steps, the entrance to which Craig had mistaken for a deep cupboard. Harkness was in front, with two men. Two more followed. All carried flashlamps.

An empty passage, concrete-floored, extended to left and to right.

"Take a party left, Harkness. I'll take the right."

Ten paces brought Smith to a metal door in the wall. He pulled up. Retreating footsteps, the sound of which echoed hollowly, as in a vault, indicated that the other party had found nothing of interest so far.

"Job for a safebreaker," Sam grumbled. "If this is the way he went, he'll get a long start."

"Quiet!" rapped Nayland Smith. "Listen."

He beat a syncopated tattoo on the metal with his knuckles. Harkness's party had apparently turned in somewhere. Their footsteps were no more than faintly audible.

Answering knocks came from the other side of the door!

"Regan!" Sam exclaimed.

Smith nodded. "This is what he called the strong room. Quiet again."

He rapped a message—listened to the reply; then turned.

"This scent is stale," he said shortly. "Regan states nobody has passed this way tonight."

"We must get Mr. Regan out, right now." Sam spoke urgently. "You, back there, O'Leary, report upstairs there's an iron door to be softened. Poor devil! Guess he's dumb for life!"

"Not at all," Nayland Smith assured him. "The effect wears off after a few days—so I was recently informed by my old friend, Dr. Fu Manchu."

He spoke bitterly—a note of defeat in the crisp voice. What had he accomplished? He could not even claim credit for saving the blueprints from Soviet hands. Some servant of Fu Manchu's had secured them before the dogs attacked Frobisher—

"Sir Denis!" came a distant, excited hail. "This way! I think we have him!"

Nayland Smith led the run back to where Harkness and two men stood before another closed door near the end of a passage which formed an L with that from which they had started.

"I think it's an old furnace room. And I saw a light in there!"

"Don't waste time! Down with it!"

Two of the party carried axes. And they went to work with a will. The door was double-bolted on the inside, but it collapsed under their united onslaughts. A cavity yawned in which the rays of Nayland Smith's lamp picked out an old-fashioned, soot-begrimed boiler, half buried in mounds of coal ash.

"Be careful!" he warned. "We are dealing with no ordinary criminal. Stand by for anything."

They entered cautiously.

The place proved to have unexpected ramifications. It was merely part of what had been an extensive cellarage system. They groped in its darkness, shedding light into every conceivable spot where a fugitive might lie. But they found nothing. A sense of futility crept down upon all, when a cry came: "Another door here! I heard someone moving behind it!"

Over the debris and coal dust of years, they ran to join the man who had shouted. He stood in what had evidently been a coal bunker, before a narrow, grimy door.

"It's locked."

Keen axes and willing hands soon cleared the obstacle.

A long, sloping passage lay beyond. Up its slope, as the door crashed open, swept a current of cold, damp air. And, halfway down, a retreating figure showed, a grotesque silhouette against reflected light from his dancing flashlamp.

It was the figure of a tall man, wearing a long coat and what looked like a close-fitting cap.

"By God!" Smith shouted, "Dr. Fu Manchu! This leads to the river—"

He broke off.

Sam had hurled himself into the passage, firing the moment he crossed the threshold of the shattered door! The crash of his heavy revolver created an echo like a thunderstorm. Nayland Smith, following hard behind, saw the figure stumble, pause—run on.

"Cease fire there!" he shouted angrily.

But Sam's blood was up. He either failed to hear the order, or wilfully ignored it. He fired again—then, rapidly, a third time.

The tall figure stopped suddenly, dropped the flashlamp, and crumpled to the damp floor.

"You fool!" Nayland Smith's words came as a groan. "This was no end for the greatest brain in the world!"

He forced his way past Sam, stooped, and turned the fur-capped head. As he did so, the fallen man writhed, coughed, and was still.

Nayland Smith looked into a face scarcely human, scarred, a parody of humanity—a face he had never seen before—the face of M'goyna . . .

He stood up very slowly. The dark, sloping passage behind him seemed to be embossed with staring eyes.

"Outmanoeuvred!" he said. "Fu Manchu played for time. This poor devil was the last of his rearguards. He has slipped through our fingers!"

645

Chapter XXII

Ten days later, Nayland Smith gave a small dinner party at his hotel to celebrate the engagement of Camille Mirabeau (Navarre) to Dr. Morris Craig. When the other guests had left, these three went to Smith's suite, and having settled down:

"Of course," said Smith, in reply to a question from Camille, "the newspapers are never permitted to print really important news! It might frighten somebody."

"Quite a lot has leaked out, though," Craig amended. "The cops gave it away. Poor old Regan has been pestered since I resigned. But although he can chatter quite acidly again, he won't chatter to reporters."

"How's Frobisher?"

"Rotten. He'll recover all right, but carry a crop of scars."

"Does his wife know the truth?"

"Couldn't say. What do you think, Camille?"

Camille, lovely in her new-found happiness and a Paris frock, shrugged white shoulders.

"Stella Frobisher is like a cork," she said. "I think she can stay afloat in the heaviest weather. But I don't know her well enough to tell you if she suspects the truth."

"The most astounding thing which the newspapers haven't reported," Nayland Smith remarked after an interval, "concerns the body of that ape man—almost certainly the creature of which I had a glimpse at Falling Waters. He's been examined by all the big doctors. And they are unanimous on one point."

"What is that?" Camille asked.

"They say the revolver bullets didn't kill him."

"What?" Craig exclaimed.

"They state, positively, that he had been dead many years before the shooting!"

And Camille (such was the strange power of Dr. Fu Manchu) simply shook her red head and murmured. "But that is impossible."

646

Yes—that was impossible. It was also impossible, no doubt, that Dr. Fu Manchu had visited New York, and perhaps, as a result of his visit, given a few more years of uneasy peace to a world coquetting with war. And so, Manhattan danced on . . .

"Our two Russian acquaintances"—Nayland Smith rapped out the words venomously—"have been quietly deported. But what I really wanted to show you was this."

From the pocket of his dinner jacket he took a long, narrow envelope. It had come by air mail and was stamped "Cairo." It was addressed to him at his New York hotel. He passed it to Camille.

"Read it together. There was an enclosure."

And so, Craig bending over Camille's shoulder, his cheek against her glowing hair, they read the letter, handwritten in copperplate script:

Sir Denis—

It was a serious disappointment to be compelled to leave New York without seeing you again. I regret, too, that M'goyna, one of my finer products, had to be sacrificed to my safety. But a little time was necessary to enable me to reach the boat which awaited me. I left by another exit. I greet Dr. Craig. He is a genius and a brave man. But his keen sense of honor is my loss. Will you, on my behalf, advise him to devote his great talents to non-destructive purposes? His future experiments will be watched with interest. I enclose a wedding present for his bride.

There was no signature.

Camille and Morris Craig raised their eyes, together.

On his extended palm Nayland Smith was holding out a large emerald. And as Camille, uttering a long, wondering sigh, took the gem between her fingers, Nayland Smith reached for his dilapidated pouch and began, reflectively, to load his blackened briar.